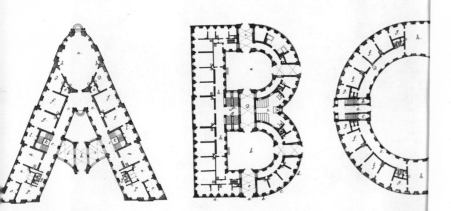

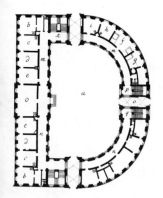
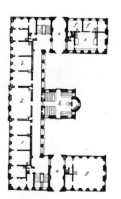
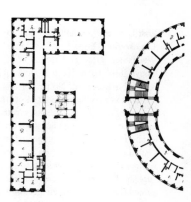

A Dictionary
of
Architecture

Nikolaus Pevsner
John Fleming
and Hugh Honour

Revised
and
enlarged

THE OVERLOOK PRESS
Woodstock, New York

First U.S. edition published 1976 by
The Overlook Press
Woodstock, New York 12498
Copyright © 1966 Hugh Honour, John Fleming and Nikolaus Pevsner

ISBN 0-87951-040-4
Library of Congress Catalog Card Number: 75-27325
Designed by Gerald Cinamon
Printed in the United States by Vail-Ballou Press, Inc.

This greatly expanded edition of the dictionary had its origins in a volume first published in 1966. In the present work Sir Nikolaus Pevsner wrote the entries about medieval and nineteenth- and twentieth-century architects, also the European and American national entries and most of the stylistic entries. He was assisted by Sabrina Longland in connection with the definition of medieval terms and by Enid Caldecott in connection with modern technical terms. The rest was written jointly by John Fleming and Hugh Honour. The three authors would like to express their gratitude to Gustav Stresow, Dr Walter Romstoeck and other members of the staff of Prestel Verlag who assembled the majority of the photographs reproduced in the present edition. The authors are indebted, as before, to many friends for suggestions and corrections, and would also like to thank Betty Ettles for her editorial help to which this edition owes a great deal. The capital letters at the head of each alphabetical section are taken from Johann David Steingruber: *Architectonisches Alphabeth* . . . Schwabach 1773 (facsimile edition, edited by Berthold Wolpe, The Merrion Press, London 1972).

AL   Alastair Laing, London
AM   Dr Alfred Mallwitz, Athens
AVR   Dr Alexander von Reitzenstein, Munich
AV   Dr Andreas Volwahsen, Cambridge, Mass.
DOE   Prof. Dietz Otto Edzard, Munich
DW   Dr Dietrich Wildung, Munich
HC   Heidi Conrad, Altenerding
HS   Dr Heinrich Strauss, Jerusalem
KG   Klaus Gallas, Munich
KW   Prof. Klaus Wessel, Munich
MR   Dr Marcell Restle, Munich
NT   Nicholas Taylor, London
OZ   Prof. Otto Zerries, Munich
RG   Prof. Roger Goepper, Cologne
RH   Dr Robert Hillenbrand, Edinburgh
WR   Dr Walter Romstoeck, Munich

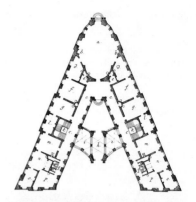

Aalto, Alvar (b. 1898), among the most important living architects, and certainly pre-eminent in his native Finland. Started neo-classically, in a typically Scandinavian idiom, *c.* 1923–5, and turned to the INTER-NATIONAL MODERN with his excellent Library at Viipuri (1927–35), Convalescent Home at Paimio (1929–33), and factory with workers' housing at Sunila (1936–9, with large additions of 1951–7). He possesses a strong feeling for materials and their characters, which, Finland being a country of forests, inspired him to use timber widely. He also invented bent plywood furniture (1932). Timber figured prominently in his Finnish Pavilion at the Paris Exhibition of 1937 and in the Villa Mairea at Noormarkku (1938). Aalto's most original works date from after the Second World War. By then he had evolved a language entirely his own, quite unconcerned with current clichés, yet in its vigorous display of curved walls and single-pitched roofs, in its play with brick and timber, entirely in harmony with the international trend towards plastically more expressive *ensembles*. The principal works are a Hall of Residence at the Massachusetts Institute of Technology, Cambridge, Mass. (1947–9), with a curved front and staircases projecting out of the wall and climbing up diagonally; the Village Hall at Säynatsälo (1951); the Pensions Institute at Helsinki (1952–7), a more straightforward job; the church at Imatra (1952–8), on a completely free plan; and the Hall of Culture at Helsinki (1958). (For illustration *see* FINNISH ARCHITECTURE.)
  Lit: G. Baird, *Alvar Aalto*, London 1971.

Abacus The flat slab on the top of a CAPITAL: in Greek Doric a thick square slab; in Greek

Abacus: Temple of Poseidon, Paestum, mid-c5

Ionic, Tuscan, Roman Doric and Ionic, square with the lower edge moulded; in Corinthian and Composite with concave sides and the corners cut off.

Abadie, Paul, *see* VAUDREMER.

Abbey, *see* MONASTERY.

Abutment Solid masonry placed to counteract the lateral thrust of a VAULT or ARCH. (For illustration *see* ARCH.)

Acanthus A plant with thick, fleshy, scalloped leaves used on carved ornament of Corinthian and Composite CAPITALS and on other mouldings.

Acanthus: Corinthian capital, Epidauros, mid-c5 B.C.

Achaemenid architecture, *see* IRANIAN ARCHITECTURE.

Acropolis The citadel of a Greek city, built at its highest point and containing the chief temples and public buildings, as at Athens.

Acroteria Plinths for statues or ornaments placed at the apex and ends of a PEDIMENT; also, more loosely, both the plinths and what stands on them.

Acroteria: c. 500 B.C.

Adam, James, *see* ADAM, ROBERT.

Adam, John, *see* ADAM, ROBERT.

Adam, Robert (1728–92), the greatest British architect of the later C18, was equally if not more brilliant as a decorator, furniture designer, etc., for which his name is still a household word. He is comparable in his chaste and rather epicene elegance with his French contemporary SOUFFLOT, but without Soufflot's chilly solemnity. He was a typically hard-headed Scot, canny and remorselessly ambitious, yet with a tender, romantic side to his character as well. Both facets were reflected in his work, which oscillates between a picturesque version of neo-classicism and a classicizing version of neo-Gothic. His work has an air of unceremonious good manners, unpedantic erudition, and unostentatious opulence which perfectly reflects the civilized world of his patrons. Appreciating that it would be bad manners, and bad business, to make any violent break with established traditions, he devised a neo-classical style lighter and more gaily elegant than that of the Palladians who preceded or the Greek Revivalists who succeeded him. He avoided startling innovations such as the Greek Doric for classical buildings or the picturesquely asymmetrical for Gothic ones. He answered the current demand for a new classicism by enlarging the

repertory of decorative motifs and by a more imaginative use of contrasting room plans derived largely from Imperial Roman Baths. In his cunning variation of room shapes and in his predilection for columned screens and apses to give a sense of spatial mystery, no less than in his neo-Gothic castles – so massively romantic outside and so comfortably classical within – he answered the taste for the picturesque. He became the architect *par excellence* to the Age of Sensibility, as BURLINGTON had been to the English Augustan period. His influence spread rapidly all over England and beyond, as far as Russia and America. His output was enormous, and only the unlucky Adelphi speculation robbed him of the fortune he would otherwise have made.

His father **William Adam** (1689–1748) was the leading architect of his day in Scotland and developed a robust, personal style based on VANBRUGH, GIBBS, and the English Palladians, e.g., Hopetoun House, near Edinburgh (1721 etc.) and Duff House, Banff (1730–39). His brothers **John** (1721–92) and **James** (1732–94) were also architects, and all three trained in their father's Edinburgh office: Robert and James attended Edinburgh University as well. Robert Adam's early work is no more than competent, e.g., Dumfries House (designed 1750–54). His genius emerged only after his Grand Tour (1754–8), most of which was spent in Rome studying Imperial Roman architecture under CLÉRISSEAU, with whom he also surveyed Diocletian's palace at Split in Dalmatia (later published by him as *Ruins of Spalatro*, 1764).

In 1758 he settled in London, where he was joined by his brother James after a similar Grand Tour with Clérisseau (1760–3). The columnar Admiralty Screen, London (1759–60), gave immediate proof of his ability and originality, but all his other early commissions were for the internal transformation of old houses or the completion of houses already begun by other architects. Nevertheless, his style rapidly matured, and the interiors of Harewood House (1758–71), Kedleston Hall (1759 etc.), Syon House (1760–9), Osterley Park (1761–80), Luton Hoo (1766–70), Newby Hall (1767–85), and Kenwood (1767–9) are perhaps his masterpieces of interior design. His meticulous attention to detail is revealed no less in the jewel-like finish of the painted decorations and very shallow stucco work than in the care he lavished on every part of each room from the carpets to the keyhole guards. No previous architect had attempted such comprehensive schemes of interior decoration. Although individual decorative motifs are often small in scale they are woven together with such skill that the general effect is rarely finicking, and although the same artistic personality is evident in each room the effect of a series is never monotonous. They perfectly illustrate those qualities for which he and James expressed their admiration in the introduction to their *Works in Architecture* (1773; 2nd vol. 1779; 3rd vol. 1822): movement or 'rise and fall, the advance and recess and other diversity of forms' and 'a variety of light mouldings'. His neo-classicism is most evident in the planning of Syon with its varied geometric shapes (basilican hall, rotunda, projected central Pantheon, etc.), and on the south front of Kedleston, modelled on a Roman triumphal arch.

His originality and ingenuity in planning culminated in his London houses of the 1770s – e.g., 20 St James's Square, 20 Portman Square – in which, however, the decoration became increasingly shallow and linear, tending towards the flippancy and frippery for which he was much criticized towards the end of his life.

Between 1768 and 1772 he and James embarked on their most ambitious enterprise, the Adelphi, a vast palatial group of houses on the banks of the Thames (now destroyed). Unfortunately the speculation failed and they were saved from bankruptcy only by the expedient of a lottery and by loans from their elder brother John in Edinburgh.

Partly as a result of the Adelphi fiasco the quality of Robert Adam's work declined sharply after 1775. But it recovered amazingly during the last decade of his life under the stimulus of large commissions in Edinburgh – the General Register House (begun 1774 and completed, with modifications, after his death), the University (begun 1789, completed by W. H. Playfair to modified designs 1815–34, the dome added by Rowand Anderson in 1887), and Charlotte Square (designed 1791). The entrance front to the University is his most monumental building and perhaps his masterpiece as an architect. To the same period belong most of his sham castles, e.g., Culzean Castle (1777–90) and Seton Castle (1789–91), which were much in advance of their date. His earlier neo-Gothic style, e.g., the interiors of Alnwick Castle (c. 1770, now destroyed), had been similar in its sophisticated elegance to his neo-

classical style. Now he developed a much bolder manner. At Culzean he took full advantage of a dramatic site on the Ayrshire coast for a martial display of round towers and battlements embracing rooms of feminine delicacy inside. The charm of the place lies in this contrast, which would have been greatly relished by the c18 Man of Sensibility, who could here enjoy the chilling horror of storms at sea from an eminently safe and civilized interior. (For illustration *see* ENGLISH ARCHITECTURE.)

Lit: A. T. Bolton, *The Architecture of Robert Adam and James Adam*, London 1922; J. Lees-Milne, *The Age of Adam*, London 1947; J. Fleming, *Robert Adam and his Circle*, London 1962; D. Stillman, *The Decorative Work of Robert Adam*, London 1966.

Adam, William, *see* ADAM, ROBERT.

Addorsed An adjective applied to two figures, usually animals, placed symmetrically back to back; often found on CAPITALS.

Addorsed head at the palace at Fulda, Germany

Adler, Dankmar, *see* SULLIVAN, LOUIS HENRY.

Adobe Unburnt brick dried in the sun, commonly used for building in Spain and Latin America, also in New Mexico, e.g. Santa Fé.

Adyton The inner sanctuary of a Greek temple whence oracles were delivered: also more loosely, any private chamber or sanctuary.

Aedicule Properly a shrine framed by two columns supporting an ENTABLATURE and PEDIMENT, set in a temple and containing a

Aedicule: Ostia Antica

statue; but also, more loosely, the framing of a door, window, or other opening with two columns, piers or pilasters supporting a gable, lintel, plaque, or an entablature and pediment.

Aeolic capital, *see* ORDER.

Affronted An adjective applied to two figures, usually animals, placed symmetrically facing each other: often found on CAPITALS.

Agger Latin term for built-up foundations of Roman roads; also sometimes applied to the banks of hill-forts or other earthworks.

Agora The open space in a Greek or Roman town used as a market-place or general meeting-place, usually surrounded by porticos as in a FORUM.

Agostino di Duccio (1418–81) was primarily a sculptor but worked with ALBERTI on the Tempio Malatestiano at Rimini where his extremely individual and exquisitely refined relief sculpture is best seen. Equally sculptural and equally masterly is the façade he designed for the small church of S. Bernardino at Perugia (1457–61). Very different in feeling is his monumental Porta S. Pietro at Perugia, begun in 1473.

Lit: L. H. Heydenreich and W. Lotz, *Architecture in Italy: 1400–1600,* Pelican History of Art, Harmondsworth 1974.

Aichel, Giovanni Santini (1667–1723). A Bohemian architect of Italian extraction born in Prague but trained in Italy, he also made visits to England and Holland. He worked sometimes in a Baroque (derived from BORROMINI and GUARINI) and sometimes in a neo-Gothic style. His speciality was the latter, a carpenter's Gothic, gay, naïve, and very personal, with a predilection for star-shaped forms (derived from Borromini) in his elegant and airy vaulting: e.g., Marienkirche, Kladrau (1712–26), and the churches at Seelau (begun 1712) and St John Nepomuk on the Green Mountain near Saar (1719–22). But he was a freak, and had no influence or followers at all. (For illustration *see* CZECHO-SLOVAK ARCHITECTURE.)

Lit: H. G. Franz, *Bauten und Baumeister der Barockzeit in Böhmen,* Leipzig 1962; E. Hempel, *Baroque Art and Architecture in Central Europe,* Pelican History of Art, Harmondsworth 1965.

Aisle Part of a church, parallel to, and divided by piers or columns – or in rare cases by a screen wall – from, the nave, choir or transept.

Akkadian architecture, *see* SUMERIAN AND AKKADIAN ARCHITECTURE.

Alan of Walsingham Sacrist of Ely Cathedral at the time when the new Lady Chapel was begun (1321) and the tower over the Norman crossing collapsed (1322) and was replaced by the celebrated octagon. From the documents it is almost certain that the bold idea of replacing the square crossing tower by a larger octagon was his. (For illustration *see* OCTAGON.)

Lit: J. Evans, *English Art 1307–1461,* Oxford 1949; J. Harvey, *English Medieval Architects,* London 1954.

Álava, *see* JUAN DE ÁLAVA.

Alberti, Leone Battista (1404–72). Playwright, musician, painter, mathematician, scientist, and athlete as well as architect and architectural theorist, he came nearer than anyone to the Renaissance ideal of a 'complete man'. Aristocratic by temperament, he was the first great dilettante architect. He confined himself to designing, and had nothing to do with the actual building of his works. But his few buildings are all masterpieces, and his *De re aedificatoria* (1452, fully published 1485) is the first architectural treatise of the Renaissance. It crystallized current ideas on proportion, the orders, and ideal (symbolic) town planning. But though he began with theory his buildings are surprisingly unpedantic and undogmatic. They progressed from the nostalgically archaeological to the boldly experimental. Perhaps his dilettante status allowed him greater freedom than his professional contemporaries. He designed only six buildings and saw only three of them completed. To some extent he was indebted to BRUNELLESCHI, whom he knew personally and to whom (among others) he dedicated his treatise *Della pittura* (1436), but whereas Brunelleschi's buildings were elegantly linear Alberti's were massively plastic. Architectural beauty he defined as 'the harmony and concord of all the parts achieved in such a manner that nothing could be added, or taken away, or altered except for the worse' and ornament as 'a kind of additional brightness and improvement of Beauty'. By ornament he meant the classical vocabulary of orders, columns, pilasters, and architraves which he always used correctly and grammatically but frequently out of context, e.g., his columns always support architraves (not arches), but are frequently merely decorative and without real structural purpose. His most notable and influential achievement was the adaptation of classical elements to the wall architecture of the Renaissance.

The illegitimate son of a Florentine exile, he was probably born in Genoa. Educated in the humanist atmosphere of Padua, he later studied law at Bologna university and visited Florence for the first time in 1428. In 1431 he went to Rome, where he joined the Papal civil service which apparently allowed him ample time for both travel and the cultivation of his various talents. As Papal inspector of monuments (1447–55) he 'restored' (with Rossellino) the C5 circular church of S. Stefano Rotondo, Rome. His first independent work appears to have been the façade of Palazzo Rucellai, Florence (executed by Bernardo ROSSELLINO and completed before 1460). With rusticated walls articulated by three superimposed orders of pilasters (Ionic and Corinthian very freely interpreted), it is indebted to Brunelleschi's Palazzo di Parte Guelfa. But it has certain novelties, e.g., square-headed door-cases, a vast cornice in-

stead of eaves, and double windows with pilasters and a central column supporting an architrave beneath the rounded cap. The exquisite adjustment of the proportions distinguishes the palace from that designed and built in emulation of it at Pienza by Rossellino. In 1450 he was commissioned to transform the Gothic church of S. Francesco, Rimini, into a memorial to the local tyrant Sigismondo Malatesta, his wife, and courtiers. It was subsequently called the Tempio Malatestiano. He designed a marble shell to encase the old building, the front freely based on a Roman triumphal arch (symbolizing the triumph over death), the side walls pierced by deep arched niches each containing a sarcophagus. The front was never finished, and it is now difficult to visualize how he intended to mask the upper part of the old Gothic façade. As it stands it is a magnificent fragment, one of the noblest and most poignant evocations of the grandeur, *gravitas*, and decorum of Roman architecture. His next work was another addition to a Gothic church, the completion of the façade of S. Maria Novella, Florence (1456–70). Entirely coated with an inlay of different coloured marbles, it owes as much to the C11–12 church of S. Miniato, Florence, as to any Roman building, though the central doorway is derived from the Pantheon. But the whole design is based on a complex geometrical arrangement of squares, and is the first instance of the use of HARMONIC PROPORTIONS in the Renaissance. The upper part of the façade is in the form of a pedimented temple front linked to the sides by great scrolls which were to be much copied in later periods. It was commissioned by Giovanni Rucellai whose name is inscribed across the top with typical Renaissance confidence. For the same patron he designed the exquisite, casket-like little marble-clad shrine of the Holy Sepulchre (1467) and perhaps also the Cappella Rucellai, Florence, in which it stands.

S. Sebastiano (1460) and S. Andrea (1470), both at Mantua, are the only buildings which he designed entire. For S. Sebastiano he chose a centralized Greek cross plan and designed the massively austere façade as a pilastered temple front approached up a wide flight of steps. But he broke the entablature with a round-headed window (derived from the Roman arch of Tiberius at Orange, *c.* 30 B.C.) and increased its severity by reducing the pilasters from six to four. This alteration and his complete rejection of columns marks his increasing tendency to stray from correct classical usage in the creation of a more logical wall architecture. The church was completed, with further alterations, after his death. At S. Andrea his plans were carried out more faithfully, though the dome he designed to cover the crossing was never executed. The façade is a combination of a pedimented temple front and a triumphal arch, with shallow pilasters in place of columns and a deep central recess framing the main door. Inside he abandoned the traditional aisle structure for a barrel-vaulted nave flanked by side chapels. Interior and exterior are carefully integrated. The sides of the nave, with pilastered solids and arched recesses alternating, repeat the rhythmical pattern and the triumphal arch of the façade on exactly the same scale. These two buildings herald a new and less archaeological attitude to antiquity. They reach forward from the Early to the High Renaissance and even beyond. (For illustrations *see* ITALIAN ARCHITECTURE and RENAISSANCE ARCHITECTURE.)

Lit: M. L. Gengaro, *L. B. Alberti*, Milan 1939; P. Portoghesi (ed.), *L. B. Alberti, L'Architettura (De re aedificatoria)*, Milan 1966; J. Gadol, *Leon Battista Alberti, Universal Man of the Early Renaissance*, Chicago–London 1969; L. H. Heydenreich & W. Lotz, *Architecture in Italy 1400–1600*, Pelican History of Art, Harmondsworth 1974.

Albini, Franco (b. 1905). Studied and lives at Milan. His interior of the Palazzo Bianco Museum at Genoa and of the treasury of Genoa Cathedral (1951 and 1954) establish him as one of the most brilliant display architects of the century. His principal building is the Rinascente department store in Rome (1961).

Aldrich, Henry (1647–1710). Dean of Christ Church, Oxford, he was a *virtuoso* and architect of distinction. Only two buildings are known to be certainly by him, or largely by him: All Saints, Oxford (1706–10, but revised 1717–20 by Hawksmoor whom Aldrich knew) and Peckwater Quad, Christ Church, Oxford (1705–6, built by William Townesend 1706–14). The former derives from WREN, the latter from Inigo JONES, and both display considerable originality. Peckwater Quad is a remarkable early example of Palladianism. Aldrich also proposed the building of Christ Church Library but the designs were recast by George Clarke (1661–1736) after Aldrich's death. The Fellows' Building, Corpus Christi College (1706–12) has been attributed to Aldrich. He wrote a treatise on Vitruvius and

Palladio which was published posthumously in 1750 as *Elementa Architecturae Civilis*. An English translation by the Rev. P. Smyth was published in 1789.

Lit: H. M. Colvin, *Biographical Dictionary of English Architects, 1660–1840*, London 1954.

Aleijadinho (António Francisco Lisboa, 1738–1814). The greatest Brazilian sculptor and architect. A mulatto (illegitimate son of a Portuguese architect), he worked in the rich goldmining province of Minas Gerais, and combined barbarically rich and contorted sculptural decoration with the more dignified architectural forms of traditional Lusitanian church design. His masterpieces are São Francisco, Ouro Preto (1766–94), and the monumental scenic staircase in front of Bom Jesus de Matozinhos, Congonhas do Campo (1800–5). (For illustration *see* BRAZILIAN ARCHITECTURE.)

Lit: G. Kubler and M. Soria, *Art and Architecture in Spain and Portugal and their American Dominions 1500–1800*, Pelican History of Art, Harmondsworth 1959.

Aleotti, Giovanni Battista (1546–1636). He was an early Baroque architect who began his career by working for twenty-two years (1575–97) as an engineer in the service of Alfonso II d'Este at Ferrara. During this period he published writings on hydraulics and also wrote a treatise on architecture (1581, unpublished). His first important building was the hexagonal S. Maria del Quartiere (1604) in Parma. For Ferrara he designed the theatre for the Accademia degli Intrepidi (1606, destroyed 1679), the imposing University façade (1610) and the elliptical S. Carlo (1623). But his masterpiece, begun when he was more than 70 years old, is the Teatro Farnese in Parma (1618–28, damaged during World War II but restored). It exceeds PALLADIO's Teatro Olimpico in both size and magnificence and has an open rectangular proscenium arch and a revolutionary U-shaped auditorium. It foreshadowed later developments in Baroque theatre design.

Lit: David R. Coffin in *Journal of Soc. of Archi. Historians*, October 1962.

Alessi, Galeazzo (1512–72). The leading High Renaissance architect in Genoa and Milan. Born in Perugia and trained in Rome where he was much influenced by MICHELANGELO, he settled in Genoa by 1548. He was adept at turning difficult sloping sites to advantage, and made great play with monumental staircases, colonnades, and courtyards on different levels. His several palaces, notably Villa Cambiaso (1548), Palazzo Cambiaso (1565, now Banco d'Italia), and Palazzo Parodi (1567), set the pattern for Genoese domestic architecture. He also built the imposing S. Maria di Carignano, Genoa (1549–52), based on BRAMANTE'S design for St Peter's. In Milan he designed Palazzo Marino (1558), now the Municipio, of which the courtyard is outstanding. The *salone maggiore* is also remarkable but was damaged in 1943 and is heavily restored. (The façade facing Piazza della Scala is by Luca Beltrami, 1889.) Other works by him in Milan include SS. Paolo e Barnaba (1561–7) and the façade of S. Maria presso S. Celso (completed by Martino Bassi after he left Milan in 1569).

Lit: E. Negri, *Galeazzo Alessi a Genova*, Genoa 1957; N. A. Houghton Brown, 'The Church of S. Barnaba in Milan' in *Arte Lembarda*, 1964, pp. 62–93, 1965, pp. 65–98.

Alfieri, Benedetto (1700–67), a Piedmontese nobleman (uncle of the poet), began as a lawyer, turned to architecture, and succeeded JUVARRA as royal architect in Turin (1739). He was largely employed in completing Juvarra's work in Palazzo Reale, Turin, and elsewhere. His main independent building is the vast parish church at Carignano (1757–64), with a severe façade and very rich interior on a peculiar kidney-shaped plan. His Royal Theatre at Turin (1738–40, destroyed) introduced the horse-shoe shaped auditorium. He also designed the noble west portico at Geneva Cathedral in a surprisingly radical classicizing style (1752–6).

Lit: R. Pommer, *Eighteenth Century Architecture in Piedmont*, New York–London 1967.

Algardi, Alessandro (1595–1654). Born in Bologna but settled in Rome, best known as a sculptor, representing the sobriety of Bolognese classicism in opposition to BERNINI. His reputation as an architect rests on the Villa Doria-Pamphili in Rome of which he had the general direction, though it seems to have been designed by G. F. Grimaldi.

Lit: R. Wittkower, *Art and Architecture in Italy, 1600–1750*, Pelican History of Art, 3rd edn, Harmondsworth 1973, paperback edn 1973.

Almonry The room in a MONASTERY in which alms are distributed.

Altar A structure on which to place or sacrifice offerings to a deity. In Greece and Rome altars took many different forms. The Christian altar is a table or slab on supports consecrated for celebration of the sacrament; usually of stone. In the Middle Ages portable altars could be of metal. After the Reformation communion tables of wood replaced altars in England.

Pergamon altar, 300 B.C.

Sarcophagus type of altar

Altar-tomb A post-medieval term for a tomb resembling an altar with solid sides but not used as one. *See* TOMB-CHEST.

Altar frontal, *see* ANTEPENDIUM.

Amadeo, Giovanni Antonio (1447–1522). Born in Pavia, and primarily a sculptor, he was working at the Certosa there by 1466; then he worked in Milan (MICHELOZZO'S Portinari Chapel in S. Eustorgio), where he encountered the Early Renaissance style. The immediate result was the Colleoni Chapel (1470–73) attached to S. Maria Maggiore, Bergamo – based on the Portinari Chapel but encrusted with Renaissance ornamentation in Gothic profusion. He designed the lower storey of the façade of the Certosa outside Pavia (1474) in a similar manner. From 1487/90 onwards he worked on Milan Cathedral (retardataire Gothic in style).

Lit: E. Arslan in *Dizionario Biografico degli Italiani*, Rome 1960.

Ambo A stand raised on two or more steps, for the reading of the Epistle and the Gospel;

Ambo, with Paschal Candlestick in foreground: S. Pietro, Sessa Aurunca near Naples, c. 1250

a prominent feature in medieval Italian churches. Sometimes two were built, one for the Epistle and one for the Gospel, on the south and north sides respectively. After the C14 the ambo was replaced by the PULPIT.

Ambulatory A semicircular or polygonal aisle enclosing an APSE or a straight-ended sanctuary; originally used for processional purposes.

Ammanati, Bartolomeo (1511–92), was primarily a Mannerist sculptor. His architectural masterpiece is the very graceful Ponte S. Trinità, Florence (1558–70, destroyed 1944 but rebuilt). With VIGNOLA and VASARI he played some part in designing Villa Giulia, Rome (1551–5). He enlarged and altered Palazzo Pitti, Florence (1558–70), building the almost grotesquely over-rusticated garden façade (1560). He completed Palazzo Grifoni, Florence (1557) and supervised the building of MICHELANGELO's vestibule stairway in the Laurenziana, Florence. Outside Florence, he designed the Tempietto della Vittoria, near Arezzo (1572). In Lucca he designed part of the Palazzo Provinciale (1578) with a handsome Serlian loggia.

Lit: M. Fossi, *B. Ammanati*, Florence 1967.

Amphiprostyle The adjective applied to a temple with porticos at each end, but without columns along the sides.

Amphitheatre An elliptical or circular space surrounded by rising tiers of seats, as used by the Romans for gladiatorial contests, e.g., the Colosseum, Rome.

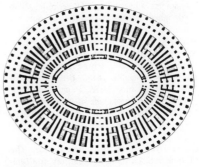

Amphitheatre, Capua, c. 200 B.C.

Colosseum, Rome, A.D. 73–80.

Anathyrosis The smooth marginal dressing of the outer contact band of a masonry joint, the central portion being left roughened and sunk so as to avoid contact.

Ancones 1. Brackets or CONSOLES on either side of a doorway, supporting a CORNICE. 2. The projections left on blocks of stone, such as the drums of a column, to hoist them into position.

Andrea di Cioni, *see* ORCAGNA.

Andrea Pisano, *see* PISANO, Nicola.

Angkor, *see* SOUTH-EAST ASIAN ARCHITECTURE.

Anglo-Saxon architecture, *see* ENGLISH ARCHITECTURE.

Angular capital An IONIC capital with all four sides alike, and the volutes turned outwards as in a Corinthian capital. A C16 innovation, probably due to SCAMOZZI and frequently employed until the late C18 when rejected as incorrect.

Annulet, *see* SHAFT-RING.

Anse de panier, *see* ARCH.

Anta A PILASTER of which the base and CAPITAL do not conform with the ORDER used elsewhere on the building; it is usually placed at the ends of the projecting walls of a portico.

Antechurch (or **forechurch**). An appendix to the west end of a church, resembling a porch or a NARTHEX, but several bays deep and usually consisting of nave and aisles.

Antefixae Ornamental blocks on the edge of a roof to conceal the ends of the tiles.

Etruscan antefixa, c. 500 B.C.

Antelami, Benedetto (active 1177–1233), a sculptor and probably an architect. Attributed to him are the Parma Baptistery (begun in 1196), the cathedral of Borgo San Donnino (1179 etc., chiefly 1214–18) and S. Andrea at Vercelli. This church already has features pointing in the direction of the French Gothic. The transition from Romanesque to Gothic is obvious in his sculpture.

Lit: G. de Francovich, *Benedetto Antelami,* Milan 1952; P. Toesca, *Il Battistero di Parma,* Milan 1960; K. W. Forster, *Benedetto Antelami,* Munich 1961.

Antependium A covering for the front of an altar, usually of metal or fabric.

Anthemion Ornament based on the honeysuckle flower and leaves, common in Greek and Roman architecture.

Anthemion ornament: Erechtheion, Athens, 421–406 B.C.

Anthemios of Tralles Geometrician and theorist rather than architect, he is known for sure to have designed only one building, but that among the greatest in the world: Hagia Sophia, Constantinople (A.D. 532–7). The dates of his birth and death are unknown. Born at Tralles in Lydia, he came of a Greek professional middle-class family; his father was a physician. In 532 Justinian chose him to design the new church of Holy Wisdom (Hagia Sophia) to replace a predecessor which had been burnt in riots. This vast undertaking was completed in the incredibly brief period of five years, to the gratification of Justinian who claimed to have surpassed Solomon. Anthemios described architecture as 'the application of geometry to solid matter', and his great work with its dome 107 ft in diameter is remarkable as a feat of engineering (even though the dome collapsed in 558). But it is also much more, for by the cunning use of screened aisles and galleries around the central area of the church he concealed the supports of the dome which thus seems to float above the building, creating an atmosphere of mystery emphasized by the contrast between the light central space and the dark aisles. He was assisted by ISIDORUS OF MILETUS.

Lit: R. Krautheimer, *Early Christian and Byzantine Architecture,* Pelican History of Art, Harmondsworth 1965, paperback edn 1974.

Anticlastic Of a surface, having curvatures in opposite senses (concave and convex) in different directions through any point, e.g. as in a HYPERBOLIC PARABOLOID ROOF.

Antis, In, *see* PORTICO.

Antoine, Jacques-Denis (1733–1801). A leading architect in the reign of Louis XVI. His masterpiece is the Mint, Paris (designed 1768, begun 1771) – huge, solemn, and very Roman, though he did not visit Italy until 1777. He used Paestum Doric for the peristyle of the Hôpital de la Charité, Paris (*c.* 1785), but his other works are less sternly neo-classical, e.g. the Palais de Justice, Paris (1778–85).

Lit: L. Hautecoeur, *Histoire de l'architecture classique en France,* vol. iv, Paris 1952.

Antonelli, Alessandro (1798–1888). Professor of Architecture at Turin from 1836 till 1857. His most famous works are the crazily high, externally classical and internally iron-supported tower of the so-called Mole Antonelliana at Turin (originally intended as a syna-gogue and about 550 ft high) and the tower of the cathedral of Novara (about 420 ft high). The former was designed in 1863, the latter in 1840.

Lit: P. Portoghesi in *Dizionario Biografico degli Italiani,* Rome 1961; C. L. V. Meeks, *Italian Architecture 1750–1914,* New Haven 1966.

Antonio da Ponte, *see* BRIDGE.

Apadana (Apadhana) In Ancient Persia a free-standing columned hall apparently serv-ing as a throne-room. Outstanding was the hundred-columned apadana built in Persepolis under Darius I (*see* PERSIAN ARCHITECTURE). The apadana often had a portico, and was itself mostly square in plan.

Apex stone The top stone in a GABLE end, sometimes called the *saddle stone.*

Apollodorus of Damascus (active A.D. 97–130). Born in Syria, he went to Rome and became official architect to Trajan (A.D. 97–117), accompanying him on his military campaigns and designing or inspiring almost all the buildings erected under him. His first recorded work is the stone-and-wood bridge over the Danube at Dobreta (A.D. 104). But his masterpieces were naturally in Rome itself: an odeon circular in plan (probably that built by Domitian in the Campus Martius), the Baths of Trajan, and Trajan's Forum. The latter, with its imposing axial planning and subtle play of symmetry, illustrates his style, a brilliant compromise between the Hellenistic and the pure Roman traditions. He also planned the markets at the extreme end of the Quirinal hill, and was probably involved in work at the port of Rome (Fiumicino) and at Civitavecchia. The triumphal arches at An-cona and Benevento have been attributed to him. Though he was on less happy terms with

Hadrian, he collaborated with him on at least one project, and dedicated to him his treatise on the construction of engines of assault, *Poliorketa.* But, according to Dio Cassius, Hadrian banished him from Rome in about A.D. 130, and later condemned him to death because of his harsh criticism of the Temple of Venus and Rome.

Lit: W. L. MacDonald, *The Architecture of the Roman Empire,* New Haven 1965; A. Boethius & J. Ward-Perkins, *Etruscan and Roman Architecture,* Pelican History of Art, Harmondsworth 1970.

Apophyge The slight curve at the top and bottom of a column where the SHAFT joins the CAPITAL or base.

Applied column, *see* ENGAGED COLUMN.

Apron A raised panel below a window-sill, sometimes shaped and decorated.

Apse Roman in origin (found in both religious and secular contexts), an apse is a usually semicircular extension to, or ending of, an-other structure, with a rounded vault. In Early Christian basilicas, the place of the clergy (PRESBYTERY) and bishop was here; it was frequently elevated, with a passage under

Apse: St Étienne, Nevers, 1063–97

the seating (Hagia Irene, Constantinople). In the ninth century, a bay was inserted between apse and TRANSEPT, reducing the former to an adjunct of the CHANCEL. AISLES might also terminate in apses, as could transepts. Double-ended churches would have a *counter-apse.* With the twelfth century, broken-ended CHEVETS became commoner; ultimately the Gothic urge toward spatial amalgamation abolished the distinction between chancel and apse in favour of a deep polygonal- or square-ended choir. *See also* CONCH, EXEDRA.

Apteral An adjective describing a classical-style building with columns at the end, but not along the sides.

Aqueduct An artificial channel for carrying water, usually an elevated masonry or brick structure; invented by the Romans.
Lit: T. Ashby, *The Aqueducts of Ancient Rome*, London 1935.

Aqueduct: Pont du Gard near Nîmes, A.D. *14*

Arabesque Intricate and fanciful surface decoration generally based on geometrical patterns and using combinations of flowing lines, tendrils, etc., covering the surface with a network of zigzags, spirals, etc. Human figures were not used. (They were in GROTESQUE decorations.)
Lit: P. Ward-Jackson in *Victoria & Albert Museum Bulletin*, 1967.

Arabesque design by
Hans Manuel Deutsch, c. 1549

Araeostyle With an arrangement of columns spaced four diameters apart. *See also* DIASTYLE; EUSTYLE; PYCNOSTYLE; SYSTYLE.

Arcade A range of arches carried on PIERS or columns, either free-standing or blind, i.e.,

Arcaded courtyard: Casa de Pilato,
Seville, c15–c16

Blind arcade: S. Giovanni Fuorcivitas,
Pistoia, late c12

attached to a wall. Also a covered shopping street, e.g. Burlington Arcade in Piccadilly. Some very large shopping arcades were built in c19 Italy, notably by MENGONI. They are called *Gallerie* in Italian, *Passagen* in German.
Lit: J. F. Geist, *Passagen: ein Bautyp des 19 Jhs*, Munich 1969.

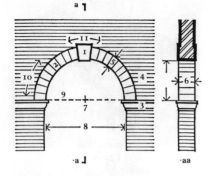

Arch *Anse de panier* is a French term for an arch whose curve resembles that of the handle of a basket; also called *basket arch*. It is formed by a segment of a large circle continued left and right by two segments of much smaller circles.

Basket arch or *three-centred arch, see above.*

Discharging arch, see relieving arch.

A *drop arch* is pointed with a span greater than its radii.

An *elliptical arch* is a half ellipse from a centre on the springing line.

Equilateral arch, see pointed arch.

A *false arch* is one constructed by progressive cantilevering or corbelling from the two sides with horizontal joints.

A *four-centred or depressed arch* is a late medieval form – a pointed arch of four arcs, the two outer and lower ones springing from centres on the SPRINGING LINE, the two inner and upper arcs from centres below the springing line.

A *horseshoe arch* is often found in Islamic buildings; it can be either a pointed or a round horseshoe.

Arch

1. Keystone
2. Voussoirs
3. Impost
4. Abutment

5. Extrados
6. Intrados or soffit
7. Centre
8. Span
9. Springing line
10. Haunch
11. Crown

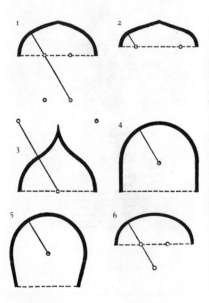

Arches:
1. Four-centred
2. Tudor
3. Ogee
4. Stilted
5. Horseshoe
6. Basket
7. Lancet

Horseshoe arch: Mosque at Cordova, 786–990

A *lancet arch* is pointed, with radii much larger than the span.

An *ogee arch* is pointed and usually of four arcs, the centres of two inside the arch, of the other two outside; this produces a compound curve of two parts, one convex and the other concave. Introduced *c.* 1300 this arch was popular throughout the late Middle Ages and in England especially in the early c14.

A *pointed arch* is produced by two curves, each with a radius equal to the span and meeting in a point at the top; also called an *equilateral arch.*

A *relieving arch* is usually of rough construction placed in a wall, above an arch or any opening, to relieve it of much of the superincumbent weight; also called a *discharging arch.*

A *segmental arch* is a segment of a circle drawn from a centre below the springing line.

A *shouldered arch* consists of a lintel connected with the jambs of a doorway by corbels. The corbels start with a concave quadrant and continue vertically to meet the lintel.

A *stilted arch* has its springing line raised by vertical piers above the IMPOST level.

A *strainer arch* is one inserted, in most cases, across a nave or an aisle to prevent the walls from leaning.

A *Tudor arch* is a late medieval pointed arch whose shanks start with a curve near to a quarter circle and continue to the apex in a straight line.

Archer, Thomas (1668–1743). The only English Baroque architect to have studied continental Baroque at first hand. His buildings are unique in England in showing an intimate appreciation of BERNINI and BORROMINI. He came of good family and made a four-year

Grand Tour after Oxford, returning home about 1693. A Whig, he was successful at Court and in 1703 obtained the lucrative post of Groom Porter. His buildings date between then and 1715, when he acquired the even more profitable post of Controller of Customs at Newcastle, whereupon he gave up architecture. The north front of Chatsworth (1704–5) and the garden pavilion at Wrest Park (1711–12) are his best surviving secular buildings, but his reputation rests mainly on his three churches – Birmingham Cathedral (1710–15); St Paul, Deptford, London (1712–30); and St John, Smith Square, London (1714–28), with its spectacular and much-maligned towers. Heythrop House, Oxon, was his most grandiloquent effort but it was burnt down and rebuilt 1870.

Lit: M. Whiffen, *Thomas Archer,* London 1950; K. Downes, *English Baroque Architecture,* London 1966.

Architects Co-Partnership A group of English architects born about 1915–17. Their principal works include: a factory at Bryn Mawr in Wales (1949); a range of students' sets for St John's College, Oxford (1956–9); a range of sets for King's College, Cambridge (1960–2); a school at Ripley, Derbyshire (1958–60) and other schools; housing at Ikoyi, Lagos (1957–9); and the Biochemistry Building of the Imperial College, London (1961–4).

Lit: M. Webb, *Architecture in Britain Today,* London 1969; R. Maxwell, *New British Architecture,* London 1972.

Architrave: Temple of Poseidon, Paestum, 500 B.C.

Architrave: Archaic temple, Naxos

Architrave The lowest of the three main parts of an ENTABLATURE; also, more loosely, the moulded frame surrounding a door or window (if this frame turns away at the top at right angles, rises vertically and returns horizontally, forming a shoulder, it is called a *shouldered architrave*). (Illustrated previous page; for further illustrations *see* DOOR, ENTABLATURE, ORDER.)

Architrave-cornice An ENTABLATURE from which the FRIEZE is elided.

Archivolt The continuous architrave moulding on the face of an arch, following its contour; also the INTRADOS or under-side of an arch.

Archivolt: Main portal,
Bamberg Cathedral, early c13

Arcuated A term applied to a building dependent structurally on the use of arches or the arch principle, in contrast to a TRABEATED building.

Arena The central open space of an AMPHITHEATRE; also, more loosely, any building for public contests or displays in the open air.

Ariss, John, the first professional architect in North America, emigrated from England in or shortly before 1751, when he advertised in the *Maryland Gazette* as being 'lately from Great Britain' and ready to undertake 'Buildings of all Sorts and Dimensions . . . either of the Ancient or Modern Order of Gibbs, Architect'.

Unfortunately his work is unrecorded, but some of the finer Virginian houses were probably designed by him, e.g., Mount Airey, Richmond County (1755–8); they are English Palladian, with Gibbsian overtones.

Lit: M. Morrison, *Early American Architecture*, New York 1952.

Ark, *see* ECHAL.

Arnolfo di Cambio A Florentine sculptor and mason of the later c13 (d. 1302?). Assistant of Nicola PISANO in 1266, he is already called a *subtilissimus magister* in 1277. He signed works of decorative architecture and sculpture combined in 1282, 1285, and 1293. The architectural forms used are truly Gothic, aware of French precedent, and include trefoil-headed and trefoil-cusped arches. In 1296 the new cathedral of Florence was begun; Arnolfo was master mason. His design is recognizable in the nave and aisles, but the present centralizing east end with its three polygonal apses is Talenti's, though it only enlarged and pushed considerably farther east the east end as intended by Arnolfo, perhaps under the influence of Cologne. It is curious that Arnolfo, in the earliest source referring to him (though as late as *c.* 1520), is called a German. Several other buildings have been attributed to Arnolfo, among them, with convincing arguments, S. Croce (begun 1295) and the Florentine Badia (begun 1284).

Lit: W. Paatz, *Die Kirchen von Florenz*, vols I–VI, Frankfurt 1940–45; H. Saalman, 'Santa Maria del Fiore, 1294–1418' in *Art Bulletin*, 1964, pp. 472–500; W. Braunfels, *Der Dom von Florenz*, Olten 1964; J. White, *Art and Architecture in Italy*, *1250–1400*, Pelican History of Art, Harmondsworth 1966; A. M. Romanini, *Arnolfo di Cambio*, Milan 1969.

Arris A sharp edge produced by the meeting of two surfaces.

Arruda, Diogo (active 1508–31). The leading practitioner of the MANUELINE STYLE in Portugal. His main work is the nave and chapterhouse of the Cristo Church, Tomar (1510–14), with its almost surrealist sculptured decoration: sails and ropes around the circular windows, mouldings of cork floats threaded on cables, buttresses carved with patterns of coral and seaweed. His brother **Francisco** (active 1510–47) was mainly a military architect, but built the exotic, almost Hindu, tower at Belem (1515–20).

Lit: F. Chueca Goitia, *Arquitectura del siglo XVI* (*Ars Hispaniae*, vol. XI), Madrid 1953; G. Kubler & M. Soria, *Art and Architecture in Spain and Portugal and their American Dominions, 1500–1800*, Pelican History of Art, Harmondsworth 1959.

Art Nouveau The name of a shop opened in Paris in 1895 to sell objects of modern, i.e., non-period-imitation, style. The movement away from imitation of the past had started in book production and textiles in England in the 1880s (*see* MACKMURDO), and had begun to invade furniture and other furnishings about 1890. Stylistically, the origins lay in the designs of William MORRIS and the

The Willow Tea-rooms, Glasgow, 1904, by Mackintosh

Interior of 4 Avenue Palmerston, Brussels, 1894, by Horta

Havana cigar shop, Berlin, 1899, by van de Velde

English Arts and Crafts Movement. One of the principal centres from 1892 onwards was Brussels (*see* HORTA, van de VELDE). In France the two centres were Nancy, where in Émile Gallé glass Art Nouveau forms occurred as early as the 1880s, and Paris. Art Nouveau forms are characterized by the ubiquitous use of undulation like waves or flames or flower stalks or flowing hair. Some artists kept close to nature, others, especially van de Velde, preferred abstract forms as being a purer expression of the dynamics aimed at. The most

Casa Milá, Barcelona, 1905–10, by Gaudí

important representative of Art Nouveau in America is Louis C. Tiffany (1848–1933), in Germany Hermann Obrist (1863–1927) and

August Endell (1871-1925). In architecture by far the greatest is GAUDÍ. It has rightly been pointed out that Art Nouveau has a source and certainly a parallel in the paintings and graphic works of Gauguin, Munch, and some others. The climax in Britain and at the same time the beginning of the end, is the work of Charles R. MACKINTOSH of Glasgow, in whose architecture and decoration the slender curves and the subtle opalescent colours of Art Nouveau blend with a new rectangular crispness and pure whiteness of framework. Vienna took this up at once, and found from it the way into the twentieth-century emphasis on the square and the cube (*see* LOOS, HOFFMANN *and* LECHNER). Art Nouveau was called *Jugendstil* in Germany and Austria, *Stile Liberty* or *Floreale* in Italy.

Lit: J. Schmutzler, *Art Nouveau*, London 1962.

Arup, Sir Ove (b. 1895). Studied Philosophy before graduating in Engineering in Copenhagen in 1922. Engaged first in civil engineering and then became involved in architecture, working with Lubetkin in London to produce Highpoint, the Penguin Pool and Finsbury Health Centre, where he applied new ideas of concrete construction and pioneered the use of load-bearing concrete walls. His own consulting practice has become known for its fresh approach to the solution of difficult structural problems, and he has collaborated closely with leading architects in England and overseas, notably with Utzon for Sydney Opera House (1956-73). A parallel partnership of architects and engineers, led by Philip Dowson, Ronald Hobbs and others, was formed in 1963. This multi-professional team aims to practise close collaboration between professions. It has been responsible for Point Royal, Bracknell, buildings for Corpus Christi, Cambridge, and Somerville, Oxford, the Mining and Metallurgy Departments at Birmingham University and the buildings for CIBA at Duxford, and Smith, Kline & French at Welwyn.

Asam, Cosmas Damian (1686-1739) and **Egid Quirin** (1692-1750), were brothers who always worked together as architects though sometimes separately as decorators (Cosmas Damian was a fresco-painter and Egid Quirin a sculptor). Sons of a Bavarian mason, they did not emerge from provincial obscurity until after visiting Rome (1711-14), where they studied under Carlo FONTANA. As a result of this Roman training they remained essentially Baroque rather than Rococo architects. They seem to have admired the juicier C17 Italians rather than their elegant and frivolous contemporaries. They decorated many important churches (e.g., Weingarten; Einsiedeln; St Jacobi, Innsbruck; Fürstenfeldbruck; Osterhofen; Freising Cathedral; St Maria Victoria, Ingolstadt; Aldersbach), but designed and built only four, in which, however, they carried to unprecedented lengths the melodramatic effects of concealed lighting, spatial illusionism, and other tricks which they had picked up in Rome. Their emotionalism is seen at its wildest in the fantastic *tableau vivant* altar-pieces at Rohr (1717-25) and Weltenburg (1717-21). They attempted something better in St John Nepomuk, Munich (1733-46), a church which is attached to their house and was entirely paid for by them. This is a tiny but sensational church, a masterpiece of German Baroque in which architecture and decoration are successfully combined to achieve an intense atmosphere of religious fervour. Their last work, the Ursulinenkirche, Straubing (1736-41), is almost equally good. (For illustration *see* SWISS ARCHITECTURE.)

Lit: A. Feulner, *Die Asam-Kirche in München*, Munich 1932; H. R. Hitchcock, *Rococo Architecture in Southern Germany*, London 1968.

Ashbee, Charles Robert (1863-1942). More a social reformer than an architect. His model was MORRIS. In 1888 he founded his Guild and School of Handicraft in the East End of London. The guild moved into the country, to Chipping Campden, in 1902. The First World War killed it. His best architectural designs are two houses in Cheyne Walk, London (1899).

Ashlar Hewn blocks of masonry wrought to even faces and square edges and laid in horizontal courses with vertical joints, as opposed to rubble or unhewn stone straight from the quarry.

Asplund, Gunnar (1885-1940), the most important Swedish architect of the twentieth century, started in the Scandinavian classicism first developed by the Danes; his principal work in that style is the Stockholm City Library (1920-8) with its high circular reading room rising as a drum above the rest of the *ensemble*. With his work for the Stock-

holm Exhibition of 1930 he changed to the
Central European Modern, but instead of treating it in the relatively massive manner then
current, he lightened up his forms by means
of thin metal members, much glass, and some
freer forms of roof, etc., thereby endowing the
style with a grace and translucency which
had a great international impact. But Asplund
was never demonstrative or aggressive. His
buildings always observe a noble restraint.
The finest of them are the extension of the
Town Hall of Göteborg (1934–7), with its
beautifully transparent courtyard, and the
Stockholm Crematorium (1935–40), which
may well be called the most perfect example
of genuine c20 monumentality and religious
architecture in existence. (For illustration *see*
SCANDINAVIAN ARCHITECTURE.)

   Lit: G. Holmdahl, S. I. Lund & K. Odeen,
Asplund Arkitekt, 1885–1940, Stockholm
1943; B. Zevi, *E. Gunnar Asplund*, Milan 1948.

Asprucci, Antonio (1723–1808). A notable
early neo-classical architect in Rome. His
masterpiece is the interior of Villa Borghese,
Rome (1777–84), and the elegant temples,
sham ruins, and other follies in the park.
   Lit: C. L. V. Meeks, *Italian Architecture
1750–1914*, New Haven 1966.

Assyrian architecture, *see* SUMERIAN AND
AKKADIAN ARCHITECTURE.

Astragal A small moulding circular in section,
often decorated with a bead and reel enrichment. (For another illustration *see* ENTABLA-
TURE.)

Astragal

Astylar A term applied to a façade without
columns or pilasters.

Atlantes Supports in the form of carved male
figures, used especially by German Baroque
architects instead of columns to support an
ENTABLATURE. The Roman term is *telamones*.
(Illustrated next column.) *See also* CARYATID.

Atrium 1. In Roman domestic architecture,
an inner court open to the sky and surrounded
by the roof. 2. In Early Christian and medieval
architecture, an open court in front of a
church; usually a colonnaded quadrangle.

*Atlantes: Upper Belvedere, Vienna,
by Hildebrandt, 1720–24*

Attached column, *see* ENGAGED COLUMN.

Attic base The base of an IONIC column consisting of two large rings of convex mouldings
(the lower of greater diameter) joined by a
spreading concave moulding, used in Athens
in the c5 and c4 B.C.

Attic base

Attic storey 1. A storey above the main
ENTABLATURE of a building and in strictly

*Attic storey: Palazzo Madama, Turin, 1718–21,
by Juvarra*

architectural relation to it, as, e.g., in Roman triumphal arches. 2. Also, more loosely, the space within the sloping roof of a house or the upper storey of a building if less high than the others.

Aumbry (or **ambry**) A cupboard or recess used to keep sacred vessels in.

Austrian architecture Austria originated in the Ostmark (Eastern Marches) established in 803 by Charlemagne after he had subdued the Bavarians in 788. When the Hungarian invasion had been halted (955), the Ostmark was renewed and remained in the hands of the Babenberg dynasty from 976 to 1246. After that Austria passed to the Habsburgs. The archbishopric of Salzburg was created in 789; additional bishoprics came much later: Gurk in 1070, Seckau in 1218, and Vienna only in 1480.

Of pre-Romanesque architecture in Austria little is known. Salzburg Cathedral (767-74) was, according to excavations, nearly 200 ft long and had a straightforward Early Christian basilica plan with one apse. The Romanesque style is an interesting mixture of elements from Bavaria and Lombardy, although West Germany (especially Hirsau, the centre of Cluniac architecture for Germany) and even France also play a part. Bavarian influence means basilican churches with pillars (Hirsau stood for columns – see St Paul im Lavanttal in Austria), no transepts, and three parallel apses, while Lombardy was the source of much of the best decoration; it is to be found at Klosterneuburg (1114-33), Gurk (1140s-c.

Church at Gurk, 1140s-c. 1200

1200; crypt of a hundred marble columns), Millstatt, and even the portal of St Peter at Salzburg (c. 1240). Another source of ornament was Normandy (zigzag, etc.) via Worms,

St Stephen's Cathedral, Vienna, C12-C15

Bamberg, and Regensburg – see St Stephen, Vienna; St Pölten; and the Karner at Tulln. Karners are charnel-houses with chapels, centrally planned, and they are an Austrian speciality. The largest church of the C12 was Salzburg Cathedral as rebuilt in 1181 etc. It was as long as Old St Peter's in Rome, and had double aisles, round towers over apses in the end walls of the transepts, two (older) west towers, and an octagonal crossing tower.

Cistercian colonization was actively pursued in Austria, and Viktring (built 1142-1202) is indeed an early and faithful follower of Fontenay, the earliest preserved house in France; it has, for example, the pointed tunnel vaults of Fontenay. On the other hand Heiligenkreuz (begun c. 1150-60) has rib vaults with heavy square ribs, a Lombard characteristic. Heiligenkreuz received a choir in 1295, of the hall type. This is of course fully Gothic, and hall churches are characteristic of the German Late Gothic. The hall choir was suggested by an earlier Cistercian hall choir in Austria: Lilienfeld (1202-30), also nearly entirely Gothic. This is an extremely early case of the hall elevation and one which established Austria as one of the sources of German hall churches. Zwettl, also Cistercian, received its splendid hall choir with ambulatory and low radiating chapels much later (1343-83). From here influences again reached out to South and South-west Germany. The friars, the most active orders of the later C13 and the C14, went in for halls too.

The principal achievement of the C14 and C15 is of course St Stephen in Vienna, not a cathedral originally. The hall chancel is of 1304–40, the glorious south tower of 1359–1433. Connections in the early C14 were principally with Bohemia (Vienna) and Bavaria (Franciscan Church, Salzburg, 1408 etc.; by Hans STETHAIMER). Developments in architecture in the later C15 and early C16 were as great and important as they were in sculpture: intricate vaults, with star, net, and even rosette motifs, are characteristic, and culminate in the stucco ribs with vegetable details of Laas (c. 1515–20) and Kötschach (1518–27) in Carinthia. Supports may be twisted piers (Salzburg Castle, 1502) or even tree-trunk piers (Bechyně Castle, just across the Moravian border). The first secular buildings are also of these late years: the Bummerlhaus at Steyr (1497), the Goldenes Dachl at Innsbruck (completed 1500), and the Kornmesserhaus at Bruck on the Mur (1499–1505). The arcading here suggests Venetian influence.

But Italian influence was very soon to mean something quite different from the Gothic of the Kornmesserhaus. The portal of the Salvator Chapel in Vienna of just after 1515 is entirely Lombard Renaissance and must be the work of a sculptor from there. Similar works, especially funerary monuments, picked up the new forms at once. In architecture the next examples are the portal of the Arsenal at Wiener Neustadt (1524) and the elegant courtyard of the Portia Palace at Spital (c. 1540); a comparison of this with the much heavier courtyard of the Landhaus at Graz (1556–65; by Domenico dell'Allio) shows a characteristic development. The stage after this is represented by the courtyard of the Schallaburg near Melk (1572–1600) with caryatids, etc. – what would in Britain be called Elizabethan. On the whole, Austria is less rich in first-rate Renaissance buildings than Bohemia. The Hofkirche at Innsbruck (1553–63) is a Gothic hall, though with slender columns instead of piers. The only fully Italian building in the ecclesiastical field is Salzburg Cathedral, by Santino SOLARI, with two west towers and a crossing dome, and this is of 1614–34. The cathedral, the Archiepiscopal Palace, and the Franciscan church show a very complete development of Italianate C17 stucco decoration.

In Vienna a remarkable number of churches were built and rebuilt, but they appear minor when one measures them by the achievements of the Austrian Baroque of c. 1690–1730. The great names are first the theatrical designer and engineer Lorenzo Burnacini (1636–1707), who designed the wildly Baroque Trinity Monument on the Graben in 1687; then Domenico MARTINELLI (1650–1718) of the two Liechtenstein palaces of the 1690s; and then FISCHER VON ERLACH and HILDEBRANDT. Little need be said about them here – of Fischer's brilliant centralizing church plans at Salzburg (Trinity, 1694–1702; Collegiate, 1694–1707), heralded by those of Gaspare ZUCCALLI of 1685; of his Karlskirche in Vienna with its fantastic Trajan's Columns;

Kremsmünster Abbey, 1606–7

Karlskirche, Vienna, 1716–37, by Fischer von Erlach

Benedictine monastery, Göttweig,
begun 1719, by Hildebrandt, after engraving
by Salomon Kleiner

1708; by CARLONE and then Prandtauer);
Göttweig (1719 etc.; by Hildebrandt); Klosterneuburg (1730 etc.; by d'Allio). Particularly
splendid are the libraries in the abbeys (Altenburg, 1740; Admont, c. 1745).

The Louis XVI or Robert ADAM style of the
later c18 is represented in Vienna by the
Academy of the Sciences (1753; by Jadot de
Ville Issey) and the Josephinum (1783; by
Canevale). The Gloriette, a large-scale eye-
catcher in the park of Schönbrunn by
Ferdinand von Hohenburg, is, in spite of its
early date (1775), in a neo-Cinquecento style.
Neo-Grecian at its most severe are the

The Upper Belvedere, Vienna, 1714–24, by Hildebrandt

The Upper Belvedere, Vienna

of his restrained and courtly decoration; and
of Hildebrandt's brilliant spatial interlocking
and his fiery decoration (Upper Belvedere,
Vienna, 1714–24). Meanwhile the great
abbeys in the country were as busy rebuilding as the towns and the nobility: Melk (1702–
14; by PRANDTAUER); St Florian (1686–

Church at Dürnstein, 1721–8,
by Munggenast and Steinl

The Temple of Theseus, Vienna, 1820–23, by Nobile

Theseustempel (1820) and the Burgtor (1821), both by NOBILE (the latter originally designed by CAGNOLA).

C19 historicism is in full swing with the perfectly preserved Anif Castle near Salzburg (1838 etc.), the church of Altlerchenfeld, Vienna (1848–61; by Eduard van der Null)

Italian and French C16 style; and, finally, the Neue Hofburg (1881 etc.; by Semper and Hasenauer), again in Renaissance. There are also large blocks of flats as parts of the monumental, strung-out composition.

Vienna was one of the most important centres in the whole world when it came to abandoning historicism and creating a new idiom for the C20. The leaders were Otto WAGNER, whose Postal Savings Bank (1904) is remarkably fresh and enterprising, his pupil OLBRICH, whose Secession (1898) blazed the trail – though more towards ART NOUVEAU than towards the C20 – and the two even younger men, HOFFMANN and LOOS. When the C20 style began to settle down and be accepted in the mid-twenties, a mild variety of it was applied to the many blocks of working-class flats, some of them vast, which the municipality of Vienna erected.

Anif Castle near Salzburg, 1838–48

Otto Wagner's villa at Vienna, 1913

in neo-Romanesque, and the Arsenal (1849–56; by Förster and others), also in a neo-Romanesque style. Shortly after, Vienna established herself as one of the centres of historicism on a grand scale with the abolition of the fortress walls of inner Vienna and the making of the Ringstrasse (begun 1859). Along this wide green belt a number of majestic public buildings were erected in various period styles: the Votivkirche (1856 etc.; by von Ferstel), in Gothic; the Opera (1861 etc.; by van der Null and Siccardsburg), in free Renaissance; the Town Hall (1872 etc.; by Ferdinand von Schmidt), in symmetrical Gothic; the Museums (1872 etc.; by SEMPER and Hasenauer), in Renaissance to Baroque; the Academy (1872 etc.; by Theophil von HANSEN), in Renaissance; the Parliament (1873 etc.; also by von Hansen), in pure Grecian; the Burgtheater (1873 etc.; again by Semper and Hasenauer), in Renaissance; the University (by Ferstel), in a mixed

Lit: Dehio-Handbuch, *Die Kunstdenkmäler Osterreichs,* Vienna 1945 onwards; E. Hempel, *Geschichte der deutschen Baukunst,* Munich 1956; E. Hempel, *Baroque Art and Architecture in Central Europe,* Pelican History of Art, Harmondsworth 1965; R. Wagner-Rieger (ed.), *Der Wiener Ringstrasse,* Vienna 1969.

Averlino, Antonio, *see* FILARETE, ANTONIO.

Axonometric projection A geometrical drawing showing a building in three dimensions. The plan is set up truly to a convenient angle,

Axonometric projection

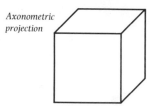

and the verticals projected to scale, with the result that all dimensions on a horizontal plane and all verticals are to scale, but diagonals and curves on a vertical plane are distorted. (*See* ISOMETRIC PROJECTION.)

Aztec architecture, *see* MESOAMERICAN ARCHITECTURE.

Azulejos Glazed pottery tiles, usually painted in bright colours with floral and other patterns, much used on the outsides and insides of Spanish, Portuguese, and Central and South American buildings.

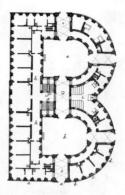

Babylonian architecture, *see* SUMERIAN AND AKKADIAN ARCHITECTURE.

Baguette (or **bagnette**). A small moulding of semicircular section, like an ASTRAGAL; also a frame with a small BEAD MOULDING.

Bähr, Georg (1666–1738). The leading Baroque architect in Dresden. He began as a carpenter and in 1705 became Ratszimmermeister (master carpenter to the city) in Dresden. But he had already begun to study mechanics (he invented a *camera obscura* and a mechanical organ) and his first building was begun the same year, the parish church of Loschwitz (1705–8) on an elongated octagonal plan. Two Greek cross plan churches followed, at Schmiedeberg (1713–16) and Forchheim (1719–26), both in the Erzegebirge. His masterpiece was the Frauenkirche in Dresden (1726–43: destroyed 1944), by far the grandest Protestant church in Germany. Bähr's first design for it dates from as early as 1722, a Greek cross plan with octagonal galleries, deriving from VISCARDI'S Mariahilfkirche at Freystadt (1700–08). But in 1726 this design was revised in favour of a square ground plan with a circular arrangement of piers, with angle turrets flanking the dome on all four sides. The dome was also re-designed to increase its height and pitch, thus producing a very bold silhouette. The interior resembled a centrally planned theatre with curving galleries and a richly decorated organ (by Gottfried Silbermann 1732–6) as the main feature. The Dreikönigskirche in Dresden Neustadt (1732–9) originally designed by PÖPPELMANN was supervised by Bähr.
Lit: F. Löffler, *Das alte Dresden*, Dresden 1955.

Bailey An open space or court of a stone-built castle; also called a *ward*. *See also* MOTTE-AND-BAILEY.

Baker, Sir Herbert (1862–1946), was born in Kent and remained an English countryman. Baker's most interesting work belongs to South Africa. He went out early, gained Cecil Rhodes's confidence, and built Groote Schuur for him in 1890 in the traditional Dutch Colonial idiom, and later private houses in Johannesburg, some very successful in an Arts and Crafts way (Stonehouse, 1902). His most prominent buildings were the Government House and Union Buildings in Pretoria (1905 onwards and 1910–13). Side by side with his friend LUTYENS he was called in at New Delhi, and was responsible there for the Secretariat Buildings and the Legislative Building (1912 etc.). His style is as imperially classical as Lutyens's, but much weaker, less original, and less disciplined. This is especially evident in his later London buildings (Bank of England, 1921; India House, 1925; South Africa House, 1930). He was more at ease where he could use a less elevated style and display a great variety of materials. This is why the War Memorial Cloister at Winchester College (1922–4) is one of his most successful buildings.
Lit: Sir Herbert Baker, *Architecture and Personalities*, London 1944.

Balcony A platform projecting from a wall, enclosed by a railing or balustrade, supported on brackets or columns or cantilevered out. (Illustrated next page.)

Baldachin or **Baldacchino** A canopy over a throne, altar, doorway, etc. It may be portable,

Balcony: Archbishop's Palace,
Lima, Peru, c18

(Right). Balcony: Bamberg Town Hall, 1744–56

Baldachin: Bamberg Cathedral, c13

(Right). Baldachin over the altar
in S. Miniato al Monte, Florence, c11–c12

suspended from a ceiling, projecting from a wall or free-standing on columns or other supports. *See also* CIBORIUM.

Balinese architecture, *see* SOUTH-EAST ASIAN ARCHITECTURE.

Balistraria In medieval military architecture, the cross-shaped opening in BATTLEMENTS and elsewhere for the use of the crossbow.

Ballflower A globular three-petalled flower enclosing a small ball; a decoration in use in the first quarter of the c14.

Ballflower

Balloon framing A method of timber-frame construction used in the U.S.A. and Scandinavia: the STUDS or uprights run from sill to eaves, and the horizontal members are nailed to them.

Ballu, Théodore (1817–85). French architect. His best-known building is Holy Trinity, Paris (1863–7), a design in the Early Renaissance style of Italy and France.

Lit: P. Sédille, *Théodore Ballu*, Paris 1886.

Baltard, Louis-Pierre (1764–1846). French architect. He built the Law Courts at Lyon (1836–41) which, with its long row of giant Corinthian columns, is a belated representative of the Empire style. Baltard taught first at the École Polytechnique, then at the École des Beaux Arts in Paris.

Baltard, Victor (1805–74). French architect. His most famous work is – or, as one must say now, was – the Market Hall of Paris (1852 etc.), all glass and iron. His church of St Augustine (1860–71) is externally a domed building of the Early French Renaissance but internally proclaims its iron construction.

Lit: M. Decouchy, *Victor Baltard*, Paris 1875.

Baluster A short post or pillar in a series supporting a rail or COPING and thus forming a *balustrade*.

Baluster

Balustrade, *see* BALUSTER.

Banded column. *See* RUSTICATED COLUMN.

Baptistery A building for baptismal rites containing the font; often separate from the church. Illustrated next column.

Bar tracery, *see* TRACERY.

Baptistery, S. Giovanni, Lenno, Lake Como, C12

Barbican An outwork defending the entrance to a castle.

Barbican: Nördlingen

Barelli, Agostino (1627–79). Born in Bologna, where he designed the Theatine church of S. Bartolomeo (1653), he later introduced the Italian Baroque style to Bavaria. He designed the Theatine church of St Cajetan, Munich (1663, completed by Enrico ZUCCALLI), on the model of S. Andrea della Valle, Rome. He also built the squarish central block of the electoral palace at Nymphenburg outside Munich (1663), completed by EFFNER in 1717–23. (For illustration *see* BAROQUE ARCHITECTURE.)

Lit: N. Lieb, *Münchner Barockbaumeister*, Munich 1941.

Bargeboards Projecting boards placed against the incline of the gable of a building and hiding the ends of the horizontal roof timbers; sometimes decorated. (Illustrated next page.)

Bargeboard

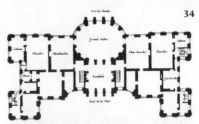

Vaux-le-Vicomte, begun in 1657, by Le Vau

Versailles, view of the château from the town

Baroque architecture The architecture of the C17 and part of the C18. It is characterized by exuberant decoration, expansive curvaceous forms, a sense of mass, a delight in large-scale and sweeping vistas, and a preference for spatially complex compositions. According to the number of these and kindred qualities present, a building or a national style of architecture may be called Baroque. The term applies fully to the C17 in Italy and to the C17 and part of the C18 in Spain, Germany, and Austria, but with limitations to the C17 in France (LE VAU, Versailles), the C18 in Italy (FONTANA, JUVARRA), and the late C17 and early C18 in England (WREN, HAWKSMOOR, VANBRUGH, ARCHER). For all these latter cases the term Baroque Classicism has been adopted to denote that they are instances of the Baroque tempered by classical elements. This is especially evident in England, where the

Scala Regia in the Vatican, Rome, 1660–70, by Bernini

Theatine church, Munich, begun in 1663 by Barelli, completed by Zuccalli

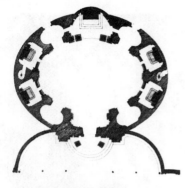

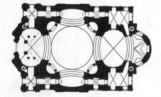

Top to bottom:

*S. Andrea al Quirinale, Rome, 1668–78,
by Bernini*

*St Lorenz, Gabel (Jablonné v Podještedí),
Czechoslovakia, 1699, by Hildebrandt*

*Blenheim Palace, Oxfordshire, begun 1709,
by Vanbrugh*

Stupinigi near Turin, begun 1719, by Juvarra

Staircase, Schloss Brühl,
near Cologne, 1743–8, by Neumann

swelling forms of Baroque plans and elevations were never favoured. *See also* ENGLISH, GERMAN, ITALIAN, SPANISH ARCHITECTURE.

Lit: E. Hempel, *Baroque Art and Architecture in Central Europe*, Pelican History of Art, Harmondsworth 1965; R. Wittkower, *Art and Architecture in Italy 1600–1750*, Pelican History of Art, 3rd edn, Harmondsworth 1973, paperback edn, 1973.

Barrel vault, *see* VAULT.

Barry, Sir Charles (1795–1860). The most versatile of the leading Early Victorian architects, an excellent planner and an energetic, tough, and hard-working man. With some inherited money he travelled in 1817–20 through France, Italy, Greece, Turkey, Egypt, and Palestine, studying buildings and doing brilliant sketches. In 1823 he won the competition for St Peter's, Brighton, and then for some years did 'pre-archaeological' Gothic churches, i.e., an inventive rather than a correct interpretation of the style. In 1824 he designed the Royal Institution of Fine Arts in Manchester – Grecian this time – and he followed this up with the Manchester Athena-

eum (1836). But the Travellers' Club in London (1829–31) was Quattrocento, and this meant the start of the neo-Renaissance for England. With the Reform Club of 1837 his Renaissance turned Cinquecento, and with Bridgewater House (1847) a free, not to say debased, Cinquecento. This development from the reticent to the spectacular and from low to high relief permeates his work in general – see, now in the Northern Renaissance field, the development from Highclere (1837), itself far busier than his early work, to the Halifax Town Hall (1859–62), which is asymmetrical and a jumble of motifs. It was completed by Barry's son Edward M. Barry (1830–80), who built the Charing Cross and Cannon Street Hotels.

But Sir Charles's *magnum opus* is, of course, the Houses of Parliament, won in competition in 1835–6 and begun in 1839; it was formally opened in 1852. Its ground plan is functionally excellent, its façade to the Thames still symmetrical in the Georgian way, but its skyline completely asymmetrical and exceedingly well balanced, with its two contrasting towers and its flèche. Most of the close Perpendicular detail and nearly all the internal detail is by PUGIN, who was commissioned by Barry for the purpose. (For illustration *see* ENGLISH ARCHITECTURE, HISTORICISM.)

Lit: A. Barry, *The Life and Works of Sir C. Barry*, London 1867; H. M. Colvin, *Biographical Dictionary of English Architects, 1660–1840*, London 1954; H.-R. Hitchcock, *Architecture: Nineteenth and Twentieth Centuries*, Pelican History of Art, Harmondsworth 1969, paperback edn 1971.

Bartizan A small turret projecting from the angle on the top of a tower or parapet.

Basement The lowest storey of a building, usually below or partly below ground level or, if beginning at ground level, of less height than the storey above.

Basevi, George (1794–1845), was articled to SOANE. In 1816–19 he was in Italy and Greece. His first buildings are Grecian, but his best-known building, the Fitzwilliam Museum at Cambridge (begun 1836), already shows the trend towards classical harmony becoming, with clustered giant columns and a heavy attic, more dramatic and indeed Baroque. It is the same trend which distinguishes the Beaux Arts style in France from the Empire style. Early in his career (*c.* 1825), Basevi also designed Belgrave Square (minus the corner mansions) and a number of country houses in various styles.

Lit: H. M. Colvin, *Biographical Dictionary of English Architects, 1660–1840*, London 1954.

Basilica A church divided into a nave and two or more aisles, the former higher and wider than the latter, lit by the windows of a CLERESTORY, and with or without a gallery. In Roman architecture, a basilica was a large meeting-hall, as used in public administration. The term indicated function and not form, but Roman basilicas were often oblong buildings with aisles and galleries and with an apse opposite the entrance which might be through one of the longer, or one of the shorter, sides. Early Christian churches evolved from Roman

Basilica at Pompeii, c. 100 B.C.

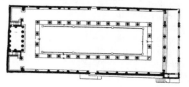

Basilica: S. Apollinare in Classe, Ravenna, early c6

Interior of S. Apollinare in Classe

basilicas of this type (not from pagan religious architecture). By the c4 the Christian basilica had acquired its essential characteristics: oblong plan; longitudinal axis; a timber roof, either open or concealed by a flat ceiling; and a termination, either rectangular or in the form of an apse.

Lit: R. Krautheimer, *Early Christian and Byzantine Architecture*, Pelican History of Art, Harmondsworth 1965, paperback edn 1974.

Basket arch, *see* ARCH.

Bastion The projecting, commonly pentagonal, part of fortifications. The coming of more accurate artillery in the fifteenth century revolutionized systems of both defence and counter-attack. High MACHICOLATED TOWERS and CURTAIN WALLS designed to provide vertical defence against assault by scaling gave way to thick scarped walls resistant to bombardment, studded with level bastions housing gun platforms and chambers, providing an interdependent system of offensive and covering fire.

*Bastion: Palmanova, near Udine,
after a plan by Scamozzi of 1593*

*Bastion: Rosenberg Castle,
Kronach, 1656–1700*

Bastions were the invention of no single person, but were evolved pragmatically in Central Italy from the middle of the fifteenth century. Architects like Baccio Pontelli and Giuliano da SANGALLO in their guise as military engineers contributed to this evolution, but the role of others who have left treatises or drawings, like FRANCESCO DI GIORGIO and LEONARDO DA VINCI, has probably been exaggerated. At first the round vied with pointed forms, but by the 1530s the angle bastion had become the norm. Further refinements were introduced over the years, notably by Daniel SPECKLE and the Comte de Pagan (1604–65; VAUBAN's originality lay more in devising means of assault by sapping), until more powerful explosives rendered the bastion obsolete.   [AL]

Lit: J. R. Hale, in *Europe in the Late Middle Ages*, London 1965; Max Jähn, *Geschichte der Kriegswissenschaften*, 1889–91.

Batter The inclined face of a wall.

Battlement A PARAPET with alternating indentations or EMBRASURES and raised portions or *merlons*; also called *crenellation*.

Baudot, Anatole de (1834–1915). A pupil of LABROUSTE and VIOLLET-LE-DUC. His St Jean de Montmartre in Paris (1894–1902) is the first building where all the structural members, including the vaulting ribs, are of exposed reinforced concrete. Yet the character remains Gothic. It can be called the most successful demonstration of the union of old and new advocated by Viollet-le-Duc in his *Entretiens*.

Lit: A. de Baudot, *L'Architecture, le passé, le présent*, Paris 1916; A. de Baudot, *L'Architecture et le béton armé*, Paris 1916; L. Hautecoeur, *Histoire de l'architecture classique en France*, vol. VII, Paris 1957.

Bauhaus The Grand-Duke of Saxe-Weimar had founded a school of arts and crafts at Weimar in 1906. He appointed van de VELDE to the directorship – a very progressive move; for van de Velde believed in teaching in workshops rather than studios. When van de Velde left Germany, he suggested GROPIUS as his successor, and Gropius took over in 1919. He re-organized the school and called it the Bauhaus. According to its first manifesto the school was to teach crafts, and all artists and architects were to work together towards the great goal of 'the building of the future'. The manifesto was enthusiastic in tone and had on its cover an Expressionist vision of a cathedral, a woodcut by Feininger. This first phase of the Bauhaus, inspired by MORRIS and sustained by the Expressionist mood of post-war Germany, did not last long. The aim now became industrial design, and stark cubic simplicity replaced the Expressionism. This fundamental change of programme was accelerated by lectures which Theo van Doesburg (1883–1931) gave in 1922, and by the appointment of Moholy Nagy (1895–1946) in 1923. The result was a memorandum by Gropius issued in 1924 and called *Art and Technology – A New Unity*. However, in the same year, political changes led to the dissolution of the Bauhaus. At that moment the Burgomaster of Dessau in Anhalt offered the school a new field of activity. A new building was designed by Gropius and built in 1925–6. In 1926 the Bauhaus received recognition as the State School of Art of Anhalt. This seemed to secure the future. A department of architecture was established, and Hannes Meyer became its head. One year later, in 1928, Gropius resigned and suggested Hannes Meyer as his successor. Meyer was politically far more radical than Gropius. He organized the department of architecture, but was dismissed for political reasons in 1930. His successor was MIES VAN DER ROHE. However, the growth of National Socialism in Anhalt led to his dismissal and, in 1932, to the closure of the school. Mies tried to carry on in Berlin, converting the school into a private enterprise. But in 1933 that also was closed by the Nazis.

The Bauhaus is the most important school of art of the C20. Its most significant achievement was that to the very end artists and craftsmen, and in the end architects, too, worked together. At the start of the Bauhaus the *Vorkurs*, as built up by Johannes Itten, comprised them all. The intention of the *Vorkurs* was to stimulate a theoretically and practically sound sense of form and colour. Later the Bauhaus became the only art school in which designs for industrial products were developed. Moreover, Gropius's own style of architecture became almost automatically a symbol of the programme of the school. But, when all is said, the most impressive fact about the Bauhaus is that Gropius succeeded in keeping together in a happy co-operation such dissimilar artists as Kandinsky, Feininger, Klee and Schlemmer. (For illustration *see* GERMAN ARCHITECTURE.)

Lit: J. Itten, *Design and Form, the Basic Course at the Bauhaus*, New York 1964; H. M. Wingler, *The Bauhaus. . . .*, Cambridge, Mass., 1969; M. Franciscano, *Walter Gropius and the Creation of the Bauhaus in Weimar*, Urbana 1971.

Bautista, Francisco (1594–1679). A Spanish Jesuit priest who built churches for his order in Madrid and Toledo. That in Madrid, S. Isidro el Real (1629), is the most interesting, based on the plan of the Gesù in Rome, with a somewhat severe façade. The church had considerable influence in Spain.

Lit: G. Kubler, *Arquitectura española 1600–1800* (Ars Hispaniae, vol. XIV), Madrid 1957; G. Kubler & M. Soria, *Art and Architecture in Spain and Portugal and their American Dominions 1500–1800*, Pelican History of Art, Harmondsworth 1959.

Bay A vertical division of the exterior or interior of a building marked not by walls but by fenestration, an order, buttresses, units of vaulting, roof compartment, etc.

Bay leaf garland Classical decorative motif used to enrich TORUS mouldings, etc.

Bay window, *see* WINDOW.

Bazar This is a Persian word meaning 'market'; its Arabic equivalent is *suq*. The *bazar*, when built as a complete entity, varies considerably from one Islamic country to another, but the most common pattern is an irregular agglomeration of covered alleys with multiple side passages, the product of continuous and largely unplanned growth over a period of centuries. Sometimes, as in the case of Aleppo, the nucleus of the *bazar* was a complex of classical colonnaded streets, gradually encroached on and altered by later buildings. Parts of medieval *bazars* survive at Tunis, Granada and elsewhere. The typical *bazar* was not intended for wheeled traffic and even the main alleys were usually rather narrow. They were lined with shops (*dukkan*) in the form of a raised platform (*mastaba*) without furniture on which the merchant or craftsman sat. The *bazar* was divided into separate quarters according to trades and, like other parts of the city, contained mosques, public fountains, and *khans* (CARAVANSERAIS) – walled rectangles enclosing a courtyard and rooms to accommodate travellers and store goods. *Bazars* were usually situated in a separate trading quarter within the city, often (but not necessarily) in the centre and near the principal mosque. Major cities might have several distinct *bazars* whose sites altered from century to century. Although open-air *bazars* exist, those with simple coverings of awnings, branches or beams are commoner, while the larger *bazars* in the cities are often vaulted, with domes over their intersections. Monumental examples are especially numerous in the Iranian world (Kashan, Kirman and Bokhara). [RH]

Bead moulding A small cylindrical moulding enriched with ornament resembling a string of beads; used in the Romanesque period.

Bead and reel, *see* ASTRAGAL.

Beakhead A Norman decorative motif consisting of a row of bird, animal, or human heads biting a ROLL MOULDING. (Illustrated next page.)

Bed moulding A small moulding between the CORONA and the FRIEZE in any ENTABLATURE.

Beehive house A primitive structure, circular in plan and built of rough stones set in projecting courses to form a dome. Prehistoric

Beakhead moulding: (St Peter, Windrush, Glos.)

examples, called *nuraghi*, have been found in Sardinia, and others of later date in Ireland and Scotland. They are still inhabited in South-east Italy (Apulia), where they are called *trulli*. The finest example of beehive construction is the tomb called the 'Treasury of Atreus' at Mycenae (C14–C13 B.C.).

Beehive construction: Treasury of Atreus, Mycenae, c14–c13 B.C.

Beer, Michael (d. 1666). He was born at Au in the Bregenzerwald and was the founder of the Vorarlberger school of architects which included, besides the Beer family, the Mos-BRUGGER family and the THUMB family. The latter intermarried with the Beer family. The long series of buildings by this school, mostly for Benedictine monasteries in S. W. Germany and Switzerland, was eventually to mark the triumph of German over Italian elements in S. German Baroque architecture (i.e., over the domination of such Italians as ZUCCALLI and VISCARDI from the Grisons). Michael Beer is known to have worked at the abbey church at Kempten until 1654 and he was probably

responsible for its design which attempted a fusion of the longitudinal and centralized types of church. It has a curious, large-domed octagon between nave and chancel. His son Franz Beer (1659–1726) became one of the leading architects of the Vorarlberg school. He began at Obermarchtal abbey church where he and Christian THUMB took over after the death of Michael THUMB in 1690. The influence of the Thumbs is still evident in his next building, Kloster Irsee (1699–1704). But he achieved an individual style and also great elegance and lightness at the abbey church at Rheinau in Switzerland (1704–11) where he emphasized verticality by setting the galleries well back from the pilaster ends of the internal buttresses which typify the Vorarlberg type of church. His style culminated in the Cistercian abbey church of St Urban in the Canton of Lucerne (1711–15) and at the Benedictine abbey church at Weingarten (1715–23) though his responsibility at the latter is uncertain. (He refused to direct the building operations, and the design was probably a collaboration with Johann Jakob Herkommer (1648–1717) and perhaps also Caspar Mos-BRUGGER.) In 1717 he reconstructed the Premonstratensian abbey church at Weissenau near Ravensburg. Two plans (unexecuted) for the abbey church at Einsiedeln are attributed to him. His eldest daughter married Peter THUMB. Johann Michael Beer (1696–1780) designed the choir and east façade at the abbey church at St Gallen (1760–69) and Ferdinand Beer (1731–89) designed the administrative block of the monastery at St Gallen. (For illustration *see* SWISS ARCHITECTURE.)

Lit: N. Lieb, *Die Vorarlberger Barockbaumeister*, Munich 1960.

Behrens, Peter (1868–1940), started as a painter but after 1890 was attracted by design and the crafts, under the direct or indirect influence of the teachings of MORRIS. He designed typefaces, was one of the founders of the Vereinigte Werkstätten at Munich, and for them designed table glass among other things. In 1900 Ernst Ludwig, Grand Duke of Hesse, called him to Darmstadt (*see* OLBRICH). The house he designed for himself there in 1901 is original, vigorous, and even ruthless. In 1907 he was appointed architect and consultant to the A.E.G. (General Electricity Company) in Berlin, and designed for them factories, shops, products, and even stationery. The factories are among the earliest anywhere to be taken seriously architecturally and designed without any recourse to period allusions. For more representational jobs he used a more representational style which has been called a 'scraped classicism' (offices in Düsseldorf for Mannesmann, 1911–12; German Embassy, St Petersburg, 1911–12). After the First World War his style paid tribute first to the then current Expressionism (offices for I. G. Farben, Höchst, 1920–4), then to the International Modern (warehouse for the State Tobacco Administration, Linz, Austria, 1930). In 1925 he designed 'New Ways', 508 Wellingborough Road, Northampton – the earliest example of the c20 style in England. (The house incorporates a room designed by MACKINTOSH in 1907.)

Lit: F. Hueber, *Peter Behrens*, Munich 1913; P. J. Cremers, *Peter Behrens, sein Werk von 1909 . . .*, Essen 1928; Catalogue, Behrens Exhibition, Kaiserlauten, etc., 1966–7.

Bélanger, François-Joseph (1744–1818). The most elegant Louis XVI architect and the leading French landscape gardener. Trained in Paris, he visited England in 1765–6. The following year he joined the Menus Plaisirs and in 1777 designed his masterpiece, the exquisite neo-classical Bagatelle in the Bois de Boulogne, Paris, which he built for the king's brother in sixty-four days to win a bet with Marie Antoinette. The garden, laid out between 1778 and 1780, was the most famous *jardin anglais* of the period. It was followed in 1784 by the *jardin anglo-chinois* at another of his pavilions, the Folie Saint James at Neuilly, and in 1786 by the last of his great landscape gardens, Méréville. He also designed the exquisite pavilion in the garden of the Hôtel de Brancas, Paris (1771) and some interiors of great elegance, e.g., Hôtel de Mlle Desvieux, Paris (1788). In 1806 he designed a remarkable glass and iron dome for the Halle au Blé in Paris to replace the hardly less remarkable glass and wood dome of Legrand and Molinos of 1782. (Bélanger had already proposed a dome of iron and glass in 1782 but his proposal was not accepted.)

Lit: J. Stern, *À l'ombre de Sophie Arnould, F.-J. Bélanger*, Paris 1930; D. Wiebenson, 'The two Domes of the Halle au Blé in Paris' in *The Art Bulletin*, June 1973.

Belfast roof, *see* ROOF.

Belfry Generally the upper room or storey in a tower in which bells are hung, and thus often the bell-tower itself, whether it is attached to

Belfry: Bruges, late c13

or stands separate from the main building. Also the timber frame inside a church steeple to which bells are fastened. Derived from the old French *beffroi* (= tower), the word has no connection with 'bell'.

Belgian architecture In the Middle Ages the Southern Netherlands belonged to the archdiocese of Cologne; hence Romanesque building drew its inspiration chiefly from Germany. The earliest building of major importance, St Gertrude at Nivelles (consecrated 1046), is, side by side with St Michael at Hildesheim, the best-preserved Ottonian church in the German orbit. The former St John at Liège was built to a central plan like Charlemagne's church at Aachen, the former Liège Cathedral had a west as well as an east chancel, St Bartholomew, also at Liège, has a typically German unrelieved façade block with recessed twin towers (cf. especially Maastricht), and the cathedral of Tournai has a trefoil east end (i.e., transepts with apsidal ends) on the pattern of St Mary in Capitol at Cologne; its group of five towers round the crossing may also be derived from Cologne.

Tournai had a great influence on the Early Gothic architecture of France (Noyon, Laon). The east end was rebuilt *c.* 1242, no longer on a German pattern but on that of such High Gothic cathedrals as Soissons and Amiens.

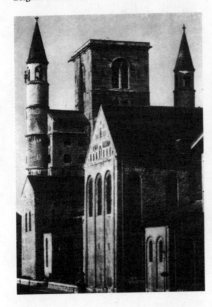

(*Left*). *St Gertrude, Nivelles, consecrated* 1046

Tournai Cathedral, interior of transept begun pre-1141

The Gothic style in present-day Belgium was, in fact, imported from France; borrowings also occurred from Normandy and Burgundy, and as in other countries the Cistercians were among the pioneers. Orval of the late C12 is still Transitional, Villers (1210–72) is fully Gothic, as are the principal church of Brussels, Ste Gudule (begun before 1226, the façade C15), the beautiful chancel of St Martin at Ypres (1221 etc.), and Notre Dame at Tongres (1240 etc.). Later Gothic architecture in the Southern Netherlands first drew mainly on French inspiration, dominant at Hertogenbosch (c. 1280–1330) and in the chancel of Hal in the C14. But in the C15 Belgium, admittedly influenced by French Flamboyant as well as German 'Sondergotik', developed a splendid style of her own. The principal buildings are Notre Dame at Antwerp (completed 1518), St Rombaut at Malines, St Peter at Louvain (1425 etc.), and the Sablon Church at Brussels. Characteristic features are complicated lierne vaults of German derivation, proud towers – that of Antwerp 306 ft high, that of Malines about 320 ft and intended to be about 530 ft – and exceedingly elaborate Flamboyant fitments, such as rood screens.

The most spectacular castle is that of Ghent (inscribed 1180), with its oblong keep and its many towers along the curtain wall. But the sphere in which Belgium is in the forefront of European building is the town halls and guild halls of her prosperous towns. The Cloth Hall at Ypres (C13–C14), 440 ft long, is the grandest such building in all Europe, and there is the town hall of Bruges (tower c. 1280–1482, 350 ft high), then, ornately and lacily decorated, those of Brussels (1402 etc.), Louvain (1447 etc.), Ghent (1517), and Oudenarde (1527). Interiors were as rich as exteriors – see, for example, the magnificent chimneypiece in Courtrai Town Hall (1526). The names of the master masons are now

Cloth Hall, Ypres, c. 1260–1380

Tournai Cathedral, mostly 1165 etc.

mostly known: the family of the Keldermans is the most familiar. There are also plenty of medieval town houses preserved; Romanesque buildings are mostly in stone (Tournai), Gothic most often in brick and frequently with crow-stepped gables (as early as the c13).

The Renaissance appeared in occasional motifs in paintings as early as 1500 and was more widely represented after 1510. The most important date for the promotion of the Renaissance spirit is 1517, when Raphael's cartoons for tapestries in the Sistine Chapel reached Brussels, where the tapestries were to be made. In the same year the Stadtholderess Margaret of Austria had additions built to her palace at Malines in the Renaissance style. Their relative purity is exceptional; the usual thing in the twenties and thirties is a happy-

Town Hall, Bruges, late c14

Bishop's Palace, Liège, 1526

go-lucky mixing of Renaissance with traditional motifs, sometimes quite restrained (The Salmon, Malines, 1530–4), but mostly exuberant (The Greffe, Bruges, with its fabulous chimneypiece, 1535–7; the courtyard of the former Bishop's Palace, Liège, 1526). In churches the Renaissance was confined to details; the proportions and the vaults remained Gothic (St Jacques, Liège, 1513–38). A very influential element in architectural decoration was introduced in Antwerp in the forties and spread all over Northern Europe – the combination of STRAPWORK, inspired by Fontainebleau, and grottesche, inspired by ancient Roman excavations. Cornelis FLORIS and later Hans Vredeman de VRIES were its most eminent practitioners.

Town Hall, Antwerp, 1561–5, by Floris

But Floris also designed the Antwerp Town Hall (1561–6), and this, though provided with a big, dominating gable in the northern style, is in its motifs entirely developed from BRAMANTE and SERLIO, i.e., the Italian (and French) Cinquecento. The former Granvella Palace in Brussels (c. 1550) is also classical Cinquecento. However, the Jesuits, in their churches, clung to the Gothic well into the c17; an exception is St Charles Borromeo at Antwerp (1615–21), with a broad Mannerist façade and a tunnel-vaulted interior with arcades on columns in two tiers. True c17 architecture came in under the influence of Italy and France (domes such as Notre Dame de Montaigu, 1609 etc.; St Pierre, Ghent, 1629 etc.; Notre Dame de Hanswyck, Malines,

Houses in the Grand' Place, Brussels, after 1697

1663 etc.), and after *c.* 1650 developed into a characteristic Belgian Baroque, inspired largely by Rubens. Church façades are without towers and covered with sumptuous and somewhat undisciplined decoration (St Michael, Louvain, 1650–66; St John Baptist, Brussels, 1657–77; St Peter, Malines, 1670–1709). Typical of the situation about 1700 are the houses round the Grand' Place in Brussels built after the bombardment of 1695 and with their gables basically still rooted in the Belgian past.

Of the C18 and early C19 little need be said; this period was dominated by French classicism (Royal Library, Brussels, *c.* 1750; Palais des Académies, Brussels, 1823–6). But in the later C19 Belgium found the way back to an exuberant Baroque. Poelaert's cyclopean Palais de Justice, Brussels (1866 etc.), is one of the most Baroque buildings of its time in Europe, though Poelaert could also work in a wild Gothic (Laeken Church, 1854, etc.). A generation later Belgium for the first time in

Palace of Justice, Brussels, begun 1866, by Poelaert

Palais Stoclet, Brussels, 1905–11, by Hoffmann

her architectural history, and only for a few years, proved herself a pioneer; this was when attempts were being made to establish ART NOUVEAU as a viable architectural style. By far the most important architect in this movement was Victor HORTA of Brussels, and the

key buildings are No. 6 rue Paul Émile Janson (designed 1892), the Hôtel Solvay (1895 etc.), and the Maison du Peuple (1896 etc.) all of them with much of the undulating-line ornament of Art Nouveau, but also with a daring use of iron both externally and internally. Henri van de VELDE, though Belgian, belongs to international rather than Belgian Art Nouveau.

Lit: A. L. J. van de Walle, *Gotischè Kunst in Belgien,* Vienna & Munich 1972; H. Gerson & E. H. Ter Kuile, *Art and Architecture in Belgium 1600–1800,* Pelican History of Art, Harmondsworth 1960.

Bell gable, *see* BELLCOTE.

Bellcote A framework on a roof to hang bells from; also called a *bell gable.*

Belvedere, *see* GAZEBO.

Bema The Greek word means a speaker's tribune or a platform. 1. Raised stage for the clergy in the apse of Early Christian churches. 2. In Eastern usage, a space raised above the nave level of a church, which is shut off by the ICONOSTASIS and contains the altar. 3. In synagogues, the elevated pulpit from which are read the Pentateuch and Torah. Rabbinical authorities differ over its correct position: Maimonides (1204) maintains that the centre is correct, so does Moses Isserles of Cracow (C16), but Joseph Karo (1575) prescribed no fixed place. In modern times it has often been moved forward near the Ark for practical reasons. It is usually wooden and rectangular, and sometimes has a curved front and back, also open sides approached by steps.

Bench-ends, *see* PEW.

Benedetto da Maiano (1442–97). He was the younger brother of GIULIANO DA MAIANO and collaborated with him at the Fini chapel in the Collegiata in S. Gimignano (1468). Though primarily a sculptor, he designed two Early Renaissance masterpieces of architecture: Palazzo Strozzi, Florence (begun 1489 in collaboration with CRONACA (Simone del Pollaiuolo) 1454–1508) and the portico of S. Maria delle Grazie in Arezzo (1490–91). Palazzo Strozzi, a vast pile of uniform rusticated masonry from the ground to the gargantuan projecting cornice, derives from MICHELOZZO's Palazzo Medici-Riccardi. (It was com-

pleted by Cronaca who designed the cornice.)
The portico of S. Maria delle Grazie in Arezzo
is supremely elegant and airy, very different
in feeling from the exterior of Palazzo Strozzi.

Lit: L. Cendali, *Giuliano e Benedetto da
Maiano*, Florence 1926.

Bentley, John Francis (1839–1902). A pupil
of Henry Clutton. Converted to Catholicism in
1861, he set up on his own in 1862. After a
number of years spent mostly on designs for
church furnishings and on additions and alterations, he built the Convent of the Sacred
Heart at Hammersmith (1868 onwards) with
a scrupulous simplicity and near-bareness;
the serried chimneys are particularly impressive. Wider success came much later. Among
the most memorable buildings are Holy Rood,
Watford, a rich Gothic church, but also most
intelligently thought out (1887 etc.), and St
Francis at Bocking, Essex (1893). In 1894 he
was commissioned to design Westminster
Cathedral in London. The style here is Byzantine, the material brick with ample stone
dressings and concrete for the domes. No iron
is used: Bentley called it 'that curse of modern
construction'. The campanile, asymmetrically
placed, is the tallest church tower in London.
The interior is superbly large in scale and extremely sparing in architectural detail, although according to Bentley's intention it
should have been covered with mosaics and
slabs of variegated marble (and this is gradually being done). However, Philip WEBB admired it bare as it was.

Lit: W. Scott-Moncrieff, *J. F. Bentley*,
London 1924.

Berlage, Hendrikus Petrus (1856–1934),
studied at Zürich Polytechnic, then worked
under CUYPERS. The building that made him
famous, and is indeed a milestone in the
development of Dutch architecture away
from C19 historicism, is his Amsterdam Exchange (begun 1897). It does not mark a
break with the past, but the treatment of
period forms, derived from the Romanesque
as well as the C16, is so free and the detail so
original that it amounted to a profession of
faith in an independent future. Specially
characteristic are certain chunky, rather
primeval details and others that are jagged
and almost Expressionist. Berlage's style, indeed, prepared the way for the Expressionism
of the so-called School of Amsterdam (*see*
OUD). Berlage designed one building for
England, the office building for Messrs Muller

in Bury Street, London (1910–14). His last
major work, the Municipal Museum in The
Hague (1919–34), is less personal in style and
rather reflects that of DUDOK.

Lit: P. Singelenberg, *H. P. Berlage, Idea and
Style . . .*, Utrecht 1972.

Berm The level area separating ditch from
bank on a hill-fort or barrow.

Bernini, Gianlorenzo (1598–1680). The dominating figure in Roman Baroque art. Primarily
a sculptor, like MICHELANGELO, he was almost
as universal a genius, being painter and poet
as well as architect. He was born in Naples of a
Neapolitan mother and Florentine father,
Pietro Bernini, a late Mannerist sculptor of the
second rank. The family settled in Rome
c. 1605. Bernini spent the whole of his working life there, and no other city bears so strong
an imprint of one man's vision and personality.
His buildings and sculpture perfectly express
the grandeur, flamboyance, and emotionalism
of the Counter-Reformation. He was already
famous as a sculptor by the age of twenty, but
his long and uniformly successful career as an
architect began with the election of Urban VIII
(Barberini) in 1624. He was appointed architect to St Peter's five years later. But most of
his important buildings belong to his middle
age, mainly during the pontificate of Alexander
VII (Chigi, 1655–67). By then his fame was so
great that Louis XIV begged him to come to
Paris to enlarge the Louvre. Unlike his neurotic
contemporary and rival BORROMINI, he was
well-balanced and extrovert in temperament,
polished and self-assured in manner. Yet he
was devout and deeply religious: an ardent
follower of Jesuit teaching, he regularly practised the Spiritual Exercises of St Ignatius. He
combined to an exceptional degree a revolutionary artistic genius with the organizing
ability of a man of affairs.

His first commissions (1624) were for the
renovation of S. Bibiana and the baldacchino
in St Peter's. Though interesting as an experiment, S. Bibiana suffers from a lack of assurance most uncharacteristic of its author and in
striking contrast to the daringly original
baldacchino (1624–33) he erected under
Michelangelo's dome in the centre of St Peter's.
With its gigantic bronze barley-sugar columns,
buoyant scrolls, and dynamic sculpture, this
showy masterpiece is the very symbol of the
age – of its grandeur, luxury, and lack of
restraint. And by its glorification of the twisted
columns used in Constantine's basilica and

traditionally connected with the Temple of Jerusalem it celebrates the continuity of the Church and its triumph over the Reformation.

Various other commissions followed: the façade and staircase of Palazzo Barberini, the remodelling of Porta del Popolo, the Cornaro Chapel in S. Maria della Vittoria. In the latter polychrome marbles, exaggerated perspective, and every trick of lighting and scenic illusion are exploited to heighten the dramatic effect of his marble group of the Ecstasy of St Teresa, placed as if behind a proscenium arch above the altar. But not until he was almost sixty did he get the chance to show his skill as a designer of churches, first at Castelgandolfo (1658–61), then at Ariccia (1662–4), and, finally and most brilliantly, at S. Andrea al Quirinale in Rome (1658–70), which perfectly realizes his conception of a church as a unified architectural setting for the religious mysteries illustrated by the sculptural decoration.

Of his two great secular buildings in Rome, Palazzo di Montecitorio (1650 onwards) and Palazzo Odescalchi (1664 onwards), the latter is by far the more important. It is composed of a richly articulated central part of seven bays with giant composite pilasters, between simple rusticated receding wings of three bays, and marks a decisive break with Roman tradition. It was very influential and became the model for aristocratic palaces all over Europe. Unfortunately, the composition was ruined by later alterations and enlargements. His gift for the monumental and colossal found supreme expression in the Piazza of St Peter's (1656 onwards). The conception is extremely simple and extremely original – an enormous oval surrounded by colonnades of free-standing columns with a straight entablature above. This not only helped to correct the faults of MADERNO's façade by giving it an impression of greater height but expressed with overwhelming authority and conviction the dignity, grandeur, and majestic repose of Mother Church. Bernini himself compared his colonnades to the motherly arms of the church 'which embrace Catholics to reinforce their belief'. The Piazza was to have been enclosed by a third arm, unfortunately never built, and the intended effect of surprise and elation on passing through the colonnades has now been idiotically destroyed by opening up the via della Conciliazione. The free-standing colonnades of the Piazza have been widely copied, from Greenwich to Leningrad. Bernini's last great work, the Scala Regia in the Vatican

(1663–6), epitomizes his style – his sense of scale and movement, his ingenuity in turning an awkward site to advantage, his mastery of scenic effects (optical illusions, exaggerated perspectives, concealed lighting), and his brilliant use of sculpture to dramatize the climaxes of his composition. He here achieved the perfect Baroque synthesis of the arts. (For illustrations *see* BAROQUE ARCHITECTURE, COLONNADE and ITALIAN ARCHITECTURE.)

Lit: R. Pane, *Gianlorenzo Bernini, Architetto,* Venice 1953; R. Wittkower, *Art and Architecture in Italy, 1600–1750,* Pelican History of Art, 3rd edn, Harmondsworth 1973, paperback edn 1973.

Berrettini, Pietro, *see* CORTONA, Pietro Berrettini da.

Bertotti-Scamozzi, Ottavio (1719–90), the leading Palladian-Revival architect in Italy, built numerous houses in and around Vicenza, notably Palazzo Pagello-Beltrame (1780) and Palazzo Franceschini (1770, now the Questura), distinctly neo-classical versions of PALLADIO. He is more important as the editor of Palladio's work: *Le fabbriche e i disegni di Andrea Palladio raccolti e illustrati* (1776–83) and *Le terme dei Romani, disegnate da A. Palladio* (1797).

Lit: F. Barbieri in *Palladio* XXI, 1962, pp. 153–9.

Béton brut 'Concrete in the raw', that is, concrete left in its natural state when the FORMWORK has been removed. Sometimes special formwork is used to show clearly the timber graining on the concrete surface.

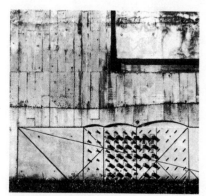

Béton brut from block of flats at Nantes, 1952–7, by Le Corbusier

Bianco, Bartolommeo (c. 1590–1657), a leading Baroque architect in Genoa, was born in Como, but was working in Genoa by 1619 when he began Palazzo Durazzo-Pallavicini. His best building is the University (1630–6), where he took full advantage of a steeply sloping site to produce a masterpiece of scenic planning with dramatic staircases and colonnaded courtyards on four levels.

Lit: L. Profumo-Müller, *Bartolomeo Bianco Architetto e il barocco genovese,* Rome 1968.

Bibiena, *see* GALLI DI BIBIENA.

Billet A Romanesque moulding consisting of several bands of raised short cylinders or square pieces placed at regular intervals.

Billet frieze: Abbey Church, Bursfelde, begun 1093

Blind (or **blank**) **tracery** Tracery applied to the surface of walls, wood panels, etc., in Gothic buildings. *See also* ARCADE.

Blind window The elements of a window (the surround, mullion, etc.) applied to a wall

Blind windows: St Kilian, Höxter, early c12

without any aperture. It was used as a decorative device and is found from the Middle Ages onwards. It was often used in later periods to give symmetry to the façade of an asymmetrically planned building.

Block capital, *see* CAPITAL.

Blocking course In classical architecture, the plain course of stone surmounting the CORNICE at the top of a building; also a projecting cornice of stone or brick at the base of a building.

Blondel, Jacques-François (1705–74). A minor architect (not related to Nicolas-François Blondel) but also a very influential writer and theorist. He ran his own school of architecture in Paris from 1743 until he became Professor at the Académie royale de l'Architecture in 1762. Conservative in taste he exalted the French tradition as exemplified by MANSART and FERRAULT and thus paved the way for Neo-classicism (*see* CLASSICISM). His publications include *Distribution des maisons de plaisance* (1737); *L'Architecture française* (1752–6) known as the 'Grand Blondel' of which only four of the projected eight volumes appeared; *Discours sur la nécessité de l'étude de l'architecture* (1754) and *Cours d'Architecture* (1771–7) which contains his public lectures and the substance of his teaching. The last two volumes were published posthumously by his pupil PATTE. Of his buildings nothing survives except three sides of the Place d'Armes at Metz (1762–75).

Lit: W. Herrmann, *Laugier and Eighteenth Century French Theory,* London 1962; J. M. Pérouse de Montclos, *É.-L. Boullée,* Paris 1969.

Blondel, Nicolas-François (1617–86), engineer and mathematician, was more interested in the theory than the practice of architecture. He expounded the rigidly classical and rationalist doctrines of the French Academy in his *Cours d'architecture* (1675, augmented ed. 1698). The Porte St Denis, Paris (1671), is his best surviving building.

Blum, Hans (fl. 1550). Blum published the most influential German treatise on the orders: *Quinque Columnarum exacta descriptio atque delineatio . . .* (Zurich 1550) and thus provided German architects with their first grammar to the classical language of architecture. It was based on SERLIO and often reprinted. Later editions (*Ein kunstrych Buoch von allerley Anti-*

quiteten . . . Zurich *c.* 1560, *Warhafte Contrafacturen etlich alt u. schoner Gebauden* . . . Zurich 1562) contain designs by Blum for churches, triumphal arches, etc. An English edition appeared in 1608.

Boasted work Stonework roughly blocked out preparatory to carving; also masonry finished with a boaster chisel.

Böblinger A family of South German masons of which the two most important members were Hans Senior and Matthäus. Hans (d. 1482) was a journeyman at Konstanz in 1435, then became foreman under Matthäus ENSINGER at St Mary, Esslingen, and in 1440 master mason of this church. Matthäus (d. 1505) was one of Hans's sons and was probably trained in Cologne. He was later at Esslingen with his father, and then at Ulm where, after three years, he became master mason of the Minster (1480). He was successor there to Ulrich and Matthäus Ensinger, and replaced Ulrich's design for the west tower with one of his own. His steeple was completed in 1481–90 and became the highest church tower in Europe (530 ft). However, Matthäus had to resign from the post and leave the town after cracks had appeared in the tower. He was called to a number of other places for consultation or to provide designs and supervise. Thieme and Becker's *Künstler-Lexikon* mentions eight more members of the family.
Lit: Thieme-Becker, *Künstler-Lexikon*, vol. IV, Leipzig 1910.

Bodley, George Frederick (1827–1907), was of Scottish descent and George Gilbert SCOTT's first pupil (1845–*c.* 1850). Mostly but not exclusively a church architect, he always worked in the Gothic style; in his earlier works he was influenced by the French C13, later by English models. His style is as competent and knowledgeable as Scott's, but distinguished by a never-failing taste and by abundant and elaborate details, including the choice of those which were used for furnishings and fitments. An early patron of MORRIS, he also started C. E. Kempe on his career. Among his earliest works are St Michael, Brighton (1859–61); St Martin, Scarborough (1861–2); All Saints, Cambridge (1863–4). In 1869 he went into partnership with Thomas Garner (1839–1906), another pupil of Scott's; the partnership lasted till 1898, though after 1884 the partners designed and supervised jobs in-

dividually. Among their most lavish works is Holy Angels, Hoar Cross, Staffordshire (1871–7). St Augustine, Pendlebury (1874), on the other hand, is one of the most monumental by virtue of its simplicity; instead of aisles, it has passages through internal buttresses, a motif derived from Albi and Spain and often repeated by the younger generation. Perhaps the noblest of all Bodley's churches is that of Clumber (1886–9), now standing forlorn in the grounds of the demolished mansion. Bodley also designed the chapel of Queens' College, Cambridge (1890–1), and buildings for King's College, Cambridge (1893). Among his pupils were C. R. Ashbee and Sir Ninian Comper.
Lit: B. F. L. Clarke, *Church Builders of the Nineteenth Century*, London 1938; H.-R. Hitchcock, *Architecture: Nineteenth and Twentieth Centuries*, Pelican History of Art, Harmondsworth 1969, paperback edn 1971.

Bodt, Jean de (1670–1745). A Huguenot who left France after the revocation of the Edict of Nantes in 1685, was trained as an architect in Holland and after working for a time in England settled in 1698 in Berlin where he soon became the most important architect after SCHLÜTER. In 1701 he built the Fortuna Portal of the Potsdam Stadtschloss (retained by KNOBELSDORFF in his rebuilding of 1744) and completed NERING's Arsenal in Berlin (*c.* 1706) and Parochialkirche, modifying both designs. About 1710 the east front of Wentworth Castle, Yorkshire, was built to his designs for the Earl of Strafford. (The Earl of Strafford was ambassador to the King of Prussia 1706–11.) In 1728 he settled in Dresden where he was appointed Superintendent of the Royal Works and thus was in charge of PÖPPELMANN's work at the Japanisches Palais. But all his own ambitious projects for buildings in Dresden and elsewhere in Saxony remained on paper.
Lit: F. Löffler, *Das alte Dresden*, Dresden 1955.

Boffrand, Gabriel Germain (1667–1754), the greatest French Rococo architect, began as a sculptor, studying under Girardon in Paris (1681), but soon turned to architecture. He became the pupil and later the collaborator of J. H. MANSART. In 1711 he became *Premier Architecte* to the Duc de Lorraine for whom he built the new château of Lunéville (1702–6) and its chapel (1720–23). He also built the large country house of Malgrange outside

Nancy (1712–15 demolished) and the main Palace in Nancy (1717–20, demolished 1745); also in Nancy the Hôtel de Beauveau or de Craon (1712–13) and the château at Haroué (1712–13). He was very prolific and made a large fortune, mainly by the speculative building of Parisian *hôtels* (e.g., Hôtels de Montmorency, 1712; de Seignelay, 1713; de Torcy, 1714), but he lost the bulk of it in the Mississippi Bubble of 1720. Like his contemporary de COTTE he had great influence outside France, especially in Germany (e.g., on the Residenz, Würzburg). His virtuosity is well seen in the Hôtel de Montmorency, Paris, built round an oval court with rooms of various shapes and sizes, including a pentagon. The elevations, as always with Boffrand, are of the utmost simplicity and reticence, while the interior is of course very luxurious. His finest interior is probably that of the two-storey pavilion he added (*c.* 1735–9) to the Hôtel de Soubise (now the Archives Nationales), Paris. His Rococo ideal of elegant informality and sophisticated simplicity was realized in his Château de Saint Ouen (*c.* 1710), a brilliant and original conception consisting of a tiny Trianon-like pavilion of three rooms, set in a spacious courtyard formed by the guests' apartment, offices, stables, etc. He published *Livre d'architecture contenant les principes généraux de cet art* in 1745. (For illustration *see* ROCOCO ARCHITECTURE.)

Lit: F. Kimball, *Le Style Louis XV*, Paris 1949; W. Graf Kalnein & M. Levey, *Art and Architecture of the Eighteenth Century in France*, Pelican History of Art, Harmondsworth 1973.

Bogardus, James (1800–74). The pioneer and publicizer in America of cast-iron fronts, he played an important part in the development of mass-production of building parts. He was a manufacturer of iron grinding machinery, not an architect or engineer. Nor was he the first to use iron in architecture. But he started a vogue for the exterior use of cast-iron in the U.S.A. His own four-storey factory in New York of 1848 had walls consisting only of cast-iron piers and lintels. His Laing Stores in New York of 1849 was built in two months. He published *Cast Iron Buildings: their Construction and Advantages* in 1856.

Böhm, Dominikus (1880–1955). One of the best German church architects of this century. Pupil of Theodor Fischer. Among his works are the church of Mainz Bischoffsheim

(1926), the Engelbertkirche at Köln-Rieth (1930) and at St Maria at Köln-Marienburg (1954).

Lit: A. Hoff, S. J. Muck, R. Thoma, *Dominikus Böhm, Leben und Werk*, 1960.

Boileau, Louis-Auguste (1812–96). French architect. One of the first to use iron construction in church architecture. His only familiar work is St Eugène in Paris (1854–5), earlier than BALTARD'S St Augustine and VIOLLET-LE-DUC'S defence of iron in the *Entretiens*. However, earlier still than St Eugène is the Ste Geneviève Library by LABROUSTE. St Eugène was the model for the church of Vésinet (1863). Boileau also wrote a book on the use of iron in architecture.

Lit: C. Beutler, 'Saint-Eugène und die Bibliothèque nationale. Zwei Eisenkonstruktionen und ihr Ideengehalt' in *Miscellanea pro arte* (Festschrift Schnitzler), Dusseldorf 1965.

Boiserie French for wainscoting or panelling, but applied more strictly to C17 and C18 panelling elaborately decorated with shallow-relief carvings.

Bolection moulding A moulding used to cover the joint between two members with different surface levels. It projects beyond both surfaces.

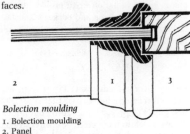

Bolection moulding
1. Bolection moulding
2. Panel
3. Frame

Bon, Giovanni & Bartolomeo, *see* BUON, Giovanni and Bartolomeo.

Bond, *see* BRICKWORK.

Bonnet tile A curved tile used for joining plain tiles along the HIPS of a roof.

Bonomi, Joseph (1739–1808). Born and trained in Italy, he came to England in 1767 at the invitation of the ADAM brothers for whom, presumably, he worked. But by the 1780s he was practising independently. His masterpiece is the small but very impos-

ing church of St James, Great Packington,
Warwickshire (1789–90). It is extremely
severe: plain brick outside, Greek Doric inside
with smooth, painted ashlar. It is the only
building in England which can be compared
with the contemporary work in France by
Ledoux and in Prussia by Gilly. Bonomi's
other work is less original. His large country-
house Roseneath (1803–6) outside Glasgow
was recently demolished. His son **Ignatius**
(*fl.* 1809–49) was an architect in Durham.

Lit: J. Mordaunt Crook, *The Greek Revival,*
London 1972.

Borromini, Francesco (1599–1667). The most
original genius of Roman High Baroque architecture and the jealous rival of his almost
exact contemporary BERNINI. A late starter,
lonely, frustrated, and neurotic, he eventually
committed suicide. Born at Bissone on Lake
Lugano, the son of a mason, he began humbly
as a stone-cutter, went to Rome in his early
twenties, and remained there for the rest of
his life. Befriended by his distant relation
MADERNO, he found employment as a stone-
carver at St Peter's, mainly on decorative
putti, festoons, etc. After Maderno's death
(1629) he continued under Bernini, later becoming his chief assistant and occasionally
contributing to the designs both at St Peter's
and at Palazzo Barberini. But their relationship was uneasy. Himself a first-rate craftsman, Borromini despised Bernini's technical
shortcomings; Bernini's success rankled. The
two men parted for good in 1633 when
Borromini's great opportunity came with the
commission for S. Carlo alle Quattro Fontane.
Despite its miniature size, S. Carlo (1638–41)
is one of the most ingenious spatial compositions ever invented and displays Borromini's
mastery of his art and revolutionary disregard
for convention. The oval plan, emphasized by
the honeycomb dome, is based on geometric
units (equilateral triangles), but the swaying
rhythm and sculptural effect of the undulating
walls and restless, intertwined plastic elements
produce an almost voluptuous effect. The
concave–convex–concave façade was added
in 1667. S. Carlo was quickly followed by S.
Ivo della Sapienza (1642–60). Borromini's
triangular planning system here produced a
star-hexagon, which he worked out vertically
with dynamic effect. The fantastic dome culminates in an extraordinary ZIGGURAT-like
spiral feature.

His style reached its zenith at S. Ivo. Later
buildings were either left unfinished or in-

hibited by complexities of site or by his having
to take over plans by previous architects.
Unfinished works include S. Maria dei Sette
Dolori (*c.* 1642–6); the interior remodelling
of S. Giovanni in Laterano (1646–9), which
still lacks the intended nave vaulting; and S.
Andrea delle Fratte (1653–65), where the
dome is still without its lantern though the
drum-like casing and three-storey tower outdo
even S. Ivo in fantasy. At S. Agnese in Piazza
Navona (1653–7) he took over from Carlo
RAINALDI, changing the character of his interior designs by seemingly minor alterations
and completely redesigning the façade on a
concave plan. The dramatic grouping of high
drum and dome framed by elegant towers is
one of his best and most typical compositions,
though he was dismissed as architect before
its completion. An awkward site cramped his
style at the Oratory of St Philip Neri (1637–
50), remarkable mainly for its ingenious dual-
purpose façade uniting chapel and monastic
buildings. His domestic architecture is frag-
mentary but no less startling – *trompe l'œil*
arcade at Palazzo Spada, river front and loggia
at Palazzo Falconieri, grand *salone* at Palazzo
Pamphili, and the library at the Sapienza. The
latter was the prototype of many great C18
libraries.

He became increasingly unorthodox, and
his last work, the Collegio di Propaganda Fide
(*c.* 1660), shows a remarkable change of style
towards monumentality and austerity, the
capitals, for example, being reduced to a few
parallel grooves. Its façade in via di Propaganda – heavy, oppressive, nightmarish – is
unlike anything before or since. Reproached
in his own day for having destroyed the conventions of good architecture, Borromini had
little immediate influence in Italy except superficially in ornamentation. (His revolutionary
spatial concepts were to bear abundant fruit
later on in Central Europe.) His style was too
personal and eccentric, especially in its
combination of Gothic and post-Renaissance
elements. His Gothic affinities were noted by
his contemporaries (e.g., Baldinucci), and indeed they went beyond a partiality for medieval
features such as the SQUINCH, for his geometrical system of planning and emphasis on
a dynamic skeleton brought him close to the
structural principles of Gothic. Yet his blending
of architecture and sculpture and his voluptuous moulding of space and mass tie him to
the Italian anthropomorphic tradition. (For
illustrations *see* BAROQUE ARCHITECTURE,
ITALIAN ARCHITECTURE and LANTERN.)

Lit: E. Thelen, *Francesco Borromini, Die Handzeichnungen*, Graz 1967; P. Portoghesi, *Borromini, Architettura come linguaggio*, Milan 1967; R. Wittkower, *Art and Architecture in Italy, 1600–1750*, Pelican History of Art, 3rd edn, Harmondsworth 1973, paperback edn 1973.

Boss An ornamental knob or projection covering the intersection of ribs in a vault or ceiling; often carved with foliage.

A boss from the Abbey Church of Mogila, near Cracow, mid-C13

Bosses: Gloucester Cathedral, c. 1335

Boullée, Étienne-Louis (1728–99). A leading neo-classical architect, he probably had more influence than LEDOUX, though he built little (the Hôtel Alexandre, Paris, 1766–8, is the most interesting survivor), and his treatise on architecture remained unpublished until as recently as 1953; for he had many and important pupils, such as J. N. L. DURAND who wrote the most influential treatise of the Empire period. His best designs date from the 1780s and 1790s and are, if anything, even more megalomaniac than Ledoux's – e.g., a 500-ft-high spherical monument to Newton – and they are also, like Ledoux's, expressive or *parlantes* in intention despite their apparently abstract, geometrical simplicity. In his treatise he pleads for a felt, as much as reasoned, architecture, and for character, grandeur, and magic. (For illustration *see* CLASSICISM.)

Lit: H. Rosenau, ed., *Boullée's Treatise on Architecture*, London 1953; J. M. Pérouse de Montclos, *Étienne-Louis Boullée (1728–1799)*, Paris 1969; A. H. Vogt, *Boullée's Newton Denkmal*, Basel–Stuttgart 1969.

Bow window, *see* WINDOW.

Bowstring roof, *see* ROOF.

Bowtell A term in use by the C15 (e.g., William of Worcester's notes; mason's contracts) for a convex moulding. A form of ROLL

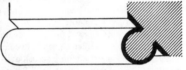

Bowtell

MOULDING usually three-quarters of a circle in section; also called *edge roll*.

Box A small country house, e.g., a shooting box. A convenient term to describe a compact minor dwelling, e.g., a rectory.

Box-frame A box-like form of concrete construction, where the loads are taken on cross walls. This is suitable only for buildings consisting of repetitive small cells, such as flats or hostels. Sometimes called *cross-wall* construction.

Box-pew, *see* PEW.

Brace, *see* ROOF.

Bracket A small supporting piece of stone or other material, often formed of scrolls or VOLUTES, to carry a projecting weight. *See also* CORBEL. (Illustrated next column.)

Bramante, Donato (Donato di Pascuccio d'Antonio, 1444–1514). The first of the great High Renaissance architects. He began under

Brackets

the shadow of ALBERTI and MICHELOZZO, and was profoundly influenced by LEONARDO DA VINCI, from whom he derived his interest in centrally-planned churches. In Rome he evolved a classic style of imposing monumentality which was to have a deep and lasting effect on the development of Italian architecture. PALLADIO declared that he 'was the first who brought good architecture to light'. He was born near Urbino, where he probably met the leading artists at the humanist court of Federigo da Montefeltro, Piero della Francesca and FRANCESCO DI GIORGIO, to whom he presumably owed his interest in the problems of perspective. He is first recorded in 1477 painting perspective decorations on the façade of Palazzo del Podestà, Bergamo, and he later (1481) made a drawing which was engraved as a perspective model for painters. He entered the service of Duke Ludovico Sforza c. 1479, for whom he worked at Vigevano as both decorative painter and architect. His first building of importance is S. Maria presso S. Satiro, Milan (begun 1482). Here he encased the tiny c9 Cappella della Pietà in a drum decorated with niches flanked by slender pilasters, and crowned it with a rather chunky octagonal lantern. He entirely rebuilt the rest of the church on a Latin cross plan. Alberti's influence is apparent in the design for the façade (never completed), the use of shallow pilasters on the side wall and the barrel-vaulted nave. There was no room for a chancel so he feigned one in *trompe l'œil* painting and relief (still deceptive if seen from the right spot). Above the crossing he built a dome with coffered interior, the first since Roman times. He also built an octagonal sacristy, very richly decorated with carvings. In 1488 he was appointed consultant to Pavia Cathedral but only the crypt was carried out according to his proposals.

He designed a centrally planned east end for the Gothic church of S. Maria delle Grazie, Milan, spacious and airy internally, but with a lavish use of elegant but rather finicking carving on the exterior of the apses and the sixteen-sided drum which encases the dome (though much of this ornament may have been added without the warrant of his designs). For S. Ambrogio, Milan, he designed the Canons' Cloister (1492, only one wing built) and a further group of four cloisters (1497, two completed after 1576 to his plans). In the Canons' Cloister he used slender Corinthian columns with high friezes and boldly projecting impost blocks, and four columns in the form of tree trunks with the stumps of sawn-off branches protruding from the cylinders.

In 1499 the French invasion of Lombardy and the fall of the Sforzas forced him to flee to Rome, then the artistic centre of Italy. Apart from some frescoes, his first work in Rome was a cloister at S. Maria della Pace (1500), astonishingly different from anything he had previously designed. It has sturdy piers and attached Ionic columns derived from the Colosseum on the ground floor, and an open gallery on the first with alternate columns and piers supporting not arches but an architrave. The effect is wholly Roman in its quiet gravity. He became still graver and more Roman in his next building, the circular Tempietto of S. Pietro in Montorio, Rome (1502), the first great monument of the High Renaissance, which has a majestic solemnity belying its small size. Surrounded at the base by a Tuscan Doric colonnade with a correct classical entablature, it has no surface decorations apart from the metopes and the shells in the niches. It was intended to have been set in the centre of a circular peristyle which would have provided the perfect spatial foil to its solidity, for it is conceived in terms of volume rather than space, like a Greek temple. Here the Renaissance came closer to the spirit of antiquity than in any other building.

The election of Pope Julius II in 1503 provided Bramante with a new and wholly congenial patron who commissioned him to draw up a vast building plan for the Vatican and St Peter's. A range of buildings later incorporated in the Cortile di S. Damaso was promptly begun, with three tiers of superimposed arcades. Though massive, this was relatively modest in comparison with the scheme for the Cortile del Belvedere, a huge courtyard on three levels measuring about

950 ft by 225 ft, flanked by arcaded buildings, with a theatre at the lower end and a museum for classical antiquities with a central exedra closing the upper court. Work began at the museum end, but only the first storey was completed to his designs (much altered later). The only one of his works in the Vatican which survives intact is the handsome spiral ramp enclosed in a tower of the Belvedere (*c.* 1505). For St Peter's he proposed a church that would have been the *ne plus ultra* in centralized planning – a Greek cross with four smaller Greek crosses in the arms, roofed by a vast central dome as large as the Pantheon's with four smaller domes and four corner towers, all standing isolated in an immense *piazza*. The foundation stone was laid in 1506 and building was begun but little was completed before the Pope's death in 1513 brought all work to a halt. The choir for S. Maria del Popolo, Rome (1505–9), is small in scale but grand in conception, with a massively coffered vault and shell-capped apse. The Santa Casa at Loreto (begun 1509) is almost as Roman as the Cortile del Belvedere, though heavily and richly decorated with sculptures by Andrea Sansovino, Tribolo, Baccio Bandinelli, G. B. della Porta and others. He also designed and began Palazzo Caprini, Rome (*c.* 1510, later altered out of recognition), with a heavily rusticated basement and five pedimented windows between coupled half-columns on the upper floor, a design which was to be widely imitated. The house was later acquired by RAPHAEL, who inherited Bramante's position as leading architect in Rome. (For illustration *see* ITALIAN ARCHITECTURE and RENAISSANCE ARCHITECTURE.)

Lit: J. Ackerman, *The Cortile del Belvedere*, Rome 1954; A. Bruschi, *Bramante Architetto*, Bari 1969; L. H. Heydenreich & W. Lotz, *Architecture in Italy 1400–1600*, Pelican History of Art, Harmondsworth 1974.

Bramantino, *see* SUARDI, BARTOLOMEO.

Brattishing An ornamental cresting on the top of a screen or cornice usually formed of leaves, Tudor flowers, or miniature battlements.

Brazilian architecture Brazil was settled by the Portuguese early in the c16 and remained a Portuguese colony till 1807. The country became an independent empire in 1822, and a republic in 1889. Architecture during the colonial centuries remained dependent on

São Francisco, São Salvador de Bahia, begun 1708

Detail of ceiling, São Francisco, São Salvador de Bahia, c. 1735

Portugal; one of the earliest Baroque churches is S. Bento at Rio of 1652. The centres of the Baroque, however, are S. Salvador de Bahia and the towns of Minas Gerais, where gold was discovered in the late c17. At Bahia the Terceiros Church of 1703 is exuberantly CHURRIGUERESQUE; so is the decoration of the church of S. Francisco (1708 etc.). The architectural climax of Brazilian Baroque, however, is Ouro Preto near Belo Horizonte, with its many churches of the second half of the c18, mostly with two façade towers and elongated central plans. To the same group belongs the church of Bom Jesus at Congonhas

Bom Jesus de Matozinhos, Congonhas do Campo,
begun 1777, by Aleijadinho

São Francisco, Ouro Preto, 1766–94

Rosario chapel, Ouro Preto, 1784

do Campo (1777): sculpture here and in
several of the Ouro Preto churches is by
ALEIJADINHO.

A revulsion from the Baroque came only
after 1815. French artists immigrated, including A. H. V. Grandjean de Montigny
(1776–1850), who finished the Customs

House at Rio in 1820. A little later, but still
French Classical, is the theatre at Recife by
Louis Vauthier (c. 1810–77), and the rather
more American-Colonial-looking theatre at
Belém do Pará (1868–78) with its attenuated
giant portico. The neo-Baroque is best illustrated by the opera house at Manáus of
1890–6.

While all this had been first colonial and
then peripheral, Brazil became one of the
leading countries of the world in architecture
after the Second World War. The Modern
Movement had been introduced by the white
cubic houses built from 1928 onwards by

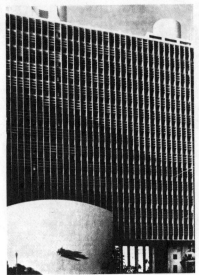

Villa in São Paulo, by Gregori Warchavchik

Ministry of Education and Health,
Rio de Janeiro, 1937–43,
by Costa and Niemeyer (and Le Corbusier)

São Francisco, Pampulha, 1943,
by Niemeyer

Gregori Warchavchik, who published his
Manifesto on Modern Architecture in 1925. LE
CORBUSIER visited Brazil briefly in 1929, and
again in 1936, in connection with the proposed new Ministry of Education at Rio. The
building was begun to an amended plan by a
group of young Brazilian architects in 1937.
Among them were both Lucio COSTA and
Oscar NIEMEYER, now the most famous

Brazilian architects. Niemeyer is especially
important for his early buildings at Pampulha,
a club, a dance hall, and a casino of 1942, and
a church of 1943. They are the earliest buildings in any country resolutely and adven-
turously to turn away from the international
rationalism then just being accepted by progressive authorities and clients in most
countries. Instead, Niemeyer introduced para-

Pedregulho flats, Rio de Janeiro, 1950–2, by Reidy

The Square of the Three Powers,
with the Parliament buildings,
Brasilia, begun 1958, by Niemeyer

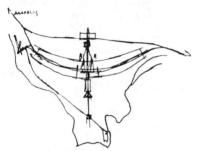

Sketch for Brasilia, by Costa, 1957

bolic curves in elevation, a tower with tapering sides, passages under canopies snaking
their way from one building to another, a
pair of monopitch roofs slanting downward
to where they meet. Other architects whose
names have become familiar are Marcelo and
Milton Roberto, Affonso Reidy, and Rino Levi.

Lucio Costa's name became a household
word overnight when in 1956 he won the
competition for the plan of Brasilia, the new
capital of Brazil (*see* COSTA). The principal
buildings there are by Niemeyer: the hotel,
the brilliant president's palace, the palaces
of the three powers, and the ministry buildings. Niemeyer's centrally planned cathedral
is not yet completed.

Lit: H.-R. Hitchcock, *Latin American Architecture,* New York 1955; H. E. Mindlin,

Modern Architecture in Brazil, Rio de Janeiro–
Amsterdam 1956: H.-R. Hitchcock, *Architecture: Nineteenth and Twentieth Centuries,*
Pelican History of Art, Harmondsworth 1969,
paperback edn 1971; S. Bracco, *L'Architettura
moderna in Brasilia,* Bologna 1967; F. Bullrich, *New Directions in Latin American Architecture,* New York 1969.

Breastsummer, *see* BRESSUMER.

Bressumer A massive horizontal beam, sometimes carved, spanning a wide opening such
as a fireplace. Also the principal horizontal
rail in a timber-framed house.

Brettingham, Matthew (1699–1769), was
undistinguished, but had a large practice and
built Holkham Hall to KENT's designs. He
later claimed to have designed it himself. Few
of his own works survive; Langley Park is
probably the best. In London he designed
several important town houses: Norfolk
House (1747–56, demolished 1938), York
House, Pall Mall (1760–67, demolished) and
No. 5, St James's Square (1748–51). His son
Matthew (1725–1803) was also an architect,
equally successful and equally undistinguished.

Breuer, Marcel, was born at Pécs in Hungary,
1902. He studied at the BAUHAUS from 1920.
In 1925 he was put in charge of the joinery
and cabinet workshop, and in that year de-

signed his first tubular steel chair. He went to London in 1935, to Harvard in 1937, and was in a partnership with GROPIUS 1937–40. His independent practice in America started effectively only after the Second World War. He was first commissioned to design private houses in New England. A sympathy with natural materials (rubble, timber), derived perhaps from his Bauhaus days, had already been apparent in some of his work in England. In the last twenty years his practice has spread to other countries (Bijenkorf, Rotterdam, with Elzas, 1953; Unesco, Paris, with Zehrfuss and NERVI, 1953), and his style has followed the rather less rational and more arbitrary trend of architecture in general (Abbey of St John, Collegeville, Minnesota, 1953 and the Lecture Hall for New York University on University Heights, Bronx, N.Y., 1961).

Lit: P. Blake, *Marcel Breuer: Architect and Designer*, New York 1949; Marcel Breuer, *Sun and Shadow*, New York 1956; L. Cranston Jones, *M. Breuer, 1921–1962*, Milan 1963.

Brickwork A *header* is a brick laid so that the end only appears on the face of the wall, while a *stretcher* is a brick laid so that the side only appears on the face of the wall.

English bond is a method of laying bricks so that alternate courses or layers on the face of the wall are composed of headers or stretchers only; *Flemish bond* is a method of laying bricks so that alternate headers and stretchers appear in each course on the face of the wall. *Heading bond* is composed of headers only.

Brickwork

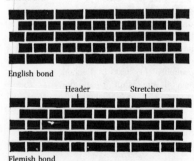

English bond

Header   Stretcher

Flemish bond

Bridge A construction spanning a stretch of water, road, railway-track or valley, and allowing their passage beneath.

1. Bridges can be categorized according to what they bear – as AQUEDUCTS, VIADUCTS or road-bridges, railway-bridges, and footbridges; according to the materials with which they are built – wood, rope, stone, iron, steel, concrete and reinforced concrete, and light alloys; or according to their type of construction – *girder bridges* (strut-framed or suspended), in which a load on the framework is exerted in compression on the end supports; *arch bridges*, where arches or arched vaults are the main load-bearers; *suspension bridges*, in which the framework is hung from high masts (PYLONS); *cantilever bridges*, whose latticed framework is mostly of iron or steel, and which like modern concrete bridges can achieve the greatest spans; and *moveable bridges*, *drawbridges* being the most familiar, but including *swing* and *bascule* bridges as well.

2. *Components.* The foundations, when free-standing supports, are called *piers*. They are of a different construction on land and in the water, where they must resist the current. The leading edge of a pier facing the current is called the *breakwater*. The superstructure of a bridge consists of the passage across and, quite commonly in the Middle Ages and Renaissance, additions like roofing, chapels, towers, and even houses. In the Middle Ages bridges were also fortified at the end by a *bridgehead*.

3. *Historical survey.* The first wooden bridges appeared in the Bronze Age around the same time as the dwellers on Lake Constance were making their huts on piles (4000 B.C.). Contemporaneously, the first primitive suspension bridges appeared in Asia and Africa; the earliest serviceable suspension and cantilever bridges capable of further development were erected in India. The arch bridge was born in Mesopotamia; from there it reached Egypt (3600 B.C.), Greece (450 B.C.) and Rome (200 B.C.). Amongst the very earliest forms of bridge were pontoon bridges, made of boats, used in military operations by the Persian kings Cyrus, Darius and Xerxes (537–480 B.C.), and still an essential part of military equipment. In Istanbul a steel pontoon bridge was laid across the Golden Horn as recently as 1939, and a concrete pontoon bridge has spanned the Derwent, near Hobart in Tasmania, since 1944 (over 1000 yards long).

The earliest Roman bridge that we know of was the wooden bridge over the Tiber (*pons Sublicius*, 691 B.C.). This bridge was maintained by the priesthood, and remained

Wooden bridge over the Serwent, Pakistan

Wooden bridge, Tirana, Albania

Suspension bridge over the Min, China

in use for 900 years. Caesar and Hannibal erected pontoon bridges of the same kind as Xerxes. Caesar left the earliest detailed description of the construction of a bridge, one that he built over the Rhine (55 B.C.). Trajan's historic bridge over the Danube in Hungary (the *pontes Trajani* built by APOLLODORUS OF DAMASCUS in A.D. 104) consisted of a series of semicircular wooden arches resting on stone piers; their approximately 200 ft span was not equalled for another twelve centuries. The Romans threw fine stone bridges across the Tiber; six erected between 200 B.C. and A.D. 260 survived into this century, among them the famous Ponte Sant'Angelo. The

most important Roman bridges outside the city itself were the Ponte di Augusto at Rimini (*c.* 5 B.C.); that of Martorell in Spain, the earliest still surviving (*c.* 219 B.C.), of dressed stone and with a centre arch measuring 130 ft across; the aqueduct of Segovia (*c.* 1000 yards long); the Puente Alcantara (A.D. 98) over the Tagus, with six semicircular arches of granite; and the Pont du Gard at Nimes (A.D. 14), the longest aqueduct of all. Every Roman arch bridge had semicircular arches; the individual piers were so solid that the collapse of one of them could never lead to the collapse of the whole bridge.

In the Middle Ages bridge-building was the task of the clergy; the Church was the repository of Roman experience, and several Orders sprang up devoted to bridge-building. The two finest medieval bridges, the arch bridge at Avignon (1178–88) by St Bénezèt, and London Bridge (1176–1209) with its 19 arches by Peter of Colechurch, which remained in use till 1831, were both built by monks. Lucerne had two fine covered wooden bridges – the Chapel Bridge (1333) and the Dance of Death Bridge (1408). The segmental arch was introduced by the beautiful Ponte Vecchio in Florence (1345); and the Charles Bridge of Prague (1348–1507) heralded the Renaissance.

In the Renaissance bridge-building became a civic responsibility, and builders had to be both artists and engineers. PALLADIO stipulated that a bridge was to be built for commodity, endurance and delight. One of the most delightful is that of the Rialto over the Grand Canal in Venice – a shallow segmental arch with six-bay arcades supporting a roof on its back, built by Antonio da Ponte 1587–91. Even more harmonious is the Ponte Santa Trinita over the Arno at Florence, with its three exquisitely curved white marble arches (1567–9). In Paris bridges were among the most important jobs of the Renaissance; the first stone bridge over

Ponte di Augusto, Rimini,
5 B.C.

Rialto Bridge, Venice,
by Antonio da Ponte, 1587–91

the Seine, the Pont Notre-Dame, was built in 1505 and the Pont-Neuf, the earliest stone bridge still to survive and be in use, between 1575 and 1606.

Whilst the role of engineering in bridge-building was recognized in the Renaissance, it was the c18, the Age of Reason, which grounded it in theory. In 1714 Hubert Gautier produced the first theoretical treatise on bridge-building; in 1716 Louis XV founded the *Corps des Pontes et Chaussées*, and 1747 saw the foundation of the first school of engineering in the world at Paris, the renowned *Ecole des Pontes et Chaussées*. Its first instructor was Jean Perronet, the 'father of modern bridge-building'. His most important bridges are the Pont Sainte-Maxence over the Oise and the Pont de la Concorde (1787–91) in Paris, both stone arch bridges with a large span. In England, John RENNIE gave Waterloo Bridge semicircular arches, not the elliptical arches used by Perronet, and began the new London Bridge, which was finished by his son (1831).

Covered wooden bridges are common to all countries rich in timber; in Switzerland Johannes and Hans Ulrich Grubenmann built noteworthy examples of the kind, such as the Reichenau (1756–7) and a bridge at Wettingen over the Limmat (1746–66). In the United States, Enoch Hale built the first wooden bridge over the Connecticut River at Bellows Falls, Vermont (1785), whilst the first to insist on covering wooden bridges as a protection against the elements was Timothy Palmer, who built the Permanent Bridge at Philadelphia in 1804–6. New techniques of strut-framing were introduced by Theodore Burr and Ithiel Town, and in 1840 William Howe patented a version using wood and iron.

The first cast iron bridge was put up over the Severn at Coalbrookdale in 1779 by Abraham Darby and John Wilkinson, with a span of over 100 feet, though cast iron had been first used in suspension bridge building some years earlier, in 1741 in the Winch suspension bridge over the Tees near Middleton.

Economic and technical developments have given bridge-building a new impetus in the last two centuries, with new fields of activity: the second half of the c19 was dominated by railway bridges (EIFFEL, the BRUNELS), and this century by the requirements of roads and motorways. The distances to be spanned and the loads to be borne have grown steadily as bridges have become the nodal points of traffic; and the challenge has given rise to new methods of construction and

Steel bridge, St André de Calzac

Steel bridge over the Truyère, 1884, by Eiffel

the use of novel materials. In 1819–26 Thomas Telford built his Menai Strait Bridge in Wales, a suspension bridge with cast iron chains, still standing in the middle of the c20. The first iron railway bridge was built by George Stephenson in 1823 for the Stockton and Darlington Railway; more famous was Robert Stephenson's Britannia Tubular Bridge over the Menai Strait (1846–50). Iron supports dominated bridge-building between 1840 and 1890, but were then overshadowed by steel. The first purely steel bridge was that over the Missouri at Glasgow, South Dakota (1878). The first modern cantilever bridge was that over the Main at Hassfurt by Heinrich Gerber (1867), with a span of about 460 ft; and the first in the U.S.A. was the Kentucký River Viaduct by C. S. Smith (1876). But up till the middle of this century the huge Firth of Forth Bridge by Sir John Fowler and Sir Benjamin Baker remained the most remarkable bridge of this type; its span was not surpassed till 1917, by the Quebec Bridge over the St Lawrence, but shortly thereafter suspension bridges took over.

One of the most important bridge-builders of the U.S.A. was John A. Roebling, who exercised a key influence on the development of the suspension bridge with his works: the Niagara Railway Bridge (1851–5), the still serviceable bridge over the Ohio (1856–7), and most notably the Brooklyn Bridge over the East River in New York (1883, completed by his son Washington Roebling).

The type of latticework suspension bridge evolved by Robert Stephenson for the Menai Strait was chiefly taken up in Germany and the U.S.A.; the two longest bridges of the kind are the two post-war bridges over the Rhine at Bonn-Beuel (1949) and Cologne (1948). The Elbe bridges at Hamburg were built as early as 1936.

The longest suspension bridge altogether, the Golden Gate Bridge at San Francisco, dates back to 1937; for the one built between the Brazilian mainland and the island of Florianopolis in 1926, Robinson and Steinmann evolved a method of partial prefabrication. The longest bridge in Europe is that over the Rhine at Rodenkirchen (1941, destroyed 1944, rebuilt 1954). Germany also boasts the longest cable bridge in the world (when opened in 1970) with a steel centre support, at Duisburg (2500 feet long, span over the river 1140 feet); and the largest modern stone bridge at Plauen; built in 1903, it was the culmination of monumental stone bridge-building.

Huge concrete bridges were created in France (Pont Albert-Louppe at Plougastel near Brest, by FREYSSINET, 1929, destroyed 1944) and Sweden (the Sando Bridge over the Angerman-Elf, 1943). The first reinforced

Reinforced concrete bridge, Sandøl, Sweden, 1943

Suspension bridge over the Rhine at Rodenkirchen, 1954

concrete bridge was built by François Hennebique in 1894 at Viggen in Switzerland, which is where MAILLART'S famous bridge of the same kind was built, and his Salginatobel bridge (1928-30) too.

A notable example of a bascule bridge is the Tower Bridge, London (1886-94). The swing bridge is well exemplified by the bridge carrying the Duke of Bridgewater's canal over the Manchester Ship Canal at Barton, Manchester (1893).   [HC]

Lit: F. Johnstone-Taylor, *Modern Bridge Construction*, Heids Courad, London 1951; H. S. Jacoby & Davis, *Foundations of Bridges and Buildings*, New York 1941; A. Schau, *Asthetik im Brückenbau*, 1928; P. Zucker, *Die Brücke, Typologie und Geschichte ihrer künstlerischen Gestaltung*, Berlin 1921; C. S. Chetto and H. C. Adam, *Reinforced Concrete Bridge Design*, London 1938.

Brise-soleil A sun-break or check; now frequently an arrangement of horizontal or vertical fins, used in hot climates to shade the window openings.

Broach spire, *see* SPIRE.

Broach-stop, *see* STOP-CHAMFER.

Brodrick, Cuthbert (1822–1905). A Yorkshire architect whose capital work is the Leeds Town Hall (1853–8), a grand edifice with a many-columned dome, influenced by COCKERELL and of course WREN. More original is his Leeds Corn Exchange (1861–3), elliptical in plan, Italian Renaissance in style, and with little in the way of enrichment. He also did the wondrously big and heavy Grand Hotel at Scarborough in a style paying tribute to the then fashionable French Renaissance (1863–7), and the Town Hall of Hull (1862–6).

Lit: T. B. Wilson, *Two Leeds Architects: Cuthbert Brodrick and George Corson*, Leeds 1937.

Brongniart, Alexandre-Théodore (1739–1813), a prominent neo-classical architect, was born in Paris and trained under J.-F. BLONDEL. In 1765 he began his very successful independent practice, designing the theatre at Caen (destroyed) and the Hôtel de Montesson, Paris (1771, destroyed). For his private houses he adopted a graceful and unpedantic neo-classical style, the nearest equivalent in architecture to the sculpture of

Clodion, who was several times employed to decorate them (e.g., Hôtel de Condé, Paris, designed 1780). But for the Capuchin convent in the Chaussée d'Antin, now Lycée Hoche (1780–82, façade rebuilt 1864), he developed a much more severe manner, designing a colonnade of Paestum Doric columns for the cloister. In 1804 he was entrusted with the new cemetery of Père-Lachaise in Paris and its *jardin anglais* layout was very influential. His last important work was the Paris Bourse, an appropriately grandiose Corinthian building in the Imperial Roman style (begun 1807, altered and enlarged 1895).

Lit: J. Silvestre de Sacy, *A.-T. Brongniart, Paris* 1940; W. Graf Kalnein & M. Levey, *Art and Architecture of the Eighteenth Century in France*, Pelican History of Art, Harmondsworth 1973.

Brooks, James (1825–1901). A Gothic-Revival church architect whose directness of approach is comparable to BUTTERFIELD'S; but where Butterfield is obstinate and perverse, Brooks excels by a simplicity which LETHABY called big-boned. His favourite material was stock brick, his favourite style that of the early C13 with lancet windows and apse. His principal churches are all in London: first a group in the poor north-eastern suburbs (St Michael, Shoreditch, 1863; Holy Saviour, Hoxton, 1864; St Chad, Haggerston, 1867; St Columba, Haggerston, 1867); and then, a little more refined, three individual masterpieces, among the best of their date in the country: the Ascension, Lavender Hill, 1874; the Transfiguration, Lewisham, 1880 (recently mutilated by the insertion of a *mezzanine* floor above the arcades); and All Hallows, Gospel Oak, 1889. The latter was intended to be vaulted throughout.

Lit: B. F. L. Clarke, *Church Builders of the Nineteenth Century*, London 1938; H.-R. Hitchcock, *Architecture: Nineteenth and Twentieth Centuries*, Pelican History of Art, Harmondsworth 1969, paperback edn 1971.

Brosse, Salomon de (1571–1626), was born at Verneuil where his maternal grandfather Jacques Androuet Du CERCEAU was building the *château*. His father was also an architect. He settled in Paris *c.* 1598, and was appointed architect to the Crown in 1608. Unlike his relations in the Du Cerceau family and his predecessor BULLANT he conceived architecture in terms of mass and not merely of surface decoration. This plastic sense is evident in his great *châteaux* of Montceaux (begun *c.* 1610), Coulommiers (1613), Luxembourg (begun 1615, enlarged and altered C19), and Blérancourt (1619, one pavilion remains). The latter was the finest, and was revolutionary in its day, being a free-standing symmetrical block designed to be seen from all sides. In 1618 he began the Palais de Justice at Rennes, to which his feeling for sharply defined masses and delicacy of classical detail gives great distinction. His frenchified classicism is epitomized in the façade of St Gervais, Paris (begun 1615), which combines VIGNOLA'S Gesù scheme with DELORME'S frontispiece at Anet with three superimposed orders. He was the most notable precursor of François MANSART, whom he anticipated in some ways.

Lit: Rosalys Coope, *Salomon de Brosse*, London 1972.

Brown, Lancelot (nicknamed Capability, 1716–83). The architect of several Palladian country houses, e.g., Croome Court (1751–2) and Claremont House (1770–2). But he is much more important as a landscape gardener. In 1740 he became gardener at Stowe where he worked on KENT'S great layout, and in 1749 he became a consulting landscape gardener. Very soon he developed an artfully informal manner and devised numerous parks with wide expanses of lawns, clumps of trees, serpentine lakes, which provided a perfect setting for the neo-Palladian country seat. Nature was not fettered, as in the formal schemes of LE NÔTRE, but tamed, and a thick planting of trees served both to conceal the bounds of the idyllic park and to protect it from the unimproved landscape beyond. His probably apocryphal remark on his lake at Blenheim, 'Thames, Thamès, you will never forgive me,' sums up his attitude. His parks were less an alternative to the formal garden than an alternative to nature which proved irresistibly appealing not only in England but also on the Continent. His best surviving parks are: Warwick Castle (*c.* 1750), Croome Court (1751), Bowood (1761), Blenheim (1765, much altered), Ashburnham (1767), Dodington Park (1764), and Nuneham Courtenay (1778).

Lit: Dorothy Stroud, *Capability Brown*, London 1957.

Bruant, Libéral (*c.* 1635–97), built the Hôtel des Invalides in Paris (1670–7), notable for the Roman gravity of its arcaded courts, and the highly original Salpêtrière Chapel in Paris (c. 1670). He was a greatly gifted architect who never achieved the success he merited.

Bruce, Sir William (d. 1710), introduced the classical style into Scotland. He came into prominence after the Restoration (for which he had vigorously intrigued), was rewarded with the lucrative Clerkship to the Bills (1660), created baronet 1668, and in 1671 appointed King's Surveyor and Master of Works in Scotland. His work at Holyrood House, Edinburgh (1671 onwards), is frenchified but still rather gauche. Kinross House (1685) and Hopetoun House (1698–1702) are more accomplished in the PRATT tradition.

Lit: J. G. Dunbar, *Sir William Bruce*, Exh. Cat., Edinburgh 1971.

Brunel, Isambard Kingdom (1806–59). The son of Sir **Marc Isambard Brunel** (1769–1849), who had been born in Normandy, had worked in the French Navy, then as city engineer in New York, and had settled in England in 1799; his most famous English work is the Thames Tunnel from Wapping to Rotherhithe (1824–43). The son was educated in Paris and trained in his father's office. In 1829 he designed the Clifton Bridge at Bristol, one of the noblest of English suspension bridges. He was also responsible for the Great Western line from London to Bristol, including the Box Tunnel. His best-known bridge is the Saltash Bridge, opened in 1859. He also built ships (the *Great Western*, which took only fifteen days to America, the even larger *Great Eastern*, and finally the *Great Britain*, recently brought back from South America by a Dutch salvage firm and now docked and being renovated at Bristol) and in addition, docks (Bristol, Monkwearmouth).

Lit: L. T. C. Rolt, *Isambard Kingdom Brunel*, London 1957.

Brunelleschi, Filippo (1377–1446), the first Renaissance architect and one of the greatest, as elegant and refined as Botticelli and as springlike. Far less dogmatic and antiquarian than his immediate successors, e.g., ALBERTI and MICHELOZZO, he was less concerned with the revival of antiquity than with practical problems of construction and the management of space. He, more than anyone else, was responsible for formulating the

laws of linear perspective, and a preoccupation with the linear conquest of space characterizes his architecture. In his buildings the horizontals are marked by thin lines which seem to follow the guides of a perspective framework, while the verticals, columns, and fluted pilasters have a spidery, linear attenuation.

Born in Florence, he began as a goldsmith and sculptor, joining the Arte della Seta in 1398, then working for a goldsmith in Pistoia (silver altar, Pistoia Cathedral, c. 1399), and competing in 1401–2 for the second bronze door of the Florence Baptistery (he tied with Ghiberti but refused to collaborate with him). In 1404 he was admitted as a master to the Goldsmiths' Guild, and in the same year his advice was sought about a buttress for the cathedral in Florence. Sometime after 1402 he made his first visit to Rome, with Donatello, to study antique sculpture. He continued as a sculptor for a while, but gradually turned his attention exclusively to architecture. In 1415 he repaired the Ponte a Mare at Pisa; in 1417 he advised on the projected dome of Florence Cathedral. His first major works, all in Florence, date from 1418 onwards – a domed chapel in S. Jacopo sopr'Arno (destroyed), the Barbadori Chapel in S. Felicità (partly destroyed), the Palazzo di Parte Guelfa (begun c. 1420, much altered, but the prototype Early Renaissance palace), and S. Lorenzo. While these were in progress he began, in 1420, to build his masterpiece, the dome of Florence Cathedral, and in 1419 the Ospedale degli Innocenti in Florence.

At S. Lorenzo he began with the sacristy (1421, finished 1428), a cube roofed by a very elegant dome with narrow ribs radiating from the central lantern, a type of construction he called *a creste e vele* (with crests and sails), which neatly expresses its appearance of canvas stretched over the quadrant ribs. The whole interior is painted white, while taut bands of grey *pietra serena* outline the main architectural members; this is the first instance of this strikingly effective decorative scheme. The church itself he designed as a basilica, adding shallow transepts and also chapels attached to the side aisles. But he drew his inspiration not from Imperial Rome so much as the Tuscan Romanesque or proto-Renaissance of the CII–12.

He was commissioned to build the cathedral dome in partnership with Ghiberti who gradually slipped out of the picture. The dome is Gothic in outline with elegantly curved white ribs springing up to the centre, but it is essentially Renaissance in its engineering technique – herringbone brickwork in the Roman manner. The skeleton was completed in 1436, and a further competition held for the lantern – won this time by Brunelleschi alone (executed 1445–67). He designed the exquisite marble octagon which is perhaps the most successful part of the whole composition. In 1438 he designed the semicircular exedrae with shell-capped niches and coupled Corinthian columns which stand beneath the drum.

The Ospedale degli Innocenti, Florence (designed 1419, built 1421–44), is often claimed as the first Renaissance building. It consists of an arcade of slender, even spindly, Corinthian columns with blue-and-white glazed terracotta plaques between the arches, and a first floor with widely spaced pedimented windows above the centre of each arch. The wide spacing of the arches harks back to c11 and c12 Tuscan work, but the detail is distinctly Roman.

In 1429 the Pazzi Chapel in the cloister of S. Croce, Florence, was commissioned. Building began c. 1433 but was unfinished when Brunelleschi died. The plan is more complex than that of the S. Lorenzo Sacristy: an atrium in the ratio of 1 : 3, the main building 2 : 3, and a square chancel. The interior decoration is more forceful than at S. Lorenzo, with virile semicircular arcs of *pietra serena*, Corinthian pilasters, and, in the spandrels, glazed terracotta reliefs. The façade is odd, closer to the tribune of a basilica than a temple portico – slender Corinthian columns supporting a blank attic storey with shallow carved rectangular panels and coupled pilasters. It seems likely that this construction, which looks uncomfortably flimsy from the side, was intended to be continued round the whole cloister. In 1433 he went again to Rome for further study of antiquity, the immediate result of which was S. Maria degli Angeli, Florence, his most archaeological design, though unfortunately building stopped after three years (1434–7) and got no further than the lower part of the walls. The rest of the building dates from five hundred years later, 1934–40. A design attributed to Brunelleschi was followed. It was the first centrally planned church of the Renaissance (an octagon with eight chapels surrounding the central space, sixteen-sided outside with flat walls and deep niches alternating). At S. Spirito, Florence (begun 1436), he reverted

to the basilican Latin cross plan, but gave it an entirely new centralized emphasis by running an aisle round the whole church (the west section never built). Once again the proportions are straightforward – an arrangement of cubes, half cubes, and double cubes – creating that balance and feeling of tranquil repose which was among the chief aims of Renaissance architects. The classical ornamentation is correct and vigorous though sometimes employed in a slightly unorthodox fashion. Several other works have been attributed to him, notably the centre of Palazzo Pitti, Florence, which he may have designed shortly before his death. Though astylar it is clearly an Early Renaissance building, with its massive rusticated stonework inspired by Roman work and with proportions governed by a simple series of ratios.

Brunelleschi became the first Renaissance architect almost by accident. He seems to have been drawn towards ancient Rome less for aesthetic than for practical, engineering reasons. An eclectic empiricist, he hit by instinct on those ideas which were to be developed by his successors. Perhaps his greatest merit was to have preserved Early Renaissance architecture from the dry pedantry of archaeology and revivalism. (For illustrations *see* DOME, ITALIAN ARCHITECTURE and RENAISSANCE ARCHITECTURE.)

Lit: P. Sanpaolesi, *Brunelleschi*, Milan 1962; E. Luporini, *Brunelleschi: Forma e ragione*, Milan 1964; H. Saalman in *Art Bulletin* XL, 1958 and December 1966; A. di T. Manetti, *The Life of Brunelleschi*, ed. H. Saalman, University Park, Pennsylvania, and London 1970; F. Prager & G. Scalia, *Brunelleschi: Studies of His Technology and Inventions*, Cambridge, Mass., 1970; L. H. Heydenreich & W. Lotz, *Architecture in Italy, 1400–1600*, Pelican History of Art, Harmondsworth 1974.

Brutalism A term coined in England in 1954 to characterize the style of LE CORBUSIER at Marseilles and Chandigarh, and the style of those inspired by such buildings: in England STIRLING & GOWAN; in Italy Vittoriano Viganò (Istituto Marchiondi, Milan, 1957); in America Paul RUDOLPH; in Japan Maekawa, TANGE, and many others. Brutalism nearly always uses concrete exposed at its roughest (BÉTON BRUT) and handled with overemphasis on big chunky members which collide ruthlessly. (Illustrated next page.)

Lit: R. Banham, *The New Brutalism*, London 1966.

(Right). Brutalism: House of Youth, Firminy, France, 1961–5, by Le Corbusier

Yale School of Art and Architecture, 1961–3, by Paul Rudolph

Bucrane (or **bucranium**) In classical architecture, a sculptured ox-skull, usually garlanded, often found in the METOPES of a Doric frieze.

Bucranium on altar found near Castel S. Angelo, Rome

Buddhist architecture, *see* CHINESE, INDIAN, JAPANESE and SOUTH-EAST ASIAN ARCHITECTURE.

Bulfinch, Charles (1763–1844), came of a wealthy, cultivated Boston family. He graduated at Harvard and was, on his European journey in 1785–7, advised by JEFFERSON. His principal works are the Beacon Monument (1789) in Boston, a Doric column, 60 ft high; the State House at Hartford, Conn. (1792); the State House in Boston (1793–1800); and the Court House, also in Boston (1810). They are perhaps the most dignified American public buildings of their time. In Boston extensive street planning and the building of terraces of houses with unified façades was also done under Bulfinch's chairmanship. In his church plans (Holy Cross, Boston, 1805; New South Church, Boston, 1814) he was influenced by WREN, in his secular work by CHAMBERS and ADAM. From 1817 to 1830 Bulfinch was in charge of work on the Capitol in Washington.

Lit: H. Kirker, *The Architecture of Charles Bulfinch,* Cambridge, Mass., 1969.

Bullant, Jean (*c.* 1520/25–78). His early, rather pedantic classical style is based on DELORME and the study of antiquity (he visited Rome *c.* 1540–5), but it rapidly acquired Mannerist complexities and, finally, in his late works for Catherine de' Medici, showed a fantasy similar to that of his rival DU CERCEAU. Much of his work has been destroyed. His additions to the Château of Écouen are early and illustrate his characteristically pedantic accuracy in classical details and no less characteristic misunderstanding of the spirit that stood behind them, as witness his most unclassical use of the colossal order. Mannerist features are striking in his bridge and gallery at Fère-en-Tardenois (1552–62) and in the Petit Château at Chantilly (*c.* 1560). Of his work for Catherine de' Medici only his additions to Chenonceaux survive – the western arm of the forecourt and gallery over the bridge (*c.* 1576). He published *Reigle générale d'Architecture* (1563) and *Petit Traicté de Géométrie* (1564).

Lit: L. Hautecoeur, *Histoire de l'architecture classique en France* II, Paris 1948; A. Blunt, *Art and Architecture in France 1500-1700*, Pelican History of Art, Harmondsworth 1970, paperback edn 1973.

Bullet, Pierre (1639-1716), a pupil of F. BLONDEL, began in the classical academic tradition and did not display much originality until towards the end of his career at the Hôtels Crozat and d'Évreux in the Place Vendôme, Paris (1702-7). Built on irregular corner sites, they foreshadow the freedom and fantasy of Rococo architects in the shape and disposition of rooms.

Lit: E. Langenskiold, *Pierre Bullet, the Royal Architect*, Stockholm 1959.

Bungalow A single-storey house. The term is a corruption of a Hindustani word, and was originally given to the light dwellings with verandas erected in India mainly for the British administrators. So many have since then been built in England by unqualified designers that certain areas have been opprobriously called 'bungaloid growths'.

Bunning, James Bunstone, *see* LABROUSTE.

Bunshaft, Gordon, *see* SKIDMORE, OWINGS & MERRILL.

Buon or **Bon, Giovanni** (1355-*c.* 1443) and **Bartolomeo** (*c.* 1374-*c.* 1467), were father and son, and the leading sculptor-builders in early C15 Venice. They are known to have worked at S. Maria dell'Orto (1392), the Ca' d'Oro (1427-34), and the Porta della Carta of the Doge's Palace (1438-42). They were probably responsible for the design as well as the carved decorations.

Lit: R. Gallo, *L'architettura di transizione dal Gotico al Rinascimento e Bartolomeo Bon*, Venice 1962.

Buontalenti, Bernardo (*c.* 1531-1608). Florentine Mannerist architect, painter and sculptor, and also a prolific designer of masques, fireworks (hence his nickname 'delle Girandole') and other entertainments for the Tuscan Grand Ducal court. He was even more sophisticated and stylish than his contemporary AMMANATI, e.g., the fantastic *trompe l'œil* altar steps in S. Stefano (1574-6), the perverse Porta delle Suppliche at the Uffizi (*c.* 1580), and the grottoes in the Boboli Gardens (1583-8), all in Florence.

But this preciosity and sense of fantasy was necessarily restrained in his major works of which the most notable are the Villa di Artimino at Signa (1594), the *galleria* and *tribuna* of the Uffizi (*c.* 1580), the façade of S. Trinità (1592-4) and the Fortezza del Belvedere (1590-95), all in Florence, and the Loggia de Banchi in Pisa (begun 1605). He also produced a fantastic design for the façade of the cathedral at Florence (1587) and carried out much engineering work for the Grand Duke, notably at the harbour of Leghorn and a canal between Leghorn and Pisa (1571-3). His grand-ducal villa at Pratolino (1569-75) was destroyed in the C19.

Lit: I. M. Botto, Exh. Cat., *Disegni di Buontalenti*, Florence (Uffizi) 1968.

Burges, William (1827-81), trained in engineering, then in the offices of Blore and M. D. WYATT. He travelled in France, Germany and Italy and was as interested in French as in English Gothic forms. In 1856, he won, with Henry Clutton (1819-93), the competition for Lille Cathedral, but in the event the building was not allotted to them. In 1859 he added the east end to Waltham Abbey, where for the first time the peculiar massiveness and heavy-handedness of his detail come out. He was a great believer in plenty of carved decoration, and specialized much less in ecclesiastical work than the other leading Gothic Revivalists. His principal works are Cork Cathedral (1862-76), still in a pure French High Gothic; the substantial addition to Cardiff Castle (1865); the remodelling of Castle Coch near Cardiff (*c.* 1875); the Harrow School Speech Room (1872); and his own house in Melbury Road, Kensington (1875-80). Hartford College, Connecticut, was also built to his designs (1873-80). (For illustration *see* ENGLISH ARCHITECTURE.)

Lit: A. Pullen, *Architectural Designs of William Burges*, London 1883-7; H.-R. Hitchcock, *Architecture: Nineteenth and Twentieth Centuries*, Pelican History of Art, Harmondsworth 1969, paperback edn 1971; M. Gironard, *The Victorian Country House*, Oxford 1971.

Burghausen, Hans von, *see* STETHAIMER.

Burlington, Richard Boyle, 3rd Earl of (1694-1753), was the patron and high priest of English PALLADIANISM and a gifted architect in his own right. He first visited Italy in 1714-15, but his conversion to Palladianism came after his return to London, which coincided with the publication of CAMPBELL'S *Vitruvius Britannicus* and LEONI'S edition of Palladio's *Four Books of Architecture*. He immediately replaced GIBBS with Campbell as architect of Burlington House and set out once more for Italy to study the master's buildings at first hand. He returned (1719) with his protégé William KENT, and for the next thirty years dominated the architectural scene in England. The widespread fashion for Palladio was largely due to his influence. He financed Kent's *Designs of Inigo Jones* (1727) and in 1730 published Palladio's drawings of Roman *thermae*. But there was a marked difference between his own and his followers' interpretation of the master. For him Palladianism meant a return to the architecture of antiquity as explained and illustrated by Palladio and he avoided, whereas his followers blindly accepted, all the non-classical and Mannerist features in the master's style. Cold, intellectual, and aristocratic, he was described by Pope as a 'positive' man, and both the strength and weakness of Palladianism derive from his obsessive, puritanical urge to preach absolute classical standards – those just and noble rules which were in due course to 'Fill half the land with imitating fools' (Pope). His fastidious but dogmatic character is equally evident in his buildings, which became increasingly dry and pedantic. They have a staccato quality – an overarticulation or overemphasis of individual features – which suggests a formula-loving mind. His *œuvre* appears to have consisted in about a dozen buildings, designed mostly for himself or friends, beginning in 1717 with a garden pavilion – the Bagno – at Chiswick, where he later built his best-known work, the ornamental villa based on Palladio's Rotonda (c. 1725). His only other important works to survive are the Dormitory, Westminster School, London (1722-30, rebuilt 1947), Northwick Park, Glos. (1730), and the Assembly Rooms, York (1731-2, refronted 1828). This latter is an exact model of Palladio's Egyptian Hall, based on VITRUVIUS. In addition to his independent work, he may be credited as part author of several buildings by his protégé Kent, notably Holkham Hall. (For illustration *see* PALLADIANISM.)

Lit: R. Wittkower, 'Lord Burlington' in *Archaeological Journal*, 102, 1945; J. Summerson, *Architecture in Britain 1530–1830*, Pelican History of Art, Harmondsworth 1969, paperback edn 1970.

Burmese architecture, *see* SOUTH-EAST ASIAN ARCHITECTURE.

Burn, William, *see* SHAW.

Burnham, Daniel H. (1846-1912), came of an old Massachusetts family. His father moved to Chicago, and there, after several false starts, the son went into an architect's office, where he met J. W. ROOT. The two went into partnership, an ideal pair: Root was poetic and versatile, Burnham practical and a skilled administrator. Burnham and Root have an important share in the evolution of the so-called Chicago School. Their best-known buildings are the Monadnock Block (1889-91), still a load-bearing masonry structure, though severely direct and unornamented; the Masonic Temple (1891), with its twenty-two storeys the tallest building in the world at the time it was built and with a complete steel skeleton (as introduced slightly before by HOLABIRD & ROCHE); and the Flat-iron Building in New York (1902). Burnham was made Chief of Construction for the World's Columbian Exposition in Chicago, which took place in 1893. Buildings were designed by HUNT, McKIM, Mead and WHITE, C. B. Atwood, POST, SULLIVAN, and others. The most monumental of them were classical and columnar, and this demonstration of Beaux Arts ideals cut short the life of the Chicago School. Later Burnham concentrated more and more on town and area planning: his plans for the District of Columbia (1901-2) are the start of comprehensive town planning in America. They were followed by the plan for Chicago (1906-9) and many others.

Lit: C. Moore, *D. H. Burnham: Architect Planner of Cities*, Boston–New York 1921; C. W. Condit, *The Chicago School of Architecture*, Chicago 1964.

Burton, Decimus (1800-81). The son of James Burton (1761-1837), a successful big London builder. As early as 1823 he designed the Colosseum in Regent's Park with a dome larger than that of St Paul's and a Greek Doric portico. It housed a panorama of London. In 1825 he began the Hyde Park Improvements which included the Hyde Park Corner Screen. He designed several housing estates (e.g., at Tunbridge Wells, 1828 etc.), the centre of Fleetwood (1835 etc.), the great Palm Houses at Chatsworth (with PAXTON) and Kew (with R. Turner), many villas (including several in

Regent's Park), the Athenaeum, London (1829–30), and a number of country houses.

Lit: H. M. Colvin, *Biographical Dictionary of English Architects, 1660–1840,* London 1954.

Bush-hammering A method of obtaining an even, rough texture on concrete after it has set, by using a bush-hammer with a specially grooved head which chips the surface.

Butterfield, William (1814–1900), a High-Church Gothic-Revivalist, was aloof in his life (a bachelor with a butler) and studious in his work. The peculiar aggressiveness of his forms – one jarring with the other – and of his colours – stone and multicoloured brick in stripes or geometrical patterns – was tolerated by the purists of the Cambridge Camden movement and their journal *The Ecclesiologist,* partly because he was their personal friend (he drew much for the *Instrumenta Ecclesiastica* of 1847), partly because he must have had a great power of conviction. His earliest church (and parsonage) of importance was Coalpit Heath (1844). This was followed by St Augustine's College, Canterbury, quieter than most of his work. The eruption of his fully developed personal style came with All Saints, Margaret Street, London (1849–59), a ruthless composition in red brick of church and accessory buildings on three sides of a small courtyard. The steeple is slender, noble, North German Gothic, and asymmetrically placed. St Matthias, Stoke Newington, London, followed in 1850–2 – yellow brick, with a nave crossed by two transverse arches; then St Alban, Holborn, London, in 1863; Keble College, Oxford, in 1867–75; the Rugby School buildings in 1870–86; and many others. Nearly all his work, apart from that for colleges and schools, was ecclesiastical. An exception is the robustly utilitarian County Hospital at Winchester (1863). His early cottages (*c.* 1848–50) are also remarkably free from historicism. They are the pattern for WEBB's Red House. (For illustration *see* ENGLISH ARCHITECTURE.)

Lit: P. Thompson, *William Butterfield,* London 1971.

Buttress A mass of masonry or brickwork projecting from or built against a wall to give additional strength.

Angle buttresses. Two meeting at an angle of 90° at the angle of a building.

Clasping buttress. One which encases the angle.

Diagonal buttress. One placed against the right angle formed by two walls, and more or less equiangular with both.

Flying buttresses. An arch or half-arch transmitting the thrust of a vault or roof from

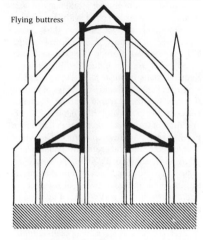

Flying buttress

the upper part of a wall to an outer support or buttress.

Setback buttress. A buttress set slightly back from the angle.

Flying buttresses: Amiens Cathedral, 1220 onwards

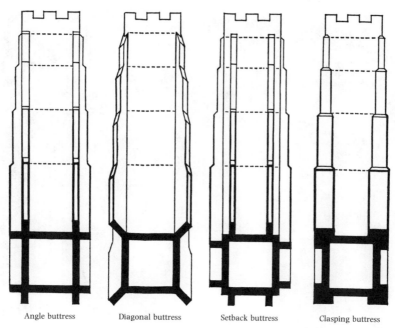

Angle buttress   Diagonal buttress   Setback buttress   Clasping buttress

Byzantine architecture The Byzantine (Eastern) Empire, which dated from the partition of the Roman Empire in A.D. 395, reached its greatest extent under Justinian I (527–65), who conquered North Africa, Italy, and part of Spain. In the c7 Syria, Palestine, Egypt and North Africa were lost to Islam. The Iconoclastic controversy (726–80 and 813–42) disrupted artistic but not architectural developments. Renewed expansion after the c8 (at the expense of the Arabs, and of the Slavs and Bulgars in the Balkans) led to a new apogee under Basil II (976–1025), succeeded by rapid decline, halted only by the accession of the Comnene dynasty in 1081. Overstrained resources, internal dissensions, and involvement in the crusading politics of the West, led to the shattering of the Empire by the Fourth Crusade in 1204 (foundation of the Latin Empire in Constantinople and Frankish fiefs in Greece). Reconstituted from the residual Nicaean Empire in 1261, Byzantium experienced a resurgence of power under Michael VIII, only to collapse into insignificance, steadily diminished by Serbian, Bulgarian and Turkish conquests, and becoming a Turkish client state before its extinction by the Turkish conquest of Constantinople in 1453.

Byzantine architecture stems directly from EARLY CHRISTIAN ARCHITECTURE in the east of the Roman Empire. No hard and fast division is possible between the two. Justinian's reign is customarily taken as the culmination of Early Christian and the seed-bed of Byzantine architecture. Vigorous Imperial patronage (cf. Procopius's 'De aedificiis') made architecture flourish remarkably; Imperial projects ranged from town walls and administrative buildings to monasteries and churches, constituting an achievement that subsequent Emperors were to seek to emulate.

Justinian's significant buildings included four churches in Constantinople: 1. H. Sergios & Bakchos (begun 526) – an irregular approximation to a square with corner niches, into which is inserted a pillared octagon bearing the umbrella dome, with arcades linking the pillars parallel to the walls, and EXEDRAE above arcades in the diagonals, GALLERIES, an enclosed sanctuary, round-apsed within and polygonal without, and a somewhat narrower NARTHEX; 2. H. Irene (begun 532) – a domed and galleried BASILICA, repeatedly altered

H. Sophia, Constantinople, begun after the fire of 532

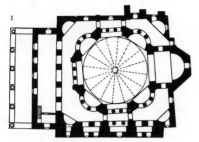

*H. Sergios and Bakchos,
Constantinople, 526–37*

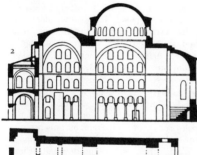

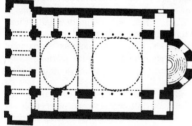

*H. Irene, Constantinople,
begun after a fire of 532*

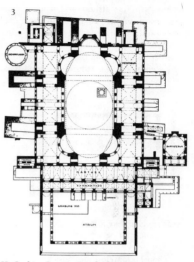

H. Sophia, Constantinople, begun 532

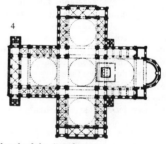

*Church of the Apostles,
Constantinople, 536–46*

subsequently; 3. H. Sophia (begun 532) – with a compartmented dome borne on four pillars, radically reconstructed in 557, buttressed by a semi-dome to both east and west, in turn diverting the thrust diagonally to ten smaller semi-domes. A sanctuary contracts to an apse with a polygonal exterior in the east, and a two-storey narthex adheres to the west. The lateral thrust is taken by broad pillars, between and beside which cross-vaulted areas on two levels form galleried aisles running through penetrations in the pillars. An ATRIUM precedes the narthex. A unique variant on the domed basilica, H. Sophia was the largest church produced before the Renaissance. It was never emulated in the Byzantine era, though Turkish architects, notably SINAN, were to create numerous

variations on it; 4. The Church of the Apostles (536–46, destroyed) – a five-domed cruciform building, probably the model chosen for St Mark's, Venice; also, in Ephesus, 5. the Church of St John – a galleried cruciform

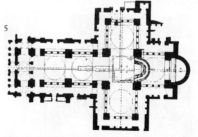

Church of St John, Ephesus, mid-c6

building with an atrium and a lengthened western arm vaulted by two transverse oval domes, and circular domes over the other parts; and 6. the church of the Monastery of St Catherine on Mt Sinai – an arcaded aisled basilica with large PASTOPHORIES, a narthex,

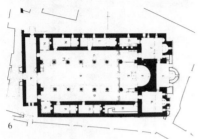

*Monastery church of St Catherine,
Mount Sinai, 561–5*

and chapels flanking the aisles. Only the architects of H. Sophia are known – ANTHEMIOS OF TRALLES and ISIDORUS OF MILETUS; Isidorus the Younger supervised the renovation of the dome after 557.

The Justinianic era employed characteristic architectural detailing: ARCHITRAVES etc. are adorned by harshly chiselled flat vegetable ornament producing deep shadows and a lace-like effect, capitals have similar ornamentation that is virtually detached from the dark painted core, playing like a diaphanous layer above its deep shadows; this kind of capital was exported ready-carved within the Empire (e.g. to Ravenna and North Africa). The dominant types of structure thereafter were: the simple basilica – less favoured later – the domed basilica, the cross-domed church, the eight-piered church, the domed cube, the TRICONCH and TETRACONCH, the domed hall,

*Euphrasian Basilica, Parenzo
(now Poreč, Yugoslavia), begun 535*

and the combination of basilica and cross-domed church (the so-called Mistra type).

The basilica had several variants. Aisled, timber-roofed basilicas are to be found, for instance, in: Sergiopolis (= Ruesafah, Mesopotamia), Basilica A, pre-520, with alternating supports, LESENES on the pillars, relieving ARCHES; Justiniana Prima (= Caričin Grad) cathedral, mid-c6; Grado, St Euphemia, 571–86, and St Mary's rebuilt about the same time, both with lesenes in the CLERESTORY above every second column – an embryonic bay-division; Parenzo (= Poreč), *c.* 540; Belovo, late c6, pillars as supports; Sybritos, Crete, post-674; H. Achilleios, Lake Prespa, c9, c10, or c11, pillars as supports; Old Metropolis, Verria, c11/12; H. Theodora, Arta, mid-c13; Metropolis, Mistra (state before 1291); Achaia (= Medzena), c13/14, alternating supports. Galleried basilicas are rarer, e.g.: Mesembria (= Nessebar), Old Metropolis, c6, two tiers of pillars as supports; Palace of the Bulgarian Tsars, Aboba (= Pliska), post-864, alternating supports; the Metropolis, Serres, c11/12. Transepts only occur in the early period, e.g. in: Basilica A, Nicopolis, c6, (tripartite), also with narthex and atrium; Tropaeum (Romania), c6; Salonika, H. Demetrios, a largely faithful reconstruction of the c5 plan in 629–34, with alternating supports and galleries. Tunnel-vaulting is commoner: first demonstrable in all post-c6 basilicas in Bin-bir-kilisse (Lycaonia), Basilica 1 with a twin-towered façade, pillars added in the c7 to take the strain, producing relieving arches; Basilica 32 with a tripartite transept, galleries, and towers flanking the porch; and subsequently, for instance, in H. Anna, Trebizond, 884/5; H. Stephanos, Mesembria (New Metropolis), c10/11; H. Anargyroi, c10/11, H. Taxiarchoi, c11 and H. Stephanos, c11/12, in Kastoria; the Koimesis Church in Zaraphona, c11/12, and the Koimesis Church in Kalambaka (= Stagi) in its first, c14, state; as well as S. Nikola Monastir, 1095, where only the nave is vaulted. The form of several of these vaulted basilicas approximates to that of an aisled hall with a slightly raised centre aisle (e.g. the Koimesis Church in Zaraphona).

The association of domes with basilicas found in the Early Christian period persisted in the Byzantine era. The domes concerned always rested on PENDENTIVES, a method of effecting the transition from the square of the supports first encountered in the c2 West Baths of Gerasa (Jordan), and taken up in the c5 in certain towers in the walls of Con-

H. Sophia, Constantinople, interior

H. Demetrios, Salonica, c6

stantinople. It derives from secular Roman architecture, and it is mistaken to regard it as an oriental feature.

Hagia Sophia was without successors, and H. Irene (in its original form) only found any in the c8 or c9. The domed basilicas of the Justinianic or immediately post-Justinianic period mostly placed the dome over a transept: Basilica B, Philippi, shortly before 540 – galleries, and a transept contained by the aisle walls; H. Sophia, Sofia, late c6 – galleries, and a projecting transept; probably also Basilica 32 at Bin-bir-kilisse. A more complex solution was found in Our Lady of the Hundred Gates at Paros, post-550 – T-shaped pillars in the oblong crossing of a transeptal basilica with continuous aisles support an oval dome (also galleries, and a CHANCEL inserted between crossing and apse). This was modified in H. Titos at Gortyna (Crete), late c6 or c7 – the aisles are no longer continuous, the galleries terminate at the apse-ended transepts, and there is a triconch choir. Only in the Middle Period did the dome recover its place over the centre of the nave: H. Nikolaos, Myra, c8 ? – almost square nave; Dere Ahsy (Lycia), late c9. In the c10 the basilica of H. Nikon in Sparta revived old practices – dome over the sanctuary, unvaulted

nave and aisles. Later examples of domed basilicas include Sv. Sofija, Ohrid, mid-c11 – dome destroyed; the Metropolis in Trebizond, 1204/22; and a recrudescence in the Latino-Byzantine churches of Cyprus. The domed basilica with the dome over the centre of the nave gave rise to a special variant in the c8, in which the supporting arches were enlarged to form a GREEK CROSS; they rested on massive pillars, and the arcades separating the nave from the aisles were thrust back to the outer edges of these, so as to accentuate the cruciform domed body in the nave; H. Sophia, Salonika, *c*. 721; the Koimesis Church in Nicaea, early c8; St Clement, Ankara, c9;

Domed basilica: H. Sophia, Salonica, c6

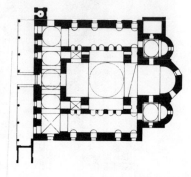

the Akataleptos Church, Constantinople, mid-c9. The church of Skripou (Boeotia), 873/4, represents a special case of the transeptal basilica with a crossing-dome: the transept intersects the aisled church almost exactly in the middle, so that nave and transept together (the tunnel-vaulted aisles are only connected by doors to the similarly vaulted nave – an *église cloisonné*) form a Greek cross.

Varieties of the basilica are far outstripped in number and importance by what might be called the standard Mid-Byzantine form – the cross-domed church (*église à croix inscrite*: quincunx). The liturgical core of the church (NAOS) forms a square, in which another square described by the four piers of the DRUMMED dome on pendentives is inscribed. Four tunnel-vaults measuring the interval between the piers form a Greek cross around the domed central space between the outer walls; the less elevated corner areas can be variously vaulted (cross-vaults, saucer domes, etc.); a three-part sanctuary (BEMA), consisting of an apse (often with chancel) and adjacent pastophories, is joined on at the east, and to the west lies a narthex, occasionally two-tiered (e.g. Theotokos the Coppersmith, Salonika, 1028). The various parts are given exterior emphasis by the varying height of the roofing, or by accentuating the spatial divisions with patterned walls. The cross-domed church spread from Byzantium into every Orthodox country, and is frequently employed to this day.

It is erroneous to derive this type of structure from Persian fire-temples, since, in the very rare instances of the latter on the same plan, the tunnel-vaults surrounding the domed square are parallel to the outer walls, and thus fail to describe a cross in space. More probable precursors are to be found in secular Roman architecture – e.g. the apparently c2

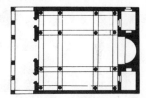

Praetorium at Musmije, Syria, probably c2

Praetorium at Musmije in Syria (central square probably still not domed), and the Audience-Chamber at Sergiopolis (Rusafah) in Mesopotamia of *c.* 560 (fully realized) – ready to be adopted in essence for the new east end of Trier Cathedral as rebuilt under Gratian. The earliest ecclesiastical example is St David's in Salonika (c5? – much altered since).

Cross-domed church: St Mark's, Venice, 1063–95

Cross-domed church: the Nea, Constantinople; from the Homilies of the Virgin by James of Kokkinobaphos, early c12

This formula was employed for the new palace church of Basil I (867–86) in Constantinople (the Nea – known only from descriptions), catching on like wildfire thereafter. The oldest surviving examples in Constantinople are the Myrelaion (Budrumdjami, built *c*. 930) and the almost contemporaneous church of the Lips Monastery. They

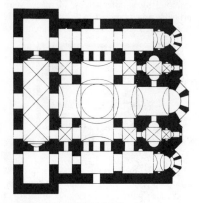

North Church of Fenari Isa Cami, Constantinople, c. 930

differ in the form of their supports: the Myrelaion has pillars, and the Lips Church columns, upholding the drum and dome. Both possibilities were equally exploited: the Katholikon of H. Meletios (CI I), the Theotokos Church of H. Lukas (*c*. 1040), and the Katholikon of H. Johannes Theologos on Hymettos (*c*. 1120) have columns, for instance, and the Kaisariani on Hymettos (late CI I) and the Çanlikilisse (nr Konya, Turkey, CI I) pillars. There are also truncated and simplified versions, e.g.: H. Asomatoi at Maina in the Peloponnese, *c*. 900, with a small portico instead of a narthex and the easterly pair of pillars fused with the dividing walls of the tripartite bema, or Burlarioi (CI I, also in the Peloponnese), east end like H. Asomatoi and corner areas no longer square but oblong – a directional tendency. The H. Asomatoi type is often encountered, e.g. in the two palaces of the first Bulgarian kingdom, Pliska and Preslav, and in numerous lesser churches.

The CI0 or CI I church of John the Baptist in Mesembria shows similar directional tendencies to H. Strategos in Burlarioi – oblong westerly corner areas, eastern ones fused with the bema and also oblong, all four tunnel-vaulted. This tendency recurs in Late Byzantine churches, e.g. H. Sophia in Trebizond

(pre-1260; elongated west end) and the Peribleptos and H. Sophia at Mistra (*c*. mid-CI4; pronounced elongation of the west end). Alternatively, the centralized character of this type of building can be accentuated by surrounding the cross-domed church on three sides with a succession of lower parts punctuated by drummed domes at the corners, e.g. H. Aikatherina and H. Apostoloi in Salonika (late CI3 and early CI4). St John Aleiturgetos in Mesembria probably represents the most elaborate cross-domed church (CI4) – saucer domes over the middle of the narthex, the corner areas, the pastophories, and the strikingly elongated bema; rich use of niches, double round-arched frieze and polychromy to calibrate the exterior.

The directional tendency helps to clarify the origin of the Mistra type (so-called because first observed in connection with three churches in Mistra). This is a singular hybrid of the basilica and the cross-domed church: the lower storey has the character of an aisled basilica, the gallery zone that of a cross-domed church. This combination seems first to have been employed in the restoration of H. Irene, Constantinople, after the earthquake of 740. It recurs in H. Nikolaos, an ancillary church of the cathedral of Paros (not earlier than CI0), and then in the Mistra churches: the Hodegetria Church of the Brontochion monastery (Aphentikon, early CI0, originally planned as a pure cross-domed church); the Pantanassa, a *c*. mid-CI5 copy of the Aphentikon; and the

Pantanassa, Mistra, c. mid-CI5

Metropolis, the CI5 rebuilding of a basilica; as well as in H. Apostoloi at Leontarion in the Peloponnese (prob. CI4). This type arose out of the necessity of equipping a cross-domed church with galleries on three sides; the combination of two heterogeneous formulae was thus deliberate.

Clearly to be distinguished from the cross-domed type of church is the eight-piered type. Here eight piers are evenly disposed about the sides of a square, reinforced by pillars at the corners; the piers on either side of the corners join with these to support SQUINCHES, which make the transition to the circular dome. This type is found in its pure form in the Katholikon of the Nea Mone on Chios (1042–56) – projections from the wall forming the piers, tripartite bema, narthex and exonarthex. More commonly, the structure is extended by the addition of high tunnel-vaulted cross arms buttressed by the pairs of piers on the sides of the square; they are clasped between other enclosed spaces, thus amplifying the plan into a rectangle. The subsidiary spaces can be groups of cross-vaulted areas interlinked with one another and with the naos, e.g. in Hosios Lukas *c.* 1020 (with galleries), or independent chapels, e.g. in Daphni, late CI I. The number of such churches is small, comprising, apart from the above, the Panagia Lykodemu in Athens (ruined by restoration); the late CI I cathedral (of the Transfiguration) of Christianou in the Peloponnese – oval domes over the lateral arms, the envelopment of the *naos* otherwise quite unique; H. Sophia in Monembassia (late CI 3); the Paregoritissa at Arta in Epirus (late CI 3); H. Theodoroi in Mistra (late CI 3); and H. Nikolaos on Lake Kopais (*c.* 1300). Of these

churches, six belonged to monasteries, two were episcopal sees (Christianou and Monembassia), and one a court church (Arta). The alien motif of a squinch is Persian in origin, and its adoption for this small group of buildings is as unexplained as the genesis of the type, which sprang into being fully-formed.

The *domed hall* is mostly regarded as a modest special case of the domed basilica. It consists of an elongated hall with an eastern apse, roughly over whose middle rises a dome on pendentives, flanked by tunnel vaults to east and west. It is most commonly found in Bulgaria (e.g. the upper storey of the Asen church in Stanimaka, post-1218; the Church

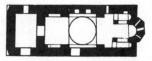

Asen church, Stanimaka (Assenovgrad), Bulgaria, c. 1218

of the Archangels in Bačkovo monastery) and in Serbia (e.g. S. Nikolaj in Kursumlija and Djurdjevi Stupovi nr Novi Pasar, both between 1168–95; Žiča, 1207/20; Mileševo, 1234), but is also frequently encountered in actual Byzantine territory, e.g. the PAREKKLESION of the Chora Church in Constantinople (early CI4); and the CI4 churches of this type in Mesembria (the Archangel Michael & Gabriel; H. Paraskeve), Mesembria alter-

Interior of dome on eight supports, Paregoritissa, Arta, late CI3

John Aleiturgitos, Nessebar (Messenbria), Bulgaria

nated between the Bulgarian and Byzantine Empires throughout the CI4, and its architecture is mostly treated as Bulgarian, but the town was largely Greek-inhabited and wholly Byzantine in culture.

There is no room for an exhaustive list of the other innumerable variations on the theme of the centralized church, but only for the important types of more than local significance: the pure cross-church (four tunnel-vaulted arms and a crossing-dome) became infrequent (one example is H. Petros in Pyrgos, Peloponnese, CIO); the square church with dome and bema is commoner, found, e.g., at Vunitsa *c.* 950, Patieina 907?, Kumani CIO, and Plataniti post-IOOO. The churches concerned are small in both cases, whereas the poly-conched (customarily triconch) variety, as already evolved for mausolea in Roman architecture, embraced major churches as well. Still, many triconch Byzantine buildings are small churches or chapels, like S. Panteleimon in Ohrid (early CIO), the Kubidilike in Kastoria (early CII), and the two Late Byzantine Peloponnesian churches of H. Nikolaos in Methana and H. Nikolaos in Platani. With the early CII Megiste Lavra on Athos, enriched by the proliferation of parts such as nartheces, chapels etc., the type achieved the status of major architecture,

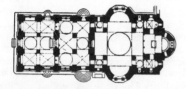

Trefoil, Katholikon, Chilandari, Mount Athos, c. 1302

and was thereafter by preference so combined with the cross-domed formula that the unified domed central square of Megiste Lavra was elsewhere elaborated with cross-arms that were then given conch endings (e.g. at Iberon, Vatopedi, Chilandar, Kutlumusiu) – a formula that long endured for monastic churches. H. Elias, Salonika (*c.* 1360, originally the Katholikon of the city's Nea Mone), is by contrast an instance of a pure monumental triconch, such as was equally favoured in Serbian architecture, e.g.: Krusevać. *c.* 1380 – a domed hall with conches to the sides of the domed square; and Ravanica, 1375–7 – an elongated cross-domed church whose side-arms are remodelled into conches.

The tetraconch is rarer. It is found in its simplest form at Veljussa (1080) for instance, whilst the earlier church at Peristera (870–71) surrounds a cross-domed church having very short arms with four triconched domed squares, each of whose outermost conches is

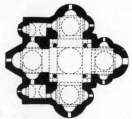

Quatrefoil, Peristera church, 870–71

larger than the others. A simpler combination of a cross-domed with a triconch church is that of, e.g., H. Apostoloi in Athens, *c.* 1020: all four arms open into conches, the spaces between the arms are reduced to triangles facing outwards as conches, and the west end is embraced by a narthex.

If Byzantium's ecclesiastical architecture exhibits experimentation with a rich gamut of tectonic and spatial themes, our knowledge of its secular architecture is a virtual blank. Little of the great palace architecture of Constantinople survives, the modest dimensions of the late ruins of the Tekfur Sarai affording scant idea of the whole palatial quarters once to be seen. Here we are dependent on the written record. The Palace of the Despots in Mistra, which prior to its destruction resembled the Doges' Palace of Venice in its façade – great arcades below, steadily diminishing windows above – did not derive from the traditions of the capital, but had more the character of a castle. The palaces and official buildings of provincial governors and the like are known only from excavations; they largely adhered to classical or late classical precedents. Other public buildings are scarcely known. Such public baths as survive, continuing the tradition of Roman thermae, were almost without exception radically reconstructed by the Turks; their use had been almost as widespread as under the Romans. Early Byzantine domestic architecture, also unearthed by excavations, largely followed Roman ways, in, for instance, multi-storey apartment-blocks (well excavated at Ephesus). Large numbers of dwellings from the Late Byzantine period survive at Mistra, but they are hardly likely to be typical, since the town was a Frankish foundation. Better known are monastic buildings, that usually form a quadrangle in whose centre stands the katholikon; all the rooms – cells, refectory, guest apartments, etc. – are up against the outer walls: a good example is H. Meletios nr

Megara. As far as practicable, this formula was used for rock monasteries (e.g. Meteora and Athos), though often transformed by later additions and alterations.

Byzantine building methods were little different from Late Roman ones. In Constantinople and large areas of Asia Minor there was from the first a love of polychrome effects produced by the alternation of materials – of broad layers of ASHLAR with layers of brick, usually large but fairly thin slabs set sparingly in bands of mortar. Only in provincial buildings might roughly-hewn rubble replace ashlar. Polychromy was intensified in the Middle Byzantine period, the alternation of stone and brick being stepped up; e.g., two layers of brick succeeding one of ashlar in which each block was separated by a vertically placed brick (Ohrid, Sv. Sofija; Daphni, etc.), or by several bricks forming a pattern (H. Anargyroi in Kastoria); and multicoloured bands of tiles placed on end could be added at clerestory level (e.g. H. Basileios in Kastoria). In the Late Byzantine period this use of building materials alone to produce polychromy and ornamentation in the exterior walling became yet more elaborate (e.g. south church of the Fenari Isa Çami, Constantinople, 1282–1304; St John Aleiturgetos. Mesembria, c14; the Paragoretissa, Arta, 1282/9; H. Apostoloi, Salonika), but small bits of coloured pottery were also used to enhance the effect (e.g. St John Aleiturgetos, Mesembria). The ruins of the Tekfur Serai reveal that this device was not restricted to ecclesiastical buildings. Such masonry was naturally not plastered, unlike perhaps churches built of rubble, probably for reasons of economy, like certain churches in Mistra. As far as vaulting techniques were concerned, Byzantine architecture was entirely derivative (from the Romans).

Byzantine churches were invariably decorated, other than during the iconoclastic controversy, with an extensive painted or mosaic pictorial programme, whose aim was

Hosios Lukas, c. 1000

to present the church as the image of the divinely-ruled cosmos. Thus the apex of the dome was normally occupied by Christ as Pantocrator (Ruler of All Things), and the apse vault by the Virgin Mary; angels were located in the dome, prophets in the drum, evangelists in the pendentives (the squinches of the eight-pier type held scenes from the cycle of the Twelve Feasts), the Communion of the Apostles in the half-cylinder of the apse, and, underneath, the Church Fathers and other saints; the rest of the pictures vary greatly in number and content (sometimes the cycle of the Twelve Chief Feasts of the Church Year, often amplified, notably in the Late Byzantine period, by cycles from the Life and Passion of Christ), though full-length depictions of saints invariably occupy the bottom row. The Last Judgement is often met with on the inner west wall or in the narthex, where there are also frequently scenes from the lives of the saints. The extensive use of painting and mosaic to clothe the walls meant the renunciation of any attempt to shape them plastically, and the undisturbed dominance of scarcely articulated surfaces.

An essential part of the internal arrangements was the separation of the presbytery (ADYTON) from the body of the church (naos) originally by an enclosure with a kind of pergola that could be made opaque with curtains (surviving thus, e.g., at Hosios Lukas); this evolved through the templon (the date of its emergence is disputed) into the pictured wall (ICONOSTASIS) with three doors.

The Bulgarians, Serbs, Rumanians, and above all the RUSSIANS adopted Byzantine forms of church architecture (at first not seldom executed by Byzantine architects – e.g., St Sophia, Kiev) and modes of decoration along with Orthodox Christianity. In the Balkans this went so far that after 1204 the further evolution of Byzantine art could shift from the Latin-held territories to the rising Serbian Empire. The architecture of the Christian peoples of the Caucasus (Armenians, Georgians) was also deeply indebted to Byzantium. Byzantine buildings are also to be found in South Italy (ITALIAN ARCHITECTURE) – Byzantine territory till the Norman conquest – especially in Calabria and Apulia. The earliest architecture of Venice derives from Byzantium, of which it was a dependency. Strong influences were exerted on the architecture of Languedoc, especially during the Crusades. To cite just one further instance of the importance of Byzantine architecture and of its resonance, BRAMANTE'S design for St Peter's, Rome, was but the classic formula of the Byzantine cross-domed church in Italian Renaissance dress.   [KW]

Lit: R. Krautheimer, Early Christian and Byzantine Architecture, Pelican History of Art, Harmondsworth 1965, paperback edn 1975.

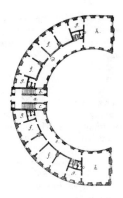

Cable moulding A Romanesque moulding imitating a twisted cord.

Cabled fluting, *see* FLUTING.

Cagnola, Marchese Luigi (1762–1833). A neo-classical architect who played a leading role in the Napoleonic transformation of Milan, designing the severe Ionic Porta Ticinese (1801–14) and the much richer Arco della Pace (1806–38). He also designed a Pantheon-like parish church at Ghisalba (*c.* 1830), a fantastic campanile crowned with CANEPHORAE supporting a dome at Urgnano (*c.* 1820), and his own many-columned Grecian villa Inverigo (begun 1813).
   Lit: G. Mezzanotte, *Architettura neo-classica in Lombardia*, Naples 1966; C. L. V. Meeks, *Italian Architecture, 1750–1914*, New Haven 1966.

Caisson 1. An air chamber, resembling a well, driven down to a firm foundation stratum in the soil and filled with concrete. It is used for construction below water (e.g., for the piers of a bridge) or on waterlogged ground. 2. A sunken panel in a flat or vaulted ceiling.

Caldarium The hot-room in a Roman bath.

Callicrates was the leading architect in Periclean Athens, and with ICTINUS designed the Parthenon (447–442 B.C.). He probably designed and built the exquisite little Ionic temple of Athena Nike on the Acropolis, Athens (448–after 421 B.C.). He also built the south and central portion of the Long Walls from Athens to Piraeus, and perhaps restored part of the city walls. (For illustrations *see* GREEK ARCHITECTURE.)

   Lit: W. B. Dinsmoor, *The Architecture of Ancient Greece*, London–New York 1950; J. M. Shear, 'Kallikrates' in *Hesperia* 32, 1963, pp. 377–88; Rhys Carpenter, *The Architects of the Parthenon*, Harmondsworth 1970.

Camarín A small chapel behind and above the high altar in Spanish churches. It is usually visible from the nave. The earliest example is in the church of the Desamparados in Valencia (1647–67).

Camber To curve (a beam) either by sawing or by bending, so that the middle is higher than the ends. This is a good remedy for sagging tie-beams (*see* ROOF), as it gives them a slightly arched form.

Cambodian architecture, *see* SOUTH-EAST ASIAN ARCHITECTURE.

Came A metal strip used for LEADED LIGHTS.

Cameron, Charles (*c.* 1740–1812), was born in Scotland, visited Rome *c.* 1768, and published *The Baths of the Romans* in 1772. Nothing more is known of him until he was summoned to Russia in about 1779 by Catherine the Great, and lived there for the rest of his life. For Catherine he decorated several apartments in RASTRELLI'S palace at Tsarskoe Selo (now Pushkino) near Leningrad (1780–85), and also designed the Agate Pavilion and Cameron Gallery there. For the Grand Duke Paul he built the great palace at Pavlovsk (1780–96) and the circular Doric peripteral Temple of Friendship (destroyed) in the English Park – the first of its kind in Russia. In about 1787 he was superseded as architect-in-chief by his pupil Brenna, and when

Catherine died in 1796 he was dismissed altogether from royal service. But he stayed on in Russia, building for private patrons, e.g., the Rasumovski Palace at Batourin in the Ukraine (1799–1802, unfinished). He returned to favour after the death of Paul I, and in 1805 designed the naval hospital and barracks at Kronstadt. He was an admirer and close follower of Robert ADAM, especially in interior decoration, though lacking his finesse. (For illustrations see PALLADIANISM and RUSSIAN ARCHITECTURE.)

Lit: G. K. Loukomski, *Charles Cameron*, London 1943; T. Talbot Rice & A. A. Tait, eds., *Charles Cameron*, Exh. Cat., Edinburgh–London 1967–8.

Campanile The Italian word for a bell-tower, usually separate from the main building. The earliest surviving Italian campanili are at Ravenna – circular and probably of the c9. The earliest recorded campanile was square and was attached to St Peter's in Rome. It went back to the mid-c8.

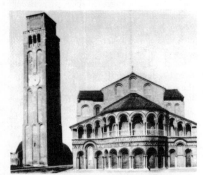

Campanile: Murano, Venice, early c13

Campbell, Colen (1673–1729). Little is known about him until 1715 when he published the first volume of *Vitruvius Britannicus* and built Wanstead House (now demolished), which became the model for large English Palladian country houses. With Baldersby Park, Yorks (1720–21) he initiated the neo-Palladian villa. He was probably responsible for Lord BURLINGTON'S conversion to PALLADIANISM and was commissioned to remodel Burlington House, London (1718–19). Mereworth Castle (1722–5) is perhaps the best of the English versions of Palladio's Rotonda design. Houghton Hall (1721, executed with modifications by Ripley) is enormous and imposing, but

Ebberston Lodge near Scarborough (1718) and Compton Place, Eastbourne (1726–7), are more elegant and refined.

Lit: H. E. Stutchbury, *The Architecture of Colen Campbell*, Manchester 1967; J. Summerson, *Architecture in Britain, 1530–1830*, Pelican History of Art, Harmondsworth 1969, paperback edn 1970.

Campen, Jacob van (1595–1657). A wealthy and erudite painter-architect and the leading exponent of Dutch PALLADIANISM, an unpretentious, placid and economic form of classicism characterized by its use of brick mixed with stone and its straightforward, almost diagrammatic use of pilasters. He studied in Italy and probably knew SCAMOZZI who certainly influenced him greatly, rather more indeed than Palladio. Van Campen's style is epitomized in his masterpiece the Mauritshuis, The Hague (1633–5), entirely Palladian in plan, with giant Ionic pilasters raised on a low ground floor and supporting a pediment, crowned with a typically Dutch hipped roof rising in a slightly concave line from the eaves. His great Town Hall in Amsterdam (now the Royal Palace: 1648–55), built entirely of stone, is heavier but very imposing – the grandest of all Dutch town halls. More original is the Nieuwe Kerk in Haarlem (1645) of the Greek-cross-in-square type. He also designed the Coymans house on the Keizergracht, Amsterdam (1625), the earliest example of Palladianism in Holland, the Noordeinde Palace, The Hague (1640) and the Accijnhuis and theatre in Amsterdam (1637). With Christian Huygens he was responsible for the general conception of decoration by Jordaens and others in POST'S Huis-ten-Bosch. His domestic style had great influence through his followers Pieter POST, Arend van 's-GRAVESANDE and Philip VINGBOONS, and it was later introduced into England by Hugh MAY and others. (For illustration see DUTCH ARCHITECTURE.)

Lit: K. Fremantle, *The Baroque Town Hall of Amsterdam*, Utrecht 1959; P. T. A. Swillens, *J. van Campen, Schilder en Bouwmeester*, Assen 1961.

Cancello In Early Christian architecture, a latticed screen or grille separating the choir from the main body of a church.

Candela, Felix (b. 1910), was born in Spain but lives in Mexico. He is one of the most resourceful concrete engineers of the age and is also important architecturally. He was inspired initially by TORROJA. Among his most significant works, both in Mexico City, are the Church of Our Lady of Miracles (1953–5), an extreme example of mid-century Expressionism, and in collaboration with the architect José Gonzáles, the Radiation Institute (1954), which is a tiny four-legged shed with a paraboloid roof only about 1 in. thick at the ridge. Later buildings by Candela are the Chapel of the Missionaries of the Holy Spirit at Coyoacán (1956, with Enrique de la Mora) with a simple saddle-shaped canopy on rough stone walls; the restaurant at Xochimilco (1958, with Joaquín Alvarez Ordóñez) placed in the water gardens like an eight-petalled flower of paraboloids; the Market Hall at Coyoacán (1956, with Pedro Ramírez Vásquez and Rafael Mijares) with the mushroom-shaped umbrellas which Candela has since used at the John Lewis warehouse, Stevenage, England (1963, with Yorke, Rosenberg and Mardall). (For illustrations *see* HYPERBOLIC PARABOLOID ROOF and MEXICAN ARCHITECTURE.)

Lit: C. Faber, *Candela, The Shell Builder*, London 1968.

Candid, Peter (or **Peter de Wit** or **de Witte**) (1548–1628). Mannerist painter and architect, born in Bruges. He was the son of a Flemish sculptor, Elias de Witte, with whom he went to Florence c. 1573. He studied painting in Italy, perhaps under VASARI, and worked as a painter both in Florence and Rome. In 1586 he settled in Munich under the patronage of Dukes Wilhelm V and Maximilian I who had already attracted thither Friedrich SUSTRIS and the Mannerist sculptor Hubert Gerhard. Candid was probably involved as an architect in the later stages of the building of the Munich *Residenz* though nothing is known about this for certain.

Canephora A sculptured female figure carrying a basket on her head.

Canopy A projection or hood over a door, window, tomb, altar, pulpit, niche, etc.

Canterbury, *see* MICHAEL OF CANTERBURY.

Cantilever A horizontal projection (e.g., a step, balcony, beam or canopy) supported by a downward force behind a fulcrum. It is without external bracing and thus appears to be self-supporting. (Illustrated next column.)

Cantilever canopy: Railway Station, Rome, 1948–50, by L. Calini and E. Montuori

Cap The crowning feature of a windmill, usually a domical roof; also an abbreviation for CAPITAL.

Capital The head or crowning feature of a column.

Aeolic capital. See ORDER.

Bell capital. A form of capital of which the chief characteristic is a reversed bell between

Basket capital, Bawit, c6

Coupled capitals: St Adalbert, Koscielec, Poland, early c13

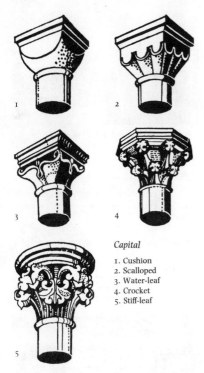

Capital

1. Cushion
2. Scalloped
3. Water-leaf
4. Crocket
5. Stiff-leaf

the SHAFT or NECKING and the upper mould-ing. The bell is often enriched with carving.

Crocket capital. An Early Gothic form, con-sisting of stylized leaves with endings rolled over similar to small VOLUTES.

Cushion capital. A Romanesque capital cut from a cube, with its lower parts rounded off to adapt it to a circular shaft; the remaining flàt face of each side is generally a LUNETTE. Also called a *block* capital.

Protomai capital. A capital with half-figures, usually animals, projecting from its four corners.

Scalloped capital. A development of the block or cushion capital in which the single lunette on each face is elaborated into one or more truncated cones.

See also STIFF-LEAF; WATER-LEAF; *and, for capitals in classical architecture,* ORDER.

Caratti, Francesco (d. 1677), was born at Bissone near Como, and went in 1652 to Prague, where he became the leading archi-tect. His masterpiece is the Czernin Palace (begun 1668), with a row of thirty giant attached Corinthian columns and a rusticated basement which breaks forward to provide bases for the columns and bulges out into a central porch. The strong chiaroscuro created by the projections makes this façade one of the most exciting of its time. He also built the Mary Magdalen Church, Prague (begun 1656), and the east wing of the palace at Roudnice (1665).

Lit: E. Hempel, *Baroque Art and Architecture in Central Europe,* Pelican History of Art, Harmondsworth 1965.

Caravanserai Otherwise known as *khan (han), ribat* and *funduq,* this building served in the Islamic world as a stopping place for caravans. Caravanserais were built both in towns and in the open country. Those in the towns (often very numerous; Isfahan, in Persia, had nearly 2,000 in the C17) served not only to house and feed travellers but also as ware-houses and centres for a particular trade or group of merchants. Certain urban caravan-serais still serve such functions; others have become markets (Khan al-Gumruk, Aleppo). Caravanserais in the open country were often built at intervals of a day's journey – about 25 km – along the major trade routes. Usually fortified, with an elaborate projecting porch, they were especially popular in Syria, Turkey and Iran. In C13 Turkey a distinctive plan developed, comprising an open courtyard with rooms for travellers and stalls for animals on two sides, an entrance complex on the third, often including a mosque, and a fourth side opposite this with a portal leading to a vaulted hall divided into nave and aisles and with a central domed lantern. Travellers and their baggage were accommodated on high platforms flanking the nave and the animals were stabled in the aisles. Fountains, baths, and kitchens were among the installations at the larger caravanserais (Sultan Hans near Aksarai and Kayseri). The combination of open courtyard and covered hall, which is found in various proportions, is a Turkish de-

*Caravanserai: Sari Khân
on the Ürgüp-Avanosa road, 1238*

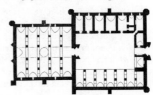

velopment; in Iran most caravanserais follow the 4-IWAN plan of mosques and MADRASAS (Ribat Mahi; most C17 caravanserais), though octagonal and circular types are also known. In Syria the caravanserais postdate the C13 and feature multi-storeyed arcaded courts, the lower rooms accommodating goods and animals while the upper rooms housed travellers. Features common to many caravanserais are a fountain or well in the centre of the courtyard; a single massive portal, with an entrance high enough to admit a loaded camel; kitchens in the corners; and, especially in the case of small caravanserais, adjoining enclosures for tethering animals. [RH]

Lit: K. Erdmann, *Das anatolische Karavansaray des 13. Jhs.,* I, 2, 1961; K. Müller, *Die Karawanserei im Vorderen Orient,* 1920; E. Pauty, *Les okelles d'époque ottomane,* 1944; M. Siroux, *Caravansérails d'Iran et petites constructions routières,* 1949.

Carlone, Carlo Antonio (d. 1708), is the most important member of a large family of Italian artists working in Austria and South Germany. His masterpiece is the richly stuccoed interior of the Italianate Priory Church of St Florian (1686–1705). Other works include the Jesuitenkirche zu den Neun Chören der Engel, Vienna (1662), with a rather secular street façade, and the charming little pilgrimage church of Christkindl (begun 1706), which was finished by PRANDTAUER, who was much indebted to Carlone.

Lit: E. Hempel, *Baroque Art and Architecture in Central Europe,* Pelican History of Art, Harmondsworth 1965.

Carolingian architecture takes its name from Charlemagne (King from 768, Emperor 800–14) and his descendants and the style extends in time from the late c8 into the C10, and in space through those countries which formed part of Charlemagne's Empire, especially France, Germany, and the Netherlands. Anglo-Saxon architecture in England and Asturian architecture in Spain stand outside this style, which is composite and the result of conflicting trends in these formative centuries of Western civilization. Charlemagne himself promoted a renaissance of Roman – i.e., Constantinian – Christianity. This is evident in poetry, in script, in illumination, and also in the plans and elevations of certain churches which follow Early Christian examples (St Denis, Fulda, etc.). But indigenous characteristics also make themselves

Gateway, Lorsch Abbey, c. 800

felt and point forward to the ROMANESQUE. In this category are prominent towers, strongly stressed west ends and east ends (Centula, plan for St Gall), and also heavier, more massive members. The most spectacular building preserved from Charlemagne's time is the cathedral of Aachen. *See also* GERMAN ARCHITECTURE, FRENCH ARCHITECTURE.

Lit: K. J. Conant, *Carolingian and Romanesque Architecture, 800–1200,* Pelican History of Art, 3rd edn, Harmondsworth 1974, paperback edn 1974.

Carr, John (1723–1807). A late and provincial exponent of PALLADIANISM, working mainly in Yorkshire. He began life as a mason in his father's quarry near Wakefield, and in his twenties built Kirby Hall to the design of Lord BURLINGTON and Roger MORRIS. He was later associated with Robert ADAM in the building of Harewood House (begun 1759). From then onwards he designed and built many large country houses. He was unoriginal, but could be refined and dignified in a quiet way, e.g., Everingham (1757–64), Denton Park (c. 1778), Farnley Hall (c. 1786) and the Buxton Assembly Rooms (1784). His largest and perhaps his best work is the Crescent at Buxton (1779–84), where he very successfully combined the younger WOOD'S invention of the monumental residential crescent with the arcaded ground floor surmounted by the giant pilaster order used by Inigo JONES at Covent Garden.

Lit: York Georgian Society, *The Works in Architecture of John Carr,* York 1973; I. Hale, *John Carr,* Ferens Art Gallery, Hull 1973.

Carrel (or **carol**). A niche in a cloister where a monk might sit and work or read; sometimes applied to BAY WINDOWS.

Cartouche An ornamental panel in the form of a scroll or sheet of paper with curling edges, usually bearing an inscription and sometimes ornately framed.

Cartouche

Caryatid A sculptured female figure used as a column to support an entablature or other similar member, as on the Erechtheum. The term is also applied loosely to various other columns and pilasters carved wholly or partly in the form of human figures: ATLANTES (male caryatids), CANEPHORAE (females carrying baskets on their heads), HERMS (three-quarter-length figures on pedestals), Telamones (another name for Atlantes), and TERMS (tapering pedestals merging at the top into human, animal, or mythical figures).

Caryatids, Erechtheum, Athens, 421–406 B.C.

Casemate A vaulted room, with EMBRASURES, built in the thickness of the ramparts or other fortifications, and used as a barracks or battery, or both.

Casement I. The hinged part of a window, attached to the upright side of the window-frame. 2. The wide concave moulding in door and window JAMBS and between COMPOUND columns or piers, found in Late Gothic architecture. The term was in use by the middle of the CI5 (William of Worcester's notes).

Casement window A metal or timber window with the sash hung vertically and opening outwards or inwards.

Casino I. An ornamental pavilion or small house, usually in the grounds of a larger house. 2. In the CI8 a dancing saloon, today a building for gambling.

Cassels, Richard, *see* CASTLE, Richard.

Castellamonte, Carlo Conte di (1560–1641), was trained in Rome. He became architect to the Duke of Savoy in 1615 and played a large part in developing the city plan of Turin, where he designed Piazza S. Carlo (1637) and several churches. He began Castello di Valentino, Turin (1633), completed in the French style with a high hipped roof (1663) by his son **Amadeo** (1610–83), who succeeded him as court architect.
    Lit: R. Pommer, *Eighteenth Century Architecture in Piedmont*, New York–London 1967.

Castellated Decorated with BATTLEMENTS.

Castle A fortified habitation. The planning and building of castles is primarily directed by the necessities of defence; it rarely extends as a whole into architecture proper, though certain features may. In the earlier Middle Ages the principal elements of a castle were the donjon or KEEP and the hall in France and England, the Bergfrid and the Palas in Germany. The keep is a tower spacious enough to act as living quarters in time of war for the lord or governor and the garrison; the Bergfrid is a tower of normal proportions; the Palas is the hall-range. The earliest dated donjon is at Langeais (*c.* 990), the earliest surviving major hall at Goslar (mid CI1).
    England built some hall-keeps, i.e., keeps wider than they are high (Tower of London). In France and Italy in the early CI3 Roman precedent led to symmetrical compositions with angle towers and a gatehouse in the

middle of one side. Some castles of Edward I in Britain took this over, and where in the late Middle Ages castles were still needed (south coast, Scottish border), they were often symmetrically composed. The rule in Britain at this time, however, was that castles could be replaced by unfortified manor houses. Towards the end of the Middle Ages the spread of firearms changed the castle into the fortress, with low BASTIONS for mounting cannon and no towers.

Fortress Elements:

Casemate. Vaulted chamber in a bastion for men and guns.

Cavalier. Raised earth-platform of a fortress used for look-out purposes or gun placements.

Counterscarp. The face of the ditch of a fortress sloping towards the defender.

Demi-Lune, see Half-Moon.

Glacis. The ground sloping from the top of the rampart of a fortress to the level of the country around.

Half-Moon. Outwork of a fortress, crescent-shaped or forming an angle.

Hornwork. Outwork of a fortress with two demi-bastions.

Ravelin. Similar to a *Half-Moon.*

Redoubt. Small detached fortification.

Scarp. The side of the ditch of a fortress sloping towards the enemy.

Sconce. Detached fort with bastions.

Lit: A. Hamilton Thompson, *Military Architecture in England during the Middle Ages,* London 1912.

Castle, Richard (c. 1690–1751). A German, formerly Cassels, who settled in Ireland in 1724, worked for PEARCE on the Parliament House, Dublin, and became the leading architect of his day in Ireland. His surviving works conform to English PALLADIANISM without any trace of his foreign origin: e.g. Tyrone House (1740–45) and Leinster House (1745) in Dublin, and his two great country houses, Carton (1739) and Russborough (1741). (For illustration *see* IRISH ARCHITECTURE.)

Lit: 'The Knight of Glin' in *The Country Seat,* ed. H. Colvin & J. Harris, London 1970; J. Summerson, *Architecture in Britain, 1530–1830,* Pelican History of Art, Harmondsworth 1969, paperback edn. 1970.

Castrum (Latin). Roman military camp, built on a common rectangular layout throughout the Empire. A castrum was surrounded by a rampart and a wall with towers, and crossed

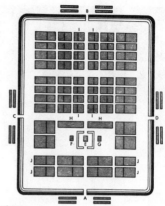

Castrum

A. Porta praetoria
B. Porta decumana
C. Porta principalis dextra
D. Porta principalis sinistra
E. Praetorium
F. Forum
G. Quaestorium
H. Tribunal
I. Cavalry
J. Auxiliary troops

by two main streets, the *cardo* and *decumanus,* running between four gates – the *porta praetoria, porta dextra, porta sinistra* and *porta decumana.* The headquarters (*praetorium*) lay at their intersection, and the barracks, armoury, and other essential military buildings in the four quarters made by the streets. Camps were strategically placed along the *limes* to secure the border.

Lit: K. D. Matthews, *Cities in the Sand,* London 1963.

Catacomb An underground cemetery, sometimes on several levels, consisting of linked galleries and chambers with recesses for tombs (*loculi*). The word *catacumbas* (of uncertain derivation) was first applied in the c5 to the Christian cemetery initiated some two hundred years earlier beneath the church of S. Sebastiano on the Appian Way outside Rome. It was later extended to cover the many similar Early Christian cemeteries in and around Rome and in Naples, Sicily and N. Africa, which vary in plan (e.g. originally gridiron in Rome and radial in Syracuse). Paintings on the walls of the Roman catacombs are among the earliest (c3–4) examples of Christian art. Christians had,

Catacomb of SS. Marcellino e Pietro, Rome,
C4–C5 A.D.

however, preferred open-air cemeteries from
the C3, and catacombs were rarely used for
burials after the C6. The term catacomb is
also applied to other and later subterranean

Cathedra Petri, St Peter's, Rome,
designed by Bernini

cemeteries (e.g. the C18 catacombs of Paris),
including those of non-Christian cults.

Lit: O. Marucchi, *Le catacombe romane*,
Rome 1933; R. Krautheimer, *Early Christian
and Byzantine Architecture*, Pelican History of
Art, Harmondsworth 1965, paperback edn
1974.

Cathedra The bishop's chair or throne in his
cathedral church, originally placed behind the
high altar in the centre of the curved wall of
the APSE. Illustrated previous column.

Cathedral Bishop's church, from CATHEDRA.

Caulcole The stalk rising from the leaves of a
Corinthian capital and supporting one of the
VOLUTES.

Cavalier In military architecture, a raised
earth-platform of a fortress, for look-out purposes or gun placements.

Cavetto moulding A hollow moulding, about
a quarter of a circle in section.

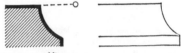

Cavetto moulding

Cell One of the compartments of a groin or rib
VAULT, in the Romanesque period usually of
plastered rubble, in the Gothic period of neatly
coursed stones; the earliest known example
is St Denis of 1140–4. Also called a *web*.

Cella The main body of a classical temple
(containing the cult image), as distinct from
the portico, etc.

Celure The panelled and adorned part of a
wagon roof (*see* ROOF) above the ROOD or the
altar.

Cenotaph A monument to a person or persons
buried elsewhere.

Centering Wooden framework used in arch
and vault construction; it is removed (or
'struck') when the mortar has set.

Central Andean architecture The formation
period (*c.* 1000 B.C.) of Central Andean
civilization took place in the northern region

of Peru. Its centre, Chavin de Huantar, has given its name to the first general style common to most regions of the Central Andes, the *Chavin style*. Chavin de Huantar was not a permanent settlement, but probably a sacred site. A temple built of massive stones and a sunken court surrounded by stone-dressed platforms belonged, as stone reliefs and sculptures applied to the buildings indicate, to the cult of some jaguar or puma god. The affinity with the La Venta culture (*see* MESOAMERICAN ARCHITECTURE) is unmistakable, and interconnections are possible. The first millennium of our era in Peru opened with a period of flourishing local cultures, and the steady refinement of styles and techniques. On the north coast the Mochica culture, from the Moche and Chicama valley, spread northwards and southwards in the course of the first eight centuries A.D. Typical of this was the stepped PYRAMID of sun-dried brick, whose best representative is the 'Huaca del Sol' from Moche, near Trujillo – a 75-ft high seven-tiered structure on a 58-ft high platform.

In the Cuzco and Lake Titicaca basin, the dawn of the heyday of the culture of the Andean Highlands (A.D. 200–800) is linked with the name of the ruins of *Tiahuanaco*, at the south end of Lake Titicaca itself (12,500 ft above sea level). Tiahuanaco was probably, like Chavin de Huantar, a kind of pilgrimage-place and religious centre for near and far. The stone remains fall into several groups, including a stepped pyramid on a roughly triangular plan, a stairway made of monoliths, lumpy stone sculptures, and a monolithic gate measuring 10 × 13 ft, called the 'Sun Gate'. Over the opening is a broad relief,

The Sun Gate, Tiahuaraco, c. 500

from whose centre a divinity advances with a raised sceptre or weapons in his hands. The builders of Tiahuanaco were most probably

the Aymara, who inhabited this region down to the time of recorded history, and survive to this day.

After the decline of cultural impulses from Tiahuanaco, which had produced the second style embracing the Central Andes, a few enlarged states were formed along the coast from the C12 onwards through the fusion of several coastal valleys. The most important was that of *Chimu* in the north, in the former territory of the Mochica. Its largely mud-brick-built capital of Chan-Chan, near the present Trujillo, is an extensive settlement covering several square miles with rectangular districts bounded by sturdy walls. The walls are often covered with geometrical or stylized figural ADOBE reliefs. A superb example is the newly restored Huaca el Dragon.

Wall frieze at Huaca El Dragon, Chan-Chan, near Trujillo, C14–C15

Paramonga, the most southerly marcher fort of the Chimu, still rises imposingly in several adobe terraces upon an 165-ft high ridge of rock, with two advanced BASTIONS commanding the coastal plain. Adobe architecture prevailed along the whole coast, including the central state of Cuismancu with its urban centre of Cajamarquilla in the hinterland of Lima.

In the Highlands, the extinction of the Tiahuanaco civilization was succeeded by a series of small independent Aymara states in the Titicaca basin, whose most noteworthy artistic creations were the *chullpas*, round or rectangular sepulchral towers of stone or adobe, which have conferred their name on the epoch.

Around A.D. 1200, simultaneously with the above-mentioned states on the Peruvian coast, the *Incas* founded their capital of Cuzco in the Highlands whence, through courage, intelligence and a gift for organization, they extended their rule over others, beginning with the linguistically and culturally related

Fortifications at Machu Picchu, Peru, c15

Quechua. But the Inca Empire only achieved its rise to the position of the greatest power on American soil prior to the coming of the Europeans following its internal consolidation around the mid-c15. The artistic gifts of the Incas were chiefly expressed in the stone architecture of the Highlands, taking up the threads of Tiahuanaco and Chavin. Rectangular stone houses with pitched roofs also supplied the paradigm for temples and palaces. Both were often associated with defensive works, which also incorporated barracks and storehouses. A typical example of such a combination is Machu Picchu, an Inca border fort discovered only in 1912, which sits 8000 ft up on a mountain ridge round which the Urubamba flows in a horseshoe bend. In the earlier Inca period polygonal blocks of stone were fitted into one another without mortar, as is the case with the three gigantic terraced zig-zag walls of Sachsayhuaman, the fortress of Cuzco.

Polygonal masonry, Sachsayhuaman, Cuzco, c13

Niches in the fortifications, Machu Picchu, Peru, c15

Granite monoliths, Ollantaytambo, Urubambatal, Peru, c. 1400

The uncompleted temple citadel of Ollantaytambo over the valley of the Urubamba is chiefly famous for the six granite monoliths forming the front face of the topmost temple hill – 12 to 14 ft high, 4 to 6 ft long, and 2 to 6 ft thick. Ollantaytambo sheltered the entrails of dead Inca rulers, whilst the mummies of the kings sat round the image of the sun-god in the great hall of the Corichanca at Cuzco. The Corichanca, or 'gold court', was the main temple of the Inca Empire; it is now occupied by the church and monastery of Santo Domingo. It has a kind of apse, whose plan is however not the arc of a circle or ellipse, but an irregular curve. This arrangement closely resembles that of the Torreon, the great tower of Machu Picchu, which envelops a sacred rock. Typical of the *Late Inca* style were small rectangularly-hewn blocks of stone, laid above one another in courses of equal width and without mortar, such as are still to be found in the Old City of Cuzco serving as the foundations of later buildings of the colonial period. A further characteristic feature of Inca architecture was the exclusive articulation of façades with trapezoid niches, windows and doors.

The sophisticated state of stonemasonry was undoubtedly connected with the belief that certain stones and cliffs were to be held sacred as the cradles of humanity or as petrified ancestors. There is a row of cliffs in the region of Cuzco into which seats, stairs, grooves and hollows have been hewn, and

Choquequilla (Gold Mount) in the Huaracondo valley near Cuzco, c15

which presumably formed part of the Inca races' cult of the dead or honouring their ancestors.

In the narrow Andean valleys, terraces held by stone walls enlarged the cultivable area for maize. Irrigation canals, water-conduits and reservoirs swelled harvests, but required considerable labour, which was compulsory for all but a few.

The greatest achievement of Inca construction are the long-distance roads, straight as a die wherever possible, 20 to 30 ft wide and bordered by walls. Only fragments survive, but the 'Royal Road of the Mountains' once extended 3750 miles, from the southern border of present-day Colombia into southern Chile. Parallel to this ran the 'Royal Road of the Coast'. Numerous transverse roads connected these two arteries, forming a network of at least 6000 miles of roads. [OZ]

Lit: H. D. Disselhof, *Geschichte der altamerikanischen Kulturen*, 1967; H. Trimbon & W. Haberland, *Die Kulturen Altamerikas*, 1969; H. Ubbelohde-Doering, *Kunst im Reiche der Inka*, 1952; *Kulturen Alt-Perus*, 1966; G. Kubler, *The Art and Architecture of Ancient America*, Pelican History of Art, 2nd edn, Harmondsworth 1974.

Chair-rail (or **dado-rail**). A moulding round a room to prevent chairs, when pushed back against the walls, from damaging their surface.

Chaitya An Indian Buddhist cave temple or prayer hall hewn out of a hill-side, in form an

Chaitya Hall, Bhaya, India, 50 B.C.

aisled basilica. Both the exterior of the wall closing the entrance and the interior are sometimes richly decorated with sculpture, as at Karli (150 B.C.) and Ajanta (c2 B.C.–c7 A.D.).

Chalet A Swiss herdsman's hut or mountain

Chalgrin

cottage. The term is now loosely applied to any house built in the Swiss style.

Chalgrin, Jean François Thérèse (1739–1811). A pupil of BOUILLÉE and Rome scholar (1758–63). He began in the rather epicene neo-classical manner then current (e.g., in the work of SOUFFLOT), and reintroduced the basilican plan in his St Philippe-du-Roule, Paris (designed pre-1765, built 1772–84), which was very influential. Also notable are his Collège de France, Paris (1780), especially the Salle des Actes, and his Pavillion de Musique de Madame at Versailles (1784). But his masterpiece, the Arc de Triomphe, Paris (1806–35), is more Romantic-Classical in the style of Boullée, with its imperial symbolism and megalomaniac scale. He did not live to see it finished, and the sculptural decoration by Rude and others gives it a distinctly C19 appearance. He rebuilt the Odéon, Paris, in 1807, following the original designs by Joseph Peyre and Charles DE WAILLY. (For illustration see TRIUMPHAL ARCH.)

Lit: L. Hautecoeur, *Histoire de l'architecture classique en France*, IV, Paris 1952.

Chamberlin, Powell & Bon A London partnership, the members of which were born about 1920. The partners won the competition in 1952 for a City of London housing estate round Golden Lane, and this extensive scheme is not completed yet. They built a fine warehouse at Witham in Essex (1953–5) and an excellent school (Bousfield School, London) in 1952–6. Their building for New Hall, Cambridge (begun 1960), is decidedly *outré* in its forms as the most recent work of the partnership tends to be. Their largest job in progress at present is for Leeds University. (For illustration, see ENGLISH ARCHITECTURE.)

Lit: R. Maxwell, *New British Architecture*, London 1972.

Chambers, Sir William (1723–96), the greatest official architect of his day in England, was born in Göteborg, Sweden, the son of a Scottish merchant. At sixteen he joined the Swedish East India Company and for nine years made voyages to India and China. His architectural training began in 1749 in Paris under J.-F. BLONDEL, and was continued in Italy from 1750 until 1755, when he settled in London. He was an immediate success. His appointment (1756) as architectural tutor to the Prince of Wales established him in royal favour, and he became successively Architect to the King, jointly with Robert ADAM (1760), Comptroller (1769), and Surveyor General (1782). He was the first treasurer of the Royal Academy and took a leading part in its foundation. In 1770 the king allowed him to assume a knighthood on receiving the Order of the Polar Star from the King of Sweden.

His career was that of a supremely successful official and his buildings are extremely competent; fastidious in ornament, impeccable in the use of orders, but rather academic, despite his famous Pagoda in Kew Gardens, and much less spectacular than those of his rival Robert Adam. His style is scholarly but eclectic, based on English PALLADIANISM smoothed out and refined by the neo-classicism of SOUFFLOT and his contemporaries, whom he had known in Paris and with whom he afterwards kept in touch. Usually best on a small scale, his scholarly finesse is well illustrated by two of his earlier works, the Casino at Marino, Dublin (1757–69), an exemplary combination of strictly classical elements to fit a Greek cross plan, and the Pagoda at Kew (1757–62), in which he aspired to similar archaeological accuracy in another manner. He was notable for his staircases, e.g. Gower House, London (c. 1769, destroyed), Melbourne House, London (c. 1772, destroyed) and Somerset House, London. His country houses are neo-Palladian in plan and composition – e.g., Lord Bessborough's villa, now a school, at Roehampton (c. 1760) and Duddingston House, Edinburgh (1762–4) – while the Strand façade of his largest and best-known work, Somerset House, London (1776–86), is a conscious imitation of a Palladian composition by Inigo JONES on the site. The courtyards and river façade display more vivacity and originality, and some of the interior decoration equals anything by Adam for elegant refinement, particularly in the Strand block in which some rooms represent the earliest examples of a mature Louis XVI style in England. Though never as fashionable as Adam, he exerted great influence both as official head of his profession and through his numerous pupils. His *Treatise on Civil Architecture* (1759) became a standard work.

Lit: J. Harris, *Sir William Chambers*, London 1970.

Chamfer The surface made when the sharp edge or ARRIS of a stone block or piece of wood, etc., is cut away, usually at an angle of 45° to the other two surfaces. It is called a *hollow chamfer* when the surface made is concave.

Champa architecture, *see* SOUTH-EAST ASIAN ARCHITECTURE.

Chancel That part of the east end of a church in which the main altar is placed; reserved for clergy and choir. From the Latin word *cancellus*, which strictly means the screen that often separated it from the body of the church. The term more usually describes the space enclosed and is applied to the whole continuation of the nave east of the CROSSING.

Chancel arch The arch at the west end of a CHANCEL.

Chantry chapel A chapel attached to, or inside, a church, endowed for the celebration of Masses for the soul of the founder or souls of such others as he may order.

Chapterhouse The place of assembly for abbot or prior and members of a monastery for the discussion of business. It is reached from the CLOISTERS, to whose eastern range it usually belongs, and in England is often polygonal.

Charnel-house An ossuary, or building in a graveyard in which are placed bones disturbed by digging up old graves. There are particularly imposing examples, often centrally planned and with the bones placed in the lower storey, in Central Europe.

Charnel house at Ják, Hungary, mid-c13

Chatri In Hindu architecture, an umbrella-shaped dome.

Chavin style, *see* CENTRAL ANDEAN ARCHITECTURE.

Chequer-work A method of decorating walls or pavements with alternating squares of contrasting materials (e.g., stone, brick, flint) to produce a chessboard effect.

Chevet The French term for the east end of a church, consisting of APSE and AMBULATORY with or without radiating chapels.

Chevron A Romanesque moulding forming a zigzag; so called from the French word for a pair of rafters giving this form.

Chevron

Chiaveri, Gaetano (1689–1770). Late Baroque architect, born in Rome but worked mainly in N. Europe – St Petersburg (1717–27), Warsaw and Dresden (*c.* 1737–48). His masterpiece was the Hofkirche in Dresden (begun 1738, badly damaged 1944), a Roman Catholic church intended to rival the grandeur of BÄHR's Lutheran Frauenkirche. It has a very elegant campanile with an open-work top section which provided the perfect foil to the solidity of Bähr's dome, as did also the exterior of the church itself with its rhythmically advancing and receding walls crowned by numerous statues. Chiaveri provided plans for the river front of the royal palace in Warsaw (1740, only partly adopted) and somewhat theatrical designs for a royal palace in Dresden (*c.* 1748, not executed). He published a volume of engraved designs: *Ornamenti diversi di porte e finestre* (1743–4).

Lit: E. Hempel, *Baroque Art and Architecture in Central Europe,* Pelican History of Art, Harmondsworth 1965; E. Hempel, *Gaetano Chiaveri,* Dresden 1955.

Chicago School, *see* BURNHAM; HOLABIRD & ROCHE; JENNEY; ROOT; SULLIVAN; UNITED STATES ARCHITECTURE.

Chicago Window A window occupying the full width of a bay and consisting of a large fixed sash flanked by a narrow movable sash

*Chicago window,
Carson Pirie & Scott Store, Chicago, by Sullivan*

on each side, as in the Marquette Building by
HOLABIRD & ROCHE (1894) and SULLIVAN'S
Carson Pirie & Scott Store (1899–1904) in
Chicago.

Chichimec architecture, *see* MESOAMERICAN
ARCHITECTURE.

Chimney bar The bar above the fireplace
opening which carries the front of the
CHIMNEY-BREAST.

Chimney-breast The stone or brick structure
projecting into or out of a room and containing the flue.

Chimney-piece, *see* MANTELPIECE.

Chimney shaft A high chimney with only one
flue.

Chimney-stack Masonry or brickwork containing several flues, projecting above the roof
and terminating in chimney-pots.

Chinese architecture Virtually nothing remains of early Chinese architecture save a
very few chance survivals. It was largely of
wood, and hence disappeared during the wars
of the Middle Kingdom.

The graves of lords and nobles were covered
with often massive mounds of earth from the
time of the Chou dynasty; that of the Ch'in
Emperor Shih-huang-ti (246–210 B.C.) had
the shape of a sawn-off square-bottomed
pyramid. A 'Spirit Road' (*shen-tao*) lined with
stone figures led to the burial plot, whose entrance was flanked by two stone towers
(*ch'ueh*). Near the grave stood two modest
shrines, occasionally of stone, a hall of offerings and a repository for the clothes of the
deceased.

The basic unit of Chinese construction was
from the first the elastic hall (*t'ang, tien*) de-

rived from domestic architecture. Excavations
near An-yang in North Honan have revealed
that wooden halls with pillars on irregular
stone bases were erected on platforms of
rammed earth, with the subsequently characteristic entrance on one of the sides. The
visual appearance of the classic Chinese hall-
structure, used for palaces and temples alike,
is established by its heavy roof, tile-covered
since at least the Han dynasty (206 B.C.–
A.D. 220), and the consistently exposed system
of supports for this. It is essentially of one
storey, but appears two-storeyed from the

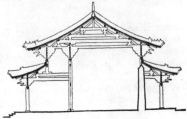

The Chinese Hall structure, section

outside, on account of the lean-to roofs over
the verandas tucked under the main roof on
all four sides. The false upper storey is taken
up within by the system of supports for the
main roof, or incorporated to the height of the
coffered ceiling over the main chamber.

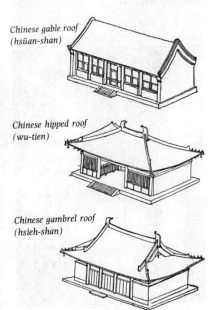

*Chinese gable roof
(hsüan-shan)*

*Chinese hipped roof
(wu-tien)*

*Chinese gambrel roof
(hsieh-shan)*

The most important forms of ROOF in China are: the gable roof (*hsüan-shan* = hanging mountain), often with parapets emphasizing the gables above the roof-line; the hipped roof (*wu-tien* = roofed veranda); the gambrel roof (*hsieh-shan* = sliced-off mountain, or *chiu-chi* = nine ridges), with hipped feet to the gables. Early on, monotonous horizontals were avoided in the massive roofs by tilting up the eaves, and sometimes both ridge-ends as well, so as to make the roofs less ponderous and as

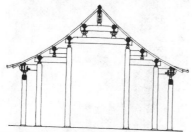

Timber-frame and beam construction

Great Hall (Chang-tien) of the Fo-kuang-szu temple on the Wu-t'ai-shan in Shansi, mid-C9

Kuan-yin-ko at Chi-hsien, A.D. 984

if but lightly poised. This was achieved by assembling small lengths of wood to form bent rafters, and using extra struts on the eaves. The system of beams under the surface of the roof transfers the weight on to the framework and pillars. In order to maximize the extent of uninterrupted flooring, pillars directly supporting the roof-ridge were dispensed with wherever possible.

The kind of timber framing adopted for these roofs is as follows: sturdy columns or pillars (*chu*) are joined horizontally by tie-beams and purlins resulting in a series of right-angles; only the struts in the ARCHI-TRAVE zone make occasional diagonals. The architrave zone mediates between the strongly projecting roof and the layer of columns and wall by means of wooden CONSOLES (*tou-kung* or *kua-tzu*), that convey the load of the projecting eaves inward on to the columns. These consoles or 'capitals' consist of an often com-

plex system of load-bearing blocks (*tou*) and bolsters (*kung*) which support the various courses of the framing, the rafters and the characteristic inward-projecting balancing-beams (*ang*) running parallel to and slightly separate from the rafters under the eaves. The elementary structure is built up out of the stepped layers of beams (*t'iao*) that run parallel to the wall and outwards and inwards at right-angles to it, as well as diagonally at the corners of the roof. This system existed in a rudimentary form by at least the Han dynasty, and, though later refined upon and elaborated, remained in essentials the same. The stylistic development of Chinese architecture can largely be seen as the elaboration of this system of supports.

The exterior and interior walls of these buildings are inserted between the columns and framing and have no load-bearing function. They are mostly of bricks or wood.

'Architrave zone' of timber frame and beam construction

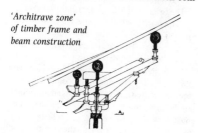

Windows and doors are likewise merely insertions, and mostly only extend through the breadth of one INTERCOLUMNIATION (*chien*).

The colouristic treatment of the halls points up the clarity of their construction. The single-coloured glaze of the roof-tiles is in each case indicative of the social standing of the building. Columns and framing are customarily lacquered or painted bright red, the beam-ends and architrave zone are painted fairly shrilly in the other primary colours. The plastered walls by contrast gleam pure white.

When it came to the interior of these halls, an enlarged rectangular central chamber for ceremonial purposes was achieved by the omission of posts under the roof-ridge. Its size is reckoned from the number of intercolumniations lengthwise and breadthwise. Generally this inner chamber has a coffered ceiling borne on consoles sitting on the frame, or a recessed, raised, often baldachin-like, one. The chamber can be aisled lengthwise or crosswise by curtain walls between the

View of Kuan-yin-ko at Chi-hsien, A.D. *984*

Interior view of a Chinese Hall

columns. This core is girded by a spatial envelope formed by the veranda-like corridor running under the projecting eaves and walled up on one or both sides. This corridor, that may surround the whole core or merely run along one side of it, may have a coffered ceiling or one may just see straight through to the rafters and supports of the eaves.

The hall with its inner chamber and envelope always remained a dwelling, and never lost its rapport with the human figure even when of large dimensions. Such complex interiors as in the West never emerged in China, where they continued to do duty chiefly as the

container or 'shrine' of an idol, which occasionally takes up almost all the room (Kuan-yin-ko at Chi-hisne, A.D. 984), or of an altar with its congeries of figures; or else the hall became the abode and ceremonial chamber of the enthroned ruler, surrounded by his most intimate retinue. The multitude, whether devout worshippers or dignitaries assembled in audience, stood in the open, in the forecourt of the hall.

The earliest evidence of the system of hall construction described above is to be found as far back as in the earthenware model houses placed in the graves of notables in the Han dynasty. It came to maturity in the T'ang dynasty (A.D. 618–906), as can be seen from the incised stone reliefs on the Great Pagoda of the Wild Goose (*Ta-yen-t'a*) of *c.* 700 in Sian-fu. The oldest actually surviving examples are the Great Hall (*Cheng-tien*) of the Fo-kuang-szu temple on the Wu-t'ai-shan in Shansi from the mid-c9, and the above-mentioned Kuan-yin-ko in the Tu-lo-szu temple at Chi-hsien east of Peking of 984.

The larger domestic complexes, and temples and palaces, were normally composed of a chain of halls that were arranged in courts one behind another along a central axis. For cosmological reasons the complexes were mostly orientated toward the south, and

The 'Hall of Seasonal Prayers' (Ch'i-nien-tien), Temple of Heaven, Peking, rebuilt 1890 following building of 1540

The Great Pagoda of the Wild Goose (Ta-yen-t'a) at Sian-fu, c. 700

thence too the way from the entry portal to the hindmost great hall is to be understood as an upward progression. The courts were surrounded by corridors or flanked by ancillary buildings, with landscaped gardens as 'built' Nature and ponds completing the complex.

Very soon halls were being transformed into circles, squares and polygons and supplied with conical or pyramidal roofs. Round this centrally-planned building other structures could be grouped with reference to the compass-points (*pao-hsia*), whence the whole complex became an image of the Earth or of the 'Middle Kingdom'. This was particularly true of the ancestral hall of the ruler, known only from literary sources, the 'Hall of Light' (*Ming-t'ang*). An echo of this type survives in the Mo-ni-tien of the Yung-hsing-szu temple at Cheng-ting in Hopei (CIO).

The most complete example of a round centrally-planned building is the 'Hall of Seasonal Prayers' (*Ch'i-nien-tien*) in the so-called 'Temple of Heaven' at Peking, which was last reconstructed in 1890 on a three-tiered stone terrace after the original of 1540.

Chinese towers were also governed by the hall concept. The look-out towers of even the early dynasties, and later the many-storeyed 'pavilions' (*lou ko*), really consisted of the superimposition of a tapering series of 'halls'.

Dodecagonal brick pagoda
of Sung-yüeh-szu, Honan, 523

Tantric pagoda at T'ien-ning-szu, near Peking,
early C12

In garden and pleasure pavilions there were often no walls between the columns in the upper storeys.

The Buddhist PAGODAS (*t'a*) of China combine ideas from various spiritual sources and artistic traditions. In the earliest example, the

Four-door pagoda (Szu-men-t'a)
at Shen-t'ung-szu, 554

dodecagonal brick pagoda of Sung-yüeh-szu in Honan of 523, the derivation from Indian temple towers of the Gupta period is unmistakable, whereas the four-door pagoda (*Szu-men-t'a*) favoured up to the c8, with a block-like body on a square plan, appears to derive from Khotan and to contain references to the mandala. The best-known example of the typically Chinese storeyed stone pagoda with a square base and simple exterior is the Great Pagoda of the Wild Goose (*Ta-yen-t'a*) at Sian-fu of around 700. Tantric Buddhism preferred octagonal stone pagodas; Lamaism, especially under the Ch'ing dynasty (1644–1911), imported the Tibetan CHORTEN (*mc'od-rten*) type of pagoda, which had more pronounced formal links with the tumulus shape of the primitive Indian STUPA. Early wooden pagodas, such as inspired the Japanese type, no longer exist in China.

Stone buildings in China readily drew on the structural features of wooden architecture, but divorced from their function, as purely decorative motifs. For obvious reasons stone was chiefly used for tombs (i.e. underground), bridges, and town walls with their defensive towers. Both true and corbelled vaults were

Chinese dynasties in the northern provinces after the mid-c5, with a second flowering under the T'ang dynasty (618–906). The façades and ceilings not uncommonly use stone to imitate timber methods of roof construction. The chambers are decorated with painting and sculpture hewn out of the living rock or made of clay. The best-known sites are those of Yün-kang (after 460), Lung-men (after about 495), Mai-chi-shan (rediscovered 1952) and Tun-huang.

The greatest fortification, the so-called Great Wall of China, was formed from already-existing earthen ramparts under the Emperor Ch'in-shih-huang-ti between 221 and 210 B.C., but only received its present form during the Ming dynasty (1368–1644; 1530 miles long, 20–26 ft wide, 36–52 ft high).

Tibetan Chorten (mc'od-rten) type of pagoda, Miao-ying-szu, Peking, 1271

The Great Wall of China, begun 221–10 B.C., completed 1368–1644

used indiscriminately from the Han dynasty onwards.

Buddhism led to the introduction to China from India via Central Asia of cave temples hewn out of the living rock, and composed of niches and chapels for worship and monks' cells. They were largely created under non-

Buddhist cave-temple at Mai-chi-shan, c5

All this was transformed by the Republican Revolution of 1911. European styles were adopted; e.g. the lecture theatre of Nanking University in pidgin-English neo-Georgian. A so-called Chinese Renaissance followed as a reaction in the 1920s. Buildings constructed after a European design were decorated with Chinese ornamental motifs; two buildings in Shanghai exemplify this at its best and worst respectively – Chung Sheng Hospital (1937) and the Government Offices (1930). Since 1949 the INTERNATIONAL MODERN style has gained in importance. The taste for one-storey houses has yielded before apartment-blocks, whose height in Peking however has been restricted to nine storeys for aesthetic reasons.

[RG]

Lit: E. Boerschmann: *Die Baukunst und religiöse Kultur der Chinesen*, 1911–31, and *Chinesische Architektur*, Berlin 1925; A.C.H. Boyd, *Chinese Architecture and Town Planning*, 1962; E. von Erdberg-Consten, in: *Propyläen Kunstgeschichte*, vol. 17, 1968; A. C. Soper, in *The Art and Architecture of China*, Pelican History of Art, Harmondsworth 1968, paperback edn 1971; N. Wu, *Chinese and Indian Architecture*, London–New York 1963.

Chinoiserie European imitations or evocations of Chinese art which first appeared in the C17, became very popular in the C18 – especially in England, Germany, France, and Italy – and lingered on into the C19. Numerous PAGODAS were built in Europe. Of the larger buildings in the style the tea-house at Potsdam (1754–7), the pavilion at Drottningholm, Sweden (1763–9), the Palazzina La Favorita, Palermo (1799), and the interior of the Royal Pavilion, Brighton (1802–21), are the most important.

Chinoiserie: Chinese Pavilion, Potsdam, 1754–6

Lit: A. Reichwein, *China and Europe*, London 1925; C. Yamada, *Die Chinamode des Spätbarock*, Berlin 1935; H. Honour, *Chinoiserie*, London 1961.

Choir The part of a church where divine service is sung.

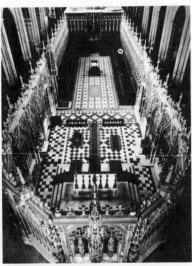

Choir: Albi Cathedral, begun 1282

Chorten (*mc'od-rten*). The Tibetan type of PAGODA which has more pronounced formal links with the tumulus shape of the primitive Indian STUPA. Illustrated previous page.

Chullpa, *see* CENTRAL ANDEAN ARCHITECTURE.

Churriguera, José Benito de (1665–1725). The eldest of three architect brothers, the others being **Joaquín** (1674–1724) and **Alberto** (1676–1750). They came of a family of Barcelona sculptors specializing in elaborately carved retables and began in this way themselves; hence their peculiar architectural style with its lavish piling up of surface ornamentation, now known as the Churrigueresque style. Some of its more fantastic and barbaric features may have been inspired by native art in Central and South America. José Benito settled early in Madrid as a carver of retables (e.g., Sagrario in Segovia Cathedral) and did not turn architect until 1709, when he laid out the town of Nuevo Baztán, the most ambitious and original urban scheme of its period in Spain. His brother Joaquín's best works date from the next decade, e.g., the patio of the Colegio de Anaya and Colegio de Calatrava at Salamanca. The youngest brother, Alberto, was the most talented, but did not emerge as an architect in his own right until after the death of his two elder brothers. The Plaza Mayor at Salamanca (begun 1729) is his first great work. San Sebastian, Salamanca, followed in 1731, but seven years later he left Salamanca and resigned as architect in charge. His last works are small but among his best: e.g., the parish church at Orgaz (1738) and the portal and façade of the church of the Assumption at Rueda (1738–47).

Lit: G. Kubler & M. Soria, *Art and Architecture in Spain and Portugal and their American Dominions 1500–1800*, Pelican History of Art, Harmondsworth 1959.

Churrigueresque style The lavish, overdecorated style named after the Churriguera family, though the term is often extended to include all the more florid, Late Baroque architecture in Spain and Spanish America, especially Mexico. Pedro de RIBERA and Narciso TOMÉ were its best practitioners in Spain where it was popular mainly in Castille.

Ciborium A canopy raised over the high altar. It is normally a dome supported on columns. *See also* BALDACHIN.

Churrigueresque sacristy: Cartuja at Granada, begun 1717

Ciborium: S. Pietro ad Oratorium, Pescara

Cimborio The Spanish term for a LANTERN admitting light over a crossing tower (*see* CROSSING) or other raised structure above a roof.

Cincture A small convex moulding round the SHAFT of a column.

Cinquefoil, *see* FOIL.

Circus 1. In Roman architecture a long oblong building with rounded ends and with tiered seating on both sides and at one end. 2. In the C18 a circular or nearly circular range of houses. 3. In modern town planning a circular road or street junction.

Cistercian architecture The Cistercian Order was founded in 1098. It was named after Citeaux in Burgundy. The third abbot, and the one to establish the rules of the Order, was the Englishman Stephen Harding. The most famous Cistercian is St Bernard of Clairvaux (1090–1153), named after Clairvaux, the second mother abbey of the Order. The other two were Pontigny and Morimond, all in Burgundy. The Order pleaded for reform, and an exacting life. One of the rules was to settle

in wild country and to colonize and cultivate it. The Cistercians became extremely successful landowners. They settled in near and far countries. At the time of the death of St Bernard there were 339 houses, in 1200 about 525 (including nunneries). Whereas the Cluniacs (*see* CLUNY) did not impose rules of architectural planning, a Cistercian house is at once recognizable by plan and elevation in whatever country it may be. Both plans and elevations, at least up to about 1150, were kept demonstratively simple. Choirs had straight ends, chapels extending east of the transepts ended straight too. The standard plan had two to each transept, but there could be up to four. Apses are rare (except in Spain). Details were simple too, but great efforts were made to achieve fine workmanship. The earliest completely preserved church is Fonte-

Cistercian abbey at Pontigny, C12

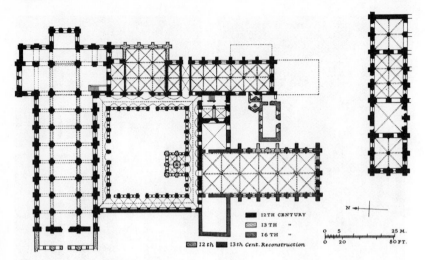

▪	12TH CENTURY
▨	13TH "
▨	16TH "

12 th ▪ 13th Cent. Reconstruction

N

0 5 .... 25 M.
0   20 .... 80 FT.

Cistercian abbey at Fontenay, 1139–47

nay in Burgundy (1139–47), the grandest preserved Burgundian church Pontigny (*c.* 1140–1200). England possesses the finest ruins: Fountains, Rievaulx, Kirkstall, Roche, Tintern, etc. The best-known Italian houses are Casamari, Fossanova, and Chiaravalle; the best-known Spanish ones Moreruela, La Oliva, Poblet and Santas Creus; the best-known in Germany Eberbach, Ebrach, Maulbronn, Bronnbach, Walkenried and Riddagshausen; in Austria Heiligenkreuz, Lilienfeld and Zwettl.

Lit: M. Aubert, *L'architecture cistercienne en France,* Paris 1947; H. Hahn, *Die frühe Kirchenbaukunst der Zisterzienser,* Berlin 1957; L. Fraccaro de Longhi, *L'architettura delle chiese cistercensi* . . . , Milan 1958.

Citadel In military architecture, a fort with from four to six bastions. It was usually sited at a corner of a fortified town but connected with it, e.g., Lille or Arras.

Cladding An external covering or skin applied to a structure for aesthetic or protective purposes. *See also* CURTAIN WALL.

Clapboard In the U.S.A. and Canada the term for WEATHERBOARD.

Clapper bridge A bridge made of large slabs of stone, some built up to make rough PIERS and other longer ones laid on top to make the roadway.

Clasp (Consortium of Local Authorities Special Programme), *see* INDUSTRIALIZED BUILDING.

Classicism A revival of or return to the principles of Greek or (more often) Roman art and architecture. The word 'classic' originally signified a member of the superior tax-paying class of Roman citizens. It was later applied, by analogy, to writers of established reputation; and in the Middle Ages it was extended to all Greek and Roman writers and also to the arts of the same period, though always with an implication of 'accepted authority'. The various classical revivals were thus attempts to return to the rule of artistic law and order as well as evocations of the glories of ancient Rome. Although most phases of medieval and later European art have to some extent been influenced by antiquity, the term 'classicism' is generally reserved for the styles more consciously indebted to Greece and Rome.

The first of these revivals was the CAROLINGIAN *renovatio* of the c8–9 – a politically, no less than aesthetically, inspired return to late Imperial Roman art and architecture. The Tuscan C11 Proto-Renaissance represents a somewhat similar attempt to revive Roman architectural forms. The few monuments produced under it exerted considerable influence on the earliest works of BRUNELLESCHI and thus the initial phase of the RENAISSANCE proper. But from the c16 onwards the Renaissance reinterpretation of antiquity was to exert almost as much influence on classicizing architects as antiquity itself. For it was during the Renaissance that writers began to evolve a classical theory of architecture based largely on the confused and confusing treatise of VITRUVIUS which had been rediscovered in 1414. Throughout the CI7 architectural theory remained essentially classical, though practising architects often paid no more than lip-service to it. But there was a practical as well as a theoretical return to classical standards in late CI7 France (notably in the work of PERRAULT and MANSART), and in early CI8 England such architects as Colin CAMPBELL, Lord BURLINGTON, and William KENT led a return to classicism by way of Inigo JONES and PALLADIO. This PALLADIANISM has sometimes been interpreted as the first phase of the late CI8 neo-classical movement.

This movement, generally referred to as Neo-classicism, began in the 1750s as a reaction against the excesses of the late BAROQUE and ROCOCO and as a reflection of a general desire for established principles based on laws of nature and reason. In art and architecture these also embodied the 'noble simplicity and calm grandeur' which Winckelmann regarded as the prime qualities of Greek art. Fresh attention was given to surviving antique buildings in Europe and Asia Minor. PIRANESI'S etchings inspired a new vision of Roman architecture, emphasizing its formal and spatial qualities. Classically 'incorrect' motifs were rejected in favour of those more archaeologically correct. But the mere copying of Greek and Roman buildings was rarely practised and never recommended. Theorists like LAUGIER and LODOLI demanded a rational architecture based on first principles, not one which imitated Roman grandeur.

These new ideas were bound up with a nascent primitivism – a belief that architecture, like society, had been at its purest and best in its simplest and most primitive form. This led to an appreciation of the severity of Greek DORIC, made possible by the publications of James STUART and others and by the discovery of the early Doric temples in Sicily and at Paestum – though for the more fundamentalist architects (e.g., C. A. Ehrensvärd in Sweden) even the latter were insufficiently plain, sturdy and masculine. It also led to the creation of an architecture of pure geometrical forms – the cube, pyramid, cylinder and sphere – which found its most extreme expression in the designs of BOULLÉE, LEDOUX and GILLY, and in buildings by SOANE in England, LATROBE in the U.S. and ZAKHAROV

Castel S. Angelo (Mausoleum of Hadrian), print by Piranesi, 1758

Design for Monument to Newton, 1784, by Boullée

Prison design for Aix-en-Provence, 1787, by Ledoux

Design for a mausoleum, by Gilly

The Brandenburg Gate, Berlin, 1789–91,
by Langhans

The Admiralty, Leningrad, 1806–15,
by Zakharov

in Russia. But if few late C18 architects took neo-classical principles to their logical conclusion equally few remained entirely immune to them.

Neo-classical buildings are solid and rather severe. Decoration, including classical enrichments, is restrained and sometimes eliminated altogether. The orders are used structurally rather than ornamentally, with columns supporting entablatures and not merely applied to the walls. Volumetric clarity is emphasized both internally and externally by unbroken

The Fredericianum, Cassel, 1769–70, by du Ry

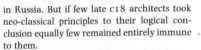

The State Capitol, Richmond, Virginia,
1785–96, by Jefferson

contours. The Baroque organic principle by which a façade is unified by interlocking its various parts (so that the wings flow out of the central block and the main storey into those above and below) is rejected in favour of an inorganic one by which the masses are rigidly defined and, sometimes brutally, juxtaposed.

In the early C19 these severe neo-classical ideals were abandoned in favour of styles richer in decoration, more picturesque in composition and more literary in their allusions to the past. In France, under the Empire, the richly luxurious and dramatically expressive Roman Imperial style was revived as propaganda for the régime. Architects once more played for effect rather than sought to express visually a high intellectual ideal. Thus the classical tradition survived, in Europe and the U.S. and in various European colonies in Asia and Africa, throughout the C19, but simply as a form of revivalism – whether Greek, Roman or Renaissance (*see* GREEK REVIVAL). And although many individual buildings in these styles are of high quality (notably those by BARRY, SMIRKE, PLAYFAIR, STRICKLAND, SCHINKEL, KLENZE, HITTORF, etc.) they show little further development. Ironically enough, the leading tenets of the neo-classicist (logical construction, truth to materials, etc.) were taken up and developed in an anti-classical way by the architects of the Gothic Revival. (*See* NEO-GOTHIC ARCHITECTURE.)

Lit: E. Kaufmann, *Architecture in the Age of Reason*, Cambridge, Mass., 1955; E. Panofsky, *Renaissance and Renascences in Western Art*, Stockholm 1960; R. Rosenblum, *Transformations in Late Eighteenth Century Art*, Princeton 1967; H. Honour, *Neo-classicism*, Harmondsworth 1968.

Clerestory (or **clearstory**). The upper stage of the main walls of a church above the aisle roofs, pierced by windows; the same term is applicable in domestic building. In Romanesque architecture it often has a narrow wall-passage on the inside.

Clérisseau, Charles-Louis (1721–1820). A French neo-classical draughtsman and architect who exerted a wide influence through his pupils and patrons, William CHAMBERS, Robert and James ADAM, and Thomas JEFFERSON. He also provided designs (not executed) for Catherine the Great. His own buildings are uninspired, e.g., the Palais de Justice, Metz (1776–89).
Lit: W. Graf Kalnein and M. Levey, *Art and Architecture of the Eighteenth Century in France,* Pelican History of Art, Harmondsworth 1973.

Clerk, Simon (d. *c.* 1489). Master mason of Bury St Edmunds Abbey from 1445 at the latest, and also of Eton College, *c.* 1455–60 (in succession to his brother John), and King's College Chapel, Cambridge, from 1477 to 1485. Of his work at Bury nothing survives; at Eton and Cambridge he continued work, that is, he did not initiate, and so his style remains unknown to us. He is named here as an example of the way distinguished masons were given responsibility in several places.
Lit: J. Evans, *English Art, 1307–1461,* Oxford 1949; J. Harvey, *English Medieval Architects,* London 1954.

Clocher The French term for a bell-tower.

Cloister vault The American term for a domical VAULT.

Cloisters A quadrangle surrounded by roofed or vaulted passages connecting the monastic

Cloister: Mont Saint-Michel, Normandy, 1203–28

church with the domestic parts of the MONASTERY; usually south of the NAVE and west of the TRANSEPT.

Cluny A Burgundian monastery founded in 910. It generated the reform of the Benedictine Order, and the militancy of the Church in the CII. Urban II, who summoned Europe to the First Crusade, was once a monk there, as were later Popes such as Gregory VII and Paschal II. In the early CI2 the abbey church of Cluny, of which little survives, was the largest in all Europe (*see* FRENCH ARCHITECTURE). It was built in the characteristic Burgundian style; but this style was not, as with the CISTERCIANS, mandatory upon its daughter-houses; these took their character from the locality. La Charité-sur-Loire, Vézelay, St Martial in Limoges, Moissac, and St Martin-des-Champs in Paris are among the best-known of them. The mother-house in England was Lewes, the chief houses in Switzerland were Romainmôtier and Payerne, and in Germany, Hirsau. Around 1200 A.D. the Order had about 1500 establishments.
Lit: J. Evans, *The Romanesque Architecture of the Order of Cluny,* Cambridge 1938; K. J. Conant, *Carolingian and Romanesque Architecture 800–1200,* Pelican History of Art, 3rd edn, Harmondsworth 1974, paperback edn 1974.

Clustered pier, *see* COMPOUND PIER.

Coade stone Artificial cast stone invented and successfully marketed in the 1770s by Mrs Eleanor Coade, and later by Coade & Sealy of London. It was widely used in the late CI8 and early CI9 for all types of ornamentation.

Coates, Wells (1895–1958). An English architect, memorable chiefly for his Lawn Road Flats in Hampstead, London (1933–4), one of the pioneer works in England in the INTERNATIONAL MODERN style of the thirties.
Lit: M. Webb, *Architecture in Britain Today,* London 1969.

Cob Walling material made of clay mixed with straw, gravel and sand.

Cockerell, Charles Robert (1788–1863), son of S. P. COCKERELL, studied under his father and assisted Sir Robert SMIRKE. From 1810 to 1817 he was abroad, first in Greece, Asia Minor, and Sicily, then in Italy. Keenly interested in archaeology, he was excellent at classical and modern languages; in Greece he worked on the discoveries of Aegina and Phigalia. However, Cockerell combined his passion for Greek antiquities with a great admiration for WREN, and the result is a style which is the English parallel of the Paris Beaux Arts style of about 1840: grander than before, fond of giant orders and sudden solecisms, yet still firmly disciplined. Cockerell is an architects' architect, and PUGIN hated him passionately. Among his buildings the following only can be referred to: the Cambridge University (now Law) Library (1836–42) with its splendid coffered tunnel vault; the Taylorian/Ashmolean Building in Oxford (1841–5); various branch buildings for the Bank of England, whose architect he became in 1833 (e.g., those in Manchester and Liverpool, both begun in 1845); and a number of insurance office buildings (e.g., the Liverpool & London and Globe Insurance, Dale Street, Liverpool of 1855–7). He was Professor of Architecture at the Royal Academy, the recipient of the first Gold Medal of the Royal Institute of British Architects, and a member of the academies of Paris, Rome, Munich, Copenhagen, etc. He also wrote on the iconography of the west front of Wells Cathedral.

Lit: H. M. Colvin, *A Biographical Dictionary of English Architects 1660–1840*, London 1954; J. Mordaunt Crook, *The Greek Revival*, London 1971.

Cockerell, Samuel Pepys (1754–1827), began in TAYLOR'S office along with NASH. He acquired numerous surveyorships – Admiralty, East India Company, St Paul's, Foundling Hospital, etc. – but is remembered for his fantastic country house, Sezincote (1803), the first Indian-style building in England. Elsewhere he showed French influence of an advanced kind, e.g., west tower of St Anne's, Soho, London. In 1792 he restored Tickencote church in the Norman style, thus anticipating C19 restorations.

Lit: H. M. Colvin, *A Biographical Dictionary of English Architects 1660–1840*, London 1954.

Coducci or **Codussi, Mauro** (*c.* 1440–1504), a leading architect in late C15 Venice, was born at Lenna near Bergamo, and had settled in Venice by 1469. Like his rival LOMBARDO he achieved (though rather less successfully) a synthesis between the Renaissance and Veneto-Byzantine style with its rich surface

decoration and mysterious spatial effects. His earliest known work is S. Michele in Isola (1469), the first Renaissance church in Venice, with a façade derived from ALBERTI'S Tempio Malatestiano but capped by a semicircular pediment of Veneto-Byzantine inspiration. Between 1482 and 1500 he completed S. Zaccaria, with its very tall façade on which columns and niches are piled up on one another, and with classical ornament in most unclassical profusion. He was more restrained in S. Giovanni Crisostomo (1497–1504), the first centrally planned church in Venice (cross-in-square). The Palazzo Vendramin-Calergi (*c.* 1500) with round-headed windows and rich marble cladding, and the Palazzo Corner-Spinelli on the Grand Canal (*c.* 1500) have been attributed to him. In 1492 he rebuilt S. Maria Formosa on the plan of its C12 predecessor (exterior and dome are C16 and C17). The great staircase of the Scuola di S. Giovanni Evangelista (1498) survives, but that of the Scuola di S. Rocco (1495) was destroyed in the C19. He also designed the clock-tower and Procuratie Vecchie in Piazza S. Marco (1496–1500).

Lit: G. Lorenzetti, *Venezia ed il suo estuario*, Venice 1926; L. Angelini, *Le opere in Venezia di M. Codussi*, Milan 1945; N. Carboneri, 'Mauro Codussi' in *Boll. del Centro Palladiano*, Vicenza 1964, p. 188.

Coffering Decoration of a ceiling, a vault, or an arch SOFFIT, consisting of sunken square or polygonal ornamental panels. *See also* CAISSON *and* LACUNAR.

Coffering: Tholos, Epidauros, 360–320 B.C.

Cola da Caprarola, *see* LEONARDO DA VINCI.

Collar-beam, *see* ROOF.

Colonia, Juan, Simon, Francisco, *see* SIMÓN DE COLONIA.

Colonnade A row of columns carrying an entablature or arches.

Colonnades: St Peter's, Rome, 1667, by Bernini

Colossal Order Any ORDER whose columns rise from the ground through several storeys, sometimes called a giant order.

Colossal Order: façade of St Peter's, Rome, 1607–14, by Maderno

Columbarium Literally a pigeon-cote, whence an ancient Roman sepulchral chamber with

Columbarium of Pomponius Hylas in the Scipione Gardens, Rome, CI

rows of small recesses like nesting-boxes to hold the urns of ashes.

Column An upright member, circular in plan and usually slightly tapering; in classical architecture it consists of base, SHAFT, and CAPITAL. It is designed to carry an ENTABLATURE or other load, but is also used ornamentally in isolation.

Columns in the cloister of S. Paolo fuori le mura, Rome, early c4

Columna rostrata (or ROSTRAL COLUMN). In Roman architecture, an ornamental column decorated with ships' prows to celebrate a naval victory.

Columna rostrata

Common rafter, *see* ROOF.

Communion table, *see* ALTAR.

Composite Order, *see* ORDER.

Compound pier A pier with several SHAFTS, attached or detached, or demi-shafts against the faces of it; also called a *clustered* pier.

Compound pier: Chapterhouse, Casamari Abbey, Frosinone, C12

Conch A semicircular niche surmounted by a half-dome.

Concrete Cement mixed with coarse and fine aggregate (such as pebbles, crushed stone, brick), sand, and water in specific proportions. In some form it has been used for more than two thousand years, especially by the Romans. The discovery of Portland Cement in 1824 led to the great developments during the C19, and its use in structures of all kinds has largely revolutionized the shape of building today. *See also* PRECAST, PRESTRESSED, and REINFORCED CONCRETE.

Conder, Josiah, *see* JAPANESE ARCHITECTURE.

Confessio In early medieval churches a subterranean chamber or recess located below or near the altar and sheltering a relic.

Console An ornamental bracket with a compound curved outline and usually of greater height than projection. *See* ANCONES, BRACKET, CORBEL, MODILLION.

Consoles: Palace, Fathepur Sikri, India

Conurbation A term used in town planning to denote a group of towns linked together geographically, and possibly by their function, e.g., the towns of the Black Country or the Potteries. The word was first used by Patrick GEDDES about 1910.

Coping A capping or covering to a wall, either flat or sloping to throw off water.

Coptic architecture The Copts, Christian descendants of the ancient Egyptians, became schismatic as Monophysites (adherents of the doctrine of the single nature of Christ) after the Council of Chalcedon in 451. Having established their own hierarchy in the C6, they conducted a bitter struggle, fed by social and national resentments, against the Imperial Byzantine Church. In the C7 they sided with the Arabs, thus preserving their existence as a church (Patriarchate of Alexandria, with its see in Old Cairo) and people up to the present, despite grave losses through conversion to Islam and often severe pressure from their Muslim overlords. They maintained close ecclesiastical contacts with the Christian kingdom of Nubia. The Abyssinian church was dependent upon the Coptic up to the Second World War, and its *Abbuna*, who was installed by the Coptic Patriarch, was generally a Coptic monk.

Coptic architecture has been little studied: secular buildings are scarcely known, but there seem to have been no planned towns or even standard types of house. Ecclesiastical architecture is known from several surviving examples, but these are mostly undated, and moreover have been frequently altered. It is as yet not possible to propose a pattern of development for Coptic church architecture; given the immense length of the Nile valley, one must expect local peculiarities of construction to have given rise to various features in different centres. Here one can only refer to a few salient types of building:

1. The so-called Sohag group was created even before the separation of the Coptic from the Byzantine Church (Deir-el-Abyâd, Deir el-

Sohag monastery, c. 440

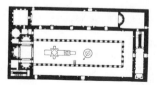

Church at Deir-el-Abyâd, c. 440

Ahmar, Dendera), and comprises aisled BASI-LICAS (perhaps once with open naves), with quite distinct triconch (clover-leaf shaped) choirs elaborately articulated within by columns, niches framed by AEDICULAS, and numerous small side-chambers (today only in the two monastery churches of Sohag). The monastery churches (built c. 440 by the reformer of Egyptian monasticism, Apa She-nuta; there is no date for Dendera) exhibit reminiscences of Ancient Egyptian archi-tecture – battered walls, mouldings evocative of temples, etc.

2. The simple aisled basilica with a gene-rally tripartite east end (rectangular or semi-circular apse with subordinate rooms on

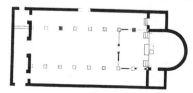

Henchir el-Atench Basilica, near Setif, Egypt

either side) stemmed from EARLY CHRISTIAN ARCHITECTURE and survived into the Middle Ages, though little new building appears to have been possible after the Arab conquest. Only in the C11/12 did significant building activity occur, with the reconstruction of earlier churches, involving the substitution of vaults for wooden roofs, the reinforcement of the load-bearing walls, and the replacement or encasement of the columns with massive masonry pillars. The vaulting was either of the continuous tunnel variety, or a succes-sion of brick domes; galleries also occur.

Typical examples are the churches of Old Cairo, where the earliest parts are in some cases relegated to undercrofts.

3. This period also witnessed the emer-gence of an utterly distinctive kind of church, apparently promoted by the proliferation of altars, which had already led to their provision in the rooms adjoining the apse and to the addition of ancillary chapels with further altars. This new type was the *broad church*, which was apparently popular with monasteries: three to six CHANCELS (haikal) of the same size lie in a row, preceded by one or more transepts broken up into sections equivalent to the chancels by transverse arches, every part being vaulted by domes on PENDENTIVES. Such broad churches are scat-tered over Upper Egypt, e.g. Medinet Habu,

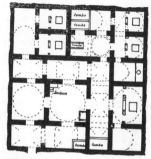

Plan of broad church at Der es Suhada, near Akhmin

Der es Suhada monastery, near Akhmin, traditionally founded c. 330, earliest surviving buildings C10–C11

Medamud, Deir Naga'a ed-Deir, the mona-steries near Akhmin (no chronological ar-rangement is yet possible).

Early monasteries (Kellia (not yet exca-vated), Monastery of Apollo in Bawit, Monas-tery of Jeremiah in Saqqâra) are like irregular mushroom growths of individual cells (com-

Carved niche, Bawit, c6

monly called chapels on account of their painted prayer-niches, some of which were the negotiable property of the monks) round the basilical monastery church. The increasing insecurity due first to Nubian nomads and then to Islamic raiders ultimately led to the creation of enclosed, fortress-like monasteries of widely differing appearance, such as those still in use in Wadi'n-Natrun. But here too a proper survey and classification remains to be done. [KW]

Lit: W. Müller-Wiener, 'Koptische Architektur' in *Koptische Kunst, Christentum am Nil*, Catalogue of the 1963 exhibition in the Villa Hügel, Essen (with bibliography of earlier literature); R. Krautheimer, *Early Christian and Byzantine Architecture*, Pelican History of Art, Harmondsworth 1965, paperback edn 1974; G. Gerster, *Kirchen im Fels*, 1968.

Corbel A projecting block, usually of stone, supporting a beam or other horizontal member.

Corbel table A range of CORBELS running just below the eaves; often found in Norman buildings.

Corbelling Brick or masonry courses, each built out beyond the one below like a series of corbels, to support a BARTIZAN, CHIMNEY-STACK, projecting window, etc.

Corbie steps (or CROW STEPS). Steps on the COPING of a gable, used in Flanders, Holland, North Germany and East Anglia, and also in C16 and C17 Scotland.

Cordemoy, J. L. de An early Neo-classical theorist about whom very little is known except that he was a priest (prior of St Nicholas at La Ferté-sous-Jouars) and was not, as is sometimes said, identical with L. G. de Cordemoy (1651–1722). His *Nouveau traité*

de toute l'architecture (1706) was the first to preach truth and simplicity in architecture and to insist that the purpose of a building should be expressed in its form. His ideas anticipated and probably influenced those of LAUGIER and LODOLI.

Lit: W. Herrmann, *Laugier and French Architectural Theory*, London 1962; R. Middleton, 'The Abbé de Cordemoy and the Graeco-Gothic Ideal' in *Journal of the Warburg and Courtauld Institutes*, xxvi, 1963.

Cordon In military architecture, the rounded stone moulding or band below the parapet of the revetment of the rampart, going all round the fort.

Corinthian Order, *see* ORDER.

Cornice In classical architecture, the top, projecting section of an ENTABLATURE; also any projecting ornamental moulding along the top of a building, wall, arch, etc., finishing or crowning it. *See also* ORDER.

Detail of cornice, Temple C, Selinus, Sicily, c. 550 B.C.

Corona The vertical-faced projection in the upper part of a CORNICE, above the BED MOULDING and below the CYMATIUM, with its SOFFIT or under-surface recessed to form a drip.

Corps de logis The French term for the main buildings as distinct from the wings or pavilions.

Cortile The Italian term for a courtyard, usually internal and surrounded by ARCADES.

Cortona, Pietro Berrettini da (1596–1669), painter and architect, second only to BERNINI in the history of Roman Baroque art, was born at Cortona, the son of a stone mason. Apprenticed to the undistinguished Florentine painter Commodi, he went with him to Rome c. 1612 and settled there. He can have received only superficial training in architecture, if any at all. First patronized by the Sacchetti family, for whom he designed the Villa del Pigneto (1626–36, now destroyed, but a landmark in villa design), he was soon taken up by Cardinal Francesco Barberini and his cultivated circle. Thereafter he had architectural and pictorial commissions in hand simultaneously. His first important building, SS. Martina e Luca, Rome (1635–50), is also the first great, highly personal, and entirely homogeneous Baroque church, conceived as a single plastic organism with a single dynamic theme applied throughout. It is notable especially for the pliable effect given to the massive walls by breaking them up with giant columns: these are not used to define bays or space, as they would have been by a Renaissance architect, but to stimulate the plastic sense. The decoration is extremely rich, even eccentric (e.g., the wildly undulating forms of the dome coffering), with here and there Florentine Mannerist traits. In contrast to Bernini he excluded figure sculpture entirely; he also excluded colour and had the interior painted white throughout.

His use of concave and convex forms in the façade of S. Maria della Pace, Rome (1656–7), is typically Baroque. More original is his application of theatre design to the *piazza*: he treated it as an auditorium, the side entrances being arranged as if they were stage doors and the flanking houses as if they were boxes. The gradual elimination of Mannerist elements from his style and his tendency towards Roman simplicity, gravity, and monumentality are apparent in the façade of S. Maria in Via Lata, Rome (1658–62). Comparison between his early and late works, notably the dome of S. Carlo al Corso, Rome (begun 1668), illustrates his remarkable progress from eccentricity and complexity, with effervescent decoration, to serene classical magnificence. Most of his grander and more ambitious schemes remained on paper (Chiesa Nuova di S. Filippo, Florence; Palazzo Chigi, Rome; Louvre, Paris). Though equally great as painter and architect he said that he regarded architecture only as a pastime.

Lit: R. Wittkower, *Art and Architecture in Italy 1600–1750*, Pelican History of Art, Harmondsworth 1973, paperback edn 1973.

Cosmati work Decorative work in marble with inlays of coloured stones, mosaic, glass, gilding, etc., much employed in Italian Romanesque architecture, especially in and around Rome and Naples, C12–13. Roman marble workers of this period were known collectively as the Cosmati from the name Cosma, which recurs in several families of marble workers.

Lit: E. Hutton, *The Cosmati*, London 1951.

Costa, Lucio, born 1902 at Toulon in France. Brazilian architect, planner, and architectural historian (in which capacity he works in the Commission for Ancient Monuments). An example of his excellent architectural work is the block of flats in the Eduardo Guinle Park at Rio (1948–54). As a planner he suddenly rose to fame by winning the competition for Brasilia, the new capital (Nova-Cap) of Brazil, in 1957. The plan is a formal one, yet not at all formal in the Beaux Arts sense. It has the shape of a bow and arrow or a bird, the head being the square with the two houses of parliament and the parliamentary offices, the tail being the railway station. Close to this are sites for light industry; nearer the head, but on the way along the straight monumental axis towards the station, follows the quarter of hotels, banks, theatres, etc., which lies at the junction of body and wings. The long curved wings (or the bow proper) are for housing; this area is divided into large square blocks, called *superquadre*, each with its freely arranged high slabs of flats, schools, church, etc. (For illustrations *see* BRAZILIAN ARCHITECTURE.)

Lit: S. Bracco, *L'Architettura moderna in Brasile*, Bologna 1967; F. Bullrich, *New Directions in Latin American Architecture*, New York, 1969.

Cottage orné An artfully rustic building, usually of asymmetrical plan, often with a thatched roof, much use of fancy WEATHER-BOARDING, and very rough-hewn wooden columns. It was a product of the picturesque cult of the late C18 and early C19 in England: an entire village of such cottages was built by NASH at Blaise Hamlet (1811). It might serve

Cottage orné, Blaise Hamlet, by Nash, 1811

merely as an ornament to a park or as a lodge or farm labourer's house, but several, intended for the gentry, were built on a fairly large scale. Papworth's *Designs for Rural Residences* (1818) includes numerous designs.

Cotte, Robert de (1656–1735), an early Rococo architect, was instrumental in the diffusion abroad, especially in Germany, of French architectural and decorative fashions. He began under his brother-in-law J. HARDOUIN-MANSART, who established him professionally and whom he eventually succeeded as *premier architecte* (1709). His main work for the Crown was the rebuilding of the choir of Notre Dame, Paris (completed 1714) with decoration by Pierre LE PAUTRE. His Parisian *hôtels* date from 1700 onwards, the most notable among those that survive being the Hôtel de Bouvallais (*c.* 1717) and the redecoration of François Mansart's Hôtel de Toulouse, now the Banque de France, in which the gallery (1718–19) is a Rococo masterpiece (the decoration is by François Antoine Vassé). He also worked extensively outside Paris (e.g., Palais Rohan, Strasbourg, 1727–8, built 1731–62), and was frequently consulted by German patrons, for extensions to the *château* at Bonn and for Schloss Clemensruhe at Poppelsdorf (1715), for example; his designs or advice were not always accepted (e.g. at Schloss Brühl, Schloss Schleissheim, and the Residenz at Würzburg).

Lit: W. Graf Kalnein & M. Levey, *Art and Architecture of the Eighteenth Century in France*, Pelican History of Art, Harmondsworth 1973.

Coupled roof, *see* ROOF.

Covarrubias, Alonso de (1488–1570), was a mason and decorative sculptor in a limpid, playful Early Renaissance style, though for structural members he still adhered to the Gothic tradition. He appears first as one of the nine consultants for Salamanca Cathedral in 1512, a sign of remarkably early recognition. From 1515 he did decorative work at Sigüenza. The church of the Piedad at Guadalajara (1526) is now in ruins, but the Chapel of the New Kings at Toledo Cathedral (1531–4) survives complete and is a delightful work. The fine staircase of the Archbishop's Palace at Alcalá is of *c.* 1530, the richly tunnel-vaulted Sacristy at Sigüenza of 1532–4. Covarrubias was master mason of Toledo Cathedral and architect to the royal castles (1537 etc.); see the courtyard of the Alcázar at Toledo.

Lit: F. Chueca Goitia, *Arquitectura del siglo XVI* (*Ars Hispaniae*, xi), Madrid 1953; G. Kubler & M. Soria, *Art and Architecture in Spain and Portugal and their American Dominions, 1500–1800*, Pelican History of Art, Harmondsworth 1959.

Cover fillet A moulded strip used to cover a joint in panelling, etc.

Coving 1. The large concave moulding produced by the sloped or arched junction of a wall and ceiling. 2. In the case of ROOD SCREENS the concave curve supporting the projecting ROOD LOFT.

Cowl A metal covering, like a monk's hood, fixed over a chimney or other vent, and revolving with the wind to improve ventilation.

Cradle roof, *see* ROOF.

Credence A small table or shelf near the altar, on which the Sacraments are placed.

Crenellation, *see* BATTLEMENT.

Crepidoma The stepped base of a Greek temple.

Crescent A concave row of houses. It was invented by John WOOD the younger at the Royal Crescent, Bath (1761–5); John CARR

Royal Crescent, Bath, by J. Wood, 1767–75

followed with his Crescent at Buxton (1779–84) which combined Wood's invention with an arcaded ground floor.

Crest, cresting An ornamental finish along the top of a screen, wall, or roof; usually decorated and sometimes perforated.

Cretan architecture, *see* MINOAN ARCHITECTURE.

Crinkle-crankle wall A serpentine or continuously snake-like curving or undulating wall.

Crocket A decorative feature carved in various leaf shapes and projecting at regular intervals from the angles of spires, PINNACLES, canopies, gables, etc., in Gothic architecture.

Crocket

Crocket capital, *see* CAPITAL.

Cronaca (Simone del Pollaiuolo) (1457–1508), was a Florentine but, like Giuliano da SANGALLO with whom he was to be closely associated, he spent several years in Rome when young (1475–85). He collaborated with Giuliano da Sangallo at the Sacristy of S. Spirito, Florence, and with BENEDETTO DA MAIANO at Palazzo Strozzi, Florence, for

which he designed the magnificent and famous cornice. His masterpiece is S. Francesco (S. Salvatore) al Monte, Florence (begun late 1480s) – extremely elegant yet robust and dignified. The Palazzo Guadagni in Florence (1504–6) has been attributed to him.

Lit: L. H. Heydenreich and W. Lotz, *Architecture in Italy, 1400–1600*, Pelican History of Art, Harmondsworth 1974.

Cross One of the most ancient symbolical and ornamental devices. As a Christian symbol it has been used in ornament and has also determined the plans of churches, the equal-armed Greek cross plan being used especially in Byzantium and in Italy during the Renaissance, but the Latin cross being more usual in Western Europe from the Middle Ages. The main types of cross are shown below.

1. Greek cross	6. Forked cross
2. Latin cross	7. Maltese cross
3. St Anthony's cross	8. Clover-leaf cross
4. St Andrew's cross	9. Cross of Lorraine
5. Double cross	10. Papal cross

Cross vault, *see* VAULT.

Cross window A window with one MULLION and one TRANSOM.

Crossing The space at the intersection of the nave, chancel, and transepts of a church; often surmounted by a crossing tower.

Crow steps, *see* CORBIE STEPS.

Crucks Pairs of large curved timbers used as the principal framing of a house. They take the place of both posts of the walls and rafters of the roof.

Crypt In a church, a chamber or vault beneath the main floor, not necessarily underground, and usually containing graves or relics. *See also* CONFESSIO. The term Ring Crypt is used for semicircular corridor crypts below the apse of a church. They are early

Crypt: St Bénigne, Dijon, 1001-18

medieval and the first seem to belong to the late c6 (St Peter's in Rome).

Cryptoporticus In Roman architecture, an enclosed gallery having walls with openings instead of columns; also a covered or subterranean passage.

Cupola A DOME, especially a small dome on a circular or polygonal base crowning a roof or turret.

Curtail step The lowest step in a flight, with a curved end which projects beyond the newel.

Curtain wall 1. A non-load-bearing wall which can be applied in front of a framed structure to keep out the weather. There are now many

Curtain walls: Lafayette Towers, 1955-63, by Mies van der Rohe

types, manufactured from a variety of materials such as aluminium, steel, and glass; sections may include windows and the spaces between. 2. In medieval architecture the outer wall of a castle, surrounding it and usually punctuated by towers or BASTIONS.

Curvilinear masonry, *see* POLYGONAL MASONRY.

Curvilinear tracery, *see* TRACERY.

Cushioned frieze A frieze with a convex profile, also called a pulvinated frieze.

Cusps Projecting points formed at the meeting of the FOILS in Gothic TRACERY, etc. (For illustration *see* FOIL.)

Cutwater The wedge-shaped end of a pier of a bridge, so constructed to break the current of water.

Cuvilliés, François (1695-1768). One of the most accomplished Rococo architects. Though he derived inspiration from the French Rococo, his decoration is much more exuberant than anything in France. His masterpiece, the Amalienburg in the park of Nymphenburg near Munich, has an easy elegance and gossamer delicacy which make it the supreme secular monument of the Rococo. Born at Soignies-en-Hainaut, he entered the service of the exiled Elector Max Emanuel of Bavaria in 1708. As court dwarf, Cuvilliés travelled in the Elector's train through Paris, and in 1714 accompanied him on his return to Munich. Too small for the army, he began by working as a military architect and showed such promise that he was sent to Paris (1720-4) to study under J.-F. BLONDEL. In 1725 he was appointed Court Architect in Munich with EFFNER. For the Elector's brother he replaced SCHLAUN as architect at Schloss Brühl near Cologne (1728) and designed the beautiful little house of Falkenlust in the park. His first work in Bavaria was the decoration of the Reiche Zimmer in the Residenz, Munich (1729-37, partly destroyed). In 1733 he provided designs for the abbey church of Schäftlarn and for Palais Königsfeld (now the Archbishop's Palace), Munich. His next work was the Amalienburg (1734-9). It is a single-storey building with a large circular room in the centre which makes the garden façade curve outwards gracefully. The carved wood and silvered decorations in the main rooms are

of exquisite refinement and the colour schemes
are remarkably subtle – a cool watery blue
background in the centre, citron yellow in
one of the side rooms, and straw yellow in
the other. In 1747 he provided plans for
Wilhelmstal, near Kassel (erected by C. L. Du
RY). His last major work was the Residenz-
theater, Munich (1751–3; partly destroyed
1944, restored 1958), one of the last insouciant extravaganzas of the Rococo, liberally
decorated with exquisitely carved *putti*,
caryatids, swags, trophies of musical instru-
ments, and those frothy cartouches which
characterize the style. In 1767 he completed
the façade of the Theatine church of St Cajetan
in Munich. He published a *Livre de cartouches*
in 1738. (For illustrations *see* GERMAN
ARCHITECTURE, ROCOCO ARCHITECTURE.)
    Lit: W. Braunfels, *F. Cuvilliés*, Würzburg,
1938; F. Wolf, *F. de Cuvilliés*, Munich 1967.

Cuypers, Petrus Josephus Hubertus (1827–
1921), the most important Dutch architect of
the C19, studied at the Antwerp Academy
and in 1850 became City Architect at
Roermond. In 1852 he set up a workshop
there for Christian art. In 1865 he went to
Amsterdam, where he built his two most
famous buildings, both in the Dutch brick Renaissance style, and both restrained and without the exuberance of others working in the
Northern Renaissance styles. The two buildings are the Rijksmuseum (1877–85) and
the Central Station (1881–9). But the majority of Cuypers's works are neo-Gothic
churches. It is hard to single out a few from
the large total: they might be St Catharina,
Eindhoven (1859); St Wilibrordus and Sacred
Heart, both Amsterdam (1864–6 and 1873–
80); St Bonifatius, Leeuwarden (1881); St
Vitus, Hilversum (1890–2); and Steenbergen
(1903). Cuypers also restored and enlarged
the castle of Haarzuylen (1894–6).
    Lit: J. T. J. Cuijpers, *Het Work van Dr
P. J. H. Cuijpers, 1827–1917*, Amsterdam
1917; H.-R. Hitchcock, *Architecture: Nineteenth and Twentieth Centuries*, Pelican History
of Art, Harmondsworth 1969, paperback edn
1971.

Cyclopean masonry In pre-classical Greek
architecture, masonry composed of very
large irregular blocks of stone; also any
polygonal masonry of a large size.

Cyma recta A double-curved moulding, concave above and convex below, also called an
ogee moulding. (For additional illustration *see*
ENTABLATURE.)

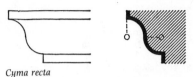

Cyma recta

Cyma reversa A double-curved moulding, convex above and concave below; also called a
reverse ogee moulding. (For additional ilustra-
tion *see* ENTABLATURE.)

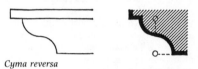

Cyma reversa

Cymatium The top member of a CORNICE in
a classical ENTABLATURE.

Czechoslovak architecture In the Middle Ages
architecture in Bohemia and Moravia formed
part of German architecture. The oldest
Christian buildings date from the C10 (Rotunda, Hradshin, Prague, excavated). The
principal Romanesque buildings of the C12
and early C13 are St George at Prague, the
crypt of Doksany and Strahov Abbey in
Prague. At Trebic in the mid-C13 French
Gothic influence begins to make itself felt. Its
climax is Prague Cathedral, begun in 1344

St Martin, Prague, C12

by Matthias of Arras and inspired by Narbonne. It was continued after Matthias' death in 1353 by Peter PARLER from Swabia, and his work is the architectural parallel to Charles IV's great epoch in Bohemian history. Charles made Prague the capital of the Empire, added large, boldly planned areas to the city, and built not far from Prague the Karlstein Castle (1348–67). Peter Parler represents a stylistic link with South Germany which was never to snap. With the flowing tracery in its windows, the complicated rib vaults, the flying ribs and the superb portrait heads on the triforium, Prague Cathedral blazed the trail for the architecture of the c15 and early c16 in Germany and Austria. Peter Parler was also the architect of the chancel of Kolin, added to a hall nave of c. 1280 – the first in Bohemia, and of course derived from Germany. Parler also began the cathedral-like church of Kutná Hora. Yet another impoitant church of Charles' time is the octagonal Karlov church in Prague.

Karlstein castle near Prague, begun 1348

Of the other Late Gothic churches the most notable are those of Třeboň, Ceský Krumlov, Olomouc, Koštice, Plseň, Brno, Most (Brüx) of 1517, and finally Louny (Laun) of 1529 etc. by Benedict Rieth.

For by then Benedict RIETH had reached his full maturity. His (though begun by M. Rajsek) are also the fabulously intertwined vaults of Kutná Hora, but Rieth's centre was of

St Barbara, Kutná Hora, by Rieth, 1512

Vaulting of choir, Prague Cathedral, 1385,
by Peter Parker

The Vladislav Hall on the Hradshin, Prague,
by Rieth, 1493–1502

it is true, than the years of King Matthias in Hungary, but earlier than the earliest pieces in Poland – and indeed in Austria and Germany. Only one generation later Italians (Paolo della Stella and others) built the Belvedere (1537 etc.) in the Hradshin gardens in the purest and most elegant Cinquecento style. It is of a precociousness as astonishing as Rieth's work. However, with the one exception of Hvezd (Stern) near Prague, a star-shaped hunting-lodge of 1555 with exquisite

Hunting Lodge, Huĕzda, near Prague,
by Wolmut and others, 1555

course Prague. On the Hradshin a predecessor, in the 1480s, had done the amazing oratory in the cathedral with its intricate decorative ribs in the form of branches and twigs. This may or may not be by Rajsek. Rieth's *magnum opus* is the Vladislav Hall on the Hradshin. This, begun *c.* 1487, combines another intertwined vault with windows of pure Italian Renaissance forms and other details in an insouciant mixture of Latest Gothic and Renaissance.

The last years of the C15 are an early date for Renaissance features in the East, later,

wholly Italian stucco decoration, it remained alone, and the common development is more similar to the German and the Polish so-called Renaissance. The number of buildings and such features as portals is great. The Schwarzenberg Palace on the castle hill has shaped gables and diamond-cut ashlar blocks (1545 etc.), the Tennis Court on the Hradshin (1565-8, by B. Wolmut) rich sgraffito decoration. The same technique of decoration appears in a house of 1555 at Telč whose crazy gable is reminiscent of Poland. Among the most characteristic features are colonnaded courtyards, in two or even three tiers (Bučovice, Velké Losiny).

Count Waldstein, the ambitious general, led architecture back to the Italian grandeur and simplicity with his vast palace in Prague and especially its loggia corresponding in height to three storeys of the palace (1623–34, by Andrea Spezza and others). Vienna has nothing to compare with it, but the two largest palaces of the second half of the C17 are in the same vein as contemporary work in Vienna (and Hungary). They are the Lobkowicz Palace at Roudnice (1652) and the Czernin Palace in Prague (1664), both by Francesco CARATTI. The Czernin Palace is twenty-nine windows wide and four storeys high, with no pavilions or other projections, but with the heaviest diamond rustication on

St Niklas, on the Mala Strana (Kleinseite), Prague, 1703-59, by Christoph and Kilian Ignaz Dientzenhofer

St Niklas, main façade, by Christoph and Kilian Ignaz Dientzenhofer, 1732-7

the ground floor and serried attached giant columns above. The change from this massed display to the splendidly curvaceous Bohemian C18 style was due to two members of the Bavarian DIENTZENHOFER family: Christoph and Kilian Ignaz. Christoph's principal work is the church of St Niklas on the Kleinseite (Malá Strana) at Prague (1708 onwards). The source of the style is GUARINI, who designed a church near Prague, and there are also close relations to HILDEBRANDT's work. The most characteristic features of Christoph Dientzenhofer's churches are façades curving forward and backward,

VON ERLACH in the early C18 (Liblice by Alliprandi, 1699 etc.). A layout of exceptional boldness was that of Kuks, built from 1707 onwards for Count Sporck. A palace, no longer extant, faced a vast block of almshouses across a valley in which was a race-course, and ex-

Abbey Church of St Margaret, Břevnov, completed 1721, by C. Dientzenhofer

Chapel at Smirice Castle, 1699, by C. Dientzenhofer

interlocked oval spaces inside, and skew or three-dimensional arches. A particularly bold motif is the diagonally set façade towers of Kilian Ignaz Dientzenhofer's St John Nepomuk on the Rock (1730). Among domestic buildings there is much influence from FISCHER

Pilgrimage Church near Saar,
1719–22, by Áichel

tremely Baroque sculpture adorns the terrace of the almshouses and extends into the
dense woods near by. The most interesting
architect of these years was AICHEL or Santini with his remodellings of Gothic churches
in a queer Baroque-Gothic all his own,
though inspired by Rieth and BORROMINI.

The best examples of the turn to Neo-
Classicism are the extensive Palladian mansion of Kačina (by C. F. Schuricht, 1802 etc.)
and the beautiful Saloon of the Rohan Palace
at Prague (by L. Montoyer, 1807). The style
carries on to the colonnade, the baths, etc.
of the Chotek gardens at Kromeřiz (Kremsier)
of the 1830s and 1840s. Little needs singling
out between 1850 and 1900, foremost the
National Theatre and the Rudolfinum of
1868 etc. and 1876 etc., both in Prague
and both by J. Zitek and J. Schulz. Both are
Italianate, the theatre richer, the Rudolfinum more restrained and refined.

For the c20 the names of J. Gočar and
J. Chochol deserve record. In c. 1910–14
they designed in a weird Expressionist or
Cubist way. The Modern Movement, inspired
by Germany, was going strong already
before 1930. The Office of the Administration
of Pensions by Havlíček and Honzik, designed
in 1928, is as good as the best German work.
So is the Electricity Company building of 1926
by A. Beneš and J. Křiž with its large, glazed
inner courtyard. Only a few years later is the
plan for Zlín (now Gottwaldov), the town of
the Bata shoe factory. The style continues without much deviation in recent housing, office
buildings and factories all over the country.

Lit: B. Knox, *The Architecture of Prague and
Bohemia,* London 1965; E. Bachmann in *Gotik
im Böhmen* (ed. K. M. Swoboda), Munich
1968, and in *Barock im Böhmen* (ed. K. M.
Swoboda), Munich 1969.

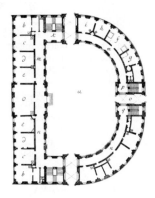

Dado 1. In classical architecture, the portion of a PLINTH or PEDESTAL between the base and CORNICE; also called a *die*. 2. In modern architecture, the finishing of the lower part of an interior wall from floor to waist height.

Dagger A TRACERY motif of the Decorated style: a lancet shape, rounded or pointed at the head, pointed at the foot, and cusped inside. When it takes a curved form it is called a MOUCHETTE.

Dais A raised platform at one end of a medieval hall, where the head of the house dined with his family circle.

Dance, George (1741–1825), son of George Dance senior (d. 1768, architect of the Mansion House, London, 1739–52), went at seventeen to Italy for seven years with his brother Nathaniel, the painter, winning a gold medal at Parma in 1763 with some surprisingly advanced neo-classical designs. His early buildings are equally original and advanced, and might almost suggest an acquaintance with his more *avant-garde* French contemporaries, LEDOUX and BOUL-LÉE, because of his use of the elements of architecture as a means of expression rather than of abstract geometrical design. His first building after his return from Italy was the exquisitely pure and restrained All Hallows, London Wall (1765–7). This was followed by his daring and highly imaginative Newgate Prison, London (1769–78, demolished), the most original and dramatic building of its period in England. His ability appears to have been quickly recognized, despite his unorthodoxy, for he was elected a founder member of the Royal Academy in 1768. His

later buildings show no decline in originality or imagination: indeed, some of them antici-pate SOANE – e.g., the Council Chamber of London Guildhall (1777, destroyed), in which the dome was treated like a parachute with fine lines radiating from the glazed opening in the centre, and the library of Lansdowne House, London (1792, completed by SMIRKE), which was lit by concealed windows in the semi-domed *exedrae* at either end of the long flat-vaulted room. After the turn of the century his style became increasingly austere and at Stratton Park (1803–4) and the College of Surgeons, London (1806–13), he foreshadowed the Greek Revival of SMIRKE and WILKINS. But his principal artistic legatee was his pupil Soane. (His unorthodoxy was exhibited in such works as the neo-Gothic south front of the Guildhall, London (1788–9) and the Tudor Gothic exterior of Ashburnham Place, Sussex (1813–17, refaced 1853).

Lit: D. Stroud, *George Dance, 1741–1825*, London 1971.

Dancing steps Shaped steps on a turn, the tapered end being widened to give a better foothold; also called *Danced stairs* or *Balanced winders*.

Danish architecture, *see* SCANDINAVIAN ARCHITECTURE.

Davis, Alexander Jackson (1803–92), was born in New York, joined Ithiel Town (1784–1844) as a draughtsman and became his partner in 1829. Town had already designed the Connecticut State Capitol with a Greek Doric portico in 1827. The partners now designed more capitols of the same type, but with domes a little incongruously rising over the middle of the longitudinal blocks (Indiana, 1831; North Carolina, 1831; Illinois, 1837; Ohio, 1839). They are among the grandest of the Greek-Revival buildings in America. The United States Custom House, New York (1833–42, now the Federal Hall Memorial Museum) should also be mentioned. But Davis could also do collegiate Gothic (New York University, Washington Square, 1832 etc.) and other versions of Gothic, and was versed in the cottage style too. At the same time he was interested in modern materials – he did an iron shop-front as early as 1835 – and was in fact an exceptionally versatile designer. He was one of the founders of the American Institute of Architects and of the villa estate of Llewellyn Park, New Jersey (1857).

Lit: R. H. Newton, *Town and Davis, Architects*, New York 1942; H.-R. Hitchcock, *Architecture: Nineteenth and Twentieth Centuries*, Pelican History of Art, Harmondsworth 1969, paperback edn 1971.

De Rossi, Giovanni Antonio, see ROSSI, Giovanni Antonio de.

De Sanctis, Francesco (1693–1740), designed the Spanish Steps in Rome (1723–5), the vast and fabulous external Baroque stairway of elegant, curvilinear design, mounting from Piazza di Spagna to S. Trinità dei Monti; a masterpiece of scenic town planning.

Lit: R. Wittkower, *Art and Architecture in Italy, 1600–1750*, Pelican History of Art, 3rd edn, Harmondsworth 1973, paperback edn 1973; W. Lotz, 'Die Spanische Treppe' in *Römisches Jahrbuch für Kunstgeschichte*, 12, 1969.

De Wailly, Charles (1730–98). Notable Louis XVI architect trained under BLONDEL, SERVANDONI and at the French Academy in Rome (1754–6). His talent ranged from interiors of a somewhat theatrical opulence (salon of Palazzo Spinola, Genoa, 1772–3) to the austerity of his most celebrated building, the Odéon in Paris (1779–85), designed in collaboration with Marie-Joseph Peyre (1730–85). It was twice burnt but little altered in rebuilding (1807 and 1818). De Wailly's later work is even more severe: château Montmusard near Dijon, château de Rocquencourt (1781–6) and various private houses in Paris.

Lit: M. Steinhauser and D. Rabreau, 'Le Theatre de l'Odéon de Charles De Wailly et Marie-Joseph Peyre', *Revue de l'Art*, 16, 1973.

Decastyle Of a PORTICO with ten frontal columns.

Decker, Paul (1677–1713), German Baroque architect famous for his book of engraved designs: *Fürstlicher Baumeister, oder: Architectus civilis* (1711, 2nd edition with supplementary plates 1716). He worked under SCHLÜTER in Berlin from 1699, later settled in Nuremberg and finally, in 1712, in Bayreuth. Little is known of his work and he appears to have built nothing of importance. But his magnificent and fantastic designs, illustrating the most extravagant type of Baroque architecture and decoration (the latter derived from Berain through Schlüter), had considerable influence on later German and Austrian architects. e.g., FISCHER VON ERLACH. Decker's posthumous *Architectura Theoretica-Practica* (1720) is a handbook to ornament.

Lit: E. Schneider, *Paul Decker der Ältere (1677–1713), Beiträge zu seinen Werk*, Düren 1937.

Decorated style, see ENGLISH ARCHITECTURE.

Deinocrates, a Hellenistic architect, contemporary with Alexander the Great, appears to have been the architect, with Paeonius, of the temple of Artemis at Ephesus (c. 356 B.C.). He is credited with the town plan of Alexandria and various other important undertakings, some of them rather fanciful, e.g., the project to transform Mount Athos into a colossal statue of the king, holding in one hand a city and in the other a huge cup into which the mountain streams would be gathered and then cascade into the sea.

Lit: R. Martin, *L'urbanisme dans le Grèce antique*, Paris 1956.

Delafosse, Jean Charles (1734–91). French architect known mainly for his ornamental designs in a rather ponderous version of the Louis XVI style, with much use of heavy swags and chunky Greek frets. Two of the houses he built in Paris survive – Hôtel Titon and Hôtel Giox (nos. 58 and 60 rue du Faubourg-Poissonnière) of 1776–80, both discreetly decorated with his favourite type of ornament.

Lit: M. Gallet in *Gazette des Beaux Arts*, LXI, March 1963.

Della Porta, Giacomo, see PORTA, Giacomo della.

Delorme, Philibert (1500/15–1570), who was born in Lyon, the son of a master mason, went to Rome for three years, probably 1533–36, where he moved in high diplomatic-humanist circles but entirely misunderstood the point of Italian architecture. He was nothing if not original and as utterly French as his friend and admirer Rabelais. His buildings are notable for their ingenuity and sometimes outrageous experimentation. Almost everything he built has been destroyed, except for parts of Anet (Diane de Poitiers's house) and the tomb of Francis I in St Denis (begun 1547). The frontispiece of Anet (begun before 1550, now in the École des Beaux Arts, Paris) is a good example of his style, correct in detail and rather more monumental than that of his contemporary LESCOT. The chapel (1549–52) and entrance front (*c.* 1552) are still *in situ*. He had a great influence on the development of French architecture, partly through his books, *Nouvelles Inventions* (1561) and *Architecture* (1567), the most practical architectural treatise of the Renaissance, containing a complete manual on the erection of a house. The decorative part of the screen in St Étienne-du-Mont, Paris, with its pierced balustrades and spiral staircase (*c.* 1545), is probably by Delorme.
    Lit: A. Blunt, *Philibert De L'Orme*, London 1958.

Demi-column (or **half-column**) A column half sunk into a wall; a type of ENGAGED COLUMN, to be distinguished from a PILASTER.

Demilune In military architecture, a detached crescent-shaped or triangular outwork, built in the moat.

Dentil A small square block used in series in Ionic, Corinthian, Composite, and more rarely Doric CORNICES. (For illustrations *see* ENTABLATURE, ORDER.)

Deutscher Werkbund The Deutscher Werkbund sprang up in Munich in 1907 as an association of artists, craftsmen, and industrialists intent on improving the appearance of everyday objects; the founders included H. Muthesius, H. van de VELDE, Th. Fischer, F. Schumacher and R. Riemerschmid; Theodor Heuss was one of its first managers. It was based on the ideas of William MORRIS with aspirations like those of the Arts and Crafts movement in England, and chiefly operated

through exhibitions (Cologne 1914, GROPIUS and TAUT; Stuttgart 1927 – the Weissenhof housing estate), publications, and courses. It served as the model for the Austrian and Swiss Werkbünde, founded in 1912 and 1913 respectively.
    At the 1914 annual meeting a clash arose between van de Velde, advocating craftsmanship and the creative individuality of the artist, and Muthesius, advocating machinery and the role of the designer in the creation of standardized products. The latter prevailed, and the Deutscher Werkbund began collaborating with industry. It was dissolved by the Nazis in 1933. SCHAROUN was elected its first president in Berlin after the war in 1946, and in 1947 it was refounded with its new seat at Düsseldorf.
    Lit: 50 Jahre Deutscher Werkbund, Frankfurt–Berlin, 1958.

Diaconicon In Byzantine architecture, a room attached to or enclosed in a church; in Early Christian times, utilized for the reception of the congregation's offerings and serving as archive, vestry and library; later used only for the latter functions (also, a sacristy).

Diaper work All-over surface decoration composed of a small repeated pattern such as lozenges or squares.

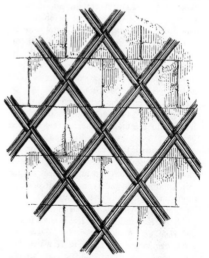

Diaper work in passage to the crypt, Canterbury Cathedral

Diaphragm arch A transverse arch (see VAULT) across the nave of a church, carrying a masonry gable. Diaphragm arches divide wooden roofs into sections and were probably used to prevent fire spreading.

Diastyle With an arrangement of columns three diameters apart. See also ARAEOSTYLE; EUSTYLE; PYCNOSTYLE; SYSTYLE.

Die The part of a PEDESTAL between the plinth and the cornice, also called the dado. (For illustration see PEDESTAL.)

Dientzenhofer, Christian or **Christoph**, see DIENTZENHOFER, Kilian Ignaz.

Dientzenhofer, Georg (d. 1689). The eldest member of an important Bavarian family of Baroque architects. His main works are the Cistercian abbey church at Waldsassen (1685–1704, with A. Leuthner); the nearby pilgrimage church at Kappel (1685–9), built on an unusual trefoil plan with three minaret-like towers to symbolize the Trinity; and the façade of St Martin, Bamberg (1681–91).

Lit: R. Kömstedt, Von Bauten und Baumeistern des fränkischen Barocks, Berlin 1963.

Dientzenhofer, Johann (1663–1726), the son of Georg, studied first in Prague then in Italy (1699–1700). His Italianate cathedral of Fulda (1704–12) reflects BORROMINI's remodelling of S. Giovanni in Laterano. His most impressive church is that of the Benedictine abbey of Banz (1710–18), where his brother Leonhard (d. 1707) had built the conventual buildings; it has a complex ground plan based on a series of ovals and derived perhaps from GUARINI. His masterpiece is Schloss Pommersfelden, one of the largest and finest of German Baroque palaces, built in the remarkably short period of seven years (1711–18), with vastly imposing staircase (for which the patron, Lothar Franz von Schönborn, sought the advice of HILDEBRANDT and also contributed ideas of his own), marble hall, gallery, hall of mirrors, and numerous richly stuccoed apartments. (For illustration see GERMAN ARCHITECTURE.)

Lit: M. H. von Freeden, Kunst und Künstler am Hofe des Kurfürsten Lothar Franz von Schönborn, Würzburg 1949; R. Kömstedt, Von Bauten und Baumeistern des fränkischen Barocks, Berlin 1963; E. Hempel, Baroque Art and Architecture in Central Europe, Pelican History of Art, Harmondsworth, 1965.

Dientzenhofer, Kilian Ignaz (1689–1751), the most distinguished member of the Dientzenhofer family, was the son of **Christian** or **Christoph** (1655–1722), and a nephew of **Johann**. He settled in Prague, where he built several churches, notably St Niklas on the Kleinseite, 1703–11, and St Margeretha, Březnow, 1708–15. Trained first under his father, then under HILDEBRANDT, Kilian Ignaz soon became the leading Baroque architect in Prague. His style is sometimes a little theatrical, and he makes much play with contrasting concave and convex surfaces. His first independent building is the pretty little Villa Amerika, Prague (1720), with an almost Chinese roof in two tiers and very elaborate window surrounds. He also built the Palais Sylva-Tarouca, Prague (1749), on a much larger scale. His originality is best seen in his churches: e.g., St Thomas, Prague (1723), with its intentionally jarring details; St Johann Nepomuk am Felsen, Prague (1730), with diagonally set towers on either side of the façade, a device he used again at St Florian, Kladno (c. 1750). His many other churches are notable for the variety of their Baroque plans – a circle at Nitzau, pure oval at Deutsch-Wernersdorf, an elongated octagon with straight sides at Ruppersdorf, and with convex inner and concave outer sides at Hermsdorf (near Hallstadt) and star shaped for the Chapel of St Mary of the Morning Star above Wockersdorf. He added a bold dome and towers to his father's St Niklas (1737–52). At the abbey church of Unter-Rotschow (1746–7) he showed for the first time a tendency towards classical restraint. (For illustration see CZECHOSLOVAK ARCHITECTURE.)

Lit: G. Frantz, Die Kirchenbauten des Ch. Dientzenhofer, Brno 1942; E. Hempel, Baroque Art and Architecture in Central Europe, Pelican History of Art, Harmondsworth 1965; Christian Norberg-Schultz, Kilian Ignaz Dientzenhofer e il Barocco Boemo, Rome 1968.

Diocletian window, see THERMAL WINDOW.

Dipteral A term applied to a building with a double row of columns on each side.

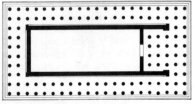

Plan of a dipteral temple

Discharging arch, *see* ARCH.

Distyle in antis In classical architecture, a PORTICO with two columns between pilasters or ANTAE.

Distyle in antis: Athenian Treasury, Delphi, c. 500 B.C.

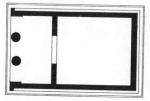

Plan of a temple with a distyle in antis portico

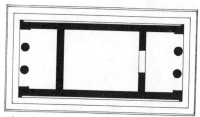

Plan of an amphidistyle temple

Dodecastyle Of a PORTICO with twelve frontal columns.

Dog-leg staircase, *see* STAIR.

Dogtooth Early English ornament consisting of a series of four-cornered stars placed diagonally and raised pyramidally. (Illustrated next column.)

Dome A vault of even curvature erected on a circular base. The section can be segmental, semicircular, pointed, or bulbous.

If a dome is to be erected on a square base, members must be interpolated at the corners to mediate between the square and the circle.

Dogtooth: Detail of a doorway, St Mary, Clymping, Sussex

They can be pendentives or squinches. A *pendentive* is a spherical triangle; its curvature is that of a dome whose diameter is the diagonal of the initial square. The triangle is carried to the height which allows the erection on its top horizontal of the dome proper.

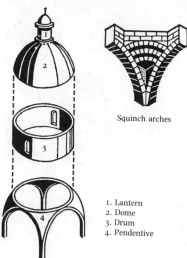

Squinch arches

1. Lantern
2. Dome
3. Drum
4. Pendentive

Sail vault

Domical vault

Umbrella dome

*Pointed dome: Florence Cathedral, 1420–34,
by Brunelleschi*

*Dome on pendentives: Theatinerkirche, Munich,
begun 1663 by Barelli, completed by Zuccalli*

*Dome on squinches:
S. Giovanni degli Eremiti, Palermo, 1132*

*Umbrella dome: Zamora Cathedral,
Spain, 1151–74*

Onion dome: House at Cabo Espichel, Portugal

A *squinch* is either an arch or arches of increasing radius projecting one in front of the other, or horizontal arches projecting in the same manner. If squinches are placed in the corners of the square and enough arches are erected on them they will result in a suitable base-line for the dome. In all these cases the dome will have the diameter of the length of one side of the square. It can be placed direct on the circular base-line, when this is achieved, or a drum, usually with windows, can be interpolated. If the dome has no drum and is segmental, it is called a *saucer* dome.

Another method of developing a dome out of a square is to take the diagonal of the square as the diameter of the dome. In this case the dome starts as if by pendentives, but their curvature is then continued without any break. Such domes are called *sail vaults*, because they resemble a sail with four corners fixed and the wind blowing into it.

A *domical vault* is not a dome proper. If on a square base, four webs (CELLS) rise to a point separated by GROINS (*see* VAULT). The same can be done on a polygonal base.

An *umbrella*, *parachute*, *pumpkin* or *melon dome* is a dome on a circular base, but also divided into individual webs, each of which, however, has a baseline curved segmentally in plan and also curved in elevation.

Domical vault, *see* VAULT.

Domus In Roman architecture, a house for a single well-to-do family, as distinct from the huts or tenements of the poor and the apartment houses (INSULAE) of the middle class.

Donjon, *see* KEEP.

Door, *see* illustration.

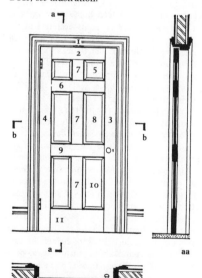

bb

1. Architrave
2. Top rail
3. Shutting stile
4. Hanging stile
5. Top panel
6. Frieze rail
7. Muntin
8. Middle panel
9. Lock rail
10. Bottom panel
11. Bottom rail

Doric Order, *see* ORDER.

Dormer window A window placed vertically in a sloping roof and with a roof of its own. The name derives from the fact that it usually serves sleeping quarters. Also called a LUCARNE.

Dormer windows: Bamberg

Dorter, *see* MONASTERY.

Dosseret The French term for an additional high block or slab set on top of an ABACUS and placed between it and the SPANDREL of

Dosseret: S. Vitale, Ravenna, c6

the arch above; also called a *super-abacus*. Common in Byzantine work, and found in some Romanesque buildings. *See* IMPOST BLOCK.

Dotti, Carlo Francesco (c. 1670–1759). A leading Late Baroque architect in Bologna.

His sanctuary of the Madonna di S. Luca, Bologna (1723–57), is a masterpiece of dramatic grouping, with a domed church built on an elliptical plan and a boldly undulating colonnade sweeping out from the main façade.

Lit: A. M. Matteucci, *F. G. Dotti*, Bologna 1968.

Double-framed roof, *see* ROOF.

Downing, Andrew Jackson (1815–52), the son of a nurseryman and from the beginning an enthusiast for landscape and plants, became America's leading writer on landscape gardening, cottages, and country houses, America's REPTON or LOUDON. His chief writings are *A Treatise on the Theory and Practice of Landscape Gardening,* 1841; *Cottage Residences,* 1842; *Notes about Buildings in the Country,* 1849; and *The Architecture of Country Houses,* 1850. For architectural commissions he was in partnership with Calvert Vaux (1824–95).

Lit: H.-R. Hitchcock, *Architecture: Nineteenth and Twentieth Centuries,* Pelican History of Art, Harmondsworth 1969, paperback edn 1971.

Dragon beam, *see* OVERHANG.

Dravidian architecture, *see* INDIAN ARCHITECTURE.

Dressings Stones worked to a finished face, whether smooth or moulded, and used around an angle, window, or any feature.

Drip A projecting member of a cornice, etc., from which rainwater drips and is thus prevented from running down the face of the wall below.

Drip-joint A joint between two pieces of metal on a roof, acting as a water conductor and preventing water from penetrating between the metal.

Dripstone, *see* HOOD-MOULD.

Drop The lower projecting end of a newel (*see* STAIR).

Drop arch, *see* ARCH.

Drop ornament A carved ornament in the form of a pendant.

Drop tracery A border of pendant tracery on the SOFFIT of a Gothic arch.

Drops English term for GUTTAE.

Drum A vertical wall supporting a DOME or CUPOLA; it may be circular, square, or polygonal in plan. Also the cylindrical blocks of stone that make up a column.

Du Cerceau A family of French architects and decorators. **Jacques Androuet** the elder (c. 1515–c. 1590) was the founder of the dynasty; he is, and always was, more famous for his engravings than for his buildings, none of which survives. The châteaux of Verneuil (1568) and Charleval (1570, abandoned unfinished 1574) were probably best. But he was essentially an inventor of ornament, not an architect, and indulged in the most wanton and grotesque designs, generally in a Late Mannerist style. His first *Livre d'architecture* (Paris, 1559) reveals his personal vein of fantasy and lack of refinement. It had considerable influence, and some of the more practical designs may even have been built. But he was best known for his *Les plus excellents bastiments de France* (1576–9). His son **Jean Baptiste** (c. 1545–c. 1590) succeeded LESCOT as architect at the Louvre in 1578. In 1584 he became *Architecte ordinaire du roi* but had to leave Paris the following year as a Protestant refugee. He provided designs for the Pont Neuf, Paris (1578) and may have designed the Hôtel d'Angoulême, Paris (1584). His younger brother **Jacques II** (1550–1614) was, with Louis MÉTEZEAU, the favourite architect of Henri IV. He became *Architecte du roi* in 1594 and probably designed the pavilions of the Place des Vosges, Paris. Baptiste's son **Jean** (c. 1590–after 1649) became *Architecte ordinaire du roi* in 1617. He built the *escalier en fer de cheval* at Fontainebleau (1634) and designed two of the most typical Louis XIII Parisian hôtels – the Hôtel Sully (1625–9) and the Hôtel de Bretonville (1637–43). They are both remarkable for the richness of their elaborately carved decoration – sculptural friezes, pediments with scrolls and masks, and allegorical figures in niches.

Lit: H. de Geymüller, *Les Du Cerceau, leur vie, leur oeuvre,* Paris 1887; R. Coope, *Saloman de Brosse,* London 1972.

Du Ry, Paul (1640–1714). He came of a family of French architects and was the grandson of Charles (*fl.* 1611–36), the son of Mathurin (*fl.* 1639) and nephew of de BROSSE. A Huguenot, he left France after the revocation of the Edict of Nantes in 1685 and settled in Kassel where he built the Oberneustadt to house other Huguenot refugees. This trim piece of urban lay-out included the simple, centrally-planned Karlskirche (1698–1710, badly damaged but restored). In his post of Oberbaumeister in Kassel he was succeeded by his son, Charles-Louis (1692–1757), who built the Mint and Militarkasino (both destroyed). Simon-Louis (1726–99), the son of Charles-Louis, was an architect of greater importance. He began under his father, then studied under the Swedish court architect Carl Harleman in Stockholm (1746–8) and Jacques-François BLONDEL in Paris before beginning a tour of Italy from which he returned in 1756. His first work was at Schloss Wilhelmstal near Kassel where he was involved in completing the building begun according to designs of CUVILLIÉS and added the two severely simple little lodges (1756–8). In Kassel he was responsible for laying out the spacious rectangular Friedrichsplatz with the austerely Palladian Fredericianum (1768–79) which is important as the first ever museum-library building designed as such. At Wilhelmshöhe, outside Kassel, he built the south and north wings of the vast and imposingly classical Schloss (1786–90), completed later by H. C. JUSSOW, and probably some of the follies in the Park (e.g., Der Mulang, a Chinese village, and the 'Felseneck'). He was also responsible for numerous buildings in Kassel most of which were destroyed in 1945. (For illustration *see* CLASSICISM.)

Dudok, Willem Marinus (1884–1974), was architect to the small town of Hilversum near Amsterdam from 1916. He designed many schools and other public buildings, and his style appears to be complete as early as 1921 (Dr Bavinck School, Public Baths): exposed brick; asymmetrical compositions of rectangular blocks, usually with a tower; long bands of low windows. The style reached its climax with the Hilversum Town Hall of 1928–30, internationally one of the most influential buildings of its date. Of Dudok's later buildings, the Utrecht Theatre (1938–41) and the Royal Dutch Steel Works at Velsen (Ijmuiden, 1948) are the most notable.

Lit: R. M. H. Magnee (ed.), *W. M. Dudok*, Amsterdam 1954.

Durand, Jean-Nicolas-Louis (1760–1834), was probably the most widely influential architectural theorist of the early C19, not only in France but also in Germany. He was trained partly under BOULLÉE and partly under the civil engineer Rodolphe Perronet (1708–94, designer of the Pont de la Concorde, Paris). He built little (Maison La Thuile, Paris, 1788, destroyed in the C19) but was employed on festival decorations during the Revolution and submitted numerous projects for public buildings to the Convention. In 1795 he was appointed professor of architecture at the new École Polytechnique, which replaced and was modelled on the royal school of military engineering, retaining this post until 1830. He published in 1800 *Recueil et parallèle des édifices en tout genre* in which public buildings of various periods and countries (including non-European) were illustrated according to his theory of modular proportions. But his major work is the two-volume *Précis et leçons d'architecture* (1802–9, frequently reprinted and translated into German) in which he stated a rationalist ideal of utilitarian functionalism. 'One should not strive to make a building pleasing, since if one concerns oneself solely with the fulfilment of practical requirements, it is impossible that it should not be pleasing', he wrote. 'Architects should concern themselves with planning and with nothing else.' Yet he abandoned neither the use of historical ornament nor the principle of strictly symmetrical planning.

Lit: L. Hautecoeur, *Histoire de l'architecture classique en France*, V, Paris 1952; E. Kaufmann; *Architecture in the Age of Reason*, Cambridge, Mass., 1955; H.-R. Hitchcock, *Architecture: Nineteenth and Twentieth Centuries*, Pelican History of Art, Harmondsworth 1969, paperback edn 1971.

Dutch architecture The oldest preserved buildings in the Northern Netherlands belong to the CAROLINGIAN fringe. They are the WESTWORK of St Mary at Maastricht and the Valkhof Chapel at Nijmegen which was built in strict imitation of Charlemagne's palace chapel at Aachen. The ROMANESQUE style proper appears first at Deventer, St Peter at Utrecht and the more impressive abbey church of Susteren (*c.* 1060 etc.), the latter clearly dependent on Werden and Essen. A little later is the grand westwork of St Servatius at Maastricht, again German in type. Even more patent is the German origin of the trefoil-

Westwork, St Mary's, Maastricht, CII

shaped early CI2 chancel of Rolduk (cf. Cologne). The mature and late Romanesque of the Rhineland is represented by St Mary at Maastricht and the splendid Roermond Abbey, begun as late as 1219–20. It was Cistercian but shows nothing of the Cistercian architectural customs. Its nearest parallel is at

Crypt of the abbey church at Rolduk, begun 1130

Neuss, and, just as in such churches of the Rhineland, a general Romanesque mood is combined with French Early Gothic motifs.

The GOTHIC style was accepted late. The cathedral of Utrecht was begun in 1254. Its style is derived from that of Soissons via the chancel of Tournai only completed in 1255. The vaulting pattern of ambulatory and radiating chapels shows the dependence. The smaller Buur Church at Utrecht has the French High Gothic type of piers and was started shortly after 1253. Halls were occasionally built on the Westphalian pattern (Zutphen), but the type of the major later medieval churches, the large number and size of which testify to the prosperity of Holland, is basilican and remarkably simple, with an inner elevation of arcade and clerestory divided by no more than a triforium, a blind triforium or a narrow wall passage. To this type belong the major churches of Breda, Delft (New Church), Dordrecht, Haarlem, The Hague (Great Church), Leiden, all begun in the late CI4. The New Church at Amsterdam followed later. All these churches have an ambulatory, but the majority leave out the radiating chapels. Some have very large transepts. The Great Church at The Hague has a specially airy hall nave, which continued to inspire architects into the CI7. The only church of richly decorated interior and exterior is St John at Hertogenbosch, started again in the late CI4. Of other typical features of the Dutch Gothic the widespread use of brick must be remembered, also with patterns in the façade (as in North Germany), and the great prominence of Late Gothic west steeples with pretty and daring open-work details (Utrecht Cathedral CI4; Zierikzee 1453 etc. mostly destroyed; Amersfoort St Mary later CI5; Rhenen 1492 etc.).

Concerning secular architecture the earliest noteworthy structures are the circular castles or enclosures of Leiden, Egmond, Teilingen, etc. They are of the late CI1 and CI2, and some have as their centre a keep. The most spectacular secular building is the Great Hall of the Binnenhof at The Hague, built in the second half of the CI3 and more akin to Westminster Hall than to Continental great halls. For the late Middle Ages the lively façades of some town halls (Middelburg, 1452 etc.) and houses with stepped gables are characteristic.

Holland has some fine Early Renaissance monuments of the 1530s built by Italians, notably the tower of Ijsselstein church (1532–5 by Alessandro Pasqualini of Bologna) and

Houses on the Heerengracht, Amsterdam,
late c16

The Mauritshuis, The Hague,
1633-5

Amsterdam (1624), and in the thirties and
forties plenty more outstanding classical buildings appeared, especially van Campen's
Mauritshuis at The Hague (1633), his magnificent Amsterdam Town Hall, now Royal
Palace (1648 etc.), and his Nieuwe Kerk at

The Knights' Hall, The Hague, c. 1280

the courtyard of Breda castle (1536 etc. by
Tommaso Vincidor also of Bologna). Buildings such as the town halls of Nijmegen (c.
1555) and The Hague (1564-5) show how
the new Renaissance motifs are absorbed
into the native traditions. Soon, however, out
of tradition and the enjoyment of the multi-
fariousness of available Renaissance motifs
and the modifications and distortions they
were capable of, a gay, boisterous national
style with ornate gables and extensive play
with brick and stone mixtures was developed.
It culminates in the work of Lieven de KEY at
Haarlem (Meat Hall 1602-3, tower New
Church 1613) and in Leiden (Town Hall
1594) and the churches by Hendrik de
KEYSER in Amsterdam which are extremely
interesting for their centralizing Protestant
plans. This style, as exemplified by buildings
like the Kloveniersdoelen at Middelburg (of c.
1607-10), had immense influence along the
German seaboard as far as Gdansk (Danzig)
and in Denmark. Architects from the Netherlands are found in most of these places.

At the same time as in England and France
classical restraint replaced these 'Jacobean'
displays. The first signs of a change were
Honselersdijk of 1621-c. 1630 and Rijswijk
of 1630, both inspired from France and both
by unknown architects. But at a time between
these two country houses of the Stadholder
Jacob van CAMPEN began his activity, and his
are the most important classical buildings in
Holland. His earliest is the Coymans House at

Haarlem (1645). Other architects also contributed to this noble and restrained style:
Pieter POST with the Weigh-House at Leiden
(1657) and the Town Hall of Maastricht (1659)
with its splendid entrance hall, Arend van
s-GRAVESANDE with the octagonal Mare

Dutch architecture

Church at Leiden (1638–48), Adriaan Dorts-man with the round Lutheran church at Amsterdam (1668–71) and Justus VING-BOONS with the ambitious Trippenhuis at Amsterdam (1662), built as a private house for two brothers. Altogether no other town in Europe is as rich as Amsterdam in pros-perous private houses. They allow us to see the whole development from the time of de Keyser into the late C18.

With the late C17 French influence be-came paramount not only in painting but also in architecture. The finest examples are William of Orange's Het Loo of c. 1685–7 by J. Roman and the French refugee Daniel MAROT, the beautiful town hall of Enkhuisen of 1686–8 by S. Vennecool, and then such remarkably ambitious private (or formerly private) buildings as the Middelburg Library of 1733 (by J. P. van Baurscheidt Jun. of Antwerp), the Royal Library at The Hague of 1734–6 (by Marot) and Felix Meritis at Amsterdam. The latter, by J. Otten Husly, is of 1778 and hence on the way to neo-clas-sicism. The Pavilion at Haarlem for Henry Hope, the banker, followed in 1785–8. The best early neo-classical church is St Rosalia at Rotterdam of 1777–9 (by Jan Giudici). This is on the pattern of the palace chapel of Versailles, while the ballroom in the Knuiter-dijk Palace at The Hague of the 1820s (by Jan de Greef) is on the pattern of the Vitruvian Egyptian Hall and of its English imitators.

The first third of the C19 was unquestion-ingly classical and more or less Grecian (Scheveningen, Pavilion 1826; Leeuwarden, Law Courts 1846). Then, about 1840, neo-Gothic made a late start (Catholic Church Harmelen 1838, Gothic Hall behind the Knuiterdijk Palace The Hague 1840, Riding School The Hague 1845, former station Rotterdam 1847). Concurrently neo-Roman-esque appears, though more rarely (Cool-singel Hospital Rotterdam 1842 etc.). As in other countries the Gothic soon turns from the romantic to the archaeologically accurate, and the best examples of this serious-minded Gothicism are the churches by CUYPERS. But Cuypers's fame is his large neo-1600 buildings, clearly disposed and resourcefully detailed (Rijksmuseum and Station Amsterdam, 1877 etc. and 1881 etc.).

From there a way into the C20 was found by the brilliant and typically Dutch BERLAGE. His Exchange at Amsterdam of 1897 etc. is in style transitional between historicism and the C20. From Berlage, whose detail tends to be arty-crafty and often very curious, one line went to J. M. van der Mey's crazy Shipping Palace at Amsterdam (of 1912–16) and then to the Expressionism of Piet Kramer and Michael de Klerk; another line went into the rationalism of the International Modern (OUD). Cubistic but fantastic is Gerrit RIET-VELD's Schroeder house at Utrecht of 1924, cubic and rational and extremely well grouped

Town Hall, Leeuwarden, C18

Schroeder House at Utrecht, 1924, by Rietveld

the buildings of DUDOK. Oud's work during and after the Second World War represents a turn away from rationalism which took place in other countries as well. The most noteworthy Dutch achievement after the Second World War is the rebuilding of the centre of Rotterdam.

*Eigen Haard Housing Estate, Amsterdam, 1921,
by M. de Klerk*

*Van Nelle Tobacco Factory, Rotterdam, 1929,
by Brinckmann and van der Vlugt*

Lit: Andreae Fockema, R. C. Hekker & E. H.
ter Kuile, *Duizend Jaar Bouwen in Nederland*,
Amsterdam 1957–8; E. H. ter Kuile in *Dutch
Art and Architecture, 1600 to 1800*, Pelican
History of Art, Harmondsworth 1966, paper-

back edn 1972; G. Fanelli, *Architettura
moderna in Olanda*, Florence 1968.

Dwarf gallery A wall-passage with small
arcading on the outside of a building; usual
in Romanesque architecture, especially in
Italy and Germany.

Dwarf gallery: Speyer Cathedral, c. 1100

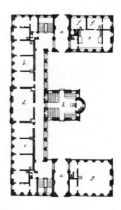

Eames, Charles (b. 1907). A universal artist. He designed furniture (the famous Eames Chair of 1940–41, developed in collaboration with Eero SAARINEN), he made films (Black Top, 1950), he made toys, organized exhibitions and built his own house at Santa Monica in California (1949). The house had a great success among architects. Windows and doors were prefabricated standard items, ordered from a manufacturer's catalogue. Yet with these standard elements Eames succeeded in achieving a light, grid-like effect of Japanese finesse. The metal frames are filled in with transparent and translucent glass and stucco.

Early Christian architecture A specifically Christian type and form of places of worship, and hence of Christian architecture, arose relatively slowly after the spread of Christianity. For a long time spacious private houses sufficed for the needs of worship (preaching and the Lord's Supper), as related in the Acts of the Apostles (Ch. xxviii, vs. 30–31): 'And Paul dwelt two whole years in his own hired house, and received all that came unto him. Preaching the kingdom of God, and teaching those things which concern the Lord Jesus Christ, with all confidence, no man forbidding him.' Domestic churches of this type continued in use far into the c3 and c4. The excavations at Dura Europos have brought to light such a church from before 256. The most important rooms were a small assembly room (with a DAIS for the bishop) for sermons and Eucharist, and a smaller room (with a tub at one end surmounted by a canopy) for Baptism. There were subsidiary rooms for charitable purposes, a

vestry, and for housing priests and church officials.

Even the hall-like churches found in Aquileia and Trier are ultimately based on the simple meeting-house, save that here their size (c. 120 × 57 ft at Aquileia) compelled the introduction of supports for the roof. Smaller but, barring the roof, virtually intact, is a hall-like church without interior supports that belonged to an early c4 villa in Kirk Bize (North Syria). This too was a

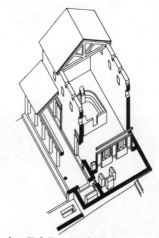

Church at Kirk Bize, North Syria, c4

simple rectangular hall with a gabled timber roof and a dais, but otherwise indistinguishable from the nearby villa. Thereafter parts were added on over the years, up to the c6, so as to keep the originally domestic church up to date (a triumphal arch at the front of the dais, formation of a second step, separation by screens and curtains, display of relics in shrines, tripartite 'choir', separate martyrs' chapel).

When Christianity became publicly avowable under Constantine the Great (306–37, sole ruler after 324) and was clearly favoured by him, it felt the need of more formal places of worship. For this the Roman market BASILICA was taken and adapted to local and liturgical needs. COLONNADES added to the long NAVE, lit by windows high up in the wall, created AISLES on either side of it. The nave was covered with a gabled timber roof, and the aisles with lean-to roofs against the wall above the columns of the nave. The west end was preceded by an ATRIUM. An APSE terminated the east end, producing a clear longitudinal emphasis in contrast to the transverse orientation of the classical basilica. Constantinian buildings mainly adhered to this basic basilical schema, e.g. old St Peter's and S. Giovanni in Laterano, Rome (*see* ITALIAN ARCHITECTURE). In large basilicas the aisles could be doubled; there was some-

times a TRANSEPT before the apse, connected with the nave by a triumphal arch (St Peter's). In place of the apse occasionally a centrally-planned termination was built (the octagon in the Constantinian Church of the Nativity, Bethlehem, and the supposed rotunda in the Holy Sepulchre).

Already in the Constantinian era centrally-planned structures – otherwise reserved for tombs, martyria and baptisteries – were employed for churches as well as the basilica; one instance was the 'Golden Octagon' (so-called on account of its gilded roof) at Antioch, which can only be reconstructed on the evidence of somewhat ambiguous literary sources. Generally, centralized plans con-

S. Lorenzo, Milan, c. 370

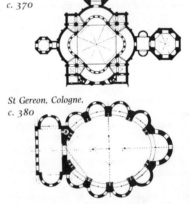

St Gereon, Cologne, c. 380

Old St Peter's, Rome, c. 400

S. Giovanni in Laterano, Rome, c4
(from a fresco in S. Martino ai Monti, Rome)

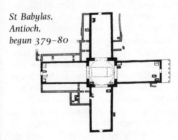

tinued to be restricted to martyrs' memorial churches (S. Lorenzo, Milan, c. 370; St Gereon, Cologne, c. 380). Cruciform structures, as a rule also martyria, likewise appeared towards the end of the c4 (S. Babylas,

St Babylas, Antioch, begun 379–80

Antioch, begun 379/80; Church of the Apostles, Milan, begun 382). Whereas in the Constantinian era building activity was largely limited to the great centres, the situation was transformed under Theodosius I (379–95) and his c5 successors. With the banning of all heathen cults in 391 Christianity became the sole official religion of the Roman Empire. Temples were closed, or even made into churches (the Parthenon, Erechtheion, and Hephaisteion in Athens; Temple of Augustus in Ankara). The completion and extension of Constantinian projects in the metropolis were paralleled by intense building activity throughout the provinces, each building imparting something distinctive to its adoption and the development of the basilica.

In Constantinople, the leading artistic centre of the Empire, the main church of Hagia Sophia, which had been damaged in the disturbances under the Patriarch John Chrysostom in 404, was renovated and given a magnificent porch resembling a classical PROPYLAEUM (consecrated 415). Smaller buildings tended, whilst adhering to the basilical schema (Chalkoprateia, basilica of the Studios monastery; galleried like the Constantinian church on Golgotha before it), to abbreviate it so as to achieve a more even relationship between length and breadth in the nave.

Roman architecture was more conservative and faithful to Constantianian models. S. Paolo fuori le mura (385–c. 400) was intended to be a copy of St Peter's. But with S. Maria Maggiore (begun under Sixtus III,

432–40) the tendency toward greater breadth and spaciousness in the nave asserted itself more strongly.

In Salonika, then the most important city in Greece, a double-aisled basilica with a notably broad galleried nave arose over the tomb of St Demetrios in the last quarter of the c5. The alternating supports (even if going back only to the first half of the c7 rebuilding) were a novelty for a basilica, whilst the transept seems to recall Rome (Salonika was then subordinate to Rome ecclesiastically). The Acheiropoietos basilica (c. 470, aisled, galleried, broad and relatively short nave) is more typical of the kind of basilica found around the Aegean, of which there are numerous examples in Greece (Epidauros, c. 400, still double-aisled; etc.). In every respect singular is the basilica of St Leonidas in

St Leonidas, Corinth,
450–60
or 518–27

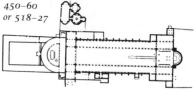

Lechaion, the dock area of Corinth. With a length of 610 ft (including atrium) it attained the dimensions of the largest Early Christian

S. Paolo fuori le mura, Rome,
begun 385 (after Piranesi)

building, the Constantinian basilica of St Peter at Rome. It is true that the nave is here broader than both aisles put together, but its elongation is still remarkable. The transept recalls Hagios Demetrios in Salonika, but the central square section is already organized as a regular crossing (as with the Ilissos basilica in Athens), and may have had some form of centralized roofing (dating not entirely certain – either 450–60, or 518–27 re-using earlier elements).

The architecture of Asia Minor was as diverse as its regions. That of the coastal areas was clearly differentiated from that of the interior, where no early churches survive anyway. The cities of the west coast produced relatively classic basilicas like St Mary's, Ephesus (pre-431), though with galleries and side-chambers right and left of the main apse. The martyrium of St John at Ephesus was exceptional, with its cruciform arrangement of four basilical arms about the central crossing over the tomb of the Apostle (cf. also a building in Salona and the Church of the Prophets and the Apostles in Jerash, Jordan, 464–5). Nor were transepts unknown along the coast (basilicas in Perge on the south coast; unexcavated basilica in Laodicaea on Lykos). As early as under the Emperor Zeno (474–91) the till then unchallenged dominance of the basilical schema seems to have been broken, with the insertion of a dome at Meryamlik (nr. Seleukeia on the south coast).

Syria's wealth of ancient monuments provides a superb picture of the development of Early Christian architecture up to the c7. Public buildings (halls with DIAPHRAGM ARCHES – supported when the span was too great by intermediate pillars creating a pseudo-aisled effect – and a stone slab ceiling, like the so-called Kaysariye and 'basilica' in Chaqqa) served as the model for domestic churches not only in North Syria (Kirk Bize), but also in South Syria (the Julianos church in Umm-idj-Djemal, with ancillary rooms off the south court, 344). Basilical features like the apse were then added. A form of basilica occurred in North Syria as early as the c4, possibly under the influence of Antioch, in carefully dressed ASHLAR, aisled, and with columnar arcades and a nearly always tripartite east end (an apse with two adjoining chambers, the southern one mostly identifiable as a martyrium with reliquaries; probably derived from Romano-Syrian temples such as Qanawat or Es Sanamein). The first to be datable is the basilica of Fafertin of 372. The group also includes the basilicas of Kharab Shems and Ruwêha. Without departing from the basic schema, these North Syrian basilicas underwent a change of character in the c5: their INTERCOLUMNIATION increased, the nave increased in breadth in relation to the aisles – the urge was thus toward greater, if still subdivided, spaces – and ornament became more pronounced. This process can be seen at work in the churches of the builder Markianos Kyris and his shop: Babiska, 390–407; Ksedjbeh, 414; St Paul and Moses, Dar Qita, 418; and Kasr-el-Benat, c. 420. These tendencies towards spaciousness and the mutual interpenetration of nave and aisles continued in the c5 and c6. Colonnades gave way to widely-spaced pillared arcades (Kalb Lauze, c. 500). On exteriors there is a noticeable enrichment of the façade (continuous string-courses carried on round windows and corners), and a deliberate counterpoint between the bare body of a basilica and the *mouvementé* roof-line produced by the eruption of distinct parts like the east end, the west and south porches and in particular the east and west towers (Kalb Lauze; Ruwêha, early c6; El Hosn near El Bara, c. 400; etc.). The martyrium of Qalat Siman (betw. 475 and

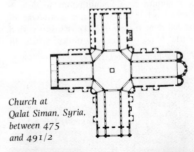

Church at Qalat Siman, Syria, between 475 and 491/2

491/2; four basilical cross-arms meeting in a timber-domed octagon over the column of St Simeon Stylites) was again *sui generis*; here

indigenous Syrian tendencies fused with
Antiochene, and to some degree Con-
stantinopolitan, elements to produce probably the most remarkable building of the c5.
Octagonal and cruciform buildings in the
Haûran (South Syria) were subsequently given
mortarwork domes (Hagios Sergios and Bakchos cathedral in Bosra, 512/13; Ezra, St
Georges, 515/16 and St Elias, 542). The
vaulting technique – using a particularly light
mortar incorporating pumice-stone – is traceable to native Roman precursors like the
Philippeion (family temple of Philip the Arab,
244–9) in Shehba.

In Palestine progress towards spaciousness
in basilicas kept pace with that of other imperial provinces. The increase in breadth of the
nave at the expense of the aisles and the enlargement of the intercolumniation is clearly
observable in the buildings of Jerash (cathedral, third quarter of the c4; St Theodore,
494–6). Influences from Constantinople are
occasionally visible (polygonally faced apses
at Emmaus, prob. c5, certainly not c4). The
Church of the Nativity in Bethlehem was rebuilt toward the end of the c5 (there is no
foundation for a Justinianic dating), and the
east end enlarged through a TRICONCH ending.

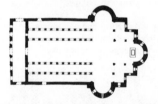

Church of the Nativity, Bethlehem, late c5

Major buildings were also built in Egypt in
the c5 to similar designs, through imperial sub-
vention and incorporating imported details,
e.g., the Menas basilica south-east of Alexandria – rebuilt with a transept not, as maintained by the sources, under Zeno (474–91),
but under Anastasios I (491–518) or after, as
revealed by a find of coins; or the basilica in
Hermopolis – with a triconch east end like
Bethlehem (COPTIC ARCHITECTURE).

In North Africa the basilica underwent
singular mutations: the aisles were often
separated from the nave by doubled columns,
the east apse was frequently balanced by
another to the west (a martyr's or bishop's
tomb), and the number of aisles might be
considerably multiplied (no less than eight in

*Mensa Cypriani (burial church
of Bishop Cyprianus, d. 258), near Carthage*

the Damous-el-Karita at Carthage). The
earliest dated building is the basilica of
Orléansville of 324 (the second apse added in
the c5). The layout of Tebessa also goes back
to the c4 (side-chambers right and left of the

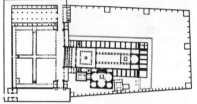

*Church and monastery at Tebessa,
North Africa, c5*

apse as in Syria). A wave of building followed
the reconquest of the province of Africa from
the Vandals by Justinian's general Belisarius
(rectangular forts with towers). Churches
were refurbished or rebuilt, thus introducing
Justinianic features (centralization of the
basilica with the aid of a domed or timber-
roofed crossing) from the capital (the Basilica
maiorum and Damous-el-Karita in Carthage;
Ss. Sylvanus and Fortunatus, Sbeitla; the Justinianic basilica No. 2 at Sabratha; basilica B
at Yunka). With such endeavours to create
unified and centralized spatial entities throughout the Roman Empire, Early Christian
architecture laid the basis of BYZANTINE
ARCHITECTURE.   [MR]

Lit: R. Krautheimer, *Early Christian and
Byzantine Architecture*, Pelican History of Art,
Harmondsworth 1965, paperback edn 1975.

Early English, *see* ENGLISH ARCHITECTURE.

Easter sepulchre A recess with TOMB-CHEST,
usually in the north wall of a CHANCEL; the
tomb-chest was designed to receive an effigy
of Christ for Easter celebrations.

Eaves The underpart of a sloping roof overhanging a wall.

Echal In a synagogue, the fitting enclosing the Ark or cupboard in which are kept the rolls of the Law; often of wood. An ornate example of the C18 exists in London at Bevis Marks, in the form of a large tripartite REREDOS.

Echinus An OVOLO MOULDING below the ABACUS of a Doric CAPITAL. Also the mould-

*Echinus: a Doric capital
from the Hephaisteion, Athens, 450–440 B.C.*

ing, covered with egg and dart, under the cushion of an IONIC capital. (For additional illustration *see* ORDER.)

Edge roll moulding, *see* BOWTELL.

Effner, Joseph (1687–1745), born in Munich, was the son of the chief gardener to Max Emanuel, Elector of Bavaria, who sent him to be trained as an architect in Paris under BOFFRAND (1706–15). In 1715 he was appointed Court Architect. He was in Italy in 1718. Between 1719 and 1725 he completed ZUCCALLI's Schloss Schleissheim and designed the magnificent monumental staircase. He also completed Agostino BARELLI's Schloss Nymphenburg outside Munich (1717–23), converting Barelli's Italianate villa into a German Baroque palace, and adding several exquisite little pavilions in the park; the Pagodenburg (1716, classical exterior with chinoiserie interior), the Roman Badenburg (1718), and the precociously picturesque Magdalenklause (c. 1726). At the Munich Residenz he was in charge of the new Grottenhof from 1715 onwards where the sparkling Ahnengalerie or Gallery of Ancestors (1726–31) was presumably designed by him. On Max Emanuel's death in 1726 he was succeeded as court architect by CUVILLIÉS and his only later building of note is the Preysing Palace in the Residenzstrasse in Munich (1727–34).

Lit: E. Hempel, *Baroque Art and Architecture in Central Europe*, Pelican History of Art, Harmondsworth 1965; F. Wolf, *Der Künstlerkreis um J. Effner*, Munich 1963.

Egas, Enrique de (d. probably 1534), was the son either of **Hanequin** of Brussels, who built the upper parts of the towers of Toledo Cathedral and the Portal of the Lions (1452), or of **Egas Cueman**, Hanequin's brother, who was a sculptor and died in 1495. In 1497 Enrique became master mason of Plasencia Cathedral – where work, however, soon stopped and was later continued by JUAN DE ÁLAVA and FRANCISCO DE COLONIA – and in 1498 of Toledo Cathedral. Enrique's masterpieces are the hospitals of Santiago (1501–11), Toledo (1504–15), and Granada (begun 1504 and soon abandoned), where the North Italian Early Renaissance appears early and at its most delightful. He was consulted at the Seo of Saragossa in 1500, and at Seville Cathedral in 1512, 1523, 1529, and 1534. He was also connected with the designs for the Royal Chapel at Granada (begun c. 1504), and was the designer of Granada Cathedral (begun 1523, but soon turned Renaissance from Enrique's Gothic by Diego de SILOE).

Lit: F. Chueca Goitia, *Arquitectura del siglo XVI (Ars Hispaniae*, vol. XI), Madrid 1953; G. Kubler & M. Soria, *Art and Architecture in Spain and Portugal and their American Dominions, 1500–1800*, Pelican History of Art, Harmondsworth 1959.

Egg and dart (or **egg and tongue**). An OVOLO MOULDING decorated with a pattern based on alternate eggs and arrow-heads.

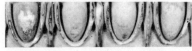

Egg and dart

Egyptian architecture Practical considerations determined the appearance of Ancient Egypt's secular architecture, as supernatural requirements did, down to the last detail, that of its funerary and religious monuments. The chief building materials were, at first, reeds, wattles (rarely timber) and unfired bricks of mud from the Nile; stone was occasionally used from 3000 B.C. onwards, and was usual in religious and funerary monuments from the time of King Zoser (c. 2600 B.C.). Limestone, granite, and a wealth of other stones were at first worked with stone and copper tools; iron and bronze came only belatedly into use. Sophisticated mathematics and astronomy lay behind the proportions and orientation of the buildings; ramps, sleds and rollers played an important role in construction, and special crafts were evolved to take heavy loads by the Nile and canals. But the key factors were an almost unlimited workforce and ample time.

The earliest architectural forms correspond to the limitations of the materials available (organic materials and sun-dried brick), and were imitated by the first buildings in stone (the stepped PYRAMID of Saqqara, c. 2600 B.C.), which then rapidly adopted abstract geometrical shapes (the pyramids of Dahshur and Giza, c. 2500 B.C.). The organic element survived as the inspiration behind such architectural details as columns (imitating papyrus sheaves, lotus-stems, and palm-trunks, or composite in form), CAVETTO and TORUS mouldings. Dried brick construction was carried over into stone, e.g. in BATTERED walls (PYLONS) and their unusual thickness.

Because of their insubstantial construction and perishable materials Ancient Egyptian secular buildings have seldom survived. Nonetheless, we have not only prehistoric round huts, and the villas of the New Kingdom

Reconstruction of pyramids at Giza c. 2500 B.C.

Deir-el-Medineh, c. 1300 B.C.

Temple façade, Saqqara, 2600 B.C.

(1600 B.C. onwards) with their portico, garden and pool, but palaces (Malkata, Medinet Habu, Bubastis) and extensive grid-like urban settlements (Illahun, Amarna, Deir-el-Medineh), whilst we know of the existence of multi-storeyed apartments.

The earliest fortifications were circular or rectangular town walls articulated by niches. Built of brick, they were superseded in the Middle Kingdom by forts with undulating walls, concentrated on the defence of Egypt's southern border, and containing townships complete with palace and temple.

Tombs were both houses for the dead and depictions of the hereafter, where the departed was to feel at home. Physically, they comprise the house of the dead man, the actual grave, and the appurtenances to supply the needs of the dead. As the permanent equivalent of the everyday, they were built of stone.

The royal tombs of the Old and Middle Kingdoms (2600–1700 B.C.) were pyramids – with a valley temple, ascent (processional way) and mortuary temple. They were a synthesis of funerary mounds and tomb-chambers (especially apparent with the early step-pyramids of e.g. Saqqara, and the hybrid blunted pyramid of Dahshur) and were both the dwelling of the dead king and the symbol of his immortality, equated with the course of the sun (OBELISKS were monuments to the sun). The chambers were hollowed out of the massive body of the pyramid, or hewn out of the bedrock beneath. With the New Kingdom this kind of tomb was superseded by the rock-cut tomb, whose often innumerable rooms penetrate several hundred yards into the cliffs, incarnating both a palace and the hereafter. They lie apart from the shrines (mortuary temples) in lonely desert valleys (Valley of the Kings at Thebes), and very occasionally inside temple precincts (Tanis). The mortuary temples emulate those of the gods or modify the type of earlier royal temples (Deir-el-Bahari).

The simplest kind of private grave was a pit in which the deceased was laid wrapped in matting. A wealthy individual in the Old Kingdom (2600–2200 B.C.) would be buried in one of the well-planned graveyards in a so-called MASTABA – a massive quadrangular stone superstructure with sloping walls containing a niched shrine with a false door and offering table, and the later ones courts and rooms decorated in relief; from this a vertical shaft led to the burial chamber deep under the surface. With the Middle Kingdom (c. 2000 B.C.) the rock tomb came to predominate. Shrine and burial chamber were hewn out of

Temple of Queen Hatshepsut, Thebes (Deir-el-Bahari), 1511–1480 B.C.

Tomb of Rameses, Valley of the Kings, Thebes (Deir-el-Bahari), c. 1130 B.C.

the rock, the façade was embellished with pillared porticoes, and a wide walled court formed the often steep forecourt (Thebes, Aswan, Middle Egypt). In the New Kingdom a small pointed pyramid rose over rock-cut tombs (Deir-el-Medineh); a pylon might emphasize the entry to tombs of the late period (Montemhet, Thebes).

Religious architecture fixed the image of the Cosmos (Underworld, Earth and Heaven) as the dwelling of the gods. The process led from the mat- and hide-hung chapels to the animal deities of the Pre- and Proto-historic period (till 2700 B.C.), via the sun shrines of the Old Kingdom (c. 2500 B.C. – the obelisk as

monument to the Sun God), to the house-like temples of the Middle and New Kingdoms. The cosmic imagery of the temple – its floor as the Earth, its star-studded ceiling as Heaven, with its columns as supports – was in keeping with its sacral function as the point of contact between the divine and earthly spheres. The floor rose gradually towards the sanctuary, whilst the ceilings of the rooms became progressively lower, so that Earth and Heaven met at the site of the divine image. The extensive courts and columned chambers (HYPOSTYLES) of temples like Karnak and Luxor were not places of prayer, but areas for processions set rigorously apart from the outer

Temple of Amon, Luxor

Small Temple, Abu Simbel, c. 1250 B.C.

I   2   3   4   5

Types of Egyptian column:

1. Saqqara, *c.* 2675 B.C.
2. 'Papyrus' type, Saqqara, *c.* 2675 B.C.

3. Temple of Queen Hatshepsut,
   Thebes (Deir-el-Bahari) *c.* 1500 B.C.
4. Temple of Amon, Karnak, *c.* 1500 B.C.
5. Temple of Hathor, Dendera, *c.* 100 B.C.

I   2   3   4

Types of Egyptian Capital:

1. Palm capital, Sahure, 2500–2350 B.C.
2. Open Papyrus capital, Luxor, *c.* 1450 B.C.
3. Composite capital, Edfu
4. Basket capital, Edfu

world. But alongside the purely religious function of the temples to the gods, chiefly expressed in the austere cycles of reliefs upon the internal walls, was their propagandist intent, as manifestations of royal power, expressed in depictions of battles on the outer walls and pylons and in the colossal statues at the temple entrances.

The basic type of the New Kingdom temples to the gods is exemplified by the temple of Amon at Karnak – a twin-towered pylon as the entrance, a colonnaded court, a columned hall like an aisled basilica in plan, anterooms, and sanctuary. The Nubian rock-temples (Abu Simbel, Bet el-Wâli) adopt this schema, only transferring it into the solid cliffs. The extent of a temple was increased by the customary provision for a holy lake, a landing-stage on the Nile or on a tributary canal, and an avenue of sphinxes linking this quay to the entrance pylon.

The best impression of what the religious architecture of Ancient Egypt was like is supplied today by the Ptolemaic temples of Dendera, Edfu and Philae (300 B.C. to A.D. 100) which adhere to the schema of the temples to the gods of the New Kingdom, perpetuating their original spatial effect, and the balanced conjunction of monumentality and graceful delicacy both overall and in detail. Whilst employing the earliest forms of building, Ptolemaic architecture created new features like composite and basket capitals that persisted in COPTIC ARCHITECTURE. *See also* ISLAMIC ARCHITECTURE.   [DW]

Lit: A. Badawy, *A History of Egyptian Architecture*, vol. I, *Ancient Egypt*, Giza 1954, vol. 2, *First Intermediate Period, The Middle Kingdom, and The Second Intermediate Period*, Berkeley and Los Angeles 1966; Stevenson Smith, *Art and Architecture of Ancient Egypt*, Pelican History of Art, Harmondsworth 1965.

Egyptian hall A hall with an internal PERISTYLE as derived by PALLADIO from VITRUVIUS. It was especially popular with Neo-Palladian architects, e.g., Lord BURLINGTON'S Assembly Rooms in York. It has no direct connection with Egyptian architecture. The 'Egyptian Hall' by P. F. Robinson in Piccadilly, London (1811-12, demolished 1904), was neo-Egyptian, i.e. not a Vitruvian Egyptian Hall.

Eiermann, Egon (1909-70), was a pupil of POELZIG. By concentrating on industrial buildings, Eiermann managed to carry the INTERNATIONAL MODERN of the thirties through the Nazi years in Germany. Of his many post-war factories one of the finest is at Blumberg (1951). His international fame was established by the German Pavilion at the Brussels Exhibition of 1958, a perfect blend of crisp, clear, cubic, transparent blocks and their grouping in a landscape setting. The solution to the problem of grouping the new Kaiser-Wilhelm Gedächtniskirche at Berlin (1959-62) with the dramatic neo-Romanesque ruin of the old is more questionable. Other recent buildings of special importance are the offices of the Essener Steinkohlen-Bergwerke, Essen (1958-60); the wholesale warehouses, etc., for Messrs Neckermann at Frankfurt (1958-61); and the German Embassy in Washington (1961-3). In 1967 he was elected chairman of the jury judging building designs submitted for the Munich Olympics. In 1968 he designed an office-block for an Italian firm in Frankfurt with towers like upright and inverted chalices.

Lit: G. K. Koenig, *Architettura tedesca del secondo dopoguerra*, Bologna 1965.

Eiffel, Gustave (1832-1923), the French engineer, is famous chiefly for the Eiffel Tower built for the Paris Exhibition of 1889. At 985 ft, the Tower was the highest building in the world until the Chrysler and then the Empire State Buildings were erected in New York. The Eiffel Tower in its immensely prominent position in the centre of Paris marks the final acceptance of metal, in this case iron, as an architectural medium. Eiffel's iron bridges are technically and visually as important as the Eiffel Tower (Douro, 1876-7; Garabit Viaduct, 1880-4). He was also engineer to the Bon Marché store in Paris (1876), and to the Statue of Liberty in New York, both of which have remarkable iron interiors. (For illustration *see* BRIDGE.)

Lit: J. Prevost, *Eiffel*, Paris 1925; Y. Igot, *Gustave Eiffel*, Paris 1961; H. Besset, *Gustave Eiffel, 1832-1923*, Paris 1957.

Eigtved, Nils (1701-54). Danish Rococo architect famous for the Amalienborg in Copenhagen, the finest C18 urban group outside France. Trained in Dresden and Warsaw under Karl Friedrich PÖPPELMANN (1725-33), he also visited Paris and Rome before settling in Copenhagen in 1735. As court architect he laid out an entire new section of the city with the octagonal Amalienborg (1750-54) and its four palaces set diagonally as its centre. He designed the Frederiks church on axis with it but his designs were greatly altered in execution. His Rococo interiors (1734 onwards) in the royal palace of Christiansborg were destroyed in 1794.

Lit: K. Voss, *Arkitekten Nicolai Eigtved (1701-54)*, Copenhagen 1971.

Elevation An external face of a building; also a drawing made in projection on a vertical plane to show any one face (or elevation) of a building.

Elias of Dereham or **Durham** (d. 1245) was Canon of Salisbury and Wells and a confidant of Archbishops Hubert Walter and Stephen Langton, Bishop Jocelyn of Wells, Bishop Hugh of Lincoln, Bishop Poore of Salisbury, and Bishop des Roches of Winchester. He was present at the sealing of Magna Carta and at the translation of the relics of Thomas à Becket in 1220. He was, in addition, in charge of the King's Works at Winchester Castle and Clarendon Palace, and '*a prima fundatione rector*' of Salisbury Cathedral. *Rector* sounds like administrator rather than designer, but he was also paid for making a vessel for Salisbury Cathedral and is called *artifex* in connection with the new shrine of Thomas à Becket; so he was certainly something of an artist, and it is likely that he was, like ALAN OF WALSINGHAM a hundred years later, a man capable also of designing buildings and of discussing details constructively with the master masons.

Lit: J. Harvey, *English Medieval Architects,* London 1954.

Elizabethan and Jacobean architecture, *see* ENGLISH ARCHITECTURE.

Ell In the U.S.A. a single-storey lean-to wing containing a kitchen. Ells were added in the C17 to WEATHER-BOARDED, timber-framed buildings in New England.

Elliptical arch, *see* ARCH.

Ellis, Peter (1804–84). A Liverpool architect now famous as a pioneer of the modern office building. His Oriel Chambers in Water Street, Liverpool, of 1864, with its façade glazed throughout in the form of angular oriels separated by very slender mullions, fore-shadows the Chicago skyscraper of twenty years later. The back is almost entirely of glass, cantilevered out in front of the frame, itself of cast iron with brick arches. The back of his office block, No. 16 Cook Street, Liverpool (1866), is even more advanced, consisting of a wall and spiral staircase entirely of glass except for the thinnest of iron mullions.

Elmes, Harvey Lonsdale (1813–47). The son of James Elmes (1782–1862), architect and writer, a champion of the Elgin Marbles, of Keats, and of Wordsworth. James wrote on prison reform, and in 1823 edited the life and works of Wren. Harvey was a pupil of his father, and in 1836 won the competition for St George's Hall, Liverpool. Even though, in its grouping and its massing of columns, it is no longer of Grecian purity, the building is convincedly classical. It was completed brilliantly by C. R. COCKERELL after Elmes's death from consumption.

Lit: H. M. Colvin, *Biographical Dictionary of English Architects, 1660-1840,* London 1954.

Ely, *see* REGINALD OF ELY.

Embrasure A small opening in the wall or PARAPET of a fortified building, usually splayed on the inside.

Encaustic tiles Earthenware tiles glazed and decorated, much used in the Middle Ages and in Victorian churches for flooring.

Enceinte In military architecture, the main enclosure of a fortress, surrounded by the wall or ditch.

Enfilade The French system of aligning internal doors in a sequence so that a vista is obtained through a series of rooms when all the doors are open. They are usually placed close to the windows. The arrangement was introduced *c.* 1650 and became a feature of Baroque palace planning.

Engaged column A column attached to, or partly sunk into, a wall or PIER; also called an *applied column* or *attached column. See also* DEMI-COLUMN.

Engel, Carl Ludwig (1778–1840). German but active from 1815 in Finland. He knew SCHINKEL'S work and had lived several years in St Petersburg. These are the two sources of his neo-classical style. His main buildings are the Senate (1818–22), the Old Church (1826), the University (1818–32), the Cathedral (1830–40) and the University Library (1836–44) all at Helsinki. The cathedral is strictly centrally planned, a Greek cross with four porticos outside, a quatrefoil inside. Above the centre is a tall dome. The university library has two splendid oblong reading-rooms with detached giant columns all round. (For illustration *see* FINNISH ARCHITECTURE.)

Lit: J. M. Richards, *A Guide to Finnish Architecture,* London 1966; N. E. Wickberg, Exh. Cat. *Engel,* Berlin 1970.

English architecture The Romans left England in 410. No datable document of English architecture exists of before the C7, but excavations have proved in places as distant from one another as Tintagel, Cornwall, Llantwit Major, Wales, and Whitby, Yorkshire, that early monastic establishments were of the Egyptian coenobitic type with separate detached huts clustered round a centre with the church and probably a refectory. At Abingdon it must have been the same, and Nendrum is an Irish example. The type reached England via Ireland. Of the same C7 are also the earliest surviving churches. They fall into two groups, one in the South-east, characterized by apses and a triple arcade dividing the choir from the nave, the other in the North, with long, tall, narrow nave and straight-ended chancel: the first group includes St Pancras and St Martin at Canterbury, Reculver, and Bradwell-on-Sea; the latter, Monkwearmouth, Jarrow, and

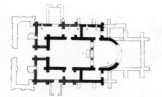

Reculver, Kent, 669 (Anglo-Saxon)

*Escomb, Durham, first half of C7
(Anglo-Saxon)*

Escomb. None of these has aisles, but instead they have side chambers, called *porticus*. Towers did not exist, but there were west porches. Between the two groups stand Brixworth in Northamptonshire, larger than the others and with aisles, and Bradford-on-Avon in Wiltshire. But the typically Anglo-Saxon decoration of Bradford, with its pilaster-strips, flat blank arches, triangles instead of arches – the whole applied like the timbering of timber-framed work – is as late as the C10 and is indeed the most prominent decorative feature of later Anglo-Saxon architecture. Towers seem to have made their appearance in the C10 too; they are either at the west end or placed centrally between nave and chancel. Highly decorated examples are to be found at

Earls Barton and Barton-on-Humber. Transepts also appear, and aisles become a little more frequent. That churches of timber which must have been the rule in the earliest centuries still went on as late as the C11 is proved by Greensted in Essex which can be dated c. 1013. Many churches of the later C11 have Anglo-Saxon side by side with Norman motifs; the mixture is called the *Saxo-Norman overlap*.

What is called Norman architecture in England is not the art of Normandy but that brought by William the Conqueror to England, i.e., really what on the Continent is called Romanesque. The Norman style in fact begins just before the Conquest, with Westminster Abbey as rebuilt by Edward the Confessor. This is a close parallel to such buildings in Normandy as Jumièges, Mont St Michel, and the churches of Caen: internally with arcade, gallery (ample or small, with large or subdivided openings towards the nave), CLERESTORY, and open timber roof; externally with two façade towers and a square crossing tower (Canterbury, Southwell). The volume of building was enormous. Nearly every cathedral and abbey church was rebuilt, and most of the bishops and abbots came from Normandy. But apart from the system of Normandy, there are also interesting variations of divers origin: the mighty single west tower of Ely on the pattern of Germany; the giant niches of the façades of Tewkesbury and Lincoln, also on German patterns; the gallery tucked in below the arch of the arcade

*Earls Barton, Northamptonshire, C10–C11
(Anglo-Saxon)*

*Ely Cathedral, c. 1090–c. 1130
(Norman)*

Durham Cathedral, 1093–c. 1130 (Norman)

(Jedburgh) and the giant round piers of Tewkesbury and Gloucester, perhaps on a Burgundian pattern (as at Tournus). Ornament is prevalently geometrical (zigzag, CRENELLATION, chain, reel and similar motifs). Figure sculpture is rarely concentrated on the portals as in the French royal domain (York, chapterhouse of St Mary); its connections are rather with the West of France and with Lombardy.

In only one respect does England appear to lead in the European Romanesque style; in the vaulting of Durham Cathedral. For while England has no parallel to the mighty tunnel vaults of so many French naves and the groin vaults of so many German naves, Durham was rib-vaulted from the beginning (1093), and hers seem to be the earliest rib vaults not only of northern Europe but possibly of Europe altogether. While it may be that some of the elementary rib vaults of Lombardy are in fact of earlier date, those of Durham are without question infinitely more accomplished, and they and their descendants in France (Caen, St Étienne; Beauvais) led to the triumphant adoption of rib vaulting at St Denis and in the whole Gothic style, first in France and then everywhere.

The Gothic style reached England first by means of the CISTERCIAN Order. Its first English buildings of c. 1130–60, however, though provided with pointed arches, have Burgundian Cistercian sources of a Romanesque kind, and where rib vaults first appear, they are derived from Durham rather than France. Cistercian churches go Gothic very gradually about 1160–80 (Roche), and a few non-Cistercian churches take part in this development (Ripon). But the real, the only fully convinced, beginning of Gothic architecture in England is the east end of Canterbury Cathedral, begun by William of Sens in 1175 and brought to completion in 1185 by William the Englishman. Sens and Paris Cathedrals are the precursors, the retrochoir at Chichester and the nave of the Temple Church the immediate successors. Also immediately follows the retrochoir at Winchester, a hall choir, and this form was liked in England (on the pattern of Anjou churches), as it reappears at Salisbury, the Temple and Barking Abbey.

But real, thoroughly English Gothic, i.e., the so-called Early English style, begins with Wells c. 1180 and Lincoln 1192. Here there is more stress on horizontals than in France, there are straight east walls (not radiating chapels), and the details also keep right away from the central French development. The chancel of Lincoln in particular with its crazy

Exeter Cathedral, nave, c. 1308–c. 1340 (Decorated)

vault has no French parallel and begins a distinguished series of figured vaults which precedes those of any other country. The first star vaults are in the Lincoln nave, and the acme of this system is Exeter of the late C13. Less original but equally impressive are Salisbury of 1220–c. 70 and the east transept of Durham.

Durham Cathedral lies on the castle hill, and late C11 as well as C12 domestic parts survive. Altogether, although English castles are primarily castles with keeps, like the French donjons (the Tower in London, Colchester, Rochester, etc.), these keeps were not normally used domestically, but great halls,

Lincoln Cathedral, the west front, C11–C13 (Early English)

The Tower of London, the keep, late C11, the concentric walls, C13–C14

chapels, etc. were also built. A reform of the defensive system was brought about by the Crusades, in England as (a little earlier) in

France. Emphasis was now laid on the defence not of one tower but of the whole wall with its many smaller towers, and often even on more than one concentric wall, on the pattern ultimately of the walls of Constantinople. Such castles are Dover, the Tower of London and the splendid late CI3 castles of Wales (Conway, Caernarvon, Harlech, Beaumaris).

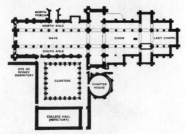

Worcester Cathedral, CII–CI4

In church architecture the late CI3 marks the change from the Early English to the Decorated style. This lasted into the second half of the CI4, and is characterized first and foremost by the OGEE, a double or S-curve, which occurs chiefly in arches and in the TRACERY of windows. The other main characteristic is a maximum of decoration covering surfaces (e.g., in foliage DIAPERS) and encrusting arches, gables, etc.; the leaves are not

naturalistic but stylized, with nobbly forms reminiscent of certain seaweeds. Spatially the Decorated style favours the unexpected vista, especially in diagonal directions. Principal works are the east parts of Bristol Cathedral (begun in 1298) and Wells Cathedral (*c.* 1290–*c.* 1340), the Lady Chapel and the famous Octagon at Ely (1321–53), and screens (Lincoln), funerary monuments (Edward II, Gloucester Cathedral; Percy Tomb, Beverley), stalls (Exeter), etc. No other country has anything as novel, as resourceful and as lavish as the English Decorated style, though when a similar direction was taken by Peter PARLER at Prague, it is likely that English influence played a determining part. The start at Prague was in 1353.

At that time, however, England was already turning her back on the Decorated. The Perpendicular style, beginning in London *c.* 1330 and reaching a full climax in the Gloucester chancel in 1337–57, is the very reverse of the Decorated. Perpendicular is characterized by the stress on straight verticals and horizontals, by slender, vertically subdivided supports and large windows, by window tracery with little fantasy and inventiveness. The signature tune is the panel motif, which is simply arched but with the arch cusped. This occurs in rows and tiers everywhere in the tracery, and almost as frequently in blank-wall decoration. In vault-

Chapter-house, Southwell Minster, late CI3 (Decorated)

Bristol Cathedral, choir aisle, 1298–1332 (Decorated)

Gloucester Cathedral, cloister, between 1351 and 1377 (Perpendicular)

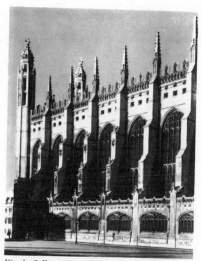

King's College Chapel, Cambridge, 1446–1515 (Perpendicular)

ing the Perpendicular first favours LIERNE VAULTS, therein following the inventions of the Decorated, and later FAN VAULTS, introduced about 1350–60 either in the cloisters at Gloucester or in the chapterhouse at Hereford. For the Early Perpendicular the chancel of Gloucester Cathedral is the most important work; for the time about 1400 the naves of Canterbury (c. 1375 etc.) and Winchester (c. 1360 etc., but mostly c. 1394 etc.), for the Late Perpendicular St George's Chapel at Windsor (1474 etc.), King's College Chapel at Cambridge (1446 etc. and 1508–15) and the chapel of Henry VII at Westminster Abbey (1502 etc.) and its predecessor, the chancel vault of Oxford Cathedral (c. 1478 etc.). But for the Perpendicular style parish churches are as significant as the major buildings so far noted. The grandest of these are in Suffolk and Norfolk, in Somerset (especially towers), and in the Cotswolds, demonstrating the riches which the wool and cloth trade made for the middle class. The Perpendicular style, once it had been established, went on without major changes for 250 years, and it can be argued that the Elizabethan style in England is more Perpendicular than it is Renaissance.

It was in Henry VII's Chapel that the first works in England in the Italian Renaissance style were put up, the tombs of the Lady Margaret and Henry VII by Pietro Torrigiani

Henry VII Chapel, Westminster Abbey, 1503–c. 1512 (Perpendicular)

of Florence (1511 etc.). Henry VIII and his court favoured the new style which was impressively promoted in the crafts by Holbein's designs. But the Renaissance in England remained till about 1550 a matter of decoration, and it was coarsened as soon as it fell into native hands. The Protector Somerset in Somerset House was the first to understand Italian or rather by then French Renaissance principles more fully, and from Somerset House the Elizabethan style proceeded. It combines the symmetry of façades, as the Renaissance had taught it, and Renaissance details, with Netherlandish decorative motifs (STRAPWORK) and the Perpendicular belief in very large windows with MULLIONS and

TRANSOMS. Longleat (mainly 1568 etc.) is the first complete example: others are Burghley House (1560s–1580s), Montacute (c. 1590 etc.), Wollaton (1580–88) and Hardwick

The Queen's House, Greenwich, 1616–c. 1635, by Inigo Jones

Hardwick Hall, Derbyshire, 1591–7 (Elizabethan)

Hatfield House, Hertfordshire, 1603–12 (Jacobean)

(1591–7). The first fifteen years of the reign of James I brought no change. Among the principal buildings are Hatfield (1608–12), Audley End (1603 etc.), Bramshill (1605–12). Plans of houses are often of E or H shape, if they do not have internal courtyards as the largest have. Windows are usually very large and may dominate the walls. Gables, straight or curved in the manner of the Netherlands, are frequent. Wood and plaster decoration is rich and often over-extravagant. Ecclesiastical architecture was almost at a standstill, and even the ample Jacobean-looking church furnishings are usually Jacobean only in style, although as late as the 1630s.

By then the greatest revolution in English architecture had, however, already taken place, the revolution achieved by Inigo JONES. His Queen's House at Greenwich was begun in 1616, his Banqueting House in Whitehall in 1619. Jones's strictly Palladian classicism was continued by John WEBB. Sir Roger

PRATT, and Hugh MAY. Another contributing factor was the domestic architecture of Holland, which influenced England first in a semi-classical form with Dutch gables. The Jones style was too pure and exacting to find favour immediately outside the most cultured circles. The universal acceptance of classical architecture came only with the time of WREN, but in domestic building the so-called Wren type of house – quite plain, with a middle pediment, a pedimented doorway, and a hipped roof – is not a creation of Wren. Stuart

Eltham Lodge, 1663–5, by May

churches are a rarity. They also become more frequent only at the time of Wren and are largely the result of the Fire of London. They are of a wide variety of plans, longitudinal or central or a synthesis of the two, and also of a wide variety of elevational features, especially in the steeples. The range of forms used by Wren is immense. It goes from the noble classical simplicity of the dome of St Paul's to the dramatic Baroque of the west towers of St Paul's and of Greenwich and the Hampton Court plans, to the brick domesticity of Kensington Palace and even to the Gothic Revival of a few of the city churches.

Prior Park, near Bath, 1735–48, by the elder Wood

Royal Hospital, Chelsea, London, begun 1682 by Wren

Blenheim Palace, Oxfordshire, 1709–24, by Vanbrugh

HAWKSMOOR, Wren's favourite pupil, and the ingenious VANBRUGH followed Wren's lead in working towards a synthesis of Baroque and Gothicism or a general Medievalism. The creation of picturesque landscaping in England about 1715–20 is closely allied to this medievalism which was much stronger than in any other country. The fact that the architects of the generation after Vanbrugh and Hawksmoor returned to the Palladianism of Jones is only at first sight a contradiction. Palladian houses and picturesque grounds must be seen as the two

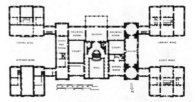

Holkham Hall, Norfolk, begun 1734, by Kent

sides of the same coin. The architects in question are men such as Colen CAMPBELL, Lord BURLINGTON, and KENT (the latter, however, much inspired by the Vanbrugh style as well). GIBBS continued rather in the Wren vein: he is chiefly remembered for his churches, which had much influence in America as well as in England. Palladianism ruled until modified by the more elegant and varied style of Robert ADAM, but essentially the Palladian tradition maintained its hold until the 1820s (NASH's Regent's Park terraces).

Georgian architecture is classical in its major exteriors; but on the smaller domestic scale it still has the sensible plainness of the

Westwell House, Tenterden, Kent, 1711 (Queen Anne)

The Library, Kenwood, London, c. 1765,
by Adam

QUEEN ANNE style. Interiors are more elaborate than exteriors; here also Palladianism was the rule at first, but it was handled with greater freedom and verve. A brief phase of ROCOCO followed about the middle of the century: then the enchantment of Robert Adam's delicate decoration captured nearly every-body. Grecian interiors were rare until about 1820, but Victorian licence and exuberance are already heralded in certain Regency interiors (Brighton Pavilion).

But Victorian architecture is not all licence and exuberance. At the other end of the scale is the respect for the past, a historicism taken

*Boodle's Club, St James's Street,
London, 1765, by J. Crunden (Georgian)*

*No. 13, Lincoln's Inn Fields, London, 1812–13,
by Soane*

very seriously, as a matter of religious or social
responsibility. The licence is usually paramount in domestic, the seriousness in ecclesiastic architecture. Not that historicism did not
dominate domestic architecture too, but there
it was taken in a less demanding way. Victorian church architecture is almost entirely
Gothic, though in the 1840s there was a
passing fashion for neo-Norman and neo-
Early-Christian or neo-Italian-Romanesque
(T. H. WYATT, Wilton). The Gothic Revival is
ubiquitous, but, in spite of this, certainly not
monotonous. SCOTT, the most successful of

*St Saviour's Vicarage, Coalpit Heath, 1844,
by Butterfield*

*The Foreign Office, London, 1862–75,
by George Gilbert Scott*

Victorian architects, was correct and knowledgeable, if not inspired. STREET had more
weight than Scott and is sometimes as original
as Butterfield, though never as perverse. For
BUTTERFIELD is at the other end of the scale;
wilful, daring and ready to give his faith (e.g.
in polychromy) preference over the motifs of
the correct Gothic. BURGES also had the

Cardiff Castle, 1865–81, by Burges

courage of his convictions (especially in favour of decorative sculpture). BROOKS on the contrary scorned decoration. His London churches fit well into poor districts. PEARSON and BODLEY got nearest perfection. Both were sensitive and so conversant with Gothic that they could handle it with originality without

Fonthill Abbey, Wiltshire, 1796–1815, (demolished), by Wyatt

St Augustine, Kilburn, London, 1870–80, by Pearson

Truro Cathedral, begun 1880, by Pearson

Houses of Parliament, London, begun 1836, by Charles Barry and A. W. N. Pugin

falling into the controversial. The phase of Gothic which inspired them all was the so-called Second Pointed or Middle Pointed, i.e. the style of c. 1250 to c. 1300. This was the style PUGIN had re-established in 1840–41. Before 1840 he had preferred the Perpendicular and this preference returned from the seventies onwards (e.g. in later Bodley). At the end of the century historicism began to break down, and Norman SHAW could use domestic C17 elements in a church (St Michael, Bedford Park) and Sedding yet freer, but always sensitively handled, elements.

In secular architecture the possibility of using Gothic side by side with Classical had been handed down from Wren and Hawksmoor via the Rococo Gothic of Horace Walpole's Strawberry Hill and the romantic Gothic

of J. WYATT's Fonthill. Other styles had also occasionally been tried, though not seriously (CHINOISERIE, also the Indian of the Brighton Pavilion). But Gothic was given publicly the same weight as Classical only with BARRY'S Houses of Parliament (1835 etc.). At the same time Barry introduced a neo-Quattrocento (Travellers' Club) and neo-Cinquecento (Reform Club) and a neo-Elizabethan (Highclere, 1837). So by c. 1840 a wide range of historical possibilities was accepted. To them in the late fifties the French Renaissance with its prominent pavilion roofs was added.

Quite separate from all this was the great engineering development. England had been first in the Industrial Revolution (and the size of the new mansions and size and frequency of the new churches bear witness to England's unprecedented industrial and consequently commercial prosperity). The first iron bridges belong to England (TELFORD, BRUNEL), and the largest iron and glass conservatories (PAXTON, BURTON). In BUNNING'S Coal Exchange (1846–9) iron and glass first appeared

St Katherine's Dock, London, 1824–8, by Telford and Hardwick

The Crystal Palace, London, 1851 (destroyed), by Paxton

with architectural ambitions, and only two years after its completion Paxton's Crystal Palace was entirely of iron and glass, the whole 1800 ft length of it. But iron and glass in architecture remained after that confined to exhibition buildings, train sheds, and, on the fringe of architecture, to warehouses and office buildings. The functional self-sufficiency of these new materials and the shunning of over-decoration which followed from their convinced use, however, made them unpopular with the High Victorian architects.

But from 1877 onwards William MORRIS fought publicly for simplicity, for truth to materials and against over-decoration, though he did so in a militant anti-industrial spirit. Hence those who were convinced by Morris's teachings were less attracted by an alliance with industry and commerce than by an application of Morris's principles to the human scale of domestic architecture. The leaders were Morris's friend Philip WEBB and the more richly endowed Norman Shaw. They, from the sixties onwards, built houses for a small section of the middle class which were fresher and aesthetically more adventurous than anything done at the same time abroad. Working-class architecture, on the other hand, i.e., housing provided by manufacturers and then by trusts (Peabody Trust), remained grim and was only humanized when HOWARD'S garden city principle had begun to be applied to factory housing (Port Sunlight, Bournville). About 1900 England was still leading both in the planning conception of the garden suburb and in the architecture of the so-called Domestic Revival. This,

House at Shackleford, Surrey, 1897, by Voysey

in the work of VOYSEY, and the early work of LUTYENS, was beginning to move out of historicism towards a greater independence of period motifs and towards that simplicity and directness which in the commercial field had already been achieved by the CHICAGO SCHOOL.

However, as soon as radical innovation became the demand of the most go-ahead architects, England ratted. The revolution remained in the hands of, apart from the Chicago School, French, German and Austrian architects, and England re-joined the party of the progressives again only very occasionally in the later 1920s, a little more frequently in the 30s (FRY, YORKE, GIBBERD, TECTON), and wholeheartedly only after the Second World War. Two phases must be distinguished for the last twenty years, the INTERNATIONAL MODERN and the new individualism and expressionism (and BRUTALISM) sparked off by LE CORBUSIER'S buildings at Marseille and Ronchamp. The former phase has its acme in housing, where the English tradition of landscaping made such a triumph as Roe-

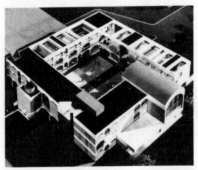

Alton East Housing, Roehampton, London, 1953–6, by LCC (now GLC) Architects Department

Sussex University, 1960 etc., by Sir Basil Spence

New Hall, Cambridge, 1966, by Chamberlin, Powell & Bon

hampton possible, and also in schools, built to fixed modules from prefabricated parts and grouped with the same trained sense of landscape. For the latter phase see LASDUN, MARTIN, SHEPPARD, SPENCE, and others. *See also* GREEK REVIVAL *and* NEO-GOTHIC ARCHITECTURE.

Lit: G. Webb, *Architecture in Britain: The Middle Ages*, Pelican History of Art, Harmondsworth 1956; J. Harvey, *Early Medieval Architects*, London 1954; J. Summerson, *Architecture in Britain 1530–1830*, Pelican History of Art, 2nd edn, Harmondsworth 1970, paperback edn 1970; H.-R. Hitchcock, *Architecture: Nineteenth and Twentieth Centuries*, Pelican History of Art, 2nd edn, Harmondsworth 1971, paperback edn 1971; P. Kidson, P. Murray, P. Thompson, *A History of English Architecture*, Harmondsworth 1965; N. Pevsner and others, *The Buildings of England*, 46 vols, Harmondsworth 1951–74.

Ensinger A family of South German masons: the two most important members are Ulrich and Matthäus. Ulrich Ensinger (d. 1419) was sufficiently distinguished by 1391 for the cathedral authorities at Milan to want to consult him; he refused the invitation. In 1392 he became master mason for Ulm Minster (begun 1377). He changed plan and elevation boldly and designed the west tower with its splendid porch. The upper parts of the tower were built to a changed design by Matthäus BÖBLINGER. In 1394 Ulrich went after all to Milan, but was not satisfied or able to convince the authorities, and so left in 1395. In 1399, in addition to his job at Ulm, he was put in charge of the continuation of the west tower at Strassburg. Here it was he who started the single tower instead of the two originally projected and built the enchanting octagon stage. The spire, however, is by his successor Johann HÜLTZ. He also worked at Esslingen from *c.* 1400 onwards, and probably designed the west tower which was carried out (and probably altered) by Hans BÖBLINGER.

Ulrich had three sons who became masons. One of them is Matthäus (d. 1463), who first worked under his father at Strassburg, then became master mason at Berne, where he designed the new minster in 1420–1. From Berne he also undertook the job of master mason at Esslingen, but was replaced there in 1440 by Hans Böblinger. From 1446 he was master mason at Ulm. Of his sons three were masons.

Lit: P. Frankl, *Gothic Architecture,* Pelican History of Art, Harmondsworth 1962; Luc Mojon, *Der Münsterbaumeister Matthäus Ensinger,* Bern 1967.

Entablature The upper part of an ORDER, consisting of ARCHITRAVE, FRIEZE, and CORNICE.

Entablature: Corinthian

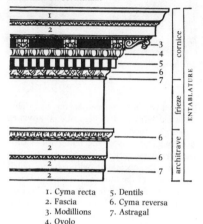

1. Cyma recta   5. Dentils
2. Fascia   6. Cyma reversa
3. Modillions   7. Astragal
4. Ovolo

Entasis The very slight convex curve used on Greek and later columns to correct the optical illusion of concavity which would result if the sides were straight. Also used on spires and other structures for the same reason.

Entresol, *see* MEZZANINE.

Equilateral arch, *see* ARCH.

Erdmannsdorf, Friedrich Wilhelm Freiherr von (1736–1800). Neo-classical architect inspired by the English neo-Palladians, then fashionable at Frederick the Great's Potsdam, rather than by Palladio himself. He decided to become an architect when travelling in England in 1763. His work is elegant and polite, very different from the radical and severe neo-classicism of his exact contemporary LEDOUX. In 1765–6 he travelled in Italy with his patron the Duke of Anhalt and met both Winckelmann and CLÉRISSEAU. He also visited England again. On his return to Germany he built the neo-Palladian country seat at Wörlitz (1768–73). His later buildings in Dessau have all been destroyed: the Schlosstheater (1777), Schloss Georgium (*c.* 1780)

and the Stables and Riding School (1790–91). (For illustration *see* PALLADIANISM.)

Lit: E. P. Riesenfeld, *F. W. von Erdmannsdorf,* Berlin 1913.

Erwin von Steinbach (d. 1318) is one of the most famous medieval architects, because Goethe wrote his prose poem on Strassburg Cathedral, and especially its façade and steeple, round Erwin's name. According to an early inscription (which is not beyond suspicion), Erwin did indeed begin the façade in 1277. Documents refer to him under 1284 (?), 1293, and 1316. But during that time the steeple was not reached anyway, and even the lower part of the façade presupposes two changes of design. It is most likely that the happily preserved drawing for the façade known as B is Erwin's. (For illustration *see* GERMAN ARCHITECTURE.)

Lit: J. W. Goethe, *Von deutscher Baukunst,* Frankfurt 1773; T. Rieger, *La cathédrale de Strasbourg,* Strasbourg 1958.

Escarp or **scarp** In military architecture, the bank or wall immediately in front of and below the rampart. It is often the inner side of the fosse or ditch.

Estípite A type of PILASTER tapering towards the base, extensively used in Spanish post-Renaissance architecture.

Etruscan architecture The main building materials were wood, rubble, clay (sometimes baked); stone was used only for the foundations of temples and secular buildings, for fortifications, and for tombs. As the Romans were anxious to erase all memory of the Etruscans very few of their buildings survive above ground level. Their most notable surviving

Terracotta decoration of temple façade, Falerii Veteres, c. 250 B.C.

Tumulus II with entrance to tomb chamber,
Cerveteri, C7–C5 B.C.

Tomba dei Rilievi, Cerveteri,
C3 B.C.

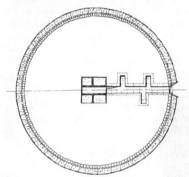

Plan of underground tomb,
S. Cerbone di Populonia

constructions are city walls dating from the
C6 to the C4 B.C. (Tarquinia, Chiusi, Cortona,
etc.) – sometimes with handsome if rather
heavy arched gateways – though most of
these are later (e.g., Falerii Novi, *c.* 250 B.C.;
Perugia, *c.* 100 B.C.). After the C5 B.C. temples
were built on a plan derived from Greece, but
with rather widely spaced, stocky, wooden,

Tomb chamber of the Volumni,
near Perugia, C2 B.C.

unfluted columns, wooden beams, and richly
modelled terracotta facings and ACROTERIA
applied to them. Underground tombs were
usually hewn out of the living rock; their
interiors were very elaborately painted and
occasionally decorated with stucco reliefs
(e.g., Tomb of the Stucchi, Cerveteri, C3 B.C.).
　　Lit: A. Boethius & J. B. Ward-Perkins,
Etruscan and Roman Architecture, Pelican History of Art, Harmondsworth 1970.

Eulalius designed the Church of the Holy
Apostles, Constantinople (536–45, destroyed),
the prototype Greek cross-plan church with
five domes. It inspired S. Marco, Venice, and
St Front, Périgueux.

Eustyle With an arrangement of columns
two and a quarter diameters apart. *See also*
ARAEOSTYLE; DIASTYLE; PYCNOSTYLE; SY-
STYLE.

Exedra In classical architecture, a semicircular or rectangular recess with raised
seats: also, more loosely, any APSE or niche
or the apsidal end of a room or a room opening full width into a larger, covered or uncovered space.

Expressionism The style dominant in Northern
Europe about 1905–25. In architecture it is
partly a continuation of ART NOUVEAU and
was itself continued after the Second World
War by BRUTALISM. Buildings should not be
confined to functioning well but create sensa-
tions of freely shaped abstract sculpture.
GAUDí in his late work was the greatest
architect of Expressionism. In Holland Expressionism is represented by the housing estates
of Michael de Klerk (1884–1923) and most

Scheepvarthuis, Amsterdam, 1911–16,
by van der Meij

Chile-Haus, Hamburg, 1923,
by Höger

wildly by van der Meij's Scheepvarthuis of 1911–16, both in Amsterdam. In Denmark the Grundtvig Church in Copenhagen (1913–26) by KLINT is gothicizing Expressionism. In Germany the most radical architectural Expressionism was never built. It is the style of Finsterlin's sketches which often do not look like buildings at all, and of POELZIG'S House of Friendship for Istanbul (1916) and sketches for the Salzburg Festival Theatre (1920). The style of the latter was only once allowed to appear in reality; in the remodelling of a circus in Berlin as the Grosses Schauspielhaus (1918–19). As Expressionism

Einstein Tower, Potsdam, 1919–20,
by Mendelsohn

also must be regarded the Einstein Tower at Potsdam by MENDELSOHN (1918–20) and the Chile-Haus in Hamburg by Fritz Höger (1922–3). Even GROPIUS and MIES VAN DER ROHE for a very short time sacrificed on the altars of Expressionism: Gropius in his monument to the revolutionaries killed in the March Riots (1921), Mies in his glass skyscrapers of 1919–21 and the monument to Liebknecht and Rosa Luxemburg (1926).

Lit: D. Sharp, *Modern Architecture and Expressionism,* London 1966; W. Pehnt, *Expressionist Architecture,* London 1973.

Extrados The outer curved face of an arch or vault. (For illustration *see* ARCH.)

Eye-catcher A decorative building usually built on an eminence in a park to terminate a view or otherwise punctuate a layout, sometimes quite large, e.g. the Gloriette at Schönbrunn which gave its name to such constructions in Austria and Germany. In English c18 landscape parks it was sometimes a sham-ruin. *See also* FOLLY.

Eye-catcher: Gloriette in the park at Schönbrunn, Vienna, 1775

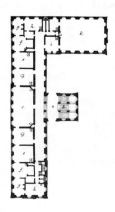

Facing The finishing applied to the outer surface of a building.

False arch, *see* ARCH.

Fan vault, *see* VAULT.

Fanlight 1. A window, often semicircular, over a door, in Georgian and Regency buildings, with radiating glazing bars suggesting a fan. 2. Also, less commonly, the upper part of a window hinged to open separately.

Fanzago, Cosimo (1591–1678), was born at Clusone near Bergamo, but settled in 1608 in Naples where he became the leading Baroque architect. Trained as a sculptor, he also worked as a decorator and painter, and was interested less in planning than in decoration though that of his finest church, S. Maria Egiziaca in Naples (1651–1717), is notable. His exuberant style is epitomized in the fantastic Guglia di S. Gennaro (1631–60), and in such effervescent façades as those of S. Maria della Sapienza (1638–41), S. Giuseppe degli Scalzi (c. 1660), and his vast unfinished Palazzo Donn'Anna (1642–4). His earlier buildings are more restrained and elegant, e.g., the arcades of the Certosa di S. Martino above Naples (1623–31).

Lit: R. Wittkower, *Art and Architecture in Italy, 1600–1750,* Pelican History of Art, 3rd edn, Harmondsworth 1973, paperback edn 1973.

Fascia A plain horizontal band, usually in an ARCHITRAVE, which may consist of two or three fasciae oversailing each other and sometimes separated by narrow mouldings.

Fenestration The arrangement of windows in a building.

Feretory A shrine for relics designed to be carried in processions; kept behind the high altar.

Festoon A carved ornament in the form of a garland of fruit and flowers, tied with ribbons and suspended at both ends in a loop; commonly used on a FRIEZE or panel and also called a *swag.*

Festoon, Palazzo Carpegna, Rome, C17

Fielded panel A panel with a plain raised central area.

Fieldstone The American word for rubble.

Figini, Luigi (born 1903) and **Pollini, Gino** (born 1903). Figini and Pollini in 1926 established with Terragni (1904–41) and a few others the Gruppo Sette, the first Italian group with an uncompromisingly modern programme. Their best-known works were done for Olivetti's at Ivrea (headquarters building 1948–50). The church of the Madonna dei Poveri at Milan (1952–6) shows the development from the rational International Style of the thirties to the freer forms of the second half of the century.

Lit: E. Gentili, *Figini e Pollini*, Milan 1959.

Figueroa, Leonardo de (*c.* 1650–1730), the creator of the Sevillian Baroque style, was the first to make use of the cut-brick construction in white or yellow walls surrounded with red trim so intimately associated with the city. His style is rich in an abundance of glazed tiles, patterned columns, SALOMÓNICAS, ESTÍPITES, tassels, foliated brackets, undulating cornices, statues of saints and caryatids and mermen. All his works are in Seville: e.g., Hospital de Venerables Sacerdotes (1687–97); Magdalena Church (1691–1709); Salvador Church (1696–1711); and the very ornate west entrance to S. Telmo (1724–34). S. Luis, the richest and finest Baroque church in Seville (1699–1731), is usually attributed to him. His son **Ambrosio** (1700–75) maintained his style in Seville (S. Catalina, 1732; chapel of the Cartuja, 1752–8; and Sacrament chapel in El Arahal, 1763–6), and the family tradition was carried on over the threshold of the neo-classical period by his grandson Antonio **Matías** (*c.* 1734–96?), who built the elegant campanile at La Palma del Condado (1780).

Lit: G. Kubler & M. Soria, *Art and Architecture in Spain and Portugal and their American Dominions, 1500–1800*, Pelican History of Art, Harmondsworth 1959.

Filarete (Antonio Averlino) (*c.* 1400–69) built little but played an important part in the diffusion of the Early Renaissance style. Born in Florence, he adopted the Greek name Filarete (lover of virtue) fairly late in life. He began as a sculptor and executed a bronze door for St Peter's (1443) in Rome. In 1451 he was commissioned by Francesco Sforza to build the Ospedale Maggiore in Milan, which

he designed on a very elaborate symmetrical plan. He built only the first storey of the central block, a sturdy basement carrying an elegant Brunelleschian arcade. While in Milan he completed his *Trattato d'architettura*, which VASARI called the most ridiculous book ever produced; it circulated widely in manuscript but was not printed until the C19. Based partly on ALBERTI, it is important mainly for its designs of ideal and hopelessly impracticable buildings and the elaborate plan for an ideal city, 'Sforzinda', which was to be blessed with every amenity, including a ten-storey tower of Vice and Virtue, with a brothel on the ground floor and an astronomical observatory on the top. But it was an attempt to treat architecture as a unified whole, as an urbanistic and even as a social challenge, and this was remarkable.

Lit: P. Tigler, *Die Architekturtheorie des Filarete*, Berlin 1963; J. R. Spencer, *Filarete's Treatise on Architecture*, New Haven 1965; A. A. Filarete, *Trattato di Architettura* (ed. A. M. Finoli & L. Grassi), Milan 1972.

Fillet A narrow, flat, raised band running down a shaft between the flutes in a column or along an arch or a ROLL MOULDING; also the uppermost member of a CORNICE, sometimes called a *listel*.

Finial A formal ornament at the top of a canopy, gable, pinnacle, etc.; usually a detached foliated FLEUR-DE-LIS form.

Finial

Finnish architecture Although Finland lies between Sweden and Russia, Eastern inspiration remained very sporadic right down to the beginning of the C19. The principal influence came throughout the centuries from Sweden and North Germany. Nothing exists that is older than the C13, and the earliest buildings are village churches. Brick soon became the favourite material – apart of course from

Belfry of church at Ruokolahti

Cathedral at Turku, C14

wood. In the village churches detail is elementary. The only large church is the
cathedral of Turku (Abo) which dates from
the C14. Star vaults and ornamented brick
gables came from Germany, detached wooden
campanili (such as also exist in England)
from Sweden. The extremely copious wall-
paintings have their parallel in Sweden too.

Gothic plan types survived very long, and
there is no Early Renaissance decoration.
The turn to a classical style came only with
the C17, and then again on Swedish patterns.
The best early example is the manor house of
Sarvlax of 1619, with giant pilasters already
of a classical kind. Then in the late C17 the
churches – being all Protestant – adopted
cruciform and other central plans, again in
connection with Swedish patterns (St Katharine, Stockholm). Wood, however, remained
the favourite material.

Square and Cathedral, Helsinki, 1830–40, by Engel

The first climax of Finnish architecture came immediately after the country had become Russian. Helsinki was made the capital in 1812, and a plan for a new centre was made in 1817 (by J. A. Ehrenstrom). Thus C19 Helsinki is a planned town with streets as wide as in the Russian provinces and a large central square. The main buildings around this square are all the work of C. L. ENGEL. They are in a neo-classical idiom mixed of SCHINKEL and Petersburg elements. They culminate in the Cathedral of 1830–40. But even as late as 1848 a large church in the country was still built of wood (Kerimaki).

The second climax falls into the years between c. 1850 and c. 1910. They are the years of a national romanticism. Like Sweden, like Russia, like Hungary, Finland looked to a romanticized and very colourful past for inspiration. Axel Gallén the painter (and of course Sibelius) are the best known representatives of this trend. In architecture it is exemplified by the National Museum at Helsinki, by SAARINEN, Lindgren and Gesellius (1901 etc.) and Tampere Cathedral of 1902–7 by Lars Spronck (1870–1956). They are quite irregular in outline, use assorted motifs of the past freely and emphasize boldly local materials. Saarinen won the competition for

Parliament Building, Helsinki, 1927–31, by J C. Sirén

had, with the Paimio Sanatorium and the Viborg Library (Viborg was taken away from Finland by Russia in 1940), achieved international fame within the current Central European modern style. But Aalto was not just one of many. His strong personality had come through already by 1937, and in his work from 1947 onwards he is one of the

Railway station, Helsinki, 1910–14, by Eliel Saarinen

Church at Vuoksenniska, 1951–8, by Aalto

the Helsinki Station, and this (1906–14) is a blend of a rational plan with motifs partly curvaceous and fantastical and partly (already) rectangular. The latter motifs come close to those used in the same years by OLBRICH and BEHRENS.

Finland achieved independence at last in 1917. AALTO was nineteen then and the much less known Erik Bryggman (1891–1955) twenty-six. A mere twelve years later Aalto

leaders of a style of free curves, unexpected skylines, bold rhythms of glass and windowless walls. He likes to use timber and hard red brick. Side by side with him there are others, first Bryggman whose Cemetery Chapel at Turku of 1939 is as bold and novel as anything by Aalto himself, and then a younger generation led by V. Rewell (1910–64; Toronto City Hall). Also among the best in Finland are T. Toiviainen, A. Ervi and K. & H.

Sirén. The place to see the high standard of present-day Finnish architecture at its most concentrated is Tapiola outside Helsinki, a 'new town' of *c.* 17,000 inhabitants.

Lit: N. E. Wickberg, *Finnish Architecture*, Helsinki 1959; J. M. Richards, *A Guide to Finnish Architecture*, London 1966.

Fischer, Johann Michael (1692–1766), the most prolific of South German Rococo architects, built no less than twenty-two abbeys and thirty-two churches. Though less gifted than his contemporaries NEUMANN and ZIMMERMANN, he had great sensitivity to spatial relationships and could obtain monumental effects. His masterpiece is the Benedictine abbey church at Ottobeuren (1744–67), with a fine soaring façade and magnificently rich interior frothing with effervescent decoration. The smaller church at Rott-am-Inn (1759–63) shows a tendency towards greater restraint and provides a perfect setting for the statues by Ignaz Günther. Other works include St Anne, Munich (1727–39, destroyed 1944); the abbey church at Diessen (1732–9); the church at Berg-am-Laim (1737–43); the Benedictine abbey at Zwiefalten (1740–65), even larger than Ottobeuren and still richer inside; and finally, the Brigittine abbey church at Altomünster (1763–6). (For illustrations *see* GALLERY and GERMAN ARCHITECTURE.)

Lit: F. Hagen-Dempf, *Der Zentralbaugedanke bei Johann Michael Fischer*, Munich 1954; E. Hempel, *Baroque Art and Architecture in Central Europe*, Pelican History of Art, Harmondsworth 1965; H.-R. Hitchcock, *Rococo Architecture in Southern Germany*, London 1968.

Fischer von Erlach, Johann Bernhard (1656–1723), a leading Baroque architect in Austria, was more restrained and intellectual than his rival HILDEBRANDT, but also more courtly and traditional. Born near Graz, he began as a sculptor and stucco worker, then went to Italy probably in 1674 and perhaps received some training in architecture under Carlo FONTANA in Rome. In 1685 he settled in Vienna. There he was eventually appointed Court Architect in 1704. His first building of note is Schloss Frain in Moravia (1690–94), with an imposing oval hall. Italian influence, especially that of BORROMINI, is very evident in his three churches in Salzburg, the Dreifaltigkeitskirche (1694–1702), Kollegienkirche (1694–1707), and Ursulinenkirche (1699–1705). His masterpiece, the Karlskirche in Vienna (begun 1716), is a unique design with no antecedents and no successors, but his Roman memories are again quite explicit, notably in the opening theme of a Pantheon portico framed by a couple of Trajan's columns, expressive of his conscious striving after imperial grandeur. His secular buildings include the façade and monumental staircase, with its monumental ATLANTES, of the Stadtpalais of Prinz Eugen, Vienna (1695–8); the Palais Batthyány-Schönborn, Vienna (*c.* 1700); the Palais Clam Gallas, Prague (1707–12); the Palais Trautson, Vienna (1710–16); and finally, the Hofbibliothek in the Hofburg, Vienna, which he began the year of his death (1723) and which was finished by his son Joseph Emanuel (1693–1742). This library is one of the most imposing interiors in Europe and illustrates his imperial manner at its grandiloquent best. He assumed the title 'von Erlach' on being knighted by the Emperor. His wide scholarship found expression in his *Entwurf einer historischen Architektur* (published Vienna 1721), which was the first architectural treatise to include and illustrate Egyptian and Chinese buildings, and which thus exerted a great influence on various later architectural exoticisms. (For illustrations *see* AUSTRIAN ARCHITECTURE.)

Lit: H. Aurenhammer, *J. B. Fischer von Erlach*, London 1973.

Flamboyant The late Gothic style in France. In Flamboyant TRACERY the bars of stonework form long wavy divisions.

Flamboyant tracery: Amiens Cathedral, C10

Flank In military architecture, the side of a BASTION returning to the courtine from the face.

Flèche A slender spire, usually of wood, rising from the RIDGE of a roof; also called a *spirelet*.

Fleur-de-lis French for lily-flower; originally the royal arms of France.

Fleuron A decorative carved flower or leaf.

Flight A series of stairs unbroken by a landing.

Flitcroft, Henry (1697–1769), was a protégé of Lord BURLINGTON, who procured him various posts in the Office of Works, where he eventually succeeded KENT as Master Mason and Deputy Surveyor. He was known as 'Burlington's Harry'. Competent but uninspired, he was little superior to the 'imitating fools' who, according to Pope's prophecy, followed Lord Burlington's just and noble rules. His colossal west front at Wentworth Woodhouse (1735 etc.), the longest façade in England, illustrates the empty pomposity into which PALLADIANISM declined: Woburn Abbey is equally derivative (*c.* 1747). His town houses are more successful, notably 10 St James's Square, London (1734). St Giles-in-the-Fields, London (1731–3), is an unflattering imitation of St Martin-in-the-Fields.
    Lit: J. Summerson, *Architecture in Britain, 1530–1830*, Pelican History of Art, Harmondsworth 1969, paperback edn 1970; H. M. Colvin, *A Biographical Dictionary of English Architects, 1660–1840*, London 1954.

Floreale, *see* ART NOUVEAU.

Floris, Cornelis (1514/20–75). Primarily a sculptor and ornamentalist but also the leading Mannerist architect in the Southern Netherlands. He visited Rome *c.* 1538. The tall, grave and classicizing Antwerp Town Hall (1561–6) is his masterpiece. Other notable works include the House of the German Hansa, Antwerp (*c.* 1566) and the rood screen in Tournai Cathedral (1572). His style was widely diffused (and debased) by the engravings of Hans Vredeman de VRIES. (For illustration *see* BELGIAN ARCHITECTURE.)
    Lit: H. Gerson & E. H. ter Kuile, *Art and Architecture in Belgium, 1600–1800*, Pelican History of Art, Harmondsworth 1960.

Flötner or **Flettner, Peter** (*c.* 1485–1546).

German Renaissance architect, sculptor, goldsmith and an influential ornamental designer. He published at Nuremberg innumerable engraved designs for furniture, arabesques, etc. In 1518 he was working at the Fugger chapel in St Anna, Augsburg, and later travelled in Italy before settling in Nuremberg in 1522. His rather fanciful version of the Renaissance style can be seen in the fountain in the marketplace at Mainz (1526), but his masterpiece as an architect was the Hirschvogelsaal in Nuremberg (1534, destroyed), the earliest and perhaps most accomplished example of Renaissance domestic architecture in Germany.
    Lit: Peter Flötner und die Renaissance in Deutschland, Exh. Cat., Nuremberg 1947.

Flush bead moulding An inset bead or convex moulding, its outer surface being flush with adjacent surfaces.

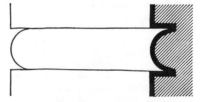

Flush bead moulding

Flushwork The decorative use of KNAPPED FLINT in conjunction with dressed stone to form patterns, such as TRACERY, initials, etc.

Fluting: Palazzo Ducale, Urbino, mid-C15

Fluting Shallow, concave grooves running vertically on the SHAFT of a column, PILASTER, or other surface; they may meet in an ARRIS or be suspended by a FILLET. If the lower part is filled with a solid cylindrical piece it is called *cabled fluting*. (Illustrated previous column.)

Flying buttress, *see* BUTTRESS.

Foil A lobe or leaf-shaped curve formed by the CUSPING of a circle or an arch. The number of foils involved is indicated by a prefix, e.g., trefoil, multifoil.

Detail of flowing tracery
showing elaborate use of cusping

Foil (aa: cusp in section)

Foil: Chartres Cathedral, c. 1225

Foliated Carved with leaf ornament.

Folly A costly but useless structure built to satisfy the whim of some eccentric and thought to show his folly; usually a tower or a sham Gothic or classical ruin in a landscaped park intended to enhance the view or picturesque effect.

> *Lit:* B. Jones, *Follies and Grottoes,* 2nd London 1974; R. A. Curtis *et al* (eds.), *Monumental Follies,* Worthing 1972.

Fontaine, Pierre François Léonard (1762–1853), the son and grandson of architects, became Napoleon's favourite architect and was largely responsible, with his partner PERCIER, for the creation of the Empire style. He studied in Paris under A. F. Peyre, then in Rome 1786–90. Percier joined him in Paris the following year, and they remained together until 1814. Their decorative style is well illustrated at Malmaison, where they worked for Napoleon from 1802 onwards, Joséphine's tented bedroom being completed in 1812. They extended the north wing of the Louvre to the Tuileries, and built the beautifully detailed Arc du Carrousel (1806–7) between the Tuileries and the Grande Galerie. Their joint works also include the rue de Rivoli, Paris (1801); the fountain in the Place Dauphine, Paris (1802); and much restoration and decoration at the royal *châteaux* (Fontainebleau, Saint-Cloud, Compiègne, Versailles) and at the Louvre, notably the Salle des Cariatides. Their influence spread rapidly throughout Europe mainly by means of their publications: *Palais, maisons, etc., à Rome* (1798) and especially their *Recueil de décorations intérieures* (1801). The most notable of Fontaine's independent works are the restoration of the Palais Royal, Paris (1814–31, including the Galerie d'Orléans), and the Hôtel-Dieu, Pontoise (1823–7).

> *Lit:* M. L. Biver, *Le Paris de Napoleon,* Paris 1963 and *P. Fontaine, premier architecte de l'empereur,* Paris 1964.

Fontana, Carlo (1634–1714), was born near Como but settled in Rome *c.* 1655. He began as assistant to CORTONA, RAINALDI, and BERNINI, working under the latter for ten years. His accomplished but derivative style is best seen in the façade of S. Marcello al Corso, Rome (1682–3), and in the many chapels he built in Roman churches: Cappella Cibo in S. Maria del Popolo (1683–7); baptismal chapel in St Peter's (1692–8). Less successful is the

Jesuit church and college at Loyola in Spain. He restored and largely rebuilt SS. Apostoli, Rome (1702), and completed Bernini's Palazzo di Montecitorio, Rome, including the main entrance (1694–7). His secular buildings are undistinguished, e.g., Palazzo Spreti, Ravenna (1700), and Ospizio di S. Michele, Rome (1700–3). By industry and perseverance he became undisputed leader of his profession in Rome and was largely responsible for the classicizing, bookish academicism into which the Baroque style declined. He had an enormous influence all over Europe through his numerous pupils who included FISCHER VON ERLACH and HILDEBRANDT in Austria, GIBBS in England, and PÖPPELMANN in Germany.

Lit: E. Coudenhove-Erthal, *Carlo Fontana und die Architektur des römischen Spätbarock*, Vienna 1930; R. Wittkower, *Art and Architecture in Italy, 1600–1750*, Pelican History of Art, 3rd edn, Harmondsworth 1973, paperback edn 1973.

Fontana, Domenico (1543–1607), was born near Lugano, settled in Rome *c.* 1563, and became architect to Sixtus V (1585–90). His *magnum opus* is the Lateran Palace in Rome (1586), followed by the Vatican Library (1587–9). He assisted Giacomo della PORTA in building the dome of St Peter's. The new Vatican Library in the Belvedere Court is also his. In 1952 he settled in Naples, where he was appointed 'Royal Engineer' and obtained many large commissions including the Royal Palace (1600–02).

Forechurch, *see* ANTECHURCH.

Formeret In a medieval VAULT, the rib against the wall, known also as a *wall rib*.

Formwork Commonly called *shuttering*, this is the temporary form that 'wet' concrete is poured into; it is constructed of braced timber or metal. When the formwork is removed, the concrete is found to have the texture of the material imprinted upon its surface. The formwork may be re-used if the type of construction is suitable, as in walls or repeating floor BAYS.

Fortress, *see* CASTLE.

Forum In Roman architecture, a central open space usually surrounded by public buildings and colonnades: it corresponds to the Greek AGORA.

Fosse A ditch or moat, whether dry or wet, used in defence.

Foundation That part of a building that meets the ground and through which all loads are transferred to it.

Foyer The vestibule or entrance hall of a theatre.

Framed building A structure whose weight is carried by the framework instead of by load-bearing walls. The term includes modern steel and REINFORCED CONCRETE structures, as well as TIMBER-FRAMED (half-timbered) buildings. In the former the frame is usually encased within a FACING (or CLADDING) of light material; in the latter the infilling may be of WATTLE AND DAUB or of brick.

Francesco di Giorgio Martini (1439–1501/2), a leading Early Renaissance theorist, wrote a treatise which, though not printed until the C19, exerted considerable influence, especially on LEONARDO DA VINCI, who owned a copy of it. He was born in Siena, the son of a poultry dealer, and trained as a sculptor and painter. Before 1477 he moved to Urbino and entered the service of Federigo da Montefeltro, who employed him as a medallist and military engineer. He wrote *c.* 1482 his *Trattato di architettura civile e militare*, based partly on VITRUVIUS (whom he translated or had translated) and ALBERTI, but showing a more practical attitude to the problems of architectural symbolism. Much of it is devoted to church planning: he produces a symbolic rationalization of the church with a long nave and centralized east end, and he also deals with the placing of the altar in a centralized church or tribune, stating the case for a central position to symbolize God's place in the universe, and for a peripheral position to symbolize his infinite distance from mankind.

His work as an architect is poorly documented. He probably contributed to the design of Palazzo Ducale, Urbino (perhaps the exquisitely beautiful loggia looking out over the surrounding hills). In 1485 he provided a model for the Latin cross church of S. Maria del Calcinaio, Cortona (completed 1516), a masterpiece of Early Renaissance clarity, harmony, and repose. He also provided a design for the austerely simple Palazzo del Comune, Jesi (1486; much altered). Many other works have been attributed to him: S. Maria degli Angeli, Siena; S. Bernardino, Urbino; and Palazzo

Ducale, Gubbio. He was also renowned as a designer of fortifications and war machinery.

Lit: A. S. Weller, *Francesco di Giorgio, 1439–1501*, Chicago 1943; *Francesco di Giorgio: Trattati di architettura, ingegneria e arti militare* (ed. C. Maltese), Milan 1967.

Freestone Any stone that cuts well in all directions, especially fine-grained limestone or sandstone.

French architecture The earliest Christian buildings in France, such as the baptisteries of Fréjus, Mélas, Aix and Marseille Cathedral, all dating from the c5, are of the same Early Christian type as baptisteries of that century in Italy and other Mediterranean countries. The origin of the plan types is Imperial Roman. Of the Merovingian period the two most interesting buildings are the so-called crypt of Jouarre near Meaux and the baptistery of St Jean at Poitiers. The former was not a crypt at all, but an attachment to a church. It was much changed in the c11 and c12, but the columns and the coarsely sub-Roman capitals are probably of the late c7. St Jean is also essentially of the c7, and still has a pediment of Roman descent, but a group of oddly triangular and semicircular windows. Chronicles tell us of more civilized and more Italo-Early-Christian buildings (Tours, Clermont Ferrand, both c5) with aisles, columns, transepts and apses. Such buildings must have continued or been revived in the Carolingian age. However, nothing of any ambition has survived. Germigny-des-Prés is tiny, though with its central plan of Byzantine origin (via

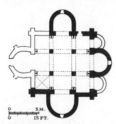

Germigny-des-Prés near Orléans, 806

Spain?) interesting enough. The excavations at St Denis have revealed a building of Early Christian type there, with aisles, transepts and apse. It was consecrated in 775. In 790–99 Centula (St Riquier) was built. All we know of it is deduced from texts and parallels with other buildings. It was of revolutionary novelty

in plan and elevation, with a WESTWORK, nave and aisles, transepts, a chancel and an apse, and with towers of identical details, perhaps of timber, over the west as well as the east crossings. They were flanked by round stair turrets. The result must have been as proud and as lively as any of the later German Romanesque cathedrals on the Rhine.

The Romanesque style can be said to have started in the c10, when two new types of plans were evolved, both to become Romanesque standard and both devised to allow for the placing of more altars. One is connected with the second building of CLUNY Abbey, the centre of a much-needed monastic reform. This was consecrated in 981 and had chancel aisles flanking the east apse, and moreover apsidal chapels on the east sides of the transept. In contrast to this so-called staggered plan is the plan with ambulatory and radiating chapels which seems to have been derived from such a crypt as that of St Pierre-le-Vif at Sens and to have been adopted in the late c10 or anyway about 1000. Early examples are Tournus and Notre Dame de la Couture at Le Mans. The building to popularize it all over present-day France was, it seems, St Martin at Tours. From here it became one of the distinguishing features of a small but important group of late c11 to early c12 churches in the country. They are or were St Martial at Limoges, St Sernin at Toulouse and to a lesser degree Ste Foy at Conques. Their other characteristics are transepts with aisles and, in elevation, galleries and tunnel vaults.

The vaulting of the main spaces of churches was a practical as well as an aesthetic need. A stone vault increases security against fire when a church is struck by lightning, and at the same time creates a spatial unity which a timber ceiling on stone walls can never achieve. Yet most French churches before the later c11 had timber ceilings (St Remi at Reims 1005–49, Jumièges in Normandy c. 1040–67, St Étienne and Ste Trinité at Caen begun c.

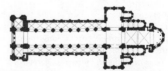

Plan of Ste Trinité, Caen, c. 1060–65

1060–65). The great exception to the rule is the fascinating church of Tournus in Burgundy which has early c11 vaults of such a

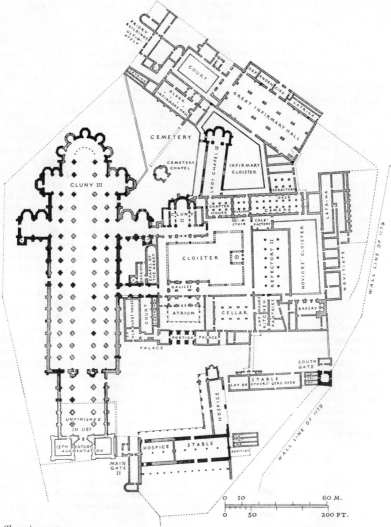

Cluny in 1157
(by courtesy of Kenneth John Conant)

variety and used in such a variety of ways that it appears to us a laboratory of vaulting. There are tunnel vaults longitudinal and transverse, groin vaults and half-tunnels.

Tournus has a separate forechurch or antechurch, two-storeyed, aisled and of three bays in depth. Such an antechurch, though single-storeyed, had already been done at Cluny and was repeated when in 1088 a new church was begun at Cluny. This was, with its antechurch and its two pairs of east transepts, to be the largest church of Europe, *c.* 600 ft long. In elevation it differed from the Tours-Toulouse type. It had a blind triforium, clere-story windows and a pointed tunnel vault. Pointed arches are by no means an invention of Gothic builders. The details at Cluny and otherwise in Burgundy show signs of an appreciation of the Ancient Roman remains in the area. Autun Cathedral, consecrated in

Ste Trinité, Caen, c. 1060–65

St Lazare, Autun, early CI2

1132, has much in common with Cluny. Vézelay on the other hand is inspired by the Rhineland. It has no gallery or triforium and groin instead of tunnel vaults.

Plan of The Madeleine, Vézalay, early CI2

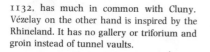

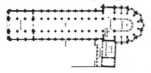

Tunnel vaults are the most usual system of vaulting in Romanesque France. The regions to which we must now turn have them as their standard. They are Auvergne (Clermont-Ferrand, Issoire), similar to the Tours–Toulouse type, but more robust in detail and built with the local volcanic materials, Poitou with HALL CHURCHES of steep and narrow proportions (the finest by far is St Savin), and Provence (Arles, St Paul-trois-Châteaux), also tall and narrow but with clerestory lighting. Provençal churches are often aisleless. Where they have aisles, groin vaults or half-tunnels are used.

Exceptions to this standard are two regions, Normandy and the Angoumois and Périgord. The former was slow in taking to major vaulting. After the Conquest anyway the weight of Norman activity and ambition

shifted to England, and here at the end of the CI1 rib-vaulting was introduced, a technically superior form of groin-vaulting (Durham). The churches of Caen took it over about 1115–20 in sexpartite forms. The Angoumois and Périgord on the other hand placed their faith in vaults of a different type, inspired, it seems, by Byzantium – either direct or via Venice. They kept away from aisles, and put on their solid outer walls domes on PENDENTIVES. Cahors, Angoulême and Périgueux are the foremost examples. Angers Cathedral, begun c. 1145, is of this type too, but in its details it is unmistakably Gothic, though a Gothic deliberately different from that of the Royal France which was the Angevins' enemy.

The Gothic of Royal France, i.e., the Gothic sooner or later for most of Europe, begins at St Denis and Sens about 1140. It is characterized by the combining of pointed arch and rib vault into a system of great logic and structural ingenuity. St Denis moreover has an ambulatory and chapels of a suppleness which makes all Romanesque east ends appear elementary additions of separate parts. Both St Denis and Sens have two-tower façades. This motif, which became Gothic standard, is derived from such Norman buildings as St Étienne at Caen, just as the rib vault with the sophisticated profiles of St Denis had its origin in Norman architecture. St Denis also possessed the first of the Gothic figure portals, with column-like figures

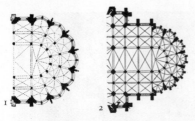

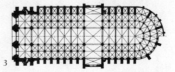

1. Plan of ambulatory and radiating chapels, east end of St Denis
2. Plan of east end of Beauvais Cathedral
3. Plan of Notre Dame, Paris

standing erect in the jambs. At St Denis they are not preserved, but they are at Chartres in the west front, *c.* 1145–50.

The great Early Gothic cathedrals are Sens, *c.* 1140 etc.; Noyon, *c.* 1150 etc.; Laon, *c.* 1160 etc.; Paris, 1163 etc. They have the sexpartite rib vaults of Caen and show a development to higher proportions, thinner members, larger openings, and less inert wall. At Noyon and Laon CROCKET capitals begin to appear, a symbol of the resilience and freshness of the Early Gothic style. Noyon and Laon have four-tier elevations inside, i.e., galleries as well as triforia. This represents a quickening of rhythm and a further opening of the wall.

Chartres, as rebuilt from 1194, turned Early Gothic into High Gothic. Its quadripartite rib vaults, tall arcades, tall clerestory windows, flying buttresses, and its replacement of the gallery by a low triforium band all convey a

sense of greater coherence, a yet quicker rhythm and yet more open walling. The system created at Chartres was taken over for the rebuilding of the cathedrals of Reims (1211 etc.) and Amiens (1220 etc.), and the abbey church of St Denis (1231 etc.), with the scale and the daring of slender supports and large openings ever increasing, until Beauvais reached a height of *c.* 155 ft. Bar

Beauvais Cathedral, c13–14

(Left). Laon Cathedral, begun c. 1160 (façade completed 1225)

Laon Cathedral, interior

Chartres Cathedral, nave and choir, 1194–1220

Ste Chapelle, Paris, c. 1245

TRACERY started at Reims; so did naturalistic foliage, the convincing concomitant of the High Gothic mood. Of the major cathedrals of these years, only Bourges stands apart, a very individual synthesis of conservative Early Gothic with the most boldly High Gothic elements. The greatest subtlety and refinement but also a first step away from High Gothic clarity appear in St Urbain at Troyes of 1262 etc. and St Nazaire at Carcassonne of c. 1270 etc. The later C13 cathedrals built as a sign of the spreading of royal power to the South and the West followed the lead of Reims and Amiens. Only in a few provinces did regional features manage to hold their own. Thus Poitou and also Anjou persisted with hall churches, even if their proportions and their spatial feeling changed in the Gothic direction. In the South a type established itself, probably on a Catalan pattern, with high proportions and chapels between internal buttresses instead of aisles (Albi, 1282 etc.).

The greatest part of the C14 in France was a period of less architectural progress, and this changed only gradually after about 1375, when Flamboyant tracery began to establish itself – more than two generations after flowing tracery had become the standard in England. The Flamboyant Style, as the French call it, i.e., French Late Gothic, got a firm foothold only in the C15, although even then it remained more a matter of decoration than of plan and elevation. The richest province is

Normandy (Caudebec, St Maclou Rouen, Pont Audemer). Other principal churches are Abbeville. Notre Dame de l'Épine near Châlons, the chancel of Moulins in Burgundy, the Trinité at Vendôme, St Nicolas-du-Port in Lorraine and the transept of Sens.

Castle building is first characterized by the KEEP or donjon, turning very early from square or oblong to round or rounded. In consequence of the experience of eastern fortification during the Crusades the keep was given up about 1200 and systems were designed instead where defence is spread along the whole CURTAIN WALL, which is sometimes doubled and has many towers. Shortly after 1200 (Louvre, Dourdan) this new system was occasionally regularized and made into a symmetrical composition of four ranges with angle towers round a square or oblong courtyard. In the course of the C15 the manor house or country house (Plessis-lès-Tours, 1463–72) began to replace the castle. The Flamboyant style created many splendid and ornate public and private buildings in the towns, such as the Law Courts of Rouen (1499–1509) and, the finest of all private houses, the House of Jacques Coeur at Bourges (1443–51).

House of Jacques Coeur, Bourges, 1443–51

The Renaissance arrived early in France, but in a desultory way. Italians were working in Marseille in 1475–81. Odd Quattrocento details in painting occur even earlier. They also appear in architectural decoration (Easter Sepulchre, Solesmes, 1496). The earliest examples of a systematic use of Quattrocento pilasters in several orders is Gaillon (1508). With François I full acceptance of such motifs

Rouen Cathedral, west façade, c16

as this is seen at Blois (1515 etc.) and in other *châteaux* along the Loire. The most monumental of them is Chambord (1519 etc.), a symmetrical composition with a square main building having an ingenious double-spiral staircase in the centre and tunnel-vaulted corridors to N., S., W. and E. with standard lodgings in the corners. The largest of the *châteaux* of François I is Fontainebleau (1528 etc.), and here, in the interior (Gallery of François I, 1532 etc.), Mannerism in its most up-to-date Italian form entered France. By the middle of the c16 France had developed a Renaissance style of her own, with French characteristics and architects. The most important of them were LESCOT, who began the rebuilding of the Louvre in 1546, and DE-LORME. Delorme introduced the dome and

Chambord, begun 1519

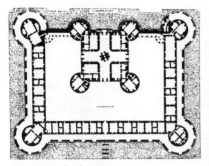

Plan of Chambord

proved himself an ingenious technician as
well as a creator of grand compositions (Anet,
c. 1547 etc.). BULLANT at Écouen (*c.* 1555
etc.) appears as Delorme's equal. His use of
giant columns, internationally very early, had
a great influence on France.

The wars of religion shook France so
violently that little on a large scale could be
built. The palace of Verneuil (begun *c.* 1565)
was built slowly, while the palace of Charleval
(begun 1573) was abandoned very soon.
Both are by the elder Du CERCEAU, and both
show an overcrowding of the façades with

Pavillon de la Reine, Place de Vosges,
Paris, 1605-12

With Henri IV things settled down. His
principal contributions are *places* in Paris, i.e.,
town planning rather than palace architecture. The Place des Vosges (1605 etc.)

Louvre, Paris, south wing, begun 1546,
by Lescot

restless and fantastical detail. The typically
French pavilion roofs make their appearance
here. Another example of the restlessness of
these years is the town hall at Arras (1572).

survives entirely, the Place Dauphine frag-
mentarily, and the Place de France, the first
with radiating streets (an idea conceived
under Sixtus V in Rome), was never built.

The elevations are of brick with busy stone DRESSINGS, a style which remained typical up to about 1630 (earliest part of Versailles, 1624). Henri IV's ideas on *places* as focal points of monumental town planning were taken up enthusiastically under Louis XIV and Louis XV, and reached their climax in the Paris of Napoleon III (Louis XIV: Place des Victoires, Place Vendôme, layout of Versailles).

The leading architects under Louis XIV were at the start François MANSART and LE VAU, then PERRAULT and Jules HARDOUIN-MANSART. François Mansart (like Corneille in literature and Poussin in painting) guided France into the classical style to which she remained faithful till beyond 1800, though it looks as if Salomon de BROSSE, the important architect under Louis XIII, had in his last work, the Law Courts at Rennes (begun 1618), preceded Mansart. Mansart is of the same fundamental importance in *châteaux* (Blois, 1635 etc.), town *hôtels* (Vrillière, 1635 etc.; Carnavalet, 1655), and churches. In church architecture de Brosse had started on tall façades crowded with Italian columns (St Gervais, 1616). Mansart toned them down to something closer to the Roman Gesù pattern, and he established the dome as a feature of ambitious Parisian churches (Visitation, 1632; Minimes, 1636). His grandest church is the Val-de-Grâce begun in 1645 and continued by LEMERCIER. But Lemercier had preceded Mansart in the field of major domed churches: his Sorbonne church with its remarkably early giant portico of detached columns was begun in 1635. Le Vau was more Baroque a

Vestibule, Maisons-Laffitte, near Paris, 1642–46, by Mansart

Vaux-le-Vicomte, 1657–61, by Le Vau

Blois, Orléans wing of the château, begun 1635.

designer than Mansart, as is shown by his
liking for curves, and particularly for ovals,
externally and internally. His first Paris house
is the Hôtel Lambert (c. 1640 etc.), his first
country house Vaux-le-Vicomte (1657–61),
with its domed oval central saloon, where
Louis XIV's team of Le Vau, Lebrun (the
painter) and LE NÔTRE appeared together for
the first time.

In 1665 Louis XIV called BERNINI to Paris
to advise him on the completion of the Louvre.
But Bernini's grand Baroque plans were dis-
carded in favour of Perrault's elegant, eminently French façade with its pairs of slender
columns and straight entablature in front of a
long loggia (1667–70). The King's architect
during Louis XIV's later years was Hardouin-
Mansart. He was not a man of the calibre of

The Panthéon, Paris, 1755–92, by Soufflot

From the middle of the c18 onwards
France turned to Classicism, first by some
theoretical writings (Cochin, 1750, LAUGIER,

*East front of the Louvre, Paris, begun 1665,
by Perrault*

the others, but he was a brilliant organizer,
and it fell to him vastly to enlarge and to complete Versailles (1678 etc.). The magniloquent
grandeur of the interiors is his but also the
noble simplicity of the Orangery and the informal layout of the Grand Trianon (1687).
He also designed the truly monumental St
Louis-des-Invalides (1680–91). In Mansart's
office the Rococo was created by younger
designers (Pierre Lepautre) about 1710–15.
It became essentially a style of interior decoration. Otherwise the difference between the
c17 and c18 *hôtel* or country house is greater
finesse and delicacy of detail, a more cunning
planning of cabinets and minor rooms, and a
decrease in scale. The most impressive major
work of the mid century is perhaps the
planning and building of the new centre of
Nancy by HÉRÉ (1753 etc.).

1753), then in actual architecture too. A
moderate, still very elegant classicism prevails
in the work of GABRIEL (Place de la Concorde
1755 etc., Petit Trianon 1763 etc.). More
radical is SOUFFLOT's Panthéon (1757 etc.)
with its exquisite dome (inspired by Wren's St
Paul's) resting on piers of Gothic structural
daring, its Greek-cross shape and its arms
accompanied by narrow aisles or ambulatories, the separation from the arms being by
columns carrying straight lintels. The last
quarter of the c18 saw even more radical endeavours towards architectural reform. They
were made mostly by young architects back
from the French Academy in Rome. There
they found inspiration not only in classical
Antiquity but even more in its bewitching
interpretation by PIRANESI. One such was
M. J. Peyre (1730–85) whose influential

Oeuvres d'Architecture came out in 1765. But
the most influential of all – BOULLÉE – had not
been in Rome. His Hôtel de Brunoy of 1772
belongs to the earliest examples of the new
simplicity and rectangularity. Others are the
Mint (1771–7) by J.-D. ANTOINE (1733–
1801), the Hôtel de Salm (1782) by Pierre
Rousseau (c. 1750–1810), and CHALGRIN's
brilliant St Philippe-du-Roule of 1772–84.
But Boullée's influence was exerted less by what
he built than by the drawings he made for a
future book. They and LEDOUX's buildings at
Arc-et-Senans and in Paris together with his

Bagatelle, Paris, 1778, by Belanger

*Saltworks at Arc-et-Senans, begun 1773,
by Ledoux*

published drawings represent a new radical-
ism of form and at the same time a megalo-
mania of scale. Boullée's most influential follower was J. N. L. DURAND (1760–1834), not
because of his buildings but because of the
publications which came out of his lecture
courses at the École Polytechnique. They were
used abroad as much as in France (see e.g.,
SCHINKEL). Durand's two books were issued
in 1800 and 1802–9. But the most successful
architects of the years of Napoleon's rulership
were PERCIER and FONTAINE. In their works
and in, e.g., the Bourse (1807) by A. T.
BRONGNIART (1739–1813), the façade of the
Palais Bourbon (1803–7) by B. Poyet (1742–
1824) and the Madeleine (1816–32) by
P. A. VIGNON (1763–1828) the style of
Boullée and Ledoux became less terse and demanding and more rhetorical and accommodating. Side by side with this classical
development from Revolution to Empire runs
the development of Romanticism in the form
of the *jardin anglais* and its furnishings.
Examples are the Bagatelle by BÉLANGER of
1778 and the part of Versailles where Marie-

Antoinette's Dairy was built in 1782–6 by
Richard MIQUE (1728–94).

The interaction between classical and
Gothic went on in the C19. The grand chapel
of Louis XVIII at Dreux was built classical in
1816–22, but enlarged Gothic in 1839. Ste
Clotilde (1846 etc.) by F. C. GAU is serious
neo-Gothic; so is Notre Dame de Bon Secours
outside Rouen (1840–7) by J. E. Barthélemy
(1799–1868), and in the 1840s also VIOLLET-
LE-DUC began his highly knowledgeable if
drastic restorations. Medieval scholarship
reached its acme with his publications. Meanwhile HITTORF completed St Vincent-de-Paul
(1824 etc.) in a classical turning Early
Christian. His later work is in a free Italianate,
and in his two circuses of 1839 and 1851 he
used glass and iron domes. The understanding
among architects of what role iron could play
was wider in France than in Britain. LAB-
ROUSTE's Ste Geneviève Library of 1843–50
is of a very pure and refined Italian Renaissance outside but has its iron framework
exposed inside. Viollet-le-Duc in his *Entretiens*
pleaded for iron, and already before their publication, in 1854–5, L.-A. BOILEAU (1812–
96) had built St Eugène essentially of iron.

Concerning façades rather than structure,
the French Renaissance was now added to the
répertoire, first in the enlargements of the
Louvre by Louis Visconti and H.-M. LEFUEL
(1852 etc.) then in the façade of St Augustin
by Victor BALTARD (1805–74). The church
(1860–67) again has iron inside. Shortly after,
the full Baroque triumphed in GARNIER's
Opéra of 1861–74. Those less ready for lush
displays now rediscovered the Romanesque
(VAUDREMER, 1864 etc.; Abadie, Sacré Coeur
1874 etc.) and with this sparked off the style
of RICHARDSON in America and with it the
great rise of American architecture.

But while Paris remained leading in the
development of iron and steel (Halles des
Machines and Eiffel Tower, both for the ex-

*Notre Dame du Raincy, Paris, 1922-3,
by Perret*

*Machinery Hall,
Paris International Exhibition, 1889*

hibition of 1889), in architecture proper she
produced nothing to emulate the English
Domestic Revival or the American Chicago
School. France came into her own again only
about 1900 with the ART NOUVEAU structures of GUIMARD and the pioneer designs of
PERRET and Tony GARNIER. From them the

*Notre Dame du Haut, Ronchamp, 1950-55,
by Le Corbusier*

Notre Dame du Haut, Ronchamp, 1950-55, by Le Corbusier

*Centre Nationale des Industries
et Techniques, Paris, 1958,
by Camelot, De Mailly and Zehrfuss*

*Fret: Double key pattern,
Ara pacis Augustae, Rome*

Fret: Key pattern

way was open to the INTERNATIONAL
MODERN of the 1920s in the hands of LE
CORBUSIER, Robert Mallet Stevens (born
1886) and André Lurçat (born 1892). Jean
PROUVÉ (born 1901) is today the most in-
teresting French experimenter in structure.
See also CISTERCIAN ARCHITECTURE, CLUNY.

Lit: P. Lavedan, *French Architecture*, Harmondsworth 1956; K. J. Conant, *Carolingian
and Romanesque Architecture, 800–1200*, Pelican History of Art, 3rd edn, Harmondsworth
1974, paperback edn 1974; P. Frankl, *Gothic
Architecture*, Pelican History of Art, Harmondsworth 1962; A . Blunt, *Art and Architecture in
France, 1500–1700*, Pelican History of Art,
2nd edn, Harmondsworth 1970, paperback
edn 1973; W. Graf Kalnein & M. Levey, *Art
and Architecture of the Eighteenth Century in
France*, Pelican History of Art, Harmondsworth 1973; H.-R. Hitchcock, *Architecture:
Nineteenth and Twentieth Centuries*, Pelican
History of Art, Harmondsworth 1969, paperback edn 1971; L. Hautecoeur, *Histoire de
l'architecture classique en France*, vols I–VI,
Paris 1943–57; M. Gallet, *Demeures Parisiennes: l'époque de Louis XVI*, Paris 1964.

French window A long window reaching to
floor level and opening in two leaves like a
pair of doors. (*See also* WINDOW.)

Fret A geometrical ornament of horizontal
and vertical straight lines repeated to form a
band, e.g., a KEY PATTERN. (Illustrated next
column.)

Freyssinet, Eugène (1879–1962). One of the
leading concrete designers of his generation.
His fame rests principally on the two airship
hangars at Orly (1916). They were of parabolic section, with a transversely folded surface
and over 200 ft high. They were destroyed in

1944. Freyssinet also designed important
concrete bridges.

Lit: P. Collins, *Concrete: The Vision of a New
Architecture*, London 1959.

Frieze 1. The middle division of an ENTABLA-
TURE, between the ARCHITRAVE and COR-
NICE; usually decorated but may be plain.
(For illustration *see* ENTABLATURE.) 2. The
decorated band along the upper part of an
internal wall, immediately below the cornice.

*Gothic frieze: Cistercian church at Megila,
near Cracow, C13*

Frisoni, Donato Giuseppe (1683–1735). He
was born at Laino, between Como and
Lugano, and began as a stucco-worker. In
this capacity he was employed in 1709 on the
vast palace at Ludwigsburg. In 1714 he
succeeded the previous architect there (Johann
Friedrich Nette) and became responsible for
the final form of the palace with its imposing
central block crowned with a double-curving
hipped roof and turret. He also designed the
elegant small banqueting house, Favorite, on
the hill opposite (begun 1718). But perhaps
his major achievement is the town plan of
Ludwigsburg, very unusual for its integration
of the palace and its garden with a regular

system of streets. (For illustration *see* TAM-BOUR.)

Lit: E. Hempel, *Baroque Art and Architecture in Central Europe*, Pelican History of Art, Harmondsworth 1965.

Frontispiece The main façade of a building or its principal entrance BAY.

Fry, Maxwell (b. 1899). One of the pioneers in England of the INTERNATIONAL MODERN of the 1930s. His early buildings are private houses, dating from 1934 onwards. From 1934 to 1936 he was in partnership with GROPIUS. The most important outcome of this is the Impington Village College (1936). Of the major post-war work of the firm (now Fry, Drew & Partners), university and other buildings for Nigeria (Ibadan University College; Co-operative Bank, Ibadan, 1947–61), housing at Chandigarh (1951–4) and the main offices for Pilkington's at St Helens (1961–4) must be mentioned.

Lit: M. Webb, *Architecture in Britain Today*, London 1969; R. Maxwell, *New British Architecture*, London 1972.

Fuga, Ferdinando (1699–1782), was born in Florence and died in Naples. But his principal works are all in Rome, e.g., Palazzo della Consulta (1732–7), the façade of S. Maria Maggiore (1741–3), and Palazzo Corsini (1736 onwards), in which his sophisticated Late Baroque style is seen at its elegant best. In 1751 he settled in Naples, where he received several important commissions (Albergo de' Poveri, Chiesa dei Gerolamini), but his early virtuosity had by then faded into a tame classicism and his late works are notable mainly for their size.

Lit: G. Matthiae, *F. Fuga e la sua opera romana*, Rome 1951; L. Bianchi, *Disegni di F. Fuga*, Rome 1955; R. Pane, *F. Fuga*, Naples 1956.

Fulcrum A support about which free rotation is possible or about which rotation occurs.

Fuller, Richard Buckminster (b. 1895). After working in a variety of commercial jobs, he started work in 1922 on structural systems for cheap and effective shelter, light in weight as well as quick to erect and capable of covering large spans. The result was his *geodesic domes* developed after the Second World War. They have been made by him on the SPACE-FRAME principle in many different materials: timber, plywood, aluminium, paper board, PRESTRESSED CONCRETE, and even bamboo. The largest is at Baton Rouge, Louisiana: it has a diameter of 384 ft and was built in 1958. (For illustrations *see* INDUSTRIALIZED BUILDING, SPACE-FRAME.)

Lit: J. McHale, *R. B. Fuller*, New York–London 1962; F. Otto, *Tensile Structures*, Cambridge–London 1967; *The Buckminster Fuller Reader*, ed. J. Miller, London 1970.

Functionalism The creed of the architect or designer who holds that it is his primary duty to see that a building or an object designed by him functions well. Whatever he wishes to convey aesthetically and emotionally must not interfere with the fitness of the building or object to fulfil its purpose.

Lit: C. A. Staellos, *Le functionalisme dans l'architecture contemporaine*, Paris 1952; E. R. de Zurko, *Origins of Functionalist Theory*, New York 1957; P. Collins, *Changing Ideals in Modern Architecture (1750–1950)*, London 1965.

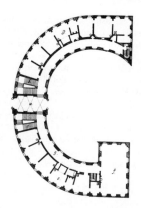

Gable The triangular upper portion of a wall at the end of a pitched roof. It normally has straight sides, but there are variants. A crow-stepped or corbie-stepped gable has stepped sides. A Dutch gable has curved sides crowned by a pediment. A hipped gable has the uppermost part sloped back. A shaped gable has multi-curved sides.

Stepped gables and Dutch gable, Lübeck

Gablet A decorative motif in the form of a small gable, as on a buttress, above a niche, etc.

Gabriel, Ange-Jacques (1698–1782). The greatest c18 architect in France and perhaps in Europe. His genius was conservative rather than revolutionary: he carried on and brought to its ultimate perfection the French classical tradition of François MANSART, by-passing, as it were, the Rococo. He resembled his great contemporary Chardin in his solid unostenta-

tious good taste, which reached its highest pitch of refinement in small intimate buildings such as his Hermitage or Pavillon de Pompadour at Fontainebleau (begun 1749) and in his great masterpiece, the Petit Trianon in the park at Versailles (1761–8). His father was a successful architect. **Jacques Gabriel** (1667–1742), who built several good Parisian *hôtels*, notably the Hôtel Peyrenne de Moras (now the Musée Rodin), and the Place Royale at Bordeaux (begun 1728), a masterpiece of Rococo urbanism. In 1735 he succeeded de COTTE as *Premier Architecte* and Director of the Academy. Ange-Jacques Gabriel was trained in Paris under his father and never went to Italy. He worked under and with his father for the Crown, and in due course succeeded him as *Premier Architecte*. In this position he built exclusively for the king, Louis XV, and Mme de Pompadour. Additions and alterations to the various royal palaces – Fontainebleau, Compiègne, Versailles – took up most of his time, but they lack inspiration, though the theatre and the projected reconstruction of the Marble Court at Versailles are extremely elegant. His largest commissions outside Versailles were for the École Militaire, Paris (1751–88), and the layout of the Place de la Concorde, Paris (1755 etc.); while the two great palaces (Hôtel de Crillon and Ministère de la Marine 1757–75) flanking his rue Royale – their façades with screens in the style of PERRAULT's great east front of the Louvre – are his most successful buildings on a monumental scale. The Pavillon Français, Versailles (1750), the small hunting-boxes or Pavillons de Butard (1750) and de la Muette (1753–4) and the Petit Château at Choisy (1754–6) foreshadow the civilized intimacy of his masterpiece. The Petit Trianon may owe something to the sober dignity of English PALLADIANISM, but the extreme elegance and refinement of this perfectly proportioned cubical composition is wholly French and achieves a serenity and distinction different in kind and quality from any other contemporary building.

Lit: de Fels, *Ange-Jacques Gabriel, premier architecte du roi*, Paris 1924; F. Kimball, *Le style Louis XV*, Paris 1949; R. Lulan, *L'Ecole militaire de Paris*, Paris 1950; Y. Bottineau, *L'Art d'Ange-Jacques Gabriel à Fontainebleau, 1735-1774*, Paris 1962; W. Graf Kalnein & M. Levey, *Art and Architecture of the Eighteenth Century in France*, Pelican History of Art, Harmondsworth 1972.

Gadrooned Decorated with convex curves; the opposite of fluted (*see* FLUTING).

Galilee A vestibule or occasionally a chapel, originally for penitents and usually at the west end of a church. Sometimes called a NARTHEX or PARADISE.

Galilei, Alessandro (1691-1737), born in Florence and trained there, went to England 1714-19 (designed portico Kimbolton Castle). In 1731 he won the competition for the façade of S. Giovanni in Laterano, Rome, with a somewhat tight, severely classical design (executed 1733-6). He also designed the elegant Corsini Chapel in S. Giovanni in Laterano (1732-5) and the façade of S. Giovanni dei Fiorentini, Rome (1734).

Lit: I. Toesca, 'Alessandro Galilei in Inghilterra' in *English Miscellany*, III, Rome 1952.

Gallery In church architecture, an upper storey over an aisle, opening on to the nave. Also called a *tribune* and often, wrongly, a

Gallery of mirrors: Schönbrunn, near Vienna, begun 1695-6, by Fischer von Erlach

TRIFORIUM. Found as an exterior feature with continuous small open ARCADING in medieval Italian and German churches, and sometimes called a DWARF GALLERY. In secular architecture, a long room, often on an upper floor, for recreation or entertainment and sometimes

Gallery: Zwiefalten Abbey church, 1739-65, by J. M. Fischer

Galleria Umberto I, Naples, 1887-91

used for the display of paintings and other works of art (hence the modern term 'Art Gallery'). In England such rooms were often called 'long galleries'. The most famous room was the *Galerie des Glaces* at Versailles (begun 1678), widely copied in palace architecture. In Italy a shopping ARCADE is called a *Galleria*, that by MENGONI in Milan being the best known.

Lit: W. Prinz, *Die Entstehung der Galerie in Frankreich und Italien*, Berlin 1970.

Galleting Inserting into mortar courses, while still soft, small pieces of stone, chips of flint, etc., sometimes for structural but usually for decorative reasons.

Galli da Bibiena The leading family of QUADRATURA painters and theatrical designers in early C18 Italy. They came from Bibiena near Bologna. Several members of the family were spirited draughtsmen and accomplished painters of *trompe l'œil* architecture; a few were architects as well. **Ferdinando** (1657–1743) designed the church of S. Antonio Abbate, Parma (1712–16), with a very effective double dome. One of his sons, **Giuseppe** (1696–1757), worked as a theatrical designer in Vienna and in Dresden (1747–53) and in 1748 designed the wonderfully rich interior of the theatre at Bayreuth; while another son, **Antonio** (1700–74), designed several theatres in Italy, of which only two survive: Teatro Comunale, Bologna (1756–63), and Teatro Scientifico, Palazzo dell'Accademia Virgiliana, Mantua. A third son, **Alessandro** (1687–1769), became Architect-General to the Elector Palatine in Mannheim, where he built the opera house (1737, destroyed) and began the fine Jesuit church (1738–56). The very elaborate stage designs by members of the family may have exerted some influence on JUVARRA and PIRANESI.

Lit: A. H. Mayor, *The Bibiena Family*, New York 1945.

Gambrel roof, see ROOF.

Gameren, Tylman van, see TYLMAN VAN GAMEREN.

Gandon, James (1743–1823). A pupil of CHAMBERS, he became the leading neoclassical architect in Dublin. He was of French Huguenot descent and his work is sometimes surprisingly advanced and close to his *avant-garde* French contemporaries, e.g., Nottingham County Hall (1770–72) of which the

façade survives. In 1781 he went to Dublin to supervise the construction of the Custom House on the Liffey (completed 1791, interior destroyed 1921). But his masterpiece is the Four Courts, also on the Liffey, where he took over from T. Cooley (1786–1802, interior destroyed 1922). Also in Dublin are his portico of the Bank of Ireland (1785) and the King's Inns (begun 1795 but later enlarged). He published, with J. Woolfe, two supplementary volumes to *Vitruvius Britannicus* in 1769 and 1771.

Lit: M. Craig, *Dublin, 1660–1860*, London 1952.

Garden city or **garden suburb** See HOWARD, Sir Ebenezer. The first garden suburbs in England were Port Sunlight and Bournville, but the finest English specimen is the Hampstead Garden Suburb in London, started in 1906. In Germany the most interesting is that planned by Richard Riemerschmid (1868–1957) at Hellerau near Dresden and begun in 1909.

Garderobe Wardrobe. Also the medieval name for a lavatory.

Gargoyle A water spout projecting from a roof, or the PARAPET of a wall or tower, and carved into a grotesque figure, human or animal.

Garner, Thomas, see BODLEY.

Garnier, Charles (1825–98), won the Grand Prix of the Academy in 1848, and went to Rome in the same year and to Athens in 1852. Back in Paris in 1854, he worked under BALLU. In 1861 he won the competition for the Opéra, and the building was completed in 1875. Prominently placed in one of HAUSSMANN's many grand *points de vue*, it is the most splendid incarnation of the Second Empire. The exterior, the ample staircase, the glittering foyer are frankly Baroque, and openly endeavour to beat the Baroque at its own game. At the same time Meyerbeer, Wagner, Verdi could not be heard in more sympathetic surroundings, since the building is most intelligently planned for its particular purpose of combining a setting for opera with a setting for social display. The same is true, in its own intentionally more meretricious way, of the Casino at Monte Carlo (1878), which, needless to say, had a universal influence in Romance countries on light-hearted resort architecture. Garnier's own villa at

T. Garnier

Bordighera (1872), with its asymmetrically placed tower, is Italianate and not Baroque. (For illustration *see* HISTORICISM.)

Lit: M. Steinhauser, *Die Architektur der Pariser Oper*, Munich 1970.

Garnier, Tony (1869–1948). When he gained the Prix de Rome in 1899 and duly went to Rome, he spent much of his time not measuring and studying ancient buildings, but working on the designs for a Cité Industrielle. These designs were submitted in 1904, exhibited, and finally published in 1917. They represent a completely new approach to town planning, in radical opposition to the academic principles of town planning as taught by the École des Beaux Arts, principles of symmetry and imposed monumentality. Garnier instead gave himself a site that was imaginary and yet realistic, since it resembled the country near his native Lyon: he decided that his town should have 35,000 inhabitants, located industry, railway lines, station, town centre, and housing, and related them rationally to each other. Moreover, he proposed that all the buildings should be made essentially of CONCRETE. He designed small houses of a quite novel cubic simplicity placed among trees, and some major buildings with the large CANTILEVERS which REINFORCED CONCRETE had just begun to make possible, with glass and concrete roofs, etc. In 1905 Garnier was called by the newly elected mayor, Édouard Hérriot, to Lyon to be municipal architect. He built the slaughterhouse in 1909–13, the stadium in 1913–16. (For illustration *see* INTERNATIONAL MODERN.)

Lit: Dora Wiebenson, *Tony Garnier: Le Cité industrielle*, London 1969.

Gärtner, Friedrich von (1792–1847), the son of an architect, studied at the Munich Academy, then for a short time with WEINBRENNER, and after that in Paris with PERCIER and FONTAINE. In 1815–17 he was in Italy, and in 1818–20 in Holland and England. After that he held a chair at the Munich Academy. On a second journey to Italy in 1828 he was introduced to King Ludwig I of Bavaria, and from then was, side by side and in competition with KLENZE, the king's favourite architect. Gärtner's speciality was what the Germans call the *Rundbogenstil*, the style of round arches, be they Italian Romanesque or Italian Quattrocento: it is said that it was King Ludwig rather than Gärtner who favoured this post-classical style. In Munich

Gärtner built the Ludwigskirche (1829–40), the State Library (1831–40), and the University (1835–40), all three in the Ludwigsstrasse, and at its south end the Feldherrenhalle, a copy of the Loggia dei Lanzi in Florence (1840–4) and an essay in the Tuscan Gothic. In 1835–6 Gärtner was in Athens, where he designed the palace of the new king, a son of Ludwig.

Lit: K. Eggert, *Friedrich von Gärtner: Baumeister König Ludwigs I*, Munich 1963.

Gau, Franz Christian (1790–1853), was born in Cologne, went to Paris in 1810, and in 1815 with a Prussian grant to Rome, where he became a friend of the Nazarenes (Overbeck, Cornelius, etc.). In 1818–20 he was in Egypt and Palestine, but returned to Paris in 1821. Gau was more widely known during his lifetime as an Egyptian scholar than as an architect. Yet his Ste Clotilde (1846–57; completed by BALLU) is the one outstanding neo-Gothic church in Paris. The style is a rich High Gothic, the façade has two towers with spires like St Nicaise at Reims, and the roof construction is of iron.

Lit: L. Hautecoeur, *Histoire de l'architecture classique en France*, vol. VI, Paris 1955.

Gaudí, Antoni (1852–1926), was born at Reus (Tarragona), where his father was a coppersmith and pot- and kettle-maker. So he grew up acquainted with metals, and it is not surprising that the savagery of his ornamental invention appeared first in metal railings and gates. Nor was the architecture of the building for which these were designed – the Casa Vicens at Barcelona – tame or imitative in the sense of C19 historicism. The house, built in 1878–80, is in fact a nightmarish farrago of Moorish and Gothic elements; indeed, Moorish and Gothic – and in addition, it seems, Moroccan – are the sources of Gaudí's style. The Casa Vicens was followed in 1883–5 by El Capricho, a house at Comillas in Northern Spain – equally crazy and less dependent on any past style.

In 1883 Gaudí was put in charge of the continuation of a large church in Barcelona, the Sagrada Familia, begun as a conventional neo-Gothic building. He did the crypt in 1884–91 and began the transept façade in 1891. By then he had been taken up by Count Güell, an industrialist who remained his faithful patron. His town house, the Palacio Güell, dates from 1885–9, and here there first appeared the parabolic arches and the wild roof excrescences which were to become part of Gaudí's repertoire. But far more fiercely extravagant than anything he or any architect had done before were the designs for the chapel of Sta Coloma de Cervelló which Gaudí began to build in 1898 for one of Count Güell's estates: it was never completed. It has an entirely free, asymmetrical, jagged plan, with pillars set at a slant, warped vaults, an indescribable interplay of exterior and interior, and ostentatiously crude benches. For the Parque Güell, a park at Barcelona, begun in 1900, similar motifs were used, and in addition the snakily undulating back of a long seat running along the sides of a large open space was faced with bits of broken tile and crockery in arbitrary patterns as effective as any invented by Picasso (who lived at Barcelona during these very years, 1901–4).

In 1903 Gaudí began the upper part of the transept of the Sagrada Familia. The lower part had gradually reached an ever freer interpretation of Gothic motifs, but the turrets at the top defeated comparison with anything architectural from the past or the present. Instead, comparisons with termite hills or with crustaceous creatures come at once to mind. The ceramic facing is similar to that in the Parque Güell. Aesthetically as surprising and socially more so than any earlier building are Gaudí's two blocks of luxury flats, the Casa Batlló and the Casa Milá (both begun 1905); for here was acceptance by wealthy Barcelonians of Gaudí's unprecedented architecture. The façades undulate, rise and fall, and are garnished with fantastical top excrescences and sharp, piercing, aggressive wrought-iron balconies. Moreover, the rooms have no straight walls, no right angles. The principles behind ART NOUVEAU (see HORTA, MACKINTOSH, MACKMURDO, van de VELDE), usually confined to decoration and mostly two-dimensional decoration, could not well be pushed further. (For illustrations see ART NOUVEAU and SPANISH ARCHITECTURE.)

Lit: G. Collins, Antonio Gaudí, New York 1960; J. J. Sweeny and J. L. Sert, Antonio Gaudí, New York & London 1963.

Gazebo A small look-out tower or summer-house with a view, usually in a garden or park but sometimes on the roof of a house; in the latter case it is also called a belvedere.

Geddes, Sir Patrick (1854–1932). If Raymond UNWIN was the greatest British town-planner of his day in practice, Geddes was the greatest in town-planning theory, a theory which he established in the present much-widened sense of the word, with emphasis laid on the necessity of preliminary surveys, on 'diagnosis before treatment', and on the dependence of acceptable town planning on sociological research bordering on biological work. Geddes was, in fact, a trained biologist and zoologist though he never took a degree. He was Professor of Botany at Dundee from 1889 to 1918, and of sociology at Bombay from 1920 to 1923. He was knighted shortly before his death. His principal work on town planning is City Development (1904).

Lit: Sir Patrick Geddes, Cities in Evolution, London 1949; Asa Briggs, Victorian Cities, London 1963.

Genelli, Christian, see GILLY.

Geodesic dome, see FULLER, RICHARD BUCKMINSTER.

Geoffrey de Noiers (active c. 1200) was called constructor of the choir of St Hugh at Lincoln Cathedral (begun 1192). The term may mean only supervisor, but more probably he is the designer of this epoch-making building. The design is, in spite of Geoffrey's name, entirely English, not merely in its proportions and the curious layout of the east chapels, but especially in its vault, the earliest vault whose ribs make a decorative (and a very wilful) pattern rather than simply express their function.

Lit: T. S. R. Boase, English Art, 1100–1216, Oxford 1953; N. Pevsner, The Choir of Lincoln Cathedral, Oxford 1963.

Georgian architecture, see ENGLISH ARCHITECTURE.

Gerbier, Sir Balthazar (1591?–1667), a Dutch-born Huguenot who settled in England in 1616, was courtier, diplomat, miniaturist, and pamphleteer as well as architect. He almost certainly designed the York Water Gate, Victoria Embankment Gardens, London (1626–7). Nothing else known to be by him survives.

Lit: H. R. Williamson, Sir Balthazar Gerbier, London 1949; J. Summerson, Architecture in Britain, 1530–1830, Pelican History of Art, Harmondsworth 1969, paperback edn 1970.

German architecture We know more about early German churches now than we did thirty years ago. Until then there were the

Gallery of Palatine Chapel, Aachen,
dedicated 805, with the throne of Charlemagne

rotunda of St Mary on the Würzburg fortress and the traces of the grand basilica of St Boniface at Fulda, both eighth century and both of Early Christian inspiration. Excavations have now told us of small aisleless churches with straight-ended chancels, much as in Northern England.

But all this is small fry compared with Charlemagne's buildings, especially the happily preserved palace chapel of Aachen and the large abbey church of Centula (St Riquier) only known from descriptions and derivations. Aachen was a palace of the Emperor, Ingelheim was another. Both were spacious, axially

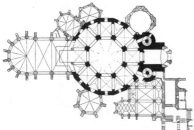

Plan of Palatine Chapel, Aachen, dedicated 805

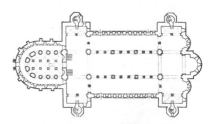

Plan of St Michael, Hildesheim

planned, and apparently aware of Imperial Roman plans. The large Aachen chapel dedicated in 805 is externally a polygon of sixteen sides, and internally has an ambulatory round an octagonal centre; above the ambulatory is a gallery and on top of the octagon a domical vault. Details are amazingly pure in the Roman tradition, as indeed is so much – script, poetry, illumination – that issued from the Emperor's circle. This applies also, e.g., to the curious gatehouse of Lorsch Abbey. At Aachen the most original feature is the WESTWORK, and as for Centula, consecrated in 799, all is original – a westwork with a tower repeating the shape of the crossing tower, transepts emanating from the crossing, and transept-like wings off the westwork, a chancel and an apse. As original is the vellum plan for St Gall Abbey, datable to

St Michael, Hildesheim, c. 1001–33

about 820. This has a west as well as an east apse and a pair of round campanili, the earliest church towers of which we have a record.

Centula can be called the pattern from which the German Romanesque style derived. The years of development are the late C10 – with the westwork of St Pantaleon in Cologne, consecrated in 980, and the nunnery church of Gernrode of 961 etc. At St Michael in Hildesheim of *c.* 1001–33 the Romanesque style is complete. Its climax is the great cathedrals and abbeys of the Rhineland dating from the mid C11 to the early C13: Speyer C11–C12, Mainz 1081 etc., Maria Laach 1093 etc.

Westwork of St Pantaleon, Cologne, 966–80

Benedictine abbey church, Maria Laach, C12–13

and Worms *c.* 1175 etc. Internationally speaking the mid C11 was the time of the great superiority of the work in the Empire over work in England, Italy and most parts of France, as it was the time of the Salians, the most powerful of the emperors. The principal buildings are the following: the hall-range of the palace of Goslar of *c.* 1050 not matched anywhere, Speyer Cathedral already mentioned, with its ruthlessly grand inner elevation and the groin vaults which the nave

received about 1080–90, the first major vault in Germany. The decoration is inspired by Northern Italy, the elevational system is

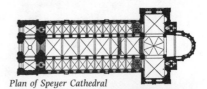

Plan of Speyer Cathedral

Speyer Cathedral, C11–C12

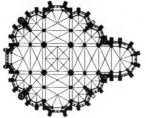

Plan of Trier St Mary, begun c. 1240

probably inspired by the Roman basilica of
Trier. Trier Cathedral is another of the masterpieces of these years – a lengthening of a
centrally planned Roman building. The west
front has the first so-called dwarf gallery, i.e.,
an arcaded wall-passage, earlier than any in
Italy. But the most coherent major building
of these years is St Mary-in-Capitol at Cologne,
built on a trefoil plan for the east end and with
tunnel vaults. The details are very severe –
BLOCK CAPITALS e.g., as had been introduced

tion exuberant – baroque, as it has been
called. The west end of Worms, completed
c. 1230, shows this at its most *outré*, but it also
shows that now the French Gothic began to
make its mark.

But we cannot leave the Romanesque
without referring to a developing liking for
HALL CHURCHES in Westphalia (Kirchlinde
c. 1175) and also in Bavaria (Waldersbach
c. 1175) and to the style promoted by the
Congregation of Hirsau, i.e., the German
Cluniacs. Their churches are not much like
French Cluniac churches. The main church
at Hirsau was begun in 1082; specially good
other Hirsau-type churches are Alpirsbach
and Paulinzella, the latter of 1112–32. The
Hirsau type had an antechurch (like Cluny)
with two west towers, nave arcades with
columns, mostly with plain block capitals, and
two slim towers over the east bays of the aisles.

Now for the relation to the Gothic in France
which had been created there about 1135–
40. Germany did not take notice of it until

Capital, St Michael, Hildesheim, c. 1001–33

Cistercian church at Altenburg, begun 1255

at St Pantaleon and at Hildesheim. Beneath is
a crypt of many short columns; Speyer has
another. The trefoil east end became the hallmark of the Romanesque school of Cologne.
Cologne before the Second World War had
more Romanesque churches than any other
city in Europe. They go on into the early C13,
when motifs tend to get fanciful and decora-

about 1200 with Gelnhausen (c. 1200–1230),
the 'PARADISE' of the abbey church of Maulbronn (c. 1210–20), St Gereon at Cologne
(1219 etc.) and Limburg on the Lahn
(consecrated 1235). The result here is a mixture, resourceful and entertaining, but impure
and not guided by any understanding of what
Gothic architecture really is about. That

Choir of Cologne Cathedral, begun 1248, dedicated 1322

Compound piers: Cologne Cathedral

changed suddenly and very dramatically with St Elizabeth at Marburg started in 1235, the church of the Virgin at Trier started a few years later (a centrally planned building making ingenious use of French elements) and Cologne Cathedral started in 1248. St Elizabeth with its rib vaults and bar-tracery presupposes Reims started in 1211, but with its trefoil east end derived from Cologne. The church after a change of plan was built as a HALL CHURCH, and that is a motif of Westphalian derivation. It became the hallmark of the Late Gothic in Germany. Cologne Cathedral is French in general and particular.

Strassburg Cathedral, the so-called 'Drawing B' of c. 1275, by Erwin von Steinbach

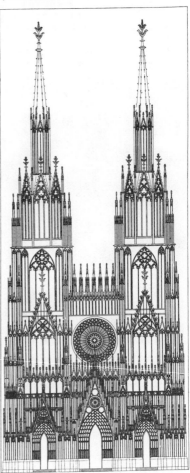

Amiens and Beauvais are closest to it. It was to be the largest and the highest of all High Gothic cathedrals, but only the east end was built, and that was consecrated only in 1322. The rest is mostly c19.

To proceed with German Gothic development one must watch for the spread of the hall church. One group is hall chancels of Austrian abbeys – Lilienfeld (consecrated 1230), Heiligenkreuz (consecrated 1295) and Zwettl (begun 1343). Meanwhile Westphalia turned from Romanesque to Gothic halls (Osnabrück 1256–92, nave Münster c. 1267 etc.). Halls also established themselves in Northeast and East Germany and especially in the architecture of the Friars. An early example (c. 1240) is the Frankfurt Blackfriars.

The full maturity of the German hall church is reached in South Germany from 1351, the

tects spreading this Late Gothic style were the PARLER family, with Peter, the greatest, who in 1353 became the Emperor Charles IV's architect of Prague Cathedral and introduced here complicated rib vaults and incidentally amazing portrait sculpture (in the triforium). A Michael Parler worked at Ulm, a Johann was called to Milan, another Johann appears at Freiburg, but the fantastic spire with its filigree tracery all over is earlier than that Parler. Altogether we hear of more architects' names now (see ENSINGER, BÖBLINGER, HEINZELMANN) and also of the statutes of masons' lodges. There are many outstanding Late Gothic parish churches in South Germany and Austria, such as St Martin at Landshut (and the Salzburg Greyfriars) by Hans STETHAIMER, Nördlingen (1427 etc.), Dinkelsbühl (1448 etc.), Amberg (1420 etc.), the Frauen-

Plan of Holy Cross, Schwäbisch Gmünd, begun 1351

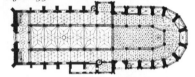

Spire of Freiburg Cathedral, c. 1350

date when the chancel of Schwäbisch Gmünd was begun, probably by Heinrich PARLER, and through the c15 into the c16. The archi-

St Martin, Landshut, begun 1387, by Stethaimer

St Lorenz, Nuremberg, 1445–72, completed by K. Roritzer

Marienkirche, Gdansk (Danzig), 1343–1502   *Vaulting of Marienkirche, Gdansk*

kirche in Munich (1468 etc.) and the chancel of St Lorenz in Nuremberg (1445 etc.). Nor is North Germany poor in Late Gothic hall churches.

But the pride of North Germany is its brick town halls such as those of Lübeck and Stralsund and the overwhelming one, mainly of the late C14, at Torun (Thorn) in the territory of the Prussian Knights. Their castles are as overwhelming, especially the C14 Malbork (Marienburg).

Altogether Germany is rich in Late Gothic secular buildings. At the castle at Meissen rebuilding of 1471–*c*. 85 demonstrates the transition from castle to palace. So does, on an even grander scale, the work of Benedict RIETH on the Hradchin at Prague. The Vladislas Hall was begun *c*. 1487. Its curvaceous rib vaults are the acme of German Late Gothic fantasy.

But the Vladislas Hall also has motifs of the Italian Renaissance. The infiltration started in fact earlier in Bohemia, Hungary and Poland than in Germany. In Germany Dürer and Burkmayr used Renaissance detail elegantly in 1508, and in 1509 the Fuggers of Augsburg founded a chapel in that city which was intended to look North Italian as an ensemble. In the second quarter of the C16 much decoration à la Como or Pavia can be found (Georgentor, Dresden 1534). Ensembles how-

ever remained rare – the purest is part of the palace of Landshut (1536) inspired by GIULIO ROMANO. Soon in any case purity was no longer the ideal. As the wholly national Elizabethan style emerges in England, so does

Knights' Hall in Marienburg Castle, near Gdansk (Danzig), 1398

Residenz, Landshut, 1536–43,
by unknown architect

Schloss Aschaffenburg, 1605–14, by Ridinger

the so-called German Renaissance in Germany, with gables, stubby columns and
coarse, more Flemish than Italian, decoration.
Examples are the Leipzig and Rothenburg
Town Halls (1556 etc. and 1572 etc.), the
former Lusthaus in Stuttgart (1580–93), the
Plassenburg near Kulmbach (1559 etc.), the
Pellerhaus in Nuremberg (1605). There are,
however, also some more international-

Wolfenbüttel (1607 etc.) and Bückeburg (1613
etc.). With Renaissance all this has little to do.
  Just as in England with Inigo Jones, a true
understanding of the High Renaissance came
only after 1600 and even then very rarely.
The key work is Elias HOLL's Augsburg Town
Hall of 1615–20. But then – and this singles
out Germany – the Thirty Years' War interrupted this organic development.

Rathausapotheke, Lemgo

Haus zum Ritter, Heidelberg, 1592

looking buildings, i.e., buildings of French
(Schloss Aschaffenburg, 1605–14) or Flemish
(Ottheinrichsbau, Heidelberg, 1556 etc.; Town
Hall portico, Cologne, 1569–70) or Italian
inspiration (St Michael, Munich, 1583 etc.).
The most original churches about 1600 are
Protestant and North German, those of

St Michael, Munich, 1592, by Sustris

portant architectural events took place in the Catholic South, and the source of inspiration was Italy, and at first even the architects were Italian, as, e.g., BARELLI and ZUCCALLI who built the Theatinerkirche in Munich (1663–88). About 1700 Germans replaced the Italians. Of the first generation are SCHLÜTER who built the Palace and the Arsenal in Berlin, the great FISCHER VON ERLACH in Vienna and PÖPPELMANN of the Zwinger in

It left the country devastated and impoverished, and when building again became possible, the situation in the country – and indeed taste – had changed. The most im-

Town Hall, Augsburg, 1610–20, by Holl

(Above). Pavilion of the Zwinger, Dresden, 1711–22, by Pöppelmann

*Amalienburg in Nymphenburg Park,
near Munich, 1734–9, by Cuvilliés*

Dresden (1709 etc.). All three were born about
1660. HILDEBRANDT in Vienna was a little
younger. While Fischer von Erlach, despite
his ingenious plans with their centralizing
tendencies and their ovals, is a classicist at
bottom, Hildebrandt represents the BORRO-
MINI and GUARINI party in Europe, as do the
DIENTZENHOFERS in Franconia and Bohemia
(Johann: Banz 1710–18; Christoph: Břevnov
near Prague 1708–15; Kilian Ignaz: the two
St Nicholases Prague 1730s). The Fischer–

Staircase at Schloss Pommersfelden, 1711–18, by Johann Dientzenhofer

Vierzehnheiligen pilgrimage church, 1743–72, by Neumann

Hildebrandt antinomy is equally patent in Dresden, but here it is a Catholic–Protestant antinomy: BÄHR's Protestant Frauenkirche of 1725 etc., the town church, v. CHIAVERI'S Catholic church of 1738 etc., the court church.

As for other Northern centres Frederick the Great's early Sanssouci at Potsdam (1745–7) looked to Rococo France (even if not with such abandon as CUVILLIÉS'S Amalienburg at Nymphenburg near Munich of 1734–9), his later buildings, including the Gothic Nauen Gate at Potsdam of 1755, to England. The Rhineland naturally looked to France, but even there – Brühl, Bruchsal – in the end the greatest German architect of the century won.

He is, needless to say, Balthasar NEUMANN, and his masterworks are the Episcopal Palace of Würzburg (1719–44), still in some elements

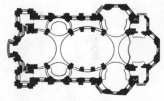

Plan of Vierzehnheiligen pilgrimage church

Plan of the Episcopal Palace, Würzburg, 1719–44, by Neumann

guided by Hildebrandt, and the splendid churches of Vierzehnheiligen (1743 etc.) and Neresheim (1745 etc.). Neumann lived at Würzburg, i.e., in Franconia. The three greatest Bavarian church builders were ASAM, ZIMMERMANN and FISCHER, all born between 1685 and 1695. The Asam brothers, also painters and sculptors, are the most Italian – influenced by Borromini, and rich in their brown and gold decoration (Weltenburg, St John Nepomuk Munich). J. M. Fischer (Ottobeuren, Zwiefalten, Rott) is all large and light in colours and ingenious in planning as well. Zimmermann is primarily remembered – rightly so – for the Wies Church (1745–54). There were two Zimmermann brothers as well, the other being a painter, and the *unisono* of all the arts is of course one of the most characteristic features of the Baroque. The

Benedictine abbey church at Ottobeuren, 1737–66, by J. M. Fischer

Schloss Benrath, near Düsseldorf, 1755–69, by Pigage

great abbeys of South Germany and even more Austria show that in all their sumptuous parts (see e.g., Melk, St Florian, Klosterneuburg).

No wonder then that the total reaction against the Rococo was a Protestant and a North German initiative, Friedrich GILLY in Berlin came from Huguenot stock. He never visited Italy, but he visited Paris and London. What London meant to him we do not know, but Paris meant the most radical innovators of Europe – the Odéon, the Théâtre Feydeau, the rue des Colonnes. Gilly died too young to build more than negligibly, but his

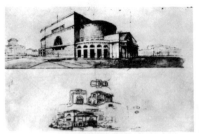

Sketch for a National Theatre in Berlin,
1798, by Gilly

designs for a National Monument to Frederick
the Great and for a National Theatre prove
him to be one of the few architects of genius
of the period.

SCHINKEL was his pupil, again one of the
greatest of the period in all Europe, less bril-

and Finland. Later in life he experimented
with more original forms – centrally planned
churches, façades of public buildings of exposed brick and functional bareness (Academy of Building of 1832–5, designs for a
library and a bazaar). When he visited
England in 1826, his principal interest was
industrial products and the new huge mills.

KLENZE, Schinkel's opposite number in
Bavaria, was more accommodating but
equally resourceful. His œuvre already comprises the full HISTORICISM of the nineteenth
century; the Greek Glyptothek and Walhalla,
the Quattrocento and Cinquecento parts of
the Royal Palace, the Early Christian of the
church of All Saints, the originality of the
Hall of Liberation above Kelheim. As for C19
historicism Germany made the Rundbogenstil
one of her specialities. In the Italian Renaissance vein SEMPER did such beautiful build-

Neue Wache, Berlin, 1816, by Schinkel

liantly endowed perhaps, but of rare competence and as resourceful as Gilly. He started
as a painter, especially as a theatrical painter,
in the romantic vein. His design of 1810 for a
mausoleum for Queen Louise is Gothic. When
after Napoleon's defeat building started again,
he built in a pure but highly original Grecian.
The Old Guard House, the Theatre, the Old
Museum (all in Berlin and all designed in
1816–22) are among the noblest of the
Greek Revival anywhere. He became Superintendent of Building in Prussia and his
influence stretched far, even into Scandinavia

ings as the Dresden Gallery (1847 etc.) and
the Dresden Opera. The difference between
the first and the second Opera (1837 etc. and,
after a fire, 1871 etc.) is that between C19 neo-
Renaissance and neo-Baroque. The neo-
Baroque appeared at its best in Paul Wallot's
Houses of Parliament (1884 etc.). Compare
then the Parliament with Ludwig von Hoffmann's Supreme Court at Leipzig (1887 etc.),
and you will get a first idea of the development from ornateness to simplicity.

Germany was indeed one of the leading
countries in overcoming historicism and

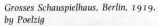

*Grosses Schauspielhaus, Berlin, 1919,
by Poelzig*

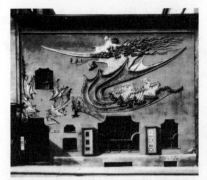

Atelier Elvira, Munich, 1897–8, by Endell

Centennial Hall, Breslau, 1912–13, by Berg

*Fagus Works, Alfeld, 1910–14,
by Gropius and Meyer*

establishing the new functional style of the c20. The key works are Peter BEHRENS's of c. 1904–14, buildings including the famous factories for the AEG and also their industrial products. For his Austrian colleagues see AUSTRIAN ARCHITECTURE. Behrens's pupils were GROPIUS and MIES VAN DER ROHE. Gropius's *magnum opus* remains the BAUHAUS building at Dessau, Mies's greatest work was done after his emigration to Chicago. Other leaders in the so-called INTERNATIONAL

Bauhaus, Dessau, 1925–6, by Gropius

Haus der Deutschen Kunst, Munich, 1933–37, by P. L. Troost

Sketch of the Philharmonic, Berlin, 1963, by Scharoun

Tent roof of Olympic Stadium, Munich, 1972, by Behnisch and others

Phönix Rheinrohr Building, Düsseldorf, 1957–60, by Hentrich and Petschnigg

MODERN were Max Berg of the Centennial Hall at Wroclaw (Breslau) of 1913 – the first (apart from bridges) to take into account the possibilities of arcuated concrete – and MENDELSOHN of the Einstein Tower of 1918–20.

But the Einstein Tower is pre-the-International-Modern of Mendelsohn. It belongs to that Expressionism which for a brief moment even Gropius and Mies fell victim to. Most convincedly Expressionist in the years about 1920 were POELZIG (Grosses Schauspielhaus Berlin 1919), Häring (Garkau farm buildings 1923) and SCHAROUN.

Scharoun's is an interesting case. His Expressionism disqualified him for the years of International Modern. Only when the neo-sculptural, individualistic, chunky-concrete style of the fifties and sixties replaced the disciplined, often neutral International Modern – and Germany was late in making the change set off originally by LE CORBUSIER – did Scharoun come into his own. The Berlin Philharmonic Hall of 1956–63 is supreme proof. Frei OTTO with his brilliant suspended roofs is now continuing in this neo-Expressionism. EIERMANN led the other, the Miesian side. He died in 1970.

Lit: G. Dehio, *Geschichte der deutschen Kunst,* Berlin 1921–31; E. Hempel, *Geschichte der deutschen Baukunst,* Munich 1949.

Giant Order, *see* COLOSSAL ORDER.

Gibberd, Sir Frederick (b. 1908). One of the first in England to accept the INTERNATIONAL MODERN style of the 1930s (Pulman Court,

Streatham, London, 1934–5). His best-known works after the Second World War are the plan and some of the chief buildings for the New Town of Harlow (1947 etc.); the Lansbury Market at Poplar, London (1950–1); and the buildings for London Airport (1950 etc.).
Lit: M. Webb, Architecture in Britain Today, London 1969; R. Maxwell, New British Architecture, London 1972.

Gibbs, James (1682–1754). The most influential London church architect of the early C18. In contrast to his predominantly Whig and neo-Palladian contemporaries, he was a Scot, a Catholic, and a Tory with Jacobite sympathies, and had the unique advantage of training under a leading Italian architect, Carlo FONTANA. Born in Aberdeen, he went to Rome c. 1703 to study for the priesthood, but left the Scots College after a year. He stayed on in Rome until 1709, and appears to have studied painting before turning to architecture. His first building, St Mary-le-Strand, London (1714–17), is a mixture of WREN and Italian Mannerist and Baroque elements. Rather surprisingly, he was then taken up by Lord BURLINGTON, though only to be dropped in favour of Colen CAMPBELL, who replaced him as architect of Burlington House. He had no further contact with the neo-Palladians and remained faithful to Wren and his Italian masters, although he absorbed into his eclectic style a few Palladian features. St Martin-in-the-Fields, London (1722–6), is his masterpiece, and was widely imitated, especially in its combination of temple-front portico and steeple rising from the ridge of the roof. The monumental side elevations of recessed giant columns and giant pilasters have windows with his characteristic GIBBS SURROUND.

His best surviving secular buildings are outside London: the Octagon, Twickenham (1720); Sudbrooke Park, Petersham (c. 1720); Ditchley House (1720–5); and the Senate House (1722–30) and King's College Fellows' Building at Cambridge (1724–49). Several of these display his ebulliently Italian Baroque style of interior decoration at its sumptuous best. His last and most original building, the Radcliffe Library, Oxford (1737–49), is unique in England in showing the influence of Italian Mannerism. He exerted great influence both in Britain and in America through his Book of Architecture (1728), one of the plates from which probably inspired the White House in Washington.

Lit: B. Little, The Life and Work of James Gibbs, London 1955; J. Summerson, Architecture in Britain, 1530–1830, Pelican History of Art, Harmondsworth 1969, paperback edn 1970; K. Downes, English Baroque Architecture, London 1966.

Gibbs surround The surround of a doorway or window consisting of alternating large and small blocks of stone, quoinwise, or of intermittent large blocks; sometimes with a narrow raised band connecting up the verticals and along the face of the arch. Named after the architect James GIBBS though used by other architects, e.g. PALLADIO, CAMPBELL.

Gil de Hontañón, Juan (d. 1526), and Rodrigo (d. 1577), father and son. Juan is the designer of the last two Gothic cathedrals of Spain, Salamanca and Segovia: at Salamanca he was consulted in 1512 (with eight others) and made master mason; at Segovia he started the new building in 1525. An earlier work of his is the cloister of Palencia Cathedral (begun 1505). He was consulted in 1513 for Seville Cathedral and designed the new lantern, etc., also still Gothic (1517–19).

Rodrigo appears first in 1521 at Santiago, probably as an assistant of JUAN DE ÁLAVA; then, in 1526, as one of the five architects consulted on the projected vast collegiate church of Valladolid (the others are his father, his master, FRANCISCO DE COLONIA, and Riaño). He was master mason at Astorga Cathedral (1530 etc.), where he built the nave; at Salamanca Cathedral (1537 etc.), where the transepts must be his; at the cloister of Santiago (1538 etc.), where he followed Álava; at Plasencia Cathedral (1537 or 1544), where the contributions of various masons are obscure; and at Segovia Cathedral (1563 etc.), where the east end is his. His finest secular work is the PLATERESQUE façade of Alcalá University (1541–53). He also wrote a book on architecture which is known only at second-hand. (For illustration see SPANISH ARCHITECTURE.)
Lit: F. Chueca Goitia, Arquitectura del siglo XVI (Ars Hispaniae, vol XI), Madrid 1953; G. Kubler & M. Soria, Art and Architecture in Spain and Portugal and their American Dominions, 1500–1800, Pelican History of Art, Harmondsworth 1959.

Gilbert, Cass (1859–1934). He designed the Woolworth Building in New York (1913) which until 1930 was the highest building in

America (792 ft). With its Gothic details it still belongs to HISTORICISM.

Gill, Irving John (1870–1936). American architect, working – after a training period in Chicago under SULLIVAN – in California. He started his own practice at San Diego in 1896. His early buildings belong to the SHINGLE STYLE, but later he created his own style, emphatically cubic and with large concrete blocks. It is the Spanish Missions Style of California that must have inspired him. The Dodge House of 1916 at Los Angeles illustrates this idiom of his. It is curiously similar to the most advanced European work of the same years.

Lit: E. McCoy, *Five Californian Architects*, New York 1966; D. Gebhard & R. Winter, *Architecture in Southern California*, Los Angeles 1965.

Gilly, Friedrich (1772–1800), came of a French Huguenot family which had moved to Berlin in 1689, and was the son of the architect David Gilly. In spite of his neo-classical convictions he started as a Gothic enthusiast, drawing the Marienburg in West Prussia (1794). The king bought one of the drawings and gave young Gilly a four-year travel grant which, because of the war, he could not take up. In 1796 the idea of a national monument for Frederick the Great was revived. The king had died in 1786, and in the following year the monument had first been suggested: Christian Genelli at once submitted a Greek Doric temple, a very early case of faith in Grecian ideals (*but see* LEDOUX and SOANE). Gilly now designed a great funerary precinct and in its centre, raised on a high platform, a much larger Greek Doric temple – a Parthenon for the Prussian king. The precinct is strikingly original and strikingly severe in its forms. It is true that Gilly leant on the most recent work of young Parisian architects and their model PIRANESI (e.g., in the tunnel-vaulted triumphal arch), but the absolutely unmoulded cubic shapes are all his.

The year after, he took up his grant, but went to France and England instead of Italy: what he drew in Paris shows the sympathies already indicated by the monument. On his return in 1798 Gilly was made Professor of Optics and Perspective at the newly founded Academy of Architecture. In the same year he did his design for a national theatre for Berlin; in spite of certain motifs derived from Paris it is perhaps the most unimitative design

of the age. It seems easier to reach the C20 from this unrelieved geometrical shape than from anything between Gilly and 1890. The functions of the various parts of the building are made perfectly clear, and the semicircular front in particular, taken from Legrand and Molinos's Théâtre Feydeau (which Gilly drew in Paris), was handed by him to Moller (Theatre, Mainz, 1829), and from there reached SEMPER. (For illustration *see* GERMAN ARCHITECTURE.)

Lit: A. Oncken, *F. Gilly*, Berlin 1935; A. Rietdorf, *F. Gilly*, Berlin 1940.

Giocondo, Fra (c. 1433–1515). A Dominican friar, born in Verona. The Palazzo del Consiglio, Verona (1476–93), with its elegant Renaissance arcade and its two-light windows on the first floor placed in a Gothic manner above the columns, has been attributed to him. He was in Paris 1495–1505. In 1511 he published the first illustrated edition of VITRUVIUS. Appointed architect to St Peter's with RAPHAEL in 1514, he produced a very elaborate plan (unexecuted).

Lit: R. Brenzoni, *Fra Giovanni Giocondo*, Florence 1960.

Giotto di Bondone (c. 1266–1337) was appointed master mason to the cathedral and city of Florence in 1334 on account of his fame as a painter. His architectural work was limited to the campanile of the cathedral, which he began in that year. The design was altered after his death.

Lit: D. Gioseffi, *Giotto architetto*, Milan 1963; M. Trachtenberg, *The Campanile of Florence Cathedral: 'Giotto's Tower'*, New York 1971.

Giuliano da Maiano (1432–90). He was the elder brother of BENEDETTO DA MAIANO. He began as a woodcarver (choirstalls in Pisa Cathedral, cupboards in New Sacristy, Florence Cathedral, 1463–5) but later worked mainly as an architect and was appointed architect to Florence Cathedral from 1477 until his death. He helped to diffuse the Early Renaissance style of BRUNELLESCHI and MICHELOZZO throughout Tuscany and beyond to the Marches and Naples. He designed the chapel of S. Fina in the Collegiata at S. Gimignano (1466), Palazzo Spannochi, Siena (c. 1473) and Palazzo Venier, Recanati (1477, much altered later). His masterpiece is the cathedral of Faenza. Palazzo Venezia, Rome, has been erroneously attributed to him. His most remarkable work was the enormous palazzo-villa of Poggioreale at Naples (1487-8, destroyed) though Francesco di Giorgio and others may have contributed to the conception. The Porta Capuana at Naples was designed by him *c.* 1485. The Palazzo Cuomo in Naples (1464-90, now the Museo Filangieri) has been attributed to him, as have the Piccolomini, Terranova and Tolosa chapels in the Chiesa di Monteoliveto in Naples.

Lit: L. Cendali, *Giuliano e Benedetto da Maiano,* Florence 1926.

Giulio Romano (Giulio Pippi or **Giulio Giannuzzi,** 1492/9-1546), who was born in Rome, began as both painter and architect in the classical shadow of RAPHAEL, but soon developed a strongly personal and dramatically forceful Mannerist style. His first building, the Villa Lante on the Gianicolo, Rome (*c.* 1518-20, now the Finnish Academy), and the Palazzo Maccarani in Piazza S. Eustachio, Rome (*c.* 1520, now Palazzo di Brazza) already display his originality, especially the Palazzo Maccarani which is extremely wilful and eccentric in its use of the classical repertory of form. (Palazzo Cicciaporci, Rome, was for long attributed to him, erroneously.) In 1524 he went to work for Federigo Gonzaga at Mantua, where all his most notable buildings were constructed. Palazzo del Te (1525-31) was designed for Federigo's honeymoon and as a summer villa. One storey high, it is built around an enormous courtyard and looks on to a garden terminated by a semicircular pilastered colonnade. Much in the plan derives from ancient Rome by way of Raphael's Villa Madama, but the careful interrelation of house and garden is new. Still more revolutionary were the façades: one of them smooth, with the SERLIAN MOTIF repeated as a blind arcade towards the garden; the others excessively rough with irregular rustication. Tuscan columns, massive keystones and wilfully misused classical details (the centre triglyph of each inter-columniation looks as if it had slipped out of place). He decorated the interior with frescoes, mainly of an erotic nature. One room gives a key to his strange personality: it has only one door and no windows and the walls and ceiling are painted to represent the Fall of the Titans, so that the shape of the room is entirely effaced and the visitor finds himself engulfed in a cascade of boulders and gigantic nude figures some 14 ft high.

On the façade of his own house in Mantua (*c.* 1544) he again indulged in a truculently licentious misuse of classical detail, but this time with a different intention. It is elegantly aloof and sophisticated instead of oppressive and neurotic. For the Palazzo Ducale, Mantua, he designed the Cortile della Cavallerizza (*c.* 1539), with coupled twisted columns on the first floor and one wing pierced by arches and square windows to afford a view across a near-by lake. He also designed S. Benedetto Po (Polizone) Abbey church, after 1540, and Mantua Cathedral (1545), with double aisles supported by sturdy Corinthian columns whose repeated drum-beat monotony draws the visitor towards the high altar – another instance of his preoccupation with the effect a building would make rather than with the perfection of its form. (For illustrations *see* ITALIAN ARCHITECTURE and MANNERISM.)

Lit: F. Hartt, *Giulio Romano,* New Haven 1958; L. H. Heydenreich & W. Lotz, *Architecture in Italy, 1400-1600,* Pelican History of Art, Harmondsworth 1974.

Glacis In military architecture, the ground sloping from the top of the parapet of the covered way till it reaches the level of the open country, so that every part of it can be swept by the fire of the ramparts.

Gloriette, *see* EYE-CATCHER.

Godefroy, Maximilien (*c.* 1760-1833). French *émigré* architect who introduced Parisian Neo-Classical ideals to the U.S. He was trained in Paris where he knew the painter J.-L. David and probably LEDOUX. His chief works are the advanced neo-classical Unitarian Church in Baltimore (1807, interior destroyed) and the Commercial and Farmer's Bank in Baltimore (1810) of which only the doorway survives. His masterpiece is the Battle Monument in Baltimore (designed 1810, built 1814-27), the first great civic monument in the U.S. and a precursor of MILLS'S Washington Monuments in Baltimore and Washington. But Godefroy's neo-classical ideals did not prevent him from indulging in neo-Gothic, e.g., the chapel of St Mary's Seminary, Baltimore (1807).

Lit: H.-R. Hitchcock, *Architecture: Nineteenth and Twentieth Centuries,* Pelican History of Art, Harmondsworth 1969, paperback edn 1971.

Gondouin or **Gondoin, Jacques** (1737-1818). French neo-classical architect trained under

J.-F. BLONDEL and at the French Academy in Rome (1761-4), then travelled in Holland and England. His masterpiece is the École de Médecine in Paris (1771-6), designed as a temple of Aesculapius. The street façade is in the form of an Ionic colonnade (correctly Greek in detail) with a triumphal arch motif in the centre giving access to a square court on the far side of which a Corinthian portico leads into the semicircular anatomy theatre covered by a half Pantheon-dome. The building also included a small hospital, library, laboratories, etc. Monumental in design and practical in plan it is one of the finest and most advanced public buildings of its period anywhere. The anatomy theatre became the

Gothic architecture: Reims Cathedral, c13

prototype for the Chamber of Deputies in the Palais Bourbon (1795–7 but rebuilt 1828–33) and for many later legislative buildings including LATROBE'S House of Representatives in the Capitol at Washington. Gondouin established a successful private practice but was ruined by the Revolution and went into hiding. Under the Empire he re-emerged and designed the column in the Place Vendôme, Paris (completed 1810), first of the giant columns to be erected in the early C19 from Baltimore to Leningrad.

Lit: M. Gallet, *Demeures Parisiennes: L'époque de Louis XVI*, Paris 1964.

Gopura The elaborate high gateway to South Indian temples, characteristic of Hindu architecture.

Gopuras at Madurai, India, C17–C18

Gothic architecture The architecture of the pointed arch, the RIB VAULT, the FLYING BUTTRESS, the walls reduced to a minimum by spacious arcades, by GALLERY or TRIFORIUM, and by spacious CLERESTORY windows. These are not isolated motifs; they act together and represent a system of skeletal structure with active, slender, resilient members and membrane-thin infilling or no infilling at all. The motifs are not in themselves Gothic inventions. Pointed arches had existed in ROMANESQUE Burgundy, Southern France, and also Durham. Rib vaults had existed in Durham too; and the principle of flying buttresses as half-arches or half-tunnel vaults under the roofs of aisles or galleries above aisles is also found in French and English Romanesque. Even the verticalism of Gothic churches is only rarely more pronounced

than that of, say, St Sernin at Toulouse or Ely (both Romanesque churches). The earliest completely Gothic building is the lower part of the east end of St Denis Abbey, dating from 1140–4. For the development of the style in France and then in all other countries, *see* FRENCH; ENGLISH; GERMAN; SPANISH; etc. ARCHITECTURE. (Illustrated previous page.)

Lit: P. Frankl, *Gothic Architecture*, Pelican History of Art, Harmondsworth 1962.

Gothic Revival, *see* NEO-GOTHIC ARCHITECTURE.

Grand order, *see* COLOSSAL ORDER.

Gravesande, Arent van 's (d. 1662). A follower of van CAMPEN and a leading exponent of Dutch classicism. His style was already well developed in his earliest known building, the Sebastiaansdoelen in The Hague (1636). His mature work is all in Leyden where he was municipal architect – the Cloth Hall (1639), the Bibliotheca Thysiana and his masterpiece the Marekerk (1638–48), an octagonal domed church with Ionic columns supporting the drum of the dome. He later began a variant of this design in the Oostkerk at Middelburg (1646).

Lit: E. H. ter Kuile in *Dutch Art and Architecture 1600–1800*, Pelican History of Art, Harmondsworth 1966, paperback edn 1972.

Greek architecture Commenting on the buildings on the Acropolis at Athens, Plutarch remarked: 'They were created in a short time for all time. Each in its fineness was even then at once age-old; but in the freshness of its vigour it is, even to the present day, recent and newly wrought.' No better description of the aims and achievements of Greek architects has ever been written. Their ambition was to discover eternally valid rules of form and proportion; to erect buildings human in scale yet suited to the divinity of their gods; to create, in other words, a classically ideal architecture. Their success may be measured by the fact that their works have been copied on and off for some 2,500 years and have never been superseded. Though severely damaged, the Parthenon remains the most nearly perfect building ever erected. Its influence stretches from the immediate followers of its architects to LE CORBUSIER. Greek architecture was, however, predominantly religious and official. Whereas temples and public buildings were of the greatest magnificence,

Parthenon, Athens, begun 447 B.C., *by Ictinus*

private houses seem to have been fairly simple single-storey affairs, built of cheap materials.

The architectural ORDERS arose in connection with temple architecture, the most prominent type of temple being PERIPTERAL. Thereafter the genius of Greek architecture lay not in the evolution of new types of building, but in the steady refinement of details, away from their original stereometric severity. Thus, a suggestion of strength was imparted to the column by making it bulge slightly (ENTASIS), and an upward curvature permeating the Parthenon and the Temple of Zeus from the CREPIDOMA to the ENTABLATURE breathes life and tension into these buildings.

There were two real Orders, in the sense of rules governing the shape and proportion of every portion of a building, Doric on the mainland and to the west, Ionic to the east. Their every detail appears to be a translation of timber construction into stone. In the Doric region the Heraion of Olympia (600 B.C.) demonstrably had wooden-shafted columns, and temples at Thermos and Delphi wooden ARCHITRAVES. VITRUVIUS explains TRIGLYPHS as the protrusion of beam-ends over an architrave. The derivation of the word METOPE indicates that it was the gap between

Metopes from Temple C at Selinus, Sicily, *c6* B.C., *now in the National Museum, Palermo*

two triglyphs. Only at Thermos and Calydon have terracotta panels used for metopes survived from early (c7 B.C.) temples. The MUTULES on the underside of the CORNICES (*geisa*) can be taken as the projecting ends of

Temple of Artemis, Ephesus, c6 B.C.

rafters; the three rows of six GUTTAE adhering to these were probably originally wooden pegs.

With the Ionic Order the columns too go back to wooden posts, and the double VOLUTES of the CAPITAL will have evolved out of bolsters. The three FASCIAE of the architrave are surmounted by DENTILS, which probably derive from the projecting ends of joists. On the Syphnian treasury at Delphi denticulation yields to a figural FRIEZE, a motif taken up by the Ionic buildings of Attica in the C5 B.C. (the Erechtheion and the Temples of Nike and Ilissos in Athens).

The two Orders also differ in plan. For reasons of symmetry the Doric peripteral temple placed a porch (the PRONAOS) not only before the main chamber, or CELLA, but also one behind it (the OPISTHODOMOS) connected with it by a door. The relationship of a cella to its PERISTYLE was not constant: the passages were narrower at the sides than at

the ends. In the classic period the PTERON placed before the pronaos excelled the others in depth (Bassae, Tegea). In the Hephaisteion at Athens and the Temple of Poseidon at Sunion the pteron is differentiated by a frieze running round the inside of it.

The peristyle and cella of an Ionic temple were by contrast rigorously subordinated to a uniform grid. Only the entry-end, the way into the ADYTUM, was distinguished by a wider centre bay. Ionia was characterized by huge DIPTERAL temples with a doubled row of columns on every side and the continuation of the front columns far into the pronaos, creating the impression of a forest of columns (as at Samos, Ephesus, Didyma, Sardis). Figural ornament was employed in Ionia both on columns (*columnae celatae*) and in the form of a frieze on the walls of a cella or on an architrave (as at Didyma). On Doric temples ornament was restricted to the PEDIMENT and to the metopes. Exceptions are the Parthenon, round the outside of whose cella ran a frieze in relief, and the Temple of Apollo at Bassae, where a frieze borne on Ionic half-columns ran round the inside of the cella.

Ignoring Sicily, where huge temples were also begun in the c6 B.C. (Temple G at Selinus and the Olympeion of Acragas (= Agrigento)), the temples of the mainland (Corinth, Delphi, Athens, etc.) in the Archaic period remained relatively small by comparison with those of Ionia. The Doric temple reached its apogee in that of Zeus at Olympia (456 B.C.) whose

Temple of Zeus, Olympia, section

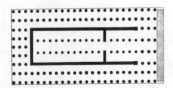

Plan of Temple of Hera IV, Samos, c. 538 B.C.

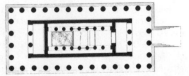

Plan of Temple of Zeus, Olympia, 470–456 B.C.

sturdy forms combined austerity and compactness to produce an incomparable whole, summing up the achievements of the Archaic period.

The only slightly later buildings on the Acropolis at Athens point by contrast far into

Temple of Athena Nike, Athens, 427–426 B.C., by Callicrates

the future. The columns of the Parthenon are slenderer, the capitals slighter, and the extension of the ends from 6 to 8 columns dispels the ponderousness inherent in the Temple of Zeus. The cella reveals a novel feeling for interior space. The base and entablature of Ionic buildings were modified in Athens, where the most complex in plan and elevation and the most richly ornamented (south porch) was the Erechtheion.

From the c5 B.C. onwards the Orders, which had evolved out of temple architecture, found increasing use elsewhere – on fountain-pavilions, gateways, theatres, *bouleuteria* (meeting or council houses), palaestrae, tombs, and most of all COLONNADES, which might

Sanctuary of Athena Pronaia, Delphi, c4 B.C.

even be two-storied in the Hellenistic period. In the late c5 B.C. (Bassae) vegetable ornament invaded columns too, with the Corinthian capital. The c4 B.C. made increasing use of peripteral ROTUNDAS (Delphi, Epidauros, Olympia) and completed the evolution of architectural members. HELLENISTIC ARCHITECTURE developed from the c3 and was thus provided with a rich gamut of components with which to resolve any architectural problem. Columns and their corresponding entablature, ANTAE, pillars, half-columns, pilasters, socles and profiles could now be used independently of their original Order, and survived as the essential components of ROMAN ARCHITECTURE, via which they were transmitted to the Renaissance and Baroque.   [AM]

Lit: D. S. Robertson, *A Handbook of Greek and Roman Architecture*, Cambridge, 2nd edn, 1943; W. B. Dinsmoor, *The Architecture of Ancient Greece*, London & New York 1950; G. Gruben, *Die Tempel der Griechen*, Munich 1966; A. W. Lawrence, *Greek Architecture*, Pelican History of Art, Harmondsworth 1974.

Greek cross A cross with four equal arms.

Greek cross plan, church at Beta Gdyorgis in Ethiopia, probably C13–C14

Greek key, *see* FRET.

Greek Revival Greek as against Roman architecture became known to the West only about 1750–60. It was at first regarded as primitive and imitated by only a few architects. The earliest example is a garden temple at Hagley by 'Athenian' STUART (1758). A Grecian fashion began only in the 1780s. Among the earliest believers in the positive value of the simplicity and gravity of the Greek c5 were LEDOUX and SOANE. The

Greek Revival: Belvedere, Schloss Klein-Glienecke, Berlin, 1836, by Schinkel

Greek Revival culminated in all countries in the 1820s and 1830s, even, with the HANSENS, in Athens itself. (*See also* GILLY, SCHINKEL, SMIRKE, WILKINS, STRICKLAND, HAMILTON, PLAYFAIR, etc.).

Lit: T. Hamlin, *Greek Revival Architecture in America*, New York 1944; P. Collins, *Changing Ideals in Modern Architecture*, London 1965; D. Wiebenson, *Sources of Greek Revival Architecture*, London 1969; J. Mordaunt Crook, *The Greek Revival*, London 1972.

Groin The sharp edge formed by the intersection of vaulting surfaces.

Groin vault, *see* VAULT.

Gropius, Walter (1883–1969). Studied at the Colleges of Technology of Berlin and Munich. He received his introduction to the C20 problems of architecture and the responsibilities of the architect in the office of Peter BEHRENS, who believed in the architect's duty to provide well-designed buildings for working in, and also well-designed everyday products. He spent the years 1907–10 with Behrens. The outcome of this was that Gropius, as soon as he had established a practice of his own (1910), submitted a memorandum to a powerful potential client on the mass-producing of housing and equipment. One year later he built, with Adolf Meyer (1881–

1929), the Fagus factory at Alfeld, one of the earliest buildings in any country to be in full command of the elements of architecture which were to constitute the INTERNATIONAL MODERN style; glass CURTAIN WALLING, unrelieved cubic blocks, corners left free of visible supports. For the Werkbund Exhibition at Cologne in 1914, Gropius produced, also with Adolf Meyer, a Model Factory and Office Building, equally radical in its statement of new principles. Apart from Behrens, Frank Lloyd WRIGHT was now a source of inspiration; for two publications about him had appeared in Berlin in 1910 and 1911. On the strength of the Werkbund Exhibition building, Henri van de VELDE, then head of the School of Arts and Crafts at Weimar, advised the Grand Duke to make Gropius his successor. Gropius accepted and, when the First World War was over, settled down at Weimar to convert the school into a completely new establishment, for which he coined the name BAUHAUS (House of Building). This name alludes to Gropius's conviction that, as with the medieval cathedral, the building ought to be the meeting-place of all arts and crafts teaching; all should work towards this ultimate unity. He also believed that all artists should be familiar with crafts, and that the initial training of artists and craftsmen should be one and the same – an introduction to form, colour, and the nature of materials. This part of the teaching programme, first worked out by Johannes Itten, was known as the Basic Course (*Vorkurs*).

Gropius, in the first years of the Bauhaus, was propelled by the ideas of William MORRIS on the one hand, by the enthusiasm of the Expressionists on the other. There are, indeed, a few works by him belonging to these first years which are entirely Expressionist in style, notably the jagged concrete monument to those killed in the March Rising (1921) and the large log-house for the timber manufacturer Adolf Sommerfeld (1921–2), the latter equipped by Bauhaus staff and students. But then in 1923, stimulated by contacts with the Dutch group of De Stijl (led by Theo van Doesburg), Gropius returned to the ideals of his early years. The Bauhaus turned from emphasis on craft to emphasis on industrial design, and Gropius's own style followed once again the line laid down by the Fagus factory. The principal monument of this change is the Bauhaus's own new premises at Dessau (1925–6), functionally planned and detailed. Other important designs of these flourishing years in Germany are those for a Total Theatre (1926) and the long slabs of 'rational' housing for Siemensstadt (1929).

The rising tide of National Socialism killed the Bauhaus, but Gropius had already left it in 1928. After Hitler assumed power, Gropius left Germany and, following a short spell of partnership with Maxwell FRY in London (1934–7) – the most influential outcome of which was the Impington Village College near Cambridge – he went to Harvard. The Impington College is the first of a type of informally grouped school buildings which after the Second World War focused international attention on England. At Harvard Gropius's principal job was once again teaching. In accordance with his faith in co-operative work he started his own firm as the Architects' Collaborative – a group of younger men working with him in full freedom. Of the achievements of this cooperative the Harvard Graduate Centre (1949) and a block of flats for the Berlin Hansa Quarter (Interbau Exhibition, 1957) may be mentioned. Foremost among Gropius's later work is the United States Embassy at Athens (1957–61). (For illustration *see* GERMAN ARCHITECTURE.)

Lit: S. Giedion, *Walter Gropius*, Milan 1954; Walter Gropius, *Scope of Total Architecture*, New York 1955; M. Franciscono, *Walter Gropius and the Creation of the Bauhaus in Weimar*, Urbana 1971; Ise Gropius & J. Marston Fitch, *Walter Gropius: Buildings, Plans, Projects, 1906–1969*, Exh. Cat. 1972.

Grotesque Fanciful ornamental decoration in paint or stucco, resembling ARABESQUE and

Detail of grotesque decoration

used by the Romans on walls of buildings which, when discovered, were underground (i.e., in 'grottoes'), hence the name. It consists of medallions, sphinxes, foliage, etc., and was much used by painters and decorators from RAPHAEL onwards, especially during the c18.

Lit: N. Dacos, *La découverte de la Domus Aurea et la formation des grotesques à la Renaissance*, London-Leiden 1971.

Grotto An artificial cavern, usually with fountains and other water-works, and decorated with rock- and shell-work. It was especially popular in the c18.

Lit: B. Jones, *Follies and Grottoes*, London 1955.

Grotto at the Villa d'Este, Tivoli, begun 1560

Grubenmann, Johannes and Hans Ulrich, *see* BRIDGE.

Guarini, Guarino (1624–83), was born in Modena and was a Theatine father, well known as a philosopher and mathematician, before he won fame as an architect. (He expanded Euclid and even foreshadowed Monge in his learned *Placita philosophica* of 1665.) Since he was first a mathematician and second an architect, his complex spatial compositions are sometimes difficult to understand by eye alone. But they are as exhilarating intellectually as artistically. All his important surviving buildings are in Turin, where he spent the last seventeen years of his life. His admiration of BORROMINI is very obvious in Collegio dei Nobili (1678) and Palazzo Carignano (1679), especially the latter with its oval saloon and undulating façade in the style of S. Carlo alle Quattro Fontane. To inflate Borromini's miniature church to palatial grandiloquence was daring enough, yet his originality had already carried him even farther in the Cappella della SS. Sindone (1667–90) and in S. Lorenzo (1668–87). Both churches are crowned with fantastic and unprecedented cone-shaped domes. That of SS. Sindone is built of superimposed segmental arches that diminish in span as they ascend, the abstract geometric poetry of this free construction being emphasized by the diaphanous light which filters through the grids. The S. Lorenzo dome is equally unusual: it is composed of interlocking semicircular arches forming an octagon on a circular drum. The inspiration for this odd conception may have come from Hispano-Moresque architecture, perhaps from the similar dome in the mosque of al Hakim at Cordova (A.D. 965). Guarini's structural ingenuity was not confined to domes, and his other experiments, notably those with banded vaults and diagonal, forward-tilted, or three-dimensional arches, were to be very influential in Germany and Austria. None of his important buildings outside Turin has survived: e.g., SS. Annunziata and Theatine Palace in Messina (1660); Ste Anne-la-Royale, Paris (1662 onwards): St Mary of Altötting, Prague (1679); and S. Maria Divina Providencia, Lisbon. His influence was greatly increased by his *Architettura civile*, published posthumously in 1737: engravings from it were known from 1668 onwards.

Lit: R. Wittkower, *Art and Architecture in Italy, 1600–1750*, Pelican History of Art, 3rd edn, Harmondsworth 1973, paperback edn 1973; G. *Guarini e l'internazionalita del barocco*, Conference papers 1968, Turin 1970.

Guas, Juan (d. 1496). A Spanish mason of French descent, probably the designer of S. Juan de los Reyes at Toledo (1476 etc.). Towards the end of his life Guas was master mason of Segovia and Toledo Cathedrals. It is likely that the wildly Late Gothic façade of S. Gregorio at Valladolid is his (1487–96).

Lit: L. Torres Balbás, *Arquitectura gótica* (*Ars Hispaniae*, vol. VII), Madrid 1952; G. Kubler & M. Soria, *Art and Architecture in Spain and Portugal and their American Dominions, 1500–1800*, Pelican History of Art, Harmondsworth 1959.

Guatemalan architecture, *see* MESOAMERICAN ARCHITECTURE.

Guêpière, Pierre-Louis-Philippe de la (*c.* 1715–73). French architect who, alongside PIGAGE, introduced Louis XVI taste and standards into Germany. In 1750 he published *Recueil de projets d'architecture* and in the same year was summoned to Stuttgart where he succeeded Leopoldo Retti as *Directeur des bâtiments* in 1752 and designed the interiors of Retti's Neues Palais (destroyed). His masterpieces are the small and exquisite La Solitude (1763–7) outside Stuttgart and Mon Repos (1760–66) near Ludwigsburg. The interior of the latter was partially modified *c.* 1804 in an Empire style. He returned to France in 1768 but built nothing of note there. His designs for the Hôtel de Ville at Montbéliard were executed after his death with considerable alterations. He published *Recueil d'esquisses d'architecture* in 1762.

Lit: H. Klaiber, *Der Baumeister P. de la Guépière*, Stuttgart 1959.

Guillaume de Sens, *see* WILLIAM OF SENS.

Guilloche A pattern of interlacing bands forming a plait and used as an enrichment on a moulding.

Guilloche moulding on the torus of columns, Erechtheum, Athens, c. 431–406 B.C.

Guimard, Hector (1867–1942), was professor at the École des Arts Décoratifs from 1894 to 1898. He is the best of the French ART NOUVEAU architects. At the beginning of his career (in 1893) he was influenced, it seems, by HORTA. His most remarkable building is the block of flats called Castel Bérenger in Paris (1894–8). The use of metal, faïence, and glass-bricks is bold and inventive, though the exterior is of less interest. On the other hand his Métro stations (1899–1904) are nothing but exterior – open metal arches in extreme Art Nouveau shapes – a daring thing for an architect to design, and perhaps an even more daring thing for a client to accept.

Lit: F. Lanier Graham, *Hector Guimard,* Exh. Cat., New York 1970; S. Cantacuzino in *The Anti-Rationalists* (ed. N. Pevsner and J. Richards), London 1973.

Gumpp, Johann Martin (1643–1739). The most important member of a family of architects working in Innsbruck where he was Hofkammerbaumeister and a pioneer exponent of the Baroque. His main works are the Fugger-Welsberg palace (1679–80), the remodelling of the old Government House (1690–92) and the Spitalkirche (1700–1701). His son **Georg Anton** (1682–1754) followed him as master mason to the Innsbruck court and was responsible for the boldly unconventional Landhaus (1725–8).

Guttae Small drop-like projections carved below the TENIA under each TRIGLYPH on a Doric ARCHITRAVE. (For illustration *see* ORDER.)

Gymnasium (from the Greek *gymnos* = naked). In Ancient Greece originally a place for games and exercise, and for the teaching and training of boys, ephebes and young men. This was soon amplified by a PORTICO, baths, wrestling-arenas (*palaestrae*), running-tracks (*stadia*), and rooms for relaxation (EXEDRAE), later enlarged into auditoria. The heyday of the gymnasium was after the Persian wars, when there were three existing at once in Athens – the Academy, the Lyceum, and the Kynosarges. There was a large one near Priene, and others, partially preserved, at Pergamon and Olympia. English has taken over the athletic, and German and Italian the educational, connotations of the word (cf. also the French *'lycée'*).

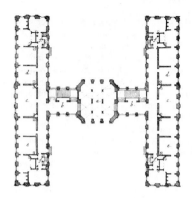

Hadfield, George (*c.* 1764–1826), was born in Leghorn and trained at the Royal Academy Schools, London, winning the Gold Medal in 1784 and studying in Italy 1790–1. In about 1794 he went to America and was appointed in 1795 to supervise the construction of the new Capitol in Washington, replacing Stephen Hallet. He disapproved of the design (by Thornton) and Hallet's revisions, but the radical alterations he suggested, such as the introduction of a colossal order, were not approved and he was dismissed in 1798. He continued to practise in Washington and impressed his neo-classical taste on the new city, e.g., the City Hall, United States Bank, Fuller's Hotel, Gadsby's Hotel, Van Ness's Mausoleum, and Arlington House (*c.* 1803–17) whose imposing Paestum portico is one of the most splendid examples of the Greek Revival in America.

Lit: T. Hamlin, *Greek Revival Architecture in America*, New York 1944; H. M. Colvin, *A Biographical Dictionary of English Architects, 1660–1840*, London 1954.

Hagioscope, *see* SQUINT.

Halfpenny, William (Michael Hoare, d. 1755). His only surviving buildings of note are Holy Trinity, Leeds (1722–7) and the Redlands Chapel, Bristol (1740–43), but he published some twenty architectural manuals for country gentlemen and builders which were enormously successful and influential. His designs are mostly Palladian but also include some rather ham-fisted attempts at Rococo sophistication, CHINOISERIE, GOTHIC REVIVAL, etc. *A New and Compleat System of Architecture* (1749) and *Rural Architecture in*

the Chinese Taste (*c.* 1750) are among the best of his books.

Lit: J. Summerson, *Architecture in Britain, 1530–1830*, Pelican History of Art, Harmondsworth 1969, paperback edn 1970; H. M. Colvin, *A Biographical Dictionary of English Architects, 1660–1840*, London 1954.

Half-timbering, *see* FRAMED BUILDING *and* TIMBER-FRAMING.

Hall church A type of church with AISLES just or virtually as high as the NAVE. The nave is thus no longer lighted from above, but from the correspondingly larger windows of the aisles. The free-ranging spaciousness characteristic of developed churches of this kind ran counter to the pull toward the SANCTUARY inherent in the BASILICA, and thus led finally to the dropping of TRANSEPTS and a distinct CHANCEL. The problems of constructing a roof over nave and aisles of

Hall church, Most (Brüx), Czechoslovakia, 1517–44

the same height produced a number of solutions, some with one monumental roof and others with one roof over the nave, and parallel roofs over each aisle or individual roofs over each bay of the aisles. Whilst isolated examples occurred very early (the first in the CI I – the Chapel of St Bartholomew in Paderborn), this type of church was only brought to a pitch of refinement by Hans STETHAIMER in the late CI4.

Lit: K. Gerstenberg, Deutsche Sondergotik 1913 (1969); E. Finck, Die gotischen Hallenkirchen Westfalens, 1934; W. Krönig, Hallenkirchen in Italien 1938; G. Weise, Die spanischen Hallenkirchen der Spätgotik und der Renaissance, Tübingen 1953.

Hall, Enoch, see BRIDGE.

Hamilton, Thomas (1784–1858), was the leading GREEK REVIVAL architect in Edinburgh alongside W. H. PLAYFAIR. His masterpiece is the Royal High School, Edinburgh (1825–9). It is as forceful and dramatic and as accomplished as any Greek Revival building anywhere. But he was never able to repeat this success and his later work lacks impetus, e.g., the Assembly Rooms, Ayr (1827–30), the Dean Orphanage, Edinburgh (1831–3), the Burns Monument on Calton Hill, Edinburgh (1830) and the ingenious, refined but unconvincing Physicians' Hall, Edinburgh (1843–6). (For illustration see SCOTTISH ARCHITECTURE.)

Lit: A. J. Youngson, The Making of Classical Edinburgh, Edinburgh 1966; J. Mordaunt Crook, The Greek Revival, London 1972.

Hammerbeam, see ROOF.

Hansen, Theophil von (1813–91). A Danish architect who became a leading exponent of CI9 Historicism in architecture, specializing in Italian Renaissance but equally at home with Greek Revival and Venetian Byzantine. He was trained in Copenhagen and travelled to Berlin, Munich, Italy and Greece and settled there, in Athens, for eight years (1838–46). His elder brother **Hans Christian Hansen** (1803–83) had been in Athens since 1833, became the Royal Architect and built Athens University (1839–50) in an appropriate Greek Revival style. Theophil Hansen's buildings in Athens, also Greek Revival, date from some years later – the Academy (1859–87) and Library (1885–92). In 1846 he had settled in Vienna where he spent the rest of

his life. In 1851 he married the daughter of Ludwig Förster, with whom he had collaborated on the Army Museum in the Arsenal in Vienna (1850) and who was mainly responsible for the Ring and the consequent urban development in Vienna. Hansen designed several of the most prominent public buildings on or near the Ring: Heinrichshof (1861–3, destroyed 1945); Musikverein (1867–9); Stock Exchange (1874–7); Academy of Art (1872–6); Parliament (1873–83).

Lit: J. Niemann & F. Feldegg, Theophilus Hansen und seine Werke, Vienna 1893; T. Paulsson, Scandinavian Architecture, London 1958; J. Travlos, Neo-classical Architecture in Greece, Athens 1967; R. Wagner-Rieger (ed.), Die Wiener Ringstrasse, Vienna 1969.

Hardouin-Mansart, Jules (1646–1708), the grand-nephew of François MANSART, by whom he may have been trained, owed more to LE VAU, whose grand manner he and Lebrun brought to perfection in the Galerie des Glaces at Versailles. He understood perfectly the artistic needs of Louis XIV's court and excelled as an official architect, being competent, quick, and adaptable. (He was appointed Royal Architect in 1675, Premier Architecte in 1685, and Surintendant des Bâtiments in 1699.) His meteoric career aroused jealousy, and Saint-Simon accused him of keeping tame architects in a back-room to do all his work for him. He was certainly lucky in having such gifted assistants as Lassurance and Pierre Le Pautre, but he had real ability himself and a vivid sense of the splendour and visual drama required for a royal setting. From 1678 onwards he was in charge of the vast extensions to Versailles. These were disastrous externally, for he filled in the central terrace of Le Vau's garden façade and trebled its length. The stables, orangery, Trianon, and chapel are more successful (the latter being finished by Robert de COTTE). His Baroque tendencies reached their height in the Invalides Church in Paris (1680–91), while the Place Vendôme (1698 etc.) illustrates his genius for the spectacular in town planning. The interior of his Primatiale at Nancy (1699–1736) is among the finest French classical church designs. Towards the end of his life, notably in a number of rooms at Versailles, Trianon, and Marly, which were redecorated under his direction in the 1690s, he veered away from Baroque splendours towards a lighter and more elegant style which marks the first step towards the Rococo. His last work, the Château Neuf at

Meudon (1706–9), combines exterior magnificence with informality and 'commodité' inside. (For illustration *see* PARTERRE.)

Lit: G. Cattani & P. Bourget, *Jules Hardouin-Mansart*, Paris 1956; A. Blunt, *Art and Architecture in France, 1500–1700*, Pelican History of Art, 2nd edn, Harmondsworth 1970, paperback edn 1973.

Hardwick, Philip (1792–1870). He stopped practising in the course of the 1840s. His son and grandson were also architects. In 1815 he was in Paris, and he spent 1818–19 in Italy. His *œuvre* does not seem to have been large, but it is of high quality and varied interest. His most famous building was Euston Station, with its majestic Greek Doric propylaea (1836–9) which became famous when it was infamously destroyed by the British Transport Commission. The station building was quite independent of the propylaea, whose spiritual function was that of a worthy introduction to that miracle of human ingenuity, the London-to-Birmingham railway. The range of stylistic possibilities open to Hardwick was great, and he was remarkably good at all of them: a monumentally plain, strictly utilitarian classicism of brick and short Tuscan columns for the St Katherine's Dock warehouses (1827–8); an at the time most unusual restrained English Baroque for the Goldsmiths' Hall (1829–35); Jacobean for Babraham Hall, Cambridgeshire (1831); and a convincing and unaffected Tudor for Lincoln's Inn Hall and Library (1842–5). On the latter, PEARSON was assistant, and it is possible that the refined detailing is his; at all events, the building is effortlessly convincing and has no longer the character of romantic make-believe of early C19 Tudor imitations.

Lit: H. M. Colvin, *A Biographical Dictionary of English Architects, 1660–1840*, London 1954; A. & P. Smithson, *The Euston Arch*, London 1968.

Harling The Scots term for ROUGH-CAST.

Harmonic proportions A system of proportions relating architecture to music. The Ancients discovered that if two cords are twanged the difference in pitch will be one octave if the shorter is half the length of the longer, a fifth if one is two thirds of the other, and a fourth if the ratio is 3:4. It was therefore assumed that rooms or whole buildings whose measurements followed the ratios 1:2, 2:3, or 3:4 would be harmonious. Early Renaissance architects, notably ALBERTI, seized on this discovery as the key to the beauty of Roman architecture and also to the harmony of the universe. The idea was further developed by PALLADIO who, with the aid of Venetian musical theorists, evolved a far more complex scale of proportions based on the major and minor third – 5:6 and 4:5 – and so on.

Lit: R. Wittkower, *Architectural Principles in the Age of Humanism*, London 1952.

Harrison, Peter (1716–75). The only architect of distinction in pre-Revolutionary America. Born in England, he emigrated in 1740, and settled in Newport, Rhode Island, as a trader in wines, rum, molasses, and mahogany. He presumably taught himself architecture but quickly acquired competence in the Palladian style, as his first work shows – Redwood Library, Newport (1749–58), a timber building imitating rusticated stone. Other buildings show Gibbsian influence: King's Chapel, Boston (1749–58); Synagogue, Newport (1759–63). But he returned to Inigo JONES and the English Palladians for inspiration in his later works: Brick Market, Newport (1761–72), and Christ Church, Cambridge, Mass. (1760). He settled in New Haven, Conn., in 1761, and became Collector of Customs there in 1768, suffering some persecution in his later years as a loyalist and government official. (For illustration *see* UNITED STATES ARCHITECTURE.)

Lit: C. Bridenbaugh, *Peter Harrison, First American Architect*, Chapel Hill, U.S.A., 1949.

Harrison, Thomas (1744–1829). A Yorkshire architect, he designed some of the best and most gravely imposing neo-classical buildings in England. He was trained in Rome (1769–76) but never went to Greece. His masterpiece is Chester Castle, a complex of public buildings on which he worked for most of his life though they were largely designed between 1786 and 1790. He won the commission in competition in 1785. The Prison, Exchequer Court, and Grand Jury Rooms were built 1788–91, the Shire Hall 1791–1801, the barracks and armoury wings 1804 onwards and the great Doric Propylaeum 1810–22. His other buildings include the Lyceum Club, Liverpool (1800–02), the former Portico Library, Manchester (1802–06), and the Knutsford Sessions House (1815–18).

Lit: J. Mordaunt Crook, 'A Most Classical Architect' in *Country Life*, CXLIX, 1971, pp. 944–7.

Hasenauer, Karl von, see SEMPER.

Haunch That part of an arch which extends for some distance above the springing at each side.

Haussmann, Baron Georges-Eugène (1809–91). A Protestant from Alsace who became a lawyer and civil servant. He was ruthless, canny, and obstinate. Napoleon III made him Prefect of the Seine Department in 1853 and entrusted to him his sweeping plans for city improvement. Haussmann kept the post till 1870, and did as much as, or perhaps more than, the emperor expected. Haussmann's improvements follow the traditional principles of French town planning as established by Henri IV and developed by Louis XIV, and finally – Haussmann's direct model – by the so-called Artists' Plan of 1797: long straight boulevards meeting at rond-points are the principal motifs. It is often said that Haussmann made these boulevards to obtain good firing-lines in case of a revolution, but he was at least as much guided by traffic considerations (e.g., the connecting of railway stations) and was also passionately devoted to vistas towards monuments or monumental buildings such as the Arc de Triomphe or the Opéra.

Lit: L. Réau, P. Lavedan, et al., L'œuvre de Haussmann, Paris 1954; G. Lameyre; Haussmann: Préfet de Paris, Paris 1958; H. Saalman, Haussmann: Paris Transformed, New York 1971.

Haviland, John (1792–1852). American architect. He was a pupil of James ELMES and went to live at Philadelphia in 1816. In 1818–19 he brought out The Builder's Assistant, the first American book to illustrate the ORDERS of columns. His magnum opus was the Eastern Penitentiary at Cherry Hill, Philadelphia (1821–9), much imitated in Europe. It has battlements, whereas Haviland's Institute for the Deaf and Dumb (1824) has classical features and The Tombs in New York (1836–8), Law Courts and Prison in one, is neo-Egyptian.

Lit: A. A. Gilchrist, 'J. Haviland before 1816' in Journal of the Soc. of Archi. Historians, vol. 20, 1961; M. Baigell, 'J. Haviland in Philadelphia, 1818–26' in Journal of the Soc. of Archi. Historians, vol. 25, 1966.

Hawksmoor, Nicholas (1661–1736), the most original of English Baroque architects except VANBRUGH, came from a family of Nottinghamshire farmers. At eighteen he became WREN'S amanuensis and was closely associated with him at Greenwich Hospital and other buildings until his death. Vanbrugh also found him an able assistant and employed him from 1690 onwards, notably at Castle Howard and Blenheim Palace. Indeed, he became more than just an assistant to both Wren and Vanbrugh, though it is impossible now to assess how much they owed to him. His independent works have great originality, and only his dour, capricious character and lack of push denied him greater opportunities and worldly success. Vigorous, odd, bookish, yet massively plastic in feeling, his style is a highly personal Baroque amalgam of Wren, classical Rome, and Gothic. Like Vanbrugh, but unlike Wren, his passion was for dramatic effects of mass, and he has been criticized for heaviness as a result. He began working on his own c. 1702 at Easton Neston, a compact rectangular building with a giant order all round; it combines Wren's grandeur and urbanity, and in some details foreshadows Vanbrugh. In 1711 he was appointed Surveyor under the Act for Building Fifty New Churches, and the six he designed himself form the bulk of his oeuvre. All of them are minor masterpieces: St Anne's, Limehouse (1712–24), with its medieval steeple in classical dress; St Mary Woolnoth (1716–27), with its square within a square plan; St George's, Bloomsbury (1720–30), the most grandiose and least odd of all his buildings; and Christchurch, Spitalfields (1723–39), as perverse and megalomaniac as anything by Vanbrugh. His other buildings are only slightly less notable – the quadrangle and hall at All Souls', Oxford (1729), and the west towers of Westminster Abbey (1734), all in his neo-Gothic manner; and finally, the grim and austere circular Doric mausoleum at Castle Howard (1729), where he returned to Rome and BRAMANTE for inspiration.

Lit: K. Downes, Hawksmoor, London 1969.

Header, see BRICKWORK.

Heinzelmann, Konrad (d. 1454), was at Ulm in the 1420s. He was called to Nördlingen in 1429 as master mason to design and build the church of St George, then to Rothenburg in 1428 to work on the church of St Jakob. In 1439 he went to Nuremberg, and designed and began the beautiful chancel of St Lorenz.

Lit: P. Frankl, Gothic Architecture, Pelican History of Art, Harmondsworth 1962.

Helix A spiral motif, especially the inner spiral of the volute of a Corinthian capital.

Helices on Corinthian capital

Hellenistic architecture This style developed in the Hellenistic kingdoms created out of the empire conquered by Alexander the Great (336–323 B.C.), and merged into ROMAN ARCHITECTURE without a definite hiatus in the CI B.C. It carried on the tradition of Classic GREEK ARCHITECTURE, but with the emphasis no longer on detailing but on the creation of larger architectural ensembles. It made great use of COLONNADES, which served to demarcate earlier shrines (Olympia, Delos) and market-places (Athens, Corinth). The succession of variously sized rectangular squares surrounded by colonnades in Miletus was typical. They recur on palaestrae, GYM-NASIA (Priene, Pergamon), heroa (Calydon, Miletus) and even houses, which now experienced an upsurge of importance by being decorated with mosaics and wall-paintings

(Pella, Delos). Even temples, like those of Zeus at Dodona, Megalopolis and Priene, were incorporated into PERISTYLE layouts.

Equally typical of this period was the combination of colonnades and PEDESTALS. The great DIPTERAL Ionic temples (Sardis, Ephesus, Didyma) are raised on many-stepped bases. The MAUSOLEA of Halicarnassus, Belevi, and *ta marmara* (near Miletus) were peripteral temple tombs on high ashlar bases. Altars were likewise often raised on pedestals and enclosed by colonnades, as at Pergamon,

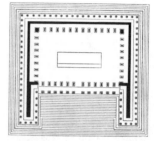

Plan of altar of Zeus, Pergamon

Magnesia, Priene and Cos. They were preceded by an imposing flight of steps – also a Hellenistic feature – and combined with colonnades of especial magnificence at the shrine of Athene at Lindos and the shrine of

Temple of Artemis, Ephesus, mid-C3 B.C.

Altar of Zeus, Pergamon, 180–160 B.C.

Aesculapius at Cos: both these were rigorously symmetrical.

The PSEUDO-DIPTERAL temple now joined those favoured in the Classic Age (Magnesia, Messene), and the Corinthian joined the Doric and Ionic ORDERS (Olympeion, Athens). Other key types of Hellenistic building were the theatre – with PROSCENIA upon colonnades; town halls (*boulesfteria*) of which the ornatest was that of Miletus on account of the peristyle and propylon preceding it; stadia with rows of stone seats; and palaestrae; whereas baths (Gortys in Arcadia, Olympia, Eretria) remained architecturally unambitious. Elaborate defensive works (the Herakleia on Latmos, Miletus, Ephesus etc.) with CURTAIN WALLS frequently punctuated by projecting towers were raised in response to the developments in siege technique in the Diadochene period.

Technical advances included the KEYSTONE ARCH and the TUNNEL VAULT. The latter was mostly used for tombs (Leukadion, Pergamon, Miletus), and very occasionally for substructures (STOA of Attalus, Delphi) or passages (Olympic stadium). [AM]

Lit: W. Zschietzschmann, *Die Hellenistische und Römische Kunst*, Handbuch der Kunstwissenschaft, Potsdam 1939; D. S. Robertson, *A Handbook of Greek and Roman Architecture*, Cambridge 1945; W. B. Dinsmoor, *The Architecture of Ancient Greece*, London & New York 1950; C. M. Havelock, *Hellenistic Art*, London 1972.

Helm roof, *see* ROOF.

Hennebique, François (1842–1921). One of the pioneers of concrete architecture. He first used REINFORCED CONCRETE in 1879. His most important patents are of 1892. In 1894 he built at Viggen in Switzerland the first bridge of reinforced concrete, in 1895 at Roubaix the first grain elevator. His concrete and glass factories begin in 1894. For an exhibition in Geneva in 1896 he built a cantilevered concrete staircase, and for a small theatre at Morges in 1899 cantilevered galleries. In a small theatre at Munich in 1903 he was allowed to leave the concrete frame exposed. His own crazy concrete villa at Bourg-la-Reine dates from 1904.

Lit: P. Collins, *Concrete: The Vision of a New Architecture*, London 1959; N. Pevsner, *Sources of Modern Design*, London 1968.

Henry of Reyns, Master of the King's Masons to Windsor Castle in 1243, and later to Westminster Abbey. He was dead, it seems, by 1253. This means he was King's Master Mason when Westminster Abbey was begun and so was probably its designer. Reyns sounds temptingly like Reims, and Reims Cathedral is, in fact, the stylistic source of much at Westminster (tracery, the wall-passages in the east chapels), together with work at Amiens, Royaumont and the Sainte Chapelle in Paris, only just completed when the abbey was begun. However, there are other features, such as the large gallery and the ridge-rib of the vault, which are entirely English and may make it more likely that Henry was an Englishman who had worked at Reims. Judging by style, Henry may also have designed the King's Chapel at Windsor Castle (built *c.* 1240).

Lit: G. Webb, *Architecture in Britain: The Middle Ages*, Pelican History of Art, 2nd edn, Harmondsworth 1965.

Hentrich, Helmut (b. 1905). Studied at Freiburg, Vienna and Berlin, and in New York under Norman Bel Geddes 1930–31. He was in partnership with Herbert Petschnigg from 1954. Among their most prominent buildings are the Thyssen Building at Düsseldorf (Dreischeibenhaus) of 1957–60, the Aweta Building at Ludwigshafen of 1960–63, the Klöckner-Humboldt Haus at Deutz of 1961–4, the Bonhoeffer Church at Düsseldorf of 1964–5 and the University buildings at Bochum begun in 1961. Their Finland House at Hamburg is the first high block in suspension construction in the whole of Europe.

Héré de Corny, Emmanuel (1705–63). The architect of the Place Royale (Place Stanislas) in Nancy, the finest example of Rococo urbanism anywhere. He was trained under BOFFRAND in Paris but returned *c.* 1740 to Nancy to become architect to Stanislas Leszczynski, ex-king of Poland and successor of the Dukes of Lorraine since 1737, for whom all his work was carried out – Hôtel des Missions Royales (1741–3), Château de Malgrange (1743). Place Royale (1752 onwards, with the Place de la Carrière leading into the Hemicycle) and the Place d'Alliance, all in Nancy. The Place Royale owes much to the superb ironwork by Lamour. Héré published his works in *Recueil des plans*, etc. (1750) and *Plans et elévations de la Place Royale de Nancy* (1753).

Lit: L. Hautecoeur, *Histoire de l'architecture classique . . .*, vols. III & IV, Paris 1950–52; J. Rau, *Emmanuel Héré . . .*, Berlin 1973.

Herland, Hugh (d. *c.* 1405). Carpenter in the king's service probably from *c.* 1350, and in charge of the king's works in carpentry from 1375, when William Herland, presumably his father, died. His *magnum opus* is the hammer-beam roof of Westminster Hall, done in the 1390s; it has a span of about 67 ft. He also worked for William of Wykeham (with WILLIAM OF WYNFORD) at New College, Oxford, and probably at Winchester College.

Lit: J. Harvey, *English Medieval Architects,* London 1954.

Herm Originally, a rectangular pillar terminating in a head or bust (usually of Hermes), used to mark boundaries, etc. in ancient Greece. The form was adopted by Renaissance and Post-Renaissance architects for decorative purposes. *See also* TERM.

Herm figures on the Zwinger, Dresden, 1711–18, by Pöppelmann and Permoser

Hermogenes (*fl. c.* 130 B.C.). Architect and apparently the most influential architectural theorist of the Hellenistic period. He was probably born at Priene where he designed an altar. Critical of the Doric ORDER, because 'the distribution of the triglyphs and metopes is troublesome and unharmonious', he designed two important Ionic temples – that of Dionysos at Teos and the large pseudodipteral temple of Artemis Leukophryne at Magnesia on the Meander. He commented on these works in writings which are lost but were known to and quoted by VITRUVIUS.

Lit: W. B. Dinsmoor, *The Architecture of Ancient Greece,* London 1950; A. W. Lawrence, *Greek Architecture,* Pelican History of Art, Harmondsworth 1974.

Herrera, Juan de (*c.* 1530–97), travelled abroad, mainly in Italy, from 1547 to 1559. He was appointed to succeed Juan Bautista de TOLEDO at the Escorial in 1563, though he did not design any additions until after 1572: the infirmary and chapel (1574–82) were his main contributions. But his majestic if sometimes rather solemn and Italianate style is best seen at the Palace of Aranjuez (1567), at the Exchange at Seville (1582), and in his designs for Valladolid Cathedral (*c.* 1585), which were only partly executed but had enormous influence, e.g., on Salamanca, Mexico, Puebla, and Lima Cathedrals. (For illustrations *see* SPANISH ARCHITECTURE.)

Lit: F. Chueca Goitia, *Arquitectura del siglo XVI* (*Ars Hispaniae,* vol. XI), Madrid 1953; G. Kubler & M. Soria, *Art and Architecture in Spain and Portugal and their American Dominions, 1500–1800,* Pelican History of Art, Harmondsworth 1959.

Herringbone work Stone, brick, or tile work in which the component units are laid diagonally instead of horizontally. Alternate courses lie in opposite directions, forming a zigzag pattern along the wall-face.

Herringbone work

Herringbone work

Hewn stone The American term for ASHLAR.

Hexastyle Of a portico with six frontal columns.

Hildebrandt, Johann Lukas von (1668–1745). The leading Baroque architect in Austria alongside FISCHER VON ERLACH, he was born in Genoa, the son of a captain in the Genoese army and an Italian mother. Italian always remained his first language. He studied with Carlo FONTANA in Rome before settling in Vienna. He was appointed Court Architect in 1700 and knighted by the emperor in 1720. He succeeded Fischer von Erlach as First Court Architect in 1723. His style is lighter than SCHLÜTER'S and more Italianate than Fischer von Erlach's, livelier too and homelier, with typically Viennese charm. He much admired GUARINI, as his early (1699) Dominican church at Gabel in North Bohemia shows. It has Guarini's characteristic three-dimensional arches and a complicated and imaginative Guarinesque plan (concave corners hidden by convex balconies etc.). The influence of BORROMINI is evident in much of the carved decoration of his masterpiece, the Lower and Upper Belvedere in Vienna, built for Prince Eugene (the former completed 1714/15, the latter built 1720–23). His secular buildings are notable for their oval and octagonal rooms (Palais Schwarzenberg in Vienna, begun 1697; Summer Palace Ráckeve in Hungary, 1701–2; Palais Starhemberg- Schönborn in Vienna, 1706–17) and for their ingeniously planned and spatially dramatic ceremonial staircases (Palais Daun-Kinsky of 1713–16 and the Upper Belvedere in Vienna, Schloss Mirabell in Salzburg of 1713–16 and his addition to the Palais Harrach in Vienna of 1727–35). In 1711 he was consulted about the great staircase at Johann DIENTZENHOFER'S Pommersfelden Palace and added the three-storey gallery there. In 1720–23 and again in 1729–44 he collaborated with NEUMANN on the rebuilding of the Residenz at Würzburg, contributing the designs for the lavishly decorated upper part of the central pavilion facing the gardens and the interiors of the Imperial hall and chapel. Though primarily a secular architect Hildebrandt built several churches including the Church of the Seminary at Linz (1717–25) with its boldly *mouvementé* façade, the parish church of Göllersdorf (1740–41) and probably the Piaristenkirche in Vienna (plan dated 1698, begun 1716 but later modified by K. I. DIENTZENHOFER), octagonal in plan and bright, rhythmical and Bor-

rominesque inside. (For illustrations *see* ATLANTES, AUSTRIAN and BAROQUE ARCHITECTURE.)

Lit: B. Grimschitz, *Johann Lucas von Hildebrandt*, Vienna 1932; E. Hempel, *Baroque Art and Architecture in Central Europe*, Pelican History of Art, Harmondsworth 1965.

Hindu architecture, *see* INDIAN ARCHITECTURE.

Hip The external angle formed by the meeting of two sloping roof surfaces. *See* ROOF.

Hipped roof, *see* ROOF.

Hippodamos of Miletus (*fl. c.* 500 B.C.). Town-planner, political theorist and philosopher interested in the problem of urbanism. According to Aristotle (*Politics*), he originated the art of town planning and devised an ideal city to be inhabited by ten thousand citizens, divided into three classes (soldiers, artisans and husbandmen) and with the land also divided into three parts (sacred, public and private). The gridiron plan associated with his name had been in use since the C7 B.C. in Ionia though not in Attica. And his social ideas were hardly forward looking. But he seems to have been the first to appreciate that a town plan might formally embody and clarify a rational social order. He taught the Athenians the value of having a clear, regular and strictly functional town plan instead of the haphazard layouts of archaic Greek towns. He lived in Athens and became a friend of Pericles whose social ideas he appears to have shared. Though not an architect and never in charge of the actual construction of any town, he was probably responsible for the layout of Piraeus (founded by Themistocles *c.* 470 B.C.) on a gridiron system with a formal, enclosed AGORA as its central feature. He possibly inspired the plan of Thourioi (founded 443 B.C.) as a Pan-Hellenic centre. The town plan of Rhodes has been less plausibly attributed to

Hippodamic town-plan, Priene, Asia Minor

him. The gridiron plan was much used in the
later classical and Hellenistic periods. Thanks
to Aristotle he has influenced writers on
urbanism since the Renaissance (e.g. Sir
Thomas More in *Utopia*).

Lit: F. Castagnoli, *Ippodamo di Mileto e
l'urbanistica a pianta octagonale*, Rome 1956;
R. Martin, *L'urbanisme dans la Grèce antique*,
Paris 1956; E. Egli, *Geschichte des Srädtebaus*,
vol. I, Zurich–Stuttgart 1959.

Hirsau School A special form of the German
Romanesque, stemming from the Abbey of
Ss. Peter and Paul at Hirsau in the Black
Forest (1082–91, destroyed), which adopted

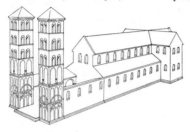

*Reconstruction of abbey church at Hirsau
(after Dehio)*

along with the Cluniac reform of the Benedictine Order, save for a few divagations, the
architecture of Cluny II as its model. The
common ideal of all the buildings in this
group is a simplified structure with minimal

*Benedictine abbey church, Alpirsbach,
begun 1095*

decoration. This took the form of a flat-roofed
columned BASILICA without a CRYPT or
GALLERIES, an extended CHANCEL with sub-
choirs opening off it, a crossing used as the
'*chorus maior*' or '*chorus psallentium*' of the
monks, and the first bay of the nave as the
'*chorus minor*' of the old and sick ones. The
last-named part is often set apart by pillars
which might support a tower (Paulinzella,
1112–32, destroyed), towers on the west
façade being dispensed with. The most important churches of this type to survive are
All Saints', Schaffhausen (from 1087), and
the abbey church of Alpirsbach (consecra-
tion of choir, 1099, finished *c.* 1125).

Lit: W. B. Hoffmann, *Hirsau und die Hirsauer
Bauschule*, 1950.

Historicism The style of architecture reigning
between the end of CLASSICISM and the out-
break of ART NOUVEAU. Its characteristic is
the use of forms of a variety of past styles not
only one after another but also simultaneously.
In fact Gothic side by side with classical,
though much more rarely, had already appeared in the c18 (Strawberry Hill), and very
occasionally some Chinese (CHINOISERIE,
Kew Pagoda). In the work of NASH who died
before Queen Victoria ascended the throne
one finds the Moorish style (Brighton Pavilion),
the Italian Villa style (Cronkhill) and the
COTTAGE ORNÉ (Blaise Hamlet). In the work
of BARRY more styles came to the fore,
and the element of playfulness, unmistakable

*Houses of Parliament, London, 1840–50,
by Barry (Neo-Gothic)*

in Nash, disappeared. The new-comers are the
Tudor Gothic of the Houses of Parliament, the
Italian palazzo style of the Travellers' and
Reform Clubs and the Elizabethan of High-
clere. The palazzo style had already been used
by KLENZE and in fact derived from LEDOUX.
Klenze is as Protean as Barry. His additions to

the Residenz in Munich are Italian, first à la palazzo, then in a free Cinquecento, and the Allerheiligen–Hofkirche in Munich is an Early Christian BASILICA. They date from 1826 etc. The Early Christian can often not easily be distinguished from the Italian Romanesque and in England the Norman. These *Rundbogen*

Sakrow church, near Berlin, 1841–4, by Persius (Rundbogenstil)

The Opéra, Paris, 1861–74, by Garnier (Neo-Baroque)

styles were also developed by SCHINKEL and his school and became a German speciality. Yet another stylistic pattern came from France, the so-called French RENAISSANCE, introduced for the additions to the Paris town hall in the thirties and culminating in the completion of the Louvre in 1852 etc. The style, or rather its most prominent motif, the pavilion roofs, was quickly taken over in England and America. The palace at Schwerin

Lindenhof, Bavaria, begun 1874 (Neo-Rococo)

Tampere Cathedral, Finland, 1902–7, by Sonck (Neo-Romanesque)

Schwerin Castle, begun 1844, by Demmler and Stüler (Neo-French-Renaissance)

of 1844 etc. is a solitary much earlier case of French Renaissancism.

The whole gamut of Historicism on the most monumental scale is the Ringstrasse in Vienna begun in 1859 (*see* AUSTRIAN ARCHI-TECTURE) with public buildings Grecian, Gothic and free Renaissance, the latter pointing forward to the neo-Baroque whose two greatest monuments are the Opéra in Paris by GARNIER (1861 etc.) and the Law Courts in Brussels by Poelaert (1866 etc.)

Late Historicism opening the way into a genuine, independent style of the c20 assumes in England the guise of QUEEN ANNE, in America that of the Romanesque. The leader of the latter style is RICHARDSON, and he had been studying the French Romanesque and architects such as VAUDREMER who worked in a neo-Romanesque.

Total refusal to come to terms with any style of the past begins between 1890 and the First World War in the CHICAGO SCHOOL, in Perret and Tony GARNIER and in WAGNER, OLBRICH, BEHRENS and GROPIUS.

Lit: N. Pevsner, L. Grote, *et al., Historismus und bildende Kunst,* Munich 1965.

Hittorf, Jakob Ignaz (1792–1867), was born at Cologne, went to Paris in 1810 with GAU and placed himself under PERCIER. He then worked under BELANGER just at the time when the latter was busy with the glass-and-iron dome of the Corn Market. In 1819–23 Hittorf travelled in Germany, England, and Italy. After that, till 1848, he was Royal Architect. His first major building, executed with his father-in-law Lepère, is St Vincent de Paul (begun 1824), still with an Ionic portico, but Early Christian rather than classical inside, with its two superimposed orders and its open roof. The exterior already shows the change from the pure classical to the new, grander, more rhetorical classical of the École des Beaux Arts as it culminated in Hittorf's Gare du Nord (1861–5). He also did extensive decorative work; laid out the Place de la Concorde in its present form (1838–40); built two Circuses (des Champs Élysées, 1839; Napoléon, 1851) with iron-and-glass domes; and, with Rohault de Fleury and Pellechet, designed the Grand Hôtel du Louvre – all of which proves his interest in new functions and new materials. Hittorf also made a name as an archaeologist, chiefly by his discovery of the polychromy of Greek architecture (1830), a 'Victorian' discovery shocking to the older generation of Grecian purists.

Lit: K. Hammer, *Jacob Ignaz Hittorf, ein Pariser Baumeister, 1792–1867,* Stuttgart 1968.

Hoban, James (c. 1762–1831), was born in Ireland, emigrated to America after the Revolution, and was advertising in Phila-delphia in 1785. But he settled in South Carolina until 1792, designing the State Capitol at Columbia (completed 1791, burnt down 1865), based on L'ENFANT's designs for the Federal Hall in New York. But he is remembered chiefly for the White House, Washington, which he designed in 1792, basing the front on a plate in GIBBS's *Book of Architecture.* He may also have had Leinster House, Dublin, in mind, though the White House is not, as has been suggested, a mere copy. It was built 1793–1801, and Hoban also supervised its rebuilding after 1814 (completed 1829). He also designed and built the Grand Hotel (1793–5) and the State and War Offices (begun in 1818), Washington. He ended his life as a solid and much respected councillor of that city.

Lit: F. Kimball, 'The Genesis of the White House' in *Century Magazine,* February 1918; W. Andrews, *Architecture, Ambition and Americans,* New York 1947.

Hoffmann, Josef (1870–1956), was a pupil of Otto WAGNER in Vienna and one of the founders of the Wiener Werkstätte (1903), based on the William MORRIS conviction of the importance of a unity between architecture and the crafts. His style developed from ART NOUVEAU towards a new appreciation of unrelieved square or rectangular forms ('Quadratl-Hoffmann') – a change not uninfluenced by MACKINTOSH, whose furniture and other work had been exhibited by the Secession (*see* OLBRICH) in 1900. The Convalescent Home at Purkersdorf outside Vienna (1903) is one of the most courageously squared buildings of its date anywhere in the world, and yet it possesses that elegance and refinement of detail which is the Viennese heritage. With his Palais Stoclet in Brussels (1905–11) Hoffmann proved that this new totally anti-period style of unrelieved shapes could be made to look monumental and lavish by means of the materials used – in this case white marble in bronze framing outside, mosaics by Gustav Klimt inside. Hoffmann later built many wealthy villas, some Austrian Pavilions for exhibitions, and also some blocks of flats, but his chief importance lies in his early works. (For illustration *see* BELGIAN ARCHITECTURE.)

Lit: A. Weiser, *Josef Hoffmann,* Geneva 1930; E. E. Sekler, 'The Stoclet House by Josef Hoffmann' in *Essays in the History of Architecture, presented to R. Wittkower,* London 1967.

Holabird & Roche William Holabird (1854–1923) went to West Point in 1873–5 and to Chicago in 1875, where he took an engineering job in the office of W. Le B. JENNEY. In 1880 he formed a partnership with Martin Roche. Their Tacoma Building (1887–9), following Jenney's Home Insurance and going decisively beyond it, established steel-skeleton construction for SKYSCRAPERS (in this case of twelve storeys) and with it the Chicago School style. Their Marquette Building (1894) has the same importance stylistically as the Tacoma Building has structurally. Its horizontal windows and its crisp, unenriched mouldings pointed the way into the c20.

Lit: C. W. Condit, *The Chicago School of Architecture*, Chicago–London 1952; C. W. Condit, *American Building Art: the nineteenth century*, New York 1960; J. Burchard & A. Bush-Brown, *The Architecture of America*, Boston–Toronto 1961.

Holford, Sir William, was born 1907 in South Africa. The leading town-planner in England, he is also widely recognized abroad, as witness his report on the development of Canberra (1957–8) and his presence on the jury for Brasilia (1957). In England his most brilliant design is that for the precinct of St Paul's Cathedral in London (1955–6), now completed, with some unfortunate modifications. He was also responsible for the post-war plan for the City of London (with Charles Holden, 1946–7).

Lit: R. Maxwell, *New British Architecture*, London 1972.

Holl, Elias (1573–1646). The leading Renaissance architect in Germany where he holds a position parallel historically to that of his exact contemporaries Inigo JONES in England and de BROSSE in France and to the slightly younger van CAMPEN in Holland. He came of a family of Augsburg masons who had risen to prominence working for the Fuggers. He travelled in Italy, visiting Venice 1600–1601 and presumably studying PALLADIO and other Italian architects. In 1602 he was appointed city architect of Augsburg where he was responsible for a large building programme including houses, warehouses, guildhalls, market halls for the various trades, schools, gates and towers for the city walls, the arsenal and the town hall. As a Protestant he suffered from the religious wars and was out of office 1630–32 and finally dismissed in 1635. His first building after his nomination as city

architect was the Arsenal, begun 1602. He believed in symmetry and classical proportions – e.g., St Anne's School (1613) with its high arcades encircling the court, regular fenestration, horizontal emphasis and remarkably well-designed classrooms lit from both sides; and the Hospital of the Holy Ghost (1626–30) which had high arcades encircling a court. But his masterpiece is the Town Hall (1615–20, damaged in the Second World War but rebuilt), a handsome, simple, rather severe building, much in advance of anything previously built in Germany. His aim was, he said, 'to obtain a bolder, more heroic appearance' and he claimed it was well proportioned. His first, unexecuted, design for it was more advanced stylistically than that built and made much play with Palladian windows almost in the manner of Palladio's Basilica in Vicenza. As built it is distinctly German in its verticality, especially in the central section of the façade which contrasts strikingly with the more classically pure bays on either side. His work outside Augsburg was less important but includes additions to the Willibaldsburg at Eichstätt (1608) and, probably, the designs for the Schloss at Bratislava (Pozsony: Pressburg, 1632–49). (For illustration *see* GERMAN ARCHITECTURE.)

Lit: J. Baum, *Die Bauwerke des E. Holl*, Strassburg 1908; Hieber, *Elias Holl*, Munich 1923; E. Hempel, *Baroque Art and Architecture in Central Europe*, Pelican History of Art, Harmondsworth 1965.

Holland, Henry (1745–1806), began under his father, a Fulham builder, then became assistant to 'Capability' BROWN, whose daughter he married. His first independent work, Brooks's Club, London (1776–8), was quickly followed by his greatest, Carlton House, London, which he enlarged and altered for the Prince of Wales (1783–5, demolished). Also for the Prince of Wales he built the Marine Pavilion at Brighton (1786–7), later transformed into the Royal Pavilion by NASH. His style owed something to both CHAMBERS and ADAM, with various Louis XVI elements added. Though lacking originality, the refined taste and 'august simplicity' of his interior decoration approached French neoclassicism in elegance. His best country houses are Southill (1795) and Berrington Hall (1778). He laid out and built Hans Town, Chelsea (1771 etc.), but this has been largely rebuilt.

Lit: D. Stroud, *Henry Holland*, London 1966.

Holy Sepulchre One of a variety of structures and sculptural groups recreating the places and incidents of Christ's Passion – in this case the tomb of Christ as rediscovered by Constantine. This was encased by Constantine in a miniature temple placed in a round (or polygonal?) church, both razed and rebuilt many times since. Imitations (sometimes only in general form) of both shrine and church inevitably followed; at first, by association, as cemetery chapels (earliest at Fulda, 820–21), and then in connection with the dramatic liturgies of Easter Week. The actual shrine was most commonly copied in Germany (notably at Constance, of the c13,

Holy Sepulchre: Minster, Constance, late c13

and Görlitz, 1481–1504) and Italy (e.g. ALBERTI'S *tempietto* in the Rucellai chapel, Florence, *c.* 1460), whilst England produced the variant of EASTER SEPULCHRES and a number of round churches (e.g. at Cambridge and Northampton), and France had a late flowering of Entombment groups. After the Reformation, only Germany kept the tradition alive up to the end of the c18, with special altars and stage sets brought out to make tableaux of the Sepulchre each Easter.

Lit: 'Das Grab des Welterlösers in seinen mittelalterlichen Nachbildungen', in *Kirchen-*

schmuck, 1895; Neil C. Brooks, *The Sepulchre of Christ in Art and Liturgy*, 1921; Ph. Halm, 'Heilige Gräber des 18 Jhs.', in *Die Christliche Kunst*, 1964/65.

Honduras architecture, *see* MESOAMERICAN ARCHITECTURE.

Hood, Raymond (1881–1934). His McGraw-Hill Building in New York (1931) is one of the first skyscrapers designed in the INTERNATIONAL MODERN style. In his Daily News Building (1930) he stressed the closely set verticals, and this must have inspired the Rockefeller Center (begun 1931).

Lit: A. H. North, *Raymond Hood*, New York–London 1931; J. Burchard & A. Bush-Brown, *The Architecture of America*, Boston–Toronto 1961; W. H. Kilham, *Raymond Hood: Architect of Ideas*, New York 1973.

Hood-mould A projecting moulding to throw off the rain, on the face of a wall, above an arch, doorway, or window; can be called *dripstone* or *label. See also* LABEL-STOP.

Hood-mould

Hornwork In military architecture, an outwork of two demi-bastions connected by a curtain and joined to the main work by two parallel wings.

Horseshoe arch, *see* ARCH.

Horta, Baron Victor (1861–1947), a Belgian architect, studied in Paris in 1878–80, then at the Brussels Academy under Balat. He appeared in the forefront of European architecture with his Hôtel Tassel in the rue Paul-Émile Janson (designed 1892). This is the same year as that of van de VELDE'S first exploration of ART NOUVEAU typography and design. The Hôtel Tassel is less startling externally, but its staircase with exposed iron supports, floral iron ornament, and much linear decoration on the wall is Art Nouveau architecture of the boldest. The Hôtel Tassel was followed by the particularly complete and lavish Hôtel Solvay (1895–1900); the Maison du Peuple (1896–

9), with a curved glass-and-iron façade and much structural and decorative iron inside the great hall (destroyed); the store L'Innovation (1901; destroyed); and several more private houses. Later Horta turned to a conventional classicism (Palais des Beaux Arts, Brussels 1922–9). (For illustration *see* ART NOUVEAU.)

Lit: F. Borsi & P. Portoghesi, *Victor Horta*, Brussels 1970.

Hôtel In France a town-house of which the standard design was established by SERLIO'S 'Grand Ferrare' in Fontainebleau (1544–6), i.e., a *corps-de-logis* with narrower wings forming a courtyard which is enclosed towards the

Le Grand Ferrare, Fontainebleau, 1544–6, by Serlio

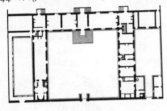

Hôtel Matignon, Paris, begun 1721, by Courtonne

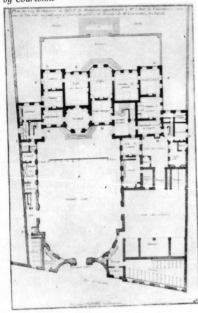

street by a wall or by a stable and kitchen block, broken in the middle by the entrance doorway. The best surviving early example is the Hôtel Carnavalet in Paris by LESCOT of c. 1545. It was usual to have a garden or small park behind the *corps-de-logis*. The latter often contained a gallery on the first floor. MANSART's Hôtel de la Vrillière, Paris (1635–45) became the model for the classical type of Parisian hôtel.

Howard, Sir Ebenezer (1850–1928), started as a clerk in the City of London, rose to be a valued shorthand writer, and remained that nearly to the end. During a stay of five years in America (1872–7), he learned to know and admire Whitman and Emerson, and began to think of the better life and how it could be made to come true. In 1898 he read Edward Bellamy's utopian work *Looking Backward*, and this gave him the idea of his lifetime: that of the garden city which is an independent city and not a suburb – this is important – and is placed in the green countryside and provided with countrified housing as well as industry and all cultural amenities. His book *Tomorrow* came out in 1898, in 1899 the Garden City Association was founded, in 1902 the book was republished as *Garden Cities of Tomorrow*, and in 1903 Letchworth was started, to the design of Parker & UNWIN. This was the earliest of the garden cities and greatly influenced the post-war SATELLITE TOWNS of Britain. Howard was knighted in 1927.

Lit: D. Macfadyen, *Sir Ebenezer Howard and the Town Planning Movement*, London 1933.

Howe, William (1886–1955). Designed in collaboration with William Lescaze (born 1896) the Philadelphia Savings Fund Building (1932), one of the first skyscrapers in the INTERNATIONAL MODERN style. Another of the *incunabula* is Raymond HOOD's McGraw-Hill Building in New York (1931). (For illustration *see* UNITED STATES ARCHITECTURE.)

Lit: J. Burchard & A. Bush-Brown, *The Architecture of America*, Boston–Toronto 1961; W. Jordy, *The Impact of European Modernism in the Mid-Twentieth Century*, New York 1972.

Huastec architecture, *see* MESOAMERICAN ARCHITECTURE.

Hueber, Joseph (1716–87). Late Rococo architect working in Styria. The son of a Viennese mason, he began as a journeyman mason in Bohemia, Saxony and Central and Southern Germany. In 1740 he took over the architectural practice of Giuseppe Carlone in Graz on marrying his widow. He built the handsome twin towers of the Mariahilfkirche in Graz (1742–4), the pilgrimage church on the Weizberg, with an elaborate interior like a stage-set (1757–76) and completed in 1774 the splendid library which Gotthard Hayberger (1699–1764) had designed for the Abbey of Admont.

Lit: E. Hempel, *Baroque Art and Architecture in Central Europe*, Pelican History of Art, Harmondsworth 1965.

Hültz, Johann (d. 1449), was master mason of Strassburg Cathedral and as such designed the openwork spire with its fabulous spiral staircase. The work was completed in 1439. Hültz was the successor to Ulrich ENSINGER, who built the octagon (the stage below the spire).

Lit: T. Rieger, *La cathédrale de Strasbourg*, Strasbourg 1958; P. Frankl, *Gothic Architecture*, Pelican History of Art, Harmondsworth 1962.

Hungarian architecture Medieval architecture in Hungary reflects the events in various centres of the West. Sometimes inspiration came from one centre, sometimes from more than one. As in other countries the beginnings are tantalizing. A building like Feldebrö of the c10 is mysterious in its stylistic pedigree. It is a square in plan with three apses in the middle of three sides. Should one link it with Germigny-des-Prés? Zalavár of the c9 has three parallel east apses like the contemporary buildings in Switzerland. The Romanesque style is, as one would expect, most closely linked with South Germany and Austria and with Lombardy. The latter appears most clearly in the grand though over-restored cathedral of Pécs with its four towers flanking the west and the

east ends of the nave. The splendid west portal of Ják has German but also North Italian and even Norman elements. The abbey churches of Ják, Lébény and Zsámbék are the most conspicuous Romanesque churches of German descent in Hungary. They have in common a relatively late date (c13), three east apses, two west towers and a west gallery.

West front of St George, Ják, 1256

Choir of St George, Ják, 1256

Plan of Pécs Cathedral, c. 1064

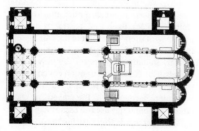

As in other countries the Cistercians and the Premonstratensians brought into Hungary a new plan and new details, all first developed in France. The finest buildings are of the C13. They are Bélapátfalva (founded in 1232), Pannonhalma, the latter (1217–24) not Cistercian, though Cistercian in style with sexpartite rib vaults, and Ócsa with polygonal instead of straight-ended east chapels. Sexpartite rib vaults are a French Early Gothic feature, and the Gothic of, e.g., Noyon is mixed with Romanesque especially Norman detail in the elegant chapel in the castle of Esztergom.

Of the High Gothic style Hungary possesses no major monument.

As for the Late Gothic, it is clearly dependent on South Germany and Austria. The

Internationally speaking the most important phase in Hungarian architecture is that of King Matthias Corvinus (1458–90) and the decades after his death. The king was a patron of Mantegna, Verrocchio, Ercole Roberti, BENEDETTO DA MAIANO and other Italians. His library of illuminated manuscripts in the Renaissance style is unparalleled north of the Alps, and he also favoured the new style in architecture. Earlier than in any country outside Italy – including even France – are the friezes from Buda Castle now in the Castle Museum and the well in Visegrád castle whose stepped terraces, still largely Gothic, are of great magnificence. In ecclesiastic art the Bakócz Chapel in Esztergom Cathedral, begun as early as 1507, is purely Italian.

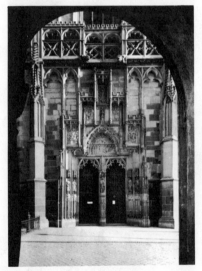

Parish Church, Košiče, 1380–1440

Bakócz Chapel, Esztergom Cathedral, begun 1507

churches are of the HALL type. They are high, with slender piers, sometimes without capitals, and they have complicated figured rib vaults. Examples are Sopron, Koloszvár, and Brassó (chancel). The friars built much in Hungary during these centuries.

Among the castles of Hungary three at least must be mentioned: Buda, where much restoration and reconstruction of the great halls and the chapel is taking place, Visegrád with its mighty keep of *c.* 1260, square with triangular projections on two opposite sides, and Diósgyör of the second half of the C14 which is oblong with an inner courtyard and four prominent angle towers.

After these years of enthusiasm Hungary settled down to a less adventurous later C16 and early C17. The fancy battlements and arcaded courtyards of houses are generally Eastern. The monuments of Turkish domination (mosques, minarets, baths and funerary chapels at Pécs, Eger, Budapest) look odd side by side with them. As a sign of the war against the Turks some fortresses were erected (Györ, etc.) by Italian engineers on the new Italian models. The Turkish occupation ended only in the late C17, and in the C18 Austrian and Bohemian Baroque held the stage. The most interesting buildings are the Eszterházy palace at Eisenstadt across the Austrian border (C. M.

Carlone, 1663–72), Prince Eugene's delightful Ráckeve (Lucas von HILDEBRANDT, 1702) and then St Anne at Budapest (1740 etc.), the

Parliament Building, Budapest, 1885–1902, by Steindl

Eszterhazy Palace, Fertöd, begun 1764

huge Eszterházy palace at Fertöd (1764 etc.) and the Lyceum at Eger (Jacob Fellner, 1765–85).

The turn away from the Baroque in the direction of Neo-classicism was taken early in Hungary. Vác Cathedral by Isidoro Canevale is of 1763–77 and yet, with its giant portico

Parliament Building (I. Steindl, 1885–1902). The revolution against eclecticism which is commonly called ART NOUVEAU had in Ödön LECHNER an exceptionally brilliant representative. The Modern Movement set in as a branch of the style of the Vienna of HOFFMANN and LOOS (B. Lajta). At present the most interesting Hungarian work is in industrial architecture.

Lit: J. Rados, *Magyar Építészettörténet*, Budapest 1961; A. Kampis, *The History of Art in Hungary*, Budapest 1966.

Cathedral at Vác, 1763–77, by Isidore Canevale

Postal Savings Bank, Budapest, 1899–1902, by Lechner

of detached columns carrying a heavy attic and not a pediment and with its central dome and coffered vaults, would be highly remarkable even if it stood in Paris. Neo-classicism culminates in the immensely impressive cathedral of Esztergom (J. S. Pack and J. Hild, 1822 to *c.* 1850) with its central plan, its many-columned dome and its eight-column giant portico, and in the competent but more conventional neo-Greek work of Mihály POLLAK (National Museum, Budapest, 1836–45).

The climax of c19 eclecticism is the richly Italianate Opera at Budapest (M. Ybl, 1875–84) and the surprisingly late Gothic-Revival

Hunt, Richard Morris (1827–95), came of a wealthy early Colonial family. They moved to Paris in 1843, and there Hunt joined LEFUEL'S *atelier* and the École des Beaux Arts. He also worked on painting with Couture and on sculpture with Barye. He travelled widely before he was made an *inspecteur* under Lefuel on the Louvre in 1854. This first-hand knowledge of the French-Renaissance Revival he took back to America in 1855. He settled in New York and, side by side with his practice, ran an *atelier* on the Parisian pattern. But he returned to Europe again in the 1860s and only in 1868 finally came to rest. He designed the Tribune Building in New York (1873, one of the first with lifts), and then rich men's residences at Newport, in New York (W. K. Vanderbilt, 1878 onwards; J. J. Astor, 1893), and elsewhere (Biltmore, Ashville, N.C., 1890). The French Renaissance remained his favourite style. Hunt was also the designer of the Administration Building at the Chicago Exposition of 1893 and the façade of the Metropolitan Museum, New York (built in 1900–2). He was one of the founders of the American Institute of Architects. (For illustration *see* UNITED STATES ARCHITECTURE.)

Lit: A. Burnham, 'The New York Architecture of R. M. Hunt' in *Journal of the Society of Architectural Historians*, May 1952.

Hurtado, Francisco (1669–1725), one of the greatest Spanish Baroque architects. His work is confined to interiors, which are of a fantasy unparalleled in Europe. Born and educated in Cordova, he became a captain in the army and possibly visited Sicily. He may have designed the *camarín* above the Monument of the Counts of Buenavista in the church of Nuestra Señora de la Victoria in Malaga (1691–3). Most of his work is in Granada, where he designed the relatively simple *sagrario* or Sacrament Chapel for the Cathedral (1704–5). The Sacrament Chapel of the Cartuja (1702–20), walled with marble, jasper, and porphyry and containing a marble tabernacle supported by red and black SALOMONICAS, is a masterpiece of polychromatic opulence. He called it 'a precious jewel', and claimed that there was nothing like it in all Europe. In 1718 he designed the very complex *camarín*, liberally decorated with grey-and-coral-coloured marble and lapis lazuli, for the Cartuja of El Paular, Segovia. He has also been credited with the design of the still more bizarrely rich sacristy of the Granada Cartuja (executed 1730–47), where the tendency to muffle the structure in a riotous welter of ornament is taken to its final extreme.

Lit: G. Kubler, *Arquitectura española, 1600–1800* (*Ars Hispaniae*, vol. XIV), Madrid 1957; G. Kubler & M. Soria, *Art and Architecture in Spain and Portugal and their American Dominions 1500–1800*, Pelican History of Art, Harmondsworth 1959.

Hypaethral Without a roof, open to the sky.

Hyperbolic paraboloid roof A special form of double-curved shell, the geometry of which is generated by straight lines. This property makes it fairly easy to construct. The shape consists of a continuous plane developing from a parabolic arch in one direction to a similar inverted parabola in the other. The surface is thus anticlastic, i.e. it has curvatures in opposite senses (concave and convex) in different directions through any point. The name 'hyperbolic paraboloid' derives from the fact that vertical cross-sections of maximum curvature are upwards – or downward – curved parabolas and its horizontal sections paired branches of hyperbolas.

Lit: E. H. Lockwood, *A Book of Curves*, Cambridge 1961.

Hyperbolic paraboloid construction

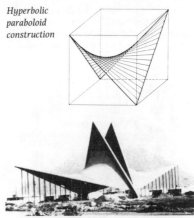

Hyperbolic paraboloid roof: San José Obrero, Monterrey, 1960, by Candela

Hypocaust The underground chamber or duct of the Roman system of central heating by means of air flues.

Hypogeum An underground room or vault.

Hypostyle A hall or other large space over which the roof is supported by rows of columns giving a forest-like appearance.

Hypotrachelium The groove round a Doric column between the SHAFT and the NECKING.

Iconostasis A screen in Byzantine churches separating the sanctuary from the nave and pierced by three doors; originally a lattice of columns joined by a decorated PARAPET and COPING. Since the C14–15 it has become a wooden or stone wall covered with icons, hence the name.

Iconostasis: Kiev, C18

Ictinus The leading architect in Periclean Athens and one of the greatest of all time. With CALLICRATES he designed and built the Parthenon (447/6–438 B.C.), about which he later wrote a book, now lost, with Carpion.

He was commissioned by Pericles to design the new Telesterion (Hall of Mysteries) at Eleusis, but his designs were altered by the three new architects who took over on the fall of Pericles. According to Pausanias he was also the architect of the Doric temple of Apollo at Bassae, begun after the Great Plague of 430 B.C. (For illustration *see* GREEK ARCHITECTURE.)

Lit: R. Carpenter, *The Architects of the Parthenon*, Harmondsworth 1970.

Imbrex In Greek and Roman architecture, a convex tile to cover the join between two flat or concave roofing tiles.

Imhotep (*c.* 2600 B.C.). Ancient Egyptian artists emerge only rarely as distinct personalities, so it is all the more remarkable that we know the name of the architect of the stepped PYRAMID of Saqqâra, the oldest monumental stone structure in history. Imhotep's name (Greek = Imuthes) with his titles of 'Chancellor, Prince, High Priest of Heliopolis, Sculptor' was contemporaneously recorded on a statue of his king Zoser and on the walls surrounding the pyramid of his successor.

He designed the huge complex of the stepped pyramid with its sham buildings, and planned its technical realization, which drew together the cultural achievements of Egypt's early and pre-history, so as to create the basis of EGYPTIAN ARCHITECTURE for the next 2½ millennia.

Owing to this achievement, and probably even more to his capacity as supreme authority over the vast workforce, he was apotheosized after his death into the patron of secular knowledge – that is, of all who were lettered save the priests – and ultimately into a popular god of healing, equated with Aesculapius by the Greeks. (For illustration *see* EGYPTIAN ARCHITECTURE.) [DW]

Lit: J. Ph. Lauer, *L'oeuvre d'Imhotep à Saqqarah*, Paris 1956.

Impluvium The basin or water cistern, usually rectangular, in the centre of an ATRIUM of a Roman house to receive the rain-water from the surrounding roofs. The term is also used, loosely, for the uncovered space in the atrium as well as the water cistern.

Impost A member in the wall, usually formed of a projecting bracket-like moulding, on which the end of an arch rests.

Impost: S. Maria Maggiore in Ferentino, CI4

Impost block A block with splayed sides placed between ABACUS and CAPITAL.

Inca architecture, see CENTRAL ANDEAN ARCHITECTURE.

Indent A shape chiselled out in a stone slab to receive a brass effigy.

Indian architecture The history of Indian architecture falls into four great epochs: (a) the Indus Valley Civilization, *c.* 2500–1500 B.C.; (b) Buddhist, Hindu and Jain, *c.* 250 B.C.– A.D. 1500; (c) Indo-Islamic, *c.* A.D. 1000– 1750; (d) European influence, from *c.* 1800.

1. *Indus Valley Civilization.* Few of the cities of this advanced prehistoric civilization have yet been excavated. Mohenjo Daro and Harappa, the two centres, are on a chequer-board plan. The primary network of main streets through the urban area is widely spaced. A closer mesh of secondary pedestrian routes subdivides the virtually square quarters of the city. The ample scale on which the identical houses were built, a complicated water-supply and drainage system, and sundry communal structures, testify to the sophistication of the inhabitants. The source of the Indus Valley Civilization is as unexplained as its decline. A connection with the civilization of the SUMERIAN cities seems possible.

2. *Buddhist, Hindu, Jain.* The architecture of the three most significant Indian religious beliefs is characterized by the marriage of differing approaches to construction: animal and plant symbolism and megalithic ways of building springing from ancient indigenous cultures and traditions, and confronting these the rigid geometry of the cosmic symbolism of the Aryan invaders. This was ultimately the determinant of the structure of the Vedic fire-altar, and subsequently of the plan of the Buddhist STUPA and the Hindu temple.

Only a few stupas and cave-temples survive from the first heyday of *Buddhist architecture* in the time of Ashoka (C3 B.C.). In origin the stupa was a hallowed sepulchral mound. Buddha instructed his disciples to raise such mounds of earth symbolically at crossroads. In India the stupa took the form of a hemisphere reinforced by gateways at the four points of the compass. Its form symbolizes the Universe, and its vertical axis the axis of the world. Pre-Buddhist solar cults were recalled by surrounding the stupa with a path, a circular railing, and gates at the points of the compass. The largest surviving stupas are those in the sanctuary of Sanchi; their figurally ornate gateways date from the CI B.C. In the cave monasteries of Mahayana Buddhism, stupas from after A.D. 500 are sometimes egg-shaped, and in Northern India bell-shaped. There and in China one part of the stupa, the many-tiered umbrella-like CHATRI on top, broke free to develop into the many-storied PAGODA on its own.

The whole of the palace and temple architecture of the early Buddhist period was of wood, so that not a fragment survives. But forms and details were adopted for the adornment of the cave temples that were built into

Stupa at Buddhist sanctuary at Sanchi, CI B.C.

rock-faces on a diminished scale in the time of
Ashoka, and on a large scale from the C2 A.D.
onwards. Such are Karli (C2 A.D.), Ajanta (C2
B.C.–C7 A.D.), and Ellora. Two types of building are to be encountered in these monastic
settlements – the square-shaped *vihara* (monastery) and the prayer- or *chaitya*-hall. In a
vihara the monastic court and its bordering
colonnades and surrounding ring of cells
were formed as if constructed traditionally in
wood. The chaitya-halls are faithful copies of
their predecessors. In plan and elevation they
resemble an aisled basilica.

By Ashoka's time Buddhism had pene-
trated *Ceylon*, where in its *Hinayana* form
(*Theravada*) it has determined the evolution
of Sinhalese architecture to this day. The
stupa-form – there called *dagoba* – inherited
from the mainland underwent various transformations. Occasionally it was enclosed by a
domical structure of wood. The earliest
monuments (Thuparama dagoba, C3 B.C.;
Ruwanweli dagoba, CI B.C.) lie in the former
capital of Anuradhapura. After a short-lived
conquest of Ceylon by South Indian Hindus,
a new heyday of Buddhist civilization began
in the C12 in the city of Polonnaruwa with the
aid of Burmese monks (Wata-da-ge dagoba
and Gal vihara). The latter monastery contains the most important monolithic statues
in Ceylon – a sitting, a standing, and a reclin-
ing Buddha (45 feet long), hewn directly from
the rockface. They were originally painted and
enclosed in spacious wooden superstructures.

Buddhist chaitya at Karli, C2

Gal Vihara, Ceylon, C12

Wata-da-ge Dagoba, Polonnaruwa, Ceylon, late C12

Up to the first centuries of our era the *Hindus* exclusively used wood and other perishable materials for building. As with Buddhist architecture, surviving evidence of Hindu architecture therefore only dates back to the time when they began to hew their temples out of the rock. From about the C8 A.D. three broad stylistic divisions emerge: (a) the Nagara style in the temples of the North; (b) the Vesara style in the temples of the central plateau; (c) the Dravidian style in the temples of the South.

The most important temples of the *Nagara style* include Bhubaneswar and Konarak

from the C8 to C13 A.D. and the twenty-to-thirty temples at Khajurao (C10–C11), famous for the pronouncedly erotic character of their figural decoration. The temples of the North usually consist of a *shikhara* (tower over the CELLA) and a *mandapa* (porch). In the cella stands the *lingam*, the phallic symbol of Shiva. Occasionally four small cells are set according to the so-called *panch-ratna* system in the diagonals of the main structure.

The *Dravidian style* originated in a few small, monolithically worked model temples – the *rathas* (cars) of Mahaballipuram near Madras (c8) – and culminated in the monumental

Hindu temple, Mukteshwara, Bhubaneswar, c8–c13 (Nagara Style)

(Right). Detail of Temple of the Sun at Konarak, C13

Detail of Gopura at Madurai, CI *(Dravidian Style)*

Hindu Kesvaha temple at Somnathpur,
c12–c13 (Vesara Style)

Colonnade in the South Indian temple city
of Madurai, c17 (Dravidian Style)

stepped pyramid of the c11 temple tower of
Tanjore. The largest sites of the Dravidian
style were the sprawling temple cities of its de-
cadent phase lasting into the c17. These
South Indian temple cities are characterized
by a small shrine in the centre enclosed by
concentric circular walls and streets, and
lofty gate-towers (GOPURA) marking the intersection of the walls with the two axes of
the temple. Such are Madurai, Srirangam and
Rameswaram.

The *Vesara style* evolved from the buildings
of the early and late Chalukya dynasty (c6–
c12) to the temples of Somnathpur, Belur and
Halebid (c12–c13), with their star-shaped
plans.

Jainism, like Buddhism an offshoot of
Hinduism, produced numerous temples in the

Dome of Temple at Mount Abu, CI1–CI3
(Jain Style)

countryside of Gujerat that defy categorization under any of the three stylistic groupings, as for instance the temples on Mount Abu, noteworthy both for the preciousness of the material they are built with – marble from a faraway source – and the exquisite workmanship of the lace-like patterns carved in it (CI1–CI3).

Scarcely any Hindu religious buildings are conceived of as a place for the forgathering of the faithful. They are rather the immanent manifestation of a transcendent design. They are chiefly intended as a depiction of some form of cosmic order. The architect therefore based his design upon a graphic representation of this order – a so-called *mandala* or *yantra*. This sign, occasionally described as a psycho-cosmogram, can either be square as a symbol of quaternity, or triangular, betokening trinity. In ancient Indian architectural theory specific mythological significance was ascribed to its points and fields. The fields were mostly the seat of particular gods. The mandala or yantra, and the canon of proportions bound up with these, determined the shape and dimensions of every part. Each stage of construction was supervised by priests. They were responsible for the harmony of the human creation with the macrocosm. Hence astrological considerations were frequently involved.

3. *Muslim* peoples from the lands west of India, who had already made a series of forays into the fertile settlements of the Indus Valley, settled in North India in the course of the CI2 and founded several sultanates, of

Mosque at Gulbarga, 1367

which Delhi was the chief. The conquerors transmitted ISLAMIC ARCHITECTURE to India. As in other countries overrun by Muslim hordes, the new rulers began by converting the temples of the infidel into mosques. In Ajmer it sufficed to screen a temple with a flat façade on the Persian model (C12). In the capital of Delhi on the other hand 27 Hindu temples were destroyed in order to build the huge mosque of Quwwat-al-Islam (victory of Islam) from the spoils. Its minaret, the *Qutub* (axle), was intended to symbolize the centre of a new Islamic imperium.

In the provincial capitals of the steadily expanding Empire a series of mosques arose whose form clearly betrayed the influence of native Hindu craftsmen, like the Jami-mesjid in Jaunpur (1407) and the Jami-mesjid in Ahmedabad (1423). Only after 1526, with the Moghul dynasty, did the development begin of that sumptuous Indo-Islamic style of architecture which quite overshadowed the evolution of independent modes of architecture in the South Indian sultanates. Moghul architecture was characterized by the marriage of Islamic, or more specifically Persian, notions of interior space with native Hindu methods of construction. The Islamic contribution embraces interiors and courts bounded by smooth walling, as well as the onion dome and four-centred arch, while the Hindu contribution includes the use of stone for walls and surfaces, as well as the constant endeavour of native builders to impart body to the space-defining screen-like walls of Islamic architecture. This urge reflects the traditional monolithic construction of Hindu architecture, in which a sense of mass played as great a role as a feeling for enclosed space.

The material, or at least the facing, used in buildings in the early Moghul style was red sandstone. PIETRA DURA work in white marble was inserted into this. In the late Moghul style the relationship of dark to light surfaces was reversed, in that the revetment was entirely of white marble, with inlays of dark semi-precious stones.

The heyday of the early Moghul style fell in the reign of the Great Moghul Akbar (1556–1605). In a matter of years he built the palace-city of Fathepur Sikri, one of the most notable attempts at urban planning in Asia. The palace area chiefly consists of a string of courts, with one- or two-storied open pavilions erected casually where needed along their walls. Only rarely does the loose aggregation of courts yield to an imposing axial ensemble; there are no street compositions.

Of the immense number of individual buildings from Akbar's time, Humayun's tomb in Delhi deserves mention as a typical example of the translation of a Persian brick

Humayun Tomb at Delhi, late C17

façade into the local red sandstone and white marble. Also prophetic of the further development of Moghul architecture was the association of buildings with formal gardens. Brightly-coloured parterres, criss-crossed by raised water-channels and paths of white marble, harmonize with similarly structured façades.

Shah Jahan (1628–66), Akbar's grandson, brought the late Moghul style to perfection. Urban designs, as for instance the Shah's palace in Delhi, the Red Fort, differ from Fathepur Sikri in the axial alignment of the various palace courts, and in the incorporation of geometrically disposed gardens into the palace area. The palaces, mosques and tombs of this time gave rise to the reports of the legendary wealth of the Great Moghuls. Palace architecture was dominated by one-storied colonnades set amidst expanses of water and flowers, traversed by narrow

Interior of the Red Fort, Delhi, late c17

runnels of water, and occasionally cooled by fine spray from water-spouts on the roof. The dazzling splendour of the white marble palaces and *mausolea* served to glorify worldly power, while the mosques proclaimed the victory of Islam. Examples of the court architecture of Shah Jahan are the halls of audience and apartments in the Forts of Delhi and Agra, and of his religious architecture the Jami Mesjid in Delhi (1644–58), the

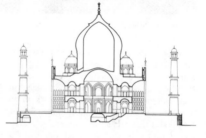

Pearl Mosque, Agra, 1647–54

Taj Mahal, Agra, 1632–52: section and plan

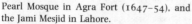

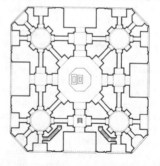

Pearl Mosque in Agra Fort (1647–54), and the Jami Mesjid in Lahore.

But all these are eclipsed in beauty and splendour by the Taj Mahal in Agra (1632–52), the tomb of Shah Jahan's wife, Mumtaz Mahal. The sequence of rooms in this is set out according to the favourite diagrammatic plan of the Moghul period – an interpenetrating square and cross. Chambers occur in

the centre, the corners, and the intersections of this figure, and between them lie – according to Indian and in contradistinction to Persian precedent – equivalent chunks of wall. The simple system of interior, dividing screen, and exterior was also expresssed in elevation. The onion dome forms an apparently distinct entity. Its chamber is the greatest space in the building, yet it is not

Taj Mahal, Agra, 1632–52

exploited. This compromise was the product of the antagonistic Islamic and Hindu
conceptions of architecture.

At the same time as the best builders and
craftsmen of North India were at work on the
Taj Mahal, in South India the Sultan of Bijapur
was realizing a project of comparable magni-
tude. His tomb, the so-called Gol Gumbaz
(with a round dome), is the largest domed
building in Asia, and only exceeded by the
Pantheon and St Peter's in Rome. It is
singular that the third largest dome in the
world should have been built in India, a
country whose native craftsmen had renounced the use of the dome and the arch on
doctrinal grounds, until the power of their
Muslim rulers forced it on them. The Islamic
architecture of South India has little in common with Moghul architecture. It occasionally
excels the latter in spatial clarity – e.g. in the
mosque of Gulbarga – but it is deficient in
the quality of its materials and detailing.

Under Shah Jahan's successor Aurangzeb
(1658–1707) the building zeal of the Moghul
dynasty expired. The architects migrated to
the courts of the provincial governors and the
maharajas. Whilst the Imperial court declined,
Indo-Islamic architecture experienced a last
resurgence in their capitals. The Hindu
maharaja Jai Singh II (1686–1743), for
instance, laid out a splendid capital on a grid
of streets, with a sumptuous palace at the
centre, in which Indian and Islamic conceptions of space were fused, and with a gigantic
observatory in one of its courts. The city he
called Jaipur (City of Victory), the observatory
Jantar Mantar (magic instrument). Altogether
Jai Singh built five such observatories in
North India. Even though he justified the
building of large stone astronomical instru-
ments on the grounds of the inaccuracy of the
traditional small ones in metal, there can be
no doubt that these striking geometrical
shapes were thought of not merely as instru-

Observatory, Jaipur, late c18

ments but as cosmic symbols expressive of the current cosmology. Indigenous Indian architecture thus ended with the same preoccupations as those with which it began.

4. With the conquest of India by the Portuguese and the English, European ideas of architecture replaced Hindu and Indo-Islamic architectural preoccupations. Religious architecture in Goa reflected the Iberian Baroque, while North India produced another variant of the English Colonial style. At the beginning of this century the English decided to move the capital from Calcutta and build a new metropolis centred on the Viceregal Residence. Sir Edwin LUTYENS and Sir Herbert BAKER designed New Delhi as a classicizing city with star-shaped squares connected by broad avenues. Those whom this design with its mixture of rectangular and hexagonal structures impressed included LE CORBUSIER, who was commissioned to design the city of Chandigarh as the new capital of the Punjab in 1951.   [AV]

Palace of Justice, Chandigarh, 1956–65

Lit: James Fergusson, *History of Indian-Eastern Architecture*, London 1910; E. B. Havill, *Indian Architecture*, 1927; B. Rowland, *The Art and Architecture of India – Hindu, Buddhist, Jain*, Pelican History of Art, Harmondsworth 1967, paperback edn 1970; A. Volwahsen, *India*, 1968; Sten Nilsson, *European Architecture in India*, London 1968.

Indo-Chinese architecture, *see* SOUTH-EAST ASIAN ARCHITECTURE.

Indonesian architecture, *see* SOUTH-EAST ASIAN ARCHITECTURE.

Industrialized building Ever since the prefabrication of the first brick, building materials have been industrial products; and ever since Thomas Cubitt in 1815 established a building firm in London which employed all trades on a permanent wage basis, industry has gradually replaced craftsmanship as the basis of European building. Until after 1945, however, the building industry was 'labour-intensive'; it could afford to employ large gangs of unskilled labourers to put up buildings quickly in a traditional way. Since 1945, a growing shortage of both skilled and unskilled labour, coupled with growing programmes of public housing and welfare building, has made it imperative to prefabricate as much as possible and thus minimize site work. It is this recent acceleration of technical development, making the industry 'capital-intensive', which is normally called Industrialized Building.

There had already been progress in mass-production of building parts long before 1945, from Abraham Darby's Iron Bridge at Coalbrookdale (1775–9) and Benyon, Bage & Marshall's iron-framed flax mill at Shrewsbury (1796) or Boulton & Watt's seven-storey cotton mill at Salford (1801) to Bunning's Coal Exchange in London (1847–9) and James BOGARDUS's repetitive cast-iron façades as well as frames (his own factory, 1848–9; Harper Brothers building, 1854). PAXTON's wholly prefabricated cast-iron and glass Crystal Palace for the 1851 Exhibition in London was the answer to a construction deadline of nine months, impossible to meet even with a massive labour force. Its linear descendant is the geodesic domes of Buckminster FULLER (Union Tank Car Co., Baton Rouge, Louisiana, 1958, 384 ft in diameter; U.S. Pavilion at Montreal Expo, 1967, c. 250 ft). This is built on the SPACE-FRAME principle which has been developed further by Jean PROUVÉ in France.

Even BARRY's Houses of Parliament in London (1839–52), an apparently craft-made building, had its bronze window-frames mass-produced by Hope's of Birmingham; and the metal window became a leitmotif of industrialized building. At GROPIUS's Fagus Works at Alfeld (1911), the structural grid was fully glazed; such window walling was used by LE CORBUSIER in the Salvation Army Citadel, Paris, and the Maison Clarté, Geneva (both 1932). In 1918 Willis Polk (1870–1924) gave the Hallidie Building at San Francisco a continuous 'CURTAIN WALL' of steel and glass which hung in front of the main frame – thus achieving a crucial separation of 'structure' from 'cladding', taken up by Gropius in the workshop wing of the Bauhaus (1925–6). Prefabricated curtain walling, often in aluminium, was made internationally acceptable by three New York skyscrapers: the United Nations Headquarters (1947–50, by Wallace K. Harrison and others, on an idea of Le Corbusier), the Lever Building (1950–52, by Gordon Bunshaft of SKIDMORE, OWINGS AND MERRILL) and the Seagram Building (1955–8 by MIES VAN DER ROHE and Philip JOHNSON). Mies had drawn a 'glass skyscraper' as early as 1920. Buckminster Fuller's Dymaxion House project (1927) derived from the techniques of aircraft and vehicle building – its relevance is becoming apparent now that

Industralized Building: a mass-producible house, 1946, designed by Buckminster Fuller

America makes more than twice as many caravans each year as static prefabricated homes. The early postwar 'prefabs' in Britain were fully made up in the factory (expensively, as production runs were not long enough); the London County Council Mobile Homes (1963–5) show how such short-life houses can continue to meet an emergency.

For permanent homes, however, Industralized Building has meant the manufacture of systems of components which can be fitted together 'dry' on site (i.e., without 'wet' cement). For reasons of fire precaution, PRECAST CONCRETE has been generally preferred to steel for housing. Following the experimental work of PERRET and NERVI, systems of precast wall and floor panels have been developed in Russia, Scandinavia and France. Steel shuttering (rather than timber) has been used to minimize applied internal finishes by giving meticulously smooth surfaces, while various methods of moulding, blasting and tamping have given external surfaces a roughness, with the aggregate exposed,

which is expected to weather attractively. Electrical conduits and other services can be inserted off the site, with preformed kitchens and bathrooms in so-called 'heart units'. Prefabrication is usually done in a special factory, close to the site. Its cost, and the cost of the expensive tower cranes necessary on site, have to be met by long and continuous production. Systems of 'battery casting' in special SHUTTERING on the site have proved more flexible for smaller housing areas. Leading concrete systems include Larsen-Nielsen and Jespersen in Denmark, Ohlsson-Skarne in Sweden, Camus and Balency in France, Wates, Reema and Bison Wall Frame in Britain.

Light steel framing has been used for schools, clinics and other single-storey structures. A British team under the Hertfordshire county architect, C. H. Aslin (1893–1959), developed a system of components from many manufacturers, on an 8 ft 3 in. grid (later altered to 2 ft 8 in.). A hundred Hertfordshire schools were built from 1946 to 1955, the year in which the CLASP (Consortium of Local Authorities Special Programme) system was developed by the then county architect of Nottinghamshire, (Sir) Donald Gibson (b. 1908). Subsequently, as Director-General of Research and Development at the Ministry of Public Building and Works, Gibson has helped to develop the NENK system for Army barracks, which has space-frame roofing, and the SCOLA system for a Second Consortium of Local Authorities building schools.

Meanwhile the National Building Agency in Britain (chief architect, A. W. Cleeve Barr) has been attempting to rationalize the 'boom' in industrialized systems for housing, of which there were said in 1964 to be 284 in various stages of production – and at various levels of quality. Concrete panel systems have tended to be suitable only for high blocks of flats, often undesirable socially. For low houses, traditional methods have been systematically rationalized: repetitive brick crosswalls can be given a prefabricated infill of timber walls and floors, and precut timber frames (on the Canadian system) can be given an infill of made-up panels of brickwork. Reinforced plastic panels, with curved-cornered windows like those of a car, have been used by the Greater London Council at Walterton Road (1967). In the Scandinavian countries 'winter building' under temporary shelters, themselves prefabricated, has speeded production.

The main doubt about industrialized building systems is whether they are sufficiently

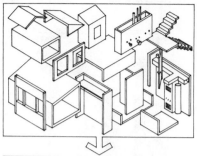

Industrialized Building: a CLASP system building for the University of York, 1965, by Matthew and Johnson-Marshall

flexible. From 1963 CLASP has been used to build the University of York, England (architects, Robert MATTHEW, Johnson-Marshall and Partners) for which non-loadbearing partition walls with good sound insulation have been devised; and in Germany, also from 1963, a sophisticated system of precast concrete beams and lightweight infill has been developed for the University at Marburg (chief

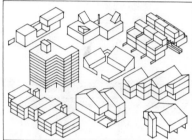

Industrialized Building: the Fibershell Kit-of-Parts by Ezra Ehrenkrantz and BSD, 1970

Industrialized Building: Takara Beautilion, Expo 70, Tokyo, by Kisho Kurokawa

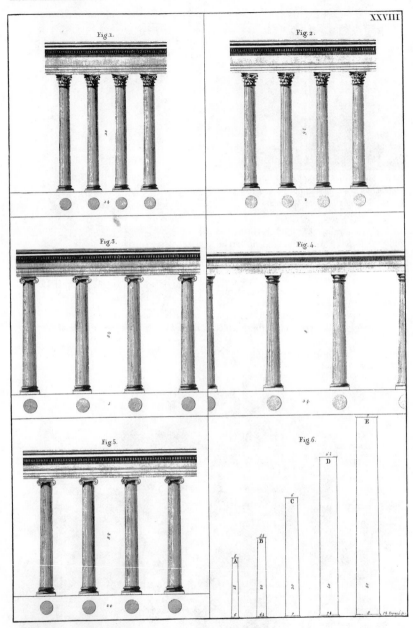

XXVIII

Fig. 1.

Fig. 2.

Fig. 3.

Fig. 4.

Fig. 5.

Fig. 6.

Intercolumniation: From Vitruvius,
De Architectura, Plate XXVIII:
Fig. 1 Pycnostyle; Fig. 2 Systyle;
Fig. 3 Diastyle; Fig. 4 Araeostyle;
Fig. 5 Eustyle

architect, Kurt Schneider). Mexico's Federal Committee for School Planning (architect-chairman, Pedro Ramírez Vásquez) has conducted an outstanding programme of cheap school building, adapted to various heights and climates – generally in concrete with steel space-frame roofing. Meanwhile in the industrially most advanced country, the U.S.A., where industrialized methods have generally been used only to perfect finishes and crane-handling techniques for tall office blocks, English types of school design have been much improved in the steel-framed SCSD system in California (1965; chief architect, Ezra Ehrenkrantz) by incorporating a sophisticated range of mechanical services in space-frame roofs.

The hope of many architects lies in Modular Co-ordination on an internationally agreed basis. It could make every prefabricated material available in related measurements, as a 'palette' from which designs could be flexibly composed. A key problem, however, is the variety of jointing at present necessary from rigid all-welded joints to the neuter non-rigid types packed with plastic.   [NT]

Lit: C. W. Condit, *American Building Art: the nineteenth century*, New York 1960; C. W. Condit, *The Rise of the Skyscraper*, Chicago 1952; E. H. L. Simon, *L'industrialisation de la construction*, Paris 1962; R. M. E. Diamant, *Industrialised Building*, London 1964; G. Blanchere, V. Chiaia, M. Petrignani, *et al.*, *Industrializzazione dell'Edilizia*, Rome 1965.

Intarsia: Detail of woodwork in Lübeck Town Hall, 1594–1613 (restored)

Inglenook A recess for bench or seat built beside a fireplace, sometimes covered by the CHIMNEY-BREAST.

Intarsia A form of mosaic or inlay made up of different coloured woods, popular in C15–16 Italy especially for the decoration of studies and small rooms in palaces and for the choir stalls of churches. (Illustrated previous column.)

Intercolumniation The space between columns measured in diameters. Vitruvius established five main ratios, 1½D. Pycnostyle, 2D. Systyle, 2¼D. Eustyle, 3D. Diastyle, 4D. Araeostyle, of which Eustyle is the commonest. (Illustrated opposite.)

International Modern A term coined in America to refer to the new architectural style of the C20, as created before the First World War by such architects as WRIGHT, GARNIER, LOOS, HOFFMANN, GROPIUS, and as accepted, at least in progressive circles, first in Central Europe in the course of the twenties and then in other countries of Europe and in America from the late twenties onwards. The style is characterized by asymmetrical composition, unrelievedly cubic general shapes,

International Modern: Sketch for a Garden City, 1901–04, by Tony Garnier

International Modern: Private house in Vienna, 1910, by Loos

International Modern: Houses at Wiesenhof,
Stuttgart, 1927, by Mies van der Rohe

International Modern:
Houses in Tashkent, 1967

an absence of mouldings, large windows often in horizontal bands, and a predilection for white RENDERING.

Lit: W. Jordy, *American Buildings and their Architects: The Impact of European Modernism in the Mid-Twentieth Century*, New York 1973.

Intrados The inner curve or underside of an arch; also called a *soffit*. (For illustration *see* ARCH.)

Inwood, Henry William (1794–1843). The son of an architect (William Inwood, *c.* 1771–1843), with whom he designed his only building of note, St Pancras Church, London (1819–22), one of the great monuments of the GREEK REVIVAL in England. Every detail is faithfully copied from the Erechtheum, Tower of the Winds, Choragic Monument, and other famous Athenian buildings. Sometimes his archaeological material is rather recondite, but he always uses it with sensibility.

Lit: J. Mordaunt Crook, *The Greek Revival*, London 1972.

Ionic Order, *see* ORDER.

Iranian architecture There are few boundaries in history that have been so mutable as those of Iran, to the extent that even former capitals are now incorporated in other states: Ctesiphon in Iraq, Herat in Afghanistan, and Merv, Bukhara and Samarkand in the U.S.S.R. Buildings falling within Iran's historic, and not just her present-day, boundaries will be dealt with here.

The Elamites (c14 to c7 B.C.). The first traces of civilization in Iran are to be found in the south-west of the country, in the delta of the Ab-e-Diz (a tributary of the Shatt-el-Arab, which is itself produced by the confluence of the Tigris and the Euphrates). Brick architecture emerged on this vast, alluvial plain as early as the c14 B.C. Urban life similar to that of neighbouring Lower Mesopotamia flourished in Susiana, where the cities of Susa and Choga Zambil formed the focus of the Elamite kingdom.

Choga Zambil, which was never brought to completion by its founder, is chiefly notable for its ZIGGURAT, the best-preserved of the whole Middle East. Built in 1250 B.C., it is a five-tiered pyramid with three containing walls, the outermost of which has a circuit of no less than 2½ miles. The ziggurat itself is shaped like a stepped pyramid with sides measuring 390 feet at the base, and with a probable original height of about 160 feet. It consists of vertical sections, each corresponding to one storey. ADOBE was used for filling, but brick for the external cladding of the walls. Within, the building contains a lower temple, 34 corbel-vaulted chambers, and partially covered-in, axially disposed stairs that used to give access to the upper sanctuary, of which no trace now remains. Choga Zambil once contained, besides the ziggurat, not only a palace with subterranean vaults but also numerous temples, which lay however outside the *temenos*, or sacred enclosure. Such is the most important group of Elamite buildings known to us, chiefly characterized by strong Mesopotamian influence. The architecture of the following period, known as Neo-Elamitic (c9 to c7 B.C.), still suffers from a want of systematic excavation, as do all the Medean cities except Tepe Nush-i Jan, near Hamadan. The ruins of the most important city, Ekbatana, are overlain by Hamadan itself.

The Achaemenids (c6 to c4 B.C.). In Pasargadae we have the tomb of Cyrus the Great (559–530), the first great king of this dynasty. It consists of an oblong chamber built of

Tomb of Cyrus the Great (died 529 B.C.)
at Pasargades (Achaemenian)

massive blocks of ashlar upon a sixfold stepped
base, with a roof whose shape probably owes
something to the gabled roofs of northern intruders. Of the city itself there remains little
trace, apart from a monumental gateway
similar to those of Persepolis and Susa.

Susa, where excavations have revealed
occupation dating back to the c5 B.C., also
preserves from the Achaemenid period a
palace that served Darius I as his winter residence. The rectangular APADANA, or hall of
audience, is a columnar structure with six
columns per bay, 36 columns in all. Double-
rowed PORTICOS face outwards on three of
the sides, and rectangular structures ensure

the stability of the building at the corners.
The marked slenderness of the columns fore-
shadows those of Persepolis, whose capitals
are adorned with a kind of double volute
topped by the coupled foreparts of bulls and
other creatures, some of them mythical. They
were designed to support a flat ceiling with
beams of Lebanese cedar. The palace is enriched by a continuous course of bas-reliefs
executed in polychrome glazed brick.

But it was in Persepolis that Achaemenid
architecture was to reach the peak of its attain-
ment. This city, the centre of the huge empire
founded by the Achaemenids, and a crucible
for the profusion of influences absorbed by the
Medes and the Persians as a result of their
distant conquests, was designed as a political
and religious manifesto, as a statement of the
might of the great king. Upon a terrace with
high ashlar walls rise platforms bearing the
Apadana of Darius and Xerxes, and its prolific
accompaniment of treasuries, magazines,
palaces and living-quarters. An imposing entrance gives access to the majestic complex of
buildings, which are laid out on a rigorously
detailed plan built up of right-angles. Two
monumental double flights of steps come
solemnly together before the Gate of Xerxes,
which is adorned by two statues of bulls with
wings and human heads, similar to those that
keep watch in front of the entrance to

Persepolis, begun 518 B.C. (Achaemenian)

Persepolis (Apadana of Darius and Xerxes), begun 518 B.C. (Achaemenian)

Assyrian palaces. To the right, the Apadana of Darius and Xerxes is an exact replica of that at Susa, only on a larger scale (245 × 245 ft). Likewise a columnar building with double porticoes on three sides, it stands upon a terrace reached to the north and east by steps encased in bas-reliefs. Guardrooms like towers at the four corners act as bulwarks to the delicate fabric of the porticoes. The 62 ft high columns, whose shafts soar aloft with a grace and charm that was not to be recaptured even in Greek art, were designed to carry not a stone but a wooden ENTABLATURE. These Achaemenid columns in fact display the typical characteristics of the Ionic ORDER, which is scarcely surprising in that it was Ionian stonemasons who carved the fluting, the volutes, and the ornamented bases. Yet their function is entirely different from those of Greek temples; whereas the latter form a PERISTYLE round a relatively small CELLA, here they create a spacious interior of easy and elegant proportions (an INTERCOLUMNIATION of more than 8 metres, resulting in over 3,600 square metres all told).

In order to glorify the unity of their empire, the Achaemenids had the stairways decorated with superb bas-reliefs showing the subject peoples as they paid tribute to the great king. These are comparable in style, as are the glazed brick panels in Susa, to Assyrian bas-reliefs. Certain of the rooms have monumental doorways which exhibit typically Egyptian COVING. The architecture of the Achaemenids as a whole therefore shows traces of influence from all the sophisticated civilizations that they subjugated: columnar halls as in Egypt, but less massive; doorways with Egyptian coving; Assyro-Babylonic bas-reliefs; columns of Ionic inspiration. Yet it is still unmistakably original in its creation of spacious, habitable interiors, light and mobile in detail. Moreover, a great transparency between interior and exterior is achieved through the use of double porticoes such as those flanking the great *apadanas*. Great importance was attached to the means of access, as witnessed by the monumental stairways, whose gentle ascent almost makes the flights of steps seem like ramps.

Another original and satisfying formulation was found by the Achaemenids for the tombs gouged out of the rockfaces at Persepolis and Naqsh-i Rustam: a cruciform façade focusing upon a palace-type colonnade hewn out of the rock, in the centre of which a door gives access to the funerary chamber.

Square stone towers with two-storeyed interiors survive at Pasargadae; it is not yet clear whether they are of cultic or funerary significance.

Parthians and Sassanids (C2 B.C. to C7 A.D.). Achaemenid art, being utterly devoted to the glorification of the dynasty, was extinguished by Alexander the Great. Now

Tomb of Darius, Naqsh-i Rustam, C5 B.C.

began the heyday of brick vaulting, which played an important role in the construction of houses in Susiana and on the high plateau from the very first. Straw-and-daub domes indeed are traceable back to prehistoric times.

The IWAN, a vaulted structure disposed round an internal courtyard, makes its first appearance in the Parthian epoch (150 B.C.). This in origin vernacular feature was subsequently adopted in Sassanid palace architecture. Broadly speaking, the whole range of DOMES and VAULTS that were henceforth to be the glory of Iranian architecture have their ancestry in Zoroastrian fire-temples. The key to further experiment was the dome upon SQUINCHES over four pillars linked by arches. Both national traditions and Roman influence played their part in the various solutions to this problem of bridging the transition between square supports and a circular dome. On their defeat by Shapur I in A.D. 260, the Emperor Valerian's legionaries were put to work in Iran erecting bridges, dams, and other structures. As we know, ROMAN ARCHITECTURE

Palace at Firuzabad, early C3

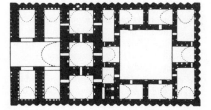

Fire Temple near Neisar, c. C2 (restored)

reached its apogee in the C3, and there was hardly a vaulting technique that was foreign to it. Shapur was builder of the palace of Bishapur in the mountains of southern Iran. The palace contains a cruciform chamber, whose iwans are embellished with mosaics. A tunnel-vaulted staircase leads up to the fire-temple.

To the Sassanid epoch belongs one of the most remarkable brick structures of antiquity, the great palace of Ctesiphon (now in Iraq).

Palace at Ctesiphon, C3 or C6 (Sassanid)

It has an 120 ft high elliptical vault unbuttressed by façades at either end. Certain historians ascribe it to the time of Shapur I, but it is more likely that it dates from the C6 A.D. and was built under Khosrau I (531–39), at the zenith of the Empire.

Islamic architecture: Iranian Islamic architecture flourished from the Arab conquest in the C7 to the fall of the Safavid dynasty in the C18. It extends beyond modern Iran to Afghanistan and Soviet Central Asia.

Mosques. Very little architecture survives before the C10. Literary sources state that the Arabs often converted the existing cultic buildings of Sassanian Persia, the fire temples,

into MOSQUES; but no incontrovertible archaeological evidence for this practice has yet been found (though the mosques of Yazd-i Khwast and Qurva may be examples). These fire temples usually consisted of a square domed chamber with four axial arched entrances; they were often placed in the centre of a large open enclosure. This model conformed admirably to the major liturgical need of Islamic worship, namely a large open space for prayer. The early mosques which the Arabs built in Iraq, Egypt and elsewhere usually consisted of large open enclosures surrounded by arcades which were deeper on the QIBLA side. Early Iranian mosques of this 'Arab plan' are Siraf and Fahraj. Soon the single domed chamber of local tradition replaced the extra aisles of the sanctuary. Sassanian architecture provided another feature which was adapted for cultic purposes – the IWAN commonly used in palaces. This too replaced the aisled sanctuary of the Arab plan. It was in the development and combination of these three features – the square domed chamber, the iwan and the courtyard – that the future of Persian architecture was to lie. It is possible that originally each of these features was used by itself as a mosque.

The Tarik Khana at Damghan, perhaps the earliest mosque in Iran, illustrates how the Persians quickly modified the Arab plan. The arcades surrounding the courtyard are executed in huge bricks of Sassanian type, the round piers are stumpy and massive and the arch profiles are elliptical. Above all, the central arch of the north façade, on the axis of the MIHRAB, rises higher than the other arches and is encased in a rectangular frame – an embryonic iwan. Another mosque type comprised a single iwan on the qibla side facing a courtyard with arcades on the other three sides (Niriz; Firdaus). It is not certain when the first attempts to combine the various types were made, but among surviving monuments the process of development can be traced most clearly in the incomparable Friday mosque of Isfahan. The original mosque was probably of Arab plan. At the end of the C11 two square domed chambers were introduced into the north and south sides. A fire destroyed much of this mosque, except the two domed chambers, in 1121, and it was probably soon after this disaster that four iwans were added on the axes of the mosque. Thus the sequence of courtyard–iwan–domed chamber, so popular in later periods, was established. Considerable variation was possible within this basic schema, for example in the size of the courtyard or the number of iwans. The Seljuks (c11-c12) introduced other types of mosque too; in Khurasan, for example, a courtyard mosque with an iwan on the north and south sides and no domed chamber was popular (Gunabad), and small domed mosques of square plan abound (Sangan-i Pa'in; Abdallahbad) as do mosques consisting simply of a low columned arcaded hall with a flat roof (Simnan; Zarand). After the Seljuk period no major innovations in mosque plans were made. The Mongols, who built mainly in the c14, added much to existing mosques (prayer hall and madrasa in Isfahan Friday mosque). When they built new mosques, they favoured established types such as the 4-iwan plan (Varamin; Hafshuya) or the isolated domed chamber (Dashti; Aziran). The mosque of Ali Shah at Tabriz is atypical, for it consists only of a courtyard and qibla iwan. It illustrates the huge scale of some Mongol foundations. The Mongol contribution lay principally in a refining and attenuation of Seljuk forms; one may compare the relationship of Gothic to Romanesque. The Timurids (c15) also added to existing mosques rather than building anew. Their winter prayer hall in the Isfahan Friday mosque comprises multiple aisles of massive pointed arches

Friday Mosque, Isfahan, c11-c19

springing directly from the ground. Large Timurid mosques survive at Mashhad and Samarkand but perhaps the most important and unusual mosque of the period is the Blue Mosque at Tabriz (1465), a large domed octagon surrounded by lesser domed chambers.

The Safavids (c16-c18) made Isfahan their capital under Shah Abbas (1587-1629). His two most famous mosques, the Lutfullah Mosque and the Masjid-i Shah, again repeat familiar schemas – the domed square chamber and the 4-iwan plan respectively. The

Dome of Masjid-i Shah, Isfahan, 1612-38

façades of both open on to the great square (Maidan) which was the centre of the new city, and both have bent entrances so that the mosques themselves are correctly orientated but do not compromise the regularity of the façades defining the square.

Courtyard of Madrasa, Madar-i Shah, Isfahan, 1706-14

Masjid-i Shah, Isfahan, 1612–38

Minarets. The earliest minarets in Iran seem to have copied the square form current in early Islam (Damghan, Siraf). But with the C11 a striking new type of tall cylindrical minaret, usually set on a polygonal plinth, was introduced. These minarets were usually built of high quality baked brick and thus have often survived, even though all trace of the mosque to which they belonged has vanished. Gradually structural variations were introduced. These included complicated flaring corbelled balconies just below the summit of the minaret (Saraban minaret, Isfahan); single and double internal spiral staircases, both with and without a central column (Simnan; Samiran); an elevation with flanges or alternating engaged columns and flanges (Zarand; Nigar); and finally a division of the elevation into three stages, each more tapering than the last (Jam; Ziar). Double minarets flanking a portal were introduced late in the C12 (Nakhchivan); later they were used to emphasize the qibla iwan in mosques (Masjid-i Shah). In the case of minarets, as in so many other building types, the innovations of the C13–C15 were limited to architectural decoration; indeed, far fewer minarets were built than in previous periods.

Mausolea. The basic forms of mausolea were also established in mediaeval times. Despite religious prohibitions, mausolea were apparently built even in the first years of Islam. In the Iranian world the earliest dated example is among the most impressive: the so-called 'Tomb of the Samanids' at Bokhara (early C10). It produces a monumental effect despite its small size. In its essentials the building scarcely differs from a Sassanian fire temple, but important new features are the engaged corner columns, the four miniature domes which crown them, and the arcaded gallery. The latter feature was retained in many later domed mausolea of square ground plan (Sangbast; mausoleum of Sanjar at Merv). In many such mausolea the PISHTAQ (a projecting rectangular iwan serving as a portal) was an important feature. In Timurid times the bulbous ribbed dome and the double dome were often used for mausolea (Shah-i Zinda complex, Samarkand). The domed mausoleum allowed for considerable variation in size and ground plan; the tomb of Uljaitu, Sultaniya, built after 1307, illustrates another popular type, the octagon with a deep niche on each side. A novel feature here is a corona of 8 cylindrical minarets crowning the corners. The octagon, especially when combined with a galleried second storey, allowed more interpenetration of exterior and interior space than did the domed square, which was often closed on three sides. A different category of mausoleum was the tomb tower. Its origins are obscure but are perhaps rather to be sought in Central Asia than in the Near East. These monuments were built from the c10 onwards and are found principally in northern Iran. Some are diminutive structures no more than 20 ft high; others tower nearly 200 ft (Gunbad-i Qabas, 1006). Few postdate the c15. Their purpose was usually only commemorative but the presence of mihrabs indicates that some were used for prayer. Their ground plans are extremely varied – circular, polygonal, square, lobed or flanged. They can be distinguished from domed square mausolea not only by these plans but also by their much lower ratio of width to height and by their roofs, which are conical or pyramidal rather than domed. Blank niches, flanges and engaged columns articulate the shafts of these towers. Under the Timurids a third type of funerary structure, the *hazira* or open courtyard, often with a tall iwan, gained popularity.

Palaces. Early surviving examples are the Ghaznavid (c11) and Seljuk palaces at Lashkar-i Bazaar and Ribat-i Sharaf, which use the 4-iwan plan. Monumental pishtaqs characterize the Mongol palace at Takht-i Suleiman and that of Timur at Shahr-i Sabz. Several Safavid palaces survive in Isfahan. They include the Ali Qapu, an arched portico crowned by a flat-roofed balcony on wooden columns, from which the Shah and his entourage could watch spectacles in the Maidan below. The formal gardens and watercourses into which it leads were once scattered with courts, 2-storey open-plan kiosks, and pavilions, of which one, Chihil Sutun, has a flat-roofed portico on wooden columns, like

Chilil Sutan Palace, Isfahan, c. 1600

an Achaemenid *talar*, preceding the Shah's throne room. The Chahar Bagh, an avenue nearly a mile long lined with trees and streams, gave access to the new capital from the south, while massive bridges (Khaju Bridge), incorporating not only sluice gates but also pavilions for the royal party, linked Isfahan with some of its suburbs.

Mediaeval Persian architecture is dominated by mosques and mausolea. They are therefore emphasized in this account. Many more types of building were erected but often too few have survived to permit generalizations about their characteristics. In other cases (MADRASAS, CARAVANSERAIS) the building type, though widespread, displays less variety than does the mosque or the mausoleum. It is significant that many buildings of very different functions rely on the same basic elements which occur in the architecture of the mosque – the domed square, the iwan and the courtyard. This can be explained as much by the versatility of these elements as by the conservatism of Persian architects. In the madrasa, for example, the 4-iwan plan, though often contracted, is modified only by the addition of cells for students; these are disposed in two storeys around the courtyard and broken by the axial iwans, here used for teaching purposes. In the caravanserais (also mostly of 4-iwan plan) single storeys are the rule; cells for travellers occupy the areas between the iwans, while the space in the corners is used for stables. A monumental pishtaq, separated from the court by a domed vestibule, defines the major axis. Sufi oratories adopt the plan of the square domed chamber, and bazaar entrances use the monumental iwan flanked by two-storey screen walls with arched recesses. Traditional elements predominated even in Safavid Isfahan, one of the most ambitious and novel schemes of town planning in Islamic history. The large public buildings of Iran display a notable preference for inner enclosed space at the expense of the exterior. This trend probably originated in the early mosques, which were usually built in the midst of bazaars on irregular sites which discouraged carefully planned façades. Even when an unencumbered site was available the Iranian architect rarely made full use of the opportunities for large-scale external display. At most he would add a monumental pishtaq (Varamin mosque; Masjid-i Shah). In the major public buildings there is less an interaction of exterior and interior space than a complete divorce between the two. In contrast to the unavoidably haphazard nature of ground plans, interiors are usually governed by a strict sense of symmetry and balance. The result is not often subtle, but the juxtaposition of powerfully defined masses – domes, vaults, iwans, arcades – and the strong contrasts of light and shade which these produce, infuse this architecture with energy and monumentality.

Khaju Bridge, Isfahan, 1665

Although building stone is available in much of the country, brick is the almost exclusive medium of construction for large buildings, rather than rubble as in Sassanian times. The versatility of this high quality baked brick soon made itself felt in the development of a wide range of vaults and domes of a scale and complexity difficult to match elsewhere in the mediaeval Islamic world. The forms included fluted and double domes, and a highly complicated system of stalactite vaulting for concave spaces such as the semi-domes of pishtaqs. The 4-centred arch was a basic element of construction, and combinations of such arches were used to articulate whole interiors. Iranian architects preferred the SQUINCH to the PENDENTIVE and used it in the octagonal and hexadecagonal zones of transition in their great domes. The numerous varieties of the trilobed squinch, a leitmotif of Seljuk architecture, illustrates the Iranian virtuosity in vaulting. The builders dispensed with centering, using instead canes bent to the desired shape, encased in plaster and then set into place once this had hardened. This technique partly accounts for the speed with which large building works were executed. Even the largest domes might be no more than one brick in thickness at their crowns. This daring vaulting is best exemplified in the scores of different domes in the Friday Mosque at Isfahan.

Decoration. Abstract and epigraphic decoration is a major component of Iranian architecture. Three basic media were used – baked brick, carved stucco and glazed tilework. From the C10 and probably earlier brick

was laid in decorative bonds which were sunken, flush or in high relief and formed geometric patterns. It blended admirably with the structure itself and with surrounding buildings, and altered its character with the changing shadows. Stucco, a more flexible medium, permitted the development of curvilinear designs, whether carved, moulded or precast. It was often painted, but was usually not robust enough to decorate exteriors. Glazed coloured tilework was used from *c.* 1100 as a means of enhancing decorative brickwork, but gradually its scope extended to the whole building. Glazed brick was succeeded by tile mosaic and entire glazed tiles, with large and small-scale patterns often reminiscent of carpet motifs. The incandescent colours of the C15 buildings of Gauhar Shad at Mashhad and Herat mark the apogee of glazed tilework. [HS & RH]

Lit: R. Ghirshman, *Persia: from the Origins to Alexander the Great*, London 1964; R. Ghirshman, *Iran: Parthians and Sassanians*, London 1962; A. U. Pope (ed.), *A Survey of Persian Art*, London 1939; A. U. Pope, *Persian Architecture*, London–New York 1965; D. N. Wilber, *The Architecture of Islamic Iran: the Il Khanid Period*, Princeton 1955; A. Godard, *The Art of Iran*, London 1965.

Irish architecture The most rewarding and original phase is that before the Normans, the phase of monastic communities where coenobites lived in round or square huts, stonevaulted by pseudo-vaults of horizontally laid

Hermitage of St Gallarus, Dingle, C7

stones corbelled forward gradually. There were several oratories in such communities, tapering round towers and the glorious High Crosses. The most famous sites are Skellig Michael, Nendrum, Glendalough, Clonmacnois, and Monasterboyce. The buildings are mostly C10–11.

(Far left). Round Tower, Ardmore

(Left). High Cross at Moon, Kildare, c9

(Below). St Kevin, Glendalough, c7

The Hiberno-Romanesque style has its most dramatic monument in Cormac's Chapel at Cashel (dated 1134); it has a tunnel-vaulted nave and a rib-vaulted chancel. There are plenty of monuments in the Norman style with only minor national characteristics. The CISTERCIANS came in the 1140s, and the east end of Christ Church Cathedral, Dublin, shows

West Portal, Clonfert Cathedral, Galway, c12

their influence. The fully Gothic style in a wholly Early English version appears in the nave of Christ Church (connected with Wells and St David's) and the largely rebuilt St Patrick's Cathedral, also at Dublin. The most conspicuous Irish contribution to Gothic architecture is her friaries, mostly rurally sited; they have the tower between nave and chancel, which is also typical of English friaries.

Medieval architecture lasted into the c17. The English promoted such new towns as Londonderry, with its Gothic cathedral of 1628–33, and such houses as Carrick-on-Suir and Strafford's Jigginstown, both of the 1630s. Gothic gradually gave place to hipped roofs or parapets, and such buildings as Beaulieu and the Kilmainham Hospital of 1679 are entirely English in style. PAL-LADIANISM also bore an ample harvest in Ireland, the chief architects being Sir Edward Lovett PEARCE, Richard CASTLE, James GANDON, and Francis Johnston. Examples are Castletown; Parliament House, Dublin, by Pearce; Powerscourt by Castle; the Customs House and the Four Courts, Dublin, by Gandon; the house of the Provost of Trinity College, Dublin; Caledon, by NASH; Townley Hall, and many others. Ireland is indeed exceedingly rich in Georgian houses, though for lack of a function they are rapidly decreasing. In Dublin very much is still preserved, and the

Castletown House, Celbridge, 1722, by Castle

city may well claim to be the finest major Georgian city in the British Isles. If any Victorian buildings are to be singled out, they would again have to be essentially English ones: Cork Cathedral by BURGES; Queen's University, Belfast, by Lanyon; and the Trinity College Museum by Deane & Woodward – all Gothic in style. The best architect today is Michael Scott, the best building up to date the new Library of Trinity College by Ahrends, Burton & Koralek, built in 1963–7.

Lit: H. G. Leask, *Irish Castles*, Dundalk 1941; H. G. Leask, *Irish Churches and Monastic Buildings*, Dundalk 1955–60.

Isidorus of Miletus assisted ANTHEMIOS OF TRALLES in the building of Hagia Sophia, Constantinople (A.D. 532–7), and was, like him, a geometrician who turned his attention to architecture. He is not to be confused with a younger Isidorus, who rebuilt the dome of Hagia Sophia in 558.

Lit: R. Krautheimer, *Early Christian and Byzantine Architecture*, Pelican History of Art, Harmondsworth 1965, paperback edn 1974.

Islamic architecture The function of most Islamic architecture is religious. This survey, which covers only the widespread Islamic building types, therefore excludes most secular architecture. Developments are best traced by schools, not personalities; even in later periods, comparatively few architects are known by name. Such countries as Egypt and Iran were of prime importance throughout the medieval period as centres of experiment

and consistent development, and greatly influenced other schools. By contrast, the distinctive architectural traditions of the Maghrib (Western North Africa and Spain) and India (*see* INDIAN ARCHITECTURE), which developed coherently for centuries, remained of only local significance and will not be treated here. Other countries were important only for brief periods (Syria in the c8; Iraq in the c9). In the early period especially, the conscription of foreign workers for building projects encouraged a uniform but eclectic art.

The pre-Islamic Arabs were nomads and had no permanent architecture. Their architectural taste was formed by the buildings they saw in the territories wrested from the Byzantines and Sassanian Persians. Thus arose the dualism which dominated early Islamic art until the oriental tradition triumphed in the c9. Thereafter Islamic architecture developed within its own religious context, isolated from both Europe – Ottoman Turkey (*see* TURKISH ARCHITECTURE) is a rare exception – and the Far East. The development of Islamic architecture virtually ceased after the early c17; thereafter it either succumbed to versions of the European Baroque or was reduced to pastiches of earlier styles.

Mosques. From the beginning the form of the MOSQUE was determined by the liturgy of Islam which is simpler than that of Christianity. Its basic features were at first few – a courtyard, since the warm climate of most Islamic countries encouraged worship in the open air; fountains or basins for ritual ablution; a MINARET; a MINBAR; a covered sanctuary on the QIBLA side and flat-roofed arcades on the other three sides to give shade. The earliest mosque, Muhammad's house at Medina (622), was a square open enclosure with a roofed area on the south side carried by columns of palm trunks. The early mosques of the Muslim armies, which were set up in open country, inflated but scarcely changed this 'Arab plan'. Many features of early mosques can plausibly be traced not only to Byzantine architecture but also to the participation of the ruler in religious ceremonies. They include the MIHRAB; the minbar; the MAQSURA; and lastly, the transept and the dome over the mihrab, both features emphasizing the importance of the sanctuary. The larger urban mosques of medieval Islam often had attached subsidiary buildings – latrines, covered prayer halls for winter worship, treasuries, MADRASAS, and even mausolea. Mosques are only rarely given a monumental exterior planned and executed as part of a single campaign – exceptions are those built in open country – though monumental entrances are common. They usually adjoin bazaars and private houses. The concept of a mosque as a major feature of a city-scape seems only rarely to have been applied by Islamic architects. Hence the architectural emphasis is usually reserved for the interior of the mosque (Fatimid, Seljuk and Ottoman architecture provide some exceptions). Many early mosques were conversions of existing cultic buildings; the Great Mosque of Damascus (706–15) was originally a pagan temple transformed into a church. The three aisles running parallel to the qibla are broken by a raised and wider central aisle, or transept, running at right angles to the qibla and marking the mihrab axis. Four minarets mark the corners of the sanctuary and the spacious courtyard north of it. For other buildings the Arabs also followed native Byzantine or Sassanian models. Thus the earliest surviving Muslim monument, the Dome of the Rock, Jerusalem (completed 691/2) – a sanctuary, not a mosque – is a domed octagonal building which echoes both Christian churches and antique mausolea. These Arab borrowings extended also to material (especially classical spoils) and decoration. The Arab mosque plan continued in use throughout the c8 and c9, but its details were refined. At Kairouan (Tunisia; mainly c9) the arcades run perpendicular to the qibla, and the extra wide central aisle

forms part of a T-shaped transept; while the contemporary mosques of Samarra (Iraq) and Ibn Tulun (Cairo) have outer enclosures containing the minaret. Extra aisles enlarg-

Ibn-Tulun Mosque, Cairo (Fostat), 876

Ibn-Tulun Mosque, Cairo (Fostat)

ing the sanctuary unfold vistas of seemingly infinite space in all directions, with rows of columns creating repeated identical units (Córdoba mosque, began 785/6). Perhaps this mirrors the long row of worshippers at

Mosque at Córdoba, 785/6–990

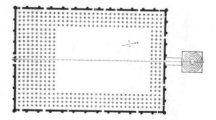

Mosque at Córdoba, 785/6–990

prayer. The Córdoba mosque shows how the basic simplicity of the Arab plan permitted indefinite extensions with no loss of direction. Arcades consisting of two superimposed tiers of columns support its parallel gable roofs. Cusped and horseshoe arches, stalactite vaults and T-shaped transepts characterize Maghribi architecture. In Fatimid Egypt (969–1171) the basic Arab plan was further elaborated by such features as the monu-

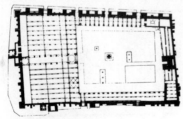

(Left and above). Sidi Okba Mosque, Kairouan, North Africa, c. 836

mental projecting entrance, domes at the angles of the qibla wall, a large square minaret at each end of the façade and numerous lateral entrances (mosques of al-Azhar and al-Hakim). The mosques of the Mamluks (1250–1517) borrowed much from Iran and Syria; many resembled local madrasas.

In Iran (*see Islamic architecture* under IRANIAN ARCHITECTURE) the numerous fire temples converted into mosques in the c7–c8 inspired one early type of mosque, the domed chamber of square ground plan, either completely isolated or placed on the south side of an enclosing courtyard. In the c12, possibly even earlier, this courtyard was enlivened by the introduction of IWANS and these were set on its major axes, thus creating the so-called 4-iwan plan which dominated later mosque architecture. The qibla iwan in front of the domed sanctuary chamber was usually the largest. One may compare the Sassanian use of the iwan as the major architectural element preceding the domed hall of audience. Other early mosques were built in the form of a courtyard with a single iwan on the qibla side, and several of Arab plan are also known.

Turkish mosques of c11–c14 date have an experimental character. Some omit the courtyard of the Arab plan, retaining only the arcaded sanctuary, often with an elaborate façade. More characteristic was the simple domed mosque, sometimes with a courtyard and iwans too but nearly always with a monumental portal. Ottoman mosques, by contrast (especially c15–c17), illustrate an integrated style, dominated by a single great dome with subsidiary domes and semi-domes.

The Blue Mosque, Istanbul, 1609–16

The influence of Hagia Sophia in this development must be stressed. For the equally important interiors of these mosques the Ottomans tried to create as extensive and unified an inner space as possible; this was lit by a multitude of windows.

Minaret. The first century of Islam saw the beginning of the evolution of the MINARET. Originally the call to prayer was given from the roof of the mosque, and this practice never totally died out; indeed it was revived in certain Islamic countries, such as Iran, in later medieval times, when minarets became increasingly rare. The earliest minarets (Kairouan, 724–7) have plausibly been derived from the massive square church towers of pre-Islamic Syria; in the c8–9 a spiral type clearly inspired by Babylonian ziggurats enjoyed a brief popularity (Samarra); and very

Selimiye Mosque, Edirne, Turkey, 1569–74, by Sinan

Great Mosque at Samarra, with minaret, mid-c8 (Abbasid)

tall cylindrical brick minarets with polygonal plinths were a feature of eastern Islamic architecture from the CII onwards. In the Maghrib, the square minarets of Syrian provenance always remained the popular type, the more elaborate being in two stages of diminishing size. Egypt developed numerous variations of a type of slender square minaret with higher octagonal and cylindrical stages articulated by balconies and twin windows, and thickly encrusted with stone carving. The Ottoman Turks adopted an extremely slender cylindrical minaret girded with two or three circular balconies and with a pencil-shaped upper part; this was probably adapted from the earlier Iranian type. Most minarets have interior staircases, usually of spiral form.

Palaces. Although mosques were the first Muslim buildings, other types of structure known from the first century of Islam are the desert residences of the Umayyad caliphs (c8). They were centres of complex agricultural and economic development as well as hunting lodges and palaces (Mshatta; Khirbat al-Mafjar). They are often fortified and contain ceremonial triple-arched entrances, throne

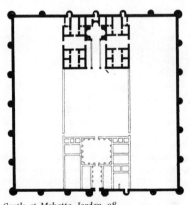

Castle at Mshatta, Jordan, c8

rooms, baths, cisterns, courtyards flanked by small non-communicating rooms (*bayts*) and larders – mostly features derived from provincial Roman and Sassanian Persian models. The palaces of the succeeding Abbasid period are more frankly Sassanian in origin, with a relentless axiality in plan geared to a strict court ceremonial designed to exalt the ruler and which itself was borrowed from Persia. A length to width proportion of 3:2 is used throughout these buildings, as in the

Samarra mosque, and imposes order on a mass of repetitive individual units, mainly courtyards with enclosing rooms similar to Umayyad types. The scale is vast – some complexes (the Jausaq al-Khaqani, Samarra) are a mile in length – but the material and execution are shoddy. Gardens and streams, perhaps connoting paradise, abound. Few palaces of succeeding periods have survived. The most notable is perhaps the Ottoman Topkapi Saray at Istanbul, a haphazard agglomeration of residential and utilitarian units, which grew up over a period of four centuries; more homogeneous is the walled Alhambra at Granada, which demonstrates better than any other surviving examples that interdependence between interior and exterior space which was a constant feature of Islamic palaces. Numerous gardens on various levels alternate informally with belvederes, open-plan pavilions, arcaded courtyards and formal domed reception halls, but an axial emphasis holds the complex together. Persian palaces, which survive almost exclusively from the c16–c17, assign an even more important role to gardens, which are laid out as formally and geometrically as the garden designs on contemporary carpets. They too contain small pleasure palaces, with columned flat-roofed porticoes which recall Persepolis. The European concept of a palace as a compact and imposing *corps de bâtiment* in which the façade played a vital role seems never to have found favour with Islamic architects.

Mausolea. In the first centuries of Islam especially, a strong body of theological opinion was implacably opposed to the building of mausolea, on the grounds that this practice was unnecessarily ostentatious. But this prohibition was soon ignored and by the CII mausolea were being built in many parts of the Islamic world, especially those areas under Turkish domination. The commonest form of mausoleum was the domed square chamber, often with four axial entrances but also found with three sides closed. This building type was widespread in Early Christian architecture, and was also used for fire temples in Sassanian Persia. The Islamic mausolea which follow this schema are usually small (Aswan), but some of very considerable size are also known, notably the Taj Mahal. Common variations of this schema are the addition of a monumental portal, minarets, high drums with concave sides and the elaboration of the internal zone of transition by multiple

SQUINCHES or by honeycomb vaulting. In Persia (and later Turkey) another type of mausoleum became popular from the C10 – a lofty slender tower with a domed or conical roof and a round, polygonal or flanged ground plan.

Madrasas. From the C11 onwards a new type of cultic building spread from eastern to western Islam – the madrasa. The early madrasas in both eastern and western Islam were simply the teachers' houses, but as the institution grew in importance and therefore in size a more formal architectural schema became necessary. In Iran the madrasa took the 4-iwan form which was popular for mosques, caravanserais and palaces; the difference was in the addition of cells for students, teachers, and officials in two storeys around a reduced courtyard. The iwans were used for teaching and for reading the Koran. The iwans (though not always the cells) were retained in the smaller but very varied madrasas built in Turkey, Syria and Egypt; sometimes a prayer hall replaced the domed chamber behind the southern and largest iwan, and a minaret emphasizes this cultic function in many later Egyptian madrasas. These madrasas often had only one or two iwans, were sometimes completely roofed, and commonly had imposing multi-recessed portals with rich carving. In Egypt they are often part of a complex including such buildings as a mosque, a mausoleum, a hospital and a khanqah (a building for Sufis), while in Syria and Turkey, too, the founder's mausoleum is often attached; but in Iran and the Maghrib madrasas were most often built as independent structures. Maghribi madrasas are characterized by a central court with a portal and an aisled mosque on one axis and two square lecture halls on the other. Although they have been compared to medieval European monasteries, madrasas were much smaller institutions and rarely had living space for more than forty students.

Caravanserais. A distinctively Islamic type of building is the CARAVANSERAI, whose function was to accommodate travellers and their animals. Those built in the first three centuries of Islam are known from literary sources only. But medieval caravanserais survive in quantities in Syria – where they often bear a striking resemblance to Roman castra (*see* CASTRUM) – and in Iran, where they adhere to the traditional 4-iwan plan with separate adjoining rooms around the courtyard and stables in the diagonal axes.

Most Iranian caravanserais are attributed to Shah Abbas (1587–1629) but are in fact datable to any period between the C16 and the C19; the majority were still in regular use a century ago. In Turkey about 100 medieval (mainly C13) caravanserais have survived. They were built at intervals of a day's journey along the major trade routes. Many are extremely elaborate, with imposing carved and projecting portals and an open domed pavilion, which served as a mosque, in the centre of the courtyard. Some are fortified; all are of stone. The courtyard, which is lined with rooms for travellers, usually leads into stables comprising a pillared vaulted hall divided into nave and aisles, the whole of surprisingly Gothic appearance.

Islamic architecture usually exhibits rich surface decoration, especially when the building materials are rubble masonry or mud brick. The aim of the decoration is sometimes to dematerialize the walls, arcades, domes and vaults it covers (Alhambra) but

Detail of the Alhambra, Granada, begun c. 1377

more often the major architectural outlines are not obscured. Figural decoration was forbidden in cultic buildings and the themes were principally vegetal, geometrical, arabesque and epigraphic, though zoomorphic decoration was popular in areas under

*Detail of façade, Castle at Mshatta,
Jordan, mid-c8*

Turkish dominance. Continual repetition of a complex decorative unit, perhaps to suggest infinity, is a common trait of Islamic ornament as of Islamic architecture. The techniques include painting; carved and moulded stucco; coloured glass and marble mosaic; carved stone, marble and wood; glazed tilework; and decorative patterned brickwork.   [RH]

Lit: K. A. C. Creswell, *Early Muslim Architecture*, Oxford 1932, 1940; K. A. C. Creswell, *The Muslim Architecture of Egypt*, Oxford 1952–9; G. Marçais, *L'architecture musulmane d'occident*, Paris 1954; O. Aslanapa, *Turkish Art and Architecture*, London 1971; A. U. Pope, *Persian Architecture*, London–New York 1965; E. Kühnel, *Islamic Art and Architecture*, London 1966; K. Otto-Dorn, *The Art of Islam*, New York 1968.

Isometric projection A geometrical drawing to show a building in three dimensions. The plan is set up with lines at an equal angle

*Isometric
projection*

(usually 30°) to the horizontal, while verticals remain vertical and to scale. It gives a more realistic effect than an AXONOMETRIC PROJECTION, but diagonals and curves are distorted.

Isozaki, Arata, *see* JAPANESE ARCHITECTURE.

Italian architecture Early Christian churches in Italy are mostly of the basilican type: nave and aisles separated by columns carrying arches or straight entablatures, and an apse, sometimes flanked by two subsidiary chambers.

S. Sabina, Rome, c. 425–30

The best preserved of the type in Rome is S. Sabina of *c.* 425–30. Transepts are rare, but occur just in the most monumental churches: Old St Peter's (324–49, with double aisles; not preserved), S. Paolo fuori le Mura (late

*Old St Peter's
(from a fresco in S. Martino ai Monti, Rome)*

271

c5, also double aisles; rebuilt after a fire of 1823), S. Maria Maggiore (c. 430–40). Centrally planned buildings also exist, but they are not frequent. S. Giovanni in Laterano (mid-c5) is octagonal. The central plan is explained here by the fact that it is a baptistery, and for baptisteries a central plan is functionally advantageous. S. Costanza (first half c4), one of the most beautiful buildings, is circular, with an ambulatory, and here the explanation is that it was a mausoleum and for mausolea the ancient Roman tradition was a round plan.

Next to Rome Ravenna was the most important centre. It became the capital of the Roman West in 404, of Odoacer in 476 and of Theodoric in 493, and of the Byzantine bridgehead in Italy in 540. Here also the majority of the churches are basilican: e.g., S. Apollinare Nuovo of c. 510–20 and S. Apollinare in Classe of c. 550. More original and varied are the centrally planned buildings: S. Vitale, completed in 547 and entirely Byzantine with its complex and ingenious octagonal plan, the Mausoleum of Galla

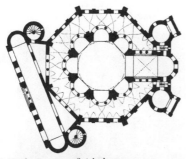

S. Vitale, Ravenna, finished 547

Placidia of c. 450 which is a Greek cross, and the two octagonal Baptisteries. The Mausoleum of Theodoric, as befitted this Gothic king, is much more massive. Moreover, it is of stone, whereas the other buildings are of brick. Characteristic features of these latter are external blank arcading or LESENES connected by a small frieze of blank arches, a motif which became typical of the North Italian Romanesque style. The earliest Italian CAMPANILI are also at Ravenna. They are circular and were probably a c9 addition. The earliest campanile of which we know is the square one once attached to St Peter's in Rome, and this went back to the mid-c8.

At least two Early Christian buildings not in Rome nor in Ravenna must be mentioned. One is S. Salvatore at Spoleto, of the late c4, with a complete façade, its details and those

Detail of the main portal,
S. Salvatore, Spoleto, late c4

of the interior still strikingly Late Roman, but with an oval dome over the chancel which is a motif of Syria and Asia Minor. The other is S. Lorenzo in Milan, remodelled in the c16, but essentially of the late c5 and already exhibiting spatial subtleties as thrilling as those of S. Vitale. Milan possesses more early churches at least in substantial parts than had been known until recently.

The transition from Early Christian to Early Medieval is imperceptible in Italy. S. Agnese in Rome of c. 630 is still entirely Early Christian, but S. Maria in Domnica and S. Maria in Cosmedin of the early c9 are in plan and elevation not essentially different. Nor is

S. Prassede, although the latter has a transept, like that at Fulda probably a self-conscious reversion to Constantinian greatness. S. Maria in Cosmedin has a hall crypt, one of the earliest ever. Both Cosmedin and Domnica end in three parallel apses, and this is so in the most important early c9 churches in North Italy too: Agliate and S. Vincenzo in Milan. But on the whole these and other North Italian churches continue the Early Christian type as well (Brescia S. Salvatore, Pomposa Abbey). Innovations are the square piers of e.g. Bagnacavallo and the small tunnel vaults of S. Maria in Valle at Cividale (which latter has also the finest early medieval sculpture in Italy). Cividale is extraordinary in plan as well, as is the interesting S. Maria at Cassino in the South, of *c.* 780–90, which introduces the Byzantine plan of the inscribed cross and has moreover groin and tunnel vaults and the three parallel apses.

It is not easy to decide where to start using the term Romanesque in Italy. The basilican plan, the columns of the arcades, the apse continuing the nave without a transept remain the Italian norm in the c11 and into the c12. The essential innovations in plan which France and Germany introduced in the late c10 and early c11 did not at once touch Italy and remained the exception even later. Ambulatories with radiating chapels for instance are rare (S. Antimo in Central and Aversa in South Italy), although vestigial ambulatories had occurred remarkably early (S. Stefano Verona, Ivrea Cathedral). The new elements which came in in the c11 seem to have been derived from the Empire. Montecassino of 1066 etc. had a transept, though one not projecting. It also still had the typically Italian three parallel apses. At Salerno Cathedral, consecrated in 1084, the transept stretches out beyond the aisle lines, and S. Nicola at Bari, the most important southern building (begun immediately after 1087), has transepts, alternating supports in the nave, a gallery, two west towers placed in Norman

Plan of S. Nicola, Bari, begun c. 1087

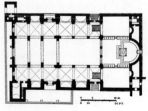

fashion outside the aisle lines and the stumps of two east towers as well. Such east towers also occur, and here clearly under German influence, at S. Abbondio at Como, consecrated in 1095. S. Fedele at Como is later and its trefoil plan is inspired by Cologne. S. Abbondio has no transept, but Aquileia of *c.* 1020 etc. already has, although for the rest it follows Early Christian tradition.

The c12 and the early c13 in Italy are hard to summarize. There is little of regional standards, at least in plans and elevations, though decorative motifs differ considerably from area to area. The great c12 cathedrals of the North Italian plain are truly Romanesque, though they also differ in many respects. But they have mostly alternating supports and galleries inside and the so-called dwarf galleries, small arcaded wall-passages, outside. Their towers are campanili, not integrated with the buildings themselves. Modena, begun in 1099, is the first, with a transept not projecting, and with the traditional three parallel apses. This is the same at S. Ambrogio in Milan with its solemn façade and its beautiful atrium. But the most important aspect of S. Ambrogio is the rib vaults with heavy ribs of plain rectangular

S. Ambrogio, Milan, first half of c12

section. This type occurs also in the South of France, and the several examples in Lombardy are probably all of the c12, i.e., later than the much more sophisticated ribs of Durham. The other principal North Italian cathedrals are Parma of after 1117, with a more German plan (far projecting transepts with apses and only one east apse), Piacenza of *c.* 1120 etc., Cremona and Ferrara. A spectacular appendix to these North Italian cathedrals is their large, detached, octagonal baptisteries. The most famous of the Italian

Cathedral and Baptistery, Pisa;
Cathedral begun 1063, finished C12 or C13

Proto-Renaissance: Baptistery,
Florence, C11–C12

baptisteries, however, is in Central Italy, that of Pisa begun in 1153. Pisa Cathedral, exceptionally large, is exceptional in other ways as well. It was started as early as 1063 (by Busceto) and has long aisled transepts with end-apses, a double-aisled nave and no vaults. The campanile, i.e., the leaning tower, arcaded in many tiers all round, was started in 1173. The same predilection for outer arcading in tiers is to be found at Lucca. Florence is different. Here already in the late C11 a movement arose which deserves the name Proto-Renaissance. It favoured ancient Roman motifs and has a graceful elegance unique in Romanesque Europe. The principal examples are the Baptistery, S. Miniato and SS. Apostoli, all in Florence, and the Badia at Fiesole, none of them exactly datable. A comparable interest in ancient Rome is found in and around Rome in the early C13 (façade, Città Castellana Cathedral, 1210; and façade, S. Lorenzo, Rome, by Vassalletto, 1220). An exception in Central Italy is the church of Chienti near Macerata which is on the Byzantine inscribed-cross plan.

S. Miniato al Monte, Florence, C11–C12

Proto-Renaissance: S. Miniato al Monte, Florence. Detail of the façade, C11–C12

St Marks, Venice, begun 1063

The relations of the the Italian Romanesque to Byzantium are manifold and interesting. The major monument, totally Byzantine, is of course St Mark's in Venice (1063 etc.) with a central plan and five domes. Domes were also placed over naves in a few major South Italian churches (Canosa Cathedral, 1071 etc; Molfetta Cathedral, *c.* 1160 etc.). The inscribed-cross plan appears here and there in different parts of Southern Italy, at Stilo, at Otranto (S. Pietro), at Trani (S. Andrea). The Byzantine elements in Sicilian architecture are fascinatingly overlaid with Saracen and Norman elements. The island had been under Byzantium from the C6, under Islam from 827, under the Normans from 1061. But during the years of the greatest Sicilian architecture, the country was one of the centres of the

Hohenstaufen Emperors. The Norman motifs of Cefalù and Monreale Cathedrals (1131 etc. and 1166 etc.) are patent to English visitors. On the other hand the Martorana at Palermo (1143 etc.) is on the Byzantine inscribed-cross plan, and S. Cataldo in Palermo looks wholly Arabic. This applies even more to the

S. Cataldo, Palermo, pre-1160

royal palaces and pavilions such as the Ziza and the Cuba at Palermo.

Romanesque Italy has much of secular architecture to offer. Here only a few buildings can be referred to – some byzantinizing palaces of Venice (especially the Fondaco dei Turchi) and the equally byzantinizing C11 Palazzo della Ragione at Pomposa, the slender towers of the nobility, especially famous those of San Gimignano and the two in the centre of Bologna, and the town halls of Como (1216), Orvieto and Massa Marittima. All these are of the C13.

But at that time the Gothic style had started on its Italian course. It had come, as in all countries, from France and, as in most countries, by means of the CISTERCIANS (Fossanova 1187 etc., Casamari 1203 etc. with rib vaults, both in Lombardy, S. Galgano in Tuscany 1227 etc.). The collegiate church of S. Andrea at Vercelli of *c.* 1220 etc. is tran-

Fossanova, c. 1140

sitional between Italian Romanesque and
French Gothic. The most original of the early
Gothic buildings in Italy is S. Francesco at
Assisi, begun in 1228 and, oddly enough,
inspired by the French West and most pro-
bably Angers Cathedral. Another early French
(Burgundian) inspiration explains the splendid
castles of Frederick II in the South of Italy and
in Sicily (Augusta; Maniace, Syracuse; Ursino,
Catania) and especially Castel del Monte of *c.*

Castel del Monte, c. 1240

1240 etc., where French Gothic structure is
fascinatingly mixed with ancient Roman detail
used in a spirit of Renaissance. The plans of
these castles are regular, mostly with angle
towers, a plan introduced at the same time in
France and then continued in both countries
(e.g., Ferrara 1389 etc.).

Altogether the Italy of the C13 and C14 is
rich in remarkable secular buildings, the public
halls of Genoa, Orvieto and Piacenza, all C13
and all continuing the Romanesque type, the
slightly later and less peacefully open town
halls of Perugia (1283 f.), Siena (1288 etc.)
and Florence (Palazzo Vecchio 1298 etc.), the
Loggia dei Lanzi in Florence of 1376 with its
strangely un-Gothic round arches, the Doge's
Palace in Venice of 1309 etc., unique in size
and composition, and some C14 palaces in

Ca' d'Oro, Venice, 1421-40

Florence and Siena, and early C15 houses in
Venice (Ca' d'Oro, 1421-40). North Italian
Late Gothic detail is more ornate, more
Northern than that further South (Porta della
Carta, Doge's Palace, *c.* 1440).

This Northern, trans-alpine character applies with much greater force to Milan
Cathedral, begun in 1386 and the work of a

Milan Cathedral, begun 1389, finished 1856

Palazzo della Ragione, Padua, c. 1300

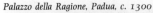

Certosa di Pavia, begun 1396

mixture of masters from Lombardy, Germany and France, all fighting each other. The scale of Milan Cathedral incited the starting on a similar scale of the Certosa of Pavia (1396 etc., built slowly) and S. Petronio, the largest parish church of Bologna (1390 etc.). But meanwhile, i.e., in the C13 and earlier C14, the Gothic style had made progress everywhere in Italy. In Bologna itself the friars' church of S. Francesco in 1236 etc. started with a French ambulatory with radiating chapels. The friars otherwise built large but without an accepted system of plan or elevation. S. Francesco at Siena of 1326 etc. has no aisles and no vault, S. Croce in Florence, the Franciscan church there, of 1294 etc. (by ARNOLFO DI CAMBIO) has aisles and no vault. The east ends of both are in the Cistercian tradition. The Frari (Franciscan) and SS. Giovanni e Paolo, Venice (Dominican; both C14) have aisles, high round piers and rib vaults. The airiness of these churches is fundamentally different from the spatial feeling of the French Gothic. This Italian-ness of Italian Gothic expresses itself most strongly in S. Maria Novella in Florence (Dominican; 1278 etc.)

S. Maria Novella, Florence, 1278–1360

and Florence Cathedral (begun by Arnolfo in 1296). The arcades are much more generously opened than in France so that nave and aisles appear parts of one space and not three parallel vessels. The measure of each bay opening of the arcades is *c.* 64 ft; at Amiens it was *c.* 25 ft. The campanile of Florence Cathedral (by GIOTTO) is the finest of all Italian Gothic campanili. The finest Gothic façades are Siena (1284 etc. by GIOVANNI PISANO) and Orvieto (*c.* 1310 etc.). As against Florence Rome had little to contribute. The only important Gothic church is S. Maria sopra Minerva of *c.* 1280 etc.

For the introduction of the Renaissance also Florence took precedence over Rome,

however much the Renaissance masters owed to ancient Rome. However, even that debt is less great than C19 scholars assumed. It is certain that BRUNELLESCHI in his churches looked more to the Tuscan Proto-Renaissance (*see above*) than to Imperial Rome. For Florence the date of the conversion to the Renaissance is *c.* 1420; for Venice, Milan and also Rome it is a generation later. For Rome ALBERTI, who was more in sympathy with the ancient Roman character in architecture than anyone else, was instrumental in establishing the Renaissance, though he had probably nothing to do with the courtyard of the Palazzo Venezia of *c.* 1470 which was the first to take up the ponderous motif of orders of attached columns to separate arched openings – such as the Romans had used in the

(Left). Colosseum, Rome, 72–80
(Right). Palazzo Venezia, Rome, c. 1470

Theatre of Marcellus and the Colosseum. But on the whole the Quattrocento prefers arcades of slender columns carrying arches, i.e., rather delicate members, and a graceful lively decoration. Examples of the former are Brunelleschi's earliest façade, that of the

Ospedale degli Innocenti, Florence, begun c. 1419, by Brunelleschi

Foundling Hospital in Florence (1419 etc.), and such palace courtyards as that of MICHELOZZO's Palazzo Medici in Florence

Pazzi Chapel, S. Croce, Florence, 1429–46, by Brunelleschi

(1444 etc.) or the Ducal Palace at Urbino (1460s), which also has some of the most exquisite Quattrocento decoration. Palace façades, especially in Tuscany, are still forbidding, in direct continuation of the Trecento. Heavy rustication was favoured (Palazzo Medici, Palazzo Strozzi), though Alberti in his Palazzo Rucellai (1446–60) used a more elegant articulation by tiers of pilasters, and this was taken up by the Cancelleria in Rome (c. 1485 etc.). Church plans are usually longitudinal: Brunelleschi's with nave and aisles and slim arcades, Alberti's S. Andrea at Mantua aisleless, but with side-chapels, a system with a great future. But both Brunelleschi and Alberti and others as well (Giuliano da SANGALLO) favoured central plans and developed them in a variety of ways (Brunelleschi, S. Maria degli Angeli, 1434 etc.; Alberti, S. Sebastiano, Mantua, 1460 etc.; Sangallo, S. Maria delle Carceri, Prato, 1485 etc.).

Central Italians (MICHELOZZO, FILARETE) had introduced the Renaissance to Milan in

Palazzo Rucellai, Florence, 1446-60,
by Alberti

Plan for St Peter's, Rome,
by Bramante, 1506

the 1450s, and at the same time it appeared
in Venice (Arsenal portal, 1457). In contrast
to Central Italy, however, the North of Italy
went in for extremely busy decoration of
façades as well as interiors (Verona and
Brescia Town Halls, Certosa of Pavia, Como
Cathedral, 1470s to 1490s and after 1500).
These façades had considerable influence on
the Early Renaissance in trans-alpine countries.
Even BRAMANTE, in his early years in Milan,
used this rich and playful decoration, though
at S. Maria presso S. Satiro it is rather Alberti
(in Mantua) who inspired him. Bramante
lived in Milan in the same years as LEONARDO
DA VINCI, but it is impossible to say what their
relationship was. Leonardo sketched architectural ideas, but did not build. Nearly all his
church plans are of central types, and he
reached unprecedented complexities. Bramante clearly was attracted by the same problem, even if none of the central churches of
Lombardy can with certainty be ascribed to
him (Lodi, Crema).

With Bramante's move from Milan to Rome
in 1499 the High Renaissance was established,
with more substantial and also more Roman
forms and character (St Peter's, Belvedere
Court Vatican, Palazzo Caprini). RAPHAEL
(Villa Madama), PERUZZI (Villa Farnesina),
and GIULIO ROMANO were Bramante's successors, but the latter two soon turned away
from his style to MANNERISM. The solecisms
of Giulio's Palazzo del Té (1525 etc.) and his
own house (1544), both at Mantua, are both
eloquent and painful. At the same time
MICHELANGELO designed in the Mannerist
way (Medici Chapel and Laurentian Library,

Mantua Cathedral, c. 1545, by Giulio Romano

Medici Chapel, S. Lorenzo, Florence,
begun 1521, by Michelangelo

Dome of St Peter's, Rome, 1588–90,
by Michelangelo and Giacomo della Porta

Florence, 1520s; exterior of St Peter's, 1546 etc.; and Porta Pia, Rome, 1561). Mannerism produced exquisite works (Farnese Palace, Caprarola, by VIGNOLA, 1547 etc.; Villa di Papa Giulio by Vignola, 1550 etc., Casino of Pius IV by LIGORIO, 1560, both Rome; Uffizi, Florence, by VASARI, 1550 etc.), as well as perverse ones (Casa Zuccari, Rome, 1590), but it never ruled unchallenged. In the north of Italy the Renaissance spirit was alive throughout the C16, as is demonstrated by

buildings such as SANSOVINO's Library of S. Marco, Venice (1532 etc.) and Palazzo Corner, Venice (1532 etc.), SANMICHELI's palaces and city gates of Verona (1520s to 1550s), and PALLADIO's palaces inside and villas outside Vicenza. Though in the work of Palladio, especially his churches in Venice, Mannerist traits are easily discovered, most of his secular work must be classed as Renaissance. The problem of Vignola in Rome is similar, but whereas Palladio, where he is not Mannerist,

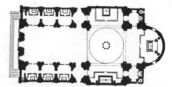

Plan of the Gesù, Rome, 1568, by Vignola

Cortile del Belvedere, Vatican, Rome, completed 1562, after design by Bramante

The Gesù, Rome, 1568–76, by Vignola

oval as early as 1573, but it became a standard element only in the CI7, varied inexhaustibly, especially by the greatest Roman Baroque architects BERNINI and BORROMINI. Bernini uses the oval transversely at S. Andrea al Quirinale, and RAINALDI uses a grouping of

S. Ivo della Sapienza, Rome, 1660, by Borromini

Villa Malcontenta, Mira, near Venice, 1571, by Palladio

belongs to the past, Vignola, where he is not Mannerist, points forward to the Baroque.

There can be no doubt that Vignola's Gesù (begun 1568) established a canon of church plan and elevation for the Baroque: chapels instead of aisles, transepts and a dome (S. Andrea della Valle, S. Carlo al Corso, etc.). The completion of St Peter's by MADERNO was also longitudinal. But the most interesting Baroque churches are those on central or elongated central plans. Vignola had used the

*S. Carlo alle Quattro Fontane, begun 1633,
by Borromini*

*Baldacchino, St Peter's, Rome, 1625,
by Bernini*

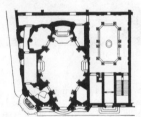

Plan of S. Carlo alle Quattro Fontane, Rome

elements which gives the impression of a
transverse oval at S. Agnese. The façade of
this church, with its two towers and its concave centre, is by Borromini, whose façade
of S. Carlino is even more complex in its use
of concave and convex parts. There the
interior carries the interaction of curves to
the highest point it achieved in Rome, but the
acme of spatial complications was reached by
GUARINI at Turin. Bernini's work at St Peter's
was concerned with decoration on the grandest
scale (Baldacchino, Cathedra Petri) and with
the forecourt in front of Maderno's façade. The
elliptical colonnades and their splaying-out
connection with the façade are aesthetically
and from the planning point of view equally
satisfying.

In the field of major urban planning Rome
had already taken the lead in the late c16,
when the long streets radiating from the

*Scala Regia, Vatican Palace, Rome, 1663–6,
by Bernini*

Piazza del Popolo had been laid out. In
secular architecture Rome contributed less,
though the open façade of the Palazzo
Barberini and the giant pilasters of Bernini's
Palazzo Odescalchi had much influence. For
Baroque palaces Genoa is the most interesting
city.

Villa Reale, Stupinigi, near Turin,
begun 1729, by Juvarra

As early as about 1700 Italy began to tone down the Baroque (FONTANA, then JUVARRA in Turin: Superga, 1717 etc.; Palazzo Madama, 1718 etc.) and in the Veneto a Palladian revival took place (Scalfarotti's S. Simeone, Venice, 1718 etc.; Preti's Villa Pisani, Strà, 1735 etc.).

The C19 is more interesting in Italian architecture than most tourists realize. The neo-classical and especially neo-Greek style has produced much outstanding work. French influence is occasionally patent (S. Carlo Theatre, Naples, by Antonio Niccolini, 1810–

Teatro San Carlo, Naples, 1810–44,
by Niccolini

44). The most monumental church is S. Francesco di Paola at Naples by Pietro Bianchi (1817–28). Neo-Greek masterpieces are JAPELLI's Caffé Pedrocchi at Padua of 1816–31, the Canova Temple at Possagno of 1819–30, the Carlo Felice Theatre at Genoa by C. Barabino of 1827 etc., the Cemetery of Staglieno (1835) by the same, and the grandiose Cisternone at Livorno by P. Poccianti of 1829 etc. A curious anachronism is the use of the classical apparatus of forms in ANTONELLI's two monster towers at Novara and Turin in 1840 and 1863. In the sixties other styles had taken the place of the classical, a Super-Renaissance in MENGONI's Galleria in Milan (1861 etc.), a Lombardo-Gothic in the Milan Cemetery by C. Maciacchini (1863 etc.) and others. As in other Continental countries Neo-Baroque followed the Neo-Renaissance (Law Courts, Rome, by

Court of Honour, Law Courts, Rome,
begun 1888, by Calderini

Palazzo Castiglioni, Milan, 1901, by Sommaruga

G. Calderini, 1888 etc.; University, Naples, by P. P. Quaglia, 1897 etc.), and Art Nouveau the Neo-Baroque. Italian Art Nouveau is inspired by Vienna in the work of Raimondo d'Aronco (Exhibition Palace, Turin, 1902); more original is that of SOMMARUGA (Palazzo Castiglioni, Milan, 1901).

The C20 style started with SANT'ELIA'S dreams of skyscrapers, but the new international style did not make itself felt until the

Palazzetto dello Sport, Rome, 1956–7, by Nervi and Vitellozzi

Design by Sant'Elia

Istituto Marchiondi, Milan, 1959, by Viganò

Restaurant at Lisanza, by Castiglioni

Casa del Fascio, Como, begun 1932, by Terragni

The Foro Mussolini, Rome, 1933

later twenties and did not get a chance of showing itself in buildings until after 1930 (G. Terragni, Casa del Fascio, Como, 1932 etc.). Today Italian architecture is characterized by much high talent (PONTI, ALBINI, FIGINI & POLLINI, Luigi Moretti) but a lack of unified direction. The most important contribution is that of NERVI to the structural and aesthetic problems of wide spans.

Lit: A. Venturi, *Storia dell'Arte Italiana*, vols. I–XI, Rome 1901–1940; R. Krautheimer, *Early Christian and Byzantine Architecture*, Pelican History of Art, Harmondsworth 1965, paperback edn 1974; K. J. Conant, *Carolingian and Romanesque Architecture 800–1200*, Pelican History of Art, 3rd edn, Harmondsworth

1974, paperback edn 1974; P. Frankl, *Gothic Architecture*, Pelican History of Art, Harmondsworth 1962; J. White, *Art and Architecture in Italy, 1250–1400*, Pelican History of Art, Harmondsworth 1966; L. H. Heydenreich and W. Lotz, *Architecture in Italy, 1400–1600*, Pelican History of Art, Harmondsworth 1974; R. Wittkower, *Art and Architecture in Italy, 1600–1750*, Pelican History of Art, Harmondsworth 1973, paperback edn 1973; C. L. V. Meeks, *Italian Architecture, 1750–1914*, New Haven–London 1966.

Iwan A vaulted hall open at one or both ends, mostly used in Islamic architecture either as an entrance portal or facing a courtyard. Mosques and mausolea consisting only of an *iwan* are also known. Usually the vault is encased in a decorative rectangular frame, and from the C13 it was often decorated with stalactite or honeycomb vaulting. While the *iwan* originated in Parthian palatial architecture, and the huge c6 *iwan* of the Sassanian palace at Ctesiphon long dominated the imaginations of Islamic architects, it was used in early Islamic architecture not only for palaces (Samarra, Merv) but also apparently in the private houses of eastern Islam. From the C11 the cruciform disposition of four axial *iwans* around a courtyard became conventional for mosques, *madrasas* and caravanserais – among other buildings – in eastern Islam, and is often found too in medieval Turkey, Syria and Egypt. In this 4-*iwan* plan, popular for a millennium in Islamic architecture, the *iwan* is used to stress axiality, to knit the ground plan together and to break up the monotony of rows of arcades. The form allows considerable variety; *iwans* can be deep or shallow and of differing width and height within a single building, and are often

Iwan: Friday Mosque, Isfahan, c. 1150, Mosaics C15, restored c. 1800

used as the principal means of articulating a façade. *Iwans* were used, depending on the type of building, for prayers, teaching, royal audiences or monumental entrances.   [RH]

Ixnard, Michel d' (1726–95), a French early neo-classical architect, worked mainly in the Rhineland. Born at Nîmes and trained in Paris, he became architect to the Elector of Trier. His main work is the large abbey church of St Blasien in the Black Forest (1764–84), with a Doric exterior and solemn Corinthian rotunda.

Lit: L. Vossnack, *Pierre-Michel d'Ixnard*, Remscheid 1938; P. du Colombier, *L'Architecture française en Allemagne au XVIIIᵉ siècle*, Paris 1956.

Jacobean architecture, *see* ENGLISH ARCHI-TECTURE.

Jacobsen, Arne (1902–71). His style is the most refined and meticulous INTERNATIONAL MODERN. He was initially influenced by ASPLUND'S Stockholm Exhibition of 1930 and appeared as an International Modern architect with work of 1931, at a time when Copenhagen was reaching the climax of a classicism as refined and meticulous in its own way as Jacobsen's architecture was to be. He built chiefly private houses and housing until shortly before the Second World War, when he was also commissioned for work on a larger scale. The Town Hall of Aarhus (with Eric Møller, 1938–42) has a concrete skeleton tower. Søllerud, an outer suburb of Copenhagen, got a town hall by Jacobsen in 1939–42. The Munkegård School at Gentofte, another outer suburb of Copenhagen, is characterized by the many small play-yards between classrooms (1952–6). The Town Hall of Rødovre, yet another outer suburb of Copenhagen, is Jacobsen's most exquisite public building (1955–6), entirely unmannered, without any cliché or gimmick, nothing really but the formal apparatus of the International thirties, yet handled with an unparalleled precision and elegance. The same is true of his cylinder-boring factory at Aalborg (1957) and the S.A.S. Hotel at Copenhagen (1960; a tower block on a podium of the Lever House type, *see* SKIDMORE, OWINGS & MERRILL). In 1964 St Catherine's College at Oxford was completed to Jacobsen's designs. During the fifties he also designed some fine and original furniture and cutlery. (For illustration *see* SCANDINAVIAN ARCHITECTURE.)
Lit: T. Faber, *A. Jacobsen*, Milan 1964.

Jadot de Ville Issy, Jean-Nicolas (1710–61). He was trained in France and became at an early age architect to the Archduke Franz I of Lorraine whom he accompanied to Vienna on his marriage to Maria Theresa. He built the Academy of Sciences and Letters in Vienna (1753) and the menagerie at Schönbrunn, both in an accomplished Louis XV style: and he probably provided the plan for the royal palace in Budapest (1749, greatly altered in the C19). He also designed the Arco di S. Gallo in Florence, erected to mark the Archduke's accession to the Grand Duchy of Tuscany in 1739.
Lit: J. Schmidt, in *Wiener Forschungen zur Kunstgeschichte*, 1929.

Jain architecture, *see* INDIAN ARCHITECTURE.

Jamb The straight side of an archway, doorway, or window; the part of the jamb which lies between the glass or door and the outer wall-surface is called a *reveal*.

James, John (c. 1672–1746), built St George's, Hanover Square, London (1712–25), with its hexastyle portico of free-standing Corinthian columns and pediment. This idea was quickly taken up by HAWKSMOOR (St George's, Bloomsbury) and GIBBS (St Martin-in-the-Fields). Wricklemarsh, Blackheath (1721), was his masterpiece, but it was demolished, like nearly all his work. He rebuilt St Mary's Church, Twickenham, except for the west tower (1713–15). He published an English edition of Andrea Pozzo's treatise on perspective in c. 1720.
Lit: H. M. Colvin, *A Biographical Dictionary of English Architects 1660–1840*, London 1954.

Japanese architecture We derive our information about the early architecture of Japan from motifs on a bronze bell of the c2–c3 A.D. and on mirrors, and from clay models (*haniwa*) from burial mounds of the c5–c7. Ordinary houses were lake-dwellings with steeply-pitched roofs whose verges projected right out beyond the gable, where they were supported by a pillar placed against the wall. The reed thatch was kept in place by battens and short cross-beams (*katsuogi*) laid over the roof-ridge.

This primitive method of building lives on in Shinto (the animistic Japanese national religion) architecture, whose deliberately simple hall-shrines (*jinja*) are notable for the clarity of their structure and clean-cut execution. Purity of worship is underlined by the custom of tearing shrines down and rebuilding them at regular intervals, mostly of twenty years. Hence the virtually unmodified survival of the old style for millennia. The earliest type of shrine (*ōyashiro-zukuri*) put the door to the

Ise Naiku, Shoden

right of the mighty central pillar against the gable, but it was later moved to the middle. The Ise school of buildings (*shimmei-zukuri*), probably under the influence of palace architecture, placed the shrine crosswise and inserted the entry in one of the sides. Cross-beams on the ridge (*katsuogi*) and crossed gable-ends (*chigi*) are idiosyncrasies of Shinto shrines whose origins are lost in the mists of time, and now have only decorative importance. The shrines proper, which are only accessible to priests, lie within a fence. The path to the shrine area is denoted by *torii* – simple, trapezoid gates with the lintel prolonged beyond the posts.

The late style (*gongen-zukuri*) preferred for ceremonial shrines since the c17 employs numerous components to create intricate roofs and interiors, clearly betraying Buddhist influence. The buildings of Nikkō are cases in point.

The spread of Chinese culture after the mid-c6 brought with it mainland, and above all Buddhist, types of building. As in CHINESE ARCHITECTURE the hall (*dō*) is the cardinal feature of the temple complex (*tera, ji*), and it rests on a platform (*kidan*) laid with stone slabs, or is later raised on piles over a plastered mound (*kamebara* = turtle's back). The load-bearing elements are wooden columns (*hashira*), with flimsy walls and doors or windows stretched between them. Above this framework lies the IMPOST zone (*kumimono*) of the roof, which extends with its supporting blocks (*masu, to*) and bolsters (*hijiki*) in one or more tiers beyond the wall to support the eaves. The roof (*yane*) is covered with tiles or with a thick layer of cypress shingles, and took one of the four shapes adopted from China: gabled (*kirizuma-*

Shinto shrines near Hiroshima, built between 1241 and 1571

Main Hall (kondô), *Tôshôdai-ji, Nara*

Nandaimon, Tôshôdai-ji, Nara

zukuri); hipped (yosemune-z.); gambrel (irimoya-z.), with hipped feet to the gables; tented (hôgyô-z). The upward slant of the eaves at the corners never attains the extreme curvature of many South Chinese examples.

In the interior the eye can either see right though the exposed framework to the rafters (taruki), or it is checked by coffering (tenjô). The interior of the hall is articulated into the core or 'mother' room (moya) defined by the main roof-posts, and the surrounding envelope made by the passages (hisashi) of the verandas, which may occasionally be surrounded by a further enclosed space (mokoshi) under its own lean-to roof (sashikake) – e.g. the main hall of Hôryû-ji at Nara, probably post-670. The surface area of a hall is reckoned according to a system already cur-

rent in the C10 (Kemmen-kihô), after the number of intercolumniations (ken), the breadth of the core, and the sides (men) of the hall with its envelope of hisashi.

The earliest forms of hall are the main hall (kondô = golden hall) and the teaching hall (kôdô) of the Nara period (646–794). The moya serves as an inner sanctuary (naijin), and the enveloping area as an outer sanctuary (gejin) for the ritual transformation of the images. The kondô customarily has a three-tiered projecting system of supports (mitesaki) for the roof, and the kôdô a simpler system, both broadly similar to the T'ang style of China (618–907), but described in Japan as Wa-yô, or 'the Japanese system'.

In the Heian period (794–1185) the functions of kondô and kôdô were united in

Main Hall (kondô) *at Tôshôdai-ji, Nara, late c8*

one hall, the 'chief hall' (*hondô*), which may be virtually square, with a transverse division into an inner and an outer sanctuary, the latter endowed with far more floor-space for the more sizable congregation of the esoteric sects. The cult of the Buddha Amida in the same period created the so-called Amida-halls, or 'halls for perpetual transformation' (*jôgyô-dô*), with a relatively small inner sanctuary (*naijin*) and a surrounding outer envelope (*gejin*) widened to two intercolumniations. Such halls can approximate to palaces in appearance, and are then architectural embodiments of paradise (Phoenix hall, *Hôô-dô*,

of the Byôdô-in at Uji, 1053). There are in addition other halls with to some extent complex plans, like the halls for the founders of sects or temples (*kaisan-dô, miei-dô*), or the refectory in Hôryû-ji already constituted as a double hall (*narabi-dô*).

Next to the hall the pagoda (*tô*) is, as reliquary monument, the most important constituent of a temple. The Japanese have favoured many-tiered pagodas of wood, which in construction and appearance resemble a series of superimposed structures each with its own roof. In fact only the ground floor is organized as a usable chapel-like

(Above), Phoenix Hall (Hôô-dô) of the Byôdô-in at Uji, near Nara, 1053; (below), detail of roof and interior

sanctuary; the upper storeys are not exploited. The whole building is arranged round a sturdy central pillar (*shimbashira*) which rises up through all the storeys to above the main roof where it supports umbrella-like ornamental bands or rings. The storeys are often structurally unconnected with the central pillar, so as to avoid stresses and possible destruction in earthquakes. The relics are buried in the ground under the stone base of this pillar. The decoration of the four chapels of the square ground floor and of the *mokoshi* used for the transformation ceremony occasionally indicates that the pagoda is an

Pagoda of Yakushi-ji, Nara, post 730

architecturally expressed mandala (pagoda of Daigo-ji near Kyôtô, 951). The timber-framing (*kumimono*) of the roofs is virtually identical with that of the halls.

There is always an uneven number of storeys – three (Hokki-ji) or five (Hôryû-ji) in the Nara period, later mostly seven, though there may be as many as thirteen (Tanzan shrine, 1532). A sense of rhythm may be imparted by the inclusion of false mezzanines (*mokoshi*), as in the Yakushi-ji (730 or somewhat later). In the variant called the *Tahô-tô*, beloved since the end of the Heian period, the square roof of the ground floor is surmounted by a stumpy cylindrical section which turns into a wooden STUPA-like dome. This is in turn surmounted by a square tent-roof on an

intricate system of supports (Ishiyamadera, 1194). Spread out alongside it is a temple composed of a cloistered court, various types of gate (*chûmon, sammon*), a bell-tower, a library (kyôzô), monks' quarters and outhouses.

The rigidly symmetrical temple complexes laid out according to mainland models in the Asuka (594–644) and Nara (645–784) periods were later relaxed to allow each building to fit freely into the landscape.

In Japan as in China stylistic development was chiefly a matter of the timber-framing of the roof. The classic 'Japanese' style (*Wa-yô*) of the Nara period was succeeded in the C12–C13 by the 'Chinese style' (*Kara-yô*) stemming from the Hang-chou region, with its serried system of supports (*tsume-gumi*). Almost contemporaneously, the so-called 'Indian style' (*Tenjiku-yô*) arrived from the coastal provinces of Southern China, with up to ten tiers of projecting eaves supports.

Japanese *palace architecture* used largely the same constructional principles for its halls as in temple architecture, but much less elaborately. The complexes are also considerably more modest than those of China or Europe. The Imperial Palace of the Heian period was reconstructed in the C19 in Kyôto. Single halls are grouped in and around courtyards, and linked by roofed corridors. The timber-framing is reduced to essentials and deliberately exposed, and the interiors are broken up by movable screens and sliding doors, and actively related to court and garden via entirely openable verandahs (*hisashi*).

Katsura Palace, Kyôto, 1620–47;
view into the garden from Ko-shoin

The character of the *residences of the nobility* (*shinden-zukuri*) in the Heian period was quite similar, but the buildings were

Silver Pavilion, Ginkaku of Jishô-ji, Kyôto, 1498 *Castle at Himeji, Hyôgo, 1609*

more loosely and less consistently arranged. Corridors (*watadono*) went from the main building (*shinden*) to ancillary ranges (*tai-no-ya*), pavilions on artificial ponds, and to outhouses. The interiors were laid with reed matting (*tatami*), had no solid furniture, and restricted the painted decoration to moveable features such as screens and sliding doors. Authentic examples of this genre do not survive; they are known only from picture-scrolls and texts.

After the still more chaste style of the knightly order (*buke-zukuri*) in the Kamakura period (1185-1333), the aristocracy indulged in a more prodigal manner of living in the C15 – the so-called 'studio system' (*shoin-zukuri*). In the end wall of the ceremonial apartments display niches (*toko-no-ma*) and shelves (*chigai-dana*) were inserted for the display of works of art. The not infrequently gilded walls and sliding-doors were painted with vigorously coloured motifs (e.g. the reception-hall of the Nishi-Hongan-ji, and that of the Nijô castle in Kyôto).

The introduction of European firearms gave rise to the construction of *fortified castles* (*shiro*) in Japan. They were built in the midst of towns, as fortresses and as

Reception Hall (ò-hiroma) of Nijô Castle, Kyôto, early C17

administration centres of the feudal duke-
doms, from the late c16 onwards. They had
moats and high sheer walls. At their heart
stood the multi-storied main tower (*tenju*),
with gun-slits in the (often plastered) wooden
walls (Himeji castle) and elaborate roofing.

At the other extreme to ceremonial architecture is the teahouse (*chashitsu*), devoted to
the aesthetic cult of tea-drinking. Its rural
hut-like style embodies Zen Buddhism's spirit
of simplicity and naturalness. One has almost
to crawl through the low entry (*nijiri-guchi*),
the interior is small, and only a few mats
(*tatami*) large. The walls are plastered grey,

*Sogo Store, Osaka, completed 1932,
by Togo Murano*

Tea House, Jo-an, Oiso, 1618

and there is a predilection for untreated wood
and bamboo. The display niche (*toko-no-ma*) is
occupied by a single *objet d'art* in isolation. [RG]

Modern Japanese architecture. With the
Meiji Restoration (1868) Japan renounced its
isolation and opened itself up to Western
influences. The English architect Josiah Conder,
a pupil of William BURGES, founded the
College of Architecture at the University of
Tokyo in 1874. Conversely, Frank Lloyd
WRIGHT's Imperial Hotel in Tokyo revealed
the influence of traditional Japanese methods
of construction on American architects (1916-
20; the treatment of the scrubbed brownish-
yellow brick and of the coarse lumps of stone
is actually more reminiscent of the art of the
Maya than of the Japanese). Wright's Czech
assistant, Antonin Raymond (b. 1890), settled
in Tokyo after the completion of this building.
His first important projects were strongly
influenced by PERRET – the St Luke Hospital
(1928) and the chapel of the Christian
Women's College (1934), both in Tokyo. The
Sogo store in Osaka, calibrated by vertical
ribs, was completed by Togo Murano (b.
1891) in 1932. It is the first important build-

ing by a Japanese architect in the INTER-
NATIONAL MODERN style.

At the end of the 1950s Japanese architecture won renown as suddenly as that of
Brazil fifteen years before it – and here as
there the decisive impulse came from LE
CORBUSIER. Some of the leading architects
had worked in his office: Kunio Maekawa (b.
1905) from 1928–30; Junzo Sakakura (b.
1904) from 1929–37, during which time he
designed the Japanese pavilion for the Paris
World Fair of 1937; Takamasa Yoshisaka (b.
1917) from 1950–53, that is, at the time Le
Corbusier was working on the Chandigarh
project. These three architects executed Le
Corbusier's design for the Museum of Western
Art in Tokyo (1955–9). But the first impor-
tant building after the Second World War was
once again by A. Raymond – the *Reader's
Digest* offices in Tokyo (1949), a one-storey
disc on reinforced concrete supports. Kenzo
TANGE (b. 1913), who worked in the office of
Maekawa, used a similar design for the
Peace Centre in Hiroshima (1950). Sakakura's
Museum of Art in Kamakura (1952) and
Maekawa's Concert Hall and Library in
Yokohama (1954) made a relatively lively
use of geometry; Tange's Town Hall in
Shimizu (1954), like that by him in Tokyo
(1956), used skeleton construction with glass
walls. In a ten-storey block composed of flat
discs in Harumi, Tokyo (1957–8), on the
other hand, Maekawa's use of salient balconies
and rough concrete surfacing was an un-
ambiguous affirmation of BRUTALISM.
Maekawa's Festival Halls (*kaikans*) in Tokyo
(1960) and Kyôto (1961) assert the distinct-
ness of their parts: free-standing concrete
columns on the ground floor, horizontally
arranged offices on the first floor (with upturned corners), from which project various
geometrically shaped blocks of greater bulk.

Hajima Town Hall, 1959, by Junzo Sakakura

Other noteworthy buildings by Maekawa include the Gakashuin University (1961) and the Setagaya Community Centre (1959), both in Tokyo. Sakakura's architecture is more finished: the Town Halls of Hajima (1959), Kure (1962) and Hiraoka (1964), the pharmaceutical laboratories in Osaka (1961), the Silk Centre in Yokohama (1959), and a department store combined with a railway station at Shibuya in Tokyo (1961). Yoshisaka's major work is the Town Hall of Gotsu (1962).

St Mary's Cathedral, Tokyo, 1964, by Tange

The foremost practitioner of recent Japanese architecture is, however, undoubtedly Kenzo Tange. All his mature works are in concrete, which is left as rough as possible and used to produce the most dramatic effects. His influence on young architects is as evident in actual buildings as in urban design. The architects of the *Metabolism Group* (founded 1961) may be seen as disciples of his. By far the most prolific of them is Kiyonori Kikutake (b. 1928). He has pushed the logic of structural expression to extreme and fantastic limits – his own star-shaped house (1958), borne on four columns; the Treasury at the great shrine of Izumo (1963), with slanting walls at the sides which shelter a stretch of about 160 feet in one direction; the Tokoen Hotel in Kaika Spa (1965), whose guestrooms are supported on freestanding columns like a bridge; the Community Centre in Miyakonojo (1966) with a wheel-shaped superstructure of steel on a concrete plinth; and the Pacific Hotel in Chigasaki (1967), in which cylindrical service-towers are girdled by bands of windows of varying height and breadth, interrupted at intervals by 'clip-on' clusters of bathrooms. The other founding members of the Metabolist Group were Furnihiko Maki (b. 1928): auditoria of the universities of Nagoya, 1961 and Chiba, 1965; Noriaki Kurokawa: the steel-framed Nitto Shokuiu factory in Sagae, 1965; and Masato Otaka (b. 1923): the prefecture-cum-cultural centre of Chiba, 1967, the Co-operative headquarters in Hananzumi, 1966, and Yamanouchi, 1967, and a housing project for the town of Sakaide, 1965, in which traffic is simply but effectively organized to run on different levels. Tange's most promising former colleagues include: Sachio Otani – Kyôto International Conference Building

International Conference Building at Kyôto, 1963–66, by Sachio Otani

Olympia Sports Stadium, Tokyo, 1963–4,
by Kenzo Tange

(1963–6); religious headquarters of the Tenso Kotai Jingu sect at Tabuse (1966); and Arata Isozaki – Girls' College and Central Library in Oita (1965–6).

Lit: R. T. Paine, A. C. Soper, in *The Art and Architecture of Japan*, Pelican History of Art, 2nd edn, Harmondsworth 1974, paperback edn 1974; W. Alex, *Japanese Architecture*, New York 1963; E. von Erdberg-Consten, *Japanische Architektur*, 1968; H. Ota, *Japanese Architecture and Gardens*, 1966; Mori & Ooka, *Pageant of Japanese Art*, vol. 6, Tokyo 1957; W. Speiser, *Oriental Architecture*, London 1965.

Japelli, Giuseppe (1783–1852), a leading Italian romantic architect and landscape gardener, was a true eclectic of a type rare in Italy. Beginning at the Caffè Pedrocchi, Padua (1816), in a very elegant version of neoclassicism, he then turned to a severe manner derived from the astylar backs of Palladian villas – e.g., Villa Vigodarzere, Saonara (1817) – then to a bold Grecian style for the Doric slaughterhouse in Padua (1821, now the Istituto d'Arte). After a visit to France and England he added a neo-Gothic wing to the Pedrocchi (1837), and finally built the neo-Rococo Teatro Verdi, Padua (1847). His landscape parks are consistently in the English manner; most of them are in the Veneto (e.g., Saonara, Ca' Minotto, Rosà), but one of the finest was at Villa Torlonia, Rome (1840).

Lit: M. Gallimberti, *Giuseppe Japelli*, Padua 1963; C. L. V. Meeks, *Italian Architecture 1750–1914*, New Haven 1966.

Javanese architecture, *see* SOUTH-EAST ASIAN ARCHITECTURE.

Jean de Chelles Architect of the south transept of Notre Dame in Paris (begun 1258). He died soon after. His successor and perhaps son, **Pierre de Chelles**, was still active in 1316, when he was called to Chartres Cathedral as a consultant.

Lit: R. Branner, *St Louis and the Court Style*, London 1965.

Jean d'Orbais Probably the designer and first master mason of Reims Cathedral (begun *c.* 1211).

Lit: R. Branner, 'Jean d'Orbais and the Cathedral of Reims' in *Art Bulletin* XLIII, 1961.

Jefferson, Thomas (1743–1826), legislator, economist, educationalist, and third President of the United States of America (1801–9), was also an able and immensely influential architect. The son of a surveyor, he inherited a considerable estate in Albemarle County, where in 1769 he chose a high romantic site for his own house, Monticello. He derived the plan from Robert MORRIS's *Select Architecture*, but modified it with reference to GIBBS and

Leoni's edition of PALLADIO. It has porticos front and back and a great forecourt with octagonal pavilions at the corners and square pavilions terminating the wings. It is very carefully thought out, both in its planning, on which he had strong personal views, and in its adaptation of Palladian elements. He was interested in Palladio mainly as the interpreter of Roman villa architecture, and looked back to Antiquity for the 'natural' principles of his architectural theory. In 1785, while he was in Europe, he was asked to design the Virginia State Capitol for Richmond. With the help of CLÉRISSEAU, he produced a temple design based on the Maison Carrée (16 B.C.) at Nîmes, but Ionic instead of Corinthian and with pilasters in place of half-columns on the flanks and rear. The Virginia State Capitol (completed 1796 with the assistance of LATROBE) set a pattern for official architecture in the U.S.A. As Secretary of State to George Washington he played a leading part in planning the new federal capital in Washington from 1792 onwards. After he became President he entrusted Latrobe with the task of completing the new Capitol (1803, burnt 1814). Latrobe also assisted him with the University of Virginia, Charlottesville – a group of porticoed houses (each containing a professor's lodging and a classroom) linked by colonnades in a formal plan, with a great Pantheon at one end of the oblong composition (1817–26). (For illustrations see CLASSICISM and UNITED STATES ARCHITECTURE.)

Lit: F. Kimball, *Thomas Jefferson Architect*, Boston 1917; F. D. Nichols, *Thomas Jefferson's Architectural Drawings*, Boston–Charlottesville, 3rd edn 1961.

Jenney, William Le Baron (1832–1907), was born in Massachusetts, studied at the École Centrale des Arts et Manufactures in Paris, was an engineer in the Civil War, and opened a practice in architecture and engineering in Chicago in 1868. In 1869 he published a book called *Principles and Practice of Architecture*. By far his most important building was the Home Insurance Building (1883–5), because its iron columns, iron lintels and girders, and indeed steel beams, prepared the way for the skeleton construction of the Chicago School (*see* HOLABIRD & ROCHE). Stylistically his work is of no interest.

Lit: C. W. Condit, *The Rise of the Skyscraper*, Chicago 1952; C. W. Condit, *American Building Art: The Nineteenth Century*, New York 1960.

Jetty The projecting floor-joists supporting the OVERHANG of a timber-framed building, sometimes called a *jettied storey*.

Jib door A concealed door flush with the wall-surface, painted or papered to correspond with the walls. The DADO and other mouldings are similarly carried across the door.

Joggle, Joggling Masons' terms for joining two stones in such a way as to prevent them from slipping or sliding, by means of a notch in one and a corresponding projection in the other. It is often seen exposed on the face of a flat arch. If the joggle is concealed it is called a 'secret joggle'.

Johnson, Philip (b. 1906), lives in Connecticut. He became an architect only in middle age. His fame was first spread by the house he built for himself at New Canaan (1949) – very much in the style of MIES VAN DER ROHE – a cube with completely glazed walls all round. The siting is romantic, and perhaps in the years about 1950 one should already have been able to guess that Johnson would not remain faithful to Mies's principles. In the guest-house (1952) close to his own house vaults began to appear, inspired by SOANE, and the synagogue at Port Chester, New York (1956), made it clear that he would prefer variety, the unexpected effect, and elegance to the single-mindedness of Mies. Buildings of more recent years are the Amon Carter Museum at Fort Worth, Texas (1961), the Art Gallery for the University of Nebraska at Lincoln (1962), the New York State Theatre for the Lincoln Center in New York (1962–4), the indianizing shrine at New Harmony, Indiana (1960), additions to the Boston Public Library (1964–73), Corpus Christi, Art Museum of South Texas (1970–72) and Minnesota I.D.S. Center, Minneapolis (1970–73). (For illustration *see* UNITED STATES ARCHITECTURE.)

Lit: H.-R. Hitchcock, *Philip Johnson*, New York 1966.

Joists Horizontal timbers in a building, laid parallel to each other with their upper edges REBATED to receive the boards of a floor. The underside either forms the ceiling of the room below or has ceiling laths nailed to it. In a large floor the main or *binding* joists are often crossed by smaller *bridging* joists which bear the floorboards. For a span exceeding about 15 ft, it was usual to insert one or more

SLEEPERS to carry the joists, which would then run longitudinally.

Jones, Inigo (1573–1652), a genius far in advance of his time in England, imported the classical style from Italy to a still half-Gothic North and brought English Renaissance architecture to sudden maturity. He was the same age as Donne and Ben Jonson, and only nine years younger than Shakespeare. Born in London, the son of a Smithfield clothworker, he appears to have visited Italy before 1603, being then a 'picture-maker'. Not until 1608 is he heard of as an architect (design for the New Exchange in London), and his earliest known buildings date from later still. Meanwhile he had become a prominent figure at Court as a stage-designer for masques in the most lavish and up-to-date Italian manner. Many of his designs survive, of fantastic Baroque costumes and hardly less fantastic architectural sets, executed in a free, spontaneous style of draughtsmanship he had presumably picked up in Italy. In 1613 he went to Italy again, this time for a year and seven months, with the great collector Lord Arundel. He returned with an unbounded admiration for PALLADIO and a first-hand knowledge of Roman monuments unique in England at that date. (He met SCAMOZZI in Venice.)

From 1615, when he became Surveyor of the King's Works, until the Civil War in 1642 he was continuously employed at the various royal palaces. Immediately he built three startlingly novel buildings which broke uncompromisingly with the Jacobean past: the Queen's House, Greenwich (1616–18 and 1629–35); the Prince's Lodging, Newmarket (1619–22, now destroyed); and the Banqueting House, Whitehall, London (1619–22). The Queen's House is the first strictly classical building in England, though there was a long break in its construction (the foundations were laid in 1616, but the elevations and interior date from 1632–5). The Prince's Lodging, modest in size, set the pattern for the red-brick, stone-quoined, hipped-roof house with dormers, so popular later in the century. The Banqueting House is Jones's masterpiece; it perfectly expresses his conception of architecture – 'sollid, proporsionable according to the rulles, masculine and unaffected' – as well as his adoration of Palladio. But though every detail is Palladian it is not a mere imitation. Everything has been subtly transmuted and the result is unmistakably English: solid, sturdy, and rather phlegmatic. The Queen's Chapel, St James's Palace, London (1623–7), was also something new for England – a classical church, consisting of an aisleless parallelogram with a coffered segmental vault, a pedimented front, and a large Venetian window. Equally striking but more elaborate was the Bramantesque temple design he used for King James's hearse in 1625.

His principal buildings for Charles I have been destroyed, except for the Queen's House, Greenwich. This is an Italian villa sympathetically reinterpreted, whose chastity and bareness must have seemed daringly original. The upper-floor loggia is very Palladian, as is also the two-armed, curved open staircase to the terrace; but, as always with Jones, nothing is a direct copy. The proportions have been slightly altered and the general effect is long and low and very un-Italian. Inside, the hall is a perfect cube and symmetry prevails throughout. Also to the 1630s belonged his great Corinthian portico at Old St Paul's, transforming the medieval cathedral into the most Roman structure in the country, and Covent Garden, the first London square, of which the church and a fragment of the square survive, both rebuilt. The square was conceived as one composition, the houses having uniform façades with arcaded ground floors and giant pilasters above (perhaps influenced by the Place des Vosges, Paris). In about 1638 he also produced elaborate designs for an enormous Royal Palace in Whitehall. These reveal his limitations and it is perhaps fortunate for his reputation that they were never executed.

1642 brought his brilliant career at Court to an end. He was with the king at Beverley, but nothing more is heard of him until 1645. Although his property was sequestrated he was pardoned in 1646 and his estate restored. From then onwards he seems to have swum quite happily with the political tide, working for the Parliamentarian Lord Pembroke. The great garden front at Wilton House was for long thought to have been built by him at about this date, but is now known to have been designed by his assistant Isaac de Caus (c. 1632). It was badly damaged by fire c. 1647 and the famous state rooms therefore date from about 1649, by which time Jones was too old to give much personal attention; he put it in the hands of his pupil and nephew by marriage, John WEBB. Nevertheless, the celebrated double-cube room, perhaps the most beautiful single room in England, epitomizes his style of interior decoration – gravity and repose combined with great opulence of heavy and rather French classical detail. Innumerable buildings have been attributed to Jones, of which a few may have had some connection with him, notably the pavilions at Stoke Bruerne Park (1629–35). Though profound, his immediate influence was confined to Court circles. In the early C18 he largely inspired the Palladian revival of BURLINGTON and KENT. (For illustrations see ENGLISH ARCHITECTURE and PALLADIANISM.)

Lit: J. A. Gotch, Inigo Jones, London 1928; J. Summerson, Inigo Jones, Harmondsworth 1966; J. Harris, S. Orgel & R. Strong, The King's Arcadia: Inigo Jones and the Stuart Court, Exh. Cat., London 1973.

Juan de Álava (d. 1537), a Spanish master mason on the verge of Late Gothic and Early Renaissance, appears first as consultant at Salamanca Cathedral in 1512 (with eight others) and Seville Cathedral in 1513 (with three others), in the latter years as master to the newly restarted work at Plasencia Cathedral (first with Francisco de Colonia, see SIMÓN DE COLONIA, who soon quarrelled with him). Then we come across him as the designer of the cloister of Santiago Cathedral (1521 onwards) and finally as master mason to Salamanca Cathedral after the death of Juan GIL DE HONTAÑÓN in 1526. S. Esteban at Salamanca (1524 etc.) is also by him; this and the work at Plasencia round the crossing are perhaps his finest.

Lit: F. Chueca Goitia, Arquitectura del siglo XVI (Ars Hispaniae, vol. XI), Madrid 1953; G. Kubler & M. Soria, Art and Architecture in Spain and Portugal and their American Dominions, 1500–1800, Pelican History of Art, Harmondsworth 1959.

Jubé The French name for ROOD SCREEN.

Jugendstil, see ART NOUVEAU.

Jussow, Heinrich Christoph (1754–1825). He was born in Kassel, was given a classical education and then studied law at Marburg and Göttingen before joining the Landgräfliches Baudepartment under Simon Louis Du RY in 1778. He later studied architecture in Paris under DE WAILLY and visited Italy and England (1784–8). He completed Du Ry's Schloss Wilhelmshöhe outside Kassel and built numerous ornamental buildings in the Roman, Chinese and Gothic tastes in the park. Among these is his masterpiece, the picturesque castle Löwenburg (1793–8), much influenced by the English Gothic Revival and the most elaborate C18 essay in the genre anywhere on the Continent. Built on a dramatic hillside site and approached by drawbridge across a moat, it is amply provided with ramparts, towers and (originally) guards in medieval costumes.

Lit: H. Vogel, Heinrich Christoph Jussow, 1754–1825: Baumeister in Kassel und Wilhelmshöhe, Kassel 1958.

Jutting, see OVERHANG.

Juvarra, Filippo (1678–1736). Born in Messina of a family of silversmiths, he was the greatest Italian C18 architect and a brilliant draughtsman. His elegant and sophisticated Late Baroque buildings are as typical of their period as Tiepolo's paintings and equally accomplished; they have a Mozartian gaiety and fecundity of decorative invention. Trained in Rome under FONTANA (1703/4–14), he first won fame as a stage-designer, and this theatrical experience was to leave a mark on nearly all his subsequent work.

In 1714 he was invited to Turin by Victor Amadeus II of Savoy, who appointed him 'First Architect to the King'. Apart from a trip to Portugal, London, and Paris in 1719–20, he remained in Turin for the next twenty years. His output was enormous, ranging from churches, palaces, country villas, and hunting-lodges to the layout of entire new city quarters in Turin – not to mention work as an interior decorator and designer of furniture and the applied arts. Of his churches the Superga (1715–31) and the chapel of the Venaria Reale (1716–21), both near Turin, are spectacular, the former being by far the grandest of all Italian Baroque sanctuaries, comparable with Melk in Austria and Einsiedeln in Switzerland. S. Filippo Neri (1715), S. Croce (1718 etc.), and the Carmine (1732–5, gutted during the war) in Turin are all very fine. His city palaces in Turin include Palazzo Birago della Valle (1716), Palazzo Richa di Covasolo (1730), and Palazzo d'Ormea (1730), while his work for the king is remarkable for the four great palaces and villas in or near Turin – Venaria Reale (1714–26), Palazzo Madama (1718–21), Castello di Rivoli (1718–21, but only partly executed), and his masterpiece Stupinigi (1719–33). In all these works he had the assistance of numerous highly skilled painters, sculptors, and craftsmen, who were summoned from all parts of Italy to execute his designs.

Though little development is discernible in his style, which is a brilliant epitome of current ideas rather than an original invention, it reached its fine flower in Stupinigi, especially in the great central hall whose scenic quality and skeletal structure suggest an influence from north of the Alps. In 1735 Juvarra was summoned to Spain by Philip V, for whom he designed the garden façade of the palace La Granja at S. Ildefonso near Segovia and the new Royal Palace in Madrid, executed with alterations after his death by G. B. SACCHETTI. He died suddenly in Madrid in January 1736. (For illustrations *see* ATTIC STOREY, BAROQUE ARCHITECTURE and ITALIAN ARCHITECTURE.)

Lit: V. Viale (ed.), *Mostra di F. Juvarra, architetto e scenografo,* Exh. Cat., Messina 1966; R. Pommer, *Eighteenth Century Architecture in Piedmont: The Open Structures of Juvarra, Alfieri and Vittone,* New York/London 1967; S. Boscarino, *Juvarra, Architetto,* Rome 1973.

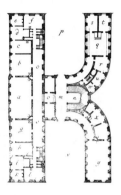

Kahn, Louis (1901–74), born on the Island of Ösel, Estonia, went to the United States in 1905. He studied and lived in Philadelphia, and was internationally noticed only fairly late in life, first with the Yale University Art Gallery (with D. Orr, 1951–3), then with the Richards Medical Research Building of the University of Pennsylvania (1958–60). The Art Gallery has for its main exhibition space a SPACE-FRAME ceiling. The Medical Research Building has all ducts gathered in a number of sheer square towers projecting from and rising above the outer walls: the reason is said to be functional, but the effect is curiously dramatic and indeed aggressive – an original version of the so-called BRUTALISM which has come to the fore in the last fifteen years. His other notable buildings include the first Unitarian Church at Rochester, N.Y. (1962), a dormitory at Bryn Mawr College, Pa. (1965) and the Salk Institute Laboratories, La Jolla, Calif. (1965).

Lit: V. Scully, Jr, *Louis Kahn*, New York–London 1962.

Kaisariya The term is of Greek origin, and in classical times meant the imperial market. In the Islamic world it simply denotes a market. Its precise meaning, however, varies considerably from one area and period to another, which renders generalization difficult. In many parts of the Muslim world the *kaisariya* was a lock-up market, often protected by guards, where the more valuable wares such as textiles and objects of precious metal were sold. The Turkish *bedesten* is of this kind. Usually sited at the centre of the BAZAR, it is a stone building closed by iron doors and often consisting of long aisles which form a grid pattern; the crossings are domed. In Egypt and elsewhere the *kaisariya* was a whole cluster of buildings comprising covered arcades and courtyards with shops, warehouses and living rooms. In Iran, the long aisles and domed crossings of Turkish *bedestens* recur, but are multiplied on a massive scale; the so-called *kaisariya* at Isfahan (1619) is in fact a full-scale *bazar*, and affords a rare example of such a complex erected during a single building campaign and comparatively free of later accretions. [RH]

Kazakov, Matvey Feodorovich (1738–1812), the leading neo-classical architect in Moscow, began in the Baroque tradition but soon adopted an Imperial Roman style, perhaps under QUARENGHI'S influence (he modified and completed Quarenghi's palace at Ostankino (Moscow) for Count Sheremetiev). He probably designed the rich Pashkov Palace, Moscow (1785–6). His main building is the Church of the Ascension on the Razumovski estate (1790–3). He also built the Petrovski Palace near Moscow (1775–82), a curious Gothic or rather Russian medieval revival fantasy.

Lit: G. H. Hamilton, *Art and Architecture of Russia*, Pelican History of Art, Harmondsworth 1954.

Keel moulding A moulding whose outline is like the keel of a ship.

Keel moulding

Keep The principal tower of a castle, containing sufficient accommodation to serve as the chief living-quarters permanently or in times of siege; also called a *donjon*.

Kent, William (1685-1748), painter, furniture designer, and landscape gardener as well as architect, was born in Bridlington of humble parents. He contrived to study painting in Rome for ten years and was brought back to London in 1719 by Lord BURLINGTON, whose friend and protégé he remained for the rest of his life. Whimsical, impulsive, unintellectual, in fact almost illiterate, he was the opposite of his patron – and as happy designing a Gothic as a classical building. Nevertheless, he allowed Burlington to guide his hand along the correct PALLADIAN lines in all his major commissions. His interior decoration is more personal, being, like his furniture, richly carved and gilt in a sumptuous manner deriving partly from Italian Baroque furniture and partly from Inigo JONES, whose Designs he edited and published in 1727.

He did not turn architect until after 1730, by which time he was well into his forties. His masterpiece Holkham Hall (1734 onwards, executed by BRETTINGHAM) was almost certainly designed largely by Burlington, whose hand is evident in the 'staccato' quality of the exterior and in the use of such typical and self-isolating features as the VENETIAN WINDOW within a relieving arch. The marble apsidal entrance hall, based on a combination of a Roman basilica and the Egyptian Hall of VITRUVIUS, with its columns, coffered ceiling, and imposing staircase leading up to the *piano nobile*, is one of the most impressive rooms in England. His lavishly gilt and damask-hung state apartments, elaborately carved and pedimented door-frames, heavy cornices, and niches for antique marbles epitomize the English admiration for Roman magnificence. The Treasury (1734), 17 Arlington Street (1741), and 44 Berkeley Square (1742-4), all in London, are notable mainly for their interior decoration, especially the latter, which contains the most ingenious and spatially exciting staircase in London. Esher Place, Surrey, was the best of his neo-Gothic works (wings, now demolished, and other alterations, c. 1730). His last building, the Horse Guards, London (1750-8), is a repetition of Holkham, with the unfortunate addition of a clock-tower over the centre: it was executed after his death by John VARDY. Through Burlington's influence Kent was ap-

pointed Master Carpenter to the Board of Works in 1726, and Master Mason and Deputy Surveyor in 1735. He is perhaps more important historically as a designer of gardens than as an architect. He created the English landscape garden, being the first to have 'leap'd the fence and seen that all nature is a garden'. This revolutionized the relation of house to landscape and led to less dramatic and forceful façades. From his time onwards the country house was designed to harmonize with the landscape, rather than to dominate and control it. (For illustration *see* NEO-GOTHIC.)

Lit: M. Jourdain, *The Work of William Kent*, London 1948; H. M. Colvin, *A Biographical Dictionary of English Architects, 1660-1840*, London 1954.

Kentish rag Hard unstratified limestone found in Kent and much used as an external building stone on account of its weather-resisting properties.

Key, Lieven de (*c.* 1560-1627), the first Dutch architect of note to work in the so-called 'Dutch Renaissance' style (similar to English Jacobean). He worked for some years in England before becoming municipal architect of Haarlem (1593), where he introduced the characteristic colourful use of brick with stone dressings (horizontal bands of stone, stone voussoirs set singly in brick above windows, etc.). His masterpieces are the façade of the Leiden Town Hall (1597), the Weigh House, Haarlem (1598), the Meat Market, Haarlem (1602-3) and the tower of the Nieuwe Kerk, Haarlem (1613).

Lit: A. Fokkema, R. C. Hekker & E. H. ter Kuile, *Duizend Jaar Bouwen in Nederland*, vol. II, Amsterdam 1958; E. H. ter Kuile in *Dutch Art and Architecture, 1600-1800*, Pelican History of Art, Harmondsworth 1966, paperback edn 1972.

Key pattern, *see* FRET.

Keyser, Hendrick de (1565-1621), the leading architect of his day in Amsterdam, where he was appointed city mason and sculptor in 1595. He worked in a style somewhat similar to English Jacobean. His plain utilitarian churches had great influence on Protestant church design in the Netherlands and Germany, especially his last, the Westerkerk in Amsterdam, built on a Greek cross plan (1620). His most important secular buildings are the Amsterdam Exchange (1608) and Delft Town Hall (1618). In domestic architecture he simplified and classicized the traditional tall, gable-fronted Amsterdam house, introducing the ORDERS and reducing the number of steps in the gables. His works were engraved and published by Salomon de Bray as *Architectura Moderna* (1631).

Lit: M. D. Ozinga, *De Protestantsche Kirchenbouw in Nederland*, Paris & Amsterdam 1929; E. Neurdenburg, *Hendrik de Keyser*, Amsterdam 1929; E. H. ter Kuile in *Dutch Art and Architecture, 1600–1800*, Pelican History of Art, Harmondsworth 1966, paperback edn 1972.

Keystone The central stone of an arch or a rib vault; sometimes carved.

Keystone

Khmer architecture, *see* SOUTH-EAST ASIAN ARCHITECTURE.

Kikutake, Kiyonori, *see* JAPANESE ARCHITECTURE.

King-post, *see* ROOF.

Kiosk A light open pavilion or summerhouse, usually supported by pillars and common in Turkey and Persia. European adaptations are used mainly in gardens, as band-stands, for example, or for small shops selling newspapers.

Klenze, Leo von (1784–1864), a North German, was a pupil of GILLY in Berlin, and then of DURAND and PERCIER and FONTAINE in Paris. He was architect to King Jérome at Cassel in 1808–13, and to King Ludwig I in Munich from 1816. Klenze was at heart a Grecian, but he was called upon to work in other styles as well, and did so resourcefully.

His chief Grecian buildings are the Glyptothek, or Sculpture Gallery (1816–34) – the earliest of all special public museum buildings – and the Propylaea, both in Munich. The Propylaea was begun in 1846, a late date for so purely Grecian a design. Grecian also, strangely enough, is that commemorative temple of German worthies, the Walhalla near Regensburg (1830–42), which is in fact a Doric peripteral temple. But as early as 1816 Klenze did a neo-Renaissance palace (Palais Leuchtenberg), the earliest in Germany, even if anticipated in France. This was followed by the Königsbau of the Royal Palace (1826) – which has affinities with the Palazzo Pitti – and the freer, more dramatic Festsaalbau of the same palace (1833). In addition, Klenze's Allerheiligen Church, again belonging to the palace (1827), is – at the king's request – neo-Byzantine. *See also* GÄRTNER. (For illustration *see* PROPYLAEUM.)

Lit: O. Hederer, *Leo von Klenze, Persönlichkeit und Werk*, Munich 1964; P. Böttger, *Die alte Pinakothek in München*, Munich 1972.

Klint, P. V. Jensen (1853–1930), is famous chiefly for his Grundvig Church at Copenhagen, won in competition in 1913 but, after further development of the design, begun only in 1919. With its steeply gabled brick façade, all of a stepped organ-pipe design, and with its interior, Gothic in feeling, it stands mid-way between the Historicism of the C19 and the Expressionism of 1920, a parallel in certain ways to BERLAGE's earlier Exchange. The surrounding buildings, forming one composition with the church, are of 1924–6. Klint's son Kaare (1888–1954) was one of the brilliant Danish furniture designers. (For illustration *see* SCANDINAVIAN ARCHITECTURE.)

Lit: K. Millech & K. Fisher, *Danske Arkitekturstrømninger, 1850–1950*, Copenhagen 1951.

Knapped flint Flint split in two and laid so that the smooth black surfaces of the split sides form the facing of a wall. *See also* FLUSHWORK.

Knight, Richard Payne (1750–1824), country gentleman and landscape-gardening theorist, began in 1774 to build Downton Castle for himself: rough, irregular (the plan is anti-symmetrical rather than asymmetrical), and boldly medieval outside, smooth, elegant, and distinctly neo-classical within, it is the prototype of the picturesque country house 'castle' which was to remain popular for half a century. In 1794 he published *The Landscape – a Didactic Poem* attacking 'Capability' BROWN'S smooth and artificial style of landscape gardening. It was dedicated to Uvedale PRICE, who published a lengthy reply differing on points of detail. Knight's much longer *Analytical Enquiry into the Principles of Taste* (1805) examines the PICTURESQUE philosophically.

Lit: N. Pevsner, *Studies in Art, Architecture and Design,* London 1968.

Knobelsdorff, Georg Wenzeslaus von (1699–1753). Court architect to Frederick the Great with whom he was on terms of close friendship and whose sophisticated, eclectic tastes he faithfully mirrored although they quarrelled over the designs for Sanssouci. He was a Prussian aristocrat and began his career in the army, but in 1729 resigned his Captain's commission to train as a painter. By 1733 he was already on friendly terms with Frederick (then Crown Prince) for whom he built a little circular temple of Apollo in his garden in the garrison town of Neu-Ruppin. Frederick then enabled him to visit Italy and after his return commissioned him to enlarge the old border house of Rheinsberg (1737). Immediately after Frederick's accession to the throne in 1740 Knobelsdorff was sent off to Dresden and Paris to prepare himself for more ambitious projects. He added a wing to Monbijou for the Queen Mother (1740–42) and a wing to Charlottenburg for the King (1742–6) with a very grand, rich, colourful interior plastered with Rococo motifs (partly destroyed in the Second World War). In 1741 he began the Berlin opera-house with a less exuberant interior and a severely Palladian exterior which owes much to English neo-Palladian models (burnt out 1843, renewed by K. F. Langhans; seriously damaged 1945 but now restored). While this was going forward he was appointed Surveyor General of Royal Palaces and Parks, Director in Chief of all buildings in the royal provinces, and a member of the Prussian Council of Ministers. In 1744 work began on the large Stadtschloss at Potsdam, colourful outside and in, and with one of the richest of all Rococo interiors (destroyed). He began Sanssouci, Potsdam, in 1745 in close collaboration with the King, who provided the general design. (Frederick's original sketch survives.) In 1746 he quarrelled with the King who dismissed him and thus ended his architectural career, though he made

posthumous amends by writing the 'Éloge de Knobelsdorff' which was read at the Berlin Academy in 1753. (His sketch design for a palace for Prince Heinrich in Unter den Linden, Berlin, was built by J. Boumann, 1748–66. It is now the Humboldt University.)

Lit: A. Streichhan, *Knobelsdorff und das friderizianische Rokoko,* Berlin 1932.

Knöffel, Johann Christoph (1686–1752). He was a contemporary in Dresden of CHIAVERI and LONGUELUNE and was much influenced by the French classicism of the latter. His Wackerbarth Palais, Dresden (1723–8, destroyed 1945) and Kurländer Palais, Dresden (1728–9, destroyed 1945) were elegant examples of restrained pilastered town architecture. In 1734 he became Oberlandbaumeister in Dresden and in 1737 began his masterpiece, the Brühl Palais (destroyed 1899). He rebuilt the large hunting-lodge, Hubertusburg, between 1743 and 1751 and completed his rival Chiaveri's Hofkirche in Dresden after Chiaveri returned to Rome in 1748.

Lit: E. Hempel, *Baroque Art and Architecture in Central Europe,* Pelican History of Art, Harmondsworth 1965; W. Hentschel & W. May, *J. C. Knöffel,* Berlin 1973.

Knotted columns A stone support carved in such a way that it appears to consist of two or four columns with their shafts tied into a knot, occasionally found in Romanesque architecture.

Knotted columns: Pieve of S. Pietro, Gropina

Korb, Hermann (1656–1735). He began as a carpenter and was promoted architect by Duke Anton Ulrich of Brunswick-Wolfenbüttel. He visited Italy in 1691, then supervised the construction of the schloss at Salzdahlum designed by Johann Balthasar Lauterbach (1660–94) – a vast building with features anticipating DIENTZENHOFER's Pommersfelden and HILDEBRANDT's Upper Belvedere, but of mainly timber construction faced to simulate stone (demolished 1813). Also of wood is the interesting library he erected at Wolfenbüttel (1706–10). It was centrally planned (on the advice of Leibniz) with an oval interior lit by windows in the dome. His only other building of note is the church of the Holy Trinity, Wolfenbüttel (1705) with two tiers of galleries creating an octagonal central space.

Lit: U. von Alvensleben, *Die Braunschweiger Schlösser der Barockzeit und ihr Baumeister H. Korb*, Brunswick 1937.

Kremlin A citadel or fortified enclosure within a Russian town, notably that in Moscow.

Krubsacius, Friedrich August (1718–89). Architect and architectural theorist, author of *Betrachtungen über den wahren Geschmack der Alten in der Baukunst* (Dresden, 1747) attacking the Baroque style and reverting to the humanist idea that 'the noblest structure, man, the perfect proportions and graceful symmetry of his figure, were the first standards for architectural invention'. Though indebted to French theorists, he thought little of French architecture. He became Royal architect and in 1764 professor of architecture at the new Academy of Arts in Dresden. But in his buildings he remained faithful to the Baroque. The most notable were the Neues Schloss at Neuwitz (1766–75; destroyed) and the Landhaus in Dresden (1770–76; burnt out 1944).

Lit: F. Löffler, *Das alte Dresden*, Dresden 1955.

Kurokawa, Noriaki, *see* JAPANESE ARCHITECTURE.

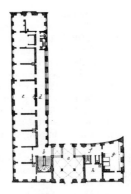

La Vallée, Simon de (d. 1642), son of an architect, settled in Sweden in 1637, becoming royal architect in 1639. He designed the Riddarhus in Stockholm (1641/2), derived from de BROSSE's Palais Luxembourg in Paris. He was succeeded as royal architect by his son **Jean** (1620–96), who travelled and studied in France, Italy, and Holland between 1646 and 1649. He completed his father's Riddarhus (with Justus VINGBOONS who designed the façades), built the Oxenstjerna Palace, Stockholm (1650), which introduced the Roman *palazzo* style, and designed the Katherinenkirka, Stockholm (1656), on a centralized plan probably derived from de KEYSER, as well as various palaces in Stockholm (e.g., for Field-Marshal Wrangel) and country houses (Castle Skokloster). (For illustration *see* SCANDINAVIAN ARCHITECTURE.)

Lit: T. Paulsson, *Scandinavian Architecture*, London 1959.

La Venta architecture, *see* MESOAMERICAN ARCHITECTURE.

Label, *see* HOOD-MOULD.

Label-stop An ornamental or figural BOSS at the beginning and end of a HOOD-MOULD.

Labrouste, Henri (1801–75), a pupil of VAUDOYER and Le Bas, won the Grand Prix in 1824, and was in Rome 1824–30. After his return he opened a teaching *atelier* which became the centre of rationalist teaching in France. His rationalism appears at its most courageous in the interior of his only famous work, the Library of Ste Geneviève by the Panthéon in Paris (1843–50). Here iron is shown frankly in columns and vault, and endowed with all the slenderness of which, in contrast to stone, it is capable. Labrouste's is the first monumental public building in which iron is thus accepted. The façade is in a nobly restrained Cinquecento style with large, even, round-arched windows, and there again, in comparison with the debased Italianate or the neo-Baroque of Beaux Arts type which just then was becoming current, Labrouste is on the side of reason. The London architect, J. B. Bunning (1802–63), in his Coal Exchange of 1846–9, now criminally demolished, was as bold in his use of iron, but as an architect was undeniably lacking in the taste and discipline of Labrouste. In the 1860s Labrouste also built the reading-room and the stackrooms of the Bibliothèque Nationale, again proudly displaying his iron structure.

Lit: S. Giedion, *H. Labrouste*, Paris 1960.

Labyrinth The most plausible theory traces this word from the pre-Hellenic *labrys*

Labyrinth from Chartres Cathedral, drawn by Villard de Honnecourt

= double axe, the ritual symbol of Minoan Crete. It originally referred to the palace of Knossos ('House of the Double Axe'), and then to other buildings with similarly tortuous plans. Amongst this and other labyrinths Pliny mentions that of Egypt, one of the Seven Wonders of the World (the giant temple of Amenemhet III in front of the pyramid near Hamara, c. 2300 B.C.). The name was extended to all embodiments of the maze in architecture, gardens, ornament and art. Epochs and civilizations with a taste for numerical symbolism and geometrical pattern-making have been especially prone to use it – Ancient Egypt, Hellenic Greece, Gothic (the cathedrals of Chartres, Sens and Amiens), Mannerism, Baroque, and even the Modern movement. By contrast with the relatively rare examples of architecture actually built on a labyrinthine plan (e.g. the maze in the *tholos* of Epidauros, the flights of steps at the Temple of Apollo in Didyma), there have been numerous architectural fantasies imagined by architects, painters and designers (PIRAN-ESI, LEDOUX, GAUDI, POELZIG, SCHAROUN, etc.). Unlike the mostly symmetrical labyrinths of Antiquity and the Middle Ages, whose intricate doubling-back nonetheless led inevitably to an exit, Mannerism introduced genuine confusion and even entrapment, through forks and the dead-end. The labyrinth enjoyed a great popularity in the Mannerist and the Baroque periods and later; there was scarcely a park that did not have a maze amongst its bosquets.

Lit: H. Ladendorf, 'Das Labyrinth in Antike und neuerer Zeit', in *Archäologischer Anzeiger*, 1963, and in *Labyrinthe* (Exh. Cat.), Berlin 1966; P. Santarcangeli, *Il Libro dei Labirinti*, Florence 1967.

Laced windows Windows pulled visually together vertically by strips, usually in brick of a different colour from that of the wall, which continue vertically the lines of the window surrounds. It was a popular motif c. 1720 in England.

Lacunar A panelled or coffered ceiling: also the sunken panels or COFFERING in such a ceiling.

Lady chapel A chapel dedicated to the Virgin, usually built east of the CHANCEL and forming a projection from the main building; in England it is normally rectangular in plan.

Lancet window A slender pointed-arched window, much used in the early C13.

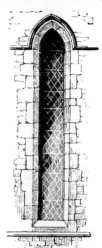

Lancet window: Witney, Oxfordshire

Langhans, Carl Gotthard (1732–1808). German neo-classical architect famous for the Brandenburg Gate in Berlin (1788–91), his one important work and the first of the Doric ceremonial gateways that were to be built all over Europe in the early C19. The Brandenburg Gate is still C18 in its elegant and rather un-Grecian proportions. His later buildings were more ponderous and cubic, e.g., the Potsdam Theatre (1795) and the theatre in Gdańsk (Danzig) (1798–1801). He also did the theatre at the Charlottenburg Schloss in Berlin (1788–91). His son **Carl Ferdinand Langhans** (1782–1869) worked under SCHINKEL in the 1830s but continued his father's style in the palace of Kaiser Wilhelm I in Berlin (1836, burnt out 1945 but now restored externally), the old Russian Embassy in Berlin (1840–41) and the theatre at Wroclaw (Breslau) (1843). (For illustration *see* CLASSICISM.)

Lit: W. Hinrichs, C. G. *Langhans*, Strassburg 1909.

Langley, Batty (1696–1751), the son of a Twickenham gardener, published some twenty architectural books, mostly manuals for the use of country builders and artisans, e.g., *A Sure Guide to Builders* (1729); *The Builder's Compleat Assistant* (1738). But his fame rests on his *Gothic Architecture Restored and Improved* (1741) in which he formalized KENT's neo-Gothic into 'orders'. He built little, and none of his works survives.

Lit: J. Summerson, *Architecture in Britain, 1530–1830*, Pelican History of Art, Harmondsworth 1969, paperback edn 1970.

Lantern A small circular or polygonal turret with windows all round, crowning a roof or DOME.

(Right). Lantern: S. Ivo della Sapienza, Rome, 1660, by Borromini

Lantern: Peterhof, near Leningrad, by Rastrelli, begun 1747

Lantern cross A churchyard cross with lantern-shaped top; usually with sculptured representations on the sides of the top.

Lasdun, Denys (b. 1914), worked with Wells COATES 1935–7. From 1938 to 1948 he was a partner in TECTON. On the strength of his fertile imagination, his directness, and the force of his forms he has become one of the most impressive English architects of the post-war years. His principal buildings to date are flats at Bethnal Green, London (1956–9); luxury flats in St James's Place, London (1957–61); the Royal College of Physicians in Regent's Park, London (1960–

64); Fitzwilliam House, Cambridge (1959 etc.), and some of the buildings for the University of East Anglia at Norwich (1963 onwards).

Lit: R. Maxwell, *New British Architecture*, London 1972.

Latin cross A cross with three short arms and a long arm.

Latrobe, Benjamin (1764–1820), the son of a Moravian minister in England, spent his boyhood and youth in England, in Germany, and again in England, where he worked under S. P. COCKERELL, as an architect, and under

Smeaton as an engineer. He must have been much impressed by SOANE's work. In 1795 he emigrated to America, where he was taken up by JEFFERSON and did the exterior of the Capitol at Richmond, Va. In 1798 he moved to Philadelphia, and there built the Bank of Pennsylvania and in 1800 the Water Works (the latter largely an engineering job). The architecture of these two buildings was resolutely Grecian – the first examples of the GREEK REVIVAL in America – the former Greek Doric, and the latter Ionic. Of the same year 1799 is Sedgeley, the earliest GOTHIC-REVIVAL house in America. In 1803 Latrobe was called in at the Capitol in Washington, and there did some of his noblest interiors, with much vaulting in stone. The work dated from 1803-11, but the majority had to be redone after the fire of 1814; so what one now sees is mostly of Latrobe's maturity. But his most perfect work is probably Baltimore Cathedral (1804-18). Its interior in particular, on an elongated central plan, with the shallow central dome and the segmental tunnel vaults is as fine as that of any church in the neo-classical style anywhere. Latrobe had at the beginning submitted designs in Gothic as well as classical forms, the Gothic being the earliest Gothic church design in America. Among his other buildings were the Baltimore Exchange (1816-20, destroyed 1904), the 'Old West' of Dickenson College, Carlisle, Pa. (after 1811) and the Louisiana State Bank, New Orleans (begun 1819). Latrobe was the first fully trained architect in the United States. Yet his engineering training made it possible for him, throughout his career, to work as well on river navigation, docks, etc. – a combination which was to become typical of American C19 architects. His pupils included MILLS, STRICKLAND and William Small. (For illustration see UNITED STATES ARCHITECTURE.)

Lit: T. Hamlin, *B. H. Latrobe*, New York/Oxford 1955.

Lattice window A window with diamond-shaped LEADED LIGHTS or with glazing bars arranged like an open-work screen: also, loosely, any hinged window, as distinct from a SASH WINDOW.

Laugier, Marc-Antoine (1713-69), was a Jesuit priest and outstanding neo-classical theorist. His *Essai sur l'architecture* (1753) expounds a rationalist view of classical architecture as a truthful, economic expression of

man's need for shelter, based on the hypothetical 'rustic cabin' of primitive man. His ideal building would have free-standing columns. He condemned pilasters and pedestals and all Renaissance and post-Renaissance elements. His book put NEO-CLASSICISM in a nutshell and had great influence, e.g., on SOUFFLOT.

Lit: W. Herrmann, *Laugier and French Architectural Theory*, London 1952.

Laurana, Luciano (c. 1420-79), was born in Dalmatia, and appeared in Urbino in 1465 at the humanist court of Federigo da Montefeltro, which included Piero della Francesca and, later on, FRANCESCO DI GIORGIO. He prepared a model for the Palazzo Ducale, Urbino, in c. 1465 and was appointed architect of the Palazzo (1468-72), for which he designed numerous chimney-pieces, doorcases, etc., of extreme refinement and elegance, anticipating and surpassing the C18 in delicacy. His masterpiece is the Florentine-style *cortile* in the Palazzo Ducale, with a light springy arcade of Corinthian columns echoed by shallow pilasters between the windows on the upper storey. The triumphal arch at the Castelnuovo in Naples has been ascribed to him.

Lit: P. Rotondi, *The Ducal Palace of Urbino*, London 1969.

Laves, Georg Friedrich (1788-1864), was a nephew of H. C. JUSSOW under whom he was trained in Kassel. After travelling in Italy, France and England he settled in Hanover in 1814. During the next fifty years Hanover was to be transformed by his romantic GREEK REVIVAL style almost as impressively as were Berlin and Munich by his great contemporaries SCHINKEL and KLENZE. The Leineschloss, later Landtag (begun 1817), Wangenheim Palace (begun 1827) and the more Italianate Opera (1848-52) are his masterpieces, together with the layout of the Waterlooplatz (1855) and other new squares and streets. But Laves was also an inventive and remarkably forward-looking engineer and submitted a startling design for the 1851 Exhibition Hall in London to be constructed largely of iron railway-track. It was an early attempt at prefabrication.

Lit: G. Hoeltje, *G. J. F. Laves*, Hanover 1964.

Le Blond, Jean-Baptiste Alexandre (1679-1719). A minor Parisian architect, he built the Hôtel de Vendôme, Paris (1705-6) and Hôtel de Clermont (1708-14) and brought out a new and influential edition of Daviler's *Cours d'architecture c.* 1710. But he is of importance mainly because he introduced the French Rococo style into Russia. His masterpiece is the vast Peterhof Palace, St Petersburg (1716), though his plans were not carried out to any great extent, and only the terrace garden has been preserved of his work there. But the interior is decorated with typically French elegance and civilized reticence.

Lit: G. H. Hamilton, *Art and Architecture of Russia*, Pelican History of Art, Harmondsworth 1954.

Le Breton, Gilles (*fl.* 1530). Master-mason who carried out Francis I's enlargements at the Château de Fontainebleau and presumably designed them. His only surviving works are the Porte Dorée, the north side of the Cour du Cheval Blanc, and the now greatly mutilated portico and staircase in the Cour de l'Ovale (begun 1531). Le Breton's simple and austere classicism, in his later works, derived from SERLIO and was to have some influence on the next generation of French architects, notably LESCOT.

Lit: L. Hautecoeur, *Histoire de l'architecture classique en France*, vol. I, 2nd edn, Paris 1963–7.

Le Corbusier, Charles-Edouard (Jeanneret) (1887–1966). Le Corbusier was born at La Chaux-de-Fonds in French Switzerland. He worked in PERRET's office in Paris in 1908–9, then for a short time in that of BEHRENS in Berlin. Le Corbusier was the most influential and the most brilliant of C20 architects, of a fertility of formal invention to be compared only with Picasso's. But he was also restless and an embarrassingly superb salesman of his own ideas. It is no doubt relevant to an understanding of his mind and his work that he was an abstract or semi-abstract painter, comparable in some ways to Léger.

In Le Corbusier's early work three strains can be followed, continually interacting. One is the mass-production of housing (Dom-ino, 1914–15, Citrohan House, 1921; the abortive housing estate of Pessac, 1925). The second is town planning. Le Corbusier published and publicized a number of total plans for cities with a centre of identical skyscrapers, symmetrically arranged in a park setting, with lower building and complex traffic routes between. They are less realistic than GARNIER's Cité Industrielle of 1901, but far

more dazzling (Ville Contemporaine, 1922; Plan Voisin, 1925; Ville Radieuse, 1935; plan for Algiers, 1930). The third strain of Le Corbusier's early thought tends towards a new type of private house, white, cubist, wholly or partly on PILOTIS, with rooms flowing into each other. The earliest is the villa at Vaucresson (1922). Many followed, including the exhibition pavilion of the Esprit Nouveau at the Paris Exhibition of 1925, with a tree growing through the building. The most stimulating and influential villas were probably those at Garches (1927) and Poissy (1929–31). In the same years Le Corbusier did some designs for major buildings: for the League of Nations at Geneva (1927; not executed) and the Centrosojus in Moscow (1928). The designs had a great effect on progressive architects everywhere. Of major buildings actually erected two must be referred to: the Salvation Army Hostel in Paris (begun 1929) with its long CURTAIN WALL; and the Swiss House in the Paris Cité Universitaire (1930–32), introducing a random-rubble baffle wall to contrast with the usual white-rendered concrete. In 1936 Le Corbusier was called to Rio de Janeiro to advise on the new building of the Ministry of Education which was subsequently executed by COSTA, NIEMEYER, Reidy (1909–64), and others. Their contribution has never been fully distinguished from his. In 1947 Le Corbusier was one of the group of architects to come to terms with the programme of the United Nations Headquarters in New York, and the Secretariat building, a sheer glass slab with solid, windowless end walls, is essentially his design.

At the same time, however, Le Corbusier began to abandon this rational smooth glass-and-metal style which until then he had been instrumental in propagating, and turned to a new anti-rational, violently sculptural, aggressive style which was soon to be just as influential. The first example is the Unité d'Habitation at Marseille (1947–52), with its heavy exposed concrete members and its fantastic roofscape. The proportions are worked out to a complicated system, called MODULOR, which Le Corbusier invented and pleaded for. The Unité was followed by another at Nantes (1953–5) and a third at Berlin (for the Interbau-Exhibition, 1956–8). Le Corbusier's most revolutionary work in his anti-rational style is the pilgrimage chapel of Ronchamp not far from Belfort (1950–4), eminently expressive, with its silo-like white tower, its brown concrete roof like the top of a mushroom, and its wall pierced by small windows of arbitrary shapes in arbitrary positions. In his villas the new style is represented by the Jaoul Houses (1954–6), whose shallow concrete tunnel vaults soon became an international cliché. Of yet later buildings the Philips Pavilion at the Brussels Exhibition of 1958 had a HYPERBOLIC PARABOLOID ROOF, a form pioneered by M. Novitzki and the engineer Dietrich in the stadium at Raleigh, North Carolina (1950–53). At Chandigarh Le Corbusier laid out the town and built the extremely powerful Law Courts and Secretariat (1951–6), the influence of which proved to be strongest in Japan. At the same time he did some houses at Ahmedabad (1954–6) which, like the buildings of Chandigarh, are of excessively heavy, chunky concrete members. In 1957 Le Corbusier designed the Museum of Modern Art for Tokyo and the Dominican Friary of La Tourette (1957–60), a ruthlessly hard block of immense force. His last important building was the Carpenter Art Centre at Harvard. (For illustrations *see* FRENCH ARCHITECTURE, INDIAN ARCHITECTURE, MONASTERY, PILOTIS.)

Lit: Le Corbusier: *The Complete Architectural Work*, 8 vols., London 1966–70; P. Blake, *Le Corbusier*, Harmondsworth 1960; C. Jencks, *Le Corbusier*, London 1973.

Le Muet, Pierre (1591–1669), a *retardataire* Mannerist, published *Manière de bien bastir pour toutes sortes de personnes* (1623), an up-to-date version of DU CERCEAU'S first book of architecture, containing designs suitable for different income groups but going farther down the social scale. His best surviving buildings are the Hôtels d'Astray, de l'Aigle and Davaux. The Hôtel Duret de Chevrey (now part of the Bibliothèque Nationale) was for long attributed to him but is now known to be by Jean Thiriot. His later buildings, e.g. Hôtel Tubeuf, Paris (1650), are more classical but never entirely free of Mannerist traits.

Lit: L. Hautecoeur, *Histoire de l'architecture classique en France*, vol. II, Paris 1948; A. Blunt, *Art and Architecture in France 1500–1700*, Pelican History of Art, Harmondsworth 1970, paperback edn 1973.

Le Nôtre, André (1613–1700), the greatest designer of formal gardens and parks, was the son of a royal gardener. He studied painting and architecture as well as garden design, and

was appointed Contrôleur Général des Bâtiments du Roi in 1657. The enormous park at Versailles (1662–90), with its vast *parterres*, fountains, sheets of water, and radiating avenues, is his masterpiece. It extends the symmetry of LE VAU'S architecture to the surrounding landscape and provides a perfect setting for the building. He began at Vaux-le-Vicomte (1656–61) and later worked at St Cloud, Fontainebleau, Clagny, Marly, and elsewhere, mostly for Louis XIV.

Lit: H. M. Fox, *André le Nôtre*, London 1962.

Le Pautre, Antoine (1621–81), designed the Hôtel de Beauvais in Paris (1652–5), the most ingenious of all Parisian *hôtel* plans considering the awkward site. It still survives. But he is best known for the engraved designs in his *Oeuvres* (first published 1652 as *Desseins de plusieurs palais*) of vast and fantastic town and country houses, which far exceed his contemporary LE VAU in Baroque extravagance. His influence is evident in the work of WREN and SCHLÜTER.

Lit: Robert W. Berger, *Antoine Le Pautre – a French architect of the era of Louis XIV*, New York 1969.

Le Pautre, Pierre (*c.* 1643–1716), the nephew of Antoine Le Pautre. He was the leading decorator at Versailles and as influential as de COTTE in the evolution of the Rococo style – notably in his Salon de l'œil de Bœuf at Versailles (1701) with its arabesque and ribbon-work decoration, in his work at the chapel at Versailles (1709–10), and in the choir of Notre Dame in Paris (1711–12) and in his interior at the Château de Bercy (1712–15).

Lit: F. Kimball, *The Creation of the Rococo*, Philadelphia 1943, revised as *Le Style Louis XV*, Paris 1949.

Le Vau, Louis (1612–70), the leading Baroque architect in France, was less intellectual and refined than his great contemporary MANSART. He was also less difficult in character and headed a brilliant team of painters, sculptors, decorators, gardeners, with whom he created the Louis XIV style at Versailles. He was a great *metteur-en-scène* and could produce striking general effects with a typically Baroque combination of all the arts. Born in Paris, the son of a master mason by whom he was trained, he first revealed his outstanding gifts in the Hôtel Lambert, Paris (1640–44), where he made ingenious use of an

awkward site and created the first of his highly
coloured, grandiloquent interiors: the staircase and gallery are especially magnificent. In
1656 he began the Hôtel de Fontenay, Paris,
and in 1657 he was commissioned by Fouquet,
the millionaire finance minister, to design his
country house at Vaux-le-Vicomte. This is his
masterpiece and by far the most splendid of all
French *châteaux*. Here grandeur and elegance
are combined in a manner peculiarly French,
and no expense was spared. The *château* was
built in about a year and the luxurious
interior, decorated by Lebrun, Guérin, and
others, and the gardens laid out by LE
NÔTRE were finished by 1661. In the same
year Fouquet was arrested for embezzlement,
whereupon his rival Colbert took over his
architect and artists to work for the king. Le
Vau was commissioned to rebuild the Galerie
d'Apollon in the Louvre (1661–2), decorated
by Lebrun (1663). In 1667 he was involved
(with PERRAULT) in the design of the great east
front of the Louvre in Paris. Work began on
the remodelling of Versailles in 1669. Le Vau
rose to the occasion, and his feeling for the
grand scale found perfect expression in the
new garden front. Unfortunately, this was
ruined a few years later by HARDOUIN-MAN-
SART's alterations and extensions, and nothing survives at all of the interiors he executed
with Lebrun; these included the most spectacular of all, the Escalier des Ambassadeurs. In
the Collège des Quatre Nations, Paris (now
the Institut de France, begun 1661), which
was built at the expense of Cardinal Mazarin,
he came closer than any other Frenchman to
the warmth and geniality of the great Italian
Baroque architects. The main front facing the
Seine is concave, with two arms curving forward from the domed centre-piece to end in
pavilions. The sense of splendour both in
planning and decoration is no less typical
than the occasional lack of sensitivity in the
handling of detail. (For illustrations *see*
BAROQUE ARCHITECTURE and FRENCH
ARCHITECTURE.)

  Lit: A. Blunt, *Art and Architecture in France,
1500–1700*, Pelican History of Art,
Harmondsworth 1970, paperback edn 1973;
Whiteley & Braham, 'Louis Le Vau's Projects
for the Louvre and the Colonnade' in
Gazette des Beaux Arts, 1964; R. W. Berger,
'Charles Le Brun and the Louvre Colonnade'
in *Art Bulletin*, December 1970.

Leaded lights Rectangular or diamond-shaped
panes of glass set in lead CAMES to form a

window. In general use in domestic architecture until the C18.

Leaf and dart An OVOLO MOULDING based on
a pattern of alternate leaf-like forms and
darts, found especially on the ECHINUS of an
Ionic capital.

Leaf and dart moulding

Lean-to roof, *see* ROOF.

Lechner, Ödön (1845–1914). One of the
most interesting of all representatives of ART
NOUVEAU architecture. He started (like Gaudí)
in a free Gothic (town hall, Kecskemét, 1892,
Museum of Decorative Art, Budapest, 1893–6)
and developed towards a fantastic style with
curvaceous gables and Moorish as well as
folk-art connotations (Postal Savings Bank,
Budapest, 1899–1902). (For illustrations *see*
HUNGARIAN ARCHITECTURE.)

  Lit: J. Kismarty-Lechner, *Ödön Lechner*,
Budapest 1961.

Ledoux, Claude-Nicolas (1736–1806), began
as a fashionable Louis XVI architect, patronized
by Mme du Barry, and developed into the most
daring and extreme exponent of neo-classicism
in France. Only BOULLÉE among his contemporaries was his equal in imagination and
originality, but most of Boullée's designs remained on paper. Neither was properly appreciated until recently. Despite its extreme
geometrical simplicity their more advanced
work is not abstract but expressive or *parlant*.
Born at Dormans, Ledoux studied under
J.-F. BLONDEL in Paris. He never went to Italy,
though he was profoundly influenced by
Italian architecture, especially by the cyclopean fantasies of PIRANESI. Though eccentric
and quarrelsome, he was immediately and
continuously successful and never lacked
commissions. His first important buildings
were the Château d'Eaubonne (1762–3),
the Hôtel d'Hallwyl (c. 1764–6), the Hôtel
d'Uzès (1764–7), the Château de Benouville
(1768–70), and the Hôtel de Montmorency,
Paris (1769–70), the last displaying his
originality in planning on a diagonal axis,
with circular and oval rooms.

In 1770 he began working for Mme du Barry and in the following year completed the Pavillon de Louveciennes, a landmark in the history of French taste. It was decorated and furnished throughout in the neo-classical style, the architectural treatment of the interior being confined to shallow pilasters, classical bas-reliefs, and delicate, honeycomb coffering. In 1776 he began the remarkable Hôtel Thélusson (demolished) in Paris, approached through an enormous triumphal arch leading into a garden laid out in the English landscape manner. This conception, in which the informality of the garden emphasized the stark simplicity and geometrical forms of the building, was repeated on a larger scale in the group of fifteen houses he built for the West Indian nabob Hosten in Paris (1792, demolished). They, too, were informally disposed in a landscape garden.

Success and official recognition appear to have stimulated rather than dulled his powers of invention, for his most advanced and original work dates from after he became an Academician and Architecte du Roi in 1773. His masterpieces include the massive and rigidly cubic theatre at Besançon (1775–84, burnt out 1957), with its unpedimented Ionic portico and, inside, a hemicycle with rising banks of seats surmounted by a Greek Doric colonnade. Odder still is his saltworks at Arc-et-Senans (1775–9), some of which still survives. It is the supreme expression of his feeling for the elemental and primeval. The glowering entrance portico is carved inside to emulate the natural rock out of which gushes water, presumably saline though also carved in stone. Even more extreme were the projects (c. 1785) he envisaged for his 'ideal city' of Chaux which were not, understandably, executed: one building was to have been a free-standing sphere and another a cylinder set horizontally.

His Paris toll-houses of 1785–9 are less extreme, but they illustrate the wide range of his stylistic repertoire. Of those that survive the most exciting is the Barrière de La Villette in Place de Stalingrad, consisting of a Greek cross surmounted by a cylinder – a very successful essay in pure architectural form. In 1783 he built a Salt Warehouse at Compiègne (only the massive arched façade survives) and in 1786 provided designs for a Palais de Justice and prison at Aix en Provence (not executed according to his designs). His career came to an end with the Revolution (he was imprisoned during the 1790s) and he

spent his last years preparing his designs for publication: *L'architecture considérée sous le rapport de l'art, des mœurs et de la législation* (1804). (For illustrations *see* CLASSICISM and FRENCH ARCHITECTURE.)

Lit: M. Raval & J. C. Moreux, *C.-N. Ledoux*, Paris 1945; E. Kaufmann, *Three Revolutionary Architects*, Philadelphia 1953; E. Kaufmann, *Architecture in the Age of Reason*, Cambridge, Mass. 1955.

Lefuel, Hector M. (1810–80), won the Grand Prix in 1839 and in the same year went to Rome. In 1854, at the death of Louis Visconti (1791–1853), he became chief architect to the Louvre, which Napoleon III had in 1851 decided to complete by large and elaborate links connecting it with the Tuileries. The neo-French-Renaissance fashion originated here and soon became international (cf. HUNT). Lefuel also designed the palace for the International Exhibition of 1855.

Lit: H. Delaborde, *Notice sur la vie et les ouvrages de H. Lefuel*, Paris 1882.

Legrand, J. B., *see* GILLY.

Lemercier, Jacques (c. 1585–1654), was the son of a master mason who worked at St Eustache, Paris. He studied in Rome c. 1607–14, bringing back to Paris the academic idiom of Giacomo della PORTA. Though he never quite succeeded in fusing this with his native French tradition, he ranks only just below MANSART and LE VAU in French classical architecture. If seldom inspired he was always more than competent. In 1624 he was commissioned by Louis XIII to plan extensions to the Louvre (the Pavillon de l'Horloge is the most notable of his additions), in harmony with LESCOT's work of the previous century. But his principal patron was Cardinal Richelieu, for whom he designed the Palais Cardinal (Palais Royal), Paris (begun 1633); the Sorbonne, Paris (begun 1626); the *château* and church of Rueil and the *château* and town of Richelieu (begun 1631). Only a small domed pavilion of the office block survives from the enormous Château Richelieu, but the town still exists as laid out by Lemercier in a regular grid with houses of uniform design built of brick with stone quoins. As a designer of *hôtels* he was remarkably ingenious, and his solution at the Hôtel de Liancourt, Paris (1623), became a prototype which was followed by nearly all his successors. His church of the Sorbonne (begun 1635) is perhaps his finest work and is one of the first purely classical churches in France. His dome at the Val-de-Grâce, Paris, where he took over from Mansart in 1646, is also most dramatic and effective.

Lit: A. Blunt, *Art and Architecture in France, 1500-1700*, Pelican History of Art, Harmondsworth 1970, paperback edn 1973; J. P. Babelon, *Demeures Parisiennes sous Henri IV et Louis XIII*, Paris 1965.

L'Enfant, Pierre Charles (1754-1825), a French architect and engineer who served as a volunteer major in the American army during the War of Independence, designed the old City Hall in New York and the Federal House in Philadelphia, but is remembered mainly for having surveyed the site and made the plan for the new federal capital in Washington, a grandiose conception based in some respects on Versailles. He would probably have been given the commission to design the Capitol and other buildings in Washington had he not become unmanageable. He was dismissed in 1792.

Lit: H. P. Caemmerer, *The Life of Pierre Charles l'Enfant*, Washington 1950.

Leonardo da Vinci (1452-1519). The greatest artist and thinker of the Renaissance. His wide-ranging mind embraced architecture as well as many other fields of human activity. Although he built little or nothing, he provided a model for the dome of Milan Cathedral (1487, not executed), and during his last years in France produced a vast scheme for a new city and royal castle at Romorantin (not executed). But his influence was great, especially on BRAMANTE, who took over his interest in centralized churches. S. Maria della Consolazione at Todi (1508), begun by Cola da Caprarola, probably derived from one of his sketches by way of Bramante. He left a large number of architectural drawings, many of them made for a projected Treatise on Architecture.

Lit: L. H. Heydenreich, *Leonardo da Vinci*, Munich 1954; L. H. Heydenreich & W. Lotz, *Architecture in Italy, 1400-1600*, Pelican History of Art, Harmondsworth 1974; C. Pedretti, *Leonardo*, London 1973.

Leoni, Giacomo (c. 1686-1746), who was born in Venice, settled in England sometime before 1715, having previously been architect to the Elector Palatine. An apostle of PALLADIANISM, he published the first English edition of Palladio's *Works* (1715) and at Queensberry House, London (1721, reconstructed 1792), provided the prototype English Palladian town house. In 1726 he published *The Architecture of L. B. Alberti*. His surviving buildings include Lyme Hall, Cheshire (1720-30); Argyll House, London (1723); and Clandon Park, Surrey (1731-5).

Lit: J. Summerson, *Architecture in Britain, 1530-1830*, Pelican History of Art, Harmondsworth 1969, paperback edn 1970.

Lequeu, Jean-Jacques (1757-after 1825). French neo-classical fantasist of neurotic power. He was born in Rouen, visited Italy in the early 1780s, and worked mainly as an architectural draughtsman until the Revolution and then as a cartographer. None of his few buildings survives. His fame rests on his drawings (Bibliothèque Nationale, Paris) in which the designs and ideas of BOULLÉE and LEDOUX appear to have gone to his head – monument to Priapus, vast and megalomaniac towers, a dairy to be built in the form of a cow, houses composed of both Gothic and Antique motifs etc., with much use of phallic and other symbols. In them he broke away from all conventions of symmetry, stylistic purity, proportion and taste.

Lit: E. Kaufmann, *Three Revolutionary Architects*, Philadelphia 1952; G. Metken, 'J. J. Lequeu ou l'architecture rêvée' in *Gazette des Beaux Arts*, 1965; J. Guillerme, 'Lequeu et l'invention du mauvais goût' in *Gazette des Beaux Arts*, 1965.

Lesbian cymatium A CYMA REVERSA moulding often decorated with LEAF AND DART.

Lescaze, William, *see* HOWE, George.

Lescot, Pierre (1500/15-78). The son of a well-to-do lawyer, who gave him a good education. His only work to survive more or less intact is part of the square court of the Louvre (1546-51), which laid the foundations of French classicism. Essentially decorative, his style is very French and entirely lacks the monumentality of his Italian contemporaries. He had the great advantage of the sculptor Jean Goujon's collaboration, and his ornamental detail is therefore of the greatest refinement and delicacy. Though much altered, parts of his Hôtel Carnavalet, Paris (c. 1545-50), survive. (For illustration *see* FRENCH ARCHITECTURE.)

Lit: A. Blunt, *Art and Architecture in France,*

1500–1700, Pelican History of Art, Harmondsworth 1970, paperback edn 1973.

Lesene A PILASTER without a base and capital often called a pilaster-strip and usually found on the exteriors of later Anglo-Saxon and early Romanesque churches. Although

Lesene: Orthodox Baptistery, Ravenna, 450–52

they were much used as decoration during the latter period, there is evidence in some Anglo-Saxon buildings to suggest that pilaster-strips as used by the Saxons were primarily functional. They served as bonding courses in thin rubble walls, and thus split up an unbroken expanse of wall, reducing cracking in the plaster and preventing longitudinal spread. The north nave wall at Breamore church shows long stones on end between flat stones, all clearly projecting some distance into the wall. This is a crude example of LONG AND SHORT WORK, but no claim can be made that the pilaster-strip and long and short work as used for QUOINS were evolved in any particular sequence. Other examples of the structural significance of the pilaster-strip are at Worth, where they are solid stone partitions, clearly of a piece with the long and short quoins, at Sompting and at Milborne.

Lethaby, William Richard (1857–1931), joined the office of Norman SHAW in 1877, became his trusted principal assistant, and set up on his own in 1889, helped on by Shaw. While he thus owed much to Shaw, as an artist and a thinker he owed more to MORRIS and Philip WEBB, on whom he wrote a book. He was as much an educator as a scholar and an architect, and indeed built very little. Foremost among his buildings are Avon Tyrrell in Hampshire (1891) and Melsetter on Orkney (1898), the church at Brockhampton in Herefordshire (1900–2) – probably the most original church of its date in the world – and the Eagle Insurance in Birmingham (1899), also of a startling originality, even if influenced by Webb.

Lethaby was the chief promoter and the first principal of the London Central School of Arts and Crafts, which was established in 1894 on Morris's principles. It was the first school anywhere to include teaching workshops for crafts. Also in 1894, Lethaby (with Swainson) brought out a learned book on Hagia Sophia in Constantinople; in 1904 a general, very deeply felt book on medieval art; in 1906 and 1925 two learned volumes on Westminster Abbey; and in 1922 a collection of brilliant, convincedly forward-looking essays called *Form in Civilisation*.

Leverton, Thomas (1743–1824), the son of an Essex builder and not highly regarded in his own day, nevertheless designed some of the most elegant interiors in London, e.g., Nos. 1 and 13 Bedford Square (1780). His 'Etruscan' hall and other rooms at Woodhall Park (1778) are equally distinguished.

Lit: J. Summerson, *Architecture in Britain, 1530–1830*, Pelican History of Art, Harmondsworth 1969, paperback edn 1970.

Libergier, Hugues (d. 1263). A French master mason whose funerary slab is now in Reims Cathedral. He is called Maistre on it and is represented holding the model of the major parish church of Reims, St Nicaise, which he designed and began in 1231. He also has a staff, an L-square, and compasses.

Lierne, *see* VAULT.

Lights Openings between the MULLIONS of a window.

Ligorio, Pirro (*c.* 1507–83). Painter and archaeologist as well as architect. In 1550 he built the Villa d'Este, Tivoli, and laid out its wonderful formal gardens with elaborate fountains and water-works. His masterpiece is the exquisite little Casino di Pio IV (1558–62) in the Vatican gardens, Rome, one of the most elegant of Mannerist buildings. Also in the Vatican, he transformed the exedra in BRAMANTE'S Cortile del Belvedere into a gargantuan niche.

Lit: D. R. Coffin, *The Villa d'Este at Tivoli*, Princeton 1966; C. Lamb, *Die Villa d'Este in Tivoli*, Munich 1966.

Linenfold Tudor panelling ornamented with a conventional representation of a piece of linen laid in vertical folds. One such piece fills one panel.

Lintel A horizontal beam or stone bridging an opening.

Lisboa, Antonio Francisco, *see* ALEIJADINHO.

Lissitsky, Eleazar Markevich, called El (1890–1941). Russian painter, typographer, designer and theorist as well as architect, Lissitsky became the apostle of Constructivism in the West in the 1920s. He trained under Joseph OLBRICH at the College of Technology, Darmstadt (1909–14). In 1919 he became Professor of Architecture at Vitebsk where he evolved his PROUN idea (PROUN = 'For the New Art') which he described as an 'interchange station' between painting and architecture – an interplay between the pictorial and structural. His ideas probably owed something to both MALEVICH and TATLIN, the latter then famous for his 1920 design for a spiral-shaped monument to the Third International. In 1920 Lissitsky designed his Lenin Tribune project which foreshadowed the prime Constructivist building, the Leningrad Pravda building projected by the VESNIN brothers in 1923. From 1922 until 1931 Lissitsky was in the West where he knew and influenced de Stijl and other *avant garde* architects. His 'Proun Cabinet' for the 1923 Berlin exhibition has recently been reconstructed at Eindhoven (Stedelijk van Abbemuseum), and his 'Abstract Cabinet', created in 1926 for Dresden and in 1927 for Hannover and intended to 'allow abstract art to do justice to its dynamic properties', has now been reconstructed in the Landesmuseum in Hanover. His most ambitious and forward-looking design – the 1924 *Wolkenbügel* project (with Mart Stam) for office blocks in Moscow on upright or splayed legs straddling roads – never got off the drawing board. In 1939 he produced designs for the Soviet Pavilion restaurant at the New York World Fair. (For illustration *see* RUSSIAN ARCHITECTURE.)

Lit: S. Lissitsky-Küppers, *El Lissitsky: Life, Letters, Text,* New York 1966; E. Lissitsky, *Russia: An Architecture for World Revolution,* reprint London 1970.

Listel, *see* FILLET.

Liwan, *see* IWAN.

Lodge The medieval term for the masons' workshop and living-quarters set up when a church, castle, or house was to be built. In the case of cathedrals and great abbeys it was often permanent, under a resident master mason, to maintain the fabric of the building.

Lodoli, Carlo (1690–1761). A Venetian priest and architectural theorist. His neo-classical and 'functional' ideas were published after his death by A. Memmo (*Elementi d'architettura lodoliana,* 1786), but they had been current for many years and were very influential, e.g., on Algarotti's *Saggio sopra l'architettura* (1753).

Lit: E. Kaufmann in *Gazette des Beaux Arts,* 1955, Pt. II, pp. 21–28; C. Semenzato in *Arte Veneta,* XI 1957.

Log-construction A form of timber construction used in regions rich in timber, in which the walls are made of tree-trunks laid horizontally on top of one another and overlapping at the corners where they are slotted together. At its most rudimentary, round boles are put on top of one another, and the joints sealed with moss and mud. At a more sophisticated level,

Types of log construction

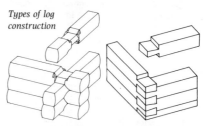

the logs are adzed down so that plane surface rests on plane surface, making the walls more solid and the joints better-fitting.

Lit: H. Phleps, *Holzbaukunst, Der Blockbau,* 1942.

Loggia A gallery open on one or more sides, sometimes pillared: it may also be a separate structure, usually in a garden.

Loggia: Villa Medici, Poggio a Caiano, c. 1480

Lombardo, Pietro (*c.* 1435–1515). A leading sculptor and architect in late C15 Venice. Though of exquisite sensitivity he stands outside the main development of Renaissance architecture. He was born at Carona in Lombardy, hence his name. He appears to have visited Florence before 1464, when he is first recorded working in Padua as a sculptor. Soon after 1467 he settled in Venice. Between 1471 and 1485 he designed and carved decorations for the chancel of S. Giobbe, Venice, a work of strongly Florentine character, His next and most important work was S. Maria dei Miracoli (1481–9), in which he successfully blended the Veneto-Byzantine and Renaissance styles – marble panelling inside and out and a Byzantine dome, combined with crisply carved Renaissance ornament. To give an illusion of greater size he resorted to various *trompe l'œil* devices which he repeated on a large scale, but with less success, on the façade of the Scuola di S. Marco (1488–90, upper storeys completed by CODUCCI). He also introduced into Venice the large architectural sepulchral monument with a classical framework and abundance of classically inspired sculpture. Here he was much assisted by his sons **Tullio** (*c.* 1455–1532) and **Antonio** (*c.* 1458–1516). Various Venetian palaces have been attributed to Lombardo, notably Palazzo Dario (*c.* 1487).

Lit: L. H. Heydenreich & W. Lotz, *Architecture in Italy, 1400–1600*, Pelican History of Art, Harmondsworth 1974.

Long and short work Saxon QUOINS, consisting of long stones on end between flat ones, all bonded into the wall. The chancel arch JAMBS at Escomb (C7 or 8) may have a bearing on the origin of the technique; it may also have been evolved simultaneously and in association with pilaster-strip work (*see* LESENE). It is the insertion of the large flat stones which makes long and short work such a good bonding technique for corners, as in many cases they extend practically through the thickness of the walls; the upright blocks alone are subject to diagonal thrust.

Superficially long and short work is of two kinds:

a. The 'upright and flat' type, where the full size of the horizontal stone is visible on both flanks;

b. the long and short strip quoin, where the horizontal stones have been cut back, making them flush with the upright blocks.

This was a refinement in the process of finding a solid cornering for stone buildings, but is not necessarily an indication of a later date (e.g., Deerhurst of the early C10 has the 'upright and flat' type). The method of construction is the same for both kinds.

Longhena, Baldassare (1598–1682), the only great Venetian Baroque architect, was born in Venice of a family of stone carvers and was trained under SCAMOZZI. In 1630 he won a competition for the design of the *ex voto* church of S. Maria della Salute, with which he was to be occupied off and on for the rest of his long life (it was not finally consecrated until 1687). Standing on an imposing site at the entrance to the Grand Canal, this church is a masterpiece of scenographic design, with a vast buoyant dome anchored by huge Baroque scrolls to an octagonal base, and a very complex façade which directs the eye through the main door to the high altar. The interior is conceived as a series of dramatic vistas radiating from the centre of the octagonal nave. Longhena realized a similarly theatrical concept in the design of his imposing double staircase for the monastery of S. Giorgio Maggiore (1643–5), which had considerable influence on later architects. In the domestic field he was less adventurous: Palazzo Rezzonico (begun 1667) and Palazzo Pesaro (begun 1676) on the Grand Canal – both completed after his death – with heavily rusticated basements, abundance of carving, and deep recesses which dissolve the surface of the exterior in patterns of light and shade, are merely Baroque variations on SANSOVINO's Palazzo Corner. (G. Massari built the top floor of Palazzo Rezzonico in 1752–6.) A tendency towards wilful exaggeration of sculptural detail in these works reaches its fantastic peak in the little church of the Ospedaletto (1670–8), with a preposterously overwrought façade bursting with *telamones*, giant heads, and lion masks. He has been credited with numerous villas on the mainland, but none is of much interest.

Lit: C. Semenzato, *L'architettura di B. Longhena*, Venice 1954; R. Wittkower, *S. Maria della Salute*, New York 1958.

Longhi, Martino the younger (1602–60), the most important member of a family of architects working mainly in Rome, was the son of **Onorio Longhi** (1569–1619) and the grandson of **Martino Longhi the elder** (d. 1591). He continued his father's work on S.

Carlo al Corso, Rome, and began S. Antonio de'Portoghesi, Rome (1638). His major achievement is the façade of SS. Vincenzo ed Anastasio, Rome (1646-50), a powerfully dramatic, many-columned composition in which Mannerist devices are used to obtain an overwhelming high Baroque effect of grandeur and mass.

Lit: R. Wittkower, *Art and Architecture in Italy, 1600-1750*, Pelican History of Art, Harmondsworth 1973, paperback edn 1973.

Longuelune, Zacharias (1689-1748). French-born painter-architect who collaborated with Matthaeus PÖPPELMANN in Dresden from 1715 onwards and in Warsaw from 1728 onwards on the designs for the vast new Saxon Palace. Very few of his own projects were executed, but his grandiose designs, which embodied French classicist theory, exerted considerable influence both in Saxony and as far away as Poland and Denmark. He designed the formal park at Gross-Sedlitz (1726), additions to the Japanisches Palais in Dresden (1729 onwards) and the Blockhaus terminating the Hauptstrasse in Dresden Neustadt (1731) (burnt out 1945 but now under reconstruction).

Lit: P. du Colombier, *L'architecture française en Allemagne en XVIII siècle*, Paris 1956.

Loos, Adolf (1870-1933), was born at Brno in Moravia, studied at Dresden, spent three crucial years in the United States (1893-6), and then worked in Vienna, strongly influenced by the doctrines just then expounded by Otto WAGNER. From the very first his designs (Goldman shop interior, 1898) refused to allow any decorative features or any curves. His most important buildings are private houses of between 1904 (house, Lake Geneva) and 1910 (Steiner House, Vienna). They are characterized by unrelieved cubic shapes, a total absence of ornament, and a love of fine materials. In his theoretical writings, or rather his journalism, he was a rabid anti-ornamentalist, an enemy therefore of the Wiener Werkstätten and HOFFMANN, and a believer in the engineer and the plumber. His famous article called *Ornament and Crime* came out in 1908. As an architect, however, he wavered. His office building in the Michaelerplatz, Vienna (1910) has Tuscan columns, his design for the Chicago Tribune competition of 1923 is a huge closely windowed Doric column; but smaller domestic jobs, such as the house for the Dadaist Tristan

Tzara in Paris (1926), remained faithful to the spirit of 1904-10. Loos was not a successful architect, but he was influential among some of the *avant-garde* in Europe. (For illustration *see* INTERNATIONAL MODERN.)

Lit: L. Münz & G. Künstler, *A. Loos*, London 1966.

Loudon, John Claudius (1783-1843), was apprenticed to a landscape gardener in Scotland and educated himself the hard way. He settled in London in 1803, and at once began writing on gardening and agriculture. He also took up farming, made money and lost it, travelled on the Continent (1814 as far as Moscow, 1819-20 in France and Italy). His *Encyclopaedia of Gardening* came out in 1822, an *Encyclopaedia of Plants* in 1829, and the architecturally important *Encyclopaedia of Cottage, Farm and Villa Architecture* in 1833. This is the standard book if one wants to see what ideals and what styles of the past English country-houses followed, chiefly in the 1840s. Loudon also started and edited the *Gardener's Magazine* (1826 etc.) and the short-lived *Architectural Magazine* (1834). He was an exceedingly hard worker, labouring under great physical disabilities, and making and losing large sums of money.

Lit: D. Clifford, *A History of Garden Design*, London 1962.

Louis, Victor (1731-1800). French neo-classical architect working in a somewhat florid style derived from ancient Rome and the city palaces (rather than the villas) of PALLADIO. Born in Paris, he was trained there and at the French Academy in Rome (1756-9). In 1765 he was called to Warsaw by Stanislas-Augustus but returned the next year without having built anything. On his return he designed the Préfecture at Besançon (1770-78). His first work of importance is also his masterpiece, the theatre at Bordeaux (1775-88), a massive structure with a dodeca-style portico (without pediment) stretching the full length of the main façade. It contains a large stage, very grand auditorium and the most monumental staircase and foyer that had been realized up to that date. He did a certain amount of other work in and around Bordeaux (e.g., Hôtel Saige, now the Préfecture, Château de Bouihl). He also had an extensive practice in Paris where his main and perhaps most appealing work was the colonnades in the Palais Royal gardens (1781-4) and the adjoining Théâtre de la Comédie-Française

(1786–90, rebuilt 1902). The original building had an iron and hollow-tile roof to reduce the danger of fires.

Lit: C. Maronneau, *Victor Louis, architecte du théâtre de Bordeaux: Sa vie, ses travaux et sa correspondence, 1731–1800,* Bordeaux 1881; W. Graf Kalnein & M. Levey, *Art and Architecture of the Eighteenth Century in France,* Pelican History of Art, Harmondsworth 1973.

Louvre 1. An opening, often with a LANTERN over, in the roof of a hall to let the smoke from a central hearth escape; either open-sided, or closed by slanting boards to keep out the rain. 2. One of a series of overlapping boards or slips of glass to admit air and exclude rain.

Lowside window A window usually on the south side of the chancel, lower than the others, possibly intended for communication between persons outside the chancel and the priest within; perhaps also for the sanctus bell to be heard outside the church.

Lozenge A diamond shape.

Lucarne 1. A small opening in an attic or a spire. 2. A DORMER WINDOW.

Ludovice, João Frederico (Johann Friedrich Ludwig, 1673–1752), the leading Late Baroque architect in Portugal, was born at Hall in Swabia, the son of a goldsmith whose craft he practised first in Rome (1697–1701) then in Lisbon. In about 1711 the King of Portugal commissioned him to build a small convent at Mafra. Gradually the size of the project was enlarged, and the building finally became one of the largest in Europe (built 1717–70). It includes a royal palace, a vast church, and conventual buildings for 300 monks. Mafra derives mainly from High Baroque Rome with a few South German and Portuguese overtones: the church, liberally decorated with Italian statues, is especially impressive. His only other works of importance are the library of Coimbra University (1717–23) with a very rich *mouvementé* façade and the apse of Évora Cathedral (1716–46).

Lit: G. Kubler & M. Soria, *Art and Architecture in Spain and Portugal and their American Dominions, 1500–1800,* Pelican History of Art, Harmondsworth 1959; A. de Carvalho, *D. João V e a arte do sen tempo,* Lisbon 1962.

Lunette A semicircular opening or TYMPANUM. The term can also be applied to any flat, semicircular surface.

Lunette: Castle chapel, Ussé, c. 1538

Lutyens, Sir Edwin (1869–1944), after a short time with George & Peto, was already in independent practice in 1889. In 1896 he designed Munstead Wood for Gertrude Jekyll, the gardener and garden designer, who helped him in his career. A number of excellent country houses in the Arts and Crafts style followed (Deanery Garden, Sonning, 1899; Orchards, Godalming, 1899; Tigbourne Court, 1899; Folly Farm, Sulhampstead, 1905 and 1912), establishing Lutyens's originality and ability for coordinating forms. However, he was very early attracted by classicism, first of a William and Mary variety (Liberal Club, Farnham, 1894; Crooksbury, east front, 1899; Hestercombe Orangery, 1905), then of a grander neo-Georgian (Nashdom, Taplow, 1905) and a semi-Palladian, semi-English-Baroque 'Wrenaissance' (Heathcote, Ilkley, 1906). Lutyens shared to the full the imperial *folie de grandeur* of the Edwardian years, and this made him the ideal architect for the last crop of really spectacular English country houses (Lindisfarne Castle, 1903; Castle Drogo, 1910–30), and of course for New Delhi. His Viceroy's House (1913 onwards) has a genuine monumentality and a sense of grandiose display which Baker in his buildings for Delhi never achieved.

However, classicism bogged Lutyens down in the end. In spite of extreme care for details of proportion and oddly impish details into which his former originality retreated, his later commercial buildings – Britannic House (1920 etc.) and the Midland Bank (1924 etc.) – stand outside the mainstream of European developments, whereas an earlier church by Lutyens such as St Jude's in the Hampstead Garden Suburb (1909–11) possessed a true originality and a sense of massing very rare in European ecclesiastical architecture of the time.

Lit: C. Hussey, *The Life of Sir Edwin Lutyens,* London 1950; A. S. G. Butler, *The Architecture of Sir Edwin Lutyens,* London 1950.

Lychgate A covered wooden gateway with open sides at the entrance to a churchyard, providing a resting-place for a coffin (the word *lych* is Saxon for corpse). Part of the burial service is sometimes read there.

Lyming, Robert, carpenter, builder, and architect, designed the loggia and frontispiece of Hatfield House (1611). At Blicking Hall (*c.* 1625) he produced the last of the great Jacobean 'prodigy' houses in which Flemish ornamentalism and asymmetrical planning were completely anglicized.

Lit: J. Summerson, *Architecture in Britain, 1530–1830,* Pelican History of Art, Harmondsworth 1969, paperback edn 1970.

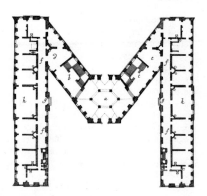

Machicolation A gallery or PARAPET projecting on brackets and built on the outside of castle towers and walls, with openings in the floor through which to drop molten lead, boiling oil, and missiles.

Machuca, Pedro (d. 1550), began as a painter, worked in Italy and returned to Spain in 1520. His masterpiece, the Palace of Charles V in the Alhambra at Granada (1527–68), is very Italian in the RAPHAEL-GIULIO ROMANO style; indeed, it is larger and more complete than any Bramantesque palace in Italy. But various Spanish or PLATERESQUE features crept into his design, e.g., the garlanded window frames.

    Lit: F. Chueca Goitia, *Arquitectura del siglo XVI* (*Ars Hispaniae*, vol. XI), Madrid 1953; G. Kubler & M. Soria, *Art and Architecture in Spain and Portugal and their American Dominions, 1500–1800*, Pelican History of Art, Harmondsworth 1959.

Mackintosh, Charles Rennie (1868–1928), studied at the Glasgow School of Art at the time when Glasgow painting had suddenly turned from a provincial past to new forms of considerable interest to people in England and even on the Continent. In 1893 and the following years he, his friend McNair, and the two Macdonald sisters, Margaret (later Mrs Mackintosh, 1865–1933) and Frances (later Mrs McNair), designed graphic work and repoussé metalwork in an ART NOUVEAU way, inspired by *The Studio* (which started in London in 1893) and especially by Jan Toorop, the Dutchman. In 1896 Mackintosh won the competition for the new building of the Glasgow School of Art and erected a building inferior to none of its date anywhere

in Europe or America – on a clear rational plan, with the basic external forms equally clear and rational (e.g., the studio windows), but with a centre-piece of complete originality and high fancifulness, influenced by VOYSEY, by the Scottish castle and manor-house tradition, and even a little by the current English 'Wrenaissance'. The metalwork of the façade and much of the interior achieve a unification of the crisply rectangular with the long, delicate, languid curves of Art Nouveau. It is in this unique harmony that Mackintosh's greatness lies, and it explains the deep impression his furniture and furnishings made on Austrian architects when they became familiar with him, first through *The Studio* and then through an exhibition at the Secession (*see* OLBRICH) in 1900. The Viennese were abandoning Art Nouveau excesses for a clearer, saner style, and Mackintosh both inspired and confirmed them.

    Mackintosh had fully evolved his style in his interior work by 1899 – white lacquered chairs and cupboards, erect, elegant, clearly articulated, and with wistfully curved inlays in metal and pink, mauve, or mother-of-pearl enamel. There was no one else who could combine the rational and the expressive in so intriguing a way. His capital works at or near Glasgow are the tea-rooms for Mrs Cranston (Buchanan Street, 1897 etc.; Argyle Sreet, 1897 and 1905; Sauchiehall Street, 1904; Ingram Street, 1901, *c.* 1906, and *c.* 1911), now alas mostly destroyed or disused; two houses (Windyhill, Kilmacolm, 1899–1901, and Hill House, Helensburgh, 1902–3); a school (Scotland Street, 1906); and the library wing of the School of Art (1907–9) with its sheer, towering outer wall and its bewitchingly complex interior. In 1901 he had won second prize in a German publisher's competition for the house of an art-lover (Baillie Scott came first), and this consolidated his reputation abroad.

However, he was not an easy man, and his erratic ways alienated clients. In 1913 he left the firm (Honeyman & Keppie) in which he had been a partner since 1904. He moved to Walberswick, then to London, then after the war to Port Vendres, and finally back to London, painting highly original, finely drawn landscapes and still-lifes, but never recovering an architectural practice. (For illustration *see* ART NOUVEAU.)

Lit: T. Howarth, *C. R. Mackintosh and the Modern Movement*, London 1952; N. Pevsner, *Studies in Art, Architecture and Design*, London 1968; D. Walker in *The Anti-Rationalists* (ed. N. Pevsner & J. M. Richards), London 1973.

Mackmurdo, Arthur H. (1851–1942), came from a wealthy family and had plenty of leisure to evolve a style of his own. In 1874 he travelled to Italy with RUSKIN. About 1880 he seems to have built his first houses. In 1882 he founded the Century Guild, a group of architects, artists, and designers inspired by Ruskin and MORRIS. The group began in 1884 to publish a magazine, *The Hobby Horse*, which anticipated some of the features of book design recovered by Morris from the medieval past in his Kelmscott Press of 1890. As early as 1883, in the design for the cover of his book on Wren's City churches, Mackmurdo introduced those long flame-like or tendril-like curves which nearly ten years later were taken up, especially in Belgium, as a basis for ART NOUVEAU. But while in such two-dimensional designs, including a number for textiles (*c.* 1884), Mackmurdo is the lone pioneer of Art Nouveau, the furniture he designed from 1886 onwards and a stand for an exhibition at Liverpool, also of 1886, established him as the forerunner of VOYSEY in clarity of structure, elegance, and originality in the sense of independence of the past. Specially characteristic, on the exhibition stand, are the long, tapering posts with a far-projecting flat cornice. In 1904 Mackmurdo gave up architecture; later he concentrated on economic thought and writing, his ideas being similar to those of Social Credit.

Lit: N. Pevsner, *Studies in Art, Architecture and Design*, London 1968; E. Pond in *The Anti-Rationalists* (ed. N. Pevsner & J. M. Richards), London 1973.

Madaleno, Juan Sordo, *see* MEXICAN ARCHITECTURE.

Maderno, Carlo (1556–1629), was born at Capolago on Lake Lugano, and had settled in Rome by 1588, beginning as assistant to his uncle Domenico FONTANA. He was appointed architect of St Peter's in 1603, when he also completed the façade of S. Susanna, Rome, a revolutionary design with which he broke away from the current rather facile and academic Mannerism and established his own lucid, forceful, and intensely dynamic style. S. Susanna and the majestic dome of S. Andrea della Valle, Rome, are his masterpieces, though he is best known for his work at St Peter's, where he had the unenviable job of altering MICHELANGELO's centralized plan by adding a nave and façade. Work began in 1607, and the façade was finished by 1612. Its excessive length is due to the later addition of towers, of which only the substructures were built and which now appear to form part of the façade. His Confessio before the high altar and his elegant fountain in the *piazza* are more successful. His secular buildings include Palazzo Mattei, Rome (1598–1618), and Palazzo Barberini, Rome (1628 onwards), though the latter was almost entirely executed after his death by BERNINI, who made various alterations, notably to the main façade. (For illustration *see* COLOSSAL ORDER.)

Lit: H. Hibbard, *Carlo Maderno*, London 1970.

Madrasa The name derives from an Arabic verb meaning 'study'; alternative forms are *medrese* and *medersa*. It denotes an Islamic building, usually erected under state patronage, which housed students of the orthodox Islamic sciences, principally law and theology, and the salaried staff which taught them there. At first such religious instruction was given in the great mosques, which always remained centres of intellectual life (al-Azhar, Cairo), or in the teachers' houses. The *madrasa* originated in the Iranian world in the later C10; the early ones were called 'Nizamiyas' after the great Seljuk vizier who founded some of the largest and most influential of them (Nishapur; Baghdad). None of these can now be identified with certainty, but the earliest surviving *madrasas*, those of Syria (Bosra, 1136), bear the marks of Iranian origin, especially in their IWANS. From Syria the fashion spread to Egypt later in the C12

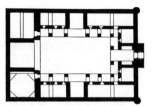

Madrasa Sahibiye at Kayseri, 1267

Madrasa Yl-Malak el-Gukander, 1319

(Nasiriya, Cairo, 1171), and thence in much reduced form to north-west Africa (Bu 'Ananiya, Fez, 1351). The form of the *madrasa* varies considerably throughout the Muslim world. Islamic law was early codified in four distinct systems or schools, and at first the precepts of only one such school were taught at a given *madrasa*. By the c13 *madrasas* which catered for all four orthodox schools were being built (Mustansiriya, Baghdad, 1233–4) and the cruciform 4-*iwan* plan was found to be particularly suitable for such buildings (Zahiriya, Cairo, 1262–3); in some Egyptian *madrasas* each school was allotted a single *iwan* for purposes of prayer and teaching (Nasiriya, Cairo, finished 1303–4). Such *madrasas* are scarcely distinguishable from 4-*iwan* mosques except by their smaller size and by their rooms for students, usually disposed behind a double tier of arcades enclosing the courtyard. These courtyards are not used for prayer and are therefore much smaller than in mosques. Turkish *madrasas* from the c13 onwards are very varied; some consist of a single dome chamber or a single *iwan* (with rooms for study in the corners), but cramped 4-*iwan madrasas* are also known, and elaborate portals flanked by minarets were popular (Çifte Minare, Sivas, 1271). In Iran 4-*iwan madrasas* were the norm (Madrasa Imami, Isfahan; Khargird). In Turkey and Egypt the *madrasa* was often part of a complex including the tomb of the founder, a mosque, a minaret, and possibly a dervish hostelry or a hospital (complex of Qalaun, Cairo, 1281; several *madrasas* at Konya and Kayseri in Turkey). Post-medieval *madrasas* were normally planned as elements of such composite foundations.   [RH]

Maekawa, Kunio, *see* JAPANESE ARCHITECTURE.

Maiano, Benedetto da, *see* BENEDETTO DA MAIANO.

Maiano, Giuliano da, *see* GIULIANO DA MAIANO.

Maillart, Robert (1872–1940), a Swiss engineer, studied at the Zurich Polytechnic (1890–4), had jobs in various engineering firms, and then set up on his own (1902). He worked on the unexplored possibilities of REINFORCED CONCRETE, and in the course of that work arrived at a new aesthetic for concrete, using it to span by curves, rather than merely as a new means of building post-and-lintel structures. His Tavenasa Bridge (1905) is the first in which arch and roadway are structurally one. He built many bridges afterwards, all of them of a thoroughbred elegance: the one across the Salginatobel has a span of nearly 300 ft (1929–30). In 1908 he also began experimenting with concrete mushroom construction, at a time when this was being done independently in the United States; the technique involves a post and a mushroom top spreading from it that are one inseparable concrete unit. Maillart's first building of mushroom construction was a warehouse at Zurich (1910).

Lit: M. Bill, *Robert Maillart*, Zurich 1962.

Maitani, Lorenzo (d. 1330), was a Sienese sculptor and architect. He was called in to advise on Orvieto Cathedral in 1310 being then described as 'universalis caputmagister' which testifies to his celebrity as an architect. From then until his death he was in complete control of all work on the façade of Orvieto Cathedral, including the sculpture, some of which is probably by him. Two drawings for the façade survive, the second being probably by Maitani (Opera del Duomo, Orvieto). In 1317 he was mentioned as working on a fountain at Perugia and in 1322 he was on the commission for the new Baptistery of Siena Cathedral.

Lit: J. White, *Art and Architecture in Italy, 1250–1400,* Pelican History of Art, Harmondsworth 1966.

Malayan architecture, *see* SOUTH-EAST ASIAN ARCHITECTURE.

Malevich, Kasimir (1878–1935). Though a painter, Malevich, like TATLIN and Gabo, designed in the mid-twenties pieces of fantastical architecture in the new modern, Constructivist manner. They were called Architectonics.

Mannerism is in its primary sense the acceptance of a manner rather than its meaning. Now Mannerism has also become a term to denote the style current in Italy from MICHEL-ANGELO to the end of the c16. It is characterized by the use of motifs in deliberate opposition to their original significance or context, but it can also express itself in an equally deliberate cold and rigid classicism. The term applies to French and Spanish architecture of the c16 as well (DELORME; the Escorial), but how far it applies to the Northern countries is controversial. Principal examples in Italy are Michelangelo's Medici Chapel and Laurentian Library, GIULIO ROMANO'S works at Mantua, VASARI'S Uffizi at Florence, and other works by these architects and LIGORIO, AMMANATI, BUONTALENTI, etc. PALLADIO belongs to Mannerism only in certain limited aspects of his work.

Fontainebleau,
stucco decoration by Primaticcio, c. 1550

Vestibule, Biblioteca Laurenziana, Florence, begun 1526, by Michelangelo

Palace at Mantua, c. 1544, by Giulio Romano

Lit: N. Pevsner, 'The Architecture of Mannerism' in *The Mint*, London 1946, reprinted in *Readings in Art History* (ed. H. Spencer), New York 1966; J. Shearman, *Mannerism*, Harmondsworth 1967.

Manor house A house in the country or a village, the centre of a manor. Architecturally the term is used to denote the unfortified, medium-sized house of the later Middle Ages.
Lit: M. Wood, *The Medieval English House*, London 1965.

Mansard roof, *see* ROOF.

Mansart, François (1598–1666), the first great protagonist of French classicism in architecture, holds a position parallel to Poussin in painting and Corneille in drama. He never went to Italy, and his style is extremely French in its elegance, clarity, and cool restraint. Though of scrupulous artistic conscience he was unfortunately both arrogant and slippery in his business relationships, and his inability to make and keep to a final plan not unnaturally enraged his clients.

As a result, he lost many commissions. For the last ten years of his life he was virtually unemployed. He was seldom patronized by the Crown and never by the great nobility; his clients belonged mainly to the newly rich bourgeoisie, who had the intelligence to appreciate and the money to pay for his sophisticated and luxurious buildings.

Born in Paris, the son of a master carpenter, he probably began under de BROSSE at Coulommiers. By 1624 he had already established himself as a prominent architect in the capital. His early work derives from de Brosse, with Mannerist overtones in the style of DU CERCEAU, but his individual style began to emerge at the Château de Balleroy (1626), where the harmonious grouping of massive blocks achieves an effect of sober monumentality. His first masterpiece, the Orléans wing of the *château* at Blois (1635–8), would have been a grander and more monumental Palais Luxembourg had it ever been completed. Only the central block and colonnades were built. But they display to the full the ingenuity of planning, clarity of disposition, and purity and refinement of detail which distinguish his work. He also introduced here the continuous broken roof with a steep lower slope and flatter, shorter upper portion that is named after him. His style reached culmination at Maisons Lafitte (1642–6), the country house near Paris which he built for the immensely wealthy René de Longueil, who apparently allowed him a completely free hand. (He pulled down part of it during construction in order to revise his designs!) It is his most complete work to survive and gives a better idea of his genius than any other. The oval rooms in the wings and the vestibule, executed entirely in stone without either gilding or colour, epitomize his suave severity and civilized reticence in decoration. His design for the Val-de-Grâce in Paris (c. 1645) is contemporary with Maisons Lafitte, but he was dismissed and replaced by LEMERCIER in 1646, when the building had reached the entablature of the nave and the lower storey of the façade. The conception appears to derive from PALLADIO's Redentore.

His other important buildings are Ste Marie de la Visitation, Paris (1632–4); the Hôtel de la Vrillière, Paris (begun 1635), wholly symmetrical and the model for the classical type of Parisian *hôtel*; the Hôtel du Jars, Paris (begun 1648, now destroyed), in which he developed a freer, more plastic disposition of rooms which was to be very influential. His last surviving work is his remodelling of the Hôtel Carnavalet in Paris (1655). He was consulted in the 1660s about the Louvre and a royal chapel, but his designs were not executed. (For illustration see FRENCH ARCHITECTURE.)

Lit: P. Smith & A. Braham, *François Mansart*, London 1972; A. Blunt, *Art and Architecture in France, 1500–1700*. Pelican History of Art, Harmondsworth 1970, paperback edn 1973.

Mansart, Jules Hardouin, see HARDOUIN-MANSART, Jules.

Mantelpiece The wood, brick, stone, or marble frame surrounding a fireplace, frequently including an overmantel or mirror above; sometimes called *chimney-piece*.

Chimney-piece: Palazzo Ducale, Urbino, mid-C15

Manueline style An architectural style peculiar to Portugal and named after King Manuel the Fortunate (1495–1521). See PORTUGUESE ARCHITECTURE.

Maqsura Originally the term denoted an enclosed space for prayer, reserved for the ruler and usually near the MIHRAB of a large urban MOSQUE. A connection with the royal box of the Byzantine court, and with the choir screen of early Christian churches, is possible. The *maqsura* comprised a metal or wooden screen, sufficient to separate the ruler from the other worshippers and thus to protect him; two of the Early Caliphs were murdered in the mosque. Its proximity to the *mihrab*, the dome over the *mihrab*, and the MINBAR, all features with princely connotations, suggests

that it also had the ceremonial function of exalting the ruler's rank, and probably for this reason *maqsuras* quickly multiplied throughout Islam. Indeed, many early *maqsuras* could be entered directly from the ruler's palace which adjoined the mosque (Baghdad, Basra, Kufa). Later the *maqsura* came to denote the detached part of the mosque set aside for communal prayer, and took the form of a domed square chamber (mosques of Baibars, Egypt; Mayyafariqin, Turkey; Isfahan, Iran). Mobile *maqsuras* of wood were also known (Kairouan, Tunisia, 1040). [RH]

Markelius, Sven (1889–1972) was a Swedish architect and town-planner. City architect and planner to the city of Stockholm 1944–54. Markelius laid out the new suburb of Vällingby. Vällingby is not a SATELLITE TOWN, as it is not meant to have a completely independent existence, but is of an exemplary plan combining a truly urban-looking centre with peripheral housing of both high blocks of flats and small houses (1953–9).

Lit: G. E. Kidder-Smith, *The New Architecture of Europe*, Harmondsworth 1962; S. Ray, *L'architettura moderna nei paesi scandinavi*, Bologna 1965.

Marot, Daniel (c. 1660–1752), was the son of a minor French architect **Jean Marot** (c. 1619–79), who is chiefly remembered for his volumes of engravings *L'architecture française*, known as 'le grand Marot' and 'le petit Marot'. Born in Paris, Daniel emigrated to Holland after the Revocation of the Edict of Nantes (1685), becoming almost immediately architect to William of Orange. He developed an intricate style of ornamentation, similar to that of Jean Berain (see his *Nouvelles cheminées à panneaux de la manière de France*), and was involved among other things with the design of the audience chamber or Trêveszaal in the Binnenhof, The Hague (1695–8), and the interior decoration and garden design at Het Loo. He followed William to England and designed the gardens (Grand Parterre) and perhaps some of the furnishings and interior decoration at Hampton Court, but though he later described himself as 'Architect to the King of England' no buildings can be ascribed to him (Schomberg House, London, c. 1698, appears to have been strongly influenced by him). He died at The Hague, where he designed part of the Royal Library (1734–8) and Stadhuis (1733–9). He published his *Oeuvres* in Amsterdam in

1715, but his main buildings date from the following years and are all in The Hague – the German Embassy (1715), the Hôtel van Wassenaar and the façade of the Royal Library (1734, wings by Pieter de Swart, 1761).

Lit: M. D. Ozinga, *Daniel Marot*, Amsterdam 1938; A. Mauban, *Jean Marot*, Paris 1944; E. H. ter Kuile in *Dutch Art and Architecture, 1600–1800*, Pelican History of Art, Harmondsworth 1966, paperback edn 1972.

Martin, Sir Leslie (b. 1908), was Architect to the London County Council from 1953 to 1956, in succession to Sir Robert MATTHEW, and then Professor of Architecture at Cambridge University (to 1973). Under Martin the finest of all L.C.C. housing estates was built, that at Roehampton for a population of about 10,000. Some of the brightest young architects in England were at that time working in the L.C.C. office, and Martin gave them full scope. In the course of building the style of the scheme changed from one inspired by Sweden to that of LE CORBUSIER at Chandigarh, and Martin's own work in partnership with C. A. St J. Wilson has moved in the same direction – see, for example, the new building for Caius College, Cambridge (1960–2). His other work includes College Hall, Leicester University (1958–61), and the outstandingly fine new Oxford libraries (1961–4).

Lit: R. Maxwell, *New British Architecture*, London 1972.

Martinelli, Domenico (1650–1718), quadratura painter and architect errant, who travelled widely and played an important part in the diffusion of the Italian Baroque style north of the Alps, was born in Lucca and ordained priest, but this did nothing to interfere with his wandering artistic career. His masterpiece is the Stadtpalais Liechtenstein in Vienna (1692–1705), which introduced the elaborate triumphal staircase which was to become an essential feature of Viennese palace architecture. He also designed the large but simpler Gartenpalais Liechtenstein, Vienna (1698–1711), and probably the Harrach Palais, Vienna (c. 1690), as well as a house for Graf von Kaunitz, Austerlitz. It is said that he also worked in Warsaw, Prague, and Holland.

Lit: H. Tietze, *Domenico Martinelli und seine Tätigkeit in Österreich*, Vienna 1922.

Martyrium A church or other building erected over a site which bears witness to the Christian faith, either by referring to an event

in Christ's life or Passion, or by sheltering the grave of a martyr, a witness by virtue of having shed his blood.

Mason's mark A symbol, monogram or initial incised in stonework by the mason responsible for the execution. Such marks are frequently found on Romanesque and Gothic buildings.

Masons' marks on the vaulting rib of Speyer Cathedral, C12

Mastaba (Arab = bench). Technical term for the shape of private tombs of the Old Kingdom in Egypt (c. 2660–2150 B.C.): a massive brick or stone mound with BATTERED walls on a rectangular base. A vertical shaft cuts through this and the surface of the rock down to the sarcophagal chamber deep in the ground. A place for sacrifices on the east side of the mastaba became a votive chamber inside it, and ultimately a house-like sequence of relief-carved and painted courts, corridors and rooms, in which rites were performed before effigies of the deceased. [DW]

Mastaba

Mathey, Jean Baptist (c. 1630–c. 1695). He was probably born in Dijon and trained as a painter, but was then taken to Prague in 1675 as architect to the Archbishop and, despite much local opposition, began to work in a classicizing French manner very different from that practised by F. CARATTI and others in Prague. He built a country house at Troya (1679–96), the quietly handsome Toscana Palace in Prague (1689–90) and, in a more exuberant style, two churches which influenced FISCHER VON ERLACH – St Francis in Prague (1679–88) and the abbey church of St Josef Malá Straná (Kleinseite).

Lit: E. Bachmann in *Barock in Böhmen* (ed. K. M. Swoboda), Munich 1969.

Matthew, Sir Robert (b. 1906), was Architect to the London County Council from 1946 to 1953, in the years in which the Council embarked on its exemplary housing and schools work. Matthew can be considered instrumental in establishing the progressive style of these buildings and the principles of variety in grouping, mixture of heights, and siting in landscape which have made the L.C.C. estates a pattern for the whole of Europe. Of recent buildings designed by the firm Robert Matthew, Johnson-Marshall & Partners the finest is New Zealand House, London (1958–63), while the most challenging is the Commonwealth Institute (1959–62), also in London, with its incorporation of the fashionable HYPERBOLIC PARABOLOID roof. (For illustration *see* INDUSTRIALIZED BUILDING.)

Lit: R. Maxwell, *New British Architecture,* London 1972.

Mausoleum A magnificent and stately tomb. The term derives from the tomb of Mausolus at Halicarnassus.

Mausoleum: Reconstruction of the Tomb of Mausolos at Halicarnassos, Turkey, mid-C4 B.C.

May, Hugh (1622–84), the son of a Sussex gentleman and prominent among the virtuosi of the Restoration, imported the placid spirit of Dutch PALLADIANISM into England and helped, with PRATT, to establish the type of house later known, erroneously, as the 'Wren' type. Eltham Lodge, London (1663–4), is his only surviving work, a rectangular brick-built house with a central pediment and stone pilasters. He may also have designed Holme Lacy House, Hereford (begun 1673–4). His work at Windsor Castle (remodelling the Upper Ward including St George's Hall and the King's Chapel, 1675–83) was important but has been almost completely destroyed. It was the most fully developed example of a Baroque scheme of decoration in Northern Europe – achieved with the aid of the painter Verrio and the sculptor Grinling Gibbons. (For illustration *see* ENGLISH ARCHITECTURE.)

Lit: J. Summerson, *Architecture in Britain, 1530–1830,* Pelican History of Art, Harmondsworth 1969, paperback edn 1970; H. M. Colvin, *Biographical Dictionary of English Architects, 1660–1840,* London 1954.

Maya architecture, *see* MESOAMERICAN ARCHITECTURE.

Maybeck, Bernard R. (1862–1937). Active chiefly at Berkeley and San Francisco. His is a curious, highly original Stick Style. Wood was his favourite material. Examples are the Faculty Club on the Berkeley campus (1899) and the First Church of Christ Scientist at Berkeley (1910–12). The mixture of vernacular, Gothic and Japanese in this building is irresistible. Many private houses show the same qualities, the interiors often being yet more stimulating than the exteriors.

Lit: J. M. Bangs, 'Bernard Ralph Maybeck', architect, comes into his own' in *Architectural Record,* January 1948; J. Burchard & A. Bush-Brown, *The Architecture of America,* Boston 1961.

McIntire, Samuel (1757–1811), was a self-trained architect of great ability and the outstanding example of the early American craftsman-builder tradition, though most of his work dates from after the end of the Revolutionary War. He was a wood-carver by trade and lived in Salem, Mass. With the help of Batty LANGLEY'S and WARE'S books and perhaps an edition of Palladio (which he owned at his death), he taught himself the PALLADIAN style, which he adopted for his first houses, e.g., Pierce-Nichols House (1782) in Salem. His most ambitious effort was Salem Court House (1785, now demolished) with superimposed orders and a dome. In the 1790s he came under the influence of BULFINCH, who provided the general design for his most important private house, the Derby Mansion (1795-9, demolished 1815), and from whom he picked up the ADAM style which he used in his later and finest houses (mostly destroyed, but there are rooms from them in the Boston and Philadelphia museums).

Lit: F. Kimball, *Mr Samuel McIntire, Carver, the Architect of Salem*, Portland, Maine, 1940.

McKim, Charles Follen (1847-1909), studied first engineering at Harvard, then, in 1867-70, architecture in Paris at the École des Beaux Arts. On his return to the States he entered the office of H. H. RICHARDSON. When he set up his own practice, he went into partnership with W. R. Mead and a little later with Stanford WHITE. In 1878 they were all interested in Colonial architecture, a highly unusual thing at the time. To this was added almost at once a liking for the Italian Renaissance which was first introduced, it seems, by Joseph Merrill Wells, who entered the office in 1879 and died early, in 1890. The Italian Renaissance meant to them the High Renaissance, not the Baroque exuberance of classical motifs then current. A first proof of this new taste was the impressively restrained group of the Villard Houses in Madison Avenue (1882), the second the Boston Public Library (1887 etc.) with its façade by McKim, inspired by LABROUSTE's Ste Genevieve Library. McKim believed in interior enrichment on a grand scale, and for the library was able to call in Sargent and Puvis de Chavannes. For the Chicago exhibition of 1893, McKim did the Agriculture Building.

Later jobs include the Germantown Cricket Club (1891), decidedly American Colonial; the lavish Madison Gardens (1891), Spanish with a tall tower reminiscent of Seville; the Washington Triumphal Arch in New York in the style of the Étoile; Columbia University in New York with its library rotunda (1893) inspired by the Pantheon in Rome and JEFFERSON's Charlottesville (1817-26); the Morgan Library in New York (1903); and the Pennsylvania Railway Station also in New York (1904-10), a grandiose scheme echoing Imperial Roman *thermae*. It was recently demolished. (For illustration *see* UNITED STATES ARCHITECTURE.)

Lit: C. H. Reilly, *McKim, Mead & White*, New York 1924; *A Monograph on the Work of* *McKim, Mead & White*, New York 1925; G. Moore, *The Life and Times of C. F. McKim*, Boston 1929; C. C. Baldwin, *Stanford White*, New York 1931; J. W. Reps, *The Making of Urban America*, Princeton 1951.

Megalithic Composed of a few very large blocks of stone, usually of irregular shape and only very roughly dressed, or used as found.

Megaron A large oblong hall, especially in Cretan and Mycenaean palaces; sometimes thought to be the ancestor of the Doric temple.

Mendelsohn, Erich or **Eric** (1887-1953). The boldness of Mendelsohn's vision of a sculptural architecture emerged early in his many small sketches for buildings that are not functionally determined but are highly expressive with their streamlined curves. In the years of German Expressionism at and after the end of the First World War, he was just once enabled actually to build such a vision (the Einstein Tower at Potsdam, 1919-20); but vigorous curves carried round corners also characterize his remodelling of the Mosse Building in Berlin (1921), and appear much tempered by the more rational spirit of the INTERNATIONAL MODERN style of the later twenties and the thirties in his excellent Schocken stores for Stuttgart (1926) and Chemnitz (1928). As expressive as the Einstein Tower, but in terms of multi-angular roof shapes instead of curves, is another early work of Mendelsohn's, a factory at Luckenwalde (1923). Mendelsohn visited the United States in 1924 and was understandably impressed by the expressive qualities of the skyscrapers. Later Berlin buildings include the headquarters of the Metal Workers' Union (1929) and Columbushaus (1929-30). In 1933 Mendelsohn went to London and joined Serge Chermayeff. Joint works are the de la Warr Pavilion at Bexhill (1935-6) and No. 64 Old Church Street, Chelsea (1936). But in 1934 he moved on to Israel, and in 1941 finally settled in the United States. In Israel he built, among other things, the Hadassah University Medical Centre on Mount Scopus, Jerusalem (1936-8), in America the Maimonides Hospital at San Francisco (1946-50). (For illustrations *see* EXPRESSIONISM and SYNAGOGUE.)

Lit: A. Whittick, *Eric Mendelsohn*, London 1964; D. Sharp, *Modern Architecture and Expressionism*, London 1966; Eric Mendelsohn, *Letters of an Architect*, ed. O. Beyer, London 1967; B. Zevi, *E. Mendelsohn: Opera completa*, Milan 1970.

Mengoni, Giuseppe (1829–77). Architect of the Galleria Vittorio Emanuele in Milan, won in competition in 1861. It was built in 1864–7 (though work on the decoration continued until 1877), and is the largest, highest, and most ambitious of all shopping arcades. It is cruciform, and the buildings through which it runs take part in the free Renaissance design of the *galleria*. Especially impressive is the façade towards the Piazza del Duomo.

Lit: G. Ricci, *La Vita e le opere dell'architetto G. Mengoni*, Milan 1930; L. Marchetti, *La Galleria di Milano*, Milan 1967; J. F. Geist, *Passagen*, Munich 1969.

Merlini, Domenico, *see* POLISH ARCHITECTURE.

Merlon, *see* BATTLEMENT.

Mesoamerican architecture In American archaeology Mesoamerica denotes the part of Central America inhabited by the Nahua and Maya peoples in the pre-Columbian period. It stretches from the line formed by Rio Panuco-Rio Lerma-Rio Sinaloa (Mexico) in the north, to Rio Ulua (Honduras) and Rio Jiboia (El Salvador) in the south, and comprises great tracts of present-day Mexico, the whole of Guatemala and British Honduras, part of El Salvador, and western Honduras.

Ancient Mexico is generally divided into six provinces, each having had a culture of its own: the south-eastern coast of the Gulf – the homeland of the Olmecs at the Spanish conquest; the middle strip of coast – homeland of the Totonacs; the northern coast of the Gulf – that of the Huastecs; the west and north-west – settled by the Tarascans at the time of the Conquista; the mountain valleys of Mexico and Puebla, which successively produced the civilizations of Teotihuacan and Tula (Toltec), and of the Chichimecs and Aztecs; and the Oaxaca highlands in the south, which was occupied by the Zapotec and Mixtec peoples.

Maya territory is divisible into the following three archaeological regions: the highlands of Guatemala and the adjacent mountainous parts of El Salvador to the south; the central plain to the north and north-west of this, whose heart embraces the Petén district of Guatemala, contiguous parts of British Hon-

duras, and the state of Chiapa in Mexico; and the northern region, consisting of the Yucatan peninsula, the bulk of Campeche, and the territory of Quintana Roo.

The periods of the great civilizations in Mesoamerica are as follows: 1. the pre-Classic or Formative period, also called the Archaic era, placed between 2000 B.C. and A.D. 300; 2. the Classic period, from A.D. 300–900; 3. the post-Classic period, from 900–1520. Each of the three periods has an early and a late, and sometimes a middle, phase.

The epitome of Mesoamerican architecture, as indeed of that of pre-Columbian America as a whole, is the PYRAMID. It differs both in shape and purpose from that of Egypt, being truncated at the top. It is stepped, with temples or altars on the upper platform which have since largely disappeared, either because they were of perishable materials, or because they were destroyed by the Spanish conquerors. Many pyramids simultaneously served as burial-places, though this was not, unlike those of Egypt, their original purpose. They were rather substitutes for natural mounds – and hence their base was at first round or oval, and only later square – and were representations of heaven, conceived of as the mountain seat of the gods, rather like the ZIGGURATS of Ancient Mesopotamia. The chief ornament of the sacrarium on the platform of Aztec pyramids was consequently the 'night sky' frieze: several rows of whitewashed hemispherical stone plugs inserted into a dark, sunken rectangular panel of the roof. Also peculiar to the Mesoamerican pyramid was the practice of 'overbuilding', i.e. at regular intervals, usually of 52 years (the date specified for the renewal of the world in the ceremonial calendar), the old temple pyramid was covered by a new sacred structure.

Another cardinal feature of Mesoamerican architecture was the sacred ball-game court

Ball-game court, Yagul CI 1–15

often closely connected with the pyramid: a rectangular, sunken or wall-girt site, with ramparts or platforms projecting inwards from the longer sides so as to leave a narrow passage, so that the playing-field seen from above resembled the Roman I, or a doubled T. In Maya, Zapotec and Totonac courts the ramparts sloped inwards; in those of the Aztecs, Mixtecs and Toltecs they were vertical, and supported large stone rings inserted vertically into the masonry in the middle, through which the ball had to pass on a main throw. The ball-game was not simply sport, but an activity vested with religious symbolism.

By the beginning of the first millennium B.C. there were already conical pyramids of alluvial stone in the Petén plain (Guatemala), whilst *La Venta* on the south-eastern coast of

Venta culture, with which the age of Meso-american civilizations begins, exerted far-reaching influences all around it, and is generally but not unquestionably associated with the *Olmec* people.

A similarly tentative connection is made between the *Totonacs* on the middle strip of the Gulf coast and the *El Tajin* culture, named after its most important ruins near Papantla. In its more restricted sense, Tajin (Totonac for 'lightning') refers to a seven-tiered pyramid on a rectangular base (82 × 114 ft, 82 ft high). The peculiarity of this building consists in the slabs of sedimentary rock covering the exterior walls, and the 364 small square niches inserted into the verticals of the tiers, with a cornice of projecting stone slabs above them. The central course of the broad stair-case is interrupted five times by dormer

Monolithic altar of basalt, Villahermosa La Venta Museum, c8–c4 B.C.

The great pyramid at El Tajin, Mexico, c7

the Gulf of Mexico, from the mid-Formative period of Mesoamerica, between 800 and 400 B.C., is the first place to have had the layout and dimensions of a ceremonial centre, with an 105 ft high mud and ADOBE pyramid approximately square in section standing in the middle. The square to the north of this main pyramid exhibits an enclosure (165 × 200 ft) formed by close-set pillars of natural columnar basalt. At the opening of the southern side of this stone fence, a jaguar's face is formed out of a mosaic of serpentine slabs on the floor of a ditch. This is the first manifestation in large-scale stone sculpture of the Mesoamerican jaguar-cult, to which La Venta indeed belonged. The squares between the earth pyramids are dotted with colossal altars and stelae bearing reliefs, human figures sculpted in the round and, most singular of all, de-tached colossal heads on stone bases. The La

window-like projections, each with three niches.

The temples of the *Huastecs* (related linguisti-cally to the Maya) on the northern Gulf coast consistently differ from others in Mexico by virtue of their round shape. Under Huastec influence circular constructions found favour in the rest of Mexico and among the Maya around the turn of the first Christian mil-lennium. They have been associated with the spread of the cult of the Huastec wind-god, a round temple in his honour having been ex-cavated for instance in Cempoala, the centre of later Totonac culture (A.D. 1200–1500). It is preceded by a rectangular structure con-taining the stairs.

The architecture of western Mexico is likewise conspicuous for temple pyramids linking together a round and a rectangular structure. Their core consists of a loose heap of stones, which is covered by a layer of volcanic stone slabs held with clay. The exterior of these *yácatas* appears not like a series of superimposed terraces, but like a sheer wall only interrupted by small breaks. The upper rectangular platform was very narrow, and there was a small tower-shaped temple on the rounded rear part of the yácatas.

Out of the lava field of the Pedregal rises the earliest datable building of the Mexican plateau, the almost circular four-tiered pyramid of *Cuicuilco* (*c.* 300 B.C.). It was originally

Pyramid at Cuicuilco, c. 300 B.C.

about 65 ft high and 440 ft in diameter. It was made of concentric rings of pounded clay with a covering of volcanic boulders. A broad ramp ascended to a repeatedly raised altar with right-angled masonry.

Teotihuacan culture centres on the eponymous and extensive pyramid site 30 miles north-west of the capital, Mexico-Tenochtitlan, and its beginnings are rooted in the close of the pre-Classic period of Central Mexico, as emerges from the finds there at the foot of the great Sun Pyramid (c3 B.C.). This is the largest structure in Mesoamerica to have been erected in a single building campaign (215 ft high and 720 ft square – 30 million cu. ft of sun-dried brick). The reputed sun-pyramid – its name derives from the Aztecs – consists of five superimposed truncated pyramids of the

same slope. Like the so-called Moon Pyramid (390 × 490 ft, 148 ft high) it is preceded by a structure consisting of several terraces. The staircase ascending from the Way of the Dead, with flights interrupted by the breaks in the pyramid, is orientated toward the west. Nothing remains of the temple once upon the topmost platform, probably consecrated to the rain-god Tlaloc. The ramparted area erroneously called the citadel by the Spaniards (1300 × 1300 ft) lies at the southern end of the Way of the Dead. It is surmounted by 15 small, regularly-spaced pyramids crowned with platforms. To the east of this area a platform extends from north to south, on to which the main temple abuts. A smaller pyramid with four tiers was built on to the front of this six-tiered temple mountain, but has recently been partially removed to reveal the fine façade of the earlier temple. Its frieze and plinth are overlaid with continuous reliefs of plumed serpents whose fully

Detail of façade of the Great Temple, Teotihuacan, c3–4

sculpted stone heads project between the equally plastic heads of the rain-god Tlaloc. Once all four sides of the pyramid were thus

Sun Pyramid, Teotihuacan, Mexico, c3 B.C.

Courtyard, Teotihuacan, Mexico

adorned; counting the twelve heads projecting from the balustrades of the staircase, no less than 366 such heads gazed down on the spectator. The head of the rain-god Tlaloc is characterized by a jaguar's jaw and eye-rings, betokening his attribute, the fabulous butterfly. There is a tendency to see the bearers of Teotihuacan culture as immigrants from the coast of the Mexican Gulf, from the region of the La Venta culture in particular.

At the beginning of the c9 A.D. Classic Teotihuacan was destroyed by fire, an event connected with the arrival on the plateau of Mexico of the *Toltecs*, who were to remain politically and culturally supreme for the next 300 years or so. Their capital was in *Tula*, where worship of the god Quetzalcoatl, the Plumed Serpent, drew on a historical personality, the priest-king Ce acatl topiltzin (b. A.D. 947). To him legend ascribes the fate of banishment to the east, which is borne out by buildings of the Toltec period in Yucatan. The pyramid of the Temple of the Morning Star at Tula, the legendary Tollan in the

Pyramid at Temple of the Morning Star, Tula, Mexico, c. 900

present-day Mexican state of Hidalgo, rises on an all but square base (roughly 140 ft square) in five stages each about 6 ft high. Each stage consists of a sloping plinth and a vertical frieze in relief, that survives in fragments. It displays an uninterrupted row of pacing jaguars and pumas – with eagles and vultures between – as well as depictions of a human face staring out of the jaw of a dragon: the image of the god of the Morning Star, Quetzalcoatl. A broad stairway leads from an extended pillared portico at the foot of the pyramid to its platform, where the work of restoration has replaced four huge ATLANTES about 16 ft high and with the features of Toltec warriors, which with the four relief-carved pillars behind once bore the timbering of the roof. The broad entrance to the portico was supported by two columns in the shape of plumed serpents. Parallel to the north and west sides of the temple, and at a slight distance from the base of the pyramid, ran a monumental wall, which ranks among the outstanding achievements of Toltec architecture, and still survives in part. It bears on both sides an artistically accomplished tripartite frieze in relief, and is crowned by a decorative row of pinnacles. The middle of the frieze exhibits a number of snakes with heads turned partly to the east and partly to the west, out of whose fangs human skeletons protrude – a symbolic representation of the planet Venus who, after her voyage through the underworld (hence the reduction to a skeleton), rises in heaven as the morning or the evening star. Two ball-game courts also form part of the site at Tula; that to the north of the Temple of the Morning Star, with its central field flanked by escarpments supporting vertical ramparts, resembles kindred layouts in Monte Albán and Xochicalco. Towards the end of the c12 Tula was destroyed and burnt by the Chichimecs.

Xochicalco, the 'Place of the Flower House', lies about 20 miles south-west of Cuernavaca on a glacis of the Mesa Central. It dates back to between the end of Teotihuacan (c9) and the beginnings of Tula (c10), and can be seen as the second Toltec centre. A 425 ft high hill was transformed into a place of worship by five artificial terraces (1150 × 650 ft). The main shrine stands on a rectangular square encompassed by other buildings, and consists of a platform and a temple, the lower part of whose walls still stands. These are open on the west side, where the broad stairway ascends to the platform. The lower part of the platform, whose core is of earth and stones, exhibits a high, sloping plinth and a lower, vertical crown, and is covered with precisely hewn and neatly fitted relief-cut slabs of andesite. Eight plumed serpents wind round the lower slope, their heads turned toward the corners, and their bodies coiled alternately round hieroglyph cartouches, and human figures sitting cross-legged with great beasts' heads as helmets. The vertical frieze shows sitting priests, and the plinth of the temple portico warrior figures in the same posture; both are linked with calendar dates whose script resembles those both of the Zapotecs and of the Maya. Maya influence is also clearly detectable in the figural reliefs of Xochicalco.

Between 1200 and 1300 A.D. the first of the pyramids, measuring only 100 × 40 ft at the base by 26 ft high, was built at *Tenayuca*, which lies on the former north shore of lake Tetzoco and was the earliest capital of the *Chichimecs*, who, like the Aztecs, belonged to the Nahua-speaking race. Over it were built at intervals of a probable 52 years, like the layers of an onion, at least five further pyramids. But at each phase the basic design, with two main stairs and two shrines on the platform, remained the same, suggesting that all the pyramids were built by the same people. On the last occasion in 1507, the base of the pyramid of Tenayuca, now occupying an area

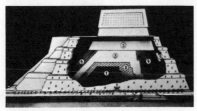

Pyramid of St Cecilia (Tenayuca), C14–15

Cross-section of pyramid at Tenayuca, begun C13

200 ft long by 164 ft wide, and almost 62 ft high to the base of the platform, was surrounded with a low stone parapet, on which lie the serried forms of 138 snakes, whose writhing bodies are of masonry whilst their heads surmounting the parapet are of hewn stone. On the north and south sides of the pyramid, which faces westwards, stand two low altars before each of which lies a coiled 'turquoise serpent' fashioned in the same way.

Coiled serpent, Tenayuca pyramid, C13–16

These snakes are embodiments of the bright day-sky, which encircles and bears the sun. There are other clear indications that the pyramid of Tenayuca served the cult of the sun.

However its special importance resides in the fact that it conveys a reliable picture (despite its small scale) of the character of the chief Aztec temple of Tenochtitlan (Mexico City), which was razed to the ground on its capture by the Spaniards in 1521. It too possessed two stairways which led to two temples, the one of the rain-god Tlaloc, the other of the tribal god Huitzilopochtli, another of whose aspects was sun-god. This temple was also surrounded by a serpent wall whose remains have been uncovered, as have two huge stone turquoise serpents' heads north and south of the arena once covered by the temple of Tenochtitlan.

In the Oaxaca Highlands traces of *Zapotec* culture are concentrated on one of the mountains, called *Monte Alban* by the Spaniards, which rises 1300 ft over the trough of the very valley in which the city of Oaxaca lies not far away. The beginnings of the 2300-ft long and 850-ft wide temple city can be traced back to Olmec influences from

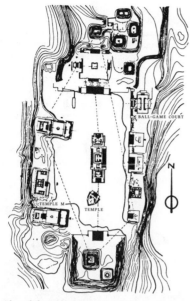

Plan of the c6–9 remains on Mount Alban

the south-eastern coast of the Gulf (La Venta) in the last centuries before the Christian era. This is chiefly evident from the revetment of the base of the earliest structure – an earth pyramid subsequently surmounted by a platform with three temples – with slabs carved with human figures of Olmec type in relief, called 'danzantes' because they probably represent priests executing ecstatic dances. The temples of Monte Alban occupy a smooth sunken area between two huge raised platforms to north and south. The northern platform attains a height of 40 ft, climbed by a striking flight of steps. Going through a vestibule with the stumps of twelve rubble columns, one reaches a sunken court

Temple 'M' on Mount Alban, c6–9

10 ft deep. Similar constructions are built on to the two square temple pyramids flanking the *danzantes* to the west of the arena. The staggered double cornice lends the walls and staircase balustrades of these, as of most buildings at Monte Alban, a characteristic profile. Three adjoining pyramids, the centre one of which has three temples and a broad staircase on its eastern side, extend for 330 ft along the long north-south axis of the temple arena. To the south of this complex is something unique in Ancient Mexican architecture, a temple with an end like a ship's bow deviating 45° eastwards from north, which was possibly used for astronomical observation. A ball-game court of Maya type adjoins the north platform on its west side. Around the turn of the first Christian millennium the centre of Zapotec culture shifted to the valley; Monte Alban became a necropolis crowded with innumerable and ornamented graves, and was finally occupied by the Mixtecs.

After the relinquishment of Monte Alban, a new centre of Zapotec culture blossomed at the east end of the Oaxaca valley, at *Mitla*, the seat of the priest-king or *Uija-tao*. This consists of five distinct palace complexes, of which three very similar ones are tolerably well preserved. They comprise three abutting parts on a square plan, an enclosed inner court, and two outer courts open on one side. All three courts are cemented, and surrounded by extended halls on low platforms, opening

The Palace of the Columns, Mitla, c15

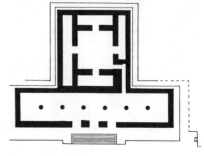

on to the courts through three centre doors. The doors are framed by massive stone beams. The most important of the palaces is the so-called Palace of the Columns, named after the vestibule serving as audience-chamber, in which six stout columns without bases or capitals once supported a flat timber roof. It was entered from a low staircase on the north side of the open central main court. A narrow twisting passage led from the columned hall to the inner court bordered by four chambers – probably the residence of the Uija-tao himself. The walls of the Palace of the Columns were revetted with about 100,000 perfectly dove-tailed slabs of trachyte, carved beforehand into a large number of alternating geometrical patterns. On the outer walls and in the courts these motifs are separated by projecting

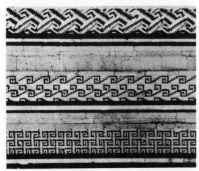

Detail of decoration
in the Palace of the Columns, Mitla

double string-courses running on two super-imposed levels, and alternately framing the rectangular fields of the friezes above and below.

Apart from roughly 200 temple-cum-tomb pyramids of clay bricks and earth at Kaminaljuyu on the edge of Guatemala City, the Formative period (1500 B.C.–A.D. 200) in the *Maya* Highlands has left behind no buildings worth mentioning. The finest surviving structure of the late Formative period on the central plain is the pyramid of Uaxactún in the Petén region. The quadrangular stump of the pyramid, which once bore a temple of some perishable material, is only 26 ft high, but it still has carved steps flanked by 16 huge masks of a jaguar god. The whole surface of the pyramid is coated with off-white stucco, as was to be the custom with all subsequent Maya buildings. Not far from Uaxactún is *Tikal*, once the greatest Maya

city, whose beginnings reach back into the Formative period, though its heyday fell in the Classic period (A.D. 200–800). Between two elongated causeways stretches a rect-angular ceremonial court, the central sanc-tuary of a built-up site covering roughly 6 square miles. Facing one another on its eastern and western sides stand two of the five steep pyramids, of anything up to 230 ft high, that belong to the centre of Tikal. They

Temple No. 1, Tikal, c6–8

bear aloft on their platforms temples with thick stone walls, sheltering cramped little corbel-vaulted shrines within. Conspicuous roof-combs are, like these pseudo-vaults, a characteristic of the Classic Maya architecture of the plain. A bevy of small pyramids, aligned behind and alongside one another, form an 'Acropolis' bordering the north side of the great arena of Tikal, whose southern side is occupied by so-called palaces – low buildings with a plethora of rooms. In front of the ramp linking the two tower-like pyramids at the foot of the Acropolis are a row of about 20 stelae, such as are usual in the Classic period of Maya culture. They bear bas-reliefs of human figures, with dates that have been deciphered.

The landmark of *Palenque* (Spanish for palisaded place), the great centre of Classic Maya culture in Chiapas, is a three-storey tower of square section, which belongs to a group of palaces embracing four inner courts, with rows of pillars forming arcades. Stucco reliefs and stone slabs sculpted with ritual representations adorn both the walls of the palaces and the interiors of the temples on the stepped pyramids. Two parallel rows of long chambers in the buildings are separated by a walled core virtually throughout, which takes both the weight of the roof-comb and the chief load of the vaults. The outer walls could hence be constructed less substantially than in other Maya cities, and the roofs be given a MANSARD-like contour. The most important structure is the Temple of Inscriptions, from within which steps descend to a richly ornamented tomb-chamber under the base of the pyramid. Instances of such a combination of tomb and temple were also found at Tikal.

Temple of Inscriptions, Palenque, c7-8

Interior of Temple of Inscriptions, Palenque

The southern outpost of Maya civilization, *Copán* in Honduras, was the leading centre of astronomy. It produced the unique Hieroglyphic Stairway. This rises to a height of 85 ft

Hieroglyphic Stairway, Copán, Honduras, c7-8

above the level of the court. The riser of each of the 63 steps is adorned with deeply and carefully incised hieroglyphs. Five over-lifesize sitting figures of gods or priests are enthroned at fixed intervals in the middle of the stairway which, with its relief-ornamented stair-rail on both sides, attains 33 ft across. Regrettably only fragments of the temple on the summit of the pyramid survive. The ball-game court of Copán, with stone pinnacles shaped like parrots – the birds of the sun – on the walls at the sides, was one of the finest in the whole Maya region. The architectural focus of Copán is the 'Acropolis', a complex of pyramids, temples and terraces elevated several feet above the city.

In the 1940s, not far from Yaxchilan in the region of Rio Usumacinta, eleven or so buildings were found on a terraced hill concealed in the jungle. One building contained murals of unique quality in its three chambers, illustrating battles with the submission of captives, ceremonial parades, and princes adorning themselves. The place was christened Bonampak (painted wall).

In the Post-Classic period, Maya architecture reached its zenith under Mexican influence in the northern region. Northern Yucatan is a parched limestone plain covered with scrub, lacking rivers and lakes, so that settlement is only feasible here and there, where there are breaches through to the water-table – the so-called *dolinen*. In Maya such *dolinen* are called (besides *ch'en* = well) *tz'onot*, whence the Spanish *zenote*. Around the turn of the first Christian millennium, a political and religious leader whom the Maya called Kukulcan (Quetzalcoatl) appeared at the head of a warrior horde. He led his tribe, the *Itzá*, to an already-existent holy place consecrated to the rain-god of the Maya, Chac, who was thought to reside there on account of the sacred *zenote*. The reinvigorated city received the name *Chichen Itzá*, i.e. 'At the Well of the Itzá'. The huge buildings put up here in the course of the next 200 years in many ways vividly recall the architecture of Tula in the Mexican highlands. The 'Temple of the Warriors', which belongs to the heart of

Castle, Chichen Itzá, CII–I2

embodies the nine heavens of Ancient Mexican tradition. Steps to the number of 364 mount the four sides, which are roughly aligned with the points of the compass. The

Temple of the Warriors, Chichen Itzá, CII–CI2

Chichen Itzá, is a largely faithful reproduction of the Temple of the Morning Star at Tula, both as to the overall design and as to details. Here too, two columns in the shape of inverted plumed serpents form the entry to the temple. As at Tula the Temple of the Warriors is preceded by a colonnade, through which the steps to the temple platform pass. A dead straight, paved processional way 300 yds long connects the sacred *zenote* with the main temple of Chichen Itzá, which was reputed to have been erected by Kukulcan himself, and whose whole design derives from the Classic Mexican temple pyramid, notably in what concerns its cosmic symbolism. The nine stages of the 80-ft high stepped pyramid – falsely called 'Castillo' by the Spaniards –

inclusion of the base makes 365 – one for each day of the year that they are scaled by the sun. The main entrance to the CELLA lies to the north, its wide portal divided by two columns in the shape of a plumed serpent such as occurs at Tula. The interior of this temple pyramid concealed inviolate an earlier Kukulcan temple, whose design was still extensively indebted to the old Maya style.

The earliest building of the Toltec phase at Chichen Itzá is the dumpy rotunda, the Caracol, which derives its name (Spanish for 'snail') from a narrow spiral staircase in the wall-mass of the interior. The Caracol is a two-storey tower on a two-tiered platform. The seven narrow rectangular openings in the remarkably thick walls of the badly damaged

The 'Caracol', or Observatory,
Chichen Itzá

upper storey face the four points of the compass and other astronomically important
directions. There can be no doubt that the
Caracol was used as an observatory. It retains many features of Maya architecture,
such as the pseudo-vaults over the upper
corridors, but as a rotunda it represents an
alien form of construction of Mexican origin.
In the eyes of many experts, the crowning
Toltec achievement at Chichen Itzá is the
sacred ball-game court, with monumental
vertical walls at the sides. At the enlarged
southern end of the east wall stands a temple
with richly ornamented exterior walls, incorporating a frieze of pacing jaguars –
whence its name of the 'Temple of the
Jaguars'. To its rear at ground level is a chapel
with a single small chamber, whose vault is
however covered up to the crown with
significant reliefs in pure Toltec style.

Yucatan also has stone testimony to
the earlier Classic period of the Maya, before
the appearance of the Toltecs. *Uxmal*, for

instance, still embodies the Late Classic Maya
style of the so-called Puuc, i.e. of the 'land of
the low chain of hills' (south-west Yucatan).
This is characterized by, amongst other things,
'veneered' walls – the mantling of rubble
fillings with a fine stone casing. This treatment of façades, like the disposal of buildings
of the palace type round rectangular courts
with open corners, exhibits parallels with
Zapotec Mitla. A good example of this is the
so-called 'Nuns' Quadrangle' (250 × 210 ft),
built some time between the C9/CII A.D. The
stone mask of the Maya rain-god Chac, with
his upturned snout, frequently appears as a
recurring motif on the façades, like that of the

*Stone masks of the Maya rain-god Chac,
Palace of Masks, Kabah, CIO–II*

temple in the style of the *'Chenes'*, i.e. of the
'land of the fishponds' (North Campeche).
This temple is one of the two shrines on the
summit of the so-called 'Pyramid of the
Soothsayer' (72 ft high). A steep stairway,
flanked by two rows of steps with superimposed masks of the rain-god, ascend to the
Chenes temple, whose roof forms a platform in
front of the topmost temple. The interior of
the elliptical-based Pyramid of the Soothsayer
contains another three virtually unaltered
temples, so that five successive phases of
building may be deciphered from it.

Two hundred yards south of the Pyramid
of the Soothsayer lies the so-called 'Governor's
Palace', of tripartite profile formed by two
recessions in the façade, with two wedge-

Governor's Palace, Uxmal, CIO–II

shaped openings, all on a 300 ft long sub-structure with a monumental stairway in front of the central range. The ten feet high frieze is composed of 20,000 tesserae. Eleven portals in the plinth of the palace give access to the twin rows of chambers. [oz]

Lit: H. D. Disselhoff, *Geschichte der altamerikanischen Kulturen,* 1967; J. E. S. Thompson, *The Rise and Fall of Maya Civilization,* 1954; George Kubler, *The Art and Architecture of Ancient America,* Pelican History of Art, Harmondsworth 1962.

Mesopotamian architecture, *see* SUMERIAN AND AKKADIAN ARCHITECTURE.

Métezeau, Louis (1559/72–1615), was closely involved with the DU CERCEAUS in Henri IV's improvements to Paris, notably the Place des Vosges (1603 onwards) and at the Louvre where he probably designed the south façade of the Grande Galerie. He also assisted in the interior decoration of the Petite Galerie, the Salle des Antiques and the Grande Galerie (1601–8). He collaborated with Dupérac on the interior decoration of the Hôtel de Jean de Fourcy, Paris (1601). His brother **Clément** or **Jacques Clément Métezeau** (1581–1652) may have been a more important architect. He was transitional between de BROSSE and LE VAU. He designed the Place Ducale at Charleville (1610), the portail of Saint-Gervais, Paris (1616), the Orangerie du Louvre (1617), the Hôtel de Brienne (1630–32) and the Château de la Meilleraye (*c.* 1630). He worked with de Brosse at the Luxembourg in Paris *c.* 1615 and in 1611 was sent to Florence by Marie de Medici to make drawings of Palazzo Pitti in connection with it, though they do not appear to have been used by de Brosse.

Lit: A. Blunt, *Art and Architecture in France, 1500–1700,* Pelican History of Art, Harmondsworth 1970, paperback edn 1973; J. P. Babelon, *Demeures Parisiennes sous Henri IV et Louis XIII,* Paris 1965.

Metope The square space between two TRIGLYPHS in the FRIEZE of a Doric order; it may be carved or left plain. (Illustrated next column.)

Meurtrière In military architecture, a small loophole, large enough for the barrel of a gun or musket and through which a soldier might fire under cover.

Metope, Temple of Hera, Paestum, late c6 B.C.

Mews A row of stables with living accommodation above, built at the back of a townhouse, especially in London. They are now nearly all converted into houses or 'mews flats'.

Mexican architecture (For earlier Mexican architecture *see* MESOAMERICAN ARCHITECTURE.) In the wake of the Spanish Conquest Mexican architecture took on a Gothic (San Miguel de Actopan, etc.) or Spanish Renaissance character until the mid c16, making thereafter in the latter part of the c16 and the early c17, as in Spain itself, the transition to the Baroque. Here as elsewhere in Central and South America (cf. BRAZILIAN ARCHITECTURE), this resulted in the most unfettered manifestations of the CHURRIGUERESQUE STYLE. The latter flourished primarily in the countryside, whereas the great city cathedrals (Mexico City 1573–1667, Puebla 1551–1664) remained more faithful to the mainstream of European Baroque. The neo-classical reaction that ensued at the end of the c18 obliterated much, and only a few churches in Tepotzotlán, Taco, Ocotlán, and Valenciana retained their Baroque furnishings intact. As to secular architecture, the Casa d'Alfeñique at Puebla is a happy survival. A favourite form of detailing in Mexico is the ESTÍPITE, with a tapered

Church at Ocotlán, c18

Detail of vaulting in S. Domingo, Puebla, c18

shaft separated by a richly sculptured cushion-block from its capital. These are to be found on the church of the Jesuit College in Tepotzot-lán, Santa Rosa in Queretaro, and many other churches.

Mexican architecture is distinguished from SPANISH ARCHITECTURE by three things: the more Moorish character of its ornament, the adoption of pre-Columbian elements (*see* MESOAMERICAN ARCHITECTURE), and the taking to extremes of certain Spanish traits – above all, that of the deliberate setting off of austerity against Churrigueresque profusion. As in the Late Gothic of Spain (San Pablo, Valladolid), the towers of a west front are often kept intentionally plain and massive, whilst the central section (the *imafronte*) and the portion of the towers above the roof-line is extravagantly subdivided and adorned. Moorish influence (*see* MUDÉJAR) is observable in the taste for smooth domes seemingly borne up by a ring of windows, and often both supported on an octagonal DRUM, and supporting an octagonal LANTERN. It is even more marked in the use of coloured glazed tiles, and stucco that often smothers whole walls and vaults with ornament. White, sometimes combined with gold, is predominantly the colour of this stucco, but there are several eruptions of crude and vivid colour, which is a legacy both native and Spanish that has gone on to

celebrate further triumphs in this century, in the University buildings of Mexico City. Coloured tiles were brought by the Arabs to Spain, and thence transmitted by the Spaniards to the New World: a good example is the late

Pilgrimage church,
El Pocito, Guadelupe, near Mexico City, c18

c18 Casa de los Azulejos in Mexico City. It is worth remarking that the great cathedral of Mexico City is raised directly over the foundations of the old Aztec temple of Tenochtitlán, and that a pilgrimage church crowns the largest Ancient Mexican pyramid, at Cholula (which has not been uncovered, though a shaft has been driven into it).

Capilla Real, Franciscan friary,
Cholula, c16

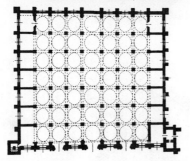

c20 Mexican architecture has made a conscious effort to reassert its pre-Columbian heritage in the use of certain forms, whilst exploiting the advances of modern European architecture. Highly influential was MIES VAN DER ROHE's demonstration, in the German pavilion at the 1929 International Fair at Barcelona, that costly materials could be

used alongside one another in a modern way. The revolutionary reversion to plainer forms from the survivals of Baroque excess occurred earlier in Mexico than anywhere else in Latin America. A fertile exponent of the INTERNATIONAL MODERN style since the mid-1920s has been José Villagrán Garcia (b. 1901), whose pupils include Juan O'Gorman (b. 1905; private housing in San Angel, 1929-30, and some schools) and Juan Legorreta (workers' housing in Mexico City, 1934). Modern architecture first gained official recognition under the regime of Lázaro Cárdenas in 1936, but it only achieved international stature after the Second World War. A new university city was built to plans by Mario Pani and Enrique del Moral on the lava slopes of the Pedregal, south of the capital, between 1950 and 1953; planned to take 20,000 students, it was the greatest architectural undertaking of the years immediately after the war, and remains a paradigm. It consists of asymmetrical pavilions loosely grouped round grassy courts, mostly more or less indebted to the International Style: Villagrán Garcia's School of Architecture and Museum of Art, Juan Sordo Madaleno's Geology Institute, Enrique Yánez's Chemistry Institute, and Pedro Ramírez Vásquez's School of Medicine. The 15-storey building put up to house the central administration by Mario Pani, Enrique del Moral and Salvador Ortega Flores, however, stands out from these by its use of variegated and polychrome materials – glazed tiles, Carrara glass, onyx, concrete, and synthetics. Even more remarkable is the Library, which Juan O'Gorman, operating as painter, sculptor and architect, used as a gigantic matrix for a profusion of vividly-coloured mosaics depicting aspects of pre-Spanish history, leaving not an inch of the windowless 12-storey bookstack uncovered. The house that O'Gorman built for himself in 1956 is close by. It is inserted into a grotto, and constructed out of a random mixture of rubble, mosaic, and reliefs. The University Stadium (by Augusto Pérez Palacios, Raúl Salinas, and Jorge Bravo) is formed out of an immense sunken bowl that, in contrast to the towering Aztec Stadium built to hold 95,000 spectators for the 1968 Olympics by Pedro Ramírez Vasquez, Rafael Mijares and Luis Martinez del Campo, requires no steps to reach it.

Jorge Gonzáles Reyna's pavilion housing the University's Centre for Research into Cosmic Radiation drew for its technical aspects

*Library of Mexico University, 1956,
by J. O'Gorman and J.M. de Velasco*

upon designs by the engineer-architect and contractor, Félix CANDELA, whose buildings have all been of world importance. Two covered markets in Mexico City – San Lucas (1956), by Villagrán Garcia, and Merced (1967), by Enrique del Moral – are structurally indebted to his work. For the 1968 Olympics Candela collaborated with Enrique Castañeda and Antonio Peyri to produce the impressive domed Palacio de los Deportes.

As chairman of a Government Committee for Educational Planning, Ramírez Vásquez presided over a remarkable campaign for the mass-production of village schools. Concrete was chosen as the basic material, with glazed tile wall-cladding, and roofs borne up by a

University Stadium, University City, 1953, by A. P. Palacios, R. Salinas and J. Bravo

Automex Factory, Poluca, by R. Legorreta

Space Research Centre, Mexico University, 1953, by J. G. Reyna, engineer F. Candela

Palacio de los Deportes, Mexico City, 1968, by Candela, Castañeda and Peyri

free-standing system of steel supports. Prefabrication played a steadily increasing role. Mexico City contains a number of prominent office-buildings that use SKELETON CONSTRUCTION: Mario Pani & Enrique del Moral's Ministry of Water Supply 1950, Pedro Ramírez Vásquez & Rafael Mijares's Ministry of Labour & Welfare (1953), Juan Sordo Madaleno's office-block in the Calle Lieja (1956), and Augusto Alvarez's Banco del Valle de Mexico (1957). Mario Pani also directed the construction of a number of low-density public housing estates on the edges of Mexico City, the most important being Nonoalco-Tlalteloco (1964–6), whose impressive SATELLITE TOWN-centre has a singular triangular office-tower. Adjoining this is the Foreign Office by Vásquez and Mijares (1966), executed in the same stark, giant

slabs as Madaleno's Ministry of Justice (1966). Altogether more appealing is Vásquez and Mijares's Anthropological Museum (1963–4), which won world-wide acclaim with its unobtrusive yet striking way of displaying ancient art. Also worth mention is Ricardo Legorreta's Automex factory in Toluca, with massive towers by the sculptor Mathias Goeritz (1958).

Lit: J. Armstrong Baird Jr., *The Churches of Mexico, 1530–1810*, Berkeley–Los Angeles 1962; Max L. Cetto, *Modern Architecture in Mexico*, London 1961.

Mezzanine A low storey between two higher ones; also called an *entresol*.

Michael of Canterbury A master mason working *c.* 1300, first at Canterbury for the cathedral, then in London, where he was the first master mason of St Stephen's Chapel (begun 1292) in the palace of Westminster and probably its designer. A **Walter of Canterbury** was in charge of work at the palace in 1322. A **Thomas of Canterbury** was working under him in 1324 and, in 1331, probably after Walter's death, was put in charge of work at St Stephen's Chapel. Thomas may have died in 1336.

Lit: J. Harvey, *English Medieval Architects*, London 1954.

Michelangelo Buonarroti (1475–1564). Sculptor, painter, poet, and one of the greatest of all architects, he was the archetype of the inspired 'genius' – unsociable, distrustful, untidy, obsessed by his work, and almost pathologically proud – in fact, the antithesis of the Early Renaissance ideal of the complete man so nobly exemplified in ALBERTI and LEONARDO. Deeply and mystically religious, he was consumed by the conflicts and doubts of the Counter-Reformation. As in his life, so in his art, he rejected all the assumptions of the Renaissance and revolutionized everything he touched. Nowhere was his influence so profound or so enduring as in architecture. He invented a new vocabulary of ornament, new and dynamic principles of composition, and an entirely new attitude to space. His few dicta and his drawings reveal that he conceived a building as an organic growth and in relation to the movement of the spectator. He made clay models rather than perspective drawings, and appears to have eschewed the type of highly finished design which could be turned over to the builders ready for execution. He usually made considerable modifications as the building went up, and it is now impossible to tell exactly how his many incomplete works would have looked had he finished them or how he would have finally realized in stone those compositions which remained on paper – the façade of S. Lorenzo, Florence (1516), or the centrally planned S. Giovanni dei Fiorentini, Rome (1556–60).

His first work in architecture is the exterior of the chapel of Leo X in Castel Sant'Angelo, Rome (1514). In 1515 he received his first major commission, for the façade of BRUNEL-LESCHI's S. Lorenzo, Florence, which he conceived as an elaborate framework for more than life-size sculpture. In 1520, before his S. Lorenzo design was finally abandoned, he was commissioned to execute the Medici family mausoleum in the new sacristy of the same church, much of which was already built. He produced a revolutionary design in which, for the first time, the tyranny of the orders was completely rejected: windows taper sharply, capitals vanish from pilasters, tabernacles weigh down heavily on the voids of the doors beneath them. But the novelty of his design is less evident in this truculent misuse of the classical vocabulary than in the revolutionary conception of architecture which inspired it. He saw the wall not as an inert plane to be decorated with applied ornaments but as a vital, many-layered organism – hence the extraordinary form of the tabernacles with their strange elisions and recessions. The fact that he developed this new conception while the sacristy was in course of construction accounts for its many inconsistencies. The work was brought more or less to its present state by 1534 but never completed.

In 1524 he was commissioned to design a library for S. Lorenzo, Florence – the famous Biblioteca Laurenziana (reading-room designed 1525, vestibule 1526). The site determined its awkward shape and also limited the thickness of the walls. But he turned both these limitations to good effect, linking the structure to the decoration in a way never before achieved or imagined. Pilasters, which had hitherto been purely decorative elements applied to a structural wall, he used as the supports for the ceiling, while the cross-beams above the pilasters are echoed in mosaic on the floor so that the eye is drawn along the length of the room through a perspective of diminishing oblongs. He counteracted this longitudinal emphasis by stressing the verticality of the vestibule. Here the columns are set like statues in niches so that they appear to be merely decorative, though in fact they carry the roof. Other features are no less perverse – blind window-frames of aedicules with pilasters which taper towards the base, consoles which support nothing, and a staircase which pours forbiddingly down from the library on to the entrance level (executed by AMMANATI). There is no figure sculpture, but the whole interior is treated plastically as if it were sculpture.

In 1528–9 Michelangelo was employed on the fortifications of Florence, which he designed, with characteristic perversity, for offence rather than defence. In 1534 he left Florence for Rome, where he spent the rest of his life. His first Roman commission was for the reorganization of the Capitol, to provide a suitable setting for the ancient statue of Marcus Aurelius and an imposing place for outdoor ceremonies (begun 1539). He laid out the central space as an oval – the first use of this shape in the Renaissance – and designed new fronts for Palazzo dei Conservatori and Palazzo del Senatore (neither finished before his death). His designs were strikingly original, e.g., in their use of a GIANT ORDER embracing two storeys, a device that was soon to become general. In 1546 he was commissioned to complete Antonio da SANGALLO's Palazzo Farnese. He converted the unfinished façade into one of the most imposing in Rome, redesigned the upper floors of the *cortile*, and planned a vast garden to link it with the Villa Farnesina on the far side of the Tiber (not executed). In the conception of this grandiose vista, as in his design for the Porta Pia (1561–5) at the end of a new street from the Quirinal, he anticipated the principles of Baroque town planning.

But his most important Roman commission was, of course, for the completion of St Peter's (1546–64). Here he was faced with the task of finishing a building begun by BRAMANTE and continued by Antonio da Sangallo. He reverted to the centralized plan of the former, but made it much bolder and stronger, and demolished part of the latter's additions. His work on the interior was entirely masked in the C17; on the exterior it is visible only on the north and south arms and the drum of the dome. (The dome itself is by della PORTA and differs substantially from Michelangelo's model.) But although his plans were much altered the church as it stands today owes more to him than to any other single architect. In his last years he designed the Cappella Sforza, S. Maria Maggiore, Rome (c. 1560), on an ingenious plan rather coarsely executed after his death. He also provided plans for the conversion of the central hall of the Baths of Diocletian into S. Maria degli Angeli (1561), but here his work was completely overlaid in the C18.

The story of his architectural career is one of constant frustration. Not one of his major designs was complete at the time of his death. Yet his influence was none the less great. The Mannerists took from him decorative details which were gradually absorbed into the European grammar of ornament. But it was not until the C17 that architects were able to appreciate and began to emulate his dynamic control of mass and space. Significantly, his true heir was to another sculptor architect, BERNINI. (For illustrations see ITALIAN ARCHITECTURE and MANNERISM.)

Lit: J. S. Ackerman, The Architecture of Michelangelo, Harmondsworth 1970.

Michelozzo di Bartolommeo (1396–1472), a sculptor and architect of extreme elegance and refinement. Nevertheless he lacked the genius of his great contemporaries Donatello and BRUNELLESCHI. Born in Florence, the son of Bartolommeo di Gherardo who hailed from Burgundy, he worked as assistant to Ghiberti (1417–24), then shared a studio with Donatello (1425–33). Between 1420 and 1427 he built the little church of S. Francesco at Bosco in the Mugello. In the mid 1430s he began to turn his attention mainly to architecture and succeeded Brunelleschi as Capomaestro at the cathedral in 1446. His first important works were for the Medici family. In the 1430s he built – or remodelled – the Medici villa at Trebbio. In 1444 he began the Palazzo Medici-Riccardi in Florence, the first Renaissance palace, with massive rusticated basement and slightly smoother rusticated upper

floors capped by a prominent cornice. Behind this slightly forbidding fortress-like exterior there is an arcaded *cortile* derived from Brunelleschi's Ospedale degli Innocenti. His Medicean villa at Caffagiolo (1451) is again fortress-like, in contrast with his Villa Medici at Fiesole (1458–61: but somewhat altered in the C18) which is exquisitely light and elegant in style. In 1457 he was working at the Medici villa at Careggi.

In 1437 he began work at S. Marco, Florence, where he designed the sacristy (1437–43), the cloisters and the light and harmonious library (1441). Between 1444 and 1455 he designed the tribune and sacristy of SS. Annunziata. The tribune (completed in 1470–73 by ALBERTI) is centrally planned, inspired no doubt by Brunelleschi's S. Maria degli Angeli, but closer to an ancient Roman model, the temple of Minerva Medica. This was the first centralized building to be erected in the Renaissance, and it reflects both a desire to revive an antique form and a pre-occupation with the circle as a symbol of the universe and eternity. At Pistoia he built the little church of S. Maria delle Grazie (1452), where he employed the Early Christian and Byzantine form of a square building with central dome and subsidiary domed chapels at the four corners. In about 1462 he was in Milan, probably working on the Medici Bank. He also built the Portinari Chapel in S. Eustorgio, Milan (c. 1462), which owes much to Brunelleschi's S. Lorenzo sacristy. With this chapel he introduced the Renaissance style to Lombardy. From 1462 to 1463 he was in Dubrovnik, where he designed the Palazzo dei Rettori.

Lit: L. Heydenreich & W. Lotz, Architecture in Italy, 1400–1600, Pelican History of Art, Harmondsworth 1974.

Mies van der Rohe, Ludwig (1886–1969), worked under Bruno Paul, and then from 1908 to 1911 in Peter BEHRENS' office in Berlin. His earliest independent designs are inspired by SCHINKEL and the Berlin Schinkel Revival of the early C20 (Kröller House, 1912). At the end of the First World War he was, like GROPIUS, caught up in the frenzy and enthusiasm of Expressionism, and he designed then his revolutionary glass skyscrapers (1919–21). When Germany settled down to its rational responsible style of the later twenties and the early thirties, Mies van der Rohe excelled in this as well (housing, Berlin and Stuttgart, 1925–7). His true greatness as an architect was first revealed in the German Pavilion for the Barcelona Exhibition of 1929, with its open plan and masterly spatial composition, its precious materials – marble, travertine, onyx, polished steel, bottle-green glass – a sign of a striving after the highest quality and the most immaculate finishes. The planning principles of the Barcelona Pavilion were tested for domestic purposes in the Tugendhat House at Brno (1930), a private house.

From 1930 to 1933 Mies van der Rohe was director of the BAUHAUS, first at Dessau and then when it moved to Berlin for its last harassed phase of existence. In 1938 he was made Professor of Architecture at the Armour Institute (now Illinois Institute) of Technology in Chicago. In 1939 he designed a complete new campus for the Institute, whose plan has since developed and whose buildings have grown. They are characterized by cubic simplicity – envelopes which easily adapt to the various requirements of the Institute – and a perfect precision of details, where every member makes its own unequivocal statement. These qualities pervade all Mies van der Rohe's work. 'I don't want to be interesting, I want to be good,' he said in an interview. The volume of his work, remarkably small until after the Second World War, later grew considerably. Among private houses the Farnsworth House at Plano, Illinois (1950), must be mentioned; among blocks of flats the Promontory Apartments (1947) with a concrete frame, and Lake Shore Drive (1951) with a steel frame, both at Chicago and Lafayette Towers at Detroit (1963); among office buildings, the Seagram Building in New York (1956–9), with a bronze and marble facing; and the new National Gallery in Berlin (1963–8). They are all a final triumphant vindication of the style created in the early C20 and assimilated gradually in the thirties, and they do not participate in the neo-sculptural tendencies of the last fifteen or twenty years. (For illustrations *see* CURTAIN WALL, INTERNATIONAL MODERN, SKELETON CONSTRUCTION.)

Lit: P. Johnson, *Mies van der Rohe*, New York 1947; L. Hilberseimer, *Mies van der Rohe*, Chicago 1956; A. Drexler, *Mies van der Rohe*, Milan 1960; W. Blaser, *Mies van der Rohe; Die Kunst der Struktur*, Zurich–Stuttgart 1965.

Mihrab A niche cut into the QIBLA wall of a mosque and acting as the focus for prayer.

Mihrab: Great Mosque, Kairouan (Sidi Okba Mosque) c. 836

Its central importance is often stressed architecturally, for *mihrabs* are generally at the centre of the *qibla* wall and at the end of an especially wide aisle or under a raised transept or dome. The earliest mosques had no *mihrabs*, which suggests that the feature was not a liturgical necessity; but some have seen it as the symbolic indication of the place where Mohammed used to pray in his house. The first *mihrabs* were erected in the later C7. The form had both honorific and holy associations in Christianity, Judaism and the classical world; it is found in synagogues, church apses and – as a throne niche – in the palaces of late antiquity. The *mihrab* thus reflects the use of the early mosques for ceremonial and political as well as religious purposes. *Mihrabs* commonly comprise one or more niches resting on pillars and in a rectangular frame, often with multiple recessions, but flat *mihrabs* – perhaps derived from the slabs which originally marked the *qibla* – also exist (Ibn Tulun mosque, Cairo). Some are externally encased in a rectangular projection (al-Hakim mosque, Cairo). Most *mihrab* niches are of semicircular, polygonal or rectangular ground plan. As the cynosure of the mosque – the *imam* stands before it to lead the Friday prayers – the *mihrab* soon attracted the most elaborate decoration of the mosque; this usually consisted of pious inscriptions and abstract ornament. The hood of the niche was at first filled with a scalloped design;

later, stalactite vaulting became popular in many areas. *Mihrabs* may be of brick, stone, marble, tilework, stucco, wood or combinations of these materials (Kairouan, Tunisia). Even portable *mihrabs* are known, and occasionally tombstones were re-used as *mihrabs*. Some large mosques, and certain mausolea (Ikhwat Yusuf, Cairo) have triple *mihrabs* or even several *mihrabs*, disposed either along the *qibla* wall or elsewhere in the sanctuary (Ardistan, Iran; Abarquh, Iran). Often each is intended for a different legal school.   [RH]

Mijares, Rafael, *see* MEXICAN ARCHITECTURE.

Milesian layout A city plan of regular gridiron pattern with streets of uniform width and blocks of houses of approximately uniform dimensions. It probably originated in the Hittite, Assyrian and Babylonian empires and developed in Ionia in the C7 B.C. It is named after the city of Miletus. Other notable examples in Antiquity are Cryne in Lydia (founded 630–24) and Paestum (built by Greek colonists in the C6 B.C.). This type of plan was advocated by HIPPODAMOS who is sometimes, incorrectly, said to have invented it.

Mills, Robert (1781–1855), who was of Scottish descent, was discovered by JEFFERSON and articled to LATROBE, with whom he stayed from 1803 to 1808. His practice started in Philadelphia in 1808 (notably Washington Hall, perhaps influenced by LEDOUX). He designed the former State House at Harrisburg in 1810 with a semicircular portico and a dome over the centre; a circular church at Charleston as early as 1804; an octagonal and a large circular one in Philadelphia in 1811–13 (the latter with 4,000 seats); and then the Washington Monument for Baltimore, an unfluted Doric column (1814–29). His principal later works are governmental buildings for Washington, all Grecian and competent (Treasury, 1836–9; Patent Office, 1836–40; Post Office, 1839 etc.), but his most famous work is the Washington Monument at Washington, won in competition in 1836 and completed only in 1884. It is an obelisk 555 ft high and was originally meant to have a Greek Doric rotunda at its foot. Mills also did engineering jobs and a number of hospitals. The Columbia Lunatic Asylum (1822) has none of the grimness of its predecessors. It is like a monumental hospital (Greek Doric portico), and has all wards to the south and a roof garden. It is of fireproof construction.

Lit: H. M. Pierce Gallacher, *Robert Mills, Architect of the Washington Monument, 1781–1855,* New York 1935; J. Burchard & A. Bush-Brown, *The Architecture of America,* Boston–Toronto 1961.

Minaret A high tower attached to a mosque and used for the call to prayer. The etymology of 'minaret' ('place of fire') has suggested to some that the Pharos of Alexandria inspired the form of the earliest minarets, and the dwelling towers of Christian ascetics have also been cited as possible models. But the tall square church towers of Christian Syria provide the closest parallel both geographically and functionally to the first surviving minarets erected in the early C8 (Damascus; Bosra). Previously the call to prayer had been delivered from the nearest roof-top; indeed, the minaret was never obligatory and many small mosques lack them. Regional variations quickly developed. Minarets in North Africa remained close to the Christian model; Egypt experimented with multi-storey minarets in which each storey had a different elevation and ground plan (square, octagonal and finally circular); Iraq and the eastern Islamic world preferred the tall cylindrical brick minaret, often with an octagonal or flanged plinth; and the Ottomans in Turkey developed slender pencil-shaped minarets girdled with tiers of balconies. Perhaps the most unusual minarets are those of Samarra, Iraq (C9), cylindrical but with an external spiral ramp clearly derived from the Mesopotamian ZIGGURAT. In

Minaret: Djerba, Tunisia

Iraq and western Islam the head of the minaret was usually domed. Most minarets have at least one balcony, sometimes of wood and generally supported by corbels or stalactite vaulting, from which the muezzin makes the call to prayer: this is reached by a single or double internal spiral staircase. Although even major mosques generally require only one minaret, it became common for Ottoman mosques to have four, and mosques with up to seven (Mecca) are known. In such mosques,

Minarets of the Suleiman Mosque (Suleimanije), Istanbul, 1550–57, by Sinan

and also in the case of portals flanked by minarets (a feature common in Turkey and Iran), the purpose of the minaret is primarily decorative. After the C11 it became common for minarets to be added, again for architectural rather than functional reasons, to mausolea and *madrasas*. For freestanding minarets, and those in isolated locations, which are often of such extravagant height that a call to prayer made from the balconies would have been inaudible, such functions as signal towers or victory monuments may be postulated (Jam, Afghanistan). In North Africa the increasingly decorative bias of later minarets finds expression in dense geometric ornament enclosing groups of windows or blank arcades; in Egypt each storey of an elaborate tiered elevation is articulated by a welter of diminutive arches, windows, blank niches and cartouches drawn together by prominent mouldings, while in eastern Islam complex brick patterning and tile mosaic dominate. The early minarets were placed at one end of the courtyard, opposite the sanctuary and on the axis of the *mihrab*, but later they were sited in a corner of the courtyard or even outside the mosque.   [RH]

Minbar The pulpit from which the sermon is preached during the Friday prayers in a mosque. It stands to the right of the MIHRAB.

Minbar in the Blue Mosque, Istanbul, 1609–16

Until the C10, possession of a *minbar* distinguished a congregational mosque, used for the Friday prayers, from other mosques. The *minbar* usually takes the form of a right-angled triangle, with a platform – often crowned by a canopy – reached by a flight of stairs. Its base is often closed by a gate. The form recalls the AMBO of Christian churches, but a similar type was apparently used by Mohammed himself and also in Sassanian Persia by commanders reviewing their armies. The *minbar* served the ruler in early Islamic times as a throne from which to address his subjects or to receive their allegiance, and thus – like the *mihrab* –was originally associated with princely and political ceremonies. Its main function as a pulpit did not develop fully until after 750. Most *minbars* are of wood, embellished with carved inscriptions and geometric decoration; they are sometimes wheeled, and therefore movable. *Minbars* of mud, stone, marble, brick, iron and tilework are also known; these tend to be structurally simpler than wooden *minbars*.   [RH]

Minoan architecture The architecture of Crete from 2000 to 1150 B.C. It is divided into the First Palace Age (Middle Minoan I & II, 2000–1700 B.C.), the Second Palace Age (Middle Minoan III and Late Minoan I & II, 1700–1400 B.C.), and the post-Palace Age

(Late Minoan III, 1400–1150 B.C.). The finds at Knossos, Phaistos, Mallia and Kato Zakro, on which the investigations into and the descriptions of Minoan architecture are based, chiefly date from the Second Palace Age; the scanty remains of the First Palace Age suggest no coherent picture. It is clear only that the palaces from both ages spring from roughly the same concept and largely feature the same type of building. Minoan architecture is above all characterized by its labyrinthine (*see* LABYRINTH) character. The ensemble is purely additive, i.e., in contrast to the free-standing MEGARON at Troy, the great assortment of rooms, each to be entered only from the one before, are shoved together at right-angles, discouraging any orientation. Underlying this apparent jumble is, however, a feeling for centralization. A large rectangular court (in Knossos 100 × 200 ft) forms the centre round which the whole complex revolves, so that

Palace at Knossos, Hall of the Queen (reconstruction by Arthur Evans)

Theatre and propylaea at Phaistos, Crete

Plan of the Palace at Knossos

the impression of a maze chiefly derives from the want of a unifying logic amongst the groups of rooms themselves. The façades of the royal apartments and the long corridors are all orientated upon the central court, thus entirely neglecting the face that the whole complex turned towards the outside world. The outer walls run irregularly, only following the loose arrangement of the successive sequences of rooms, and making no façades. Looking at the layout as a whole, a powerful interplay between lengthwise and transverse tendencies emerges; the cunning distribution of light-wells to achieve illumination is also striking.

Minoan palace architecture is conspicuous for the absence of warlike elements; it was ultimately indebted to a refined taste for gracious living, whose prime considerations were practical and ritual, furthering not just a courtly but also an intimate style of existence. In other words, Minoan palaces are in no way to be seen as monuments intended as expressions of power.

For their TOMBS, the Minoans took and improved upon the megalithic manner of construction deriving from North Africa, to make BEEHIVE domes by laying courses of only slightly projecting blocks of stone upon one another.   [KG]

Lit: A. J. Evans, *The Palace of Minos*, 4 vols., London 1921–36; J. D. S. Pendlebury, *The Archaeology of Crete*, London 1939; A. W. Lawrence, *Greek Architecture*, Pelican History of Art, 2nd edn, Harmondsworth 1974.

Minster Originally the name for any monastic establishment or its church, whether a monastery proper or a house of secular canons, it came to be applied to certain cathedral churches in England and abroad (e.g., York, Strassburg) and also other major churches (Ripon, Southwell, Ulm, Zürich).

Minute In classical architecture a unit of measurement representing one sixtieth part of the diameter of a column at the base of its shaft. It may be either one sixtieth or one thirtieth part of a MODULE.

Mique, Richard (1728–94). Leading Louis XVI architect and the last of the royal architects at Versailles. He was trained under J.-F. BLONDEL in Paris, then employed by ex-King Stanislas at Nancy who ennobled him (1761). On Stanislas's death in 1766 he returned to Paris. He built the Ursuline convent, now Lycée Hoche, at Versailles (1767–72) with quietly elegant conventual buildings and a church inspired by Palladio's Villa Rotonda, and in 1775 the Carmelite church at Saint-Denis (now Justice de la Paix) with an Ionic portico and cupola. The same year he succeeded GABRIEL as first architect to Louis XVI and in this capacity was responsible for numerous minor works at Versailles – the decoration of the Petits Appartements of Marie Antoinette in the main palace, the theatre at the Petit Trianon, the exquisite circular Temple de l'Amour, the Belvédère, and, his best known work, the picturesquely rustic Hameau of imitation farm buildings, cottages, etc. (1783–5) with exposed beams and irregular roofs. He was finally guillotined.

Lit: L. Hautecoeur, *Histoire de l'architecture classique en France*, vol. IV, Paris 1952.

Misericord (or **miserere**). A bracket on the underside of the seat of a hinged choir stall which, when turned up, served as a support for the occupant while standing during long services.

Mixtec architecture, *see* MESOAMERICAN ARCHITECTURE.

Mnesicles A prominent architect in Periclean Athens. He designed the Propylaea, Athens (437–432 B.C., but never finished).

Lit: J. A. Bundgaard, *Mnesikles*, Copenhagen 1957; C. Tiberi, *Mnesicle, l'architetto dei Propilei*, Rome 1964.

Modillion A small bracket or CONSOLE of which a series is frequently used to support

Modillion: Temple of Clitummus, near Spoleto

the upper member of a Corinthian or Composite CORNICE, arranged in pairs with a square depression between each pair. (For illustration *see* ENTABLATURE.)

Module A unit of measurement by which the proportions of a building or part of a building are regulated. 1. In classical architecture, either the diameter or half the diameter of a column at the base of its shaft, in either case divided into minutes so that the full diameter represents 60 minutes. 2. In modern architecture, any unit of measurement which facilitates prefabrication.

Modulor The system of proportion advanced by LE CORBUSIER in his *Le Modulor* (1951). It is based upon the male figure and is used to determine the proportions of building units.

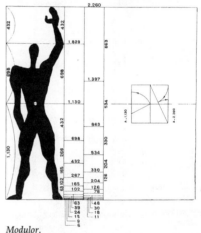
Modulor, devised by Le Corbusier, 1951

Moghul architecture, *see* INDIAN ARCHITECTURE.

Molinos, *see* GILLY, Friedrich.

Moller, Georg, *see* GILLY, Friedrich.

Mollet, Armand-Claude, *see* COURTONNE, Jean.

Monastery Monasticism originated in Egypt, where the first men to choose a monastic life were hermits. A more organized monastic existence was conceived by St Pachomius (346): monks now still lived on their own like hermits, but so close together that they had a

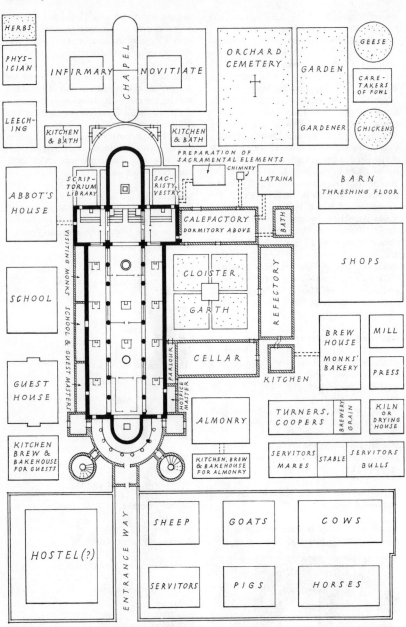

Plan for a monastery, c. 820,
based on a diagram in the Chapter Library, St Gall.
After Conant

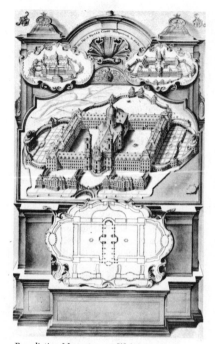

Benedictine Monastery at Weingarten,
engraved 1723

joint chapel and a joint refectory. Such monks
are known as coenobites. This form of
monasticism reached Europe by way of the
South of France and from there entered Ireland
(Skellig Michael). But the monastic architecture of medieval England and the Continent
is that created in the c6 as the expression of
the rule of the order established by St Benedict
at Montecassino. Its first surviving complete
expression is the plan of *c.* 820 made by a
cleric of Cologne for St Gall in Switzerland;
here we have the axial arrangement of

La Tourette friary, Eveux, near Lyon,
1956–60, by Le Corbusier

ranges – the coenobites' layouts were haphazard – the cloister with its arcaded walks,
the chapterhouse and dormitory in the east
range, the refectory in the range opposite the
church, the stores in the west range. Abbots
or priors usually lived near the west end as
well, while the infirmary was beyond the
claustral parts to the east. There were also a
guest house, kitchens, brewhouse, bake-
house, smithy, corn-mills, stables, cowsheds,
pigsties, etc., and workshops. In terms of
architectural composition the monastery is
infinitely superior to the medieval castle.

Monolith A single stone, usually in the form
of a monument or column.

Montferrand, August Ricard (1786–1858).
French Empire architect who emigrated to
Russia and became, with ROSSI and STASSOV,
a leading post-Napoleonic architect in Leningrad. He was trained under PERCIER and
worked at the Madeleine in Paris under
VIGNON. His masterpiece is the vast and
sumptuous St Isaac's Cathedral in Leningrad
(1817–57). The dome (completed *c.* 1842)
is framed in iron – an early example of the use
of metal structure, preceding the dome of the
Capitol in Washington by a decade. His enormous granite Alexander Column in Winter
Palace Square (1829) is imposing though less
original in conception than MILLS'S almost
contemporary Washington Monument in
Washington.
    Lit: G. H. Hamilton, *Art and Architecture of
Russia,* Pelican History of Art, Harmondsworth
1954.

Moral, Enrique del, *see* MEXICAN ARCHI-
TECTURE.

Morris, Robert (1701–54), a relation of Roger
MORRIS, was a gifted writer on architectural
theory. His books include *An Essay in Defence
of Ancient Architecture* (1728), *Lectures on
Architecture* (1734), and the posthumous
Select Architecture (1755) which had a wide
influence, e.g., on JEFFERSON'S Monticello.
    Lit: See Lit. for Roger Morris below.

Morris, Roger (1695–1749). One of the most
gifted and original exponents of PALLADIAN-
ISM, though of the CAMPBELL rather than the
BURLINGTON school. Most of his work was
done in association with the 9th Earl of
Pembroke, an amateur architect whose share
in his designs is difficult to assess; works in-

clude Marble Hill, Twickenham (1728), and the ornamental Palladian Bridge at Wilton (1736). Towards the end of his life he turned neo-Gothic at Inveraray Castle, Argyllshire (1746 etc.).

Lit: H. M. Colvin, *Biographical Dictionary of English Architects 1660–1840*, London 1954; J. Summerson, *Architecture in Britain, 1530–1830*, Pelican History of Art, Harmondsworth 1969, paperback edn 1970.

Morris, William (1834–96), was not an architect, but holds an unchallengeable place in a Dictionary of Architecture because of his great influence on architects. This influence acted in three ways. Morris had begun by studying divinity, then for a short time turned to architecture and worked in the Oxford office of STREET, and subsequently in a desultory way learnt to paint under Rossetti. When he furnished his digs in London, and more so when, after his marriage, he wanted a house, he found that the architecture as well as the design of his day were not to his liking. So he got his friend Philip WEBB to design Red House for him, and this straightforward, red-brick, made-to-measure house had a great deal of influence. Secondly, as the result of the search for satisfactory furnishings, Morris and some friends created in 1861 the firm Morris, Marshall & Faulkner (later Morris & Co.), for which enterprise Morris himself designed wallpapers, the ornamental parts (and, rarely, the figure work) of stained glass, chintzes (i.e., printed textiles), and later also carpets, tapestries and woven furnishing materials, and in the end (1890–6) even books and their type and decoration (Kelmscott Press).

All his designs shared a stylized two-dimensional quality which contrasted with the then prevailing naturalism and its unbridled use of depth; but they also possessed a deep feeling for nature which itself contrasted with the ornamental work of a few slightly older English reformers (PUGIN; Owen Jones). These qualities impressed themselves deeply on younger architects of Norman SHAW'S office and school, so much so that some of them took to design themselves. However, they might not have gone so far, if it had not been for Morris's third way of influencing architects, his lectures, which he began in 1877 and continued till his death. They were impassioned pleas not only for better, more considered design, but for abolishing the ugliness of towns and buildings and of the things made to fill buildings, and for reforming the society responsible for towns, buildings, and products. Morris was a socialist, one of the founders of organized socialism in England. That he was also a poet would not be of relevance here, if it were not for the fact that his poetry and his prose romances developed from an avowed medievalism to a strongly implied social responsibility for the present. At the same time the medievalism, displayed, for example, by the self-conscious use of obsolete language, is a reminder of the medievalism – admittedly adapted and even transmuted – of all his designs. There is, indeed, a medievalism even in Morris's theory, for his socialism is one of labour becoming once more enjoyable handicraft. And although Morris fervently believed, harking back again to the Middle Ages, that all art ought to be 'by the people for the people', he could never resolve the dilemma that production by hand costs more than by machine, and that the products of his own firm therefore (and for other reasons) were bound to be costly and not 'for the people'. It needed a further reform and a revision of this one essential tenet of Morris's to arrive at the C20 situation, where architects and artists design for industrial production and thereby serve the common man and not only the connoisseur. But Morris started the movement, and it was due to him that artists such as van de VELDE or BEHRENS turned designers, and that architects like VOYSEY did likewise. It was also due to him that the criteria of two-dimensional design rose from C19 to C20 standards. Webb's work for Morris had the same effect on furniture design.

Lit: J. W. Mackail, *The Life of William Morris* (The World's Classics), Oxford 1950; E. P. Thompson, *William Morris, Romantic to Revolutionary*, London 1955; P. Henderson, *William Morris: his life, work and friends*, London 1967; P. Thompson, *The Works of William Morris*, London 1967.

Mosaic Surface decoration for walls or floors formed of small pieces or *tesserae* of glass, stone, or marble set in a mastic. The design may be either geometrical or representational. Mosaic reached its highest pitch of accomplishment in Roman and Byzantine buildings. (Illustrated next column.)

Lit: E. W. Antony, *A History of Mosaics*, London 1935; P. Portoghesi, *Mosaico e Architettura*, Ravenna 1959.

Mosbrugger or **Moosbrugger, Caspar** (1656–1723), was born at Au in the Bregenzerwald –

Detail of Mosaic at Thysdrus, Tunisia, early c3

the headquarters of the Vorarlberg masons' guild – and was a founder of the Vorarlberg school of architects which included the BEER and THUMB families. He was apprenticed to a stone-cutter, then became a novice at the Benedictine monastery of Einsiedeln in 1682 and remained there as a lay-brother for the rest of his life. He became the greatest Swiss Baroque architect. Already in 1684 he was asked for advice at Weingarten Abbey, though building did not begin there until many years later. His masterpiece is the abbey church at Einsiedeln (begun 1704), a spatial composition of unusual complexity even for a Baroque architect. He did not live to see it completed. He also designed the parish church at Muri (1694–8). He probably played some part (even if only an advisory one) in the design of the vast Benedictine abbey church at Weingarten (1714–24) with a façade much like that at Einsiedeln, and he probably built the church at Disentis (1696–1712). (For illustration *see* SWISS ARCHITECTURE.)

Lit: E. Hempel, *Baroque Art and Architecture in Central Europe*, Pelican History of Art, Harmondsworth 1965; N. Lieb & F. Dieth, *Die Vorarlberger Barockbaumeister*, Munich–Zurich 1967.

Moslem architecture, *see* ISLAMIC ARCHITECTURE.

Mosque This is the principal religious building of Islam and the place for communal prayer. A distinction must be made between the cathedral or Friday mosque (*jami*) – which from the beginning served to hold the entire adult Muslim community assembled to perform the ritual Friday prayers and to hear the preacher's sermon – and the simple oratory (*masjid*) which sufficed for daily prayer. The lack of sacraments and ceremonies and a hostility to figural representation in a religious context kept the furnishings of the mosque to a minimum. Naturally the major experiments and the finest realizations of mosque architecture have been reserved for the *jami*, which is usually of considerable size and whose components (such as the MIHRAB, MINBAR, and MAQSURA) derive largely from Christian models. Moreover, the *jami* alone betrays the influence of court ceremonial, principally in the elements just cited and in such architectural features as the wide central aisle, the raised and gabled transept and the dome over the *mihrab*. This pronounced secular element helps to explain why the early *jami*, like the Roman forum, was used for many public functions, including those of school, law court, place of assembly, parade ground, hostelry, treasury and community centre. From the C10 onwards the custom grew of celebrating the Friday prayers in the *masjid* and concurrently such secondary places of worship as shrines, MADRASAS, mausolea and dervish establishments assumed some of the functions of the mosque. The forms of the *masjid* thus became more varied. Neither the Koran nor the Traditions ascribed to Mohammed specify the form of cultic buildings. The earliest mosques mirror, but on a much larger scale, Mohammed's own house, in which he worshipped. This comprised a square, largely open enclosure with a covered sanctuary on the QIBLA side and rooms disposed along the east. From the c8 onwards most mosques were given at least one MINARET. Gradually mosques which reflected the influence of non-Islamic cultures were built; the Umayyad mosque at

Mosque at Samarra, c9

Damascus (finished 715), like a basilica, has three aisles, whilst some early mosques in Iran are square domed chambers with three axial openings and thus very similar to pre-Islamic fire temples. The mosque of 'Arab plan', comprising an open courtyard surrounded by arcades with a deeper arcaded sanctuary on the *qibla* side, often marked by a raised transept or domes, was the most popular model in medieval Islam and is found from Spain to India. A pronounced feature of such mosques is the stress on the interior, with a corresponding lack of interest in an elaborate façade. In the Iranian world this plan was elaborated from the CII, possibly owing to the influence of the *madrasa*, by the addition of an IWAN on the main axes of the courtyard, with a domed chamber as the focus of the sanctuary; at the same time the arcades surrounding the courtyard were disposed along two tiers. This is the classic form of the 4-iwan plan. In Turkey, mosques consisting of covered HYPOSTYLE halls were gradually supplanted from the CI4 by domed mosques in which the courtyard became a secondary feature. This trend culminated in the Ottoman mosques of the CI6 with their pronounced centrality of plan and their multiplicity of domes and vaults surrounding the central domed space. [RH]

Motte A steep mound, the main feature of many CII and CI2 castles. *See* MOTTE-AND-BAILEY.

Motte-and-bailey A post-Roman and Norman defence system consisting of an earthen mound (the *motte*) topped with a wooden tower, placed within a BAILEY with enclosure ditch, palisade, and the rare addition of an internal bank.

Mouchette A curved DAGGER motif in curvilinear TRACERY, especially popular in England in the early CI4. (Illustrated next column.)

Mouldings The contours given to projecting members. *See* Bead, Cable, Keel, Ogee, Roll, Wave moulding; Beakhead; Billet; Bowtell; Chevron; Dogtooth; Hood-mould; Nailhead.

Mozarabic The style evolved by Christians under Moorish influence in Spain from the late c9 to the early CII, e.g., San Miguel de Escalada near León (consecrated in 913) with its arcade of arches of horseshoe shape, Santiago de Peñalba (931-7) and Santa

Two pairs of mouchettes,
Chapelle du Saint-Esprit, Rue (Somme), c16

Maria de Lebeña (also CIO). The style is Christian in inspiration but Islamic in conception and has many Islamic features such as the horseshoe arch. Mozarabic churches are usually small and stand in the open countryside. They form the largest and best preserved group of pre-Romanesque buildings in Europe.

Lit: J. F. Arenas, *Mozarabic Architecture,* Barcelona 1972.

Mozarabic: S. Miguel de Escalada,
near Léon, consecrated 913

Mudéjar Spanish Christian architecture in a purely Moslem style. (Literally, the term refers to Moslems who remained in Christian Spain after the reconquest.) The style was evolved by Moslems in Spain or by Christians working within the Spanish Moslem tradition. Notable examples are Alfonso VIII's early C13 chapel at the monastery of Las Huelgas, Burgos, and the C14 Alcázar, Seville, which

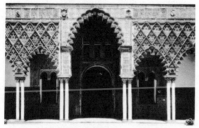

Mudéjar: Patio de las Doncellas, Alcazar, Seville, C14

has Kufic inscriptions extolling Christian rulers. Mudéjar motifs persisted in Spanish Gothic architecture and may also be found in PLATERESQUE buildings of the C16. (For illustration *see* SPANISH ARCHITECTURE.)

Lit: M. Gomez Moreno, *Arte mudéjar Toledana,* 1916; E. Kühnel, *Maurische Kunst,* 1924; G. G. King, *Mudejar,* Bryn Mawr 1927.

Mullion A vertical post or other upright dividing a window or other opening into two or more LIGHTS.

Munggenast, Josef (d. 1741). Cousin and pupil of PRANDTAUER for whom he worked as foreman and whom he succeeded as architect at Melk. In collaboration with the Viennese sculptor, engineer and architect Matthias Steinl (1644–1727) he built the church for the Augustinian canons at Dürnstein, with a boldly *mouvementé* interior and outstandingly handsome tower (1721–7). His main independent work is the reconstruction of the monastery of Altenburg where he provided a richly coloured, exuberantly Baroque casing for the Gothic church and created one of the best of all Baroque libraries (1730–33). (For illustration *see* AUSTRIAN ARCHITECTURE.)

Lit: E. Hempel, *Baroque Architecture in Central Europe,* Pelican History of Art, Harmondsworth 1965.

Muntin The vertical part in the framing of a door, screen, panelling, etc., butting into, or stopped by, the horizontal rails. (For illustration *see* DOOR.)

Murano, Togo, *see* JAPANESE ARCHITECTURE.

Musalla In pre-Islamic times this was a walled precinct used for prayer, and thus had obvious affinities with the early mosques. In Islam it denotes simply an area for prayer, but is most commonly used both for the sanctuary of a mosque and for an open-air place for mass prayer used on the occasion of the two great Muslim religious feasts, occasionally for prayers for the dead, and in time of drought. Although it need comprise no more than a MIHRAB in front of which the ruler or his representative, often installed on a platform, leads the prayer, it may take such monumental forms as a high wall with a central *mihrab* (commonly found in India); a large domed chamber with wide openings on three sides giving on to an open esplanade (Sabzavar, Iran); and a large complex combined with a MADRASA, comprising an enclosed courtyard, multiple minarets and a monumental portal (Herat, Afghanistan).   [RH]

Mushrabeyeh work Elaborate wooden lattices used to enclose the upper windows in Islamic domestic architecture.

Mushrabeyeh work

Mutule The projecting square block above the TRIGLYPH and under the CORONA of a Doric CORNICE.

Mycenean architecture Mycenean architecture, centring on the Peloponnese with the Argolis, was strongly influenced by the MINOANS in both its tombs and its royal residences. But in contrast to the Minoans' well developed taste for fine living and domestic comfort, as expressed in their unfortified palaces with a succession of small, intimate rooms, the Helladic warriors erected defiant, defensive royal citadels (Mycenae, Tiryns). The only things adopted were the haphazard exteriors, the types of plan and

The Lion Gate, Mycenae, c. 1450 B.C.

Entrance to the Treasury of Atreus, Mycenae, c. 1350 B.C.

Interior of fortifications at Tiryns, c. 1300 B.C.

structure, and the additive manner of arrangement round a court; virtually every other principle of Minoan architecture was transmuted. The Mycenean MEGARON, the heart of the complex, was now conceived of as a wholly autonomous and clearly articulated structure. Large-scale architecture was created, where the transition from entrance-gateway to megaron represented a climactic and imposing progress, no longer comparable with the labyrinthine and abruptly terminating passages and corridors of Minoan palaces. Yet Mycenean architecture could never entirely emancipate itself from Minoan influences, and thus never existed fully in its own right.

The Mycenean *tholos* or domed tomb, whose precursors were probably the shaft-tomb and the somewhat later tomb-chamber, an underground 'House of the Dead', is likewise traceable to Minoan influences. The most imposing tholos, the so-called 'Treasury of Atreus', or 'Tomb of Agamemnon' (*c.* 1350 B.C.), is prefigured by the roughly 350 years earlier Minoan ossuaries, that resemble it closely both in construction and design.   [KG]

Lit: A. J. B. Wace, *Mycenae*, Princeton 1949; G. E. Mylonas, *Ancient Mycenae, Capital City of Agamemnon*, Princeton 1957; A. W. Lawrence, *Greek Architecture*, Pelican History of Art, Harmondsworth 1974.

Mylne, Robert (1734–1811), a contemporary and rival of Robert ADAM, descended from a long line of Scottish master masons. He was trained by his father in Edinburgh, then went to Paris (1754) and Rome (1755–8), where he had amazing success by winning First Prize at the Accademia di S. Luca in 1758. But he did not fulfil this early promise. His first work after settling in London (1759) was to be his most famous, Blackfriars' Bridge (1760–9, demolished), in which he introduced elliptical arches. Thereafter he worked extensively both as architect and engineer. His largest country house, Tusmore (1766–9, altered by W. Burn 1858), was neo-Palladian. More elegant and original is The Wick, Richmond (1775), a small suburban 'box', while his façade of the Stationers' Hall, London (1800), shows him at his most neo-classical.

Lit: R. S. Mylne, *The Master Masons to the Crown of Scotland*, Edinburgh 1893; J. Summerson, *Architecture in Britain, 1530–1830*, Pelican History of Art, Harmondsworth 1969, paperback edn 1970.

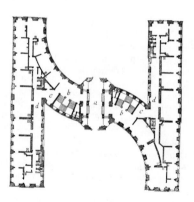

Nagura architecture, *see* INDIAN ARCHITEC-TURE.

Nailhead An Early English architectural enrichment consisting of small pyramids repeated as a band.

Naos The sanctuary or principal chamber of a Greek temple, containing the statue of the god. In Byzantine architecture, the core and sanctuary of a centrally planned church, i.e., the parts reserved for the performance of the liturgy.

Narthex 1. In a Byzantine church, the transverse vestibule either preceding nave and aisles as an inner narthex (esonarthex) or preceding the façade as an outer narthex (exonarthex). An esonarthex is separated from the nave and aisles by columns, rails or

Narthex: St John Studios, Constantinople, late c5

a wall. An exonarthex may also serve as the terminating transverse portico of a colonnaded ATRIUM or quadriporticus. 2. In a general medieval sense, an enclosed covered ANTECHURCH at the main entrance, especially if the direction is transverse and not east-west

and several bays deep; sometimes called a GALILEE.

Nash, John (1752–1835), London's only inspired town-planner and the greatest architect of the PICTURESQUE movement. He was the exact opposite of his contemporary SOANE, being self-confident and adaptable, socially successful and artistically conservative, light-handed and slipshod in detail, but with an easy mastery of general effects on a large scale. Again unlike Soane, he was an architect of exteriors rather than interiors. The son of a Lambeth millwright, he was trained under TAYLOR, but quickly struck out on his own and by 1780 was building stucco-fronted houses, then a novelty in London. In 1783 he went bankrupt, retired to Wales and recovered, then joined the landscape gardener REPTON, with whom he developed a fashionable country-house practice. His output was enormous and in every conceivable style – classical (Rockingham, Ireland, 1810(demolished)), Italian farmhouse (Cronkhill, *c.* 1802), castellated Gothic (Ravensworth Castle, 1808 (demolished); Caerhays Castle, 1808), even Indian and Chinoiserie (Brighton Pavilion, 1815). He also built thatched cottages (Blaise Hamlet, 1811). With their fancy-dress parade of styles and irregular planning and silhouettes, these buildings epitomize the Picturesque in architecture. The same picturesque combination of freedom and formality marks his greatest work, the layout of Regent's Park and Regent Street in London (1811 onwards), a brilliantly imaginative conception foreshadowing the garden city of the future. He was already sixty, but still had the enthusiasm and organizing ability to carry the whole scheme through, and he lived to see it finished. The park is sprinkled with villas and surrounded by vast terraces and crescents of private houses built palatially with grandiose stucco façades. There are also cottage terraces and make-believe villages of barge-boarded and Italianate villas. Of his Regent Street frontages nothing now remains except the eye-catcher, All Souls, Langham Place (1822–5). During the 1820s he planned Trafalgar Square, Suffolk Street, and Suffolk Place, built Clarence House and Carlton House Terrace, and began Buckingham Palace, all in London. But he shared in his royal patron's fall from public favour, was suspected of profiteering and sharp practice, and his career came to an abrupt end when George IV died in 1830. He was dismissed from Buckingham Palace (completed by Edward Blore) and from the Board of Works of which he had been one of the Surveyors General since 1813. His reputation remained under a cloud for the next fifty years or more. (For illustration *see* TOWN PLANNING and COTTAGE ORNÉ.)

Lit: J. Summerson, *John Nash*, London 1935; T. Davis, *John Nash*, London 1960.

Nave The western limb of a church, that is, the part west of the CROSSING; more usually the middle vessel of the western limb, flanked by AISLES.

Nazzoni or **Nasoni, Niccolo** (d. 1773). He was born near Florence and settled in Portugal (1731), where he became one of the leading Baroque architects. His main work is São Pedro dos Clérigos, Oporto (1732–50), a large and impressive church on an oval plan with a very richly decorated façade, embraced by a bold pattern of ascending staircases.

Lit: R. C. Smith, *Nicolae Nasoni, arquitecto de Porto*, Lisbon 1966.

Necking A narrow MOULDING round the bottom of a CAPITAL between it and the shaft of the column.

Needle spire, *see* SPIRE.

Neo-classicism, *see* CLASSICISM.

Neo-Gothic architecture The movement to revive the Gothic style belongs chiefly to the late C18 and the C19. Before the late C18 it must be distinguished from the Gothic Survival, an unquestioning continuation of Gothic forms, which is of course largely a matter of

out-of-the-way buildings. Of major buildings mostly churches are concerned, and St Eustache in Paris and the chapel of Lincoln's

Gothic Survival: St Eustache, Paris, 1532–1637

Early Gothic Revival: The Library, St John's College, Cambridge, 1624

Gothic Survival: Jesuit Church, Cologne,
1621–29

Design for mausoleum for
Queen Luise of Prussia, 1810, by Schinkel

Inn in London were completed well within
the c17. By then, however, the new attitude
of Revival had also appeared – the conscious
choice of the Gothic style in contrast to the
accepted current style. The first cases are those
of the finishing of Gothic buildings, cases of
Gothic for the sake of conformity (flèche, Milan
Cathedral; façade, S. Petronio, Bologna), but
soon the choice was also made for new buildings, though rarely before c. 1720. Then cases
multiply, at least in England (HAWKSMOOR),
and with Horace Walpole's Strawberry Hill (c.
1750–70) the Gothic Revival became a
fashion. It affected France and Germany in

Strawberry Hill, Twickenham, 1750–77

Gateway, Hampton Court, 1732, by Kent

the later c18, and a little later also Italy,
Russia, America, etc. With the growth of
archaeological knowledge, the Gothic Revival
became more competent but also more
ponderous. For churches Gothic remained the
accepted style well into the c20. Of public
buildings, the epoch-making one was the
Houses of Parliament in London (1834 etc.):
other major examples are the Town Hall in

*Hohenzollern Castle, Württemberg, 1850–67,
by Stüler*

*Votivkirche, Vienna, 1856–79,
by Ferstel*

Vienna, the Houses of Parliament at Budapest,
the Law Courts in London, the University at
Glasgow.

Lit: K. Clark, *The Gothic Revival*, London
1950; A. Kamphausen, *Gotik ohne Gott: ein
Beitrag sur Deutung der Neugotik des 19
Jahrhunderts*, Tübingen 1952; P. Frankl, *The
Gothic. Literary Sources and Interpretations
through Eight Centuries*, Princeton 1966; P. B.
Stanton, *The Gothic Revival and American
Church Architecture: An Episode in Taste,
1840–1856*, New York 1968.

Nering, Johann Arnold (1659–95). Prussian
architect who, despite his early death, laid
the foundations for architectural developments in c18 Berlin. He was trained as a
military architect, sent to Italy and made
Oberingenieur in 1680, later Oberbaudirektor.
He was much employed on urban planning
and built the Leipziger Tor (1683), the

covered arcade with shops on the Mühlen-
damm in Berlin and the Friedrichstadt suburb
with 300 two-storey houses, all in military
order (1688 onwards). He enlarged the
Burgkirche at Königsberg, on the model of
the Nieuwe Kerk in The Hague (pre-1687),
gave the Oranienburg Palace its present appearance (1689–95), began the Charlottenburg Palace, Berlin, the Arsenal, Berlin (1695
completed by SCHLÜTER and de BODT), and
the Reformed Parish Church on an interesting
quatrefoil plan. His style is severe and owed
much to PALLADIO by way of the Dutch Neo-
Palladians.

Lit: Thieme-Becker, *Künstler Lexikon*, vol.
XXV, Leipzig 1931.

Nervi, Pier Luigi (b. 1891), took his degree in
civil engineering in 1912, but had a long
wait before he was allowed to establish himself as what he undoubtedly is, the most

brilliant concrete designer of the age. Nervi is as inventive and resourceful a technician as he is aesthetically sensitive an architect. He is, moreover, an entrepreneur and a university professor, a combination which would be impossible, because it is not permitted, in Britain.

The stadium in Florence was built in 1930-2; it seats 35,000, has a cantilever roof about 70 ft deep and an ingenious flying spiral staircase sweeping far out. In 1935, for a competition for airship hangars, he produced his idea of a vault of diagonally intersecting concrete beams with very massive flying-buttress-like angle supports. Such hangars were built at Orbetello from 1936 onwards (destroyed). A second type with trusses of precast concrete elements was carried out at Orbetello in 1940. 1948 is the date of Nervi's first great exhibition hall for Turin. The concrete elements this time are corrugated, an idea which went back to experiments of 1943-4. The second hall followed in 1950, again with a diagonal grid. The building of 1952 for the Italian spa of Chianciano is circular, and has a grid vault. By this time Nervi's fame was so firmly established that he was called in for the structure of the Unesco Building in Paris (1953-6). His also is the splendid structure of the Pirelli skyscraper in Milan (1955-8; see also PONTI) – two strongly tapering concrete pillars from which the floors are cantilevered.

With Jean PROUVÉ as the other consultant engineer, Nervi was responsible for the enormous new exhibition hall on the Rondpoint de la Défense in Paris (1958): a triangle, each side 710 ft long, with three triangular sections of warped concrete roof, rising to a height of 150 ft.

Nervi's most recent buildings are the Palazzetto dello Sport in Rome (1959), circular with V-shaped supports for the dome all round; the Palazzo dello Sport, also in Rome (1960), with a 330-ft span and seating 16,000; yet another exhibition hall for Turin (1961), a square with sides 520 ft in length, supported on sixteen enormous cross-shaped piers; and the vast audience hall for the Pope in the Vatican (1970-71). (For illustration see ITALIAN ARCHITECTURE.)

Lit: The Works of Pier Luigi Nervi (ed E. N. Rogers & J. Jödicke), London 1957; A. L. Huxtable, Pier Luigi Nervi, New York 1960; A. L. Huxtable, Aesthetics and Technology in Building, Cambridge, Mass. 1965.

Nesfield, Eden, see SHAW.

Neumann, Johann Balthasar (1687-1753), the greatest German Rococo architect, was a master of elegant and ingenious spatial composition. He could be both wantonly sensuous and intellectually complex, frivolous and devout, ceremonious and playful. His churches and palaces epitomize the mid-C18 attitude to life and religion. But despite their air of spontaneity, few works of architecture have been more carefully thought out. His designs are as complex as the fugues of Bach; and for this reason he has been called an architect's architect.

The son of a clothier, he was born in Bohemia but worked mainly in Franconia where he began in a cannon foundry and graduated to architecture by way of the Prince Bishop's artillery. He visited Vienna and Milan (1717-18) and soon after his return began the Bishop's new Residenz in Würzburg, consulting HILDEBRANDT and Maximilian von Welsch in Vienna and de COTTE and BOFFRAND in Paris about his designs. The influence of Hildebrandt is very evident in the finished palace, which was executed under a succession of five bishops over some sixty years, though it was structurally complete by about 1744. Outstanding here are the Hofkirche or Bishop's Chapel (1732-41, Hildebrandt collaborating on the decoration) and the magnificent ceremonial staircase leading up to the Kaisersaal (designed 1735, ceiling decoration by Tiepolo 1752-3). This staircase is one of his most original and ingenious conceptions, second only to his superb staircase at Bruchsal (1731-2, damaged in Second World War but restored). He later designed the imposing staircase at Schloss Brühl near Cologne (1743-8). These ceremonial staircases formed the most important single element in each palace and are at the same time masterpieces of engineering ingenuity and exhilarating spatial play. At Schloss Werneck (1734-45) he again collaborated with Hildebrandt, but this time impressed his own stamp on all parts of the building. His secular work was by no means limited to palace architecture: he was engaged in town planning and laid out whole streets of town houses, e.g., the Theaterstrasse at Würzburg. The house he built for himself in the Kapuzinergasse (No. 7) at Würzburg, reveals his ability to work in a minor key.

He was much employed as a church architect, designing the parish church at

Wiesentheid (1727), the pilgrimage church at Gössweinstein (1730–39), the church of St Paulinus, Trier (begun 1734), the church of Heusenstamm near Offenbach (1739–40), the Holy Cross Chapel at Etwashausen (1741) and additions to St Peter, Bruchsal (1738) and the Dominican church at Würzburg (1741). In 1743 he began his great masterpiece, the pilgrimage church of Vierzehnheiligen, near Banz where the foundations had already been built by a previous architect. His first task was to accommodate his own ideas to a somewhat inconvenient plan and this provided a spur to his genius. He worked out a remarkably complicated scheme based on the grouping of ovals, both in the vaulting and ground plan, which provides a breathtakingly exciting spatial effect, enhanced by the foaming and eddying Rococo decoration. Nowhere did the *mouvementé* quality of Rococo architecture find better expression: not only the statues but even the columns seem to be executing an elegant minuet. (The central altar, pulpit and much of the plasterwork were not completed until after Neumann's death.)

In the larger abbey church at Neresheim (begun 1747) he had a much freer hand and his plan is much simpler, though again based on ovals. By the use of very slender columns to support the large central dome he achieved an almost Gothic airiness. His last work of importance, the Marienkirche at Limbach (1747–52), is on a much smaller scale, but is unusual for him in being no less elaborately decorated on the exterior than inside. (For illustrations *see* BAROQUE ARCHITECTURE, GERMAN ARCHITECTURE, ROCOCO ARCHITECTURE.)

Lit: M. H. von Freeden, *Balthasar Neumann*, Munich–Berlin 1950; H.-R. Hitchcock, *Rococo Architecture in Southern Germany*, London 1968.

Neutra, Richard (1892–1970). He was Austrian by birth and studied in Vienna. In 1912–14 he worked under LOOS, and in 1921–3 he was with MENDELSOHN in Berlin. In 1923 he emigrated to Chicago, but finally settled down at Los Angeles in 1925. He became one of the chief propagators of the new European style in America. His work is predominantly domestic, and mostly of a wealthy and lavish kind. His forte is a brilliant sense for siting houses in landscape and linking building and nature; many of his houses are indeed on a scale rarely matched in Europe: Desert House, Colorado, 1946; Kaufmann House, Palm Springs, 1947; and his own house at Silverlake, Los Angeles, 1933 and 1964. Neutra also designed some excellent schools and, towards the end of his life, some religious and commercial buildings. His style remained essentially that of his youth; it was unchanged in its direction by the anti-rational tendencies of the last ten or fifteen years. (For illustration *see* UNITED STATES ARCHITECTURE.)

Lit: E. McCoy, *R. Neutra*, New York 1960; R. Spade, *Richard Neutra*, London 1971.

New Towns Those towns designed in the British Isles under the Act of 1946 – fifteen in the first phase of development, including Crawley, Harlow and Cumbernauld, six in the second (from 1961), including Telford and Skelmersdale, and eight in the third (from 1967), including Milton Keynes and, most recently, Stonehouse (Scotland). Although most of them have an existing town or village as a nucleus, they are entirely independent units, with populations of about 60,000 to 80,000. The development of these planned towns over the years has been of great interest from sociological, architectural, and planning points of view.

Newel, *see* STAIR.

Nicola Pisano, *see* PISANO, Nicola.

Niemeyer, Oscar (b. 1907), studied in his home town Rio de Janeiro, then worked in the office of Lucio COSTA and received his diploma in 1934. In 1936 he belonged to the team of Brazilian architects working with LE CORBUSIER on the new building for the Ministry of Education at Rio. He built the Brazilian Pavilion for the New York World Fair of 1939 with Costa, but only came fully into his own with the casino, club, and church of St Francis at Pampulha outside Belo Horizonte (1942–3). Here was a completely new approach to architecture, admittedly for non-utilitarian purposes: parabolic vaults, slanting walls, a porch canopy of a completely free double-curving form – a sculptural, frankly anti-rational, highly expressive style. The style suited Brazil with its past of the extremest Baroque; it also became one of the elements in that general turn away from rationalism which is principally familiar in Le Corbusier's buildings after the Second World War.

Niemeyer was made architectural adviser to Nova Cap, the organization instituted to create Brasilia, the new capital, and in 1957 became its chief architect. He designed the hotel in 1958 and the exquisite president's palace in the same year. The palace has a screen of freely and extremely originally shaped supports in front of its glass façade, and Niemeyer has varied this theme in other buildings at Brasilia as well (Law Courts). The climax of the architectural composition of the capital is the Square of the Three Powers, with the Houses of Parliament – one with a dome, the other with a saucer-shaped roof – and the sheer, quite unfanciful skyscraper of the offices between. The slab blocks of the various ministries are also deliberately un-fanciful. Niemeyer certainly varies his approach according to the spiritual function of buildings. Thus the cathedral of Brasilia, circular, with the excelsior of a bundle of curved concrete ribs rising to the centre, is highly expressive; the block of flats for the Interbau Exhibition in Berlin (Hansa Quarter, 1957) is rational, without, however, lacking in resourcefulness; and Niemeyer's own house outside Rio (1953) is a ravishing interplay of nature and architecture. (For illustration see BRAZILIAN ARCHITECTURE.)

Lit: S. Papadaki, *Oscar Niemeyer*, New York 1960; R. Spade, *Oscar Niemeyer*, London 1971.

Nobile, Pietro (1773–1854), a neo-classicist of a rather archaeologizing tendency, worked in Vienna (Theseustempel, a miniature of the Haiphesteion, Athens, built to house a statue by Canova, 1820–3; the Burgtor, 1824) and in Trieste (S. Antonio, 1826–49). (For illustration *see* AUSTRIAN ARCHITECTURE.)

Lit: H.-R. Hitchcock, *Architecture: Nineteenth and Twentieth Centuries*, Pelican History of Art, Harmondsworth 1969, paperback edn 1971.

Nogging, *see* TIMBER-FRAMING.

Nook-shaft A shaft set in the angle of a PIER, a RESPOND, a wall, or the JAMB of a window or doorway.

Norman architecture, *see* ENGLISH ARCHITECTURE.

Norwegian architecture, *see* SCANDINAVIAN ARCHITECTURE.

Nymphaeum Literally a 'temple of the nymphs' but generally a Roman pleasure-house, especially one containing fountains and statues.

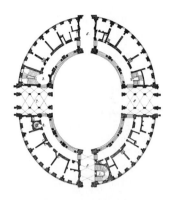

Obelisk In Ancient Egypt this symbol of the primeval mound rising up out of the primeval waters, and of the rising sun, nearly always stood in pairs at the entrance to tombs (in the Old Kingdom, *c*. 2660–2150 B.C.) and temples (from the Middle Kingdom onwards, *c*. 2000

Obelisks at Karnak,
Upper Egypt, 1500–1200 B.C.

B.C.), but also singly, as the central cult object in shrines to the sun (Abu Gurôb, Karnak). It was a usually granite MONOLITH (maximum height *c*. 100 ft), square in section and tapering pyramidally to a once gilded apex. Only four obelisks stand today on their original sites in Egypt; since Antiquity over 30 have been plundered and brought to Europe, e.g. Cleopatra's Needle on the Embankment, London. Renaissance, Baroque, and nineteenth century architects employed the striking form of the obelisk both as a monument

in its own right, and as a decorative termination on pediments, attic storeys etc.   [DW]

Lit: R. Engelbach, *The Problem of the Obelisks*, London 1923.

Octagon An eight-sided figure frequently used as a ground plan – e.g. in military architecture from an early period, in Roman architecture for the very influential atrium of Nero's Golden House (late 60s A.D.), in Carolingian architecture for the Palatine Chapel at Aachen (c9), in medieval architecture for the Karlskirche in Prague (c14) and for small buildings such as chapter-houses (e.g. at York and Salisbury), and sometimes as a central element in the plan of a Gothic church, e.g. at Ely Cathedral. In Renaissance and later domestic architecture rooms and sometimes whole buildings were erected on octagonal plans,

Octagon: Ely Cathedral, 1323–c. 1330

e.g. the Octagon, Twickenham, by James
GIBBS.

Octastyle Of a portico with eight frontal
columns.

Oculus A round window.

Oeil-de-bœuf window A small circular window, similar to that which lights the small
octagonal vestibule at Versailles known as
the *Oeil-de-bœuf.*

Oeil-de-Boeuf: Rosenburg Castle, Kronach,
1656-1700

Oeillet In medieval architecture, a small opening in fortifications through which missiles
could be discharged.

Off-set The part of a wall exposed horizontally
when the portion above it is reduced in
thickness; often sloping, with a projecting
drip mould on the lower edge to stop water
running down the walls, e.g., in Gothic buttresses. Also called the *water-table.* See
WEATHERING.

Ogee A double-curved line made up of a convex and a concave part (s or inverted s).

Ogee arch, *see* ARCH.

Ogee moulding, *see* CYMA RECTA and CYMA
REVERSA.

Ogive The French name for a pointed arch;
hence *ogival,* a term applied to French Gothic
architecture, but no longer used.

O'Gorman, Juan, *see* MEXICAN ARCHITEC-
TURE.

Olbrich, Joseph Maria (1867-1908), studied
at the Vienna Academy, gained the Rome
prize in 1893, returned to work under Otto
WAGNER, and in 1897-8 built the Secession
in Vienna, the premises of a newly founded
society of the young progressive artists of
Austria and the work which immediately
established Olbrich's reputation. The little
building, with its strongly cubic walls and its
delightful hemispherical openwork metal
dome, is both firm in its basic shapes and
fanciful in its details. It is this unusual combination of qualities which attracted Ernst
Ludwig Grand Duke of Hessen to Olbrich. So
in 1899 Olbrich was called to Darmstadt and
there, on the Mathildenhöhe, built the studio
house (Ernst Ludwig Haus) and some private
houses, including one for himself. The group
of houses, some of them by other members of
the group of artists assembled at Darmstadt
(e.g. BEHRENS), was first built and furnished
and then, in 1901, presented as an exhibition,
the first of the kind ever held. Later Olbrich
added another exhibition building and a
tower, the Hochzeitsturm (1907). His last
major building was the Tietz department
store at Düsseldorf, the closely set uprights of
whose façade, deriving from Messel's Wert-
heim store in Berlin, were very influential.

Olbrich's historical role is among those
who succeeded in overcoming the vegetable
weakness of ART NOUVEAU by providing it
with a firmer system of rectangular co-
ordinates. The other leading architects working in this direction were HOFFMANN and
MACKINTOSH. Both Mackintosh and Olbrich
succeeded in preserving the fancifulness of
Art Nouveau sinuosity within this new, more
exacting framework, whereas Hoffmann, and
of course Behrens to a still greater extent,
moved right away from Art Nouveau.

Lit: R. J. Clark, *et al., J. M. Olbrich: Das
Werk des Architekten,* Darmstadt–Vienna–
Berlin 1967; K. H. Schreyl, *Joseph Maria
Olbrich: Die Zeichnungen in der Kunstbibliothek
Berlin,* Berlin 1972.

Olmec architecture, *see* MESOAMERICAN
ARCHITECTURE.

Olmsted, Frederick Law (1822-1903), the
principal landscape architect of America after
DOWNING'S death and America's leading
park designer, studied engineering and travel-

led widely in America, Europe, and even China, before being made superintendent for the Central Park to be formed in New York (1857). He visited European parks in 1859, then for a while supervised a mining estate in California (1863–5) and at that time suggested making the Yosemite area a reserve, and finally returned to the Central Park job in 1865. Olmsted also planned the parks system of Boston, the Niagara reserve, millionaires' estates, and the campus of the newly founded Leland Stanford University at Palo Alto. Among his pupils the most important was his nephew John Charles Olmsted (1852–1920).

Lit: B. Mitchell, *Frederick Law Olmsted*, Baltimore 1924; C. W. Condit, *American Building Art*, New York 1960; H. Fein, *Landscape into Cityscape: Frederick Law Olmsted. Plans for a greater New York*, Ithaca 1967.

Opisthodomos The enclosed section at the rear of a Greek temple, sometimes used as a treasury.

Optical refinements Subtle modifications to profiles or surface to correct the illusion of sagging or disproportion in a building. *See* ENTASIS.

Opus Alexandrinum Ornamental paving combining mosaic and OPUS SECTILE in guilloche design.

Opus incertum Roman walling of concrete faced with irregularly shaped stones.

Opus incertum

Opus listatum Walling with alternating courses of brick and small blocks of stone.

Opus quadratum Roman walling of squared stones.

Opus reticulatum Roman walling of concrete faced with squared stones arranged diagonally like the meshes of a net.

Opus reticulatum

Opus sectile Ornamental paving or wall covering made from marble slabs cut in various, generally geometric, shapes.

Orangery A garden building for growing oranges, with large windows on the south side, like a glazed LOGGIA.

Orangery at Endsleigh, late c18, by Repton

Oratory A small private chapel, either in a church or in a house.

Orcagna (Andrea di Cione) (active 1343–68). He was primarily a painter – the most important in Florence after Giotto's death – but also a sculptor and architect. He was admitted to the Guild of Painters in 1343/4 and to the Guild of Stonemasons in 1352. By 1356 he was *capomaestro* at Orsanmichele, Florence, and by 1358 at Orvieto Cathedral where he is frequently mentioned until 1362, though mainly in connection with the restoration of mosaics on the façade. In 1350 he became adviser on the construction of Florence Cathedral and until 1366 was active as a leading member of various commissions including that which evolved the definitive design. (For illustration *see* TABERNACLE.)

Lit: K. Steinweg, *Andrea Orcagna*, Strassburg 1929; J. White, *Art and Architecture in Italy, 1250–1400*, Pelican History of Art, Harmondsworth 1966.

Orchard, William (d. 1504), master mason, was probably the designer of Bishop Waynflete's Magdalen College at Oxford (1468 etc.). The initials W.O. in the ingenious vault of the Divinity School, completed in the 1480s, allow this to be attributed to him, and if so, the similarity in design of the vaults of the Divinity School and the chancel of Oxford Cathedral make him a likely candidate for this even more ingenious vault. Both are characterized by the pendants which look like springers built on non-existing piers between a nave and aisles. It is a technically daring, highly original, and visually most puzzling solution.

Lit: J. Harvey, *English Medieval Architects*, London 1954; G. Webb, *Architecture in Britain: The Middle Ages*, Pelican History of Art, 2nd edn, Harmondsworth 1965.

Order 1. In classical architecture, a column with base (usually), shaft, capital, and entablature, decorated and proportioned according to one of the accepted modes – Doric, Tuscan, Ionic, Corinthian, or Composite. The simplest is the Tuscan, supposedly derived from the Etruscan-type temple, but the Doric is probably earlier in origin and is subdivided into Greek Doric and Roman Doric, the former having no base, as on the Parthenon and the temples at Paestum. The Ionic Order originated in Asia Minor in the mid c6 B.C. The Ionic capital probably developed out of the earlier Aeolic capital, of Semitic origin. (The Aeolic capital has an oblong top supported by two large volutes with a PALMETTE filling the space between.) The Corinthian

Orders	F. Capital	3. Triglyph
	G. Shaft	4. Abacus
A. Entablature	H. Base	5. Echinus
B. Column	I. Plinth	6. Volute
C. Cornice		7. Fluting
D. Frieze	1. Guttae	8. Dentils
E. Architrave	2. Metope	9. Fascia

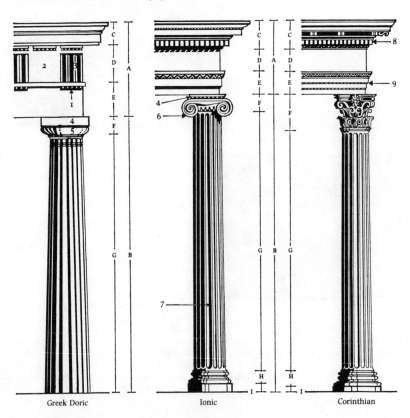

Greek Doric   Ionic   Corinthian

Order was an Athenian invention of the C5 B.C., but was later developed by the Romans, who provided the prototype for the Renaissance form. The Composite Order is a late Roman combination of elements from the Ionic and Corinthian Orders. The Doric, Tuscan, Ionic,

Aeolic capital: Larissa, early C8 B.C.

Corinthian Order: Olympieion, Athens, begun 175 B.C., completed A.D. 131–2

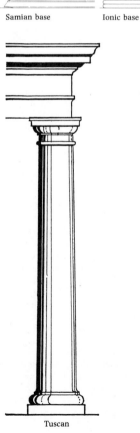

Samian base   Ionic base

Tuscan   Roman Doric   Composite

and Corinthian Orders were described by VITRUVIUS, and in 1540 SERLIO published a book on the Orders which established the minutiae of the proportions and decorations for Renaissance and later architects.
2. Of a doorway or window, a series of concentric steps receding towards the opening.
Lit: J. Summerson, *The Classical Language of Architecture*, London 1964.

Oriel, see WINDOW.

Orientation The planning of a building in relation to the rising sun, especially of West European churches which are usually orientated east-west with the altar at the east end. But there are many exceptions, e.g., St Peter's, Rome, which is orientated west-east.

Østberg, Ragnar (1866-1945). His international fame derives entirely from his Stockholm City Hall (begun 1909, completed 1923), a building transitional – like BERLAGE'S and KLINT'S work – between C19 historicism and the C20. The City Hall makes extremely skilful use of elements of the Swedish past, Romanesque as well as Renaissance. Its exquisite position by the water suggested to Østberg certain borrowings from the Doge's Palace as well. But these motifs are converted and combined in a highly original way, and the decorative details, rather mannered and attenuated, are typical of the Arts and Crafts of Germany, Austria, and Central Europe in general about 1920. The City Hall was very influential in England in the twenties. Østberg had studied in Stockholm (1884-91) and travelled all over Europe as well as in America (1893-9). He was professor at the Stockholm Konsthögskola in 1922-32.
Lit: R. Østberg, *En Architekts Anteckningar*, Stockholm 1928; H.-R. Hitchcock, *Architecture: Nineteenth and Twentieth Centuries*, Pelican History of Art, Harmondsworth 1969, paperback edn 1971.

Otaka, Masato, see JAPANESE ARCHITECTURE.

Otani, Sachio, see JAPANESE ARCHITECTURE.

Otto, Frei (b. 1925). Brilliant operator of suspended roofs, e.g. Garden Exhibition, Cassel (1955); Garden Exhibition, Cologne (1957); German Pavilion, International Exhibition, Montreal (1967). The shapes he creates are what architects in the sixties got enthusiastic about, but they are the results of technological thinking.
Lit: L. Glaesar, *The Work of Frei Otto*, New York 1972.

Ottonian architecture, see GERMAN ARCHITECTURE.

Oubliette In medieval architecture, a secret prison cell reached only through a trapdoor above, and into which a prisoner could be dropped and, presumably, forgotten.

Oud, Jacobus Johannes Pieter (1890-1963), worked for a short time under Theodor Fischer in Germany in 1911. In 1915 he met Theo van Doesburg and with him and RIETVELD he became a pillar of the group De Stijl. Architecturally this group stood for an abstract cubism in opposition to the fanciful School of Amsterdam with its Expressionist compositions (de Klerk, Piet Kramer). There exist designs by Oud in a severely cubic manner which date from as early as 1917 and 1919. In 1918 he was made Housing Architect to the City of Rotterdam, a position he retained until 1927. His most important estates are one at Hoek van Holland (1924-7) and the Kiefhoek Estate (1925-30). Later Oud mellowed, abandoned the severity of his designing, and helped to create that curiously decorative, somewhat playful Dutch style which was nicknamed locally Beton-Rococo. The paramount example is the Shell Building at The Hague (1938-42).
Lit: G. Veronesi, *J. J. P. Oud*, Milan 1953; H. L. C. Jaffe, *De Stijl 1917-1931*, London 1956; K. Wiekart, *J. J. P. Oud*, Amsterdam 1965.

Overdoor, see SOPRAPORTA.

Overhang A system of timber construction, popular in the C15, in which the upper storey is thrust out over the lower by weighting the overhang of the JOISTS with the upper wall and thereby strengthening them. Overhanging is also known as *oversailing* or *jutting*. An overhang on all four sides of a building needs strong corner posts. Upon each is projected the *dragon beam* from the centre of the house, which in turn receives the shortened rafters on both sides. All the rafters are mortised into the main beams. On their outer projecting ends is placed the sill of the walling for the next storey. Sometimes curved braces are slotted into the lower framing to strengthen the rafters. *See also* ROOF.

Oversailing, *see* OVERHANG.

Oversailing courses A series of stone or brick courses, each one projecting beyond the one below it.

Ovolo moulding A wide convex moulding, sometimes called a quarter round.

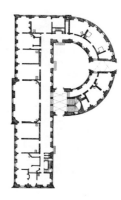

Pad stone, *see* TEMPLATE.

Pagoda A Buddhist temple in the form of a tower, usually polygonal, with elaborately ornamented roofs projecting from each of its many storeys; common in India and China and, as CHINOISERIE, in Europe.

Pagoda at Nanking, c. 1880

P'ai lou A Chinese type of ornamental arch or gateway. It was usually commemorative or triumphal in function, e.g. to celebrate the

virtue of a widow on not remarrying or to stand at the entrance to a processional way. *P'ai lou* are almost always built of stone but in imitation of wooden prototypes and carpentry technique (e.g. the stone beams are tenoned through the columns). They have one, three or five openings. *P'ai lou* closely resemble in

P'ai-lou of Chang Ling, Ming Dynasty (1368–1644)

form the Indian *torana* and may therefore be Indian in origin though the architectural and decorative details are all conspicuously Chinese.

Paine, James (*c.* 1716–89), was born and lived in London, but worked mainly as a country-house architect in the Midlands and North. Solid and conservative, he carried on the neo-Palladian tradition of BURLINGTON and KENT: he and Sir Robert TAYLOR were said to have 'nearly divided the practice of the profession between them' during the mid-century. His houses are practically planned and very well built, with dignified conventional exteriors and excellent Rococo plasterwork, e.g., Nostell Priory interior (begun *c.* 1733) and the Mansion House, Doncaster (1745–8). Later on he showed more originality. At Kedleston (begun 1761, but soon taken over by ADAM) he had the brilliant idea of placing in sequence an antique basilica hall and a Pantheon-like circular saloon. At Worksop Manor (begun 1763, but only a third built) he envisaged a gigantic Egyptian Hall, and at Wardour Castle (1770–6) he designed a magnificent circular staircase rising towards a Pantheon-like vault. But by this date he had been superseded in the public eye by Robert Adam, and his reputation and practice declined rapidly. As a result of some domestic trouble during his last years he retired to France, where he died. Most of his work is illustrated in his two volumes of *Plans, Elevations and Sections of Noblemen's and Gentlemen's Houses* (1767 and 1783).

Lit: J. Summerson, *Architecture in Britain 1530–1830*, Pelican History of Art, Harmondsworth 1969, paperback edn 1970.

Palaestra In Ancient Greece a wrestling school, which usually formed part of a GYMNASIUM. The term is sometimes extended in English usage to describe the whole gymnasium.

Palladian window, *see* SERLIANA.

Palladianism A style derived from the buildings and publications of PALLADIO. Its first exponent was Inigo JONES, who studied Roman ruins with Palladio's *Le antichità di Roma* and his buildings in and around Vicenza (1613–14), and introduced the style

Villa Trissino, Meledo, by Palladio

Palazzo Chiericati, Vicenza, 1551–7, by Palladio

buildings – temple fronts, the SERLIANA window, etc. – but here the leading influence was SCAMOZZI rather than Palladio. The great Palladian revival began in Italy and England in the early C18: in Italy it was confined to Venetia, but affected churches as well as secular buildings; in England it was purely domestic. The English revival, led by CAMPBELL and Lord BURLINGTON, was at the same

Villa Capra (Rotonda), Vicenza, begun c. 1550, by Palladio

Chiswick House, near London, begun c. 1720, by Lord Burlington

into England. Elsewhere in Northern Europe, especially Holland (van CAMPEN) and Germany (HOLL), Palladian elements appear in

time an Inigo Jones revival. Numerous books were published under Burlington's aegis and these provided a set of rules and exemplars

Schloss Wörlitz, near Dessau, 1769-73, by Erdmannsdorf

which remained a dominant force in English architecture until late in the c18. From England and Venetia, Palladianism spread to Germany (KNOBELSDORFF) and Russia (CAMERON and QUARENGHI). At Potsdam accurate copies of Palladio's Palazzo Valmarana and Palazzo Thiene were built in the 1750s under the influence of Frederick the Great and his courtier, the Paduan Count Algarotti. From England the style also spread to the U.S.A. in the 1760s (JEFFERSON). Outside Italy the Palladian revival was concerned mainly with the use of decorative elements. Little attention was paid to Palladio's laws of HARMONIC PROPORTIONS except in Italy, where his ideas on this subject were examined by BERTOTTI-SCAMOZZI and elaborated by a minor architect, Francesco Maria Preti (1701-84).

Lit: N. Pevsner in *Venezia e l'Europa*, Venice 1957; E. Forssmann, *Palladios Lehrgebäude*, Stockholm 1965.

Palladio, Andrea (1508-80). The most influential and one of the greatest Italian architects (*see* PALLADIANISM). Smooth, elegant, and intellectual, he crystallized various Renaissance ideas, notably the revival of Roman symmetrical planning and HARMONIC PROPORTIONS. An erudite student of ancient Roman architecture, he aimed to recapture the splendour of Antiquity. But he was also influenced by his immediate predecessors, especially BRAMANTE, MICHELANGELO, RAPHAEL, GIULIO ROMANO, SANMICHELI, and SANSOVINO, and to some extent by the Byzantine architecture of Venice. His style is tinged with MANNERISM, and it was understandably thought to be 'impure' by later neo-classical architects and theorists.

The son of Piero dalla Gondola he was born in Padua and began humbly as a stone mason, enrolled in the Vicenza guild of bricklayers and stone masons in 1524. Then, in about 1536, he was taken up by Giangiorgio Trissino, the poet, philosopher, mathematician, and amateur architect, who encouraged him to study mathematics, music, and Latin literature, especially VITRUVIUS, and nicknamed him Palladio (an allusion to the goddess of wisdom and to a character in a long epic poem he was then writing). In 1545 Trissino took him to Rome, where he studied the remains of ancient architecture for two years. On returning to Vicenza he won a competition for the remodelling of the Early Renaissance Palazzo della Ragione or Basilica and work began in 1549. He surrounded it with a two-storey screen of arches employing a motive derived from SERLIO but henceforth called Palladian. This columned screen gives to the heavy mass of the old building a grandeur wholly Roman and an airy elegance no less distinctively Palladian. It established his reputation, and from 1550 onwards he was engaged in an ever-increasing series of overlapping commissions for palaces, villas, and churches.

The first of his palaces in Vicenza was probably Palazzo Porto (begun *c.* 1550), on a symmetrical plan derived from ancient Rome, with a façade inspired by Raphael and Bramante but much enriched with sculptured ornament. Soon afterwards he began the more original Palazzo Chiericati (completed in the late c17). This was built not in a narrow street but looking on to a large square; so he visualized it as one side of a Roman forum and designed the façade as a two-storey colonnade of a light airiness unprecedented in c16 architecture. In Palazzo Thiene (begun *c.* 1550, but never completed) he used a dynamic combination of rectangular rooms with a long apsidal-ended hall and small octagons similar to those of the Roman *thermae*. For the convent of the Carità in Venice (planned 1561, but only partly executed) he produced what he and his contemporaries supposed to be a perfect reconstruction of an ancient Roman house; it also contains a flying spiral staircase, the first of its kind. But while his plans became ever more archaeological, his façades broke farther away from classical tradition towards Mannerism, probably the result of a visit to Rome in 1554. Thus the façade of Palazzo Thiene gives an impression of massive power, emphasized by the rustication of the whole wall surface. It has rusticated Ionic columns on either side of the windows – barely emerging from chunky bosses – heavy quoins and *voussoirs* which contrast with smooth Corin-

thian pilasters. Palazzo Valmarana (begun
1566) is a still more obviously Mannerist
composition with a mass of overlapping
pilasters and other elements which almost
completely obscure the wall surface. The end
bays are disquietingly weak, no doubt intentionally. But only in the Loggia del Capitano
(1571) did Palladio wilfully misuse elements
from the orders. The Loggia is by far his
richest building, with a mass of *horror vacui*
relief decoration. His last building in Vicenza
was the Teatro Olimpico (begun 1589 and
finished by SCAMOZZI) – an elaborate reconstruction of a Roman theatre.

His villas show no similar process of
development. In the 1550s he evolved a
formula for the ideal villa – a central block of
ruthlessly symmetrical plan, decorated externally with a portico and continued by long
wings of farm buildings, either extended horizontally or curved forwards in quadrants, as at
La Badoera (*c*. 1550–60), and linking the villa
with the surrounding landscape. On this theme
he composed numerous variations – from the
elaboration of La Rotonda (begun *c*. 1550),
with its hexastyle porticos on each of its four
sides, to the simplicity of La Malcontenta
(1560) and Fanzolo (*c*. 1560–5), where the
windows are unmarked by surrounds and the
decoration is limited to a portico on the main
façade, to the stark severity of Villa Poiana,
where columns are replaced by undecorated
shafts. The use of temple-front porticos for
houses was a novelty (Palladio incorrectly supposed that they were used on Roman houses).
Sometimes they are free-standing but usually
they are attached; and at Quinto (*c*. 1550) and
Maser (1560s) he treated the whole central
block as a temple front. The relation of the portico to the rest of the building and the sizes of
the rooms inside were determined by HAR-
MONIC PROPORTIONS.

Temple fronts and harmonic proportions
also play an important part in his churches,
all of which are in Venice: the façade of S.
Francesco della Vigna (1562), and the
churches of S. Giorgio Maggiore (begun 1566)
and Il Redentore (begun 1576). The latter
two appear inside to be simple basilicas, but
as one approaches the high altar the curves
of the transepts opening out on either hand
and the circle of the dome overhead produce
a unique effect of expansion and elation. Both
churches terminate in arcades screening off
the choirs and adding a touch of almost Byzantine mystery to the cool classical logic of the
plan.

In 1554 Palladio published *Le antichità di
Roma* and *Descrizione delle chiese . . . di Roma*,
of which the former remained the standard
guide-book for 200 years. He illustrated Bar-
baro's *Vitruvius* (1556) and in 1570 published
his *Quattro libri dell'architettura*, at once a
statement of his theory, a glorification of his
achievements, and an advertisement for his
practice. (His drawings of the Roman *thermae*
were not published until 1730, by Lord
BURLINGTON.)

He was the first great professional architect. Unlike his most notable contemporaries,
Michelangelo and Giulio Romano, he was
trained to build and practised no other art.
Though he was erudite in archaeology and
fascinated by complex theories of proportions,
his works are surprisingly unpompous and
unpedantic. But the rules which he derived
from a study of the ancients, and which he
frequently broke in his own work, came to be
accepted almost blindly as the classical canon,
at any rate for domestic architecture. (For
illustrations *see* ITALIAN ARCHITECTURE,
PALLADIANISM and SERLIANA.)

Lit: R. Wittkower, *Architectural Principles
in the Age of Humanism*, London 1952; J.
Ackerman, *Palladio*, Harmondsworth 1966;
Corpus Palladianum, Vicenza 1968 onwards.

Palmette A fan-shaped ornament composed
of narrow divisions like a palm leaf.

Palmette and anthemion frieze

Pani, Mario, *see* MEXICAN ARCHITECTURE.

Pantheon dome A dome similar to that of the
Pantheon in Rome, though not necessarily
open in the centre.

Pantile A roofing tile of curved S-shaped
section.

Paradise 1. An open court or ATRIUM surrounded by porticos in front of a church (some
medieval writers gave this name to the atrium
of Old St Peter's). 2. The garden or cemetery
of a monastery, in particular the main cloister
cemetery (e.g., Chichester Cathedral, where
the cloister-garth on the south side is called

*Paradise: Abbey church at Maulbronn,
c. 1215*

the 'paradise'). PARVIS seems to be a corruption of *paradisus*.

Parapet A low wall, sometimes battlemented, placed to protect any spot where there is a sudden drop, for example, at the edge of a bridge, quay, or house-top.

Parclose A screen enclosing a chapel or shrine and separating it from the main body of the church so as to exclude non-worshippers.

Parekklesion In Byzantine architecture, a chapel, either free-standing or attached.

Pargetting Exterior plastering of a TIMBER-FRAMED building, usually modelled in designs, e.g., vine pattern, foliage, figures; also, in modern architecture, the mortar lining of a chimney flue.

Parker, Barry, *see* UNWIN.

Parler The most famous family of German masons in the C14 and early C15. The name is confusing, as *Parlier* is German for the foreman, the second-in-command, in a masons' lodge and can thus occur in reference to masons not members of the family. The family worked in South Germany, chiefly Swabia, and in Bohemia, chiefly Prague. More than a dozen members are recorded. The most important ones are **Heinrich I** and his son **Peter.** Heinrich I was probably *Parlier* at Cologne, and then became master mason at Schwäbisch-Gmünd, one of the most important churches in Germany for the creation of the specifically German Late Gothic style (*Sondergotik*). It is likely that he designed the operative part, the chancel, a design on the HALL CHURCH principle which had great influence. A Heinrich of the same family, quite

possibly he, also designed the chancel at Ulm (begun 1377).

Peter (d. 1399) was called to Prague in 1353, aged only twenty-three, to continue the cathedral begun by Matthias of Arras (*c.* 1340). He completed the chancel and went on to the west, working first on a synthesis of the French cathedral plan with the hall principle of Gmünd and its consequences. In the chapels farther west he developed interesting and fanciful lierne vaults, curiously similar to English ones built a generation and more earlier. He probably designed and worked also at Kutná Hora (Kuttenberg) and Kolin.

The Parlers, and especially Peter, also exercised great influence through the sculptural work of their lodges. Another member of the family, **Johann**, was master mason of the town of Freiburg from 1359 and perhaps designed the chancel of the minster there (1354–63). Yet another, again called **Heinrich of Gmünd**, was at Milan Cathedral in 1391–2 ('Enrico da Gamondia'), but left under a cloud, having been unable to win the authorities over to his ideas. The **Hans of Freiburg** ('Annes de Firimburg') who, also in vain, made a report to the Milan authorities earlier in 1391 may be yet another Parler. (For illustration *see* CZECHOSLOVAK ARCHITECTURE.)

Lit: K. M. Swoboda, *Peter Parler*, Vienna 1941; E. Bachmann, *P. Parler*, Vienna 1952.

Parquet Flooring of thin hardwood (about ¼ in. thick) laid in patterns on a wood subfloor and highly polished. Inlaid or plated parquet consists of a veneer of decorative hardwood glued in patterns to squares of softwood backing and then laid on a wood subfloor.

Parterre In a garden, a level space, usually adjacent to the main house, laid out in low, formal beds of flowers as at the Grand Trianon, Versailles. In a theatre, that part of the auditorium on the ground floor lying behind the orchestra.

Parvis(e) 1. In France the term for the open space in front of and around cathedrals and churches; probably a corruption of *paradisus*, *see* PARADISE. 2. In England a term wrongly applied to a room over a church porch.

Pastophory A room in an Early Christian or Byzantine church serving as a DIACONICON or PROTHESIS; as a rule, flanking the apse of the church.

Patera A small, flat, circular or oval ornament in classical architecture, often decorated with ACANTHUS leaves or rose petals.

Patera

Patio In Spanish or Spanish American architecture, an inner courtyard open to the sky.

Pavilion An ornamental building, lightly constructed, often used as a pleasure-house or summerhouse in a garden, or attached to a cricket or other sports ground; also a projecting subdivision of some larger building, usually square and often domed, forming an angle feature on the main façade or terminating the wings.

Chinese Pavilion at Kew, London, mid-c18

Paxton, Sir Joseph (1801–65), the son of a small farmer, became a gardener and in 1823 worked at Chiswick in the gardens of the Duke of Devonshire. The Duke discovered his exceptional ability and in 1826 made him superintendent of the gardens at Chatsworth. He became a friend of the Duke, with him visited Switzerland, Italy, Greece, Asia Minor, Spain, etc., and in 1854 became Liberal M.P. for Coventry. He designed greenhouses for Chatsworth, the largest being 300 ft long (1836–40), tried out a new system of glass and metal roof construction in them, laid out the estate village of Edensor (1839–41), and so, in 1850–1, moved into architecture proper by submitting, uninvited, his design for a glass-and-iron palace for the first international exhibition ever held. The Crystal Palace was truly epoch-making, not only because this was the most direct and rational solution to a particular problem but also because the detailing of this 1,800-ft-long building was designed in such a way that all its parts could be factory-made and assembled on the site – the first ever example of PREFABRICATION. Paxton was also nominally responsible for a few large country houses (Mentmore, Ferrières, for members of the Rothschild dynasty), but they were partly or largely designed by his son-in-law. He was, further, one of the founders of the *Gardener's Chronicle*, and was interested in public parks as well as private grounds (Birkenhead, 1843–7). (For illustration *see* ENGLISH ARCHITECTURE.)

Lit: G. F. Chadwick, *The Works of Sir Joseph Paxton*, London 1961.

Pearce, Sir Edward Lovet (*c.* 1699–1733). He was the leading exponent of PALLADIANISM in Ireland. His father was first cousin to VANBRUGH, like whom he began his career in the army. Nothing is known of his architectural training – if he had any – but he became one of the most interesting and original architects of the BURLINGTON school. His masterpiece is the Parliament House (now the Bank of Ireland) in Dublin (1728–39) with its remarkable colonnaded approach. The octagonal House of Commons was burnt in 1792 and later demolished. He also built the south front of Drumcondra House (1727) and Cashel Palace (*c.* 1731). He became Surveyor-General for Ireland in 1730.

Lit: H. Colvin & M. Craig, *Architectural Drawings in the library of Elton Hall by Sir John Vanbrugh and Sir Edward Lovett Pearce*, 1964.

Pearson, John Loughborough (1817–97), was a pupil of Ignatius BONOMI, SALVIN, and HARDWICK. Under Hardwick he worked on the Hall of Lincoln's Inn, where one may well discover his hand in the niceness of the detailing. In 1843 he set up practice, and almost at once was commissioned to design small churches. His first important church is St Peter, Kennington Lane, Lambeth, London (1863–5), French Gothic and vaulted throughout, the ribs of stone, the webs of brick. This building displays his faith in truth in building and in a nobility to fit the religious purpose. Pearson also designed country houses – e.g., Quar Wood, Gloucestershire (1857), which is Gothic, and Westwood, Sydenham, London (1881), which is French Renaissance – but essentially he is a church architect and a Gothicist. His best churches of the 1870s and 1880s are among the finest of their day not only in England but in Europe. Their style is C13 Franco-English, their decorative detail extremely sparing, and their spatial composition quite free and unimitative. Examples are St Augustine, Kilburn Park, London (1870-80); St Michael, Croydon (1871); St John, Red Lion Square, London (1874, demolished); Truro Cathedral (1880-1910); St John, Upper Norwood, London (1880-81); Cullercoats, Northumberland (1884). He was also surveyor to Westminster Abbey. (For illustrations *see* ENGLISH ARCHITECTURE.)

Lit: B. F. L. Clarke, *Church Builders of the Nineteenth Century*, London 1938.

Pebbledash, *see* ROUGHCAST.

Pedestal In classical architecture, the base supporting a column or colonnade; also, more loosely, the base for a statue or any superstructure.

Pedestal: Corinthian

1. Torus
2. Scotia
3. Plinth
4. Die or dado

Pediment Not a Greek or Roman term but signifying in classical architecture a low-pitched GABLE above a PORTICO, formed by running the top member of the ENTABLATURE along the sides of the gable; also a similar feature above doors, windows, etc. It may be straight-sided or curved segmentally. The terms *open pediment* and *broken pediment* are confused and have been employed to describe pediments open or broken either at the apex or base. For clarity, a pediment where the sloping sides are returned before reaching the apex should be called an *open-topped* or *broken-apex pediment*; and one with a gap in the base moulding an *open-bed* or *broken-bed pediment*.

Pele-tower A term peculiar to Northern England and Scotland, signifying a small tower or house suitable for sudden defence.

Pendant A BOSS elongated so that it hangs down; found in Late Gothic vaulting and, decoratively, in French and English C16 and early C17 vaults and also stucco ceilings.

Pendants: Parish church at Ingolstadt, begun 1407

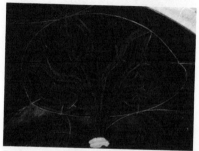

Pendants: Parish church, Needham Market, C15

Pendentive A concave SPANDREL leading from the angle of two walls to the base of a circular DOME. It is one of the means by which a circular dome is supported over a square or polygonal compartment (*see also* SQUINCH), and is used in Byzantine (Hagia Sophia, Istanbul) and occasionally Romanesque archi-

Pendentive: S. Maria della Consolazione, Todi, begun 1508

tecture (Périgueux), and often in Renaissance, Baroque, and later architecture.

Penthouse A subsidiary structure with a lean-to roof (*see* ROOF); also a separately roofed structure on the roof of a high block of flats.

Percier, Charles (1764–1838), studied in Paris under A. F. Peyre and in Rome (1786–92) with his future partner P. F. L. FONTAINE. They worked together from 1794 until 1814, becoming the leading architects in Paris under Napoleon and creating the Empire style in decoration. For their joint works and publications, *see* FONTAINE.
    Lit: M. L. Biver, *Pierre Fontaine, premier architecte de l'empereur,* Paris 1964.

Pergola A covered walk in a garden usually formed by a double row of posts or pillars with JOISTS above and covered with climbing plants.

Peripteral Of a building, surrounded by a single row of columns.

Plan of a peripteral temple

Peristyle A range of columns surrounding a building or open court.

Peristyle: Casa dei Vettii, Pompeii

Perpendicular style, *see* ENGLISH ARCHITECTURE.

Perrault, Claude (1613–88), a doctor by profession and amateur architect, was partly if not mainly responsible for the great east front of the Louvre in Paris (begun 1667), one of the supreme masterpieces of the Louis XIV style, LE VAU and the painter Lebrun were also members of the committee appointed to design this façade. It owes something to BERNINI'S rejected project for the Louvre, and is notable for its great colonnade or screen of paired columns. He also designed the Observatoire, Paris (1667), and brought out an edition of VITRUVIUS (1672). In 1683 he published *Ordonnance des cinq espèces de Colonnes.* His brother **Charles** (1626–1703) was a theorist and Colbert's chief assistant in the Surintendance des Bâtiments. (For illustration *see* FRENCH ARCHITECTURE.)
    Lit: W. Herrman, *The Theory of C. Perrault,* London 1973.

Perret, Auguste (1874–1954). The son of the owner of a building and contracting firm. After studies under Guadet he and two brothers joined the firm which was known from 1905 as Perret Frères. His first outstanding job was the house No. 25b rue Franklin near the Trocadéro in Paris, a block of flats on an interesting plan; it has a concrete structure with the concrete members displayed and ART NOUVEAU faience infillings. Next came a garage in the rue Ponthieu (1905), even more demonstratively expressing its concrete frame. The Théâtre des Champs Élysées (1911–14) was originally designed by van de VELDE, but in its final form it is essentially Perret's, and its distinguishing feature is again the proud display of its concrete skeleton. Details, however, are decidedly classical, even if with a minimum of traditional motifs, and Perret was subsequently to develop in that direction.

Nevertheless, until the mid-twenties bold concrete experiments still prevailed: the 65-ft arches across the vast workroom of the Esders tailoring establishment (1919), and the decorative concrete grilles of the windows and the slender concrete steeple on the churches of Notre Dame du Raincy (1922–3) and of Montmagny (1926). Some examples of Perret at his most classical – basically the successor to the most restrained French C18 style – are the Museum of Public Works (1937, though with a brilliant curved flying concrete staircase inside) and the post-war work for Amiens (skyscraper 1947) and Le Havre (1945 etc.). The latter includes Perret's last work, the strange centrally planned church of St Joseph. (For illustration *see* FRENCH ARCHITECTURE.)

Lit: E. N. Rogers, *A. Perret*, Milan 1955; P. Collins, *Concrete: The Vision of a New Architecture*, London 1959; E. Goldfinger, *Auguste Perret: Writings on Architecture*, London 1971.

Perron An exterior staircase or flight of steps usually leading to a main, first-floor entrance to a house.

Perronet, Jean, *see* BRIDGE.

Persian architecture, *see* IRANIAN ARCHITECTURE.

Peruvian architecture, *see* CENTRAL ANDEAN ARCHITECTURE.

Peruzzi, Baldassare (1481–1536). One of the best High Renaissance architects in Rome. His works are much indebted to BRAMANTE and RAPHAEL, but have an almost feminine delicacy which contrasts with the monumentality of the former and the gravity of the latter. Born in Siena, he began as a painter under Pinturicchio. In 1503 he went to Rome, where he was employed by Bramante and assisted him with his designs for St Peter's. He probably built S. Sebastiano in Valle Piatta, Siena (*c*. 1507), a centralized Greek cross church derived from Bramante. His first important work was the Villa Farnesina, Rome (1508–11), one of the most exquisite of all Italian houses both for its architecture and for its interior decoration (frescoes by Peruzzi himself, Raphael, GIULIO ROMANO, Sodoma, and Ugo da Carpi), which combine to make it the outstanding secular monument of the High Renaissance. The plan is unusual: a square

block with an open loggia in the centre of the garden front and projecting wings. The main rooms are on ground level. The façade decoration is rich with two superimposed orders of pilasters crowned with a boldly carved frieze of *putti* and swags in which the attic windows are set.

On Raphael's death (1520) Peruzzi completed his S. Eligio degli Orefici, Rome, and succeeded him as architect of St Peter's. In 1527 he fled from the Sack of Rome to Siena, where he was appointed city architect. In Siena he was mainly engaged on fortifications (near Porta Laterina and Porta S. Viene) but he also built Palazzo Pollini and, outside Siena, the Villa Belcaro (now much altered). His last work, Palazzo Massimo alle Colonne, Rome (1532–6), is perhaps his most interesting, for its unorthodox design seems to echo the uneasy atmosphere of Rome in the years after the Sack. The façade is curved; there is a disturbing contrast between the ground floor with its deeply recessed loggia and the papery-thin upper part, with shallow window surrounds on the first floor and curious flat leathery frames round those on the floors above. In the *cortile* the sacrosanct orders are wilfully misused. The self-confidence of the High Renaissance has here given way to the sophisticated elegance and spiritual disquiet of Mannerism.

Lit: C. L. Frommel, *Die Farnesina und Peruzzis architektonisches Frühwerk*, Berlin 1961; H. Wurm, *Der Palazzo Massimo alle Colonne in Rom*, Berlin 1965; L. Heydenreich & W. Lotz, *Architecture in Italy, 1400–1600*, Pelican History of Art, Harmondsworth 1974.

Pew A fixed wooden seat in a church, in use at least by the C14. In medieval times pews were partially enclosed at the ends next to the aisles with *bench-ends*, which sometimes rise above the WAINSCOT and terminate in carved FINIALS (*see* POPPYHEAD). A *box-pew* is one with a high wooden enclosure all round and a small door; it is essentially a Georgian type.

Peyre, Marie-Joseph, *see* DE WAILLY, Charles.

Pharos A Roman lighthouse.

Piano nobile The main floor of a house, containing the reception rooms. It is usually loftier than the other floors, with a basement or ground floor below and one or more shallower storeys above.

Piazza

Piazza 1. An open space, usually oblong, surrounded by buildings. 2. In C17 and C18 England, a long covered walk or LOGGIA with a roof supported by columns.

Picturesque Originally a landscape or building which looked as if it had come out of a picture in the style of Claude or of Gaspar Poussin. In the late C18 it was defined in a long controversy between Payne KNIGHT and Uvedale PRICE as an aesthetic quality between the sublime and the beautiful, characterized in the landscape garden by wild ruggedness (chasms, dark impenetrable woods, rushing streams, etc.), and in architecture by interesting asymmetrical dispositions of forms and variety of texture – as in the COTTAGE ORNÉ and the Italianate or castellated Gothic country houses of John NASH.

Lit: C. Hussey, *The Picturesque*, London 1927; N. Pevsner, *Studies in Art, Architecture and Design*, London 1968.

Pier 1. A solid masonry support, as distinct from a COLUMN. 2. The solid mass between doors, windows, and other openings in buildings. 3. A name often given to Romanesque and Gothic pillars varying from a square to a composite section (*see* COMPOUND PIER).

in 1769. His most famous work is the façade of Teatro della Scala, Milan (1776-8). He also built several vast palaces, all rather severe with long façades on which ornament is reduced to a bare minimum, e.g., Palazzo Reale, Milan (1773), Palazzo Belgioioso, Milan (1779), and Villa Reale, Monza (1780).

Lit: C. L. Meeks, *Italian Architecture, 1750-1914*, New Haven 1966.

Pierre de Montereau (or Montreuil) (d. 1267) was master mason of Notre Dame, Paris, in 1265. The High Gothic work at St Denis Abbey, begun in 1231, is ascribed to him. On his tombstone he is called *doctor lathomorum*.

Lit: P. Frankl, *Gothic Architecture*, Pelican History of Art, Harmondsworth 1962; R. Branner, *St Louis and the Court Style in Gothic Architecture*, London 1965.

Pigage, Nicolas de (1723-96), was born at Lunéville and trained in Paris, visited Italy and probably England, and in 1749 became architect to the Elector Palatine Carl Theodor in Mannheim, for whom all his best work was executed. His masterpiece is Schloss Benrath near Düsseldorf (1755-69), a large pavilion, apparently of one storey (but in fact of three), somewhat similar to Sanssouci at Potsdam,

Alternating columns and piers: Abbey Church, Bursfelde, begun 1093

Pier and half column: Madeleine, Vézelay, early C12

Piermarini, Giuseppe (1734-1808), the leading neo-classical architect in Milan, trained in Rome under VANVITELLI and settled in Milan

and decorated internally in the most exquisitely refined and restrained Rococo manner that hovers on the verge of Louis XVI classicism. At Schwetzingen he laid out the Elector's garden (1753 onwards), and built a miniature theatre (1752) and various follies (1753–95), including a mosque, a romantic water castle, and a bath-house with a mirror ceiling. (For illustration *see* GERMAN ARCHITECTURE.)

Lit: P. du Colombier, *L'architecture française en Allemagne en XVIIIe siècle*, Paris 1956.

Pilaster A shallow PIER or rectangular column projecting only slightly from a wall and, in classical architecture, conforming with one of the ORDERS.

Pilasters: Episcopal Palace, Bressanone (Brixen), 1764–71

Pilaster-strip, *see* LESENE.

Pilgram, Anton (d. *c*. 1515), was mason and sculptor first at Brno and Heilbronn (at Heilbronn he did the high-spired tabernacle for the Holy Sacrament), and later at St Stefan in Vienna, where the organ foot (1513) and the pulpit (1514–15) are his, both very intricate in their architectural forms and both including a self-portrait of the master.

Pillar A free-standing upright member which, unlike a COLUMN, need not be cylindrical or conform with any of the orders.

Pillar piscina, *see* PISCINA.

Pilotis A French term for pillars or stilts that carry a building, thereby raising it to first-floor level and leaving the ground floor open.

Pilotis: Swiss Hostel, Cité Universitaire, Paris, 1932, by Le Corbusier

Pinnacle A small turret-like termination crowning spires, buttresses, the angles of parapets, etc.; usually of steep pyramidal or conical shape and ornamented, e.g., with CROCKETS.

Pinnacles: Regensburg Cathedral, C13–14

Piranesi, Giovanni Battista (1720–78) was mainly an engraver of views of Roman antiquities and an architectural theorist. He exerted a profound influence on the development of the neo-classical and Romantic movements. Born in Venice, he was trained as an engineer and architect, and settled in Rome *c*. 1745. His highly dramatic views of Roman ruins and imaginative reconstructions of ancient Rome helped to inspire a new attitude to Antiquity. In *Della magnificenza ed architettura dei Romani* (1761) he championed the supremacy of Roman over Greek architecture and in *Parere sull'architettura* (1765) advocated a free and imaginative use of Roman models for the creation of a new architectural style. He put his theories into practice only once, not very successfully, at S. Maria del Priorato, Rome (1764–6), which combines an antique flavour with allusions to the Knights of Malta, who owned the church; but it lacks the power and imagination of his engravings.

Lit: H. Focillon, *Piranesi*, Paris 1918; A. H. Mayor, *Giovanni Battista Piranesi*, New York 1928; R. Wittkower, *Piranesi*, Smith College Museum of Art, Northampton, Mass., 1961; M. F. Fischer, 'Die Umbaupläne des G. B. Piranesi für den Chor von S. Giovanni in Laterano' in *Münchner Jahrbuch der bildenden Kunst*, xix, 1968.

Pisano, Nicola (d. *c.* 1280), and his son **Giovanni** (d. shortly after 1314), the greatest Italian sculptors of their generations, are also recorded as architects. In the case of Nicola we have no documents, but tradition (VASARI) and some stylistic arguments; in the case of Giovanni we are on firmer ground. He appears as master mason of Siena Cathedral in 1290 and at Siena some years earlier, during the time when the cathedral received its Gothic façade. About 1296 he moved to Pisa and was there probably also master mason. **Andrea Pisano** (d. 1348–9) was not a relation of Giovanni. He is the finest Italian sculptor of the generation following Giovanni's and was also an architect. As such he is traceable in records of Florence Cathedral as master mason probably after Giotto's death in 1337, and at Orvieto Cathedral also as master mason from 1347. However, at Orvieto by that time the most important sculptural and architectural work on the façade was over, and at Florence also nothing architectural can be attributed to him with certainty.

Lit: J. White, *Art and Architecture in Italy, 1250–1400*, Pelican History of Art, Harmondsworth 1966.

Piscina A stone basin in a niche near the altar for washing the Communion or Mass vessels; provided with a drain and usually set in or against the wall south of the altar. A freestanding piscina on a pillar can be called a *pillar piscina*. (Illustrated next column.)

Pishtaq A Persian word literally meaning 'fore-arch'. The term denotes a monumental façade comprising a central vaulted porch or

Piscina: Tarrant Rushton, Dorset

arch enclosed by a rectangular frame. This element, possibly developed in mausolea (Tim, Uzbekistan), was used in eastern Islamic architecture from the C10 onwards either to mark the principal entrance to a building – such as a mosque, mausoleum, *madrasa* or caravanserai – or for *iwans* disposed in a cruciform arrangement on the axes of an arcaded courtyard. In both cases, therefore, the *pishtaq* helps to articulate otherwise monotonous façades and to give them a focus. The early *pishtaqs* are rather flat but are enlivened by the multiple recessions of the rectangular frame. Later the arch opened into a deep vaulted vestibule and was encased in an increasingly lofty and attenuated frame (Turbat-i Jam, Iran; Gazur Gah, Afghanistan). Although such vestibules have seating in the form of benches, a major purpose of the *pishtaq* was to display ornament and epigraphy, and they therefore serve as an index of the changes in these fields during the medieval period. The creative development of the genre had ceased by the C16.   [RH]

Plaisance A summerhouse or pleasure-house near a mansion.

Plateresque Literally 'silversmith-like'. The name is given to an ornate architectural style popular in Spain during the C16. It is characterized by a lavish use of ornamental motifs – Gothic, Renaissance, and even Moorish – unrelated to the structure of the building to which they are applied. The main practi-

Plateresque gateway:
University of Salamanca, early C16

tioners, many of whom were sculptors as well
as architects, included Diego de SILOE, Alonso
COVARRUBIAS, Rodrigo GIL DE HONTAÑÓN.
    Lit: J. Camón Aznar, *La arquitectura
platersca*, Madrid 1945; F. Chueca Goitia,
Arquitectura del siglo XVI (Ars Hispaniae, XI),
Madrid 1953.

Playfair, William Henry (1789–1857), was
the leading GREEK REVIVAL architect in
Edinburgh alongside T. HAMILTON. He was
the son of James Playfair (d. 1794) who designed Melville Castle (1786) and Cairness
House (1791–7) the latter in an advanced neo-
classical style with neo-Egyptian features
inside. W. H. Playfair may have studied under
SMIRKE in London but returned to Scotland
in 1817 on being commissioned to complete
R. ADAM's Edinburgh University. This established him professionally. He followed Adam's
designs closely, but the interiors are his,
notably the Library (*c.* 1827) which is among
his finest works. In 1818 he also began the
Academy at Dollar and the New Observatory
on Calton Hill, Edinburgh, where he also
built a Doric monument to his uncle John
(1825) and another to Dugald Stewart (1831)
based on the Choragic Monument to Lysicrates. His best known works are the Royal
Scottish Academy (1822, enlarged and modified 1831) and the National Gallery of
Scotland (1850), both Doric and rather dour.
The Surgeons' Hall (begun 1829), with its
elegant and crisp Ionic portico, is perhaps his
masterpiece. Though essentially a Greek

Revival architect Playfair worked in other
styles as well, e.g., neo-Gothic at New College,
Edinburgh (1846–50) and neo-Elizabethan
at Donaldson's Hospital, Edinburgh (1842–
51).
    Lit: A. J. Youngson, *The Making of Classical
Edinburgh*, Edinburgh 1966.

Plinth The projecting base of a wall or column
pedestal, generally CHAMFERED or moulded
at the top. (For additional illustration *see*
PEDESTAL.)

Plinth

Plinth block A block at the base of the architrave of a door, chimney-piece, etc., against
which the skirting of the wall is stopped.

Podium 1. A continuous base or plinth supporting columns. 2. The platform enclosing
the arena in an ancient amphitheatre.

Poelaert, Joseph, *see* BELGIAN ARCHITEC-
TURE.

Poelzig, Hans (1869–1936), studied at the
College of Technology in Berlin, and in 1899
was appointed to a job in the Prussian
Ministry of Works. In the next year, however,
he became Professor of Architecture in the
School of Arts and Crafts at Breslau (Wroclaw),
and in 1903 its director. He stayed till 1916,
then became City Architect of Dresden (till
1920), and after that Professor of Architecture in the College of Technology and the
Academy of Arts in Berlin. In 1936 he accepted
a chair at Ankara, but died before emigrating.
    His first building of note was the water
tower at Posen (Poznan), built in 1910 as an
exhibition pavilion for the mining industry.
It is of iron framing with brick infilling and
details of exposed iron inside. Of 1911–12
are an office building at Breslau, with the
motif of bands of horizontal windows curving
round the corner – a motif much favoured in
the 1920s and 1930s – and a factory at Luban,

equally advanced in its architectural seriousness and its grouping of cubic elements.
During and immediately after the First World
War Poelzig was one of the most fertile in-
ventors of Expressionist forms, chiefly of a
stalagmite or organ-pipe kind. These fantastic
forms characterize his House of Friendship
(1916), designed for Istanbul, his designs for
a town hall for Dresden (1917), and those for
a Festival Theatre at Salzburg (1919–20),
none of which was executed. However, he did
carry out the conversion of the Grosses
Schauspielhaus in Berlin (1918–19), with its
stalactitic vault and its highly Expressionist

Crypt of Cracow Cathedral, CII *and* CI2

corridors and foyer. Later buildings were
more conventionally modern (the enormous
office building of 1928 for the Dye Trust, I. G.
Farben, at Frankfurt and the equally enormous building (1929) for the German Broadcasting Company in Berlin). (For illustration
see GERMAN ARCHITECTURE.)

Lit: T. Heuss, *H. Poelzig, Lebensbild eines
Baumeisters,* Tübingen 1939; D. Sharp, *Modern Architecture and Expressionism,* London
1966; B. Miller Lane, *Architecture and Politics
in Germany, 1918–1945,* Cambridge, Mass.,
1968; *Hans Poelzig, Gesammelte Schriften und
Werke* (ed. J. Posener), Berlin 1970.

Point-block housing A point-block is a high
block in which the centre is reserved for staircases, lifts, etc. and the flats fan out from that
centre.

Pointed arch, *see* ARCH.

Pointing In brickwork, the strong mortar
finishing given to the exterior of the joints.

Polish architecture The oldest surviving
building in Poland is the small quatrefoil
Chapel of St Mary on the Wawel Hill at

*Cistercian Monastery Church, Mogila,
near Cracow, 1243*

Dominican Church, Cracow, CI3–CI4,
restored 1850

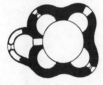

*Plan of quatrefoil Chapel of St Mary,
Cracow, late* CIO

Cracow. It is of the CIO and in this and all the
rest the exact parallel to the oldest building of
Bohemia, on the Prague Hradshin. The
Romanesque style in Poland is part of that of

Germany. Italian connections are largely explicable *via* Germany. The best preserved cathedral is at Plock (1144 etc.). Its rounded transept ends indicate inspiration from Cologne. The cathedral on the Wawel has its (German) crypt and parts of the west towers. At Gniezno splendid bronze doors survive, at Strzelno some columns decorated with small figures under arches.

As in other countries the way was paved for the Gothic style by the CISTERCIANS. Their first abbey was at Jedrzejow near Wroclaw (Breslau) in Silesia (1140 etc.), and there are a number of other abbeys. More determinedly Gothic are the buildings of the friars, starting with that of the Blackfriars at Sandomierz (1227 etc.). The east part of Wroclaw Cathedral, of 1244–72, has the straight ambulatory of Cistercian tradition. The nave followed in the c14, the century in which Cracow Cathedral on the Wawel was also rebuilt. Gniezno Cathedral of *c.* 1360 etc. has an ambulatory and a ring of straight-sided radiating chapels on the pattern of Cistercian architecture.

Late Gothic Polish churches have the high proportions and the ornate figured rib vaults of Germany. Wroclaw, Gdańsk (Danzig), Torun (Thorn), the Cistercian abbeys of Oliva and Pelplin, were of course all German. A characteristic Eastern feature however – though even this originated in Germany – is the so-called folded vaults, i.e., complicated space frames without ribs. Basilican sections are more frequent than halls. There are also a few two-naved halls. The church at Goslawice is an octagon with four cross-arms.

Town Hall at Torun (Thorn), late c14.
Tower is c13

Of secular buildings by far the proudest is the town hall at Torun of 1259 etc. but mainly the late c14, a bold oblong with blank giant arcading, an inner courtyard and one mighty tower. The surviving early buildings of Cracow University are also among the most interesting buildings of their kind anywhere in Europe.

The Renaissance reached Poland early, and probably by way of Hungary and Czechoslovakia. The Early Renaissance parts of the Wawel (castle) of Cracow were begun as early as 1502 and the domed chapel of King Sigismond attached to Cracow Cathedral in 1517; the architects in both cases were Italians. Yet closest to the windows of the Wawel palace is the Vladislav Hall at Prague, closest to the chapel that of 1507 at Esztergom. Specially characteristic of the indigenous later c16 and early c17 style are lively top crestings instead of battlements (Cracow, Cloth Hall, 1555) and courtyards or façades with arcading on two or three levels (Poznan, i.e., Posen, Town Hall, 1550–61). The former also occurs in the other East European countries, the latter in them and Germany. Castles

Town Hall at Poznan (Posen), 1550–61

The Cloth Hall at Cracow, 1555

in the country were often square or oblong with courtyard and with or without angle towers (Niepolomice, 1550 etc., Baranów, 1579 etc., Ujazdow, 1606 etc.).

Baranów, 1579–1602

Much interesting church work went on as well, with stuccoed tunnel vaults, their decoration being either Gothic Survival or simple geometrical patterns (Pultusk, 1556–63) or strap-work. Architects continued to be Italian, and that remained so in the C17 as well. Poland has proportionately more churches of Italian inspiration in the C16 and early C17 than Germany.

The Italian church type of the Gesù in Rome was taken over before 1600 (Jesuit Church, Cracow, 1597 etc. by J. M. Bernardone and J. Trevano); and Poland contributed much to the Italianate Baroque of the later C17 (Cracow University Church, 1689 etc.). Besides longitudinal there are central churches. Klimontov, 1643 etc., is oval, Gostyn, 1677 etc., octagonal, and the church of the Perpetual Adoration in Warsaw, 1683 etc., round with four short arms. The latter is by the Dutch TYLMAN VAN GAMEREN who

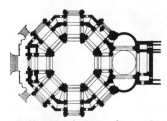

Plan of Abbey Church, Gostyn, begun 1677

became the leading Polish architect about 1700.

The plans of the C18, with their predilection for elongated central themes, show affinities with Bohemia and once more South Germany (Lwow, Dominicans, 1744 etc., Berezwecz with its curvaceous twin-tower façade, 1750 etc.). The principal country house of the first half of the C17 is Podhorce of 1635–40, still square with angle towers,

Church at Lipka, 1687–1730

and with the pedimented windows and superimposed orders of pilasters which one would find at the same time in Austria and Czechoslovakia. The full-blown Baroque came with Wilanów near Warsaw of 1681 etc. (by

Wilanów, begun 1681

A. Locci). In opposition to it was van Gameren's Franco-Dutch style (Warsaw, Krasinski Palace 1689 etc.). This however did not apply to his ecclesiastical architecture throughout. St Anne at Cracow (1689 etc.) is thoroughly Italian and Baroque. The c18 saw a large activity both by the Saxon court and the native nobility. They culminated in PÖPPELMANN'S designs for the Royal Palace. Style again varies from his exuberant Baroque to the classical French restraint.

Neo-classicism came early, and its earliest and finest phase corresponds with the reign of King Stanislaw Augustus Poniatowski (1764–85). Earlier still is the chapel belonging to the country palace of Podhorce. This is of 1752–66, by an architect signing himself C. Romanus. It is round, with a giant portico and a dome. Round and domed also, with a Roman Doric portico and decidedly French, is the Protestant Church at Warsaw of 1777 by S. B. Zug (1733–1807). The lead-

ing court architects of Stanislaw were Giacomo Fontana (1710–73) and Domenico Merlini (1730–97). Theirs is the Ujazdow Palace of 1768 etc. and by Merlini and the younger Kamsetzer, Jan Baptist (1753–95), are the remodelling of the Lazienki Palace of Ujazdow (1788) and the excellent interiors of the Royal Palace (1780–85). Kamsetzer's church at Petrykosy of 1791 is wholly of the French Revolution type. At the same time the grounds of the country houses were converted in the English picturesque way (Arcadia, 1778 etc., Natolin, Warsaw Belvedere). Between c. 1780 and c. 1825 Poland produced a number of spacious country houses in the classicist style and also the two town halls of Wilno and Grodno with detached giant porticos. But the

Vilna Cathedral, 1753–98

Lazienki Palace, Warsaw, after 1788

most monumental of the giant porticos is that of Wilno Cathedral of 1777–1801, and that is by the Polish architect W. Gucewicz (1753–98). The leading early C19 architect in Warsaw was Antonio Corazzi (1792–1877). He designed the Polish Bank (1828–30), which is very French, and the Grecian Grand Theatre (1826–33). The later C19 went through the same historicist motions as all European countries, but in the early C20 Poland had a kind of national romanticism which is more characteristic of Russia, Finland and Sweden than of the West. It is exemplified by the church of St James at Warsaw of 1909 etc. by Oscar Sosnowski (1880–1939).

Church at Bialystok, begun 1927, by Sosnowski

Lit: Z. Dmochowski, *The Architecture of Poland*, London 1956; B. Knox, *Polish Architecture*, London 1971.

Polish parapet A decorative device consisting of a large-scale cresting of blind arcades, pinnacles, pyramids, etc., used to crown the façades and mask the roofs of many Polish buildings, notably the Cloth Hall at Cracow (1555) and the Town Halls of Poznań (c. 1550–61) and Culm (1567–97). It also occurs in Czechoslovakia.

Pollack, Mihály (1773–1855), the leading Hungarian classicist, was born in Vienna. His father was an architect, and his step-brother was Leopoldo POLLAK. He studied under his brother in Milan and settled in Budapest in 1798. His style is moderate, never *outré*, and not very personal. Occasionally he also used Gothic features (Pécs, or Fünfkirchen, Cathedral, 1805 etc.). He built large private houses

and country houses, but his *chefs-d'œuvre* are public buildings at Warsaw, notably the Theatre and Assembly Room (completed 1832), the Military Academy (Ludoviceum, 1829–36), and the National Museum with its Corinthian portico and its splendid staircase (1836–45).

Lit: A. Zádor, *Mihály Pollack*, Budapest 1960.

Pollak, Leopoldo (1751–1806). He was born and trained in Vienna, settled in Milan in 1775 and became an assistant to PIERMARINI. His masterpiece is the Villa Belgioioso Reale (1793), now the Galleria d'Arte Moderna, a very large and very grand but strangely frenchified version of PALLADIO, with a rusticated basement, giant Ionic order, and lavish use of sculpture. He also built several villas near Milan and laid out their gardens in the English style, e.g., Villa Pesenti Agliardi, Sombreno (c. 1800).

Lit: C. L. V. Meeks, *Italian Architecture, 1750–1914*, New Haven 1966.

Pollini, Gino, *see* FIGINI.

Polygonal masonry Masonry composed of blocks of stone dressed to fit one another with irregular polygonal exposed faces rather than rectangular ones as in ASHLAR masonry. If some of the edges are curved the masonry is described as 'curvilinear'.

Ponti, Gio (b. 1891), designer and architect, was also a painter and draughtsman in the twenties. His drawing reflects the style of the Vienna Secession (*see* OLBRICH), and his designs for porcelain of around 1925 may also be inspired by the Wiener Werkstätte. Ponti is a universal designer: his *œuvre* includes ships' interiors, theatrical work, light fittings, furniture, and products of light industry. Most of his best work in these fields dates from after the war, e.g., the famous very delicately detailed rush-seated chair (1951). His fame as an architect rested for a long time on three buildings: the Faculty of Mathematics in the Rome University City, dated 1934 and one of the *incunabula* of INTERNATIONAL MODERN architecture in Italy (though preceded by Terragni's few buildings); and then the twin office buildings (1936 and 1951) designed for the Montecatini Company, both in Milan. The first, with its subdued modernity and its elegant detail, was a pioneer work and at the same time very personal, the second is more conventional. Ponti's finest building is the Pirelli skyscraper in Milan (1955-8), built round a hidden structural concrete core by NERVI; the building is 415 ft high, a slender slab of curtain walling with the long sides tapering to the slenderest ends.

Lit: J. S. Plant, *Espressione di Gio Ponti,* Milan 1957.

Ponzio, Flaminio (1560-1613), official architect to Pope Paul V (Borghese), was able but rather unadventurous; he never developed far beyond the Late Mannerist style in which he was trained. His most notable work is the Cappella Paolina in S. Maria Maggiore, Rome (1605-11), very richly decorated with sculpture and panels of coloured marbles and semi-precious stones. He also built the very long façade of Palazzo Borghese, Rome (1605-13), and the handsome Acqua Paola fountain on the Janiculum (1612). Early in the C17 he rebuilt, with a new dome, RAPHAEL and PERUZZI'S S. Eligio degli Orefici, Rome.

Lit: H. Hibbard, *The Architecture of the Palazzo Borghese,* Rome 1962.

Pöppelmann, Matthaeus Daniel (1662-1736). He was the architect of the Zwinger at Dresden, a Rococo masterpiece. He was born at Herford in Westphalia and settled in Dresden in 1686, being appointed Kondukteur in the Landbauamt in 1691, and eventually, in 1705, succeeded Marcus Conrad Dietze as Landbaumeister to the Elector of Saxony and King of Poland, Augustus the Strong. In 1705-15 he built the Taschenberg Palais in Dresden for the Elector's mistress. For a state visit in 1709 he built a temporary wooden amphitheatre which the Elector then decided to replace with a stone construction (the Zwinger) which would be incorporated in the great new royal palace which Pöppelmann was commissioned to design. In 1710 he was appointed Geheim Cämmeriere and sent off to study and gather ideas in Vienna and Italy. His designs for the palace show some influence from both the Viennese Baroque of HILDEBRANDT and the Roman Baroque of Carlo FONTANA. But the Zwinger itself could hardly be more original in general conception – a vast space surrounded by a single-storey gallery linking two-storey pavilions and entered through exuberant frothy gateways – the whole composition resembling a giant's Meissen table-centre. Only a section was ever built (1711-20; the Kronentor in 1713, the Wallpavillon in 1716. It was damaged in 1944 but is now rebuilt). The sculptural decoration was executed by Balthasar Permoser and the brilliance of the total effect is largely due to the successful collaboration between sculptor and architect. Pöppelmann's other buildings are far less exciting: the 'Indian' Wasserpalais at Schloss Pillnitz on the Elbe (1720-23) with Chinoiserie roofs and painted figures of Chinamen under the eaves; the Bergpalais at Schloss Pillnitz (1724); Schloss Moritzburg, begun 1723 but executed under the direction of LONGUELUNE; and, from 1727 onwards, extensions to the Japanisches Palais in Dresden, executed under the direction of de BODT. Pöppelmann's designs for the Dreikönigskirche in Dresden Neustadt (1732-9) were executed by Georg BÄHR. From 1728 onwards Pöppelmann collaborated with Longuelune in Warsaw on the designs for a vast new Saxon Palace of which only the central section was built (c. 1730). His son Carl Friedrich (d. 1750) succeeded him in Warsaw. (For illustration *see* GERMAN ARCHITECTURE.)

Lit: J. L. Sponsel, *Der Zwinger, die Hoffeste und die Schlossbaupläne zu Dresden,* 2 vols., Dresden 1924; B. A. Döring, *Matthes Daniel Pöppelmann,* Dresden 1930; E. Hempel, *Baroque Art and Architecture in Central Europe,* Pelican History of Art, Harmondsworth 1965.

Poppyhead An ornamental termination to the top of a bench or stall-end, usually carved with foliage and fleur-de-lis-type flowers, animals, or figures. A poppyhead is in fact a FINIAL.

Porch The covered entrance to a building; called a PORTICO if columned and pedimented like a temple front.

Porta, Giacomo della (c. 1533-1602), a Mannerist architect of Lombard origin working in Rome, is notable mainly as a follower of MICHELANGELO, whom he succeeded as architect of the Capitol. Here he finished the Palazzo dei Conservatori to Michelangelo's design with slight alterations (1578) and also built the Palazzo del Senatore (1573-98) with rather more alterations. He followed VIGNOLA as architect of the Gesù, Rome, designing the façade (1573-84), which was destined to be copied for Jesuit churches throughout Europe. In 1573-4 he became chief architect at St Peter's, where he completed Michelangelo's exterior on the garden side and built the minor domes (1578 and 1585) and the major dome (1588-90), rather more ornate and nearer in outline to the dome of Florence Cathedral than Michelangelo intended. He also built the Palazzo della Sapienza (begun c. 1575); S. Maria ai Monti (begun 1580); the nave of S. Giovanni dei Fiorentini (1582–92); S. Andrea della Valle (1591, completed by MADERNO 1608–23); S. Maria Scala Coeli (begun 1582); the façade of S. Atanasio dei Greci; Palazzo Marescotti (c. 1590), and the very splendid Villa Aldobrandini, Frascati (1598–1603). (For illustration see ITALIAN ARCHITECTURE.)

Lit: L. H. Heydenreich & W. Lotz, Architecture in Italy 1400–1600, Pelican History of Art, Harmondsworth 1974.

Portcullis A gate of iron or iron-reinforced wooden bars made to slide up and down in vertical grooves in the JAMBS of a doorway; used for defence in castle gateways.

Porte-cochère A porch large enough for wheeled vehicles to pass through.

Portico A roofed space, open or partly enclosed, forming the entrance and centrepiece of the façade of a temple, house, or church, often with detached or attached columns and a PEDIMENT. It is called prostyle or in antis according to whether it projects from or recedes into a building; in the latter case the columns range with the front wall. According to the number of front columns it is called tetrastyle (4), hexastyle (6), octastyle (8), decastyle (10), or dodecastyle (12). If there are only two columns between pilasters or antae it is called distyle in antis.

Portuguese architecture Until about 1500 Portugal participates in the development of Spanish architecture: there are Roman remains (temple at Évora); S. Frutuoso de Montélios is a c7 church on a Greek cross plan with horseshoe apses and domes, clearly inspired by Byzantium; Lourosa is MOZARABIC of 920; and the principal monuments of the Romanesque style also have their closest parallels in Spain. They are the cathedrals of Braga (begun c. 1100) and Coimbra (begun after 1150), inspired by

Portico: Pantheon, Rome

Engaged portico: Schloss Belvedere, Berlin, 1768

Old Cathedral, Coimbra, begun after 1150

Lisbon Cathedral, begun 1147

Santiago de Compostela, in the style of the so-called pilgrimage churches of France: high tunnel-vaulted naves, arcades and galleries, and no clerestory lighting. On the other hand, they have no ambulatories. Individual buildings of special interest are the Templars' church of Tomar of the late c12, with a domed octagonal centre and a lower sixteen-sided ambulatory, and the Domus Municipalis of Braganza, a low irregular oblong with rows of short arched windows high up.

The Romanesque style died hard; the cathedral of Évora (begun 1186) is still pre-

Gothic. The Gothic style was introduced by the Cistercians, and the outstanding Early Gothic building is Alcobaça (begun 1178) on the pattern of Clairvaux and Pontigny, i.e., with ambulatory and radiating chapels forming an unbroken semicircle. Its tall rib-vaulted interior is one of the noblest of the order in all Europe. The monastic quarters are well preserved and very beautiful too. But Alcobaça is an exception; for, generally speaking, the Gothic style does not begin in Portugal until the mid c13. Among the most important buildings are a number of friars'

(Above). Dominican friary at Batalha:
(Left). Cloister begun 1388. (Right). Octagon and radiating chapels, begun 1420

churches (S. Clara, Santarém) and a number of cathedral cloisters (Coimbra, Evora, Lisbon – all early C14).

But Portuguese architecture comes properly into its own only with the great enterprise of Batalha, a house of Blackfriars commemorating the battle of Aljubarrota. It was begun in 1388 with a vaulted nave of steep Spanish proportions and an east end of the type peculiar to the Italian friars. But in 1402 a new architect appeared, called Huguet or Ouguete, and he introduced a full-blown Flamboyant, i.e., a Late Gothic style, mixed with many reminiscences of the English PERPENDICULAR. The façade, the vaults of cloister and chapterhouse, and the chapel of

João I are his work. He also began a large octagon with seven radiating chapels east of the old east end, but this was never completed. Here, as in the link with the old east end, the vaults are of complex English types. The climax of the Late Gothic in Portugal is the MANUELINE STYLE, named after King Manuel I (1495–1521). It is the parallel to the Spanish style of the Reyes Católicos and, like it, springs from the sudden riches pouring in from overseas. But whereas the Spanish style is essentially one of lavish decoration, the most significant works of the Manueline style show a transformation of structural members as well, especially a passion for twisted piers. These appear at Belém, a house

Cloister of the Jeronymite Monastery at Belém, begun 1502

Church of the Jeronymite Monastery at Belém, begun 1502

Doorway, Abbey of Alcobaça, early c16

of the order of the Jeronymites (1502 etc.) – together with richly figured vaults and ample surface incrustation – and also at Setúbal (1492 etc.). In addition there are the wildly over-decorated doorways and windows of Golegã and Tomar (1510 etc.). The portal to the unfinished east chapels of Batalha suggests East Indian inspiration. The leading masters were one Boytac, a Frenchman, at

Setúbal and Belem, Mateus Fernandes in the portal of Batalha, and Diogo de ARRUDA in the nave and the windows of Tomar.

But Tomar also contains the most important examples in Portugal of the Italian Renaissance in its Roman Cinquecento forms. The buildings in question are the cloister and the church of the Conception (both *c.* 1550). But, as in Spain, the Renaissance had arrived

Main Cloister, Monastery of Christ, Tomar, 1557, by Diogo de Torralva

Courtyard of the former Jesuit university
at Évora, late c16

earlier and in playful Quattrocento forms. Among cathedrals the Cinquecento style is represented by Leiria (1551 etc.), the work of Afonso Álvares. His nephew Baltasar designed the Jesuit church of Oporto (c. 1590–1610) with its typically Mannerist, high and restless twin-tower façade. Also as in Spain, the Baroque was long in coming, but when it came it was less wild than in the neighbouring country; it influenced Brazil considerably (e.g., the Seminary at Santarém, 1676). The leading Baroque architects are João Turriano (1610–79) and João Antunes (1683–1734), and the most completely Baroque town is Aveiro. Octagonal and round plans are

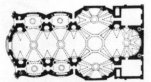

Plan for Santa Maria Divina Providência
in Lisbon, c. 1650, by Guarini

typical of Portuguese Baroque churches. The climax of the Baroque is well within the c18. It appears in the buildings of Niccolò NASONI (d. 1773), a native of Italy – such as the palace of Freixo and several churches at

Oporto – and the buildings of J. F. LUDOVICE (c. 1670–1752), a native of Germany – such as the grand abbey of Mafra (1717–70) and the chancel of Évora Cathedral (1716–46).

Santos Passos Church, Guimarães,
1767–98, by da Silva

Church of the Misericordia, Viseu, c18

Opposition to the Baroque set in about the middle of the c18. There were two centres: Oporto, where the large hospital is by John CARR of York (design 1796) and the Terceiros Church has decoration inspired by Robert ADAM; and Lisbon, where rebuilding (to a plan) after the disastrous earthquake of 1755 was done on French principles. The most

HUNT's office. He conducted his own practice from 1860 and started again after the war in 1868. Post was an eclectic, without commitment to any one style in particular. He was interested in structure and planning, and late in life was partly responsible for evolving the standard American hotel plan with a bath to every room, a system which is complete in the Statler Hotel at Buffalo (1911–12). He did a number of millionaires' residences (Cornelius Vanderbilt, 1889 and 1895) and several prominent office buildings in New York, e.g., the Equitable Building of 1869 (the first with lifts), the New York Times and Pulitzer Buildings (both 1889), and the St Paul Building (1897–9) which, with its twenty-two storeys, was the tallest in New York at that time.

Lit: C. W. Condit, *American Building Art, the Nineteenth Century*, New York 1960.

Praça do Commercio
(formerly Terreiro do Paço), Lisbon, c. 1755

spectacular piece of the rebuilding is the Terreiro do Paço, the large square facing the Tejo.

Lit: G. Kubler & M. Soria, *Art and Architecture in Spain and Portugal and their American Dominions, 1500–1800*, Pelican History of Art, Harmondsworth 1959; R. C. Smith, *The Art of Portugal, 1500–1800*, London 1968.

Post, George Browne (1837–1913), graduated in civil engineering and then worked in

Post, Pieter (1608–69), began as van CAMPEN's right-hand man at the Mauritshuis and Amsterdam Town Hall. He became a leading exponent of Dutch PALLADIANISM, an unpretentious, placid, and economic form of classicism, characterized by its use of brick with stone dressings and straightforward, almost diagrammatic use of pilasters. His masterpiece was the Huis-ten-Bosch near The Hague (1645–51, exterior ruined by c18 additions: interior decoration supervised by van Campen and C. Huygens), but the small Weigh-House at Leiden (1657), with its Tuscan pilasters on a rusticated base and supporting a simple pediment, is more typical. The Town Hall of Maastricht (begun 1659) is more ambitious. His style had great influence, and was imported into England by Hugh MAY and others.

Lit: G. A. C. Blok, *Pieter Post*, Siegen 1937; Fockema Andreae, R. C. Hekker, & E. H. Ter Kuile, *Duizend Jaar Bouwen in Nederland*, Amsterdam 1957–8.

Post and lintel construction, *see* TRABEATED.

Postern A small gateway, sometimes concealed, at the back of a castle, town, or monastery.

Powell & Moya (A. J. Philip Powell and John Hidalgo Moya, b. 1921 and 1920) established themselves by winning the City of Westminster competition for the large housing estate in Pimlico, later named Churchill Gardens (1946). The clarity, precision, and directness of their style have been maintained in all their later work, such as the Mayfield School in Putney, London (1956), the Princess Margaret Hospital at Swindon (1957 etc.), the ingenious sets for Brasenose College, Oxford (1956 etc.), the Festival Theatre at Chichester (1962), large additions to St John's College, Cambridge (completed 1967), and Christ Church, Oxford (completed 1968), and Wolfson College, Oxford (begun 1971).

Lit: R. Maxwell, *New British Architecture*, London 1972.

Pozzo, Andrea (1642–1709). Erroneously known as 'Padre Pozzo', he was a lay brother who entered the Jesuit order in 1665. Architect and painter, he was famous for his illusionistic ceiling paintings, notably that in S. Ignazio, Rome (1691–4) and also those in the Chiesa delle Missione, Mondoví (1676–7) and the Palais Liechtenstein, Vienna (1704–8). Born in Trento, he was trained in Milan and from 1681 worked in Rome (for a time in RAINALDI's studio) until 1702 when he settled in Vienna. He was extremely influential in the spread of the Baroque style from Italy to central Europe, through his engraved designs. His *Perspectivum pictorum et architectorum*, Rome 1693–1702, was frequently reprinted and had several foreign language editions as well. He designed the S. Ignazio altar in the Gesú, Rome (1697–8). His build-

ings are unexciting compared to his engraved designs. They include S. Ignazio, Dubrovnik (1699–1725), the Gesú and the interior of S. Maria dei Servi at Montepulciano (1702), the university church at Vienna (1705), and S. Francesco Saverio at Trento (begun 1708).

Lit: M. Carboneri, *A. Pozzo architetto, 1642–1709*, Trento 1961; B. Kerber, *Andrea Pozzo*, Berlin–New York 1971; R. Wittkower, *Art and Architecture in Italy, 1600–1750*, Pelican History of Art, Harmondsworth 1973, paperback edn 1973.

Prandtauer, Jakob (1660–1726), was the architect of Melk (1702–14), perhaps the most important of all Baroque abbeys. The church, with its undulating façade, many-pinnacled towers, and bold dome, is clasped between two long ranges of monastic buildings which stretch forward to form a courtyard. Prandtauer took every advantage of the unusually dramatic site above the Danube to create a picturesque group of buildings which seems to rise out of the rock. The interior of the church (completed by other architects) is rich and *mouvementé*, with an almost Gothic sense of height. Prandtauer's other works are less exciting: the church at Sonntagberg (1706–17), a smaller version of Melk; completion of CARLONE's church at Christkindl; the magnificent open stairway (1706–14) and Marmorsaal or Marble Hall (1718–24) at St Florian near Vienna; the priory of Dürnstein (begun 1717); the little hunting-lodge of Hohenbrunn (1725–9); alterations to the Gothic cathedral (1722) and townhouses at St Pölten. He belonged to an ancient tradition of master masons and (unlike HILDEBRANDT) supervised every stage of the works entrusted to him. Close sympathy with his religious patrons is suggested by his buildings no less than by his personal piety. He was a member of a lay confraternity and contributed handsomely to the expense of building his parish church (1722) and townhouses in St Pölten.

Lit: H. Hantsch, *J. Prandtauer*, Vienna 1926; *J. Prandtauer und sein Kunstkries*, Exh. Cat., Vienna 1960.

Pratt, Sir Roger (1620–84), a gentleman architect, learned and widely travelled, was the most gifted of JONES's followers. His few buildings were very influential, but have all been destroyed or altered. At Coleshill (1650, now destroyed), Kingston Lacy (1663–5, altered by BARRY), and Horseheath (1663–5, destroyed) he invented the type of house later erroneously called the 'Wren' type. Clarendon House, London (1664–7, destroyed), was the first great classical house in London and was widely imitated and copied, e.g., at Belton House, Lincolnshire, by Stanton (1684–6).

Lit: J. Summerson, *Architecture in Britain, 1530–1830,* Pelican History of Art, Harmondsworth 1969, paperback edn 1970.

Precast concrete Concrete components cast in a factory or on the site before being placed in position.

Lit: K. Billig, *Precast Concrete,* London 1955.

Pre-Columbian architecture, *see* MESOAMERI-CAN ARCHITECTURE.

Prefabrication The manufacture of whole buildings or components in a factory or casting yard for transportation to the site. *See also* INDUSTRIALIZED BUILDING.

Presbytery The part of the church which lies east of the choir and where the high altar is placed.

Prestressed concrete A development of ordinary REINFORCED CONCRETE. The reinforcing steel is replaced by wire cables in ducts, so positioned that compression can be induced in the tension area of the concrete before it is loaded. This is done by stretching or tensioning the cables before or after casting the concrete. It results in more efficient use of materials and greater economy.

Lit: Michael Chi & Frank A. Biberstein, *The Theory of Prestressed Concrete,* New Jersey 1953; M. R. Hollington, *ABC of Prestressed Concrete,* London; R. J. Libby, *Modern Prestressed Concrete; Design Principles and Construction Methods,* London 1971.

Price, Sir Uvedale (1747–1829), landscape gardening theorist, was a friend of REPTON and R. P. KNIGHT, whom he joined in a revolt against the 'Capability' BROWN style. In reply to Knight's poem *The Landscape* he published a three-volume *Essay on the Picturesque* (1794), which defined the PICTURESQUE as an aesthetic category distinct from the Sublime and the Beautiful as defined by Burke. His approach was more practical than Knight's and laid great stress on the need for landscape gardeners to study the works of the great landscape painters.

Lit: N. Pevsner, *Studies in Art, Architecture and Design,* London 1968.

Primaticcio, Francesco (1504/5–70), was primarily a decorative painter and sculptor and, as such, head of the First School of Fontainebleau. His few buildings date from towards the end of his career, notably the Aile de la Belle Cheminée at Fontainebleau (1568) and the Chapelle des Valois at St Denis, largely built after his death by BULLANT and now destroyed. (For illustration *see* MANNERISM.)

Lit: L. Dimier, *Le Primatice,* Paris 1928.

Principal, *see* ROOF.

Profile The section of a MOULDING or, more generally, the contour or outline of a building or any part of it.

Pronaos The vestibule of a Greek or Roman temple, enclosed by side walls and a range of columns in front.

Propylaeum The entrance gateway to an enclosure (usually temple precincts), as on the Acropolis at Athens.

Propylaeum, Munich, begun 1846, by Klenze

Proscenium 1. In a Greek or Roman theatre, the stage on which the action took place. 2. In a modern theatre, the space between the curtain and orchestra, sometimes including the arch and frontispiece facing the auditorium.

Prostyle Having free-standing columns in a row, as often in a PORTICO. (Also illustrated next page.)

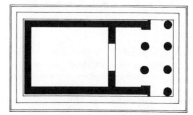

Plan of a prostyle temple

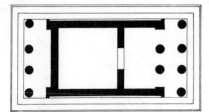

Plan of a prostyle temple

Prothesis In Byzantine architecture, the room attached to or enclosed in the church and serving for the preparation and storage of the species of the Eucharist before Mass; generally used for the storage of the Eucharist after Mass.

Proto-Renaissance, *see* ITALIAN ARCHITEC-TURE.

Prouvé, Jean (b. 1901). Trained as a metal-craftsman and now one of the masters of light-metal construction, a fervent believer in industrialized production not only of parts but of whole buildings (housing estate of small units made of aluminium, at Meudon, 1949). He has worked as a consultant and collaborator with Baudouin, Lodz, Lopez, Zehrfuss and others, but is on his own capable of great architectural elegance (Buvette, Evian, 1957).
    Lit: Architecture, nos. 11–12, 1954; *Cimaise,* nos. VI –VIII, 1961.

Pseudo-dipteral In classical architecture, a temple planned to be DIPTERAL but lacking the inner range of columns.

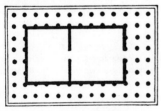

Plan of a pseudo-dipteral temple

Pseudo-peripteral In classical architecture, a temple with porticos at either end and EN-GAGED COLUMNS or pilasters along the sides.

Pteroma In a Greek temple, the space between the walls and colonnades.

Pteron An external colonnade as in a Greek temple.

Pugin, Augustus Welby Northmore (1812–52). His father, **Augustus Charles** (1762–1832), came from France to London in 1792, became a draughtsman in the office of NASH and later a draughtsman and editor of books on Gothic architecture (*Specimens*, 1821 onwards; *Gothic Ornaments*, 1831). The son helped on these, but soon received decorative and then architectural commissions. He designed furniture for Windsor Castle and stage sets for the theatre (*Kenilworth*, 1831) before he was twenty. He found himself shipwrecked off the Firth of Forth in 1830, got married in 1831, lost his wife one year later, got married again in 1833, lost his second wife in 1844, got married once more in 1849, and lost his mind in 1851.

He had a passion for the sea, and, after his conversion to Catholicism in 1834, a greater, more fervent passion for a Catholic architecture, which had to be Gothic of the noblest 'Second Pointed', i.e., late C13 to early C14 in style. He leaped to fame and notoriety with his book *Contrasts* (1836), a plea for Catholicism illustrated by brilliant comparisons between the meanness, cruelty, and vulgarity of buildings of his own day – classicist or minimum Gothic – and the glories of the Catholic past. Later he wrote more detailed and more closely considered books (*The True Principles of Pointed or Christian Architecture*, 1841, etc.), and in them showed a deeper understanding than anyone before of the connections between Gothic style and structure and of the function of each member. From these books he even appears a founder father of FUNCTIONALISM, though this is true only with qualifications.

His buildings mostly suffer from lack of means. He was rarely allowed to show in stone and wood the sparkling lavishness he could achieve on paper. He was as interested in furnishings, altars, screens, stained glass, metalwork, as in the building itself. This is how BARRY got him to work for the Houses of Parliament, where not only the Gothic details of the façades but even such fitments as inkstands and hatstands were designed by Pugin. He was a fast and ardent draughtsman. Perhaps his best churches are Cheadle in Staffordshire (1841-6), the cathedral of Nottingham (1842-4), and St Augustine, Ramsgate (1846-51), which he paid for himself and which stands next to his own house.

As against earlier neo-Gothic churches, Pugin's are usually archaeologically correct, but often have their tower asymmetrically placed, and this started the calculated asymmetry of most of the best English c19 church design. (For illustration *see* ENGLISH ARCHITECTURE.)

Lit: M. Trappes-Lomax, *Pugin: A Medieval Victorian*, London 1932; D. Gwynn, *Lord Shrewsbury, Pugin and the Catholic Revival*, London 1946; H.-R. Hitchcock, *Early Victorian Architecture in Britain*, New Haven–London 1954; P. Stanton, *Pugin*, London 1971.

Pulpit An elevated stand of stone or wood for a preacher or reader, which first became general in the later Middle Ages (the AMBO was used in the early Middle Ages). Often elaborately carved, and sometimes with an acoustic canopy above the preacher called a sounding board or TESTER. Occasionally found against the outside wall of a church.

Pulpit in the abbey church at Weingarten 1762–5

Pulpitum A stone screen in a major church erected to shut off the choir from the nave. It could also be used as a backing for the retrochoir stalls. *See also* ROOD SCREEN.

Pulvin In Byzantine architecture, a DOSSERET above the capital supporting the arch above.

Pulvinated Convex in profile; a term usually applied to a FRIEZE.

Purbeck marble A dark conglomerate from the Isle of Purbeck capable of receiving a high polish. In fashion in England from the later c12 onwards and favoured particularly in the c13. Used for COMPOUND PIERS in churches. Purbeck shafts in conjunction with shafts of normal limestone give a striking effect of light and dark. Also used for effigies all over England.

Purlin, *see* ROOF.

Pycnostyle With an arrangement of columns set $1\frac{1}{2}$ times their diameter apart. *See also* ARAEOSTYLE; DIASTYLE; EUSTYLE; SYSTYLE.

Pylon In ancient Egyptian architecture, the rectangular, truncated, pyramidal towers flanking the gateway of a temple; also, more

Pylon: Temple of Horus, Edfu, c. 300 B.C.

loosely, any high isolated structure used decoratively or to mark a boundary.

Pyramid The Greek word pyramid denotes the classic form of royal Egyptian tomb in the Old and Middle Kingdoms (*c.* 2260–1750 B.C.) – a solid construction on a square base with inclined triangular sides meeting at a point. Its earliest manifestation in stepped form at Saqqâra (*c*, 2600 B.C.) – the product of a number of superimposed MASTABAS – was succeeded by transitional examples like the pyramid of Medûm (*c.* 2595 B.C.), and the 'bent' pyramid – a cross between a pyramid and a mastaba – and 'red' pyramid at Dahshûr (*c.* 2590–2570 B.C.). The pyramid of Cheops at Gizeh has both the ideal shape – with a 52° inclination – and the largest

Stepped pyramid of King Zoser, Saqqâra, c. 2600 B.C.

Stepped pyramid, end of the Third Dynasty, c. 2620 B.C.

dimensions of any pyramid in Egypt (750–ft sides, 475 ft high); it was originally surfaced from head to toe with blocks of polished limestone, and it contains a system of passages and chambers – entrance shafts, a great hall (housing the giant block sealing the former), the tomb chamber with contrivances for distributing the load above it, and unused chambers. In the Middle Kingdom (2050–1750 B.C.) pyramids were of brick with a limestone casing (since plundered). In the

The 'bent' pyramid at Dahshûr, c. 2580 B.C.

The Red Pyramid at Dahshûr, c. 2570 B.C.

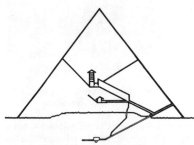

Section: Pyramid of Cheops, Gizeh

Pyramids at Gizeh, c. 2500–2400 B.C.

Ruinous pyramid of the Middle Kingdom period, Dahshûr, c. 1800 B.C.

Pyramids near Gebel-Barkal, late C2–C1 B.C.

New Kingdom (1600–1185 B.C.) they were used for private tombs, but they reverted to royal use in the Sudan after about 700 B.C. and in the Kingdom of Meroë (300 B.C.–A.D. 300). The relatively steep Meroitic pyramids house not only a tomb chamber, but also rooms for worship, adorned with reliefs. Pyramids are later to be found outside Egypt: in Asia Minor they crowned tomb-structures (e.g. Halicarnassus), and in Rome they were sometimes used for tombs (Pyramid of Cestius). China independently evolved earthen pyramids housing stone tomb-chambers. Ancient American stepped pyramids were (with one exception) not tombs but temple substructures, and are hence mountable by steps and not pointed, ending instead in a platform carrying the actual building to which they were subordinate (*see* MESO-AMERICAN ARCHITECTURE).   [DW]

Lit: I. E. S. Edwards, *The Pyramids of Egypt*, Harmondsworth, 1967.

Pythios (*fl.* 353–334 B.C.). Architect and theorist working in Asia Minor. With Satyros he designed and wrote an account of the most famous and elaborate sepulchral monument of antiquity, the richly sculptured Mausoleum built for the Carian satrap Mausolos at Halicarnassus and numbered among the seven wonders of the world (begun before 353 B.C. and finished after 350; sculptured fragments now in the British Museum). He was also the architect of the large temple of Athena Polias at Priene (dedicated 334; fragments now in Berlin and in the British Museum) in which the Ionic Order was thought to have achieved its canonical form. In a treatise on this building (known to Vitruvius but now lost) he extolled the perfection of its proportions, criticized the Doric Order and, apparently for the first time, recommended a wide training for the architect who, he said, 'should be able to do more in all the arts and sciences than those who, by their industry and exertions, bring single disciplines to the highest renown'.

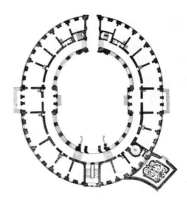

Qibla The direction in which every Muslim must turn when praying. Originally this was Jerusalem, but in 624 Mohammed changed it to the Kaʿaba or Black Stone in Mecca. Although it could be marked by a ceremonial spear or ʿanaza, in a mosque this direction is always indicated by the so-called *qibla* wall; shrines, MADRASAS and often mausolea are similarly orientated. Since the entire *qibla* wall marks the direction of the Kaʿaba a MIHRAB or prayer niche is not strictly necessary, but it serves the function of singling out the *imam*, who stands before it to lead the prayer. Often the *qibla* wall was given supplementary *mihrabs*. Errors in calculating the *qibla* have sometimes necessitated major rebuilding in a mosque, though it is commoner for the *mihrab* alone to be realigned. The *qibla* is rarely marked on the outer walls, although some *mihrabs* do project externally.

Quadrangle A rectangular courtyard enclosed by buildings on all sides and sometimes within a large building complex. The arrangement is often found in colleges and schools.

Quadratura *Trompe l'œil* architectural painting of walls and ceilings. In the C17 and C18 it was frequently executed by travelling painters who specialized in it and were known as *quadraturisti*.

Quadriga A sculptured group of a chariot drawn by four horses, often used to crown a monument or façade.

Quarenghi, Giacomo (1744–1817), a very prolific architect, was much admired and patronized by Catherine II of Russia. Born near Bergamo, he went to Rome in 1763 to study painting, but soon turned to architecture. He designed the interior of S. Scolastica, Subiaco (1771–7), in a light, elegant vein of neo-classicism. In 1776 he accepted an invitation to St Petersburg where he spent the rest of his life. His first important building is the English Palace, Peterhof (1781–9, destroyed), a sternly aloof Palladian house with no decoration apart from a vast projecting portico on one side and a recessed loggia on the other. He employed a similar formula for the State Bank (1783–90) and the Academy of Sciences (1783–9), both in Leningrad. The Hermitage Theatre, Leningrad (1783–7), is smaller and richer. His later work is more accomplished and excellent in its precision and clarity of mass, e.g., Imperial Pharmacy, Leningrad (1789–96), Alexander Palace, Tsarkoe Selo (1792–6), the Riding School (1805–7) and Smolny Institute (1806–7), both in Leningrad.

Lit: V. Zanella, *Disegni di G. Quarenghi*, Exh. Cat., Venice 1967; G. H. Hamilton, *The Art and Architecture of Russia*, Pelican History of Art, Harmondsworth 1954.

Quarry (or **Quarrel**). A small, usually diamond-shaped pane, or a square one placed diagonally, with which medieval leaded windows were glazed. The term can also apply to any small quadrangular opening in the TRACERY of a window. The word probably derives from the French *carré*. Various devices and patterns were painted on quarries, particularly during the Perpendicular period.

Quatrefoil, *see* FOIL.

Queen Anne architecture, *see* ENGLISH ARCHITECTURE.

Queen-post, *see* ROOF.

Quirk A sharp v-shaped incision in a mould-ing and between mouldings.

Quoins The dressed stones at the corners of buildings, usually laid so that their faces are alternately large and small. From the French *coin* (corner).

Quoins

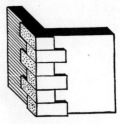

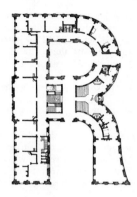

Rabbet A rectangular recess made along an ARRIS: any channel or groove cut along the face of a piece of stone, wood, etc., so as to receive a tongue or edge of another piece.

Rabirius (*fl.* 81–96 A.D.). Roman architect who, according to Martial, was employed by Domitian to build the palace on the Palatine in Rome which became the permanent residence of Roman emperors (the word palace is derived from it) and was still in use in the late c6. Enough survives to reveal the grandeur of this vast building or complex of buildings, erected on two levels of the hill and incorporating a hippodrome, libraries and courtyard gardens as well as innumerable state and private apartments. It was both a symbol of the Emperor's power and a perfect setting for the ceremony of his court (poets were quick to associate the several domes above the official rooms with the arc of the heavens). With its rich decorations and many fountains splashing in marble lined courtyards it was the epitome of luxurious opulence. Rabirius has been credited with many other buildings, without evidence, but was probably responsible for Domitian's villa near Albano, of which little survives.

Lit: L. Crema, *L'Architettura Romana (Enciclopaedia Classica* XII, part I), Turin 1959; W. L. MacDonald, *The Architecture of the Roman Empire*, New Haven–London 1965.

Radburn planning A planning idea conceived in the United States after the First World War by a group including Lewis Mumford, Clarence Stein, Henry Wright, and others. It was first tried out at Radburn, New Jersey. The main object of the plan is the complete segregation of traffic and pedestrians.

Areas known as superblocks are ringed by roads from which cul-de-sac service roads lead to the interior. All paths and walks linking the blocks with each other and the town centre pass over or under the roads. Examples of towns planned under some such system are Vällingby, near Stockholm, and Cumbernauld, one of the NEW TOWNS in Scotland.

Lit: L. Mumford, *The Culture of Cities*, New York 1938; C. Tunnard, *Man-Made America: Chaos or Control*, New Haven 1963.

Raguzzini, Filippo (d. 1771). The most original and spirited Rococo architect in Rome, where he built the hospital and church of S. Gallicano (1725–6) and Piazza di S. Ignazio (1727–8). The latter is a masterpiece of scenic town planning.

Lit: M. Rotili, *F. Raguzzini e il Rococo Romano*, Rome 1951.

Rainaldi, Carlo (1611–91), was born and lived in Rome. Son of a minor architect, **Girolamo Rainaldi** (1570–1655), he came into his own only after his father's death. He evolved a typically Roman grand manner notably for its lively scenic qualities and for its very personal mixture of Mannerist and North Italian features with the High Baroque style of his great contemporaries, especially BERNINI. With his father he began S. Agnese in Piazza Navona, Rome, on a conservative Greek cross plan in 1652, but was dismissed in the following year when BORROMINI took over the work. His principal buildings are all in Rome – S. Maria in Campitelli (1663–7); the façade of S. Andrea della Valle (1661–5); the exterior apse of S. Maria Maggiore (1673); and the artfully symmetrical pair of churches in Piazza del Popolo, S. Maria in Monte Santo and S. Maria de' Miracoli (1662 etc.), which punctuate the beginning of the three main streets radiating into the centre of the city (Bernini replaced him as architect of the former in 1673).

Lit: R. Wittkower, *Art and Architecture in Italy, 1600-1750*, Pelican History of Art, Harmondsworth 1973, paperback edn 1973.

Rainwater head A box-shaped structure of metal, usually cast iron or lead, and some-times elaborately decorated, in which water from a gutter or parapet is collected and dis-charged into a down-pipe.

Ramp 1. A slope joining two different levels. 2. Part of a staircase handrail which rises at a steeper angle than normal, usually where winders (*see* STAIR) are used.

Rampart A stone or earth wall surrounding a castle, fortress, or fortified city for defence purposes.

Ramsey, *see* WILLIAM OF RAMSEY.

Raphael (Raffaello Sanzio, 1483-1520). The greatest exponent of High Renaissance clas-sicism in architecture as well as in painting. His buildings are few, but they quickly took their place beside ancient Roman buildings and the late works of BRAMANTE as archi-tectural models. Though he owed much to Bramante, his style is sweeter, softer, and simpler. Born in Urbino, he was trained as a painter under Pietro Perugino at Perugia. An early painting of *The Betrothal of the Virgin* (1504, Brera Gallery, Milan) is dominated by a domed building, which reveals an exquisite sensitivity to architecture and a particular interest in centrally planned structures. In 1508 he settled in Rome, where he was almost immediately employed by Pope Julius II to paint the Stanza della Segnatura in the Vatican, including *The School of Athens* with its wonderful architectural perspective of coffered vaults. His first building was S. Eligio degli Orefici, Rome (designed *c.* 1511-12, construction begun 1514. The dome was begun, probably under PERUZZI, in 1526 and completed in 1542: but the whole church was rebuilt, with a new dome, by Flaminio PONZIO in the early C17). He designed the Palazzo Bresciano-Costa, Rome (*c.* 1515, now demolished) and Palazzo Pandolfini, Florence (*c.* 1517, but executed by Giovanni Francesco

Sangallo and, after 1530, by Aristotile Sangallo). These derive from Bramante's Palazzo Caprini with notable variations, e.g., unbroken horizontal lines of rustication on the basement, and at Palazzo Costa alternate triangular and segmental pediments above the windows on the first floor, between clusters of three pilasters. (Palazzo Vidoni-Caffarelli, Rome, of *c.* 1525 has often been attributed to Raphael but is not by him.)

In 1515 he was appointed Superintendent of Roman Antiquities and probably proposed a scheme (also attributed to Bramante) for measuring and drawing all the Roman re-mains and restoring a large number of them. The most notable result of his archaeological interests was the design for Villa Madama, Rome (begun 1517, but never completed), with a circular courtyard and numerous apsed and niched rooms inspired by the Roman *thermae*. The only part completed was decorated with exquisitely subtle stucco reliefs and GROTESQUE paintings by Giovanni da Udine and GIULIO ROMANO, derived from such Imperial Roman buildings as Nero's Golden House. Here Raphael re-created the elegance of Roman interior decoration as effectively as Bramante had reproduced the solemnity and monumental grandeur of Roman architecture. He was appointed archi-tect of St Peter's (1514) with Fra GIOCONDO and A. da SANGALLO, and drew up a basilican variant to Bramante's plan. His centrally plan-ned Chigi Chapel in S. Maria del Popolo, Rome, of 1512-13 was completed by BERNINI.

Lit: T. Hoffmann, *Raffael in seiner Bedeutung als Architekt*, Zittau 1904-14; J. Shearman, 'Raphael as Architect' in *Journal of Royal Society of Arts*, April 1968.

Rastrelli, Bartolommeo Francesco (1700-71), the leading Rococo architect in Russia, was the son of an Italian sculptor who went to St Petersburg with LE BLOND in 1716. He studied in Paris under de COTTE and his style is, with occasional Russian overtones, purely French. In 1741 he was appointed official architect to the Tsarina Elizabeth Petrovna, for whom all his main buildings were designed: Summer Palace, St Petersburg (1741-4, destroyed); Anichkov Palace on the Nevski Prospekt, St Petersburg (1744); Peterhof (1747-52), a colossal enlargement of Le Blond's building with lavish if slightly over-ripe Rococo decoration inside; the Cathedral of St Andrew, Kiev (1747-67); and the curious Russo-Rococo Smolny Convent, St Petersburg

(1748–55). His masterpieces are the Great Palace, Tsarskoe-Selo, now called Pushkino (1749–56), and the Winter Palace, St Petersburg (1754–62), both with immensely long façades, and both painted turquoise-blue, with white trim. But he is seen at his best in the delicate little pavilions he designed for Tsarskoe-Selo. He was an exquisite miniaturist, usually forced to work on a heroic scale. (For illustrations *see* LANTERN and RUSSIAN ARCHITECTURE.)

Lit: J. Denisov & A. Petrov, *B. F. Rastrelli*, Leningrad 1963.

Ravelin In military architecture, an outwork formed of two faces of a salient angle and constructed beyond the main ditch and in front of the CURTAIN WALL.

Raymond, Antonin, *see* JAPANESE ARCHITECTURE.

Raymond du Temple (active *c.* 1360–1405). Master of the King's Works in Masonry, and also master mason of Notre Dame in Paris. The king was godfather to his son.

Lit: Thieme-Becker, *Künstlerlexikon*, vol. XXXII, Leipzig 1938.

Rear arch The arch on the inside of a wall spanning a doorway or window opening.

Rear vault The small vaulted space between the glass of a window and the inner face of the wall, when the wall is thick and there is a deep SPLAY.

Rebate A continuous rectangular notch or groove cut on an edge, so that a plank, door, etc. may be fitted into it.

Redan A small RAVELIN.

Redman, Henry (d. 1528), was the son of the master mason of Westminster Abbey, and is first found working there in 1495. He succeeded his father at the Abbey in 1516 and also worked for the king, holding the post of King's Master Mason from 1519, jointly with William VERTUE, and in the end alone. He was called in with Vertue for an opinion at King's College Chapel, Cambridge, in 1509, and again appears with him at Eton for the design of Lupton's Tower in 1516. He was also Cardinal Wolsey's architect, and may have designed Hampton Court. At Christ Church, Oxford (Cardinal College), he was, jointly with John Lebons or Lovyns, in charge from the beginning (1525).

Lit: G. Webb, *Architecture in Britain, The Middle Ages*, Pelican History of Art, Harmondsworth 1965.

Reeding Decoration consisting of parallel convex mouldings touching one another.

Reginald of Ely (d. 1471). First master mason, and so probably the designer, of King's College Chapel, Cambridge (begun 1446). However, his design did not include the present fan vaulting; it seems that he intended a lierne vault (*see* VAULT). Reginald in all probability designed Queens' College too (1446 etc.), and perhaps the archway of the Old Schools (begun 1470), now at Madingley Hall.

Lit: J. Harvey, *English Medieval Architects*, London 1958.

Regulus The short band between the TENIA and GUTTAE on a Doric ENTABLATURE.

Reidy, Affonso, *see* BRAZILIAN ARCHITECTURE.

Reinforced concrete Since concrete is strong in compression and weak in tension, steel rods are inserted to take the tensile stresses which, in a simple beam, occur in the lower part; the concrete is thus reinforced.

Renaissance The Italian word *rinascimento* (rebirth) was already used by Renaissance writers themselves to indicate the restoration of ancient Roman standards and motifs.

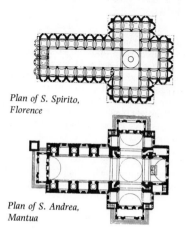

Plan of S. Spirito, Florence

Plan of S. Andrea, Mantua

S. Francesco (Tempio Malatestiano), Rimini,
begun 1450, by Alberti

Sant'Andrea, Mantua, begun 1470,
by Alberti

S. Spirito, Florence, begun 1436,
by Brunelleschi

S. Maria della Consolazione, Todi, 1508–1607

Today the term means Italian art and architecture from c. 1420 (BRUNELLESCHI) to the early C16. It was replaced by MANNERISM and BAROQUE, though the old mistaken custom is still occasionally found of extending Renaissance to include the Baroque. In countries other than Italy the Renaissance started with the adoption of Italian Renaissance motifs, but the resulting styles – French Renaissance, German Renaissance, etc. – have little in common with the qualities of the Italian Renaissance, which are details of ancient Roman derivation and a sense of stability and poise. See also CLASSICISM, and BELGIAN, CZECHOSLOVAK, DUTCH, FRENCH, GERMAN, HUNGARIAN, ITALIAN, POLISH, RUSSIAN, SPANISH and SWISS ARCHITECTURE.

Palazzo Riario (Cancelleria), Rome,
1486–1511. After an engraving by Specchi

Cloister of S. Maria della Pace, Rome, 1504, by Bramante

Rendering The plastering of an outer wall.

Rennie, John (1761–1821), son of a farmer, was trained by an inventive millwright and then at Edinburgh University. In 1784 he was put in charge of installing the new Boulton & Watt steam engine at the Albion Works in London. In 1791 he set up in business on his own. He was first interested in canals (Kennet and Avon), later also in fen drainage, harbours and docks, lighthouses, and also bridges. He designed the Plymouth Breakwater (begun 1806) and Waterloo Bridge (1810), as well as other London bridges. His sons **George** (1791–1866) and **Sir John** (1794–1874) were both famous engineers too.

Lit: C. T. G. Boucher, *John Rennie, 1761–1821: The Life and Work of a Great Engineer,* Manchester 1963.

Renwick, James (1818–95), the son of an English engineer who emigrated to America and became the most prominent man in his field in the United States, graduated at Columbia College, New York, and became famous as an architect of churches (Grace Church, Broadway, 1843 etc., St Patrick's Cathedral, 1853–87). His other best-known buildings are the sweetly picturesque neo-Norman Smithsonian Institution in Washington (1846), and Vassar College, an essay in a free Renaissance mixture (1865).

Lit: R. T. McKenna, 'James Renwick Jr and the Second Empire Style' in *Magazine of Art,* March 1951.

Repton, Humphry (1752–1818), the leading English landscape gardener of the generation after BROWN, was a contemporary of PRICE and KNIGHT, with whose defence of wildness and ruggedness, however, he did not agree. The innovation of his layouts, an innovation which pointed forward into the C19, is the treatment of the garden close to the house not naturally and picturesquely, but formally with parterres and terraces, to which in his late work he added such 'Victorian' motifs as rose-arbours, aviaries etc. He also was responsible for a certain amount of architectural work though this was mostly left to his sons **John Adey** (1775–1860) and **George** (1786–1858). Repton had lived as a country gentleman until a financial setback forced him to make a living out of his passion for gardening. He was at once successful, and the total of parks and gardens treated by him is in the neighbourhood of two hundred. He wrote *Sketches and Hints on Landscape Gardening* in 1795, *Observations on the Theory and Practice of Landscape Gardening* in 1803, *An Inquiry into the Changes of Taste in Landscape Gardening* in 1806, and *Fragments on the Theory and Practice of Landscape Gardening* in 1816. The term 'landscape gardening' is his. (For illustration *see* ORANGERY.)

Lit: D. Stroud, *H. Repton,* London 1962.

Reredos A wall or screen, usually of wood or stone, rising behind an altar, and as a rule decorated.

Respond A half-PIER bonded into a wall and carrying one end of an arch; often at the end of an ARCADE.

Retable (Latin, *retabulum* = rear wall). A superstructure, found since the C11, either placed upon the rear of the mensa (*see* ALTAR), or on its own pedestal behind the altar. The former was favoured in the Middle Ages, and the latter in the Renaissance and Baroque. Romanesque retables were of stone or stucco (with reliefs), metal (repoussé or enamelled), or wood (painted), and had a straight or semicircular termination, or a semicircular termination to the middle portion only. From the painted retable developed, especially in Central Europe, those with a fixed central shrine of wood or stone and a pair of (triptych), or several (polyptych) movable wooden wings with carved or painted images. With the C15 the retable came to stand upon a *predella,* a base about a third the height of the shrine, so that the wings could be moved without having to clear the mensa. Late Gothic retables sprouted their own architectural framing of

Retable: Gothic winged altarpiece, St Sigmund, Pustertal, c. 1430

Revetment, *see* RETAINING WALL.

Reyns, *see* HENRY OF REYNS.

Rib A projecting band on a ceiling or vault, usually structural but sometimes purely decorative, separating the CELLS of a groined VAULT.

Arco del Vescovo, Rieti, 1298

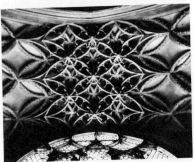

Flying ribs: Frauenkirche, Ingolstadt, 1509–24

pillars, gables and pinnacles. From the C16 onwards, culminating in the Baroque, the fixed retable usual in Italy also prevailed in Central Europe and notably in Spain – wings being renounced, and the altarpiece receiving an architectural frame in the form of an AEDICULA peopled by statues. South German Rococo strove to achieve the incorporation of the retable into a decorative schema embracing the whole church (*see* the ASAM church in Munich).

Retaining wall A wall, usually battered, which supports or retains a weight of earth or water; also called a *revetment*.

Reticulated, *see* TRACERY.

Retrochoir The space behind the high altar in a major church.

Return The side or part which falls away, usually at right angles, from the front or direct line of a structure. Two particular uses of the term are: *a.* that part of a dripstone or HOOD-MOULD which, after running downwards, turns off horizontally; *b.* the western row of choir stalls which runs north–south, set against the screen at the west end of the choir.

Reveal That part of a JAMB which lies between the glass or door and the outer wall surface. If out diagonally, it is called a SPLAY.

Ribbon development The construction of continuous strings of houses along main roads. This was responsible for much spoliation of the English countryside during the first quarter of this century, but was largely halted by the passing of the Ribbon Development Act of 1935.

Ribera, Pedro de (*c.* 1683–1742), the leading Late Baroque architect in Madrid, carried the CHURRIGUERESQUE style to its ultimate point of elaboration. In the neo-classical period he was held up for derision by one authority, who published a complete list of his buildings as an object lesson to students, with the result that his *œuvre* is unusually well documented. Of Castilian origin, he began working for the city council of Madrid in 1719, and became its official architect in 1726. With the exception of the tower of Salamanca Cathedral (*c.* 1738) and a chapel attached to S. Antonio, Ávila (1731), all his buildings are in Madrid. His most celebrated work is the doorway to the Hospicio S. Fernando (*c.* 1722), an overpowering extravaganza of boldly and somewhat coarsely carved draperies, festoons, top-heavy *estípites*, urns, and flames rising in staccato leaps above the roof-line. In 1718 he built the little church of the Virgen del Puerto, which has an exterior like a garden pavilion, with a picturesque bell-shaped spire, and an octagonal interior with a *camarín* behind the altar. Other works include the Toledo Bridge (designed 1719, built 1723–4), with elaborately carved tabernacles perched above the arches; the Montserrat Church (1720, incomplete); and S. Cayetano (1722–32, incomplete).

Lit: G. Kubler, *Arquitectura española, 1600–1800* (*Ars Hispaniae*, vol. XIV), Madrid 1957; G. Kubler & M. Soria, *Art and Architecture in Spain and Portugal and their American Dominions, 1500–1800*, Pelican History of Art, Harmondsworth 1959.

Ricchino, Francesco Maria (1583–1658). The most important Lombard architect of the early Baroque. His S. Giuseppe in Milan (1607–30) broke away from the prevailing academic Mannerism as decisively as did MADERNO'S S. Susanna in Rome (1603). Both in its plan (a fusion of two centralized units) and in its aedicule façade S. Giuseppe is entirely forward-looking. Nearly all his later churches have been destroyed. Of his surviving works the best are the concave façades of the Collegio Elvetico, Milan (1627), and the Palazzo di Brera, Milan (1651–86), with its noble courtyard. His vast central cortile of the Ospedale Maggiore, Milan, was designed with G.-B. Pessina (1625–49, restored 1950s).

Lit: P. Mezzanotte in *Storia di Milano*, vol. XI, Milan 1958; E. Cataneo, *Il San Giuseppe del Ricchino*, Milan 1957.

Richardson, Henry Hobson (1838–86), studied at Harvard, and then studied architecture at the École des Beaux Arts in Paris (1859–62), where, after the Civil War, he returned to work under LABROUSTE and then HITTORF. Back at Boston he started a practice, and in 1870 won the competition for the Brattle Square Church, in 1872 that for Trinity Church. These established him as an original, and at the same time a learned, architect. His favourite style was a very massive, masculine Romanesque, inspired by architects such as VAUDREMER. But the tower of the Brattle Square Church, with its frieze of figures right below the machicolated top, is Romanesque only in so far as it is round-arched. In 1882 Richardson travelled in Europe, and only then saw French and North-Spanish Romanesque buildings at first hand. The Romanesque suited him as a style: it was direct and powerful, and thus capable of fulfilling American requirements. Rockfaced rustication was also a favourite with him. In fact, he was always attracted by utilitarian jobs. The most monumental of these is the Marshall Field Wholesale Building in Chicago (1885). He also designed small railway stations in the eighties. Before then he had done some small libraries (North Easton, 1877; Quincy, 1880), two buildings for Harvard (Sever Hall, 1878, which is remarkably independent of any stylistic imitation; Austin Hall, 1881, which is Romanesque), and also some private houses (the shingle-faced, very original and forward-pointing Stoughton House at Cambridge, 1882–3; the Glessner House at Chicago, 1885). Richardson was a *bon vivant*, a designer of zest and conviction. His Romanesque was soon widely imitated – to its detriment – but helped greatly in liberating America from the indiscriminate imitation of European revivals. Among his pupils were MCKIM and WHITE, and he also influenced ROOT and SULLIVAN decisively. (For illustrations *see* SHINGLE STYLE, UNITED STATES ARCHITECTURE.)

Lit: H.-R. Hitchcock, *The Architecture of H. H. Richardson and his Times*, New York 1961.

Rickman, Thomas (1776–1841), moved late from medicine and business into architecture. From sketching and writing about old churches he went on to open a practice as an architect. This was in 1817, the year in which he also published some lectures under the title *An Attempt to discriminate the Styles of Architecture in England*. This little book established our terms Early English, Decorated, and Perpendicular. As a church architect Rickman could be remarkably conscientious in trying to create credible Gothic interiors. Such churches as those at Hampton Lucy (1822–6) and Oulton (1827–9) must have struck his contemporaries as archaeologically convincing. They were done in partnership with **Henry Hutchinson**, his former pupil (1831), who was also largely responsible for Rickman's most familiar building: New Court, St John's College, Cambridge (1826–31), with the attached so-called Bridge of Sighs. Rickman was a Quaker, but late in life turned Irvingite.

Lit: A. Jones, 'Rickman and the Fitzwilliam competition' in *Architectural Review*, 1957

Ridge The horizontal line formed by the junction of two sloping surfaces of a roof. (For illustration *see* ROOF.)

Ridge-rib, *see* VAULT.

Ridinger or **Riedinger, Georg** (1568–after 1616). Leading German Renaissance architect, a contemporary of Elias HOLL, Heinrich SCHICKHARDT and Jacob WOLFF. His masterpiece was Schloss Aschaffenburg (1605–14, destroyed but rebuilt) built for the Archbishop of Mainz, Ulrich von Gemmingen (the patron of Matthias Grünewald) and his successor Johann Schickard von Kronberg. The square ground-plan of four wings and corner towers round a central courtyard was probably derived from French château design through Du CERCEAU's engravings. Though still rather medieval and fortress-like, the elevations were articulated with strong horizontal mouldings and occasional Netherlandish ornamentation. Ridinger thought it 'heroic'. It had great and long-lasting influence in Germany, e.g., on Petrini's (1624–1701) Marquardsburg of almost a hundred years later. (For illustration *see* GERMAN ARCHITECTURE.)

Rieth (or **Ried**) of Piesting, Benedikt (*c.* 1454–1534). The most important architect and vaulting engineer of the Dürer period and the creator of the three-dimensionally curved rib. In 1518 he presided over the stonemasons' chapter at Annaberg. Springing from the Austro-Bavarian guild tradition, the formative influences on him came from Nuremberg, the scene of activity of his immediate precursors in vaulting techniques (former Augustinian church 1479–84, the Ebracher Hof 1489), who in their turn had drawn on English VAULT construction. In 1489 he was summoned to Prague by King Vladislav II, where he was at first engaged as fortifications expert (ramparts of Prague Castle), without making any significant advances.

In 1490–93 he built the Organ Gallery in the Cathedral of St Vitus, Prague; vaulted beneath with a large PENDANT, with ribs and TRACERY interpreted as branches and foliage, in an extreme manifestation of Late Gothic naturalism.

The vast Vladislav Hall in Prague Castle (1493–1502) is the most impressive Gothic interior north of the Alps. It has a lierne VAULT with remarkable curving ribs. However, the exterior detailing (doors and windows) of the Hall, like the Ludwig wing erected at right angles to it in 1500–09, already employs Renaissance features picked up by Rieth from the Hungarian palaces of his royal master. There is also documentary evidence for his participation in improvements to the Castles of Schwihau (1504–5) and Blatná (1530) in Bohemia. With the quadrangular layout of Schloss Frankenstein in Silesia (1514–30), he completed the transition from the irregular, defensible castle of the Middle Ages to the symmetrical showpiece of later times.

The most important of Rieth's religious buildings is the HALL-CHURCH nave of St Barbara, Kutná Hora, begun by the PARLERS as a cathedral in 1388. For this he devised what must be the most exquisite lierne vault of the time (only executed after his death by his foreman Nikolaus, 1540–48). His last work, and also his burial-place, was the City Church of Laun, a hall-church with octagonal pillars and a three-APSED choir in the Parler tradition. But here the ribs of the lierne vault are broken off and devoid of tension, the pattern is fragmented and movement absent. The exteriors of his naves are characterized by the use of a row of spiky tent-roofs, instead of the huge saddleback roofs usual over hall-churches.

Rieth and his pupils represent the culmination of more than a century of exploitation of the lierne vault in Central Europe, as initiated by Peter Parler. Rieth's strikingly early adoption of Renaissance details is of secondary importance by comparison with this. (For illustration *see* CZECHOSLOVAK ARCHITECTURE.)

Lit: G. Fehr, *Benedikt Rieth*, Munich 1961; W. Schadendorf, *Benedikt Rieth und seine Bedeutung, Zeitschrift für Ostforschung*, vol. II, 1962.

Rietveld, Gerrit Thomas (1888–1964), was the son of a joiner to whom he was apprenticed. He was later in the cabinet-making business. He came into contact with De Stijl in 1919. His most famous design for a build-ing is the Schroeder House at Utrecht (1924). With the growth of rationalism in architec-ture he was eclipsed, but once more received work when, in the fifties, the style of the twenties began to be revived. (For illustration *see* DUTCH ARCHITECTURE.)

Lit: T. M. Brown, *The Work of G. Rietveld, Architect*, Cambridge, Mass., 1970; *G. Riet-veld, Architect*, Exh. Cat., Hayward Gallery, London 1971-2.

Rinaldi, Antonio (*c.* 1709-94). One of the leading Late Rococo architects in Russia. His main works are the Chinese Palace, Oranien-baum (1762-8), with a pretty CHINOISERIE interior, and the Marble Palace, Leningrad (1768-72), derived from JUVARRA's Palazzo d'Ormea, but rather more austere and classical, faced with red granite and grey Siberian marble. It is of interest also as the first ever example of the use of iron beams in architecture.

Lit: G. H. Hamilton, *The Art and Architecture of Russia*, Pelican History of Art, Harmonds-worth 1954.

Rinceau An ornamental motif consisting of scrolls of foliage.

Rise Of an arch or vault, the vertical distance between the SOFFIT at the crown and the level of the SPRINGING LINE.

Riser, *see* STAIR.

Robert de Luzarches The master mason who began Amiens Cathedral in 1220.

Lit: G. Durand, *Monographie de la cathédrale d'Amiens*, Amiens & Paris, 1901.

Rococo architecture The Rococo is not a style in its own right, like the BAROQUE, but the last phase of the Baroque. The great breaks in European art and thought take place at the beginning of the Baroque and again at the beginning of NEO-CLASSICISM. The Rococo is chiefly represented by a type of decoration initiated in France, by lightness in colour and weight, where the Baroque had been dark and ponderous, and, in South Germany and Austria, by a great spatial complexity, which, however, is the direct continuation of the Baroque complexity of BORROMINI and GUARINI. The new decoration is often asym-metrical and abstract – the term for this is *rocaille* – with shell-like, coral-like forms and many c- and s-curves. Naturalistic flowers,

Rocaille decoration

Rococo: Hôtel de Soubise, Salon de la Princesse, Paris, 1736-9, by Boffrand

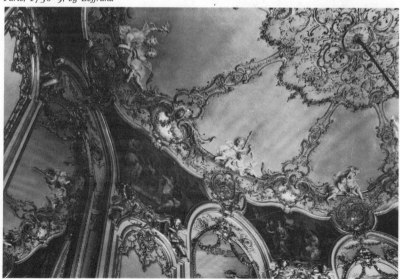

Wieskirche, Bavaria, 1745–54,
by Zimmermann

Vierzehnheiligen, near Banz, 1743–72,
by Neumann

branches, trees, whole rustic scenes, and also
Chinese motifs are sometimes playfully introduced into *rocaille*. In French external
architecture the Rococo is only noticeable by

a greater elegance and delicacy. England has
no Rococo, apart from occasional interiors.
But the playful use of Chinese, Indian, and also
Gothic forms in garden furnishings can well
be ascribed to Rococo influence.

Lit: F. Kimball, *The Creation of the Rococo,*
Philadelphia 1943, revised as *Le Style Louis
XV,* Paris 1949.

Rodríguez, Ventura (1717–85), the leading
Spanish Late Baroque architect, began under
SACCHETTI at the Royal Palace, Madrid, and
was employed by the Crown until 1759. His
first important work was the Church of S.
Marcos, Madrid (1749–53), built on an oval
plan derived from BERNINI'S S. Andrea al
Quirinale, Rome. In 1753 he built the Tras-
parente in Cuenca Cathedral. In 1760 he
became professor at the Madrid academy and
his work began to assume a more dogmatic
appearance. The Royal College of Surgery,
Barcelona (1761), is almost gaunt in its
severe renunciation of ornament. His noblest
work is the façade of Pamplona Cathedral
(1783), with a great Corinthian portico
flanked by square towers, archaeologically
correct in detail yet still reminiscent of early
C18 Rome.

Lit: L. Pulido & T. Diaz, *Biografía de don
Ventura Rodrigues,* Madrid 1898; G. Kubler,
Arquitectura española, 1600–1800 (*Ars His-
paniae,* vol. XIV), Madrid 1957; G. Kubler &
M. Soria, *Art and Architecture in Spain and
Portugal and their American Dominions, 1500–
1800,* Pelican History of Art, Harmondsworth
1959.

Roebling, John A., *see* BRIDGE.

Roll moulding Moulding of semicircular or
more than semicircular section.

Roman architecture Whereas GREEK ARCHI-
TECTURE is tectonic, built up from a logical
series of horizontals and verticals (the Doric
temple has been called 'sublimated carpentry'), Roman architecture is plastic with much
use of rounded forms (arch, vault, and dome),
so that buildings tend to look as if they had
been made of concrete poured into a mould.
In Greek and HELLENISTIC ARCHITECTURE
the column was the most important member;
in Rome the column was frequently degraded
to merely decorative uses, while the wall became the essential element. Hence the Roman
predilection for the PSEUDO-PERIPTERAL
temple (Temple of Male Fortune, Rome, mid

Maison Carrée, Nîmes, begun c. 19 B.C.

and in the palace buildings by RABIRIUS for Domitian on the Palatine in Rome (late CI A.D.). Later vaulted buildings of importance include the Baths of Caracalla (c. A.D. 215), Baths of Diocletian (A.D. 306), and the Basilica Nova of Maxentius (A.D. 310–13), all in Rome.

Roman architecture reached its apogee in the Pantheon, Rome (c. A.D. 100–25, with a dome 141 ft in diameter), which is both a feat of engineering and a masterpiece of simple yet highly satisfying proportions – it is based on a sphere, the height of the walls being equal to the radius of the dome. Comparison of the Pantheon with the Parthenon reveals the

CI B.C.; Maison Carrée, Nîmes, begun c. 19 B.C.), for the Corinthian ORDER, and for elaborately carved ENTABLATURES and other ornamentation. It was the development of concrete used in conjunction with brick that made possible the construction of the great Roman domes and vaults. Concrete proved as

The Pantheon, Rome

Cryptoporticus, the Forum, Arles, late CI B.C.

The Pantheon, interior, 27 B.C.–A.D. 120–24

economical of material as of labour, since the masons' rubble could be used for filling. Surfaces were either stuccoed or clad in marble. The earliest concrete dome is of the C2 B.C. (Stabian Baths, Pompeii), while the earliest large-scale concrete vault is that of the Tabularium in Rome of 78 B.C., where the half-columns are used ornamentally – the first important instance of the divorce of decoration and function. The concrete barrel vault on a large scale appears in Nero's Golden House, Rome, by the architect SEVERUS (mid CI A.D.)

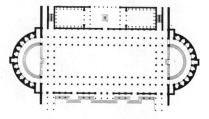

Plan of Basilica of Trajan, Rome, early C2, by Apollodorus

Arch of Constantine, Rome, A.D. *315*

contrast between the tectonic and extrovert nature of Greek and the plastic, introvert nature of Roman architecture. This is equally evident in the most typically Roman of all buildings, the BASILICA, which, with its interior colonnades, is like a Greek temple turned outside in. Other typically Roman buildings are: THERMAE, with their rich decoration and complicated spatial play; AMPHITHEATRES, of which the Colosseum, Rome (A.D. 72–80) is the largest; TRIUMPHAL ARCHES, a purely decorative type of building of which the earliest recorded examples were temporary structures of the C2 B.C. Always of the Corinthian or Composite Order, these arches vary from the relative severity of that at Susa near Turin to

Colosseum, Rome, 72–80

the elaboration of that at Orange in the south of France (*c.* 30 B.C.). City gateways were hardly less profusely decorated, e.g., Porta Nigra at Trier (late c3 or early c4 A.D.).

In domestic architecture three types were developed; the *domus* or town-house; the *insula* or multi-storey apartment house or tenement block; and the *villa* or suburban or country house. The *domus* derived from the Greek and Hellenistic house and was usually of one storey only and inward-looking, the rooms being grouped axially and symmetrically around an atrium and one or more peristyle courts. The street façade was plain and without windows, or was let off as shops, as can still be seen at Pompeii. The *insula* had

symmetrically along arcaded streets and round public squares. The *villa* derived from the traditional farm-house and was more casual and straggling in plan than the *domus*. It was also more outward-looking, and great variety in planning and room shapes was attained in the more luxurious examples. The exteriors were enlivened with porticos and colonnades, rooms were designed to catch the view, or the sun in winter or the shade in summer, as at Pliny's villa at Laurentum.

Hadrian's fantastic sprawling villa at Tivoli (*c.* A.D. 123) illustrates almost the whole range of Imperial Roman architecture at its sophisticated best. Indeed it is perhaps over-sophisticated already. The last great architec-

Villa dei Misteri, Pompeii, C2 B.C.

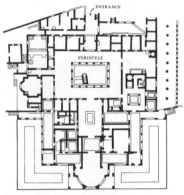

Incised plan of Rome, showing insulae, C2 *or* C3

several identical but separate floors and was often vaulted throughout with concrete construction. A decree of Augustus limited their height in Rome to 75 ft. During the Neronian rebuilding of Rome after the fire of A.D. 64 new quarters of *insulae* were laid out

Hadrian's Villa, Tivoli, c. 123–135

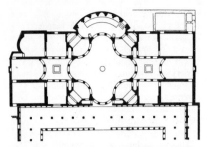

Plan of Nymphaeum, Hadrian's Villa at Tivoli

tural monument of the Roman Empire is Diocletian's Palace at Split in Yugoslavia (c. A.D. 300), built after the Pax Romana had begun to disintegrate. Yet even here the Roman genius for experimentation was still at work. Certain decorative elements, e.g., engaged columns standing on isolated corbels, anticipate the language of BYZANTINE ARCHITECTURE.

Lit: D. S. Robertson, *A Handbook of Greek and Roman Architecture*, Cambridge 1943; W. L. MacDonald, *The Architecture of the Roman Empire*, New Haven–London 1965; A. Boëthius & J. B. Ward-Perkins, *Etruscan and Roman Architecture*, Pelican History of Art, Harmondsworth 1970.

Romanesque architecture The style current until the advent of GOTHIC. Some experts place its origins in the c7, others in the c10: the former view includes CAROLINGIAN in Romanesque architecture, the latter places the beginning of Romanesque at the time of the rising of the Cluniac Order in France and the Ottonian Empire in Germany. The first view also includes Anglo-Saxon architecture, the second identifies the Romanesque in Britain with the Norman.

The Romanesque in the Northern countries is the style of the round arch. It is also characterized by clear, easily comprehended schemes of planning and elevation, the plan with staggered apses (*en échelon*) at the east end of

Plan of S. Maria,
Ripoll (Catalonia), c. 1020–32

churches, the plan with an ambulatory and radiating chapels, plans (mainly in Germany) with square bays in nave, transepts, and chancel, and square bays in the aisles one quarter the area. The compositions of the

Santiago de Compostela, begun 1075

Notre Dame, Paray-le-Monial, c12

Main Portal, La Madeleine, Vézelay

La Madeleine, Vézelay, early CI2

walls also stress clearly marked compartments, e.g., in the shafts which in Norman
churches run from the ground right up to the
ceiling beams.

The Early Romanesque had not yet the skill
to vault major spans. Experiments began
about 1000, but remained rare till after 1050.
Then various systems were developed which

differentiate regional groups: tunnel vaults in
France, often pointed (Burgundy, Provence),
and also in Spain; groin vaults in Germany;
domes in the South-west of France; rib vaults
at Durham and in Italy. The spread of the rib
vault and the pointed vault, however, is
usually a sign of the approaching Gothic style.
In the exteriors the two-tower façade plus a

Worms Cathedral, CI I *(the round towers)*
to early CI3

tower over the crossing is most typical of
England and Normandy, whereas screen
façades with no towers are characteristic of
the South of France, and a multitude of towers
over the west as well as the east parts is
typical of Germany. *See also* ENGLISH, GER-
MAN, ITALIAN and SPANISH ARCHITECTURE.

Lit: R. de Lasteyrie, *L'architecture religieuse
en France à l'époque romane*, Paris 1929; A. W.
Clapham, *Romanesque Architecture in Western
Europe*, Oxford 1936; K. J. Conant, *Carolingian
and Romanesque Architecture, 800–1200*, Pelican History of Art, 2nd edn, Harmondsworth
1974, paperback edn 1974.

Romano, *see* GIULIO ROMANO.

Rood Originally the Saxon word for a cross
or crucifix. In churches this was set up at the
east end of the nave, flanked by figures of the
Virgin and St John. It was usually wooden,
and fixed to a special beam stretching from
RESPOND to respond of the CHANCEL ARCH,
above the ROOD LOFT. Sometimes the rood is
painted on the wall above the chancel arch.

Rood loft A gallery built above the ROOD
SCREEN, often to carry the ROOD or other

images and candles; approached by stairs
either of wood or built in the wall. Rood lofts
were introduced in the CI5, and many were
destroyed in the Reformation.

Rood screen A screen below the ROOD, set
across the east end of the nave and shutting
off the chancel. *See also* PULPITUM.

*Rood screen in Lauterbach Church,
near Offenburg, late* CI5

Roof
  Elements:
    Braces. Diagonal subsidiary timbers in-
serted to strengthen the framing of a roof.
They can be straight or arched (the arched
brace is a refined version of the CRUCK), and
connect either a tie-beam with the wall below,
or a collar-beam with the rafters below.
    Collar-beam. A tie-beam applied higher
up the slope of the roof.
    Crown-post. A post standing on a tie-
beam and supporting a collar-purlin running
immediately under the collar-beam of a rafter
roof. Frequently four braces or struts spring
from the crown-post to the collar-purlin and
the collar-beam.
    Hammerbeam. A horizontal bracket, usu-
ally projecting at the wall plate level, to carry
arched braces and struts, and supported by
braces. Hammerbeams lessen the span and
thus allow shorter timbers. They also help to
reduce lateral pressure.
    King-post. A post standing on a tie- or
collar-beam and rising to the apex of the roof
where it supports a ridge-piece.
    Principals. The main rafters of a roof,
usually corresponding to the main bay divisions of the space below.
    Purlin. A horizontal timber laid parallel
with the wall plate and the ridge beam some
way up the slope of the roof, resting on the
principal rafters and forming an intermediate
support for the common rafters.

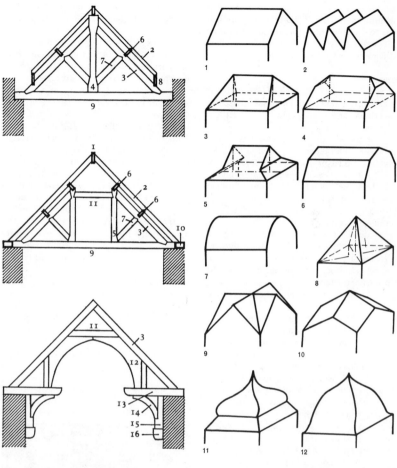

Roof elements:

1. Ridge
2. Common rafter
3. Principal rafter
4. King-post
5. Queen-post
6. Purlin
7. Strut
8. Sole plate
9. Tie-beam
10. Wall plate
11. Collar-beam
12. Arched brace
13. Hammerbeam
14. Brace
15. Wall post
16. Corbel

Roof types:

1. Saddleback
2. Saw
3. Hipped
4. Half-hipped
5. Gambrel
6. Mansard
7. Wagon
8. Pyramid
9. Cross
10. Helm
11. Onion-dome
12. Bell

Queen-posts. A pair of upright posts placed symmetrically on a tie-beam (or collar-beam), connecting it with the rafters above.

Rafter or *common rafter.* A roof timber sloping up from the wall plate to the RIDGE.

Strut. A timber, either upright, connecting the tie-beam with the rafter above it, or sloping, connecting a king- or queen-post to the rafter.

Tie-beam. The horizontal transverse beam in a roof, connecting the feet of the rafters, usually at the height of the wall plate, to counteract the thrust.

Wall plate. A timber laid longitudinally on the top of a wall to receive the ends of the rafters.

Wind-braces. Short, usually arched, braces connecting the purlins with the principal rafter and the wall plate, and fixed flat against the rafters. Wind-braces strengthen the roof area by increasing resistance to wind pressure. They are often made to look decorative by foiling and cusping.

Types:

A *Belfast* or *bowstring roof* is constructed with curved timber trusses and horizontal tie-beams, connected by light diagonal lattices of wood.

A *coupled* roof is constructed without ties or collars, the rafters being fixed to the wall plates and ridge pieces.

A roof is *double-framed* if longitudinal members (such as a ridge beam and purlins) are used. Generally the rafters are divided into stronger ones called principals and weaker subsidiary rafters.

A *gambrel roof* terminates in a small gable at the ridge; in America the name is given to a roof with a double pitch like a *mansard* roof.

A *helm roof* has four inclined faces joined at the top, with a gable at the foot of each.

A *hipped roof* has sloped instead of vertical ends.

A *lean-to roof* has one slope only and is built against a higher wall.

A *mansard roof* has a double slope, the lower being longer and steeper than the upper; named after François MANSART.

A *saddleback roof* is a normal pitched roof. The term is most usual for roofs of towers.

In a *wagon roof*, by closely set rafters with arched braces, the appearance of the inside of a canvas over a wagon is achieved. Wagon roofs can be panelled or plastered (ceiled), or left uncovered. Also called a *cradle roof.*
See also HYPERBOLIC PARABOLOID ROOF.

Root, John Wellborn (1850–91), was born in Georgia, went to school near Liverpool and studied at Oxford. He then took an engineering degree at the University of New York. In 1871 he went to live at Chicago. There he met BURNHAM and went into partnership with him, a suitable partnership to which Burnham contributed his organizational acumen and interest in planning, Root his resourcefulness and his aesthetic accomplishments, which included not only drawing but also music. On the work of the partnership *see* BURNHAM.
Lit: The Meanings of Architecture: Buildings and Writings by John Wellborn Root (ed. D. Hoffmann), New York 1967; D. Hoffmann, *The Architecture of John Wellborn Root*, Baltimore 1973.

Roriczer (or **Roritzer**) A family of C15 German masons, master masons of Regensburg Cathedral for three generations. **Wenzel** died in 1419. His style was so clearly influenced by Prague and the PARLERS that he must have been trained in their lodge. The surviving drawing of the west front of the cathedral may be his, **Konrad**, his son, is mentioned as master mason to the cathedral in 1456 and 1474. Concurrently, he had the same job at St Lorenz in Nuremberg (*see* HEINZELMANN) from *c.* 1455 onwards. At Regensburg he probably designed the triangular porch. He was consulted for St Stefan in Vienna in 1462, and for the Frauenkirche in Munich in 1475. He must have died *c.* 1475. His son **Matthäus** was Konrad's second-in-command at Nuremberg from 1462 to 1466. He wrote an important small book on how to set out Gothic finials (published 1486), was also master mason of Regensburg Cathedral, and died shortly before 1495, whereupon his brother **Wolfgang** was appointed his successor. Wolfgang was executed for political reasons in 1514. (For illustration *see* GERMAN ARCHITECTURE.)
Lit: P. Frankl, The Gothic: Literary Sources and Interpretations through Eight Centuries, Princeton 1960; P. Frankl, *Gothic Architecture,* Pelican History of Art, Harmondsworth 1962.

Rose window (or **wheel window**) A circular window with FOILS or patterned TRACERY arranged like the spokes of a wheel.

Rose window: S. Maria Maggiore, Tuscania, C12

Rosette A rose-shaped PATERA. (Illustrated next column.)

Rossellino, Bernardo (1409–64), was primarily a sculptor. As an architect he began

Rosettes: Baal-Schamin Temple, Palmyra, 131

by completing the façade of the Misericordia at Arezzo and in 1433 designed the chapel of the Sacrament in the Vatican (destroyed). He was in Rome 1450–59 and knew ALBERTI there, and carried out his designs for Palazzo Rucellai, Florence, and his restoration and alterations to S. Stefano Rotondo, Rome. In 1451 he was appointed architect to Pope Nicholas V, for whom he designed the east end of a completely new St Peter's (never completed). His chief works are the palace and cathedral at Pienza (1460–3), commissioned by Pope Pius II (Piccolomini). The former is a heavier and much less subtle version of Palazzo Rucellai, the latter a not unattractive cross between Alberti's Tempio Malatestiano, Rimini, and S. Maria Novella, Florence.

Lit: M. Tysskiewiezowa, *Bernardo Rossellino*, Florence 1928; E. Carli, *Pienza, la città di Pio II*, Rome 1967.

Rossetti, Biagio (*c.* 1447–1516). Architect and town-planner, he was responsible for the expansion of Ferrara under Duke Ercole I by a planned extension to the north on a site enclosed by a wall – the Addizione Erculea. It is the most important piece of systematic Renaissance town-planning in Italy, and contains four churches and eight palaces by Rossetti. He is first recorded working at Palazzo Schifanoia, Ferrara, under Pietro Benvenuti (d. 1483) whom he succeeded as ducal architect. In 1492 he began work on the Addizione Erculea. His most important building is the Palazzo dei Diamanti (after 1498) but the Casa Rossetti and the Palazzi Bevilacqua and Rondinelli in Piazza Nuova (1490s) are very accomplished too. His Palazzo di Lodovico Moro is *c.* 1500. S. Francesco and S. Cristoforo are the best preserved of his four churches, S. Maria in Vado and S. Benedetto being much altered or damaged.

Lit: B. Zevi, *Biagio Rossetti*, Turin 1960.

Rossi, Giovanni Antonio de' (1616–95). A prolific Roman High Baroque architect. His most important work is in the domestic field, e.g., the grandiose Palazzo Altieri, Rome (1650–4 and 1670–6), and the smaller, more elegant Palazzo Asti-Bonaparte, Rome (*c.* 1665), which set a pattern for C18 architects in Rome. In his ecclesiastical work he showed a preference for oval plans and lavish sculptural decoration. His Cappella Lancellotti in S. Giovanni in Laterano, Rome (*c.* 1680), and S. Maria in Campo Marzo, Rome (1676–86), are minor masterpieces of Roman High Baroque.

Lit: G. Spagnesi, *G. A. de Rossi*, Rome 1964; R. Wittkower, *Art and Architecture in Italy, 1600–1750*, Pelican History of Art, Harmondsworth 1973, paperback edn 1973.

Rossi, Karl Ivanovich (1775–1849). The leading architect in post-1815 St Petersburg where he was responsible for replacing the Greek Revival style of THOMON, VORONIKHIN and ZAKHAROV with a much jucier Rome-inspired brand of classicism. The son of an Italian ballerina, he was trained in Russia and visited Italy only in 1802. Until 1816 he worked mainly in Moscow, but his principal buildings are in Leningrad: the New Michael Palace (now the Russian Museum, 1819–28) together with the square and surrounding buildings, the huge and richly Roman General Staff Arch and the vast hemicycle of office buildings on either side; the Alexander, now Pushkin, Theatre (1827–32); and the Senate and Synod (1829–34). But he is perhaps less important for these buildings than for the town planning around them.

Lit: G. H. Hamilton, *The Art and Architecture of Russia*, Pelican History of Art, Harmondsworth 1954.

Rostral column, *see* COLUMNA ROSTRATA.

Rotunda A building (often surrounded by a colonnade) or room circular in plan and usually domed, e.g., the Pantheon.

Roughcast An external rendering of rough material, usually applied in two coats of cement and sand on to which gravel, crushed stone, or pebbles are thrown before the second coat is dry; also called *pebbledash*.

Rubble masonry Rough unhewn building stones or flints, generally not laid in regular courses. *Coursed rubble* is walling with the

Rubble masonry: Bori, near Gordes, Provence

Rubble work

stones or flints roughly dressed and laid in deep courses. *Speckled rubble* is walling with stones of varying sizes with small rectangular fillings or snecks between them.

Rudolph, Paul (b. 1918), was a pupil of GROPIUS at Harvard. In 1958 he became head of the school of architecture at Yale University, New Haven, for which he designed the new building (1961–3), but shortly after left Yale. The building for the school unmistakably belongs to the trend often termed BRUTALISM, but Rudolph – like SAARINEN and Philip JOHNSON – is one of those who do not feel compelled to adhere to one style in all their designs, even those of the same year, though this in no way impairs his sincerity. Rudolph's other principal buildings are the Sarasota High School (1958–9), Cocoon House, Siesta Key, Florida (1960–1), and the fortress-like Endo Laboratories at Garden City, New York (1961–4). (For illustrations *see* BRUTALISM and UNITED STATES ARCHITECTURE.)

Lit: R. Spade, *Paul Rudolph*, London 1971.

Ruf, Sep, *see* EIERMANN, Egon.

Rundbogenstil, *see* GERMAN ARCHITECTURE.

Running dog A classical ornament often used in a frieze, similar to the wave ornament. It is sometimes called a *Vitruvian scroll.*

Running dog

Ruskin, John (1819–1900), was not an architect, but the source of an influence as strong on architecture as it was on the appreciation of art. This influence made itself felt in two ways: by the principles which Ruskin tried to establish, and by the styles whose adoption he pleaded for.

As for the former, they are chiefly the principles of the *Seven Lamps of Architecture*, which came out in 1849: Sacrifice (architecture, as against mere building, takes into account the venerable and beautiful, however 'unnecessary'); Truth (no disguised supports, no sham materials, no machine work for handwork); Power (simple grand massing); Beauty (only possible by imitation of, or inspiration from, nature); Life (architecture must express a fullness of life, embrace boldness and irregularity, scorn refinement, and also be the work of men as men, i.e., handwork); Memory (the greatest glory of a building is its age, and we must therefore build for perpetuity); Obedience (a style must be universally accepted: 'We want no new style', 'the forms of architecture already known are good enough for us'). From this last point, Ruskin proceeded to list the styles of the past which are perfect enough to be chosen for universal obedience. They are the Pisan Romanesque, the Early Gothic of West Italy, the Venetian Gothic, and the earliest English Decorated. This last, the style of the late C13 to early C14, had in fact been the choice of PUGIN, of the Cambridge Camden Movement (*see* BUTTERFIELD), and of SCOTT. But Ruskin's next book on architecture was *The Stones of Venice* (1851–3), which, being in praise of the Venetian Gothic, led admirers of Ruskin to imitate that style – J. P. Seddon, J. Prichard, early STREET, early E. Godwin. But *The Stones of Venice* also contains the celebrated chapter *On the Nature of Gothic*, which for the first time equated the beauties of medieval architecture and decoration with the pleasure taken by the workman in producing them. This was the mainspring that released the work of MORRIS as creator of workshops and as social reformer.

Lit: H.-R. Hitchcock, *Early Victorian Architecture in Britain*, New Haven–London 1954; J. D. Rosenberg, *The Darkening Glass*, London 1961; K. Clark, *Ruskin Today*, Harmondsworth 1964; N. Pevsner, *Some Architectural Writers of the Nineteenth Century*, Oxford 1972.

Russian architecture Russian architecture sets out as a branch of BYZANTINE ARCHITECTURE: stone churches from the C11 to the C16 have the characteristic motifs of the inscribed cross and the five domes (Chernigov, 1017 etc.). The principal apse is flanked by subsidiary apses, and occasionally there are also subsidiary outer aisles (Novgorod, St Sophia, 1045 etc.). Occasionally also churches carry

St Dimitri, Vladimir, c. 1200

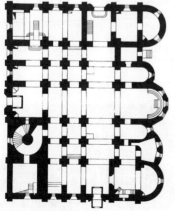

St Sophia, Novgorod, 1045–52

a lavish display of external relief sculpture (Vladimir, St Dimitri, *c.* 1200). There must also have been many log-built churches, but none is preserved earlier than the C17.

The Renaissance came to Russia remarkably early. Ivan the Great (1462–1505) was married to a Byzantine princess educated in Rome. Aristotile Fioravanti, an architect of Bologna, went to Moscow from Hungary in 1474, and another Italian, Alevisio Novi, arrived shortly before the death of Ivan. Fioravanti built the Church of the Dormition in the Kremlin, Moscow, on the accepted Byzantine plan, but with modifications for the sake of greater spatial clarity. Novi, in St Michael in the Kremlin, Moscow (1505–9), went much further in Renaissance detail such as the Venetian semicircular shell-gables. But in plan and elevation – inscribed cross and five domes – the Russian tradition was retained by Novi and by others building in the C16. However, a new indigenous type, derived probably from early wooden churches, appeared at Kolomenskoe in 1532, a type with a much simpler central plan and a tall, octagonal, central tower with spire. This type was made more and more decorative in the course of the C16, and invaded the Kremlin precincts in the shape of the fabulous Cathedral of St Basil (1555–60), which is overcrowded with motifs, just as contemporary buildings of Renaissance-Mannerism in Germany and England can be. The plan, with eight instead of four domed subsidiary spaces round the central tower, is novel too.

(Left): Wooden church at Kolomenskoje, 1532

Cathedral of St Basil, Moscow, 1555–60

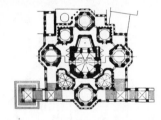

Mannerism like this continued throughout most of the c17 (Nativity, Moscow, 1649–52; Trinity, Ostankino, 1668), until the next foreign assault, that of the Baroque, brought final westernization. The church of the Virgin of Vladimir in Moscow (1691–4) has Baroque detail, the church of the Intercession at Fili (1693) a quatrefoil plan, the church at Dubrovitsi (1690 etc.) decoration as wild as if it were in Spain. With the former State Pharmacy (late c17), and the Menshikow

Tower, both in Moscow (1704–7), more structural Baroque elements came in.

But it was Peter the Great's St Petersburg that was intended to be the wide open gate for the West to enter Russia. SCHLÜTER was called to Russia in 1713, but died in 1714. In 1713 the German Gottfried SCHÄDEL (d. 1752) began the Menshikow Palace at Oranienbaum. The Cathedral in the Fortress (1714 etc.) is by the Italo-Swiss Domenico TREZZINI (1670–1734), the Library and

Palace at Pushkino (Tsarskoe-Selo), near Leningrad, begun 1749, by Rastrelli

Smolny Cathedral, Leningrad, begun 1748, by Rastrelli

Cabinet of Rarities (1718 etc.), by the German Georg Johann Mattarnovi (1719). With the Empress Elizabeth Russian architecture finally reached above the provincial level. RASTREL-LI'S Summer Palace (1741 etc.), Peterhof (1747 etc.), Tsarskoe-Selo (1749 etc.) and Winter Palace (1754 etc.) and also his Smolny Cathedral (1748 etc.) are in a grand and glorious Rococo. Yet the plan of the cathedral is unmistakably Russian. The

Bedroom at Pushkino (Tsarskoe-Selo), near Leningrad, 1780-85, by Cameron

The Summer Palace, Pushkino (Tsarskoe-Selo), near Leningrad, 1780-85, by Cameron

interiors of the palaces are decorated with almost overdone luxury.

The turn to the neo-classical style came no later than in most other countries, with the Academy and the Marble Palace at Leningrad, the former (1765 etc.) by the Frenchman Vallin de la Mothe (1729-1800), the latter (1768 etc.) by the Italian RINALDI. Only a little later Russian architects began to replace foreigners, and STAROV'S round tower at Nikolskoe (1774-6) is as severely neo-classical in the new Parisian sense as anything of the same date in the West. Starov had, in fact, studied in Paris and Italy.

Concurrently QUARENGHI began to build in the style of PALLADIO and CAMERON in that of Robert ADAM. Grecian in design, again influenced by France, are the Exchange of 1804 by Thomas de THOMON (1754-1813), ZACHAROV'S Admiralty (1806), and VORONI-

The Admiralty, Leningrad, begun 1806, by Zakharov

KHIN'S Mining Academy (1811). Altogether, Leningrad can be considered of all cities the one with the most consistent and the most sweeping classicist character. Meanwhile, churches remained less exactingly classical, and the Cathedrals of the Virgin of Kazan (by Voronikhin, 1801 etc.) and of St Isaac (1817 etc. by August Ricard MONTFERRAND, 1786-1858), both at Leningrad, carry their domes as a token of classicism as well as of the Russian tradition. The Picturesque in garden furnishings (ruins, etc.) hit Russia in the late C18 (QUARENGHI and especially V. I. Bazhenov, 1737–99) and produced the Historicism of the C19, as in other countries. What is peculiar to Russia is an Ancient Russian Revival starting, it seems, in the 1830s and culminating in the Moscow Historical Museum of 1874 etc. by V. O. Sherwood (1832–97).

Events of the C20 are the short-lived adherence of Russia to the most advanced architectural concepts of the early 1920s (LISSITSKY, TATLIN, VESNIN, Leonidov, Ladov-

ski), and then (after 1932) the enforced return to a grandiloquent classicism (Red Army Theatre, Moscow; University, Moscow; Moscow Underground). Recently this classicism has been disavowed, and large-scale housing programmes with prefabricated elements show Russia at one with Western interests and viewpoints.

Lit: G. H. Hamilton, The Art and Architecture of Russia, Pelican History of Art, Harmondsworth 1954; O. A. Shvidovsky, Building in the U.S.S.R., 1917–1932, London 1971.

Wolkenbügel project for Moscow, by El Lissitsky, 1924

Stadium, Krasnoyarsk, 1968

Palace of the Communist Party, Kiev, 1936–41

Rusticated column A column whose SHAFT is interrupted by plain or rusticated square blocks.

Hostel at Alma-Ata, 1967

Rusticated columns: Palazzo Pitti, Florence

Rustication Masonry cut in massive blocks separated from each other by deep joints, employed to give a rich and bold texture to an exterior wall and normally reserved for the lower part of it. Various types have been used: *banded* with only the horizontal joints emphasized; *chamfered* with smooth stones separated by V joints, as in *smooth* rustication described below; *cyclopean* (or *rock-faced*),

Cyclopean rustication:
Palazzo Pitti, Florence, c. 1458

Diamond-pointed rustication:
Palazzo dei Diamanti, Ferrara, 1493

with very large rough-hewn blocks straight from the quarry (or artfully carved to look as if they were); *diamond-pointed*, with each stone cut in the form of a low pyramid; *frosted*, with the surface of the stones carved to simulate icicles; *smooth*, with blocks neatly finished to present a flat face, and chamfered edges to emphasize the joints; *vermiculated*, with the blocks carved with shallow curly channels like worm tracks. Sometimes it is simulated in stucco or other compositions, e.g. by PALLADIO.

Ry, Paul du, *see* DU RY, Paul.

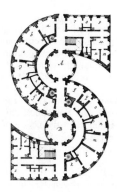

Saarinen, Eero (1910–61), the son of Eliel SAARINEN, went with his father to the United States, but spent part of his study years in Paris (1929–30). In 1931–4 he was at Yale, in 1935–6 back in Finland. His important works are all of the post-war years, and taken together they are admirable for their variety and their sense of visual and structural experiment. The General Motors Research Laboratories at Warren, Michigan (1948–56), has severely rectangular buildings in the style of MIES VAN DER ROHE, plus a circular auditorium with a shallow aluminium-roofed dome, and a highly original water-tower 132 ft high as a vertical accent. The Kresge Auditorium of the Massachusetts Institute of Technology at Cambridge (1953–5) has a warped roof on three supports, and the chapel there has undulating inner brick walls and a central opening in a dome whose top is of an abstract sculptural form. The chapel of Concordia Senior College (1953–8) has a steeply pointed, decidedly Expressionist roof, while the Yale University Hockey Rink (1953–9) has a central arch of double curve spanning the length, not the width of the building. The Trans-World Airline's Kennedy Terminal, New York (1956–62), with its two dramatically outward-swinging arches, is consciously symbolic of flight and has elements inside of almost GAUDÍ-like heavy curving. After that the T. J. Watson Research Centre at Yorktown, New York (1957–61), is, with its 1000-ft curved shape, perfectly crisp and unemotional; but the Ezra Stiles and Morse Colleges at Yale (1958–62), a unified composition, have the stepping-forward-backward-and-upward movement so characteristic of Louis KAHN's Medical Research Building in Philadelphia, begun one year earlier. Saar-inen's last fling was the Dulles Airport for Washington (1958–63), with a long down-curving roof ridge on lines of closely set, heavy and outward-leaning concrete supports. Saarinen also designed the United States Embassies in London (1955–61) and Oslo (1959 etc.). (For illustration *see* UNITED STATES ARCHITECTURE.)

Lit: A. A. Temko, *Eero Saarinen*, London 1962; Exh. Cat., *Eero Saarinen on his work*, New Haven 1968.

Saarinen, Eliel (1873–1950). His most famous building is the railway station at Helsinki, which was built in 1905–14 after a competition he won in 1904. The style is inspired by the Vienna Secession (*see* OLBRICH), but in a highly original version, and the building takes its place in the series of outstanding Central European railway stations characteristic of the years from the end of the C19 to the First World War (Hamburg begun 1903; Leipzig, 1905; Karlsruhe, 1908; Stuttgart, 1911). Saarinen took part in the Chicago Tribune competition of 1922, and his design, though placed second, was much admired. As a result he left Finland and emigrated to the United States, where his best-known buildings are Cranbrook School (1925 etc., 1929 etc.) and Christ Church, Minneapolis (1949). (For illustration *see* FINNISH ARCHITECTURE.)

Lit: A. Christ-Janner, *Eliel Saarinen*, Chicago 1948.

Sacchetti, Giovanni Battista (1700–64). A pupil of JUVARRA, whom he followed to Spain and whose designs he executed for the garden façade of the palace La Granja at S. Ildefonso (1736–42). His main work is the Royal Palace, Madrid (begun 1738), where

he greatly enlarged Juvarra's scheme by reference to BERNINI'S Louvre project: the result is imposing, almost overpowering and rather top-heavy. He also laid out the area of the city surrounding the palace.
Lit: E. Battisti in Commentari, IX, 1958.

Sacconi, Count Giuseppe (1853–1905). His magnum opus is the National Monument to Victor Emmanuel II in the centre of Rome, won in competition in 1884. Among other works the Assicurazioni Generali in Piazza Venezia, Rome (1902–7) might be mentioned.
Lit: C. L. V. Meeks, Italian Architecture, 1750–1914, New Haven–London 1966; F. Borsi, L'architettura dell'Unità d'Italia, Florence 1966.

Saddle bars In CASEMENT glazing, the small iron bars to which the lead panels are tied.

Saddle stone, see APEX STONE.

Saddleback roof, see ROOF.

Sakakura, Junzo, see JAPANESE ARCHITECTURE.

Sally-port A POSTERN gate or passage underground from the inner to the outer works of a fortification.

Salomónica The Spanish word for a barley-sugar or SOLOMONIC column, a feature much used in Spanish Baroque architecture.

Salvi, Nicola (1697–1751), designed the Trevi Fountain in Rome (1732–62), a Late Baroque masterpiece. It consists of a classical palace-façade, based on a Roman triumphal arch; this is set on an enormous artificial outcrop of rock out of which fountains gush into a lake-size basin at the bottom. Marble tritons and Neptune in a shell preside over the whole fantastic composition.
Lit: A. Schiavo, La Fontana di Trevi e le altre opere di Nicola Salvi, Rome 1956.

Salvin, Anthony (1799–1881), came of an old North Country family and was the son of a general. A pupil of NASH, he became an authority on the restoration and improvement of castles, and his work in that field included the Tower of London, Windsor, Caernarvon, Durham, Warwick, Alnwick, and Rockingham Castles. But he by no means devoted himself exclusively to castles, though he

was emphatically a domestic rather than an ecclesiastical architect. The range of styles used by him includes the sober Tudor of Mamhead in Devon (1828, a remarkably early use of the Tudor style), the lush Italian Renaissance interiors of Alnwick (1854 etc., not designed but approved by him), and the elaborate Jacobean of Thoresby, Nottinghamshire (1864–75). But his most stunning building is quite an early one: Harlaxton in Lincolnshire (1834 etc.), which is in an elaborate, indeed grossly exuberent, Elizabethan. The building was carried on by W. Burn.
Lit: H.-R. Hitchcock, Early Victorian Architecture in Britain, New Haven–London 1954; M. Girouard, The Victorian Country House, Oxford 1971.

Sambin, Hugues (1515/20–1601/2). French Mannerist architect, sculptor and furniture designer. He worked in Burgundy where he led a school of gifted provincial architects who indulged in rich surface effects with elaborately cut rustication (e.g., Petit Château at Tanlay, c. 1568) or with high relief sculpture (e.g., Maison Milsand, Dijon, c. 1561). Sambin also built the Palais de Justice at Besançon and his style had considerable influence, even in Paris, e.g., Hôtel de Sully. He published Termes dont on use en architecture (1572).
Lit: A. Castan, L'Architecture de Hugues Sambin, Besançon–Dijon 1891.

Sanctuary Area around the main altar of a church (see PRESBYTERY).

Sanfelice, Ferdinando (1675–1750), a leading Neapolitan architect of his day, was spirited, light-hearted, and unorthodox. He is notable especially for his ingenious scenographic staircases, e.g., Palazzo Sanfelice, Palazzo Serra Cassano.
Lit: R. Pane, Architettura a Napoli nell'Età barocca, Naples 1939.

Sangallo, Antonio da (Antonio Giamberti), the Elder (1455–1534), was born in Florence. He was the brother of Giuliano da Sangallo. His only notable building is one of the great masterpieces of Renaissance architecture, S. Biagio, Montepulciano (c. 1518–26). It was inspired by BRAMANTE's plan for St Peter's, i.e., a Greek cross with central dome and four towers (only one of which was built) between the arms. His earlier church of S. Maria di Monserrato in Rome is of 1495.

Lit: G. Clausse, Les San Gallo: Architectes, peintres, sculptures médailleurs, XVᵉ et XVIᵉ siècle, Paris 1900-02; L. H. Heydenreich & W. Lotz, Architecture in Italy, 1400-1600, Pelican History of Art, Harmondsworth 1974.

Sangallo, Antonio da (Antonio Giamberti), the Younger (1485-1546), who was born in Florence, was the most notable member of the Sangallo family: nephew of Antonio the elder and Giuliano. He became the leading High Renaissance architect in Rome for two decades after RAPHAEL's death. He began as an architectural draughtsman, employed first by BRAMANTE then by PERUZZI. In 1516 he became Raphael's assistant as architect at St Peter's, and was employed there to strengthen Bramante's work. He designed Palazzo Palma-Baldassini, Rome, c. 1520. His masterpiece is Palazzo Farnese, Rome (begun 1534, completed after 1546 by MICHEL-ANGELO), the most monumental of Renaissance palaces. The façade is astylar and the walls are smooth except for string courses dividing the storeys and bold quoins, which combine to give a horizontal emphasis stressing the gravity of the composition. It is at once sober, elegant, and restful. Several other palaces have been attributed to him, notably Palazzo Sacchetti, Rome (begun 1542). In 1539 he became chief architect of St Peter's, and supplied designs for the alteration of Bramante's plan (not executed). He designed the interior of the Cappella Paolina in the Vatican (1540). For many years he was employed as a military engineer on the fortifications around Rome. On his death he was succeeded as architect of St Peter's by Michelangelo, whose dynamic style makes a striking contrast to Sangallo's suave, self-confident classicism.

Lit: G. Giovannoni, Antonio da San Gallo, Florence 1942; L. H. Heydenreich & W. Lotz, Architecture in Italy, 1400-1600, Pelican History of Art, Harmondsworth 1974.

Sangallo, Giuliano da (Giuliano Giamberti, 1445-1516), military engineer and sculptor as well as architect, was born in Florence, the brother of Antonio da Sangallo the elder. He was one of the best followers of BRUNELLESCHI, and maintained the Early Renaissance style into the age of BRAMANTE and RAPHAEL. He was in Rome for seven years (1465-72) and may have worked at Palazzo Venezia. Most of his buildings are in and around Florence: Villa del Poggio a Caiano (1480-5, later altered internally); S. Maria delle Carceri, Prato (1485), the first Renaissance church on a Greek cross plan, with a marble-clad exterior and Brunelleschian interior; the atrium of S. Maria Maddalena de Pazzi, Florence (c. 1490-95); the sacristy of S. Spirito, Florence (in collaboration with CRONACA, 1492-4); probably Palazzo Corsi, Florence (now the Museo Horne); and Palazzo Gondi, Florence (1490-94), with a rusticated façade deriving from Palazzo Medici-Riccardi and a monumental staircase rising from the interior courtyard. Between 1489 and 1490 he made a model for Palazzo Strozzi, Florence, and though the palace was executed by Benedetto da Maiano and Cronaca its conception was probably his. He left Florence after the death of Lorenzo the Magnificent. His Palazzo Rovere at Savona (now much altered) dates from these years. He also worked in Rome, where he built S. Maria dell' Anima (1514) and provided a project for St Peter's (c. 1514).

Lit: G. Marchini, Giuliano da San Gallo, Florence 1942; L. H. Heydenreich & W. Lotz, Architecture in Italy, 1400-1600, Pelican History of Art, Harmondsworth 1974.

Sanmicheli, Michele (c. 1484-1559), the leading Mannerist architect in Verona, was famous as a military engineer; most of his works have a rather fortress-like appearance, and the façade he designed for S. Maria in Organo, Verona (1547), might almost be mistaken for one of the fortified gateways to the city. He is often compared with PALLADIO, who was indebted to him and succeeded him as the leading architect in the Veneto, but there is a striking contrast between the massive muscularity of Sanmicheli's works and the far more intellectual and polished buildings of Palladio.

Born in Verona, the son of an architect, he went to Rome c. 1500. He supervised work on the Gothic façade of Orvieto Cathedral (1510-24), where he also designed the Petrucci Chapel (1515). In 1526 he was employed by the Pope on the fortifications of Parma and Piacenza, and in the following year he settled in Verona. He was much in demand as a military architect, fortifying Legnago (1529), in charge of the fortifications at Verona (from 1530) and Venice (from 1535), and also in Corfu and Crete. The buildings he designed in this capacity are among his best – boldly rusticated gateways and whole fortresses with robust Doric columns and a few strongly effective ornaments such as coats of arms and giant heads frowning out of keystones, e.g., Porta Nuova, Verona (1533–40), Forte di S. Andrea a Lido, Venice (1535–49), Porta S. Zeno, Verona (1542), and most forceful of all, the Porta Palio, Verona (1557).

His palaces begin in the tradition of BRAMANTE and RAPHAEL with Palazzo Pompei, Verona (c. 1529), but he soon developed a more individual style, making much play with strong contrasts of light and shade. Palazzo Canossa, Verona (c. 1530), has a very high rusticated base and simplified Serlian windows on the first floor; Palazzo Bevilacqua, Verona (c. 1530), is richer, with an elaborate pattern of windows, spiral columns, and a rather oppressive use of sculpture. Here he adopted a device which later became very popular, projecting the triglyphs of the order to form consoles for a balcony. In his later palaces he strove towards the elimination of the wall surface, and at Palazzo Grimani, Venice (begun 1556, later altered), he almost entirely filled the spaces between the pilasters and columns with windows. He was little employed for churches, but the Cappella Pellegrini, S. Bernardino, Verona (c. 1528), and Madonna di Campagna, Verona (1559), are of interest for their peculiar domes, rather squat, on high drums decorated with alternating groups of two blank arches and three windows.

Lit: G. Fiocco *et al., Michele Sanmicheli, Studi Raccolti*, Venice 1960; P. Gazzola, ed., *Michele Sanmicheli*, Exh. Cat., Verona 1960; L. H. Heydenreich & W. Lotz, *Architecture in Italy, 1400–1600*, Pelican History of Art, Harmondsworth 1974.

Sansovino, Jacopo (1486–1570), who was primarily a sculptor, introduced the High Renaissance style of architecture to Venice. Born in Florence, the son of Antonio Tatti, he was trained under Andrea Sansovino, whose name he took. From 1505 he worked mainly in Rome as a sculptor and restorer of antique statues. At the Sack of Rome (1527) he fled to Venice, intending to go to France, but he was commissioned to repair the main dome of S. Marco, appointed Protomagister of S. Marco in 1529, and then stayed on in Venice for the rest of his life. Friendship with Titian and Aretino introduced him into the Venetian 'establishment'; he soon became the leading architect, a position he maintained until the arrival of PALLADIO, who owed much to him.

His main buildings are all in Venice: the Library and Mint (1537–54) facing the Doge's Palace, and the nearby Loggetta (1537–40) at the base of the Campanile. They show a happier combination of architecture and figure sculpture than had previously been achieved in Venice. Palladio called the Library the richest building erected since classical times. Sansovino built several churches, notably S. Francesco della Vigna (1534, completed by Palladio) and the façade of S. Giuliano (1553–5). In Palazzo Corner on the Grand Canal he adapted a Roman-type palace to Venetian requirements (before 1561). On the mainland he built Villa Garzoni, Pontecasale (c. 1530), a somewhat severe structure surrounding a wide courtyard, where he came nearer to the feeling of an antique villa than any other c16 architect.

Lit: M. Tafuri, *Jacopo Sansovino e l'architettura del'500 a Venezia*, Padua 1972; L. H. Heydenreich & W. Lotz, *Architecture in Italy, 1400–1600*, Pelican History of Art, Harmondsworth 1974.

Sant'Elia, Antonio (1888–1916), the architect of Italian Futurism. He was killed in the war, too early to have had a chance to do any actual building. However, his drawings, chiefly of 1913–14, are a vision of the industrial and commercial metropolis of the future, with stepped-back skyscrapers, traffic lanes at different levels, factories with boldly curved fronts. The forms are influenced by the Vienna Secession (*see* OLBRICH), but are also curiously similar to those of MENDELSOHN'S sketches of the same years. The metropolitan content, however, is Futurist.

Lit: U. Apollonio, *Antonio Sant'Elia*, Milan 1958; L. Caramel, *Antonio Sant'Elia, Catalogo della Mostra Permanente*, Como 1962.

Santini, *see* AICHEL.

Saracenic architecture, *see* ISLAMIC ARCHITECTURE.

Sash window A window formed with sashes, i.e., sliding glazed frames running in vertical grooves; imported from Holland into England in the late c17.

Satellite town A self-contained town which is nevertheless dependent upon a large centre nearby for certain facilities, such as higher education.

Scagliola Material composed of cement or plaster and marble chips or colouring matter to imitate marble; known in Antiquity but especially popular in the C17 and C18.

Scallop An ornament carved or moulded in the form of a shell.

Scamozzi, Vincenzo (1552–1616), the most important of PALLADIO's immediate followers was a conservative and rather pedantic formalist who maintained the principles of the C16 Mannerist style in the age of the Baroque. But he designed a handful of buildings of outstanding merit. Born in Vicenza, he was the son of a carpenter-cum-architect, from whom he received his training. Before 1576 he built his masterpiece, the Rocca Pisana at Lonigo, a villa perched on a hilltop and commanding spectacular views which the windows were designed to frame in an unprecedented manner. The villa is a simplified version of Palladio's Rotonda with an inset portico on the main façade and Venetian windows on the other. (Lord BURLINGTON took elements from both villas for Chiswick House.) His later houses, e.g., Villa Molin alla Mandria near Padua (1597), tended to be enlargements and elaborations of Palladian themes. From 1578 to 1580 he travelled in South Italy, visiting Naples and Rome, where he gathered material for his *Discorsi sopra le antichità di Roma* (1582). After Palladio's death he took over several of his unfinished works, notably S. Giorgio Maggiore, Venice. At the Teatro Olimpico, Vicenza, he added the elaborate permanent stage set (1585). In 1588 he designed a similar theatre at Sabbioneta. In 1582 he began the somewhat overweighted church of S. Gaetano, Padua. The same year he won the competition for the Procuratie Nuove in Piazza S. Marco, Venice, with a design based on Sansovino's Library – much elongated and heightened by a third storey. Also in Venice, in 1595, he began S. Nicola da Tolentino, a derivation from Palladio's Redentore. In 1599 he went to Prague, then across Germany to Paris, returning to Venice in 1600; four years later he visited Salzburg, where he made designs for the cathedral (not executed), a cross between the Redentore and S. Giorgio Maggiore. The fruits of these travels were incorporated in his *L'idea dell'architettura universale* (1615), the last and most academic of the theoretical works of the Renaissance and the first to mention medieval as well as classical and Renaissance buildings. It also provided the final codification of the ORDERS and thus exercised a wide and lasting influence especially in North Europe.

Lit: F. Barbieri, *V. Scamozzi*, Vicenza 1952; L. H. Heydenreich & W. Lotz, *Architecture in Italy, 1400–1600*, Pelican History of Art, Harmondsworth 1974.

Scandinavian architecture The beginnings are auspicious: the ship-shaped houses of *c.* 1000 near Trelleborg in Denmark, sixteen of them, each nearly a hundred feet long, and with an outer veranda all round, arranged in four squares of four, all in one round enclosure, and

Reconstruction of a house at Trelleborg, Sweden, c. 1000

Houses at Trelleborg, Sweden, c. 1000

the superb and frightening decoration of the Oseberg ship, cart and sledges, all superb Viking work of *c.* 800. The Vikings were heathens and intrepid explorers. They conquered parts of England, settled down in Normandy, and reached Iceland, Greenland and America. At the same time the Swedes conquered Russia and reached the Dnieper. The Christianization of Denmark and Sweden took place from North Germany in the C9 and C10, of Norway only at the end of the C10. The style of the intricate Viking ornamentation continued in the next outstanding contribution of Norway, the STAVE CHURCHES of the C12 (Urnes, Borgund, Lom) with their timber arcading structurally as ingenious as it is visually fascinating. Apart from stave churches there were also straightforward log churches of the type of Greensted in Essex. The best examples are Hedared and St Mary Minor at Lund in

Stave church at Borgund, Norway,
c. 1150

Stave church at Lom, Gudbrandsdal, Norway,
C12 (choir decoration, c. 1700)

Carved decoration from stave church at Urnes,
Norway

Sweden of *c.* 1020. But the most impressive
Swedish contribution to timber architecture
is her detached bell-towers of unboarded
skeletal construction. Where stone was used,
the northern countries looked primarily to
Germany for guidance (cf. for an early example
the C11 WESTWORK of Husaby). Another
source, though less pronounced, is Anglo-
Saxon England (e.g. Sigtuna, St Peter). The
principal C12 cathedrals were Lund (in
Sweden) which became an archbishop's see
in 1104. Viborg (in Finland) and Ribe (in
Denmark). Their twin west towers, their projecting transepts, their hall crypts and their
details all derive from Germany. Lund is the
most interesting. Its origin is Speyer in Germany and *via* Speyer, Lombardy. A master
Donatus working at Lund may well have been
Italian himself. At Ribe, the dome over the
crossing seems S.W. French in origin, but the
mid-C13 sexpartite rib vaults of the nave are
Early French Gothic. Brick may have reached
Denmark from Lombardy and was at once
adopted (Ringsted, 1160 etc., the Cistercian
Sorø, 1161 etc.). The most interesting Danish
building of the Middle Ages is of brick: the

Østerlars, Bornholm, Denmark, C12

Crypt of Lund Cathedral, Sweden, CI2

Trondheim Cathedral, Norway, begun CI2

Kalundborg Cathedral, Seeland, Denmark,
c. 1170

church of Kalundborg, a centrally planned late CI2 building with a centre on the Byzantine (Russian?) inscribed-cross plan, but with four arms of equal length, projecting and crowned by four towers, which with the broader and higher central tower creates a splendid skyline.

Roskilde Cathedral, Seeland, Denmark,
begun c. 1190

Of brick also is Roskilde Cathedral, much changed by picturesque later additions. Its ambulatory is French Romanesque, but other elements mark the transition to the Gothic style. The two most important Norwegian cathedrals point unmistakably to England. Stavanger has a nave of *c.* 1130 etc. with typically English short round piers and a Gothic chancel of 1272 etc., equally English. Trondheim has a singular east end in which the straight-ended chancel is continued by an octagon to house the shrine of St Olav. The corona of St Thomas at Canterbury, evidently the source for the centrally planned east shrine, had been completed in 1185. Trondheim must have been begun just about then. The details of octagon and choir are derived from Lincoln, begun in 1192. The screen between chancel and octagon is of *c.* 1330 and has its parallels also in England. The west front, left incomplete, is entirely English too, of the screen type with late CI3 sculpture and two west towers set outside the aisle fronts. The finest secular building of the Middle Ages in Scandinavia is King Haakon's Hall at Bergen, completed in 1261. The largest Scandinavian cathedral is that of Uppsala, begun *c.* 1270 and with a French Gothic ambulatory and radiating chapels, and continued from 1287 by Étienne de Bonneuil. Linkøping Cathedral, also CI3, has a nave of hall type more probably derived from English hall choirs such as those of Salisbury and the Temple Church than from Germany. But German HALL CHURCHES, more and more the favourite church type in that country, also had an impact on the North, and an increasing impact (Malmö St Peter, Aarhus Cathedral). The friars, settling from the 1230s onwards, preferred halls. One of the earliest friars' churches is that of the Dominicans at Sigtuna (c. 1240), one of the finest is that of the Carmelites at Elsinore (Helsingborg) of the late C15. Both have brickwork in the decoratively enriched patterns so dear to the North German builders. Altogether the churches of the Late Gothic period depend on North Germany and especially Westphalia. Examples are the cathedrals of Strängnäs and Västerås in Sweden with their figured rib vaults. Swedish parish churches are notable for the survival of a large number of Late Gothic wall paintings.

The Renaissance made itself felt late and slowly. A house like Hesselagergaard in Denmark of c. 1550 has semicircular gables on the Venetian pattern, but otherwise shows little of a true understanding of the Renaissance. The two great castles or country palaces of the Danish kings, Frederick II's Kronborg and Christian IV's Frederiksborg, date from 1574–85 and c. 1602–20 respectively. In style they derive from the Netherlands, and Antonis van Opbergen and Hans Steenwinckel Sen., working at Kronborg, and Hans and Laurens

Frederiksborg, Denmark, 1602–20

Steenwinckel, the architects of Frederiksborg, were in fact Dutchmen. Rosenborg in Copenhagen, a summer palace, dates from 1606–17, the delightful Exchange in Copenhagen by the Steenwinckels, from 1619–25. Its spire, which is in the form of three entwined dragons' tails, is a landmark of the city. The style of all these buildings is close to that of the Netherlanders who built at Danzig or Emden, and not too distant from that of Jacobean England. The same style in ecclesiastical architecture appears in Holy Trinity, Kristianstad in Sweden of 1618 etc., probably by the Steenwinckels. The church is a hall church with very slim piers and still has the shaped gables of the Netherlandish style. The burial chapel of Christian IV attached to Roskilde Cathedral was begun even a few years earlier (1614) and has

The Exchange, Copenhagen, 1619–25

Netherlandish gables of a slightly more advanced type and in addition Gothic windows, a case of Revival rather than Survival.

Kristiansstad was founded by Christian IV and is laid out regularly with a grid of streets and oblong blocks. The king laid out other towns as well. One of them is Oslo (1624), but the most regular is Kristiansand in Norway (1641). In Sweden shortly after 1625 the present-day centre of Stockholm was laid out as a grid. Kalmar was built on a grid plan after 1647. Karlskrona, also a planned town, was founded in 1679. In 1662 the area of Copenhagen east of Kongens Nytorv and towards the new Citadel was laid out with a grid of straight streets, and in the course of the late C17 and the C18 this area filled up with private palaces and houses as stately as those of the best quarters of Paris during the same period. Their style throughout is the classical style which by then had begun to dominate Denmark and Scandinavia.

The classical style also reached the Northern countries from the Netherlands. Justus VINGBOONS visited Sweden in 1653-7. But already before then the style of van CAMPEN and POST had been developed. The de Geer House in Stockholm of 1646 is a perfect example of it. The initiator may have been Simon de LA VALLÉE, who had arrived in 1637 and died in 1643, or his son Jean de la Vallée. Their work (and Vingboons') is the Riddarhus in Stockholm of 1652-65. Jean at the same time provided in the Oxenstjerna Palace of 1650 an example of the Roman palazzo façade. In Denmark the former Vordingsborg of 1671 by Lambert van Haven is entirely Dutch. The Charlottenborg Palace, also in Copenhagen (1672-83), and forming part of the new area already referred to, is essentially Dutch too. The former Sophie-Amalienborg in Copenhagen of 1667-73 on the other hand is an attempt at the Italian villa in Denmark.

Churches are of course all Protestant and hence all variations on Dutch types. There are a remarkable number of them, starting with St Katharine in Stockholm by the younger LA VALLÉE, begun in 1656. It is a Greek cross with a dome and four corner turrets. Kalmar Cathedral by Nicodemus TESSIN the Elder of 1660 etc. is also basically a Greek cross with corner turrets, but the west and east arms are lengthened and apsed. Our Saviour at Copenhagen by Lambert van Haven is again a Greek cross, but has a west tower and a centre with an inscribed cross. To the churches must be added the Kagg Mausoleum at Floda in

Skokloster, near Stockholm, 1646-68, by La Vallée

Drottningholm, Sweden, garden front, begun 1662, by Tessin the elder, and completed 1700, by Tessin the younger

Sweden of 1661, again a Greek cross, and the grand Carolean Mausoleum attached to the Riddarholm Church at Stockholm by the elder Tessin with its splendid columnar exterior. This was designed in 1671.

Openness to influences from several countries remained characteristic of Scandinavia in the C18, or rather of Denmark and Sweden; for Norway had been left behind ever since the Middle Ages. Much Norwegian domestic architecture was still of wood even in the C18. (The largest wooden building is Stiftsgården at Trondheim of 1774-8, nineteen windows wide, the finest is Danisgård at Bergen of the 1770s too, with its Rococo details.)

The most monumental building of Scandinavia, the Royal Palace in Stockholm by the younger TESSIN, begun in 1697, reflects more powerfully than any other palace in Europe the impact made by BERNINI'S plans for the Louvre in Paris. In 1693 Tessin had made for the King of Denmark a similar design. Tessin knew both Rome and Paris. His country house Steninge of 1694-8 has an entirely French plan, derived from Vaux-le-Vicomte. His father's Drottningholm of the 1660s and Eriksberg had been French throughout.

*Fredensborg, Seeland, 1719-26,
by J. C. Krieger*

About and after 1700 Frederiksborg (1699 etc.) and Fredensborg (1719 etc.), both in Denmark and both much altered, were Italian in inspiration; Christiansborg, the former Royal Palace of Copenhagen, of 1733 etc. (by E. D. Häusser; 1687–1745) is South German. So is the charming Hermitage in the Deer Park

*Hermitage, Deer Park, Copenhagen,
1734-6, by Thura*

north of Copenhagen of 1734–6 (by Laurids Thura; 1706–59). Svartsjö in Sweden on the other hand of 1735–9 (by Carl Hårleman) is a French *maison de plaisance*. The East India Company Warehouse at Göteborg of c. 1740 (by the same architect) is a paramount example of early commercial architecture, nineteen windows wide and four storeys high. About the middle of the C18 the Picturesque movement made its mark in Scandinavia too, inspired by England which had been visited by F. M. Piper (1746–1824) before he designed the landscape park of Haga, and followed an English *jardinier* in dealing with the landscape park of Drottningholm. The finest mid-C18 work in the Northern countries is Amalienborg in Copenhagen, built by Nils EIGTVED in 1750–54 as an octagon with four palaces in the diagonals and four streets branching off in the main directions. The style is French, the

quality of the highest. Eigtved also designed the Frederiks-Church, magnificent, with a dominating dome on a high drum. But this was not carried out; Laurits Thura made another, more classical, design, and Nicolas-Henri Jardin, called in from France, a third, in its details even more classical, with a giant

*Frederiks Church, Copenhagen, mid-C18,
by Jardin, completed 1876–94, by Meldahl*

portico of detached columns and columns round the drum.

The Classical Revival or neo-classicism indeed began remarkably early in Denmark, and C. H. Harsdorff's Moltke Chapel at Karise of 1761–6 and his Chapel of Frederik V in Roskilde Cathedral (final design 1774) are

Frederiks Chapel, Roskilde Cathedral,
Denmark, 1774, designed by Harsdorff

among the purest works of their date anywhere on the Continent. The paramount neo-
classical buildings in Sweden are the theatre of
Gripsholm Castle (1782) by Erik Palmstädt
(1741–1803) and the works of Jean-Louis
Desprez (1743–1804), who had belonged to
the most advanced Parisian circle and settled
down in Sweden in 1784. Between that year
and the tragic death of Gustavus III in 1792
he was the centre of the strictest Scandinavian
classicism. However, such was the mood of
the later c18 that he also designed in the
Chinese style for the park of Haga.

The neo-Greek leaders are C. F. HANSEN
(1756–1845) in Denmark and the Danish F.
Linstow and C. H. Grosch in Norway. The
principal works are the Law Courts on the
Nytorv of 1803–16 and the Church of Our
Lady of 1810–26, both in Copenhagen, and
in Oslo the Royal Palace of 1824–48 (Norway in 1814 had at last broken free of Denmark and become linked by common monarchs
with Sweden) and the University of 1840 etc.,
the former by Linstow, the latter by Grosch.
All on his own is Gottlieb Bindesbøll (1800–
1856) whose Thorwaldsen Museum in Copenhagen of 1839–47 is as original within the
Greek Revival as the work of Greek THOMSON
in Glasgow.

For 'Victorian' historicism the best examples are the castellated and turreted
Oskarshall outside Oslo of 1848 and then the

Copenhagen University Library (1855–61) by
J. D. Herholdt (1818–1902) in the 'Rund-
bogenstil', but with elegant exposed iron
members inside, the Royal Theatre at Copen-
hagen (1872–4) by V. Dahlerup in the Italian
Renaissance, the University at Uppsala (1879–
87) by H. T. Holmgren in a grander Renais-
sance, the Magasins du Nord (1893 etc.) at
Copenhagen by A. Jensen with French pavilion
roofs, the Nordisk Museum (1890–1907),
Stockholm, by I. G. Clason in the Northern
Renaissance and the finally completed Frederik
Church (1876–94) at Copenhagen by F.
Meldahl in a surprisingly early grand French
Baroque following the style of the original
design of Jardin.

From the 1890s onwards, however, some
Danish architects joined the vanguard of those
who endeavoured to get away from Victorian
obtrusiveness and from historicism. The
Copenhagen Town Hall by Martin Nyrop
(1849–1921) was begun in 1893 and is as
important as BERLAGE'S Exchange in Amsterdam as an example of the imaginative treatment of elements from various styles of the
past to achieve an original whole. ØSTBERG'S
City Hall (1911–23) in Stockholm belongs
to the same category; so does L. I. Wahlman's
Engelbrecht Church (1906–14) in Stockholm,
externally a homely Renaissance, internally
with parabolic arches, KLINT'S Grundvig
Church, begun finally only in 1919, straddles
the gap between latest traditionalism and the
Expressionism after the First World War. But
the Grundvig Church is an exception in Denmark. The way to c20 liberty was as a rule not
via a free Gothic but via Classicism. The paramount examples are the Fåborg Museum of
1912–15 by Carl Petersen (1874–1923) and
the Copenhagen Police Headquarters of 1918

Stockholm Exhibition, 1930, by Asplund

Grundvig Church, Copenhagen,
designed 1913, begun 1919, by Klint

etc. by Hack Kampmann (1856–1920) and the brilliant Aage Rafn (1890–1953). From then Denmark entered its moderate, sensitive C20 style, illustrated at its most Danish in Aarhus University by Kay Fisker (1893–1965), C. F. Møller and P. Stegmann (1932 etc.), at its most international by the impeccable work of Arne JACOBSEN and others such as H. Gunnløgsson (Kastrup Town Hall 1961) and Jørgen Bo & V. Wohlert (Louisiana Museum 1957–8). Only Jørn Utzon (b. 1918) has broken the perfect Danish restraint with his rhapsodic design for the Sydney Opera House (1956–73).

Denmark reached the INTERNATIONAL MODERN later than Sweden. Sweden had been

Crematorium, Stockholm, 1935–40,
by Asplund

Town Hall, Rødovre, Denmark, 1956,
by Jacobsen

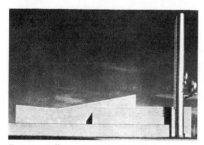

Factory, Aalborg, 1957, by Jacobsen

Design for Sydney Opera House, 1956,
by Utzon

inspired to classicism by Denmark, and Teng-
bom, Sigurd Lewerentz and ASPLUND belonged to it. But Asplund in the buildings for
the Stockholm Exhibition of 1930 broke away
from it and introduced a brand of the International Modern, more delicate, with thinner
steel and more glass than heretofore. Examples
of the International Modern of the thirties at

its best are the schools by P. Hedqvist and by
N. Ahrbom and H. Zimdahl, the Göteborg Concert Hall by N. E. Erikson (1931–5), the point-
block housing by e.g. S. Backstrøm and L.
Reinius (c. 1945 etc.), Eskil Sundahl's factory
and housing among the trees on an island
near Stockholm, and Vällingby, an outer
suburb of Stockholm, not a satellite town. The
excellent plan by MARKELIUS was drawn up
in 1949. Building began in 1953. Compared
with the freshness of all this Swedish and
Danish architecture, the Oslo Town Hall of
1933–50 by A. Arneberg and M. Poulsson is
heavy and uncouth.

Lit: G. E. Kidder-Smith, *Sweden Builds,* New
York 1957; G. Kauli, *Norwegian Architecture,*
Oslo 1958; T. T. Faber, *A History of Danish Art,*
Copenhagen 1967; *Danmarks Byggningskunst*
(ed. H. Lund & K. Millech), Copenhagen 1963;
A. Lindblom, *Sveriges Konsthistoria,* 3 vols.,
Stockholm 1944–6.

Scarp or **escarp** In military architecture, the
bank or wall immediately in front of and
below the rampart. It is often the inner side
of the ditch or fosse.

Schädel, Gottfried (d. 1752). A German working in St Petersburg, where his masterpiece
was the vast, exuberantly Baroque palace for
Prince Menshikov at Oranienbaum (1713–
25), the first large Western-style palace to be
built in Russia. Its scale was immense, a central
block with long curving wings which terminated in domed pavilions, built on an
escarpment faced with decorative niches to
give the appearance of two storeys below the
ground floor.

Lit: G. H. Hamilton, *The Art and Archi-*
tecture of Russia, Pelican History of Art, Harmondsworth 1954.

Scharoun, Hans (1893–1972), presents us
with the curious case of an architect who, because of his style, stood in the forefront when
he was thirty; who through a shift in style
among others fell into oblivion, and who, with
a return to something approaching the style
which had been his in his youth and which he
had never felt compelled to change, found
himself in the forefront once again at the age
of sixty-five to seventy. Scharoun belonged
among the Expressionists and fantasts of post-
1918 Germany; like them he freely penned
his dreams. In the later twenties he built some
houses and flats, but major jobs were offered
him only in the post-Second-World-War

mood, in which sympathy with the twenties plays such an important part; then the *Wirtschaftswunder* made it possible to build what had remained on paper forty years earlier. His chief recent jobs are an estate at Charlottenburg-North, Berlin (1955–61); Romeo and Juliet, a twin scheme of flats at Stuttgart (1955–9); and the Berlin Philharmonie (1956–63). (For illustration *see* GERMAN ARCHITECTURE.)

Lit: H. Lauterbach, *H. Scharoun*, Exh. Cat., Berlin 1967.

Schickhardt, Heinrich (1558–1634). One of the first German Renaissance architects, less well known than Elias HOLL because none of his buildings survive, but of great historical importance. He was trained by Georg Beer (d. 1600) whom he helped to design the Neues Lusthaus at Stuttgart (1584–93, demolished). In 1590 he became official architect to the Duke of Württemberg with whom he visited Italy (1598–1600). His newly acquired knowledge of Italian Renaissance architecture was manifested in the new wing he added to the Schloss at Stuttgart on his return (1600–1609, destroyed 1777) – a symmetrical building with some sixty Tuscan columns in the ground floor stables. He also designed and laid out the small town of Freudenstadt around a large central arcaded square with church, town hall, market hall and hospital at the corners (destroyed in the Second World War but rebuilt) – an unusually progressive example of North European town planning. The church is L-shaped, with altar and pulpit in the corner.

Lit: J. Baum, *H. Schickhardt*, Strassburg 1916; E. Hempel, *Baroque Art and Architecture in Central Europe*, Pelican History of Art, Harmondsworth 1965.

Schindler, Rudolf M. (1887–1953). Born and trained in Vienna. In 1913 he emigrated to America, where in 1918 he began to work under Frank Lloyd WRIGHT. In 1921 he started practising on his own in Los Angeles. About 1925 he had developed his personal style inspired by Wright and the INTERNATIONAL MODERN, especially of OUD. Cubism also must have inspired him. From 1925 onwards, for a few years, he worked in partnership with NEUTRA. Like Neutra, Schindler specialized in expensive houses. His *magnum opus* is Beach House (Lovell House) at Newport Beach (1925–6).

Lit: D. Gebhard, *R. Schindler*, London 1971.

Schinkel, Karl Friedrich (1781–1841), the greatest German architect of the C19, was Prussian and worked almost exclusively in Prussia. He was the son of an archdeacon, went to school in Berlin, and received his architectural training there too, under GILLY, in whose father's house he boarded, and at the newly founded Academy. He was powerfully influenced by the original and francophile style of Gilly. He stayed in Italy and in Paris in 1803–5, then worked as a painter of panoramas and dioramas, and a little later (chiefly *c.* 1810–15) did independent paintings too, in an elevated Romantic style (landscapes and Gothic cathedrals). This led on to theatrical work, and Schinkel designed for the stage from 1816 right into the thirties (forty-two plays, including *The Magic Flute*, *Undine*, *Käthchen von Heilbronn*). Meanwhile, however, he had begun to submit architectural designs, hoping to attract attention to himself. The first was for a mausoleum for the much beloved Prussian Queen Luise. This was eminently romantic in the Gothic style, with coloured glass in the windows and life-size white angels by the head of the sarcophagus. It was followed by church designs, e.g., a cathedral in the trees, centrally planned with a steep Gothic dome. In 1810 Schinkel had secured a job in the administration of Prussian buildings, with the help of Wilhelm von Humboldt. In 1815 he was made Geheimer Oberbaurat in the newly created Public Works Department, a high title for so young a man, and in 1830 he became the head of the department.

All his principal buildings were designed between 1816 and 1830. The earliest are pure Grecian, yet always serviceable, functionally planned, and with the motifs of the façade, in the spirit of Gilly, modified with originality to ensure that the stylistic apparatus does not interfere with the use of the building. The Neue Wache or New Guard House in Unter den Linden, Berlin, came first (1816; Greek Doric portico, transformed internally in 1966), then the Theatre (1818–21), large, with a raised Ionic portico and excellent interiors (badly damaged 1945 but being restored), and after that the Old Museum (1823–30, interior partly destroyed 1945), with its unbroken row of slender Ionic columns along the façade, its Pantheon-like centre rotunda, taken obviously from DURAND, and its staircase open to the portico and picturesquely introducing a degree of interpenetration of spaces not to be expected from outside. This is the first sign of hidden resources in Schinkel, making it impossible to label him a Grecian and leave it at that. Side by side with these major buildings, Schinkel designed the War Memorial on the Kreuzberg (1818), Gothic and of cast iron, Tegel, Humboldt's country house (1822-4), in a characteristic domestic Grecian, and the Werdersche Kirche (1821-31). The design for this last was submitted in a classical and a Gothic version, both vaulted; the Gothic version won, evidently inspired by the English type of Late Gothic Royal Chapels with their four angle turrets.

Schinkel was, indeed, keenly interested in England and in 1826 travelled through the country, after staying for a while in Paris. It was not his first major journey since Italy: in 1816 he had been to the Rhine, where he developed an interest in the preservation of monuments, and in 1824 he went again to Italy. In England he was more interested in industrial developments than in architecture proper, the promotion of crafts and industry being part of his official responsibilities.

His principal late works show a remarkable change of style and widening of possibilities. They include unexecuted designs for a bazaar (1827) and for a library (1812-5), both utilitarian without any period trimmings. Among executed works, the Nikolaikirche at Potsdam (1830-37, badly damaged 1945 but being restored) is classical, whereas the building for the Academy of Architecture is only vestigially period (North Italian Quattrocento), but essentially also unenriched functional. A widening in another direction led to projects for centrally and longitudinally planned churches in arcuated styles, vaguely Early Christian or Italian Romanesque (the so-called *Rundbogenstil* of Lombardy; *see* GÄRTNER), while a broadening of yet another kind is represented by two small buildings in the park of Potsdam – Charlottenhof and the Roman Bath (1826 and 1833) – and the costly projects for a palace on the Acropolis (1834) and in the Crimea (1838), in all of which Grecian motifs are applied to picturesquely irregular compositions where architecture and nature collaborate. (For illustrations *see* GERMAN ARCHITECTURE, GREEK REVIVAL, NEO-GOTHIC ARCHITECTURE.)

Lit: A. Grisebach, *Carl Friedrich Schinkel*, Leipzig 1929; *Karl Friedrich Schinkel: Lebenswerk* (ed. P. O. Rave, and now G. Kühn), Berlin 1929-62; P. O. Rave, *K. F. Schinkel*, Munich 1953; H. G. Pundt, *Schinkel's Berlin*, Cambridge, Mass. 1972.

Schlaun, Johann Conrad (1695-1773). A Westphalian Baroque architect who began with small and simple churches for Capuchin friars, e.g., Brakel (1715-18). He then studied under NEUMANN at Würzburg (1720-21), travelled to Rome and returned to Münster by way of France and Munich (1724). In 1725 he was appointed architect to Clemens August, Elector of Cologne, for whom he began Schloss Brühl (later altered by CUVILLIÉS) and the very elegant little cruciform hunting-lodge Clemenswerth near Sögel (c. 1736-50). For the Elector's minister, Graf von Plettenberg, he designed various buildings for the park at Nordkirchen, notably the Oranienburg (from 1726). Still clinging to the Baroque style, by then rather *démodé*, he built the Clemenskirche, cleverly inserted into a corner of the House of the Brethren of Mercy at Münster (1744-54), restored 1973, the Erbdrostenhof in Münster (1753-7) and the Schloss at Münster (1767-73). The two houses he built for himself are remarkably original: the Rüschhaus outside Münster (1745-8) in the Westphalian rustic tradition with a few sophisticated Baroque flourishes, and a town-house in Münster (1753-5) stylistically similar.

Lit: T. Rensing, *J. C. Schlaun*, Munich–Berlin 1954; *Johann Conrad Schlaun*, Exh. Cat., 2 vols., Landesmuseum, Münster 1973.

Schlüter, Andreas (c. 1660-1714). He was equally distinguished as sculptor and architect. As an architect he ranks slightly below his great contemporaries HILDEBRANDT and FISCHER VON ERLACH. He was trained in Danzig (and was probably born there) but is first heard of in Warsaw in 1689-93 as the sculptor of pediments on the Krasiński Palace. He does not seem to have worked as an architect in Poland. In 1694 he was called to Berlin by the Elector Friedrich III who sent him to France and Italy to study. On his return in 1696 he was commissioned to carve the very elaborate sculptural keystones for windows and doors on the Berlin Arsenal designed by NERING. He succeeded Nering as architect at the Arsenal in 1698. In the same year he was put in charge of the building of the Royal Palace in Berlin, and in 1698 became its Surveyor General. The Royal Palace (bombed 1945, demolished 1950) was his masterpiece. Some of his sculptural decoration on the Lustgarten façade, on the great staircase and Baronial Hall, was fortunately removed before demolition in 1950. The influence of BERNINI and LE PAUTRE is evident in the design, as well as that of Fischer von Erlach and Nicodemus TESSIN the younger, both of whom were in Berlin while it was being built. In 1701-4 he also built the Old Post Office in Berlin (demolished 1889), but he fell into disgrace shortly afterwards as a result of the collapse of the Münzturm water-tower at the north-west corner of the Royal Palace. He was dismissed from his appointments in 1707. In 1711-12 he built the Villa Kamecke in Dorotheenstadt, Berlin (destroyed 1945, but fragments preserved in the Bode Museum, E. Berlin). After the king's death he left Berlin and settled in St Petersburg in 1714, dying there the same year.

Lit: H. Ladendorf, *Das Bildhauer und Baumeister Andreas Schlüter*, Berlin 1935; E. Hempel, *Baroque Art and Architecture in Central Europe*, Pelican History of Art, Harmondsworth 1965.

Schoch, Johannes or **Hans** (*c.* 1550-1631). His masterpiece is the Friedrichsbau in Heidelberg Castle (1601-7) in which the architectural elements are closely knit and vigorously moulded though still somewhat heavy-handed as compared with later and more accomplished German Renaissance buildings, e.g., Jacob WOLFF's Pellerhaus in Nuremberg of the same years. Schoch may have worked with Speckle (1536-89) on the Neuer Bau at Strassburg (1582-5) and perhaps also on the Grosse Metzig in Strassburg (1586). The Fleischhalle at Heilbronn (*c.* 1600) and the south wing of the Arsenal at Amberg (1604) may derive from designs by Schoch.

Schwarz, Rudolf (1897-1961). He was predominantly a designer of churches. Architectural symbolism meant much to him, e.g. in planning, a closed ring, an open ring, a chalice, a path forward. He was a pupil of POELZIG. Among his works are the Fronleichnamskirche at Aachen (1928-30, with Hans Schwippert), St Maria Königin at Frechen (1952-54), Holy Cross at Botrop (1955-57). He wrote two books on church architecture (1938, 1960).

Lit: Rudolf Schwarz in *Das Münster* X, 1957.

Sconce In military architecture, a small fort or earthwork, usually built as a counter-fort or to defend a pass, castle gate, etc.

Scotia A concave moulding which casts a strong shadow, as on the base of a column

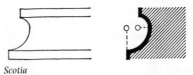
Scotia

between the two TORUS mouldings. (For additional illustration *see* PEDESTAL.)

Scott, Sir George Gilbert (1811-78), the son of a clergyman and himself an evangelical, regarded himself as an architect of the multitude, not of the chosen few, and his sturdy stand on the *juste milieu* secured him an unparalleled multitude of buildings. He started with workhouses – a speciality of Sampson Kempthorne, the architect under whom he had worked – and he did them in partnership with W. B. Moffatt. The Royal Wanstead School at Wanstead, Essex, formerly an Orphan Asylum, is their first important work; it is Jacobean in style. But one year later they built St Giles, Camberwell, London, and here Scott found his feet. This is a Gothic church which was substantial, no longer papery as the earlier neo-Gothic churches had been, and which was, moreover, both knowledgeable and, with its properly developed chancel, ritualistically acceptable to the Cambridge Camden group. In the same year Scott began to restore Chesterfield church, and so started on his career as a busy, undaunted restorer. In the next year, 1844, he won the competition for St Nicholas at Hamburg with a competent German Gothic design which established him internationally. He restored more cathedrals and parish churches than can be remembered, was made surveyor of Westminster Abbey in 1849, and built – to name but a few – the grand Doncaster parish church (1854 onwards), the chapels of Exeter College, Oxford (1856), and St John's College, Cambridge (1863-9), and the parish church of Kensington, London (1869-72). His style is mixed Anglo-French High Gothic (late C13 to early C14).

He was also active as a secular architect. Examples are Kelham Hall, Nottinghamshire (1857, etc.), the St Pancras Station and Hotel in London (1865, etc.), the Albert Memorial (1864, etc.), and the group of houses in Broad Sanctuary, just west of Westminster Abbey (1854). Scott even wrote a persuasive book to prove that the Gothic style was as suited to secular as to clerical C19 tasks (*Remarks on Secular and Domestic Architecture*, 1858), and was deeply hurt when he found himself forced by Lord Palmerston to do the new Government offices in Whitehall in the Renaissance style (final design 1861). Scott was ambitious and fully convinced he was as good an architect as any; this comes out clearly in his *Personal and Professional Recollections* (1879). He was, in fact, a highly competent architect, but he lacked genius. As a restorer he believed in careful preservation, but was ruthless in action. In spite of this he was quite a medieval scholar, as is demonstrated by his *Gleanings from Westminster Abbey* (1862).

His sons **George Gilbert** (1839–97) and **John Oldrid** (1842–1913) were both Gothicists too, competent and careful like their father, but they had in addition a sensitivity which belongs to the Late as against the High Victorian milieu. George Gilbert's *chef d'œuvre* was St Agnes, Kennington, London (1877), remarkably bare and grand; John Oldrid, following his brother, did the noble Catholic church of Norwich (1884–1910). (For illustration *see* ENGLISH ARCHITECTURE.)

Lit: G. G. Scott, *Personal and Professional Recollections by the late Sir G. G. Scott*, London 1879; B. F. L. Clarke, *Church Builders of the 19th Century*, London 1938; P. Ferriday, 'Syllabus in Stone. The Albert Memorial by G. G. Scott' in *Architectural Review*, 135, 1964; N. Pevsner, *Some Architectural Writers of the Nineteenth Century*, Oxford 1972.

Scott, Sir Giles Gilbert (1880–1960), rose to sudden and very early fame with his design for Liverpool Cathedral, won in competition in 1904 and very evidently inspired by BODLEY. This means that it is still Gothicist in the C19 manner. However, it has an originality of plan and a verve of verticals which promised much. Scott's early ecclesiastical buildings, such as St Joseph, Lower Sheringham, Norfolk (1910–36), and the Charterhouse School Chapel (1922–7), are indeed both original and bold, and in addition much less dependent on a style from the past. Scott exploited a surprising variety of possibilities. The results included Battersea Power Station in London (1932–4), which became the pattern for post-war brick-built power stations all over England, and the new Waterloo Bridge (1939–45). However, his official representational architecture lost the early tensions and turned commonplace: Cambridge University Library (1931–4), the new building for the Bodleian Library, Oxford (1936–46), Guildhall Building, London (1954–8).

Scottish architecture Prehistory is characteristically represented by Neolithic chamber-tombs (Maes Howe, Orkney), a Bronze Age stone circle (Callanish), hut circles and round houses, and Iron Age *brochs*, that is, round stone houses built without mortar. Roman occupation lasted from A.D. 58 to 100 and from 140 to 200 and was superficial. Several forts were built, but the most familiar monument is the Antonine Wall of 143. The Dark Ages produced bee-hive huts and high crosses. The Ruthwell Cross of c. 700 is the most accomplished in Britain. The figure sculpture surpasses anything of the same date in all Europe. Round church towers, an Irish feature, begin in Scotland as in Ireland in the C10 (Brechin, Egilsay). The Romanesque style starts in the C11, but the major Norman works belong to the C12: Dunfermline (c. 1150) under Durham influence, Jedburgh Abbey of the same date with the so-called giant arcading of Romsey and Oxford, and Kelso of the late C12 with the west transept of Ely and Bury St Edmunds. Castles of stone appeared in the late C12; but Scotland did not go in for keeps. To the Transitional from Norman to Gothic belong the Cistercian Dundrennan Abbey and the elegant nave of Jedburgh. Fully Gothic are the choir of Glasgow Cathedral with its vaulted undercroft, the beautiful west end of Elgin and the nave of Dunblane. The paramount example of the C14 and C15 is Melrose, which has some French features. We shall find such direct inspiration from France again later. As for the C15 and early C16 the climax in ecclesiastic architecture is Rosslyn Chapel (c. 1450), in its superabundance of decoration reminiscent of Spain, and in secular architecture Borthwick (c. 1430) with its majestic Great Hall covered by a pointed tunnel vault. In the C15 and C16 secular architecture is on the whole more eventful than church architecture. As for the latter, it is enough here to mention St Giles at Edinburgh with a fine tierceron vault and a so-called crown on its tower and a few other town parish churches (Linlithgow, Stirling, Dundee). Concerning castles, Inverlochy of the C13 has a nearly square *enceinte* with four round corner towers, Caerlaverock has a big C13 to C15 gatehouse, and there are the many tower houses. They are high and forbidding. Characteristic of them are the many tourelles, a French not an English feature. Elphinstone, the oldest part of Glamis and Affleck represent the type. The Great Hall of Edinburgh Castle dates from c. 1505 and has a wooden roof.

Of about the same date is the impressive gate-house of Stirling Castle.

As in England the Renaissance comes in the first half of the c16 as a mode of decoration applied to indigenous buildings or elements. Such is the case of the Great Halls of Edinburgh Castle and Stirling Castle and later of Falkland Palace (c. 1540). In all these cases the source is not the Renaissance of Italy but

Fyvie Castle, Aberdeenshire, 1600–3

of France and her Loire châteaux. Equally French is, for example, Huntly Castle (1602), whereas Crichton Castle (1581–91) derived its façade of diamond-cut ashlar blocks from Ferrara or Spain. The castles and tower-houses of the Elizabethan and Jacobean decades are Scotland's most memorable contribution to pre-Victorian architecture. Half-a-dozen names are all that can be given here. Kellie of 1573, Balmanno of about the same time, Dundarave of 1596, Cawdor of about the same time, Crathes of 1595 and Fyvie also mostly late c16. Jacobean and after are the north quarter of Linlithgow Palace (1618–21) and the east quarter of Caerlaverock (c. 1620–35). Inside such buildings is often good plasterwork and far more often than in England ceiling painting (mostly of folk quality). The most monumental Scottish building of the mid-c17 is Heriot's Hospital in Edinburgh of 1628–59. This has a large courtyard and four sturdy angle towers.

A Scottish c17 speciality is reformed churches of more monumental intentions than they are in England. Burntisland is square with a square tower above the middle (1592), Lauder is a Greek cross (1673); Dairsie (1621) and several others are Gothic Survival.

The Inigo Jones-Christopher Wren style took some time to get entry into Scotland. The interpreter was William BRUCE. An early ex-

ample is Holyrood House (1671 etc.). It has superimposed pilasters and a pediment, once again more French than English. A pedimented centre was also introduced by Bruce at Hopetoun House in 1703. This part of the mansion and also a house like Kinross belong to the English group round Coleshill. After Scotland had thus submitted to the London taste, Scottish Georgian is on the whole the same as English Georgian. The ADAMS worked in the north as they did in the south – see the major parts of Hopetoun and Robert Adam's Mellerstain (1778) and his Edinburgh University (1789–94). His Culzean (1771–92) is the most dramatically sited of the several remarkable, almost astylar, castles which he designed towards the end of his life for Scottish clients, e.g., Seton Castle near Edinburgh. (They are very different from his earlier neo-Gothic work in England.) The most important architectural event in c18 Scotland however is the laying out of Edinburgh's New Town. The design is of 1767, by James Craig. But Charlotte Square was built to designs by Robert Adam (1791).

So to the c19. Scotland was stronger in the Grecian than in the Gothic mode. Of Gothic buildings reference might be made to the gorgeous Taymouth of 1806–10 (by A. & J. Elliot) and St John at Edinburgh of 1816–18 (by W. Burn). As for Grecian, the Edinburgh High School of 1825 (by T. Hamilton) is one of the most serious Doric compositions in Britain. Also at Edinburgh are PLAYFAIR'S

The High School, Edinburgh, begun 1825, by Thomas Hamilton

Royal Scottish Academy (Doric, 1823–36) and National Gallery (1850). The Perth Waterworks of 1832 (by W. Anderson) deserve to be better known. But the most interesting neo-Greek phenomenon in Scotland is the work of Greek THOMSON, who expressed himself in that style at a time when it was thoroughly unpopular all over Europe (but

*The Caledonian Road Church, Glasgow, 1856,
by Alexander Thomson*

Partners, the controversial town-centre colossus of Cumbernauld, 1963 etc., by Sir Hugh Wilson, St Bride at East Kilbride, 1958 etc.,

*St Andrew's Residence, Scotland, 1964-9,
by James Stirling*

cf. the Vienna Parliament of 1873-83 by HANSEN). His churches handle the Greek amazingly freely, with a dash of Egyptian, whereas his terraces of well-to-do houses such as Moray Place, Glasgow, of 1859 are clearly derived from SCHINKEL. Thomson also did commercial premises, though in that field the most interesting building is the house at the corner of Argyll Street and Jamaica Street, Glasgow, which is of 1855-6 (by J. Baird) and has an arcuated cast-iron front. Other styles used in the mid-C19 are the Gothic (Glasgow Stock Exchange, 1877, by J. Burnet) and the Elizabethan (Edinburgh Donaldson's Hospital, 1854, by Playfair). Nothing in such buildings would have led anybody to expect that by the 1890s Scotland would possess the most brilliant architect of Europe, Charles Rennie MACKINTOSH. His synthesis of sinuous Art Nouveau decoration with precisely rectangular panels, his synthesis (in the Glasgow School of Art of 1896-1909) of functional considerations with freely playing ornament, his synthesis of sympathy for the Scottish past and daring innovation, his sense of spatial interpenetrations – all this was nowhere else to be seen combined in one man. Today on the other hand Scotland is part of Britain, and no national traits can be discovered. Recent examples are Stirling University, 1966 etc., by Sir Robert Matthew, Johnson-Marshall &

by J. A. Coia, and a factory at Galashiels, 1970 etc., by Peter Womersley.

Lit: D. MacGibbon & T. Ross, *Castellated and Domestic Architecture of Scotland*, 5 vols., Edinburgh 1887-92; D. MacGibbon & T. Ross, *The Ecclesiastical Architecture of Scotland*, 3 vols., Edinburgh 1896; S. Cruden, *The Scottish Castle*, Edinburgh 1960; J. G. Dunbar, *The Historic Architecture of Scotland*, London 1966; T. W. West, *The History of Architecture in Scotland*, London 1967; A. Gomme & D. Walker, *Architecture of Glasgow*, London 1968; G. Hay, *Architecture in Scotland*, Newcastle on Tyne 1969.

Screens passage The space at the service end of a medieval hall between the screen and the buttery, kitchen, and pantry entrances.

Scroll 1. An ornament in the form of a scroll of paper partly rolled. 2. In classical architecture, the VOLUTE of an Ionic or Corinthian

*Scroll:
Dorchester,
Oxfordshire*

CAPITAL. 3. In Early English and Decorated Gothic architecture, a moulding in such a form.

Sedilia Seats for the clergy, generally three (for priest, deacon, and sub-deacon), and of masonry, in the wall on the south side of the CHANCEL.

Sedilia: Chesterton, Oxfordshire

Segment Part of a circle smaller than a semicircle.

Segmental Of an arch or other curved member, having the profile of a circular arc substantially less than a full semicircle.

Selva, Antonio (1751–1819), a leading neo-classical architect in Venice, trained under TEMANZA, then visited Rome, Paris, and London (1779–83). His early works are in a simplified neo-Palladian style, e.g., Teatro La Fenice, Venice (1788–92, burnt down but re-built to his design). But he developed a much stronger neo-classical manner later on, e.g., Duomo, Cologna Veneta (1806–17), with its vastly imposing octastyle Corinthian portico.
Lit: E. Bassi, *Giannantonio Selva, architetto veneziano*, Padua 1936; C. L. V. Meeks, *Italian Architecture, 1750–1914*; New Haven–London 1966.

Semper, Gottfried (1803–79), the most important German architect of the Early and High Victorian decades, was born at Ham-burg and studied at Göttingen, and then in Munich (under GÄRTNER). In 1826, after fighting a duel, he fled to Paris, where he worked under GAU and HITTORF. The years 1830–33 were spent in Italy and Greece, and after that journey Semper published a pam-phlet on polychromy in Greek architecture, immediately influenced by Hittorf. In 1834 he was appointed to a chair at the Dresden Academy and there built his finest buildings. The Opera came first (1838–41). It was, in its original form, neo-Cinquecento, with subdued ornamentation and an exterior that expressed clearly its interior spaces. The semicircular front was inspired by Moller's theatre at Mainz (*see* GILLY). After that followed the synagogue, a mixture of Lombard, Byzantine, Moorish, and Romanesque elements (1839–40); the Quattrocento Villa Rose (1839); and the Cinquecento Oppenheim Palace (1845). Then came the Picture Gallery, closing with its large arcuated façade the Baroque Zwinger at the time left open to the north (1847–54), and the Albrechtsburg, a grand terraced Cinquecento villa above the river Elbe (1850–5), sym-metrical, yet the German equivalent of, say, Osborne. After the revolution of 1848 Semper fled Germany and went first to Paris (1849–51) – an unsuccessful time, which made him contemplate emigration to America – and then to London (1851–5), where he did cer-tain sections of the 1851 Exhibition and advised Prince Albert on the tasks for the museum which is now the Victoria and Albert.

Semper was, in fact, keenly interested in art applied to industry, and his *Der Stil* (1861–3, only two volumes published) is the most interesting application of materialist principles to craft and design, an attempt at proving the origin of ornament in certain techniques peculiar to the various materials used. In architecture Semper believed in the expression of the function of a building in its plan and exterior, including any decorative elements.

In 1855 Semper went to the Zürich Poly-technic and taught there till 1871. During that time he made designs for the Wagner National Theatre (1864–6) which considerably in-fluenced the building as it was erected at Bayreuth (by O. Brückwald, 1841–1904; opened 1876). Semper's last years were spent in Vienna. His style then, as is clearly seen in the Dresden Opera (redesigned 1871 after a fire), was more Baroque, less disciplined, and looser. This is also evident in the two large identical museum buildings for Vienna, forming a forum with the Neue Hofburg (1872 etc., and 1881 etc.), and in the Burgtheater (1873). These last buildings were executed by Karl von Hasenauer (1833–94), but the well-thought-out, clearly articulated plans are Semper's.

Lit: H. Semper, G. Semper, Berlin 1880; L. D. Ettlinger, G. Semper und die Antike, Halle 1937; C. Z. von Manteuffel, Die Baukunst G. Sempers, Freiburg 1952; H. Quitzsch, G. Sempers Ästhetische Anschauungen, Berlin 1962; N. Pevsner, Some Architectural Writers of the Nineteenth Century, Oxford 1972; M. Fröhlich, Kritischer Katalog, Gottfried Semper, Basel 1973.

Sens, see WILLIAM OF SENS.

Sepulchre, see EASTER SEPULCHRE, HOLY SEPULCHRE.

Serliana (or Serlian motif) An archway or window with three openings, the central one arched and wider than the others: so called because it was first illustrated in SERLIO'S Architettura (1537), though it probably derived from BRAMANTE. It was much used by PALLADIO, and became one of the hallmarks of PALLADIANISM, especially in C17-18 England. It is more commonly known as a Venetian or Palladian window.

Serliana or Palladian or Venetian opening: Basilica, Vicenza, 1549–1614, by Palladio

Serlio, Sebastiano (1475–1554), painter and architect, was more important as the author of L'Architettura, which appeared in six parts between 1537 and 1551 (augmented from his drawings 1575). This was the first book on architecture whose aim was practical rather than theoretical, and the first to codify the five ORDERS: it diffused the style of BRAMANTE and RAPHAEL throughout Europe, and provided builders with a vast repertory of motifs. Born and trained in Bologna, Serlio

went to Rome c. 1514, and remained there until the sack of 1527 as a pupil of PERUZZI, who bequeathed him plans and drawings used extensively in his book. He then went to Venice until 1540, when he was called to France, and advised on building operations at Fontainebleau. Here he built a house for the Cardinal of Ferrara, known as the Grand Ferrare (1544–6, destroyed except for the entrance door) and the château at Ancy-le-Franc, near Tonnerre (begun 1546) which survives. The Grand Ferrare established the standard form for the HÔTEL or town-house in France for more than a century. The fantastic designs, especially for rusticated portals, in the later parts of his book, which were published in France, were much imitated by French Mannerist architects.

Lit: W. B. Dinsmoor in Art Bulletin, XXIV 1942; M. Rosci, Il Trattato di architettura di Sebastiano Serlio, Milan 1967; L. H. Heydenreich & W. Lotz, Architecture in Italy, 1400–1600, Pelican History of Art, Harmondsworth 1974.

Sert, José Luis (b. 1902). He comes from Barcelona, worked from 1929 to 1932 for LE CORBUSIER and emigrated to America in 1939. He became GROPIUS'S successor at Harvard. He designed Students' Halls of Residence for Harvard in 1962 – a restless design. Other works of his are the U.S. Embassy at Baghdad and the Fondation Naeght at St Paul near Nice.

Lit: K. Bastlund, J. L. Sert 1927–1965, Zurich–London 1967.

Servandoni, Giovanni Niccolò (1695–1766), born in Florence and trained as a painter under Pannini, began as a stage designer in France in 1726, but soon turned to architecture. In 1732 he won the competition for the west façade of St Sulpice, Paris. Though not executed until 1737, and revised meanwhile, this is among the earliest manifestations of a reaction against the Rococo. He later worked in England, designing the gallery of R. MORRIS'S Brandenburg House, Hammersmith (1750, demolished 1822).

Lit: L. Hautecoeur, Histoire de l'architecture classique en France, vol. III, Paris 1950.

Severus (fl. A.D. 64). Roman architect employed by Nero to build the Domus Aurea on the Esquiline after the disastrous fire of A.D. 64. Tacitus and Suetonius testify to the grandeur of the whole concept, the spacious gardens with which the buildings were integrated, the size, number and richness of the rooms decorated with gold, gems, mother of pearl and ivory, the baths of sea water and sulphur water, the dining-rooms fitted with devices for sprinkling the guests with scent from the ceiling. Nero is reported to have remarked that he was 'beginning to be housed like a human being'. The parts which survive reveal the architect's genius in designing a large series of rooms of contrasting forms and creating ingenious systems of indirect lighting. He was assisted by the engineer Celer in this work and also in a project to build a canal from Lake Avernus to the Tiber. It is probable that he was also in charge of the rebuilding of Rome after the fire and the author of the new city building code.

Lit: Chr. Hülsen, *Forum und Palatin*, 1926; A. Boethius, *The Golden House of Nero*, Ann Arbor 1960.

Severy A compartment or bay of a vault.

Sexpartite vault, *see* VAULT.

Sgraffito Decoration on plaster of incised patterns, the top coat being cut through to show a differently coloured coat beneath.

Shaft The trunk of a column between the base and CAPITAL (*see also* ORDER). Also, in medieval architecture, one of several slender columns attached (in a cluster) to a pillar or pier, door jamb or window surround. *See* COMPOUND PIER.

Shaft-ring (or **annulet**). A motif of the C12 and C13 consisting of a ring round a SHAFT.

Sharawadgi Artful irregularity in garden design and, more recently, in town planning. The word, probably derived from the Japanese, was first used in 1685 to describe the irregularity of Chinese gardens: it was taken up again and popularized in mid-C18 England and, in connection with town planning, some forty years ago.

Shaw, Richard Norman (1831–1912), was a pupil of William Burn (1789–1870), a very successful, competent, and resourceful architect of country houses, and won the Academy Gold Medal in 1854, after having travelled in Italy, France, and Germany. He published a hundred of the travel sketches in 1858 and in the same year went as chief draughtsman to STREET, following WEBB in this job. He started in practice with a friend from Burn's office, Eden Nesfield (1835–88), but they mostly worked separately. Shaw began in the Gothic style, and did a number of churches, some of them remarkably powerful (Bingley, Yorkshire, 1864–68; Batchcott, Shropshire, 1891–92), and one at least partaking of his happily mixed, mature style (Bedford Park, West London, 1880). But this style was not reached by Shaw and Nesfield at once. A few years intervened of highly picturesque, still somewhat boisterous country mansions, timber-framed as well as of stone (Leys Wood, Sussex, 1868; Cragside, Northumberland, 1870 etc.). At the same time, however, a change took place to a more intimate style, simpler details, and local materials (Glen Andred, Sussex, 1868). This both architects have entirely in common.

Shaw and Nesfield's mature style is much more subdued, and its period sources are mid-C17 brick houses under Dutch influence and the William and Mary style, rather than Gothic and Tudor. Decoration is more refined than was usual, and interior decoration was here and there left to MORRIS's firm. Which of the two architects really started this style is not certain. Nesfield is the more likely – see his Dutch C17 Lodge at Kew Gardens (1866) and his William-and-Mary-cum-Louis-XIII Kinmel Park (c. 1866–8) – but Shaw made an international success of it. That some inspiration from Webb stands at the beginning is indubitable. The key buildings were New Zealand Chambers in the City of London (1872), Lowther Lodge, Kensington (1873, now Royal Geographical Society), Shaw's own house in Ellerdale Road, Hampstead (1875), and the exquisite Swan House, Chelsea Embankment (1876). At the same time Shaw designed Bedford Park, Turnham Green, London, as the earliest garden suburb ever. About 1890 (Bryanston, Dorset) Shaw turned away from the dainty elegance of this style towards a grand classicism with giant columns and Baroque details (Chesters, Northumberland, 1891; Piccadilly Hotel, 1905).

Lit: R. Blomfield, *R. N. Shaw*, London 1940; N. Pevsner, 'R. N. Shaw' in *Victorian Architecture*, ed. P. Ferriday, London 1963; M. Girouard, *The Victorian Country House*, Oxford 1971.

Shell A thin, self-supporting membrane on the eggshell principle; used for roofing in timber or concrete.

Shepheard, Edward, *see* WOOD, John the Elder.

Sheppard, Richard (b. 1910). The most interesting buildings by R. Sheppard, Robson & Partners to date are Churchill College, Cambridge (1959 etc.), with a number of small and medium-sized courts grouped loosely round the towering concrete-vaulted hall; hostels for Imperial College, London (1961–3); the School of Navigation of Southampton University (1959–61); Digby Hall, Leicester University (1958–62); and the West Midland Training College at Walsall (1960–3).

Lit: R. Maxwell, *New British Architecture,* London 1972.

Shingle style The American term for the Domestic Revival of the 1870s and 1880s, influenced initially by Norman SHAW, but replacing his tile-hanging by shingle-hanging. The pioneer building is the Sherman House at Newport, Rhode Island, by H. H. RICHARDSON (1874). MCKIM, Mead & WHITE also participated. The masterpiece is Richardson's Stoughton House at Cambridge, Massachusetts

Shingle Style: Stoughton House, Cambridge, Mass., 1882, by H. H. Richardson

(1882). The shingle style is almost exclusively a style of the medium-sized private house, and its most interesting and most American feature, not implied in the name, is open internal planning.

Lit: V. Scully Jr, *The Shingle Style,* New Haven–London 1955.

Shingles Wooden tiles for covering roofs and spires.

Shinto architecture, *see* JAPANESE ARCHITECTURE.

Shouldered arch, *see* ARCH.

Shute, John (d. 1563), the author of the first English architectural book, *The First and Chief Groundes of Architecture* (1563), described himself as a painter and architect, and was a member of the household of the Duke of Northumberland who sent him to Italy about 1550. His book included illustrations of the five orders, derived mainly from SERLIO. It went into four editions before 1587 and must have been widely used.

Lit: M. Girouard, *Robert Smythson and the Architecture of the Elizabethan Era,* London 1966.

Shuttering, *see* FORMWORK.

Sill The lower horizontal part of a window-frame.

Siloe, Diego de (c. 1495–1563), was a sculptor as well as an architect, and one of the main practitioners of the PLATERESQUE style. Born in Burgos, he studied in Italy (Florence and possibly Rome), where he acquired a Michelangelesque style of sculpture and picked up the vocabulary of Renaissance architecture. His finest work as both sculptor and architect is the Escalera Dorada in Burgos Cathedral (1519–23) – a very imposing interior staircase rising in five stages and derived from that designed by BRAMANTE to link the terraces of the Belvedere Court. To decorate it *putti,* portraits in roundels, winged angel heads, and other Renaissance motifs are used with a still Gothic profusion. In 1528 Siloe began his masterpiece, Granada Cathedral, where his main innovation was a vast domed chancel very skilfully attached to the wide nave. Here he adopted a purer and more severe manner which was to have wide influence in Spain. His other buildings include the tower of S. Maria del Campo, near Burgos (1527); the Salvador Church, Ubeda (1536); Guadix Cathedral (1549); and S. Gabriel, Loja (1552–68), with its unusual trefoil *chevet.* (For illustration *see* STAIR.)

Lit: F. Chueca Goitia, *Arquitectura del siglo XVI* (*Ars Hispaniae,* vol. XI), Madrid 1953; G. Kubler & M. Soria, *Art and Architecture in Spain and Portugal and their American Dominions 1500–1800,* Pelican History of Art, Harmondsworth 1959.

Sima recta, *see* CYMA RECTA.

Sima reversa, *see* CYMA REVERSA.

Simón de Colonia (d. *c.* 1511). Son of **Juan de Colonia** (d. 1481), and father of **Francisco de Colonia** (d. 1542). Juan no doubt came from Cologne, and, indeed, the spires of Burgos Cathedral (1442–58) look German Late Gothic. Juan was also the designer of the Charterhouse of Miraflores outside Burgos (1441 etc.). Simón, sculptor as well as architect, followed his father at Burgos Cathedral and Miraflores and designed, in a typically Spanish wild Late Gothic, the Chapel of the Constable of the cathedral (1486 etc.) and the façade of S. Pablo at Valladolid (1486–99). He became master mason of Seville Cathedral in 1497. Francisco, who probably completed the façade of S. Pablo, is responsible (with Juan de Vallejo) for the crossing tower of Burgos Cathedral (1540 etc.), still essentially Gothic, though Francisco had done the Puerta de la Pellejería of the cathedral in the new Early Renaissance in 1516. Francisco was made joint master mason with JUAN DE ÁLAVA at Plasencia Cathedral in 1513, but they quarrelled over the job and also over Álava's work at Salamanca Cathedral. Álava commented on Francisco's *'poco saber'*. (For illustration *see* SPANISH ARCHITECTURE.)

Lit: L. Torres Balbás, *Arquitectura gotica* (*Ars Hispaniae*, VII), Madrid 1952; G. Kubler & M. Soria, *Art and Architecture in Spain and Portugal and their American Dominions, 1500–1800*, Pelican History of Art, Harmondsworth 1959.

Sinan (1489–1578 or 1588), the greatest Turkish architect, was supposedly of Greek origin. He worked for Suleiman 'the Magnificent' throughout the Ottoman Empire, from Budapest to Damascus, and, according to himself, built no less than 334 mosques, schools, hospitals, public baths, bridges, palaces, etc. His mosques developed from Hagia Sophia, the most famous being the enormous Suleimaniyeh in Istanbul (1550–57), though he himself considered his masterpiece to be the Selimiye at Edirne (Adrianople) (1569–74). (For illustrations *see* ISLAMIC ARCHITECTURE, MINARET, TURKISH ARCHITECTURE.)

Lit: E. Egli, *Sinan*, Zurich & Stuttgart 1954; O. Asplanapa, *Turkish Art and Architecture*, London 1971; A. Stratton, *Sinan*, New York–London 1972.

Sinhalese architecture, *see* INDIAN ARCHITECTURE.

Sitte, Camillo (1843–1903), Austrian townplanner and architect, was director of the Trades' School of Salzburg (1875–93), and then of Vienna (1893 onwards). His fame rests entirely on his book *Der Städtebau* (1889), which is a brilliant essay in visual urban planning. Sitte, with the help of a large number of diagrammatic plans, analyses open spaces in towns and the many ways in which irregularities of plan can cause attractive effects. His subject is really 'townscape', in the sense in which this term is now used by the *Architectural Review* and such critics as Gordon Cullen.

Lit: G. R. Collins, *C. Sitte and the Birth of Modern City Planning*, New York 1965.

Skeleton construction A method of construction consisting of a framework (*see* FRAMED BUILDING) and an outer covering which takes no load (*see* CLADDING). The skeleton may be visible from the outside. (Illustrated next column.)

Skewback That portion of the ABUTMENT which supports an arch.

Skidmore, Owings & Merrill (Louis Skidmore, 1897–1962; N. A. Owings, b. 1903; and J. O. Merrill, b. 1896). One of the largest and at the same time best architectural firms in the United States. They have branches in New York, Chicago, and other centres, each with its own head of design. Gordon Bunshaft (b. 1909), a partner in 1945, is an especially distinguished designer. Outstanding among the works of the firm are the following: Lever House, New York (completed 1952), which started the international vogue for curtainwalled skyscrapers rising on a podium of only a few storeys, and which has, moreover, a garden-court in the middle of the podium; the Hilton Hotel at Istanbul (begun 1952); the United States Air Force Academy at Colorado Springs (begun 1955). Other important buildings are the Manufacturers' Trust Bank in New York (1952–4), memorably low in a city of high buildings and (although a bank and in need of security) largely glazed to the outside, the Connecticut General Life Insurance at Hartford (1953–7), a beautifully landscaped and detailed, Brunswik Corporation Offices (Chicago, 1965), Hartford Fire Insurance Com-

Skeleton construction:
Rheinstahl-Hochhaus, Essen

Skeleton construction: Crown Hall,
Illinois Institute of Technology, Chicago,
1952–6, by Mies van der Rohe

pany (San Francisco, 1967), John Hancock
Center (Chicago, 1968), and Sears Tower
(Chicago, completed 1974), the highest SKY-
SCRAPER (1,454 ft) in the world. Skidmore's
style is developed from that of MIES VAN DER
ROHE and, until recently, rarely departed from
its crispness and precision. For some years
now the firm has gone in for concrete used in
pre-cast members. In this field their Banque
Lambert in Brussels of 1959 has proved as influential as Lever House less than a decade

before. In some others of their recent buildings
a playfulness – even though a structural
playfulness – has appeared which is less
convincing. (For illustration *see* UNITED
STATES ARCHITECTURE.)

  Lit: H.-R. Hitchcock (ed.), *Architecture of
Skidmore, Owings & Merrill 1950–1962*, London 1963; C. Woodward, *Skidmore, Owings &
Merrill*, London 1970; A. Drexler, *Architecture of Skidmore, Owings & Merrill*, London
1974.

Skirting The edging, usually of wood, fixed
to the base of an internal wall.

Skylight A window set into a roof or ceiling
so as to provide top-lighting.

Skyscraper A multi-storey building constructed on an iron and later a steel skeleton
provided with high-speed elevators and combining extraordinary height with ordinary
room-spaces such as would be used in low
buildings. The term originated in the United
States in the late 1880s, about ten or twelve
years after office buildings in New York had
reached the height of ten or twelve storeys or
c. 250 ft. To go much beyond this was impossible with traditional building materials, and
further development was based on the introduction of metal framing. This took place at
Chicago in 1883 (*see* JENNEY). Steel skeleton
construction for skyscrapers was first established in 1890 by BURNHAM & ROOT'S Rand
McNally Building. Architecturally the finest
achievements are HOLABIRD & ROCHE'S
Tacoma and Marquette Buildings of 1886 etc.
and 1894 etc. and SULLIVAN'S Wainwright
Building, St Louis, and Guaranty Building,
Buffalo, of 1890 and 1894. The highest skyscraper before the First World War was C.
Gilbert's Woolworth Building in New York
(792 ft). The Empire State Building of 1930–
32 is 1,250 ft high; the twin towers of the
World Trade Center, New York (1970–74; by
YAMASAKI) are 1,350 ft. The Sears Tower,
Chicago (completed 1974; by SKIDMORE,
OWINGS & MERRILL) is the highest to date at
1,454 ft. The Eiffel Tower is 985 ft.

  Lit: C. W. Condit, *The Rise of the Skyscraper*,
Chicago 1952; E. Schultz & W. Simmons,
Offices in the Sky, Indianapolis 1959.

Slate-hanging A wall covering of overlapping
rows of slates on a timber substructure.
(Illustrated next page.)

Slate-hanging

Sleeper wall An underground wall either supporting SLEEPERS, or built between two PIERS, two walls, or a pier and a wall, to prevent them from shifting. The foundation wall of an ARCADE between nave and aisle would thus be a sleeper wall.

Sleepers In a building, strong horizontal beams on which the JOISTS rest. The term can apply to: *a.* beams laid lengthwise on the walls under the ground floor, supporting the floor joists; *b.* in buildings of more than one storey, the beams between the principal posts, marking the divisions and carrying the joists and any other similar cross-beams. With a span of more than 15 ft or so, transverse sleepers are inserted to carry longitudinal joists. The modern term comes from the medieval *dormant*, so called because lesser timbers 'slept' on them.

Slype A covered way or passage, especially in a cathedral or monastic church, leading east from the cloisters between transept and chapterhouse.

Smirke, Sir Robert (1780–1867), the leading GREEK REVIVAL architect in England, nevertheless lacked the genius of his almost exact contemporary in Germany, SCHINKEL, by whom he may have been influenced. The son of a painter and Academician, he was articled to SOANE, but quarrelled after a few months. From 1801 to 1805 he travelled in Italy, Sicily, and Greece, sketched most of the ancient buildings in the Morea, and on his return to London published the first and only volume of his projected *Specimens of Continental Architecture* (1806). His first buildings were medieval in style – Lowther Castle (1806–11) and Eastnor Castle (*c.* 1810–15). He made

his name with Covent Garden Theatre (1808, destroyed), the first Greek Doric building in London and as such very influential. It showed with what simple means gravity and grandeur might be achieved. His cool business-like efficiency quickly brought him fame and fortune, and in 1813 he reached the head of his profession when he joined Soane and NASH as Architect to the Board of Works. His masterpieces came in the next decade, first the British Museum (1823–47), then the General Post Office (1824–9, demolished), both large in scale and massively Grecian in style. Though less uncompromising and less impressive than Schinkel's Altes Museum in Berlin (1825) the British Museum with its tremendous Ionic colonnade has a noble dignity and illustrates his admirable directness and scholarly detailing at their best. Knighted in 1832, he retired in 1845.

Lit: J. Mordaunt Crook, *The British Museum*, London 1972; J. Mordaunt Crook, *The Greek Revival*, London 1972.

Smithson, Peter and Alison (b. 1923 and 1928). Their school at Hunstanton in Norfolk (1954) was one of the most controversial buildings of the time; it is not informal but a symmetrical group, and in its details is inspired by MIES VAN DER ROHE. The Smithsons then turned in the direction of BRUTALISM, but their biggest and most mature building, for the *Economist* in London (1962–4), has none of the quirks of that trend. It is a convincingly grouped scheme of various heights, with a façade to St James's Street that succeeds in establishing a *modus vivendi* with the C18 clubs around, and with two high blocks of different heights behind.

Lit: E. Maxwell, *New British Architecture*, London 1972; A. & P. Smithson, *Without Rhetoric; An Architectural Aesthetic, 1955–72*, London 1973.

Smythson, Robert (*c.* 1536–1614), the only Elizabethan architect of note. He perfected the spectacular if rather outlandish country-house style developed by the courtiers and magnates of the period. First heard of at Longleat, where he worked as principal freemason (1568–75), he built his masterpiece, Wollaton Hall, during the next decade (1580–8). This was a revolutionary building – a single pile with corner towers and a central hall, planned symmetrically on both axes. The plan probably derives from SERLIO and the whimsical Flemish carved ornamentation of banded shafts, strap-work, etc., from de VRIES, but the fantastic and romantic sham-castle silhouette is his own invention and wholly English. He settled near Wollaton, acquiring property there and the style of a 'gentleman'. But he almost certainly had a hand in the design of three later houses of note, Worksop Manor (c. 1585, now destroyed), Hardwick Hall (1590–7) and Burton Agnes (1601–10). His son **John** (d. 1634) designed Bolsover Castle (1612 etc.), perhaps the most romantic of all the sham castles.

Lit: M. Girouard, *Robert Smythson and the Architecture of the Elizabethan Era*, London 1966.

Soane, Sir John (1753–1837). The most original English architect after VANBRUGH. His extremely personal style is superficially neo-classical but, in fact, romantic or 'picturesque' in its complicated and unexpected spatial interplay. Intense, severe, and sometimes rather affectedly odd, his buildings reflect his tricky character. He was always slightly uncertain of himself and, despite his genius, never achieved complete confidence and authority even in his own style. The son of a Berkshire builder, he trained under DANCE and HOLLAND, then studied for three years in Italy, where he probably knew PIRANESI; but French influence, especially that of Peyre and LEDOUX, was more profound. He returned to London in 1780, but his career only really began with his appointment as Surveyor to the Bank of England in 1788. His work at the Bank, now destroyed, was among the most advanced in Europe. The Stock Office (begun 1792) and Rotunda (begun 1796) must have seemed shockingly austere, with their shallow domes and general emphasis on utility and structural simplicity, not to mention his reduction of classical ornamentation to rudimentary grooved strips and diagrammatic mouldings. The romantic or picturesque element in his work is felt increasingly after 1800, notably in Pitshanger Manor (1800–1803; now Ealing Public Library) and in the Dulwich College Art Gallery (1811–14, restored 1953), a 'primitivist' construction in brick with each element curiously detached by some slight break or recession, and, above all, in his own home, No. 13 Lincoln's Inn Fields, London (1812–13), now Sir John Soane's Museum. This is highly eccentric and personal to the point of perversity, especially inside, with its congested, claustrophobic planning, complicated floor-levels, in-

genious top-lighting, hundreds of mirrors to suggest receding planes and blur divisions, and hanging, Gothic-inspired arches to detach ceilings from walls. The exterior perfectly illustrates his linear stylization and emphasis on planes rather than masses. His last buildings of note are the astylar utilitarian stables of Chelsea Hospital (1814–17), St Peter's, Walworth (1822), and Pell Wall (1822–8) a villa-type gate-lodge with curious features reminiscent of VANBRUGH. He was made Professor of Architecture at the Royal Academy in 1806 and knighted in 1831. He published *Designs in Architecture* (London, 1778, re-issued 1790). (For illustrations *see* ENGLISH ARCHITECTURE.)

Lit: J. Summerson, *Sir John Soane*, London 1952; D. Stroud, *Sir J. Soane*, London 1961.

Socle A base or pedestal.

Soffit The underside of any architectural element, e.g., an INTRADOS.

Soffit cusps Cusps springing from the flat soffit (*see* INTRADOS) of an arched head, and not from its chamfered sides or edges.

Solar An upper living-room in a medieval house; from the Latin *solarium* (a sunny spot or a sun-roof).

Solari, Guiniforte (1429–81), a Milanese 'last-ditch' Gothic conservative, completed FILARETE's Renaissance Ospedale Maggiore, built the simplified Gothic nave of S, Maria delle Grazie, Milan (1463–90, completed by BRAMANTE), and worked on the Gothic Milan Cathedral. He began S. Pietro in Gessate, Milan, c. 1475. From 1459 he assisted his father **Giovanni** (b. 1410) at the Certosa di Pavia where the crossing and the choir were designed by him. The Certosa was begun by Giovanni Solari c. 1429 and finished by 1473.

Lit: G. C. Bascapé & P. Mezzanotte, *Milano nell'Arte e nella Storia*, Milan 1948.

Solari, Santino (1576–1646), one of the first Italian architects to work extensively in Germany and Austria, came of a large family of artists from Como. His main work is Salzburg Cathedral (1614–28), an entirely Italian basilican church with dome and with twin towers flanking the west façade. For the Bishop of Salzburg he built the Italianate *Lustschloss* at Hellbrunn, outside Salzburg (1613–19). He also designed (c. 1620) the solemn little shrine of the black-faced Virgin at Einsiedeln, Switzerland, later surrounded by MOSBRUGGER'S fantastic Baroque abbey church.

Lit: E. Hempel, *Baroque Art and Architecture in Central Europe*, Pelican History of Art, Harmondsworth 1965.

Solarium A sun terrace or LOGGIA.

Solea In an Early Christian or Byzantine church, a raised pathway projecting from the BEMA to the AMBO.

Solomonic column A barley-sugar or twisted column, so called from its supposed use in Solomon's temple. *See also* SALOMÓNICA.

Sommaruga, Giuseppe (1867–1917), a native of Milan, was a pupil at the Brera Academy and of Boito and Beltrami, but turned to ART NOUVEAU and became, with Raimondo d'Aronco (1857–1932; buildings for the Turin Exhibition, 1902), its most important representative in Italy. His principal works are the Palazzo Castiglioni on the Corso Venezia, Milan (1901) and the Hotel Tre Croci at Campo dei Fiori, Varese (1909–12). (For illustration *see* ITALIAN ARCHITECTURE.)

Lit: E. Catto & L. Mariani Trani in *L'architettura*, XIII, 1967–8, pp. 340–44, 410–14, 480–84, 550–54, 620–24.

Sopraporta A decorative panel, usually a painting, above the door of a room, usually framed in harmony with the doorcase to form a decorative unit.

Sopraporta: Schloss Benrath, near Düsseldorf, 1755–69, by Pigage

Soufflot, Jacques-Germain (1713–80), the greatest French neo-classical architect, was the son of a provincial lawyer against whose wishes he went off to Rome to study architecture in 1731. He stayed seven years, settling on his return in Lyon, where he was commissioned to build the enormous Hôtel Dieu (1741 etc.). This made his reputation, and in 1749 he was chosen by Mme de Pompadour to accompany her brother, M. de Marigny, to Italy, where he was to spend two years preparing himself for his appointment as Surintendent des Bâtiments. The tour was very successful and may be regarded as marking the beginning of Neo-Classicism in France, of which the great masterpiece was to be Soufflot's Ste Geneviève (called the Panthéon since the Revolution) in Paris (begun 1757). This was a revolutionary building for France and was hailed by the leading neo-classical critic and theorist, LAUGIER, as 'the first example of perfect architecture'. It perfectly expresses a new, more serious, not to say solemn attitude towards Antiquity, and combines Roman regularity and monumentality with a structural lightness derived from Gothic architecture. Soufflot himself said (1762) that one should combine the Greek orders with the lightness one admired in Gothic buildings. He continued working on his masterpiece to the end of his life, but did not live to see it finished. His other buildings are of much less interest, e.g., École de Droit, Paris (designed 1763, built 1771 onwards) and various follies in the park of the Château de Menars (1767 etc.) including a rotunda, nymphaeum, and orangery, all in an elegant but rather dry neo-classical style.

Lit: J. Mondain Monval, *Soufflot, sa vie, son oeuvre, son ésthetique, 1713–1780*, Paris 1918; H. Petzet, *Soufflots Sainte-Geneviève*, Berlin 1961.

Sounding board, *see* PULPIT.

South American architecture, *see* BRAZILIAN and CENTRAL ANDEAN ARCHITECTURE.

South-East Asian architecture: Java, Bali, Indo-China, Burma and Thailand. Even before the beginning of our era Indian civilization, notably its art and religions, had been transmitted to neighbouring lands. But further afield, i.e. in the countries in question, Indian influence only becomes apparent in the early centuries of our era. The motive force behind the diffusion of Hindu and Buddhist teachings in the whole of South-east Asia was the trade in exotic products between the Roman Empire and the Far East. The connections established during this period between India and the countries of the Far East outlasted the cessation of trade by several centuries. There is a clearly definable division of influence between India and China in this part of the world – whence the name Indo-China. On this peninsula, split up by the great Menam and Mekong rivers, Khmer, Thai, and Cham civilizations flourished. To the north-east, the delta of the Red River and North Vietnam had become provinces of Imperial China, and so fell under its cultural aegis. To the north-west, the Irrawaddy Delta in the Gulf of Bengal was fruitful soil for Indian influence.

Java and Bali. Indonesia first merits our closer attention; for very early on this region produced first-rate architecture, whose influence was in turn to be felt in Indo-China. There are two main strands in Javanese art, inspired by Buddhism and Hinduism respectively. Javanese art began to blossom in the c3 A.D. under the auspices of the powerful Shailendra dynasty, which adopted Buddhism as the state religion and erected several buildings, of which Borobudur (*c.* 800) is the finest.

The hemispherical Buddhist STUPA – derived from that of Sanchi in India – served the architect of Borobudur as the basis for his monumental work (140 ft square). The structure is composed of five stepped square

Aerial view of the Buddhist temples and stupas at Borobudur, Java, 760–847

View from the upper level of the stupa at Borobudur, Java, 760–847

platforms, over which rise three further stepped but circular platforms, crowned by a tall stupa. The whole thing forms an artificial mound 150 ft high, ascended by four axially set stairways partly with CORBELLED vaults. Seventy-two small pierced stupas perch on the three topmost circular platforms. It is designed for Buddhist ritual processions, and symbolizes the cosmic mountain, the centre of the world. Its considerable importance is underlined by the presence of countless reliefs decorating the lower tiers.

Towards the middle of the c9 the Shailendra dynasty ceded its place to the descendants of an earlier dynasty, who vigorously imposed Shaivite Hinduism. From this period stems the Hindu temple city of Prambanam, dependent upon earlier c8 examples on the Dieng Plateau, and still marked by strong Indian influence. The temples are ASTYLAR CELLAS on a square plan, containing an idol

Bima Temple, Dieng, Java, c. 700

(a statue or *lingam*). The corbelled roofing is produced by upper storeys tapering by tiers, such as is found in Hindu architecture all over Indo-China. This type of structure, which goes back to the South Indian stone temple of Mahaballipuram, was to become a characteristic feature of South-East Asian art. The indented plan and the soaring roofing – incarnating the heavenly city erected on the summit of Mount Meru – are leitmotifs of Hindu architecture, as are the concentrically superimposed ring walls, whose portals and corner-towers are a religious transposition of an urban theme.

All Javanese temples – from Borobudur to the sanctuaries of Prambanam – are built of stone. Religious complexes underwent a spectacular development during the Hindu period. The temple of Tjandi Lara Djongrang for instance is composed of three tower-shaped shrines, the most important of which is 155 ft high. They are enclosed by a square wall with 360-ft sides. A second and concentric wall with 720-ft sides in turn encloses 224 small temples identical to the shrines between it and the first wall. The whole complex faces the four points of the compass. It displays a remarkable feeling for the organization of large units. As in India, these sanctuaries are profusely adorned with divinities in high relief. They also contain bas-reliefs, which as regards style and quality scarcely differ from the Buddhist examples at Borobudur.

These temple sites in Central Java were followed by various buildings in the east of the country – a region that appreciably accentuated its own style in the c13. East Javan architecture is notable for its thick cornices separating the tiers of the high roofs from one another, and for the exaggerated projections that give the buildings such striking silhouettes. The plentiful horizontal mouldings are generally executed in brick – especially in the region of Trawulan. This style also

Schiwa Temple at Mengwi, Bali

gives rise to the singular 'cloven gates', of which the finest examples were to be produced in Bali in the c14–15. These are *chandi bentars* – towers which have the appearance of having been cut vertically in two and the halves set apart, in order to provide access to the axially situated entry. In vernacular Balinese architecture, which is chiefly of wood and straw (as was in all probability once the case in India), the diminishing repetition of the stages reaches such a point that one can count 7, 9 or even 11 storeys piled on top of one another. The results are high, slender towers, with accentuated points called *'meru'* – proving that they symbolize the heavenly mountain.

Indo-China: from Funanese to Early Khmer (c3–8). Indian influence in Indo-China is evident down the middle reaches of the Mekong from the first centuries of our era. But architecture first makes its appearance with the foundation of the cities of the Bassac delta, and of the capital, Oc-eo, in particular, which is within a rectangular enclosure 3000 × 1500 yds in extent. It consists of five earth ramparts separated by moats. The buildings of this city were probably not executed in lasting materials. Funanese shrines were of wood and straw, in this like their South Indian models antecedent to the stone Hindu structure at Mahaballipuram of the c6–7.

Amongst the earliest monuments that we know are the shrines of the city of Sambor Prei Kuk, whose square wall had sides over a mile in length, and is ascribed to the beginning of the c7. This was the first in a series of important works in this capital, the focal point of the united kingdom of Chen-la. The brick shrines are disposed inside large concentric quadrangular walled enclosures, and given tiered corbelled roofs. They may be rectangular or octagonal in plan. The jagged articulation of the wall with pilasters, the sandstone supports flanked by colonnettes, and the gables shaped like the Indian *kudu*, all prefigure Khmer architecture.

In the c8, after the obscure course of events leading to the bifurcation of the kingdom of Chen-la, architecture hardly seems to have made any progress. There were Javanese incursions into Indo-China and the Malay peninsula, and these were not to be without effect on the principles of true Angkoran architecture.

Pre-classic Angkoran works. Before tracing the course of Khmer art, we must pursue its embryonic stage to the end – to Kulên, 30 miles to the north-east of the Great Cambodian Lake. In the period between 800 and 850, the architectural essentials of the style that was to break upon the world at Roluos, near Angkor, were forged. For it was at Rong Chên in Kulên that the temple mountain, which was to be so characteristic of Khmer architecture, made its appearance. This was a kind of hybrid between two features adopted from India and Java: on the one hand the stupa (as in Borobudur), which formed the supporting plinth, on the other hand, the shrine, which (like those of Dieng or Prambanam) consists of a square cella surmounted by tapering stages above. A step in the same direction was made in the early c9 at the sanctuary of Ak Yum, to the north-west of Angkor. It seems to have been the work of Jayavarman II, who had lived for several years at Shailendra's court in Java.

But it was only with the foundation of Roluos by King Indravarman (877–89) that these techniques were refined into the Khmer style. For the first time in the history of Indo-China properly planned cultivation was introduced, leading to improved harvests of rice. It was thanks to the prosperity that this produced that the vast complexes of Angkor could be created. Indravarman had grasped the fact that the Angkoran plain could only be fully exploited by breaking the vicious cycle of the rainy seasons, through which the land was alternately flooded for four months, and parched for the next eight. His answer was to have made a great artificial lake, called a *baray*.

The first baray of which we know was that of Lolei in Roluos, to which the name of Indratataka was given. It was $2\frac{1}{2}$ miles long by $\frac{1}{2}$ a mile wide. Barrages held the water above the level of the plain, so that it sufficed to open the sluices to irrigate the paddy-fields. The Indratataka held six million cubic metres of water. This was later augmented by the Eastern Baray ($4\frac{1}{2} \times 1$ mile), constructed by Yasovarman around 900, and the Western Baray ($5 \times 1\frac{1}{2}$ miles), constructed around 1050 and holding more than forty million cubic metres of water. The Khmer system of cultivation was now established.

But to return to Roluos, where Indravarman was not merely content with the construction of his baray. He began by erecting the sanctuary of Preah Kô, which became Jayavarman II's memorial temple in 879. This building scarcely shows any advance on those of Sambor or Kulên. But shortly after,

in 881, he began building the temple-mountain of Bakong, situated in the centre of the city of Hariharalaya. This is in sandstone, and consists of five square terraces or platforms. It measures 218×212 ft at its foot, and attains pyramidally a height of 50 ft. The main shrine then rises upon this vast base. Twelve

Bakong Temple, Roluos, Cambodia, begun 881

lesser shrines are placed round the penultimate platform of the monument, and eight large brick *prasate* (tower-shrines) are disposed ringwise about the interior of a 520×390 ft walled enclosure round the pyramid. The whole thing is cordoned off by a moat 5000 ft in circumference. The city was built round this moat, and in turn confined by another moat 72 ft wide making a huge rectangle 2600 ft long by 2300 ft wide. The city is divided into four equal quarters by axial streets leading to the central temple, and spanning the moats on earthen ramparts. This system was to be the key to Khmer projects: a baray supplying running water to the moats of a city, in whose centre lies the royal sanctuary in the form of a temple mountain. The whole complex represented an intricate system of hydraulics, dependent upon a flourishing economy based upon the intensive cultivation of rice. Its basic elements remained the same, even when it was expanded fourfold or fivefold. The architecture is only secondary to the hydraulics, which its monuments are designed to protect and hallow through a special cult. For the Khmer temple, whether sacred to Hindu gods like Shiva, Vishnu or Brahma, or, at the end of the Angkoran period, to the Buddha-King, symbolized the centre of the world, Mount Meru, the dwelling-place of the gods.

The square plan and its geometrical subdivisions were based on a great *mandala* (a magic diagram) which brought the temple into harmony with cosmic order and the forces governing the world. When applied to domestic architecture, the mandala permitted the identification of the royal city with the centre of the universe. So too, the Angkoran plain is subdivided like a mandala by the axes of the two roads at right angles to one another leading to the sanctuaries, whose perspectives affirm the boundlessness of the Khmer kingdom, which is thus likewise made sacred to the gods.

This bi-polar symmetry, exemplified by the right-angled system of roads centred on the main shrine, is the underlying principle of centrally-planned temples in India. But it was never so consistently employed – from sacred monuments to human settlements, down even to field-systems – as by the Khmers. The ingenuity of the Khmers lay precisely in their ability to combine this thorough and self-sufficient panoply of symbolism, and its magico-religious application, with their practical genius for the conservation and distribution of water. To this remarkable gift for synthesis are attributable works like Phnom-Bakheng (a temple complex set on a natural hill, selected as the centre of Yasovarman's new capital), Pre Rup, Takeo, and lastly, the classic perfection of Angkor Wat.

Phnom Bakheng Temple, Angkor, Cambodia, late c9

Pre Rup Temple, Angkor, mid-c10

Classic Khmer architecture. Architecture made steady advances after the construction of Roluos; it became both more diverse, and more homogeneous. Thus for instance, the long ancillary buildings that had fringed the main shrine since the foundation of Preah Kô and Bakong became increasingly numerous, so as even to extend along the platform of the temple mountain (Pre Rup). One by one, these long chambers encircled whole stages of the pyramid. Inspired progress toward the simplification of this kind of structure finally led, at Phineanakas and Takeo, to the birth of one of the vital features of classic Khmer architecture – the continuous gallery. There was no longer any division into separate chambers, and the outer wall of the galleries thus produced became one with the enclosing wall of each storey. Ultimately both the axial gates (*gopuram*) and the corner towers were incorporated too. The next step was to substitute a more lasting material for the timber and tile roofing of the pre-classic period. Corbelled courses of dressed stone or brick were used for this.

Angkor Wat. With the great temple of Angkor Wat, erected in the reign of the most famous of the Angkoran kings, Suryavarman II (1113–50), Khmer architecture reached its apogee – both in the perfection of forms and mastery of space, and in the quality of its execution. This is not only the largest, but also the finest, of all the temples to have been built in Indo-China. At Angkor Wat the 650-ft wide moat describes a rectangle of 5000 × 4250 ft, thus covering an area of almost a square mile. The temple was the centre of a city, of which only those buildings erected in imperishable materials remain. In total,

Temple at Angkor Wat, Cambodia, early c12

Aerial view of temple at Angkor Wat,
Cambodia, early C12

Angkor Wat afforded an area inhabitable by
17,000–20,000 people. The banks of the
moat are stepped in stone.

Confronting the broad western access-
road is a large 775-ft long columned hall,
interrupted by a triple, cruciform gopuram
half way down it. This ample construction,
which serves as the main entrance, is an
imitation of the main façade of the temple,
which is only visible after passing through
this majestic ceremonial gateway. A further
1150-ft long causeway on the same axis runs
to the foot of the temple. It is raised, and
bordered by superb *naga* balustrades, as well

Temple balusters, Angkor Wat

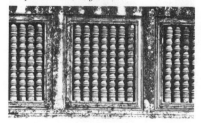

as being accessible by six flights of steps on
either side. It gives on to a terrace with the
role of a temenos (a kind of sacred platform),
1100 ft long by 700 ft wide, at whose centre
stands the temple.

The front of the temple of Angkor Wat
rises from a high and elaborately profiled base.
The arms of the huge circulating gallery (608 ×
700 ft) which opens outwards extend symmetrically to either side of it. The columned
hall, which rests on square sandstone pillars,
has a vaulted main gallery and cruciform
pavilions at the corners. A band of fantastic
reliefs runs for more than 1600 ft along the
whole inner wall of the gallery round the
temple. It marvellously depicts both a whole
mythology and a kind of chronicle of the
kingdom.

Pursuing the same axis, we penetrate the
distinguishing feature of classic Angkoran
architecture – the cruciform monastic court.
The court connects the gallery of the reliefs
with the gallery of the second perimeter wall.
Three galleries, uniting with three gopurams
on their second storey, lie upon the axis of
the main entrance and upon the two axes

of the side-entrances. A further gallery at right angles to these three then bisects the whole thing, so as to produce a cross-shaped plan. As a result there are four small open courts. The galleries of this 'cloister' introduce the first true vault of sandstone, supported on a quadruple row of columns, which make a central nave buttressed by double aisles on either side. This cruciform complex is again hemmed by galleries with a roof protecting a veritable garland of sculpture: a whole ballet of alluring *apsaras* and *devatas* in deeply cut relief pass before our eyes.

The three parallel galleries of the cloister follow the upward movement of the stairs, and give access to the second storey with the aid of a stacked system of vaulting. The circulating gallery of the second floor is only open, with balustered windows, toward the inside. This second enclosure, measuring 325 × 375 ft, contains the huge 42-ft high substructure from whose topmost platform a quincunx of towers rears aloft.

The third tier of the temple mountain, supporting the sanctuary, is formed by a circulating gallery whose balustered windows this time open outwards. The inner colonnades are supported on pillars. Passages run at right angles towards the central shrine from the middle of each of the four sides of this gallery. With vaults borne on a quadruple row of pillars, these passages largely repeat the galleries of the floor below. The chief difference lies in the presence of the quintuple tower, with its dramatically soaring sanctuary accompanied by four corner-towers, all in the form of a tiara. The central shrine is preceded by four gates resting on pillars, and mounts 138 ft to the lotusbud-shaped pinnacle of its roof, rising 212 ft above the Angkoran plain. From here the vast mandala described by the whole layout in its setting is clearly apparent – the image of the heavenly palace of the gods on the summit of Mount Meru.

The last resurgence under Jayavarman VII. After the death of Suryavarman II around 1150, the Cham exploited the confused state of affairs in order to execute a bold raid on Angkor in 1177, and to set fire to it. King Jayavarman VII succeeded in expelling the intruders, restoring the might of the Khmer, and having himself crowned King of Angkor in 1181. He set about the complete reconstruction of the city forthwith.

He renounced the Hindu faith of his predecessors and professed Buddhism. The consequence of this conversion was a wholly new style with a singular baroque flavour. The severe, clean lines of Angkor Wat vanished, and space was treated in a new way. We are abruptly confronted by an art that fudged the distinction between sculpture and architecture. The towers of the monuments are studded with huge sculpted faces, embodying at once the Buddha's portrait and that of the ruler, Jayavarman VII.

King Jayavarman founded a temple city. This was Ta Prohm, with a perimeter wall measuring 3250 × 1950 ft. The actual temple was built according to a schema that served as model for most of the Buddhist monasteries built or begun by Jayavarman VII. In essence this kind of flat temple, which had been prefigured by the shrines of Banteay Samre and Beng Mealea at the time of the foundation of Angkor Wat in the classic period, consisted of a triple enclosure of concentric galleries. The gradual elision of the steps of the pyramid and the circulating galleries foreshadowed earlier has here been taken to its logical conclusion.

The temple of Preah Khan, which is surrounded by a broad rectangular moat 130 ft across, with sides of 3250 × 2450 ft, closely resembles that of Ta Prohm. But the finish of the building betrays the haste with which it was built. The bonding of the wall is mediocre, not to say botched, and much of the sculptural decoration appears perfunctory and coarse.

The masterpieces of Angkor Thom and the Bayon. Founded around 1200, the capital of Angkor Thom (= the great, or regal, city) gave a new accent to Angkoran architecture. It was then that the markedly baroque style emerged which preceded the decay of the kingdom. It declares itself even in the peri-

North Gate, Angkor Thom, Cambodia, early C13

meter wall. On the five dikes traversing the moats there is a remarkable phenomenon – the causeway of the giants. This is an access-road bordered by high balustrades on both sides. These are composed of 54 giants, each carrying the body of an enormous *naga* in his powerful arms. This allusive allegorical composition illustrates one of the favourite themes of Indian mythology – the churning of the sea of milk, symbolizing the creation of the world. This mythical episode is further commented on by the towers.

This symbolic art attains the height of its expressive power at Bayon, a further master-piece of Jayavarman VII's. It is an unbeliev-ably complex work, ornate and tangled, yet still imposing. The galleries open outwards,

Bayon Temple, Angkor Thom, Cambodia, early c13

and their inside walls are overlain with narra-tive reliefs. Towers emerge at the corners and from the triple gopurams, adding incident to each side of the square complex. These towers reveal sculpted faces. There are so many of them they resemble a forest, dwarfed by the high cylinder of the central tower. They represent giant heads with four faces looking towards the cardinal points of the compass. These faces with their benevolent, tranquil features, the utter composure suggested by their closed eyes and their graceful, smiling mouth, embody the divine-cum-royal visage of the Bodhisattva-King. The Bayon is thus a monument of profound new significance. The faces of the Buddha-King, turned towards the four points of the compass, express the benevolence and solicitude of the god poured out on the universe, but also the omnipresent power of the ruler.

During the c14 various insignificant kings succeeded to the Angkoran throne, but towards the mid-c15 the city was forsaken altogether.

Champa architecture. Simultaneously with the rise of Angkor civilization, Cham art was

evolving on the eastern side of Indo-China. It likewise was under vigorous Indian influence, and reveals no great divergences from the first Khmer sanctuaries like Sambor and Kulên. Its *prasate* are generally executed in brick, with a sparing use of stone for decora-tive purposes, as in the supports and reliefs. In Mison (c7–11) they rise on classic plans. But in Bin-dinh (c11) we also find an octagonal tower resembling certain shrines at Sambor Prei Kuk. With the last Cham constructions, the Brahminical hegemony in Indo-China reached its term.

This was the period when the Hindu faith was being driven out of Angkor by Buddhism. Henceforth it was these Mahayana Buddhists who perpetuated the art of the stupa – as it had been born in Sanchi twelve centuries be-fore – whilst in India itself the Buddha had had no following for centuries.

Burma and Thailand. When the Thais con-quered Angkor in the c14, they brought with them traditions that they had directly in-herited from the north-west, i.e. from Burma and the Irrawaddy valley. It is therefore pre-ferable to treat the Kingdom of Burma before Siam.

Burma had profited from contact with Indian civilization from the very first centuries of our era, and the countryside was sprinkled

Kubyankgyi Temple, Pagan, Burma, 1113

with stupas. But the works that remain seldom
date from before the period of the overlord-
ship of the city called Pagan, 'the City of the
Four Million Pagodas', whose history began
in 849. In 1044 its king undertook the conquest of Lower Burma. He took the city of
Thaton, and conveyed the 30,000 highly
civilized inhabitants – they had long-standing
contacts with India – to his city of Pagan.

Shwe Dagon Pagoda, Rangoon, Burma,
begun 1372

Thatbyinnyu Temple,
Pagan, Burma, 1144

This was the beginning of Pagan's rise to
prominence. In two centuries, on a site
covering 150 square miles, the kings built
more than 5000 pagodas and stupas in a
style initially inspired by Tibetan art. The
singularity of this architecture consisted in
its use of true vaults of brick, or of stone
VOUSSOIRS – perhaps under Persian influence.
As a result of Muslim raids, Persian refugees
were apparently driven down the Ganges as
far as Bengal, which would explain this. Very
unusual buildings were erected in Pagan
between the CII and C 13 – temples of brick
and stucco, often with spacious interiors.
They combine the vaulting technique which
they had adopted with ornamental gables in
the shape of the Indian *kudus* flame. These vast
structures, which resemble reliquary shrines,
often contain a colossal statue of the Buddha.
They are scattered over the whole Pagan
plain, forming a veritable forest of stupas.
The invasion of Kubla Khan at the head of
Mongol hordes brought the country to its
knees, which meant the end of architectural
florescence in this region.

Between the C14 and the C18 the centre of
gravity shifted to Pegu, Mingun, Mandalay
and Rangoon. There the erection of round
and quadrangular stupas, often of huge dimensions, was continued. The pagoda of Shwe
Dagon in Rangoon for instance has been repeatedly enlarged from 1372 to the present
day, and has now attained a height of 342 ft.

It is particularly conspicuous for its gilding
with gold leaf.

The Thais experienced influences from
Burma, and later from Ceylon: the tall,

Wat Sri Samp'et, Ayuthia, Thailand, C15–16

pointed silhouette of the stupas, which is
akin to late buildings in Burma, seems to derive from there. The Sukhothai style flourished
in the C13–C14, yielding to the U-Thong and
Ayuthia styles, especially noted for their

sculpture and bronze statues, from the c14 to the c18. What is of interest in these styles, leaving aside the erection of stupas and pagodas, is the wooden construction employed for palaces in the period of the Bangkok style. Its details – crossed gables and layered roofs – are likely to have closely resembled the princely constructions of the late Angkoran rulers, of which alas nothing remains.   [HS]

Lit: J. Boisselier, *Manuel d'Archéologie d'Extrême-Orient, Asie du Sud-Est*, I, 1966; G. Coedès, *Les États hindouisés de l'Indo-chine*, 1964; L. Frédéric, *Sud-Est Asiatique*, 1964; B. P. Groslier, *Hinterindien*, 1961; P. Stern, *Les monuments khmers du style du Bayon et Jayavarman VII*, 1965; M. Gleize, *Les monuments du groupe d'Angkor*, 1963.

Space-frame A three-dimensional framework for enclosing spaces, in which all members are interconnected and act as a single entity, resisting loads applied in any direction. Systems can be designed to cover very large spaces, uninterrupted by support from the ground, and the surface covering can be integrated to play its part in the structural whole. Some types have the appearance of egg-boxes (pyramidal in their elements), others are based on hexagonal or other geometric figures. The chief exponents to date are Z. Makowski (*space-grid*), Le Ricolais, Konrad Wachsmann, and Buckminster FULLER, whose dome, designed for the Union Tank Car Co., Baton Rouge, U.S.A. (1958), has a diameter of 384 ft.

Space-frame: Union Tank Car Company, Louisiana, 1958, by Buckminster Fuller

Spandrel The triangular space between the side of an arch, the horizontal drawn from the level of its apex, and the vertical of its spring-

ing; also applied to the surface between two arches in an arcade, and the surface of a vault between adjacent ribs.

Spanish architecture After the Roman aqueducts, etc., the first noteworthy monuments in Spain are a few relics of the Visigothic age, notably S. Juan de Baños (661), originally

S. Juan de Baños, Palencia, consecrated 661

with a very odd plan with a square chancel and square chapels of the same size attached to the long narrow transepts. The plan of S. Miguel at Tarrasa (c9 or earlier) – Tarrasa being one of the rare surviving examples of a 'church family' – is of the Early Christian and Byzantine inscribed-cross plan, that of S. Pedro de Nave (c7) a composition of square or

S. Pedro de Nave, near Zamora, c. 690

oblong compartments like the English *porticus*. This latter scheme became that of the eminently interesting Asturian churches of the c9 such as Sta Cristina de Lena and S. Miguel de Liño.

S. Miguel de Liño, Oviedo, 842–50

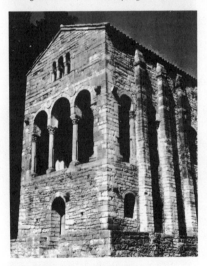

Aula Regia of Ramiro I, now Sta Maria de Naranco, near Oviedo, 842–50

One of them, now a church, was originally a royal hall (Sta Maria de Naranco).

Meanwhile the Mohammedans had captured most of Spain (711 etc.), and the Mosque of Cordoba had been begun in 786. It grew to be in the end a vast rectangle of *c.* 550 × 420 ft, filled with a forest of columns so as to form nineteen parallel naves. The most ornate parts date from *c.* 970. The vaults of these parts with their intersected ribs must have inspired certain Gothic and certain Baroque vaults. However, Islam's architecture also immediately inspired Spanish Christian archi-

tecture. The term MOZARABIC means such mixtures of Mohammedan and Christian elements as are exemplified by S. Miguel de Escalada (consecrated in 913), with its arcade arches of horseshoe shape, Santiago de Peñalba (931–7) and Santa Maria de Lebeña (also c10). The term MUDÉJAR refers to Christian architecture in a purely Moslem style, and this remained characteristic of secular architecture in Spain nearly to the end of the Middle Ages. No wonder, considering the glories and luxurious comforts of the Alhambra of Granada which – in the one remaining Moslem part of the peninsula – was built as late as the c14. Among the Christians such Mudéjar towers of the c13 as those of Teruel look back at the splendour of the

The Alhambra, Granada, begun c. 1377

Giralda at Seville of *c.* 1185–90, and palaces of Christian rulers established Mohammedan forms of decoration, of plan and of life. The palace of Tordesillas is of the 1340s, the Alcázar at Seville of the years of Pedro the Cruel (1349–68), and at Seville the so-called House of Pilate carried Mudéjar right into the c16, even if the last-built parts of the house (which was completed in 1553) take full note of Gothic as well as developed Renaissance motifs.

But this anticipates the story by several centuries. The Romanesque style had started in the early cii in Catalonia in a version similar to that of Lombardy (Ripoll, 1010–32, desperately restored; Cardona, consecrated 1040). The cii in Spain is particularly important for decorative sculpture. It seems that ever since S. Pedro de Nave in the cio the Spanish were ahead of the French in this field. There is certainly nothing in France to compare with the capitals of Jaca. The French Romanesque of the great pilgrimage churches has an outstanding representative in the far north-west corner of Spain in the celebrated church of Santiago de Compostela (begun *c.*

1075 and completed with the splendidly sculptured Pórtico de la Gloria in 1188). Other Romanesque churches are S. Martin de Frómista of *c.* 1060 etc., S. Isidro at León with its antechurch known as the Panteón de los Reyes also of *c.* 1060, and Lugo Cathedral, a direct descendant of Santiago, and S. Vicente at Ávila, both of the ci2. The Late Romanesque of Spain is best represented by the Old Cathedral of Salamanca and the Cathedral of Zamora, both with curious domes of West and South-West French affinities, but essentially original.

Santiago de Compostela, Cathedral, begun 1075

Dome of the Old Cathedral, Salamanca, ci2

S. Isidro, León, Panteón de los Reyes, 1054–67

To determine the date when the Gothic style arrived is as difficult for Spain as for England. The Old Cathedral of Salamanca for instance has pointed arches almost entirely. But pointed arches are not necessarily Gothic. The CISTERCIANS who came directly or indirectly from Burgundy brought the pointed arch as a Burgundian Romanesque motif. The Cistercians arrived in Spain in 1131, and soon large buildings were erected by them in many places: Moreruela, Meira, La Oliva, Huerta, Veruela, Poblet, Santas Creus have the standard French plan with chancel and transeptal east chapels. But while these are mostly straight-ended it is also usual in Spain to have the chancel apsed (Oliva, Huerta, Meira) or even an ambulatory and apsed radiating chapels (Moreruela, Poblet, Veruela). Whereas in many of these churches one may doubt what to regard as Romanesque, what as Gothic, La Oliva must clearly be considered Gothic, and the date of the beginning is 1164.

With the C13 the North French cathedral style entered Spain. The most French cathedrals of the C13 are those of Burgos (1221 etc.), Toledo (1226 etc.), and León, but the most

León Cathedral, C13–C15

original version of the Spanish Gothic is Catalan (Barcelona Cathedral, 1298 etc.; Sta María del Mar, Barcelona, 1329 etc.; Palma Cathedral, Majorca), with very wide and high naves and very high aisles or with aisles replaced by chapels between internal buttresses (Sta Catalina, Barcelona, 1223 etc.; Sta María del Pino, Barcelona, *c.* 1320 and Gerona

Gerona Cathedral, begun 1312

Cathedral whose nave with a span of 74 ft is the widest in Europe). The Late Gothic style was much influenced by Germany and the Netherlands, as is shown by such works as the towers of Burgos Cathedral by Juan de Colonia (*see* SIMÓN DE COLONIA) (begun 1442). Late

Capilla Real, Cordova Cathedral, 1371

Gothic vaults with their lierne rib patterns also have German origins. Spatially, however, Spain was entirely Spanish: the vast rectangles of her cathedrals hark back to the mosques of Islam, but their height and the height of the aisles are her own. Seville Cathedral was begun in 1402 and is 430 ft long and 250 ft wide, with a nave 130 ft high and aisles 85 ft high. Spain continued to embark on new cathedrals on this scale right up to the time of the Reformation. Salamanca was started in 1512, Segovia in 1525. In Spain those were the years of greatest wealth, resulting in the many funerary monuments and

New Cathedral, Salamanca, begun 1512, from plans by Gil de Hontañón

*New Cathedral, Salamanca, begun 1512,
from plans by Gil de Hontañón*

*Capilla del Condestable, Burgos Cathedral,
1482–1532*

the excessively lavish decoration of such buildings as the Constable's Chapel at Burgos
Cathedral (1482 etc.) and S. Juan de los Reyes,
Toledo (1476 etc.), or of such façades as
those of S. Pablo (1486 etc.) and S. Gregorio
(c. 1492), both at Valladolid. No square inch
must remain without its complicated and lacy
carving. The spirit of Islam re-asserted itself
in this, and the desire to over-decorate surfaces
was carried on with Renaissance details in the
C16 (PLATERESQUE style) and with Baroque
details in the C18 (CHURRIGUERESQUE style).

West front of S. Pablo, Valladolid,
begun c. 1486, by Simón de Colonia

Vaulting of Capilla Mayor
in the New Cathedral, Salamanca, c. 1525

(1509–12) or the staircase of the Hospital of
Toledo (1504 etc.) are pure and perfectly at
ease. But almost at once the crowding of
motifs started again, and the façade of the
University of Salamanca (c. 1515 etc.) is no

View of interior courtyard
and ground plan of Charles V's unfinished palace,
Granada, 1526, by Machuca

S. Gregorio, Valladolid, c. 1492

Spain is the country of the most spectacular
castles. For the c12 the most magnificent
display is the walls of Avila, for the c13 the
castle of Alcalá de Guadaira, for the c14
Bellver on Majorca (1309–14) which is round
and has a round courtyard, for the c15 Coca,
vast and all of brick.

The Italian Renaissance had actually
reached Spain early, and such monuments as
the courtyard of the castle of La Calahorra

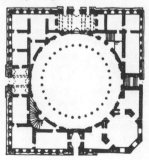

Royal Palace at Aranjuez, begun 1561,
completed c18 by Bonavia

more than a furnishing of the Late Gothic façade with new motifs. Soon, however, the pure Italian High Renaissance also entered Spain. The first and for a while the only example is Charles V's unfinished palace on the Alhambra (1526 by MACHUCA), with its circular courtyard and its motifs reminiscent of RAPHAEL and GIULIO ROMANO. The severest and vastest palace in the Italian style is Philip II's Escorial (1563 etc. by Juan Bautista de TOLEDO and HERRERA). Ecclesiastical architecture in the c16 reached its climax in the east end of Granada Cathedral by SILOE (1528 etc.), and the parts of 1585 etc. of Valladolid Cathedral by Herrera. But such

austerity remained rare, and Spain came once again into her own when, in the late c17, she developed that style of excessive Baroque surface decoration which culminated in such buildings as the façade of Santiago de Compostela (1738 etc.), the sacristy of the Charterhouse of Granada (1727 etc.), the Transparente in Toledo Cathedral (1721–32), the portal of the Hospital of S. Ferdinand in Madrid (1722) and that of the Dos Aguas Palace at Valencia (1740–44). Great sobriety in an Italian and French sense characterizes the circular Sanctuary of St Ignatius of Loyola, begun in 1689 and designed by Carlo FONTANA, the Royal Palace in Madrid by

The Escorial, begun 1563,
by Toledo and Herrera

Pilar Church, Saragossa, begun 1681

Casa de Dos Aguas, Valencia, 1740–44

G. B. SACCHETTI begun in 1738, the Royal Palace of La Granja, partly by Filippo JUVARRA (1719 etc.), and the Royal Palace of Aranjuez, by another Italian, Bonavia (1748 etc.). Among the Spanish academics Ventura RODRIGUEZ was the most conspicuous figure; his giant portico for Pamplona Cathedral was built in 1783. Of 1787 is the even more neo-classical design for the Prado in Madrid by Juan de VILLANUEVA.

The Prado, Madrid, designed in 1787, by Villanueva

The Sagrada Familia, Barcelona, begun 1882, taken over by Gaudí 1884

To the C19 and C20 Spain has not made any essential contributions except for the fabulous work of GAUDÍ at Barcelona which

Race course at Zarzuela, Madrid, 1935, by Torroja

Silo, Institute for Concrete Construction, Costillares, Madrid, 1951, by Torroja

is the international climax of ART NOUVEAU in architecture.

Lit: Ars Hispaniae, Madrid 1947 onwards; B. Bevan, A History of Spanish Architecture, London 1938; G. Kubler & M. Soria, Art and Architecture in Spain and Portugal and their American Dominions, 1500–1800, Pelican History of Art, Harmondsworth 1959.

Spence, Sir Basil (b. 1907), before the war designed mostly large country houses in Scotland; after the war he made his name in England as well by exhibition work (Sea and Ships, Festival of Britain, 1951). In 1951 he won the competition for Coventry Cathedral, and the building was consecrated in 1962. It is outstanding in the use made of the steeple of the old Perpendicular cathedral as its one vertical accent; in the use of the shell of the old nave and chancel as a landscaped atrium; in the saw-tooth side walls treated so that only those sides have windows which face towards the altar; and in the ample opportunities given to artists and craftsmen

(Graham Sutherland, John Piper, Geoffrey Clarke). Since 1954 Sir Basil Spence and his firm have done much university work (Edinburgh, Southampton, Nottingham, Liverpool, Sussex) and most recently the Barracks in Knightsbridge, London, and the Chancellery of the British Embassy in Rome (completed 1971).

Lit: R. Maxwell, *New British Architecture*, London 1972.

Spere-truss A wooden arch with PIERS – the latter attached with trusses to the side walls – which stood, at least at wall-plate height, at the kitchen end of a medieval timber-framed hall, marking the division between the hall proper and the SCREENS PASSAGE; so-called from the screen or *spere* which separated the hall from the kitchen.

Spire A tall pyramidal, polygonal, or conical structure rising from a tower, turret, or roof (usually of a church) and terminating in a

point. It can be of stone, or of timber covered with SHINGLES, or lead. A *broach* spire is usually octagonal in plan, placed on a square tower and rising without an intermediate parapet. Each of the four angles of the tower not covered by the base of the spire is filled with an inclined mass of masonry or broach built into the oblique sides of the spire, carried up to the point, and covering a SQUINCH. A broach spire is thus the interpenetration of a lower-pitch pyramid with a much steeper octagon. A *needle* spire is a thin spire rising from the centre of a tower roof, well inside a parapet protecting a pathway upon which scaffolding could be erected for repairs.

Spirelet, *see* FLÈCHE.

Splay A sloping, chamfered surface cut into the walls. The term usually refers to the widening of doorways, windows, or other wall-openings by slanting the sides. *See also* REVEAL.

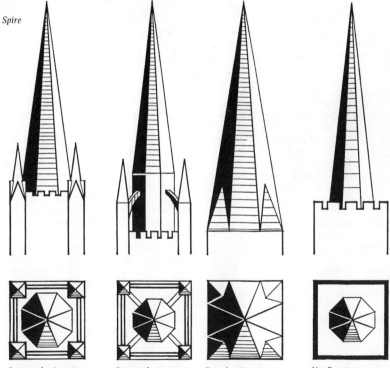

Spire

Octagonal spire over tower with pinnacles

Spire and octagon over tower with flying buttresses

Broach spire

Needle spire

Springing line The level at which an arch springs from its supports. The bottom stone of the arch resting on the IMPOST each side can thus be called a *springer. See also* ARCH, SKEWBACK.

Spur An ornament, usually of foliage, on the corner of a square plinth surmounted by a circular PIER; also called a *griffe*.

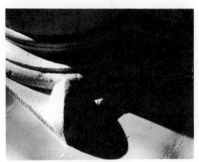

Spur: St Michael, Altenstadt, pre-1200

Spur stone A stone projecting from the angle of a corner or arch to prevent damage by passing traffic: it is usually circular in section.

Squinch An arch or system of concentrically wider and gradually projecting arches, placed diagonally at the internal angles of towers to fit a polygonal or round superstructure on to a square plan. (For illustration *see* DOME.)

Squint An obliquely cut opening in a wall or through a PIER to allow a view of the main altar of a church from places whence it could not otherwise be seen; also called a *hagioscope*.

Staddle stones Mushroom-shaped stones used as bases to support timber-built granaries or hay barns, especially in Sussex.

Stadia, *see* GYMNASIUM.

Stair, staircase There are special names for the various parts of a stair: the *tread* is the horizontal surface of a step; the *riser* is the vertical surface; a *winder* is a tread wider at one end than the other. A *newel staircase* is a circular or winding staircase with a solid central post in which the narrow ends of the steps are supported. The *newel* is also the principal post at the end of a flight of stairs;

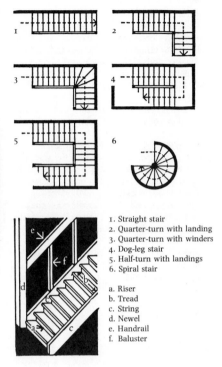

1. Straight stair
2. Quarter-turn with landing
3. Quarter-turn with winders
4. Dog-leg stair
5. Half-turn with landings
6. Spiral stair

a. Riser
b. Tread
c. String
d. Newel
e. Handrail
f. Baluster

it carries the *handrails* and the *strings* which support the steps. A *dog-leg staircase* consists of parallel zigzag flights without a central well. A *geometrical staircase* is composed of stone steps each of which is built into the wall at one end and rests on the step below; generally built on a circular or elliptical plan.

Staircases seem to have existed as long as monumental architecture: a staircase of *c.* 6000 B.C. has been discovered in the excavations of Jericho. Monumental staircases also existed at Knossos in Crete and Persepolis in Iran. The Greeks and the Romans were not apparently much interested in making an architectural feature of the staircase, and medieval staircases were also utilitarian as a rule. In the Middle Ages the accepted form was the newel staircase, which could assume a monumental scale (Vis du Louvre, Paris, late C14), but only did so to any extent after 1500 (Blois). The standard form of the Italian Renaissance is two flights, the upper at an angle of 180° to the lower, and both running up between solid walls. However, a few architects, notably FRANCESCO DI GIORGIO and LEONARDO DA VINCI, worked out on paper a

Escalera Dorada, Burgos Cathedral, c. 1520,
by Siloe

Stadium, Florence, 1930–32,
by Nervi

Staircase, Schloss Pommersfelden, 1711–18,
by Johann Dientzenhofer

number of other, more interesting types, and these seem to have been translated into reality in the c16, mostly in Spain. There is the staircase which starts in one flight and returns in two, the whole rising in one well; the staircase which starts in one and turns at right angles into two (BRAMANTE's Belvedere Court in the Vatican; Escalera Dorada, Burgos); and, the most frequent type, the staircase which runs up in three flights at right angles round an open wall, i.e., a squared spiral stair with intermediate landings. But Bramante in the Vatican still built a normal spiral stair, though also with an open well, and BERNINI (Palazzo Barberini) made this oval, a characteristically Baroque turn, PALLADIO invented the geometrical or flying staircase (Academy, Venice), a spiral staircase without any support other than the bonding of the steps into the outer wall.

The Baroque is the great age of monumental and inventive staircases. The finest of all are in Germany (Würzburg, Brühl, and especially Bruchsal, all by NEUMANN), but there are excellent ones also in France (MANSART at Blois) and in Italy (Naples).

In c20 architecture the staircase has assumed a new significance as the element in a building which is most expressive of spatial flow. The earliest staircase in a glass cage is GROPIUS's at the Cologne Werkbund exhibition (1914). Since then much has been made of flying staircases, staircases without risers, and similar effects.

Stalactite work Ceiling ornament in ISLAMIC ARCHITECTURE formed by corbelled SQUINCHES made of several layers of brick scalloped out to resemble natural stalactites. (For illustration *see* next page.)

Stall A carved seat of wood or stone in a row of similar seats; if hinged, often carved on the underside (*see* MISERICORD).

Stanchion A vertical supporting member, nowadays mainly of steel.

*Stalactite work: Mosque of the Shah,
Isfahan, 1612–38*

Starling A pointed projection on the PIER of a bridge to break the force of the water. *See* CUTWATER.

Starov, Ivan Yegorovich (1743–1808), the first Russian-born architect to work successfully in the West European manner, was born in Moscow and trained at the St Petersburg Academy of Fine Arts. He then went to Paris, where he was trained under DE WAILLY (1762–8). His works are neo-classical and rather solid, e.g., church and columned rotunda belfry at Nikolskoe (1774–6, destroyed 1941), Cathedral of the Trinity, Leningrad (1776). His masterpiece is the vast Tauride Palace, Leningrad (1783–8), built for Potemkin and very rich in columns inside and out but later remodelled by Luigi Rusca.

Lit: L. Hautecoeur, *L'architecture classique à St Pétersbourg à la fin du XVIIIe siècle*, Paris 1912; G. H. Hamilton, *The Art and Architecture of Russia*, Pelican History of Art, Harmondsworth 1954.

Stassov, Vasili Petrovich (1769–1848). The best-known Russian architect of the later neo-classical period in Leningrad, i.e., after the great period of THOMON, VORONIKHIN and ZAKHAROV. His bell-tower of the village church in Gruzino (1815) is geometric almost in the LEDOUX manner. His masterpiece is the Triumphal Gate in Leningrad (1833–8), a trabeated Greek Doric propylaeon entirely constructed in cast iron. His earlier Church of the Transfiguration (1826–8) and Trinity Cathedral (1828–35), both in Leningrad, have Greek cross plans and five domes.

Lit: G. H. Hamilton, *The Art and Architecture of Russia*, Pelican History of Art, Harmondsworth 1954.

Stave church A timber-framed and timber-walled church; the walls are of upright planks with corner-post columns. The term is applied exclusively to Scandinavian churches built from the early or mid CII onwards. Later stave churches usually have inner rows of posts or piers, sometimes an external covered arcade, and roofs arranged in tiers. A third system was also used from *c*. 1200, incorporating a central column from the floor to the roof. (Illustrated next column; *see also* SCANDINAVIAN ARCHITECTURE.)

Lit: A. Bugge, *Norwegian Stave-churches*, Oslo 1953.

Steeple The tower and spire of a church taken together.

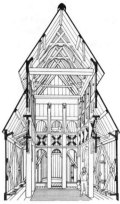

*Section of stave church
at Borgund, Norway, c. 1150*

Stephenson, Robert, *see* BRIDGE.

Stereobate A solid mass of masonry serving as a base, usually for a wall or a row of columns.

Stereobate of the Parthenon, Athens

Stethaimer, Hans (d. 1432), worked at Landshut in Bavaria. He came from Burghausen, is usually called Hans von Burghausen and may not have been called Stethaimer. He began St Martin's, the chief parish church of Landshut, in 1387. On his funerary monument other works of his are mentioned: they include the chancel of the Franciscan Church at Salzburg (begun 1408). He was one of the best of the German Late Gothic architects, believed in the 'HALL CHURCH', in brick as a material, where he could use it, and in a minimum of decoration. At Salzburg the most fascinating motif is that of the long slender piers of the chancel with one of them placed axially, due east, so that the eye faces not an interstice but a pier with the light from the east playing round it.

Stethaimer's monument may indicate that he was also concerned with sculpture. His source is the style of the PARLER family. (For illustration *see* GERMAN ARCHITECTURE.)

Lit: E. Hanfstaengl, *H. Stethaimer*, Leipzig 1911.

Stiff-leaf A late C12 and early C13 type of sculptured foliage, found chiefly on CAPITALS and BOSSES, a development from the CROCKETS of crocket capitals; almost entirely confined to Britain. (For illustration *see* CAPITAL.)

Stijl, De, *see* OUD, Jacobus Johannes Pieter.

Stile Liberty, *see* ART NOUVEAU.

Stilted arch, *see* ARCH.

Stirling & Gowan (James Stirling and James Gowan, b. 1926 and 1924). Their small housing estate at Ham, near London (1958), established their sympathy with the trend influenced by LE CORBUSIER and often called BRUTALISM. Their Department of Engineering, Leicester University (1959–63), is their most complete statement. After James Stirling had separated from James Gowan, he designed the building for the History Faculty for Cambridge (1965–8), and a new building for the Queen's College, Oxford (1968–70). They have a ruthlessness which militates against their achieving a more than passing success. (For illustration *see* SCOTTISH ARCHITECTURE.)

Lit: R. Banham, *The New Brutalism*, London 1966; R. Maxwell, *New British Architecture*, London 1972.

Stoa In Greek architecture, a detached colonnade. In Byzantine architecture, a covered hall, its roof supported by one or more rows of columns parallel to the rear wall; in Latin, porticus.

Stoep The Dutch term for veranda.

Stone, Edward (b. 1903). Successful American architect who likes to clothe his façades with an ornamental veil, usually including arched elements. He designed his own house, 7 East 67th Street in New York, in 1956. Other buildings of his are the U.S. Embassy at New Delhi (1954–8), the U.S. Pavilion at the Brussels International Exhibition (1958) and the former Huntington Hartford Museum in Columbus Circle in New York (1958–9) (now the New York Cultural Center).

Stop-chamfer An ornamental termination to a CHAMFER, common in the Early English period and very much favoured by Victorian architects, bringing the edge of the pared-off stone or beam back to a right angle; also called a *broach-stop*.

Stop-chamfer

Stops Projecting stones at the ends of HOOD-MOULDS, STRING COURSES, etc., against which the mouldings finish; often carved. *See also* LABEL-STOP.

Storey (or **story**) The space between any two floors or between the floor and roof of a build-ing. In England the ground-level storey is usually called the ground floor, in America the first floor, in France the *rez-de-chaussée*.

Storey-posts The principal posts of a timber-framed wall.

Stoup A vessel to contain holy water, placed near the entrance of a church; usually in the form of a shallow dish set against a wall or pier or in a niche.

Strainer arch, *see* ARCH.

Strapwork Decoration originating in the Netherlands *c.* 1540, also common in Eliza-bethan England, consisting of interlaced bands and forms similar to fretwork or cut leather; generally used in ceilings, screens, and funerary monuments. (Illustration previous column.)

Street, George Edmund (1824–81), a pupil of George Gilbert SCOTT, was in practice in 1849. after having already designed some churches in Cornwall. In 1850–1 he travelled in France and Germany, in 1853 in North Italy (result-ing in a book on the marble and brick build-ings of North Italy which came out in 1855), in 1854 in Germany again, in 1861–3 three times in Spain (his important book on Spanish Gothic architecture was published in 1865). In 1852 Street started a practice at Oxford, and among his first assistants were WEBB and MORRIS. The first important build-ing is the Cuddesdon Theological College. Street was a High Church man much ap-preciated by the Cambridge Camden group (*see* BUTTERFIELD), a tremendous worker and a fertile draughtsman who liked to design all details himself. His first large church was St Peter, Bournemouth (1853 etc.).

The practice was moved to London in 1855, and there Street's most characteristic early church is St James the Less, off Vauxhall Bridge Road (1860–1), a very strong design encouraged no doubt by Butterfield but not in imitation of him, and inspired by RUSKIN. The Gothic is Continental rather than English. Among Street's most notable churches are Oakengates, Shropshire (1855); Boyne Hill, Berkshire (1859); St Philip and St James, Oxford (1860–2); All Saints, Clifton, Bristol (1863–8); St John, Torquay (1861–71); St Mary Magdalen, Paddington, London (1868–78); and Holmbury St Mary, built at his own expense (1879). Street is always unconven-

Strapwork: St Luzen, Hechingen

tional and inventive, yet hardly ever as aggressive as Butterfield. His principal secular work is the Law Courts, won in competition in 1866. It is a high-minded essay in C13 Gothic, yet picturesque in grouping. The Great Hall inside is particularly impressive. (For illustration *see* ENGLISH ARCHITECTURE.)

Lit: B. F. L. Clarke, *Church Builders of the Nineteenth Century,* London 1938; H.-R. Hitchcock, *Architecture: Nineteenth and Twentieth Centuries,* Pelican History of Art, Harmondsworth 1969, paperback edn 1971.

Stressed-skin construction A form of construction in which the outer skin acts with the frame members to contribute to the flexural strength of the unit as a whole.

Stretcher, *see* BRICKWORK.

Strickland, William (1788–1854), a pupil of LATROBE in Philadelphia, rose to fame with the Bank of the United States, Philadelphia, now the Portrait Gallery. This had first been designed by Latrobe, but was then built to a modified design by Strickland (1818–24). It is Grecian in style, whereas Strickland's earlier Masonic Temple (1810) had been Gothic. His finest building is the Philadelphia Merchants' Exchange (1834 etc.), with its elegant corner motif crowned by a copy of the Lysicrates Monument. He also built the United States Mint, Washington (1829–33), in a style similar to MILL'S, and the United States Naval Asylum (1827) with an Ionic portico and tiers of long balconies left and right. Strickland was a very versatile man: in his early days he painted and did stage design, and he was also throughout his later life engaged in major engineering enterprises (canals, railways, the Delaware Breakwater).

Lit: A. A. Gilchrist, *W. Strickland, Architect and Engineer,* Philadelphia 1950; A. A. Gilchrist, 'Additions to William Strickland' in *Journal of the Society of Architectural Historians,* XIII, October 1954.

String course A continuous projecting horizontal band set in the surface of an exterior wall and usually moulded.

Strings The two sloping members which carry the ends of the treads and risers of a STAIRCASE.

Strut, *see* ROOF.

Stuart, James 'Athenian' (1713–88), a minor architect, is nevertheless important in the history of GREEK REVIVAL architecture for his temple at Hagley (1758), the earliest Doric Revival building in Europe. He and Revett went to Greece in 1751–5 and in 1762 published the *Antiquities of Athens* (2nd vol. 1789), which had little immediate influence except on interior decoration. Indolence and unreliability lost him many commissions, and he built very little. He designed several first floor rooms at Spencer House, London (1760 onwards). His No. 15 St James's Square, London (1763–6) was later altered internally by James WYATT (*c.* 1791). The Triumphal Arch, Tower of the Winds, and Lysicrates Monument in the park at Shugborough are his best surviving works. They date from between 1764 and 1770. His chapel at Greenwich Hospital (1779–88) seems to have been designed largely by his assistant William Newton. (For illustration *see* GREEK REVIVAL.)

Lit: L. Lawrence, 'Stuart and Revett: their literary and architectural careers' in *Journal of the Warburg and Courtauld Institutes,* 1938; J. Summerson, *Architecture in Britain, 1530–1830,* Pelican History of Art, Harmondsworth 1969, paperback edn 1970.

Stuart architecture, *see* ENGLISH ARCHITECTURE.

Stucco Plasterwork.

Studs Upright timbers in TIMBER-FRAMED houses. (For illustration *see* TIMBER-FRAMING.)

Stupa (Sanskrit) The simplest form of Buddhist religious monument, often designed to receive relics. In origin the stupa was a hallowed sepulchral mound. Buddha instructed his disciples to raise such mounds of earth symbolically at crossroads. In India the *stupa* took the form of a hemisphere reinforced by gateways at the four points of the compass. Later, in South-east Asia, stupas are often bell-shaped. They are built of stone on a terraced base, and crowned with a square top supporting a CHATRI. The stupa is often surrounded by a fence or row of columns with four imposing gates. The name for the stupa in Ceylon is *dagoba,* and in Bhutan, Nepal and Tibet, *chorten.* (For illustrations *see* CHINESE ARCHITECTURE, CHORTEN, INDIAN ARCHITECTURE and SOUTH-EAST ASIAN ARCHITECTURE.)

Stylobate The substructure on which a colonnade stands; more correctly, the top step of the structure forming the CREPIDOMA.

Suardi, Bartolomeo, called Bramantino (fl. 1503–36). He was primarily a painter but was responsible for one outstanding building in his native Milan, the octagonal Trivulzio chapel in S. Nazaro. It is a masterpiece of classical restraint and geometrical purity. It was begun in 1512.
   Lit: W. Suida, *Bramante e il Bramantino*, Milan 1955.

Suger, Abbot (1081–1151), was not an architect; neither does he seem to have been responsible, even as an amateur, for any architectural work. But as he was abbot of St Denis, outside Paris, when the abbey church was partly rebuilt (c. 1135–44), and as this was the building where the Gothic style was to all intents and purposes invented, or where it finally evolved out of the scattered elements already existing in many places, his name must be recorded here. He wrote two books on the abbey in which the new building is commented on, but nowhere refers to the designer or indeed explicitly to the innovations incorporated in the building.
   Lit: E. Panofsky, *Abbot Suger on the Abbey Church of St Denis and its Art Treasures*, Princeton 1946; M. Aubert, *Suger*, Paris 1950; E. Panofsky, *Meaning in the Visual Arts*, New York 1965.

Sullivan, Louis Henry (1856–1924), was of mixed Irish, Swiss, and German descent. He was born in Boston, studied architecture briefly at the Massachusetts Institute of Technology, and moved to Chicago in 1873. He worked there under JENNEY, then, after a year in Paris in VAUDREMER'S *atelier*, returned to Chicago. In 1879 he joined the office of Dankmar Adler, and the firm became Adler & Sullivan in 1881. Their first major building, and no doubt the most spectacular in Chicago up to that time, was the Auditorium (1886–90), which was strongly influenced by RICHARDSON. The auditorium itself is capable of seating more than 4000. Sullivan's interior decoration is exceedingly interesting, of a feathery vegetable character, derived perhaps from the Renaissance but at the same time pointing forward into the licence of ART NOUVEAU. His two most familiar skyscrapers, the Wainwright Building, St Louis (1890), and the Guaranty Building, Buffalo (1894), have

not the exclusively functional directness of HOLABIRD & ROCHE's Marquette Building of 1894, but they do express externally the SKELETON structure and the cellular interior arrangements. However, Sullivan, though pleading in his *Kindergarten Chats* (1901) for a temporary embargo on all decoration, was himself as fascinated by ornament as by functional expression, and this appears even in the entrance motifs of his major building, the Carson, Pirie & Scott Store (1899–1904), which is most characteristic of the 'Chicago School'. For the Chicago Exhibition of 1893 Sullivan designed the Transportation Building, with its impressively sheer giant entrance arch. He recognized the setback which the classicism otherwise prevailing at the exhibition would mean to the immediate future of American architecture.
   Adler died in 1900, and after that time Sullivan's work grew less until it dried up almost entirely. He was a difficult man, uncompromising and erratic, but his brilliance is undeniable – see the passages which his pupil WRIGHT has devoted to his *Lieber Meister*. (For illustrations *see* CHICAGO WINDOW, UNITED STATES ARCHITECTURE.)
   Lit: H. R. Hope, 'Louis Sullivan's architectural ornament' in *Magazine of Art*, March 1947; H. Morrison, *L. Sullivan, Prophet of Modern Architecture*, New York 1952; C. W. Condit, *The Chicago School of Architecture*, Chicago 1964.

Sumerian and Akkadian (Babylonian, Assyrian) architecture The architecture of the land between the Tigris and the Euphrates, from the Persian Gulf up the former to Nineveh and up the latter to Mari, covers three pre-Christian millennia. It is largely, and in the south almost exclusively, of sun-dried brick of constantly changing format. Stone in southern Mesopotamia is a luxury, only to be found in the desert. The trunks of date-palms had to serve as the local timber. Despite the poverty of materials, Sumerian architecture was capable of great achievements by the turn of the fourth millennium B.C.: ample temples with sophisticated articulation (pillars, niches), high temples on terraces presaging the ZIGGURAT. The extreme weather-proneness of the unfired brick led to the frequent renovation of buildings, and hence to great mutability in their appearance. Consequently their present state of preservation is mostly poor; it is often impossible to grasp more than the plan.

After about 2700 B.C. another type of large-scale architecture makes its appearance – the ruler's palace. Particularly impressive are the Babylonian palace of Mari (1700 B.C.)

Plan of the palace at Mari, 1700 B.C.

and the Late Assyrian palace of Sargon II at Dur Sharrukin (Khorsabad). Save with the ziggurats, architecture tended chiefly to the horizontal: complexes of gatehouses, ranges of apartments, internal courts, temple *cellae*, perimeter walls – all, as far as we can judge from hypothetical reconstructions, were of the same height. An important feature of the walls was not only their articulation, but also their adornment with murals, reliefs, friezes, and glazed tiles.

The principle behind domestic architecture was arrangement round a central court. In the cities there was a jumble of tightly packed houses of irregular plan, with narrow alleys

Plan of Ur,
c. 2000 B.C.

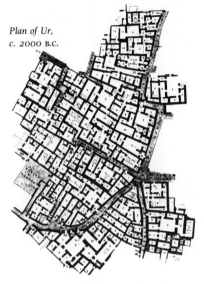

Ishtar Gate, Babylon, 600 B.C.

between them. It is true that there have only been a few cases of residential quarters as yet being systematically excavated, but the general effect is not likely to have differed greatly from that of the medieval city in the Near East.

Among the technically most remarkable achievements of Mesopotamia was the aqueduct of King Sennacherib of Assyria (704–681 B.C.), of which there are fragments near Jerwan, in Iraqi Kurdistan.

Ground-plans with indications of scale are found on clay tablets dating back to 2200

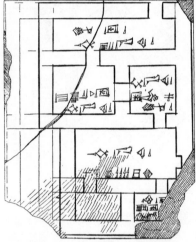

Ground plans on a clay tablet of c. 2150 B.C.

B.C. Also renowned is the slightly later statue of Gudea as architect; the sitting ruler is depicted with the plan of a great building on his lap. [DOE]

Lit: W. Andrae, *Das Gotteshaus und die Urformen des Bauens im Alten Orient,* 1930; *Das wiedererstandene Assur,* 1938; E. Stromenger, *Fünf Jahrtausende Mesopotamien,* 1962; H. Frankfort, *The Art and Architecture of the Ancient Orient,* Pelican History of Art, Harmondsworth 1970, paperback edn 1970.

Sustris, Friedrich (1524–99 or 91 ?). Netherlandish Mannerist painter and architect working in Munich at the same time as Peter CANDID and the Mannerist sculptor Hubert Gerhard. Sustris studied in Italy where he acquired a sophisticated Mannerist style derived from VASARI. His main work in architecture is the chancel and transept of St Michael's Church in Munich (1592, built after the collapse of a tower in that year). He prob-

ably designed the Grotto Court (*c.* 1581) in the Residenz, very Florentine Mannerist in style. In 1584 he remodelled the parish church of Dachau. His design for the interior decoration of Schloss Landshut survives (1577) and the Akademie der Wissenschaften (formerly the Jesuit College) in Munich is attributed to him. (For illustration *see* MANNERISM.)

Lit: M. Hock, F. *Sustris,* Munich 1952.

Swag A FESTOON in the form of a piece of cloth draped over two supports.

Swan-neck An OGEE-shaped member, e.g., the curve in a staircase handrail where it rises to join the newel post.

Swedish architecture, *see* SCANDINAVIAN ARCHITECTURE.

Swiss architecture Switzerland has all the architectural advantages and disadvantages of a position between three larger countries (Germany, France and Italy): the advantage of variety of styles, the disadvantage of little visual identity.

The country is uncommonly rich (given its small size) in early buildings. At Romainmôtier a small, aisleless c5 church with two transeptal porticos (in the English sense of the word) has been excavated, and a larger church consecrated in 753 and still of the same archaic plan. Chur has the c8 east end of St Lucius with a ring-crypt and above it three parallel apses on Italian Early Christian precedent. The same east end is to be found at St Martin at Chur and at Müstair and Disentis.

St Peter, Müstair

The earliest Romanesque churches are inspired by Burgundy and especially the second church of Cluny. They are the third building of Romainmôtier with a typically Burgundian antechurch, and Payerne. Both are CI I.

At that same time the cathedral of Lausanne had already been begun, and this as well as Geneva Cathedral are again orientated towards France and now a Gothic France. Lausanne Cathedral in particular actually belongs to the Burgundian school of the CI 3. The principal Late Gothic churches on the other hand are an outlier of South Germany: Berne Minster (1421 etc.), St Oswald at Zug (1478 etc.) and St Leonard at Basel (1489 etc.).

It is understandable that the Renaissance appears first in the cantons bordering on Italy. The portal of St Salvator at Lugano of 1517 is close to Como in style. Of later CI6 buildings it is enough to refer to the three-

Abbey church, Payerne, CI I–CI 2

St Leonard, Basel, begun 1489

Schaffhausen on the other hand of the late CI I and early CI 2 looks to Germany and the chief German Cluniac centre Hirsau. The Romanesque style culminates in the cathedral of Basel, connected closely with Alsace. It contains a little of the early CI I, but dates mostly from *c.* 1180 and later.

storeyed courtyard arcades of the Ritter House at Lucerne (1556–61) and to the Geltenzunft (1578) and Spiesshof (late CI6) at Basel, both more classical than such buildings usually are in Germany. The Spiesshof in particular with its SERLIANA windows is indeed closely dependent on SERLIO.

Château Chillon near Montreux, mid-CI2 and after

The C17 gives a mixed impression. There is the fascinating Gothicism of the church of the Visitandes at Fribourg, a quatrefoil in plan but with the most intricate rib vaults (1653-6), there is the Zürich Town Hall, still Renaissance rather than Baroque, though as late as 1694-8, and there are the beginnings of a German Baroque in such a church as that of Muri, designed by MOSBRUGGER and begun in 1694. Its centre is a spacious octagon. Mosbrugger then designed the spatially complex Einsiedeln (1703).

St Gall Abbey Church, 1755-69

1755-69) and the cool restrained French Dixhuitième (private houses, Geneva). There is in this of course also a contrast between Catholic and Protestant. Typically Protestant churches of unusual interior are the entirely French Temple at Geneva (1707-10 by Vennes), and Holy Ghost, Berne (1726-9 by

View of interior and ground plan, Abbey church, Einsiedeln, 1704-17, by Caspar Mosbrugger. Interior by the Asam brothers

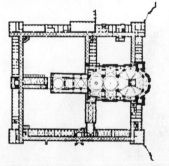

Holy Ghost, Berne, 1726-9, by Schildknecht

The C18 in Switzerland stands under the sign of the contrast between the dazzling and melodramatic South German Baroque (St Gall

Schildknecht). The church at Berne is oblong and has four entries in the middles of the four sides and as its only asymmetrical accents a (German) west tower and the pulpit inside close to the east end. The cathedral of Solothurn of 1762 etc. (by G. M. Pisoni) is mildly classicist, the noble west portico of Geneva

Cathedral of 1752–6 (by Count ALFIERI) much more radically so. But the most exactingly neo-classicist building of the late C18 in Switzerland is the town hall of Neufchâtel of 1782–90 (by P. A. Pâris).

For the C19 the most interesting series of buildings are the hôtels, but they have not yet been sufficiently studied. For the C20 Switzerland contributed good architecture in the pre-first-war years (Badischer Bahnhof, Basel, by Curjel & Moser, 1912–13), outstanding Expressionism of the same and the immediate post-first-war years (Goetheanum Dornach by Rudolf Steiner 1913 and again after a disastrous fire 1923–8) and much good and early

Goetheanum, Dornach, 1923–8,
by Rudolf Steiner

work in the International Modern of the twenties and thirties. Some of the churches were highly influential abroad (e.g., St Anthony, Basel, by Moser 1925–31). LE CORBUSIER who was born at La Chaux-de-

St Anthony, Basel, 1925–31, by Moser

Fonds contributed one block of flats at Geneva (1931–2). The standard of architecture in Switzerland has remained high, and even the newest buildings keep away from extremism and irrationalism – a Swiss trait no doubt.

Terraced housing at Zug,
by Fritz Stucky and Rudolf Meuli

Lit: J. Gantner & A. Reinle, *Kunstgeschichte der Schweiz*, 4 vols., 1936–62; J. Bachmann & S. von Moos, *New Directions in Swiss Architecture*, New York 1969.

Synagogue The very meaning of the Greek *'synagogos'* (= 'meeting' or 'community', in Hebrew *'knesset'*, whence the building, *'Bet ha-Knesset'*) reveals that the synagogue was originally no house of prayer, but a place of assembly and instruction (hence the German *'Schul'* and Italian *'scuolá'*), that had nothing to do with the ancient Temple, the abode of the divinity.

This difference of function also occasioned a divergence in form from the classical temple. Excavations in and beyond Palestine frequently reveal the adoption and adaptation of the secular Roman BASILICA (often aisled, as at Capernaum), with a flat ceiling and often a dais and benches along the walls. The building would mostly be oriented in the direction of prayer, towards Jerusalem. The Ark of the Covenant (*Aron Hakodesh*) for the Scrolls of the Law had no fixed position at first, but later a niche (e.g. at Dura-Europos on the Upper Euphrates) or an apse (as at Beth Alpha in Israel) was provided, whose place was mostly on the front end wall.

This type of synagogue is chiefly found in the C3–7, i.e. in the Late Roman and Byzantine periods, in Galilee, which, after the destruction of the Temple (A.D. 70) and the crushing of the rebellion under Hadrian, became the centre of the Jewish colony in Palestine, with Tiberias as the then residence of the Jewish Patriarchs. But there were also important synagogues outside Palestine; written accounts suggest that the great one in Alexandria destroyed in the rising against Trajan was particularly splendid; that recently excavated at Sardis in Asia Minor, not one of the major Jewish communities, was nonetheless half as long as the present St Peter's in Rome.

It is typical of synagogues to borrow the stylistic vocabulary of their time. We find Hellenistic and Roman ornament and mosaic in classical synagogues; that in Worms, the oldest in Germany until its destruction by the Nazis and subsequent reconstruction, is Romanesque; the Altneuschul in Prague (with quinquepartite vaults to avoid cross-vaulting) and the synagogue in Kasimierz (Cracow) are Gothic, just like the one in Regensburg recorded in two etchings by Altdorfer. This latter was twin-naved like some friars' churches, in whose case too the central row of columns was not disruptive, because preaching and the active participation of the congregation was regarded as more important than an uninterrupted view of the mystery of the ritual. The Renaissance, and above all the Baroque, styles occur in many Italian examples (e.g. Padua and Venice), the Rococo at Cavaillon near Avignon, the usual historicizing styles in many of those of the CI9 – the neo-Gothic synagogue at Budweis in Bohemia even has two church towers. In the CI9 a 'Byzanto-Moorish' style was particularly popular in the West. probably with the intention of asserting the Oriental heritage of the Jews (e.g. Dresden by SEMPER and Oranienburgerstrasse, Berlin).

In likely imitation of the Christian High Altar, the place of the Ark with the scrolls and the reading-desk is up nine steps against the end wall in more recent synagogues; whereas in earlier ones (Prague, Amsterdam) the reading-desk (*Almenor, see also* BEMA) was placed in the middle (with obvious acoustic advantages). In Italian synagogues, in the two early ones near Avignon (Carpentras and Cavaillon), and in distant Cochin (India), the place of the reading-desk is at the opposite end to the Ark, and often up about ten steps as the architectural counterpart of this.

In earlier synagogues the women's section (*Esrat Naschim*) was set off from that of the men by a curtain; now women sit in galleries.

A special form of synagogue, of which today there are only fragments in museums,

was the Polish wooden synagogue, which, like the Slavonic wooden-churches, was built in the CI7–CI8 where wood was plentiful, and permission for such wooden structures was easier to obtain. The interiors were painted by local folk artists. Prior to the Nazi destructions, there were a few such painted synagogues in the Main region, done by artists whose families had fled from Polish pogroms.

Modern architecture gave synagogues the same aesthetic fillip as it had given to churches, especially in the U.S.A., where more

Synagogue at Cleveland, 1945, by Mendelsohn

than 500 have been built since the War, but also in Europe and in Germany in particular, with the opportunities afforded by the reconstruction of what the Nazis destroyed.

In accordance with the original purpose of the synagogue, these are not only houses of prayer, but also contain assembly- and club-rooms. Often furnished with stained-glass windows and sacred vessels in the modern style, there are everywhere signs of a resurgence in both the architecture and the interior design of synagogues.   [HS]

Lit: Cecil Roth (ed.), *Jewish Art*, London 1971; Samuel Krauss, *Synagogale Altertümer*, Berlin–Vienna 1922; Richard Krautheimer, *Mittelalterliche Synagogen*, Berlin 1927; Avram Kampf, *Contemporary Synagogal Art*, New York 1966.

Synclastic Of a surface, having curvatures in the same sense (concave or convex) in all directions through any point as in a simple DOME and in contrast to an ANTICLASTIC surface.

Synthronon In Early Christian and Byzantine churches, the bench or benches reserved for the clergy in the semicircle of the apse or in rows on either side of the BEMA.

Systyle With an arrangement of columns spaced two diameters apart. *See also* ARAEO-STYLE; DIASTYLE; EUSTYLE; PYCNOSTYLE.

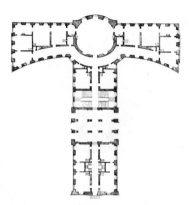

Tabernacle 1. An ornamented recess or receptacle to contain the Holy Sacrament or relics. 2. A free-standing canopy.

Tabernacle in Orsanmichele, Florence, by Orcagna, 1349–59

Tablinum In Roman architecture, a room with one side open to the ATRIUM or central courtyard.

Taenia, *see* TENIA.

Talman, William (1650–1719), WREN'S most distinguished contemporary, was the leading country-house architect until eclipsed by VANBRUGH. Little is known about him personally, though he seems to have been difficult and quarrelsome. His country houses are by far the largest and most lavish of their period in England, and display a mixed French and Italian Baroque character. They were very influential, e.g., in the use of giant pilasters with architrave and frieze to frame a façade, the cornice alone continuing across. Thoresby (1683–5, destroyed), the east front of Chatsworth (1687–96), Dyrham Park (1698–1700), Dorchester House, Surrey (*c.* 1700), and the new front at Drayton (*c.* 1701) were his main works, all country houses. He designed the state apartments at Burghley House, Northants (1658, destroyed). He succeeded Hugh MAY as Comptroller of the Office of Works in 1689, serving under Wren, whose design for Hampton Court he probably revised and altered in execution.

Lit: M. Whinney & O. Millar, *English Art, 1625–1714,* Oxford 1957; J. Summerson, *Architecture in Britain 1530–1830,* Pelican History of Art, Harmondsworth 1969, paperback edn 1970.

Tambour 1. The core of a Corinthian or Composite CAPITAL. 2. The circular wall carrying a DOME or CUPOLA (*see* DRUM). (Illustration next page.)

Tange, Kenzo (b. 1913), studied at Tokyo University 1935–8 and 1942–5, then joined the office of Kunio Maekawa (*see* JAPANESE ARCHITECTURE). His mature buildings are all dramatically plastic: the Kagawa prefectural offices at Takamatsu (1958), with a ruthlessly expressed post-and-beam structure; the waterfront Dentsu offices at Osaka (1960); the Atami Gardens Hotel at Atami (1961), meticulously furnished by Isamu Kenmochi; the challenging, somewhat sombre City Hall at Kurashiki (1960), standing four-square and

*Tambour: Dome of the abbey church
at Weingarten, 1717–19, by Frisoni*

quakeproof; St Mary's Roman Catholic Cathedral, Tokyo (1965), a cruciform arrangement of paraboloids; and the joyful Golf Club at Totsuka (1962), in which an upswept traditional roof is typically contrasted with aluminium curtain walls. With Yoshokatsu Tsuboi as engineer, Tange designed the magnificent tensile catenary roof spanning the 15,000 seat National Gymnasium, ready for the Tokyo Olympic Games in 1964. Tange's leadership of the younger generation principally results from his research work into town planning at Tokyo University, the absence of which has reduced Japan's expanding industrial cities to a critical state of congestion. Tange's plan for Tokyo (1960) shows a logical hierarchy of rapid transit roads within connecting ring roads, enclosing environmental areas of high density housing; his idea was to extend the city in this way on piles over Tokyo Bay. He won the international competition for replanning Skopje in Yugoslavia (1965), with a system of multi-purpose blocks. He has designed prototypes of these for the Dentsu building and Tsukiji area, Tokyo (1965), with flying bridges clad in criss-cross concrete grilles (an alternative, much reduced design will be carried out), and for the Yamanashi broadcasting centre, Kofu (built 1966–7), which is held together by sixteen cylindrical towers of lifts and services. Tsuboi was engineer for Dentsu, and Fugaku Yokoyama for the astonishing Yamanashi project. In 1967 Tange was also appointed (with Uzo Nikiyama) master planner of the international exhibition of 1970 at Osaka. (For illustrations *see* JAPANESE ARCHITECTURE.)

Lit: R. Boyd, *Kenzo Tange*, New York 1962; K. Tange & U. Kultermann, *Kenzo Tange: Architecture and Urban Design*, 1970.

Tarsia, *see* INTARSIA.

Tas-de-charge The lowest courses of a vault or arch, laid horizontally and bonded into the wall.

Tatlin, Vladimir (1885–1953). Tatlin was a painter with special interest in certain crafts, especially ceramics. He also did theatrical work. In 1913 he visited Paris. After the Revolution he turned to the same kind of abstract, Constructivist architectural fantasies as did Gabo occasionally. The Memorial to the Third International, a skew spiral composition, made in 1919–20, is his one and only famous design. It was meant to be 1300 ft high, i.e. higher than the Eiffel Tower.

Lit: *Vladimir Tatlin*, Exh. Cat., Modern Museet, Stockholm 1968; V. Quilici, *L'architettura del costruttivismo*, Bari 1969.

Taut, Bruno (1880–1938), a pupil of Theodor Fischer in Munich, settled in Berlin in 1908. He was professor at the College of Technology, Berlin, in 1931, and at Ankara in 1936; between these posts he visited Russia in 1932 and Japan in 1933. Taut was first noticed for his highly original glass pavilion at the Werkbund Exhibition of 1914 in Cologne (*see* GROPIUS, van de VELDE), a polygonal building with walls of thick glass panels, a metal staircase inside, and a glass dome, the elements set in lozenge framing (a SPACE-FRAME). In the years of the wildest Expressionism in Germany, Taut wrote his frantic *Die Stadtkrone* (1919) and designed fantastic buildings for imprecisely formulated purposes.

Lit: B. Miller Lane, *Architecture and Politics in Germany, 1918–1945*, Cambridge, Mass., 1968; K. Junghanns, *B. Taut, 1880–1938*, Berlin 1971.

Taylor, Sir Robert (1714–88), son of a mason-contractor, trained as a sculptor under Cheere and visited Rome *c.* 1743. Though sufficiently successful to be commissioned by Parliament to design and carve the monument to Captain Cornewall in Westminster Abbey (1744), he soon abandoned sculpture for architecture and by assiduity and businesslike methods quickly built up a large practice. He and PAINE were said to have 'nearly divided the practice of the profession between them' during the mid-century. He was conservative and uninspired but highly competent, and worthily carried on the neo-Palladian tradition of BURLINGTON and KENT. Most of his work has been destroyed, notably that in the Bank of England which included his last and by far his most original work, the Reduced Annuities Office, a top-lit hall with circular clerestory carried on segmental arches. It anticipated SOANE. Asgill House, Richmond (1758–67). and Stone Building, Lincoln's Inn, London (begun 1775), are the best of his surviving buildings. He was knighted when sheriff of London, 1782–3, and left the bulk of his large fortune to found the Taylorian Institution in Oxford for the teaching of modern languages.

Lit: J. Summerson, Architecture in Britain, 1530–1830, Pelican History of Art, Harmondsworth 1969, paperback edn 1970.

Tebam A dais or rostrum for the reader in a SYNAGOGUE. Adjoining it to the east is the Chief Rabbi's seat.

Tecton A team established by Berthold Lubetkin (b. 1901) to which among others Denys LASDUN belonged. The team did the Highpoint Flats I and II at Highgate, London, in 1936 and 1938, the Finsbury Health Centre in 1938–9, and the blocks of flats in Rosebery Avenue in 1946–9. Their most popular work was for the London Zoo (1934–8). The details here of freely moulded concrete are prophetic of the 1950s.

Telamones, see ATLANTES.

Telford, Thomas (1757–1834), son of a Scottish shepherd, trained as a mason, worked in Edinburgh, then in London, and by 1784 had been made supervisor of works on Portsmouth Dockyard. In 1788 he became surveyor to the county of Shropshire. He built several churches in the county, notably Bridgnorth (1792), and several bridges, notably the brilliant Buildwas Bridge (1795–8), which was of iron (the Coalbrookdale Bridge had been built in iron in 1777) and had a 130 ft span. In 1793 work started on the Ellesmere Canal, and Telford was put in charge. He built the Chirk Aqueduct at Ceiriog, 700 ft long and 70 ft high (1796 etc.), and the Pont Cysylltau Aqueduct, 1000 ft long and 120 ft high (1795 etc.). In 1800 he suggested the rebuilding of London Bridge with a single span of 600 ft. Telford was responsible for other canals (Caledonian, 1804 etc.; Göta, 1808 etc.), for the St Katherine's Docks (1825; see HARDWICK), for fen drainage, for roads, and for further bridges, including the beautiful Dean Bridge, Edinburgh, of stone (1831), the Menai Straits Suspension Bridge, of iron, with a 530 ft span (1819 etc.), and the Conway Suspension Bridge, also of iron (1826). (For illustration see ENGLISH ARCHITECTURE.)

Lit: L. T. C. Rolt, Thomas Telford, London 1958.

Temanza, Tommaso (1705–89). The most sensitive of Venetian neo-Palladians. His masterpiece is the little church of the Maddalena, Venice (c. 1760), with its interior freely derived from PALLADIO's chapel at Maser. He wrote Le vite dei più celebri architetti e scultori veneziani (1778).

Lit: C. L. V. Meeks, Italian Architecture, 1750–1914, New Haven–London 1966.

Template The block of stone set at the top of a brick or rubble wall to carry the weight of the JOISTS or roof-trusses; also called a pad stone.

Tenia The small moulding or fillet along the top of the ARCHITRAVE in the Doric ORDER.

Teotihuacan architecture, see MESOAMERICAN ARCHITECTURE.

Term A pedestal tapering towards the base and usually supporting a bust; also a pedestal merging at the top into a sculptured human, animal, or mythical figure; also called terminal figures or termini.

Terrace 1. A level promenade in front of a building. 2. A row of attached houses designed as a unit.

Terracotta Fired but unglazed clay, used mainly for wall covering and ornamentation as it can be fired in moulds.

Terragni, Giuseppe, see ITALIAN ARCHITECTURE.

Terrazzo A flooring finish of marble chips

mixed with cement mortar and laid *in situ*; the surface is then ground and polished.

Tessellated A cement floor or wall covering in which TESSERAE are embedded.

Tesserae The small cubes of glass, stone, or marble used in MOSAIC.

Tessin, Nicodemus, the elder (1615–81), a leading Baroque architect in Sweden, was born in Stralsund and began by working under Simon de LA VALLÉE. In 1651–2 he made a tour of Europe and in 1661 was appointed city architect of Stockholm. His main work is Drottningholm Palace (begun 1662), built in an individual Baroque style derived from Holland, France, and Italy. His other works include Kalmar Cathedral (1660), Göteborg Town Hall (1670), the Carolean Mausoleum attached to the Riddarholm Church, Stockholm (designed 1671), and numerous small houses in Stockholm. His son **Nicodemus the younger** (1654–1728) succeeded him as the leading Swedish architect. Trained under his father, he travelled in England, France, and Italy (1673–80), and completed his father's work at Drottningholm. His main building is the vast royal palace in Stockholm (begun 1697), where he adopted a Baroque style reminiscent of, and probably influenced by BERNINI's Louvre project. (For illustration *see* SCANDINAVIAN ARCHITECTURE.)

Lit: A. Lindblom, *Sveriges Kunsthistoria,* Stockholm 1946; E. Lundberg, *Arkitekturens Formsprak 1629–1715,* Stockholm 1959.

Tester A canopy suspended from the ceiling or supported from the wall above a bed, throne, pulpit, etc.

Tetraconch A building composed of four 'conchs' (i.e. of four semicircular niches surmounted by half-domes).

Tetrastyle Of a PORTICO with four frontal columns.

Thai architecture, *see* SOUTH-EAST ASIAN ARCHITECTURE.

Thatch A roof covering of straw or reeds, Norfolk reeds being the best in England.

Thermae In Roman architecture public baths, usually of great size and splendour and containing libraries and other amenities as well as every provision for bathing. Their remains in Rome were closely studied by architects from PALLADIO onwards and had great influence on planning.

Thermal window A semicircular window divided into three lights by two vertical mullions, also known as a Diocletian window because of its use in the Thermae of Diocletian,

Thermae of Diocletian, Rome, 298–306, reconstruction

Rome. Its use was revived in the C16 especially by PALLADIO and is a feature of PALLADIAN-ISM.

Tholos The dome of a circular building or the building itself, e.g., a domed Mycenaean tomb.

Thomon, Thomas de (1754–1813). Leading NEO-CLASSICAL architect in Russia. He was born in Nancy, probably studied under LEDOUX in Paris and completed his training in Rome c. 1785. In 1789 he followed the Comte d'Artois into exile to Vienna where he found a patron in Prince Esterhazy. From there he went to Russia. His designs for the Kazan Cathedral were rejected (1799) but in 1802 he became architect to the court of Alexander I in St Petersburg and immediately obtained important commissions – the Grand Theatre (1802–5, demolished) and the Bourse (designed 1801–4, built 1805–16), a Tuscan Doric temple with blank pediments, great segmental lunettes and flanking *columnae rostratae*. The Bourse is his masterpiece and a major neo-classical building of the most severe and radical kind, more advanced than anything in Paris at that date. In 1806–10 he built a Doric mausoleum to Paul I in the park at Pavlovsk. He published *Recueil de plans et façades des principaux monuments construits à St Petersburg* (1808, republished in Paris 1819 with an amended title).

Lit: G. H. Hamilton, *The Art and Architecture of Russia*, Pelican History of Art, Harmondsworth 1954.

Thomson, Alexander (1817–75), lived and worked at Glasgow, and was in practice from about 1847. He was known as 'Greek' Thomson, and rightly so, for to be a convinced Grecian was a very remarkable thing for a man belonging to the generation of PUGIN, SCOTT, and RUSKIN. The formative influence on his style was SCHINKEL rather than English Grecians. This comes out most clearly in such monumental terraces as Moray Place (1859), where the purity of proportion and the scarcity of enrichment suggest a date some thirty years earlier. His churches, on the other hand, though essentially Grecian, are far from pure: they exhibit an admixture of the Egyptian, even the Hindu, as well as a boldness in the use of iron, which combine to produce results of fearsome originality. His three churches – all United Presbyterian – are the Caledonian Road Church (1856), the Vincent Street Church (1859), and the Queen's Park Church (1867). All three are among the most forceful churches of their date anywhere in Europe. Equally interesting are Thomson's warehouses, especially the Egyptian Halls. (For illustration *see* SCOTTISH ARCHITECTURE.)

Lit: A. Gomme & D. Walker, *Architecture of Glasgow*, London 1969; J. Mordaunt Crook, *The Greek Revival*, London 1972.

Thornton, William (1759–1828), was an English physician who emigrated from the West Indies to the U.S. and became an American citizen in 1788. He designed the Philadelphia Library Company building in 1789 and in 1793 won the competition for the Capitol, Washington, though his runner-up, Stephen Hallet, was put in charge of the execution of his designs. The foundation stone was laid by George Washington in the same year. Hallet modified Thornton's designs and was replaced in 1795 by James HOBAN who proposed further alterations and was dismissed in 1798. But by 1800 the north wing containing the Senate had been completed substantially to Thornton's designs. In 1803 LATROBE took charge and completed the south wing by 1807. He also supervised the rebuilding after the Capitol had been sacked and burnt by British troops in 1814. Latrobe followed Thornton's designs for the exterior though not for the interior. In 1827 BULFINCH connected the two wings, again following the original design. (The dome and further extensions were added by T. U. WALTER, 1857–63.) Thornton also designed the Octagon House, Washington (1800) and Tudor Place, Washington (1815).

Lit: G. Brown, *History of the U.S. Capitol*, Washington 1900–1903.

Thorpe, John (c. 1565–1655), an unimportant clerk in the Office of Works and later a successful land surveyor, was not, as is sometimes thought, the architect of Longleat, Kirby, Wollaton, Audley End, and other great Elizabethan and Jacobean houses. Plans and a few elevations of these and many other Elizabethan buildings are in a volume of drawings by him in the Sir John Soane Museum, London.

Lit: J. Summerson, *Architecture in Britain, 1530–1830*, Pelican History of Art, Harmondsworth 1969, paperback edn 1970; J. Summerson, 'The Book of Architecture of John Thorpe' in *Walpole Society*, XL, 1966.

Thumb, Michael (d. 1690). He was born at Bezau in the Bregenzerwald and was a founder of the Vorarlberge school of architects which included, besides the Thumb family, the MOSBRUGGER family and the BEER family. The latter intermarried with the Thumb family. The long series of buildings of this school, mostly for Benedictine monasteries in S.W. Germany and Switzerland, was eventually to mark the triumph of German over Italian elements in S. German Baroque architecture (i.e., over the domination of such Italians as ZUCCALLI and VISCARDI from the Grisons). Michael Thumb's pilgrimage church of Schönenberg near Ellwangen (begun 1682) is a prototype of the *Vorarlberger Münsterschema* – a pillared HALL CHURCH, the internal buttresses being faced with pilasters and projecting so deep as to form chapels, usually connected above by a gallery. He continued the type at the Premonstratensian abbey church of Obermarchtal (1686–92). Both churches are notable for their plainspoken dignity. His son **Peter** (1681–1766) worked as a foreman for Franz BEER from 1704 and married his daughter. He later occupied an influential position at Constance. As an architect he developed a much more sophisticated manner than his father and achieved a wonderfully light and sparkling Rococo unity of effect in his best interiors. In 1738 he built the library of the monastery of St Peter in the Black Forest, successfully adapting the Vorarlberger Münsterschema of internal buttresses with columns and a balcony swirling round them. His masterpiece is the pilgrimage church of Birnau on Lake Constance (1746–58) where he had the collaboration of Feuchtmayer on the decoration. At the great Benedictine abbey of St Gall he worked for eleven years (1748–58) but the extent of his contribution to the abbey church is uncertain. He was probably mainly responsible for the great central rotunda and he probably influenced the design of the two-towered east façade, built by Johann Michael BEER in 1771–8. For the library in the monastery of St Gall (1758–67) he employed the same system as at St Peter in the Black Forest. (For illustration *see* SWISS ARCHITECTURE.)

Christian Thumb (d. 1726) worked with Michael Thumb at Schönenberg and at Obermarchtal, where he continued after Michael's death in 1690. His masterpiece is the Schlosskirche at Friedrichshafen (1695–1701). He probably collaborated with Andreas Schreck at the abbey church at Weingarten (1716–24).

Lit: H.-R. Hitchcock, *Rococo Architecture in Southern Germany,* London 1968.

Tibaldi, Pellegrino (1527–96). He began as a painter in Bologna but became the protégé of St Carlo Borromeo who established him in Milan where he worked mainly as an architect from 1564 onwards, succeeding ALESSI as the leading architect. His more notable works include the Collegio Borromeo at Pavia, begun 1564; the austere Canonica cortile in the Archiepiscopal Palace in Milan, commissioned 1565 and begun *c.* 1572; S. Fedele in Milan, begun 1569 (the year after the Gesù in Rome) and S. Sebastiano, Milan, begun 1576. He was appointed chief architect of Milan cathedral in 1567 and built the crypt under the choir and the high barriers between the choir and the ambulatory. From 1586 to 1594 or 1595 he was in Spain, working as a painter at the Escorial.

Lit: W. Hiersche, *Pellegrino de'Pellegrini als Architekt,* Parchin 1913; A. Peroni, 'Architetti manieristi nell'Italia settentrionale: Pellegrino Tibaldi e Galeazzo Alessi', *Bollettino Centro Internazionale Studi Architteture Andrea Palladio,* IX, Vicenza 1967; L. H. Heydenreich & W. Lotz, *Architecture in Italy, 1400–1600,* Pelican History of Art, Harmondsworth 1974.

Tie-beam, *see* ROOF.

Tierceron, *see* VAULT.

Tilehanging A wall covering of overlapping rows of tiles on a timber structure.

Timber-framing A method of construction (also called *half-timbering* or *half-timber construction*) where walls are built of timber framework with the spaces filled in by plaster

Little Moreton Hall, Cheshire, C16 *and* C17

Timber-framing

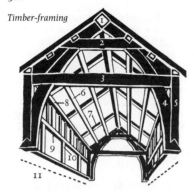

1. Ridge piece
2. Collar-beam
3. Tie-beam
4. Arched brace
5. Post
6. Purlins
7. Rafters
8. Wall plate
9. Bressumer
10. Studs
11. Line of ground wall

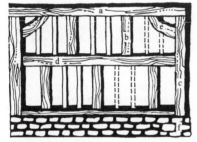

a. Wall plate
b. Stud
c. Post
d. Bressumer
e. Bracing
f. Ground wall

or brickwork (known as nogging). Sometimes the timber is covered with plaster or boarding laid horizontally (*see* WEATHERBOARDING).

Toledo, Juan Bautista de (d. 1567), philosopher and mathematician as well as architect, spent many years in Italy and for some time before 1559 was architect to the Spanish Viceroy in Naples. In 1562 he was appointed architect of the Escorial, drew up the entire ground plan, but built only the two-storeyed Court of the Evangelists, modelled on SANGALLO's Palazzo Farnese, Rome, and the vast severe south façade. (For illustrations *see* SPANISH ARCHITECTURE.)

Lit: F. Chueca Goitia, *Arquitectura del siglo XVI* (*Ars Hispaniae*, vol. XI), Madrid 1953; G. Kubler & M. Soria, *Art and Architecture in Spain and Portugal and their American Domi-*

nions, *1500–1800*, Pelican History of Art, Harmondsworth 1959.

Toltec architecture, *see* MESOAMERICAN ARCHITECTURE.

Tomb The largest and best-known tombs are the PYRAMIDS of the Old Kingdom in Egypt (Gizeh, 4th Dynasty, *c.* 2500 B.C.). They evolved out of the MASTABA, of which a number were superimposed to form a stepped pyramid (Saqqara, Imhotep's stepped pyramid for Zoser, 3rd Dynasty). The Middle Kingdom gave up such conspicuous monuments, which had already been subject to plundering during the Old Kingdom. The dead were instead buried in concealed rock- and passage-tombs, from among which that of Tut-ankh-amon survives virtually inviolate, giving us, since the distinguished dead were buried with their household goods in all old civilizations, a thorough insight into Egyptian art and culture of the middle New Kingdom (*c.* 1350 B.C.). Toward the end, stone chapels were set up, with subterranean chambers.

Persia (*see* IRANIAN ARCHITECTURE) and certain rocky districts of Asia Minor (Lycia) were familiar with the rock-cut tomb with a sham façade. There were also house-sarcophagi (the Kyros tomb) on high stepped plinths, and pyramidally topped tower-tombs related to Greek architecture. In the case of the MAUSOLEUM of Halicarnassus (begun by Pytheos of Priene and Satyros of Paros *c.* 350 B.C.) all these themes were orchestrated into one structure whose size and splendour made it into one of the Seven Wonders of the World.

The early Greeks had shaft and THOLOS tombs, both found in Mycenae, the grandest of the latter being the so-called Treasury of Atreus. The mainland progressed from mounds of earth to table-tombs ornamented with stelae, vessels, and sculpted beasts. Rock tombs recurred amongst the ETRUSCANS; they had several chambers and were decorated with architectural depictions within. They co-existed with constructed tombs with a block-like body and a pyramidal helm (*cippus*); it was chiefly this form that was adopted by the Romans for their larger tombs (e.g. that of Cecilia Metella in Rome), and further elaborated into centralized buildings (the tomb in Diocletian's palace at Split and the Tomb of Theodoric at Ravenna). But the funerary culture of the Romans also made use of all the other forms evolved in Greece, the Orient,

Tomb of Theodoric, Ravenna, early c6

and Egypt (the Pyramid of Cestius), as well as of sepulchral avenues (Pompeii), and of the *columbarium* for the display of cinerary urns. Catacombs should also be instanced here amongst these already cemetery-like complexes.

Churches or mosques were raised over the graves of holy men, but they scarcely differed from ordinary buildings of the kind. This is in striking contrast to the tombs of India and China, particularly those of the Moslem Mogul Emperors of the former, which were often of fabulous size and splendour (notably the Taj Mahal). In Europe, sculptural elements in tombs increased steadily in importance, and although attempts were made during the Renaissance and later to revive the tomb as architecture, they only repeated past forms or borrowed the form of the temple. Nevertheless, these attempts produced several very remarkable buildings, most notably, of course, Michelangelo's Julius monument, which was never fully realized, and the Medici Chapel in Florence, and Primaticcio's Valois Chapel in St Denis, also never completed. In the nineteenth century, the Orleans Chapel at Dreux, with stained glass by Ingres, and the Royal Chapel in the park at Windsor Castle should be mentioned. Of modern tombs, that of Lenin in Moscow is of course by far the most famous, and, architecturally, the most interesting. *See also* TÜRBE.

Lit: E. Panofsky, *Tomb Sculpture*, New York–London 1964.

Tomb-chest A chest-shaped stone coffin, the most usual medieval form of funerary monument. *See also* ALTAR-TOMB.

Tomé, Narciso (active 1715–42), began as a sculptor with his father and brothers on the

façade of Valladolid University (1715). His famous TRANSPARENTE in Toledo Cathedral (1721–32) is the most stupefying of all Baroque extravaganzas in spatial illusionism. It goes farther than anything invented by Italian Baroque architects and is exceptional even for Spain.

Lit: G. Kubler, *Arquitectura española, 1600–1800* (*Ars Hispaniae*, vol. XIV), Madrid 1957; G. Kubler & M. Soria, *Art and Architecture in Spain and Portugal and their American Dominions, 1500–1800*, Pelican History of Art, Harmondsworth 1959.

Torralva, Diogo de (1500–66), the leading Portuguese Renaissance architect, was the son-in-law of ARRUDA but abandoned his rich MANUELINE style for one much simpler, sterner, and more Italianate. His main work is the cloister of the Cristo Monastery, Tomar (1557), with the SERLIAN MOTIF used as an open arcade on the upper floor. He designed the apse for the Jeronimite Church at Belem (1540–51). Several other buildings have been attributed to him, notably the octagonal church of the Dominican Nuns at Elvas (1543–57). (For illustration *see* PORTUGUESE ARCHITECTURE.)

Lit: G. Kubler & M. Soria, *Art and Architecture in Spain and Portugal and their American Dominions, 1500–1800*, Pelican History of Art, Harmondsworth 1959; R. C. Smith, *The Art of Portugal*, London 1968.

Torroja, Eduardo (1899–1961). Concrete engineer and architect in Spain. His principal works are the grandstand of the Zarzuela racecourse near Madrid (1935), and the Algeciras market hall (1933). (For illustration *see* SPANISH ARCHITECTURE.)

Lit: E. Torroja, *Philosophy of Structure*, University of California 1958; E. Torroja, *The Structures of Eduardo Torroja*, New York 1958; F. Cassinello, *Eduardo Torroja, Cuadernos de Arquitectura*, 1961; J. Joedicke, *Shell Architecture*, New York 1963.

Torus A large convex moulding of semicircular profile, e.g., at the base of a column. *See also* ASTRAGAL. (For illustration *see* PEDESTAL.)

Totonac architecture, *see* MESOAMERICAN ARCHITECTURE.

Touch A soft black marble quarried near Tournai, used chiefly for monuments.

Tourelle A turret CORBELLED out from the wall.

Tower Definable as a structure whose height is very great in ratio to its extent. The original 'Tower' – that of Babel – would not, now that it is known to have been a stepped pyramid (ZIGGURAT), any longer qualify as one. Ambitiously tall towers were foreign to Antiquity, save for lighthouses, whose most famous representative, that on Pharos near Alexandria (c. 280 B.C.), became the epitome of its kind; but that it was reckoned one of the Seven Wonders of the World indicates how exceptional it was. Used early on in association with walls and gates as part of the defences, but restricted in height by their function, towers in Antiquity had no unusual or symbolic role: they assumed the latter in the Early Christian period, when they became rather more symbolic than practical adjuncts to churches. They were often built, as CAMPANILES, beside the early churches of the West (S. Apollinare in Classe, Ravenna,

Tower at Alsum, Ethiopia, c2–c4

c9); but in the East (Syria) they were soon incorporated in the church and this led to a variety of architectural solutions; similarly in the West, from the Carolingian period onwards, towers increasingly formed part of church design. The two most important Carolingian cases, both only recorded in illustrations, are St Gall and Centula, the former, an ideal plan of c. 820, with two campanili symmetrically set at the west end and thereby heralding two-tower façades, the latter with a profusion of towers – two over the CROSSINGS, and two flanking both the east and west ends, all round in section and of moderate height. The west group looks like a crossing and transepts but was almost certainly a WESTWORK (cf. Corvey). The grouped towers of Centula became the model for major German Romanesque buildings: first St Michael at Hildesheim of c. 1000–1073 and then Speier, Laach, Mainz and Worms. A parallel development was that of the two-tower façade. This is first met in the early CI I on the Upper Rhine (Strasbourg), and in Burgundy (Cluny) and Normandy (Jumièges, Caen). After that the arrangement of two façade towers and a crossing tower was widely accepted in England (e.g. Durham, Southwell) and also in France. For CI 2 and CI 3 French Gothic cathedrals and abbeys this composition was canonical (St Denis, Chartres, Paris, etc.). Progressive Gothic thereafter often did away with the second tower, so as to have only one that much higher soaring above the façade. Famous instances are: the towers of Freiburg (CI4) and Strasbourg Minsters (CI5; at 462 ft unsurpassed till the CI9), and of the Stefansdom, Vienna (CI5).

While ecclesiastical architecture led the tower to its greatest triumphs, in the Late Middle Ages the tower in its secular forms – as a municipal BELFRY, or as part of private or public defences – made a conspicuous contribution to the townscape, e.g., at Bologna and S. Gimignano in Italy. This is also the place to mention the great castles of the High Middle Ages, at whose core was first the donjon, or tower-KEEP, and then the less spectacular towers along a wall which now formed the chief protection. The increasing efficacy of artillery in the CI6 put an end to these, and they shrank to bulwarks and BASTIONS. The early country houses which took the place of castles still had projecting towers, but mostly only as stair-turrets and gatehouses, and in the CI7 they disappeared completely.

Two-tower façades like those of the Middle Ages were not often used by Italian Renaissance and Baroque architects. Examples are SANGALLO's model for St Peter's (*c.* 1540), ALESSI's S. Maria in Carignano at Genoa (1552), and BORROMINI's Baroque S. Agnese in Rome. BERNINI wanted to add two towers to the front of St Peter's, but the plan was soon given up. Wren's St Paul's has two Baroque west towers apart from the dome, but for Britain that remained an exception. The German and Austrian Baroque on the other hand favoured the scheme of St Paul's. Specially early is Kempten, specially fine are Fulda, Melk and Vierzehnheiligen. As for single towers the best sequence is Wren's city churches with their never exhausted variety of styles and motifs.

In the C19 several buildings begun in the Middle Ages were completed to their planned heights (Cologne 510 ft, Ulm 525 ft), but C19 architects also exploited new techniques to build towers that were nothing other than symbolic affirmations of faith in technology (the Eiffel Tower 985 ft). Telecommunications masts and skyscrapers, products of the engineer and the steel frame, are the towers of the C20.

Tower-shaped structures occur in other cultures – the Indian STUPA, the Far Eastern PAGODA, and the Islamic MINARET – the latter being in its post-Omayyad form the one most closely approximating to the European conception. *See also* SPIRE.   [AVR]

Lit: H. Thiersch, *Pharos, Antike und Islam,* Berlin 1909; M. Revész-Alexander, *Der Turm als Symbol und Erlebnis,* Berlin 1953.

Town, Ithiel, *see* DAVIS, ALEXANDER JACKSON.

Town-planning *The concept.* Town planning is the prior control of future construction and land use in a given area. Whereas up until the middle of the last century this activity was chiefly limited to the design of the physical framework best suited to the needs of a community, today town-planning is also increasingly understood as an instrument of social policy.

The concept of town or urban planning, first given currency towards the end of the C19 by Joseph Stübben and Camillo SITTE, superseded earlier ideas of *urban expansion.* Of its various aspects, the measures used to sweep away insanitary living conditions are called *slum clearance,* and those used to remedy the shortcomings of existing areas, *redevelop-*

ment. The fashionable expression of recent years, *community development,* means by contrast the coordination of the provision of homes with policies for the direction of investment and the creation of an economic infrastructure. The legal powers vested in a planning body cover on the one hand *land use,* by means of which it lays down in broad detail the uses to which land within its jurisdiction may be put, in the light of the foreseeable needs of the community, and on the other hand *planned development,* through which it lays down what is to be built and where.

In Great Britain the terms 'town and country planning' or 'town planning' have replaced 'improvement' and 'civic design', whilst in the U.S.A. the following terms are currently used: 'Urbanismo', 'city planning', 'community planning', 'urban planning' and 'urban design'. Recently 'environmental planning' and 'environmental design' have been used to refer to the wider urban context. The French have only the all-embracing word *urbanisme,* which extends to research into urban life as does the Italian word *urbanismo,* whilst the Germans talk of *Stadtplanung* or *Städtebau.*

History. The earliest evidence of urban construction dates to as far back as between 7000 and 5000 B.C., but the first towns of which we have detailed knowledge are those round the Mediterranean, notably those of Greek and Roman Antiquity, which were to leave a lasting imprint on Western civilization.

As both strongholds and settlements, the earliest Greek cities for the most part followed the example of the hill-top cities of the Peloponnese and Asia Minor (Mycenae, Troy) in their choice of situation. Subsequently, the upper town (ACROPOLIS) was complemented by further quarters on the slopes or at the foot of the hill (as at Athens). Not only does the occasional virgin foundation on the mainland have a planned layout (Piraeus), but so, conspicuously, do the colonial cities planted in South Italy, Sicily, and on the coast of Asia Minor (Selinus, Priene, Miletus, Syracuse), with their characteristic system, ascribed to the architect HIPPODAMOS, of streets intersecting at right angles, even on an uneven site. The heart of these cities, which were often overlooked by a detached temple precinct, was the porticoed market-place (AGORA); the streets on to which the courtyarded houses backed were merely traffic-routes, and not planned ensembles.

Here Roman town-planning brought a decisive change; a Hippodamic regularity of layout centring upon the *cardo* and *decumanus* (see CASTRUM) indeed persists, but the main streets, squares, temples, and FORA are lent a wholly new distinction by the symmetry and axiality of their stately architecture, especially in the Late Roman period (Rome itself, Palmyra, Baalbek).

Urban life in Europe shared in the decline of the Roman Empire, almost totally to disappear when the Arab conquests severed trade within the Mediterranean. Where Roman cities continued to be occupied, it was by basically rustic populations huddled at random for defence within their walls, so that their layout has but rarely survived intact (e.g. Turin). Forts and monasteries were the only forms of human aggregation. Trade and, with trade, urban life did not revive till the C10. Unplanned towns sprang up at the intersections of trade routes and at the mouths of rivers – often as settlements outside the walls of abbeys, forts, or former cities, subsequently to absorb these. In the C11–12 enlightened rulers recognized and fostered towns, especially along the Channel and down the Rhine, by the bestowal of freedoms and privileges, whilst in Italy urban communes asserted their independence. Some rulers, like Conrad of Zähringen (Freiburg, etc.) and Louis VI (Lorris), proceeded to found towns for the wealth they would generate; but there was no thought of planning their layout or fabric till the C13, when the brothers Alphonse, Count of Poitiers (Villefranche-de-Rouergue) and St Louis (Aigues-Mortes, Carcassonne) in the Languedoc, and Edward I in Gascony (Monpazier, Lalinde) and N. Wales (Flint, Conway) planted their *villeneuves* and *bastides* to settle and hold down conquered regions. Such

bastides (and the rare cases of new, or rather transferred, towns like Salisbury or Winchelsea in England) were on an elementary chequerboard plan dictated by apportionment; one lot was left vacant for the (often arcaded) central *place d'armes*. Physical planning was otherwise the exception in the Middle Ages, save in Tuscany, where civic pride was expressed both in the erection of public buildings and in regulating the siting and appearance of private ones. Awareness of the visual appearance of cities is reflected in the emergence of townscapes in Late Medieval painting.

With the Renaissance, perspective demonstrations furthered awareness of the street as a vista and of the square as an ensemble – whether the revived classical vocabulary was used to give the latter a uniform facing (first insisted on by Lodovico Il Moro at Vigevano, 1492–94) or in integrating distinct buildings (MICHELANGELO's Capitol). At the same time, the popularity of VITRUVIUS inspired a wealth

Ideal town-plan, by Vitruvius

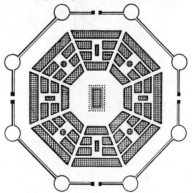

of ideal plans of cities, usually radial in design (e.g. by FILARETE, FRANCESCO DI GIORGIO, Speckle, Perret), but only exceptionally realized (Palmanova, Coeworden).

Palmanova, near Udine,
after a plan by Scamozzi of 1593

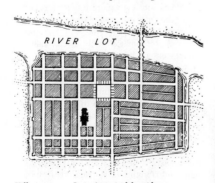

Villeneuve-sur-Lot: A typical bastide

Other new towns that in the C17 were still being founded by a single figure for reasons of religion or profit drew on such ideal cities to give prominence to the square as the core of the town, crossroads, and focal point (Freudenstadt, Henrichemont, Livorno, Charleville).

It was these visual aspects of planning that seized the imagination of the absolutist princes of North Europe in the C17 and C18; giving rise both to the French series of *places royales* focused on a statue of the king (beginning in Paris with the Place Dauphine 1607–14 and the Place des Vosges 1605–12), and to towns laid out, sometimes upon the same principles as a formal garden, as complements to royal palaces (Versailles, Karlsruhe, Ludwigsburg).

to be called such) in 1661 which inaugurated London's characteristic expansion through the leasehold development of aristocratic estates, focusing upon squares with gardens in the middle, that persisted up until the mid-C19 (by e.g. the Harleys, Cavendishes, Russells, and Grosvenors). At Bath, the WOODS enriched the vocabulary of squares and streets with a CIRCUS and CRESCENTS, and whole blocks, each designed to look like a single palazzo; and the principles of Bath and London were extended to the New Town of Edinburgh by Craig and the ADAMS. NASH introduced elements of the PICTURESQUE in his development of the Crown Estates, exploiting the irregular course of his Regent Street thoroughfare and incorporating Regent's Park with its villas.

Town-plan of Karlsruhe, engraving 1739

Though in Germany towns and quarters were still created *de novo* to receive religious refugees as the generators of new wealth and industry (Erlangen, Neuwied, Kassel; and vainly proposed by Defoe for the New Forest), elsewhere urban growth was largely unsystematic. The rulers of France and England at first responded to the surge of population in their capitals in the C16 simply by attempting to prohibit their expansion by decree, only to capitulate in the C17 before the large-scale schemes of speculators like Le Barbier and Barbon, and monasteries and aristocrats eager to develop their estates. The new *quartiers* then created, the Faubourgs of Paris and the West End of London, met the desire of the upper classes for more space and fresher air; but whereas the French preferred to build private *hôtels* with gardens on their own terrain, the English accommodated themselves to leasehold properties behind the uniform façades of streets and squares. Covent Garden, designed by Inigo JONES for the Earl of Bedford in 1630, was the first project with uniform façades, but it was the Earl of Southampton's creation of Bloomsbury Square (also the first

Cumberland Terrace, Regent's Park, London, begun 1811, by Nash

Such schemes made minimal provision for the rapidly increasing numbers of urban poor driven or attracted from the countryside by the Agricultural and Industrial Revolutions, and forced into ever more intensive occupation of the older quarters of towns. Industrialists might provide housing and even build new towns (Middlesbrough, Decazeville) to obtain workers, but they built only to minimum standards, creating spaceless rows of back-to-back terraces. To advanced thinkers like Robert Owen (who had attempted to make a community out of the factory settlement he acquired at New Lanark) and Fourier, the only remedy appeared to be the creation of entirely new communities in the countryside, planned down to the last detail (like LEDOUX's project for Chaux), self-sufficient, and communal. No such venture ever became viable; instead it was cholera and political upheaval which, by leaping the physical separation of the classes, compelled attention to the plight of the urban poor. The Public Health Act of 1848 in England, and the Loi de Melun of 1850 in France, initiated the legislation forging the powers necessary for socially motivated planning; the acceptance of the most crucial of these, expropriation, was facilitated by its use in railway-building.

Railways, especially in England, fostered the flight of the better-off away from the dirt and crowding of industry to villas in the suburbs and resorts. The need for space and more pleasant surroundings for all was recognized in the creation of public parks (PAXTON's Princes' Park, Liverpool 1842; Recreation Grounds Act 1859), and by whole towns set in open country with generous provision of space, and even gardens, for their employees by more enlightened industrialists (Titus Salt's Saltaire, Price's Candles' Bromborough, Cadbury's Bournville, Lever Brothers' Port Sunlight; and abroad notably by Krupp at Essen and Pullman at Chicago).

On the Continent, considerations of prestige and national security led to the 'sanitation' of whole areas of towns and the provision of great traffic arteries in the course of schemes of civic improvement (HAUSSMANN in Paris 1853–69, Poggi in Florence 1864–77); the arteries often took the place of redundant fortifications (already razed to provide walks in Paris in the C17), whence their name of *boulevards* or *circonvallazioni*; in Vienna the whole GLACIS was converted into the architectural showpiece of the Ring (begun 1858).

All these measures were seen in isolation as specific improvements, until, towards the end of the century, the fundamentals of modern town-planning as a discipline were established by such books as Reinhard Baumeister's *Stadterweiterungen in technischer, baupolizeilicher und wirtschaftlicher Beziehung* (1876), and Joseph Stübben's *Handbuch des Städtebaus* (1890). Camillo SITTE's *Der Städtebau nach seinen künstlerischen Grundsätzen* (1899) influenced the course of discussion about the basic principles of town-planning for at least the next two decades, with its call for a return to the aesthetic qualities of medieval town-planning, as he deduced them from surviving medieval centres. In the last decade of the C19 the publications of two social reformers, Ebenezer HOWARD (1898) and Theodor Fritsch (1896), threw up the idea of the *garden city* – a scheme for decen-

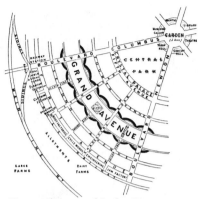

Diagram of segment of Garden City, by Howard

tralized urban expansion which was quickly taken up, if more often for *dormitory suburbs* than for autonomous settlements as its authors had intended (1899, foundation of the Garden City Association; 1903 Letchworth; 1907 Hampstead Garden Suburb; 1902 German Garden City Association – Dresden-Hellerau, Essen-Margarethenhöhe; the Green Belt Towns in the U.S.A.)

Just as important as the garden-city movement, but standing entirely on its own, is Tony GARNIER's *Cité industrielle*, a book on which he worked mostly in 1899–1904 and which was published in 1917. Here was the practical approach to a normal, if fictitious, town, and the demonstration of answers to such questions as location of industry, location of housing and location of the town centre. It did not for some time influence town-planners.

Yet by around 1910 town-planning was defined as a discipline; professorships in housing and town-planning were established and planning bodies set up. Exhibitions (London and Berlin 1910) promoted a wealth of experiment and theory in the field (Theodor Fischer, Ludwig Hilberseimer, Ernst May, LE CORBUSIER). Increasing appreciation of the necessity of situating the growth of urban communities in a regional context (Raymond UNWIN, Fritz Schumacher) led in the 1920s to numerous attempts at cooperation between authorities (1920, foundation of the Housing Union of the Ruhr), out of which regional planning authorities evolved. The basic statement of the principles of town-planning of the time is set out in the Athens Charter of 1933, produced by the International Congress for Modern Architecture (CIAM). With their goal of the articulated yet loose-knit town, these ideas have made a lasting contribution not just to the expansion and reconstruction of towns after 1945, but also to the planning of the English *New Towns* and the Greater London area, as well as to the plethora of Scandinavian *satellite towns*. Among the several suggested ways of structuring a community, the *neighbourhood unit* and the concept of the *linear city* (first evolved by Soria y Mata in 1882 and later most notably elaborated in Le Corbusier's projects for ideal cities, and

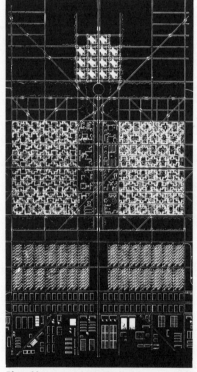

Plan of linear city, by Le Corbusier

those of L. Hilbersheimer, O. E. Schweitzer, etc.) merit especial mention. The current desire for compactness, flexibility, and mixed zoning may be seen as a reaction against the sprawl caused by rigid zoning and the much-lamented loss of the urban 'community'.

Since the sixties it has been evident that politicians and the public have come to appreciate what has long been known to the

experts, that town-planning, as a set of policies to do with the environment and the quality of human life, is of far more than technical and aesthetic concern. It is hence foreseeable that the public will come to play an increasing role in the decision-making process. [KB & AL]

Lit: Pierre Lavedan, *L'histoire de l'urbanisme*, Paris 1925–7; T. F. Tout, *Medieval Town Planning*, London 1927; Wolfgang Braunfels, *Mittelalterliche Stadtbaukunst in der Toscana*, Munich 1953; Colin & Rose Bell, *City Fathers*, London 1969; Leonardo Benevolo, *The Origins of Modern Town Planning*, London 1967; Lewis Mumford, *The Culture of Cities*, London 1938; John Summerson, *Georgian London*, London 1969.

Trabeated The adjective describing a building constructed on the post-and-lintel principle, as in Greek architecture, in contrast to an ARCUATED building.

Post-and-lintel construction: Temple of Hera, Paestum, mid-c6 B.C.

Tracery The ornamental intersecting work in the upper part of a window, screen, or panel, or used decoratively in blank arches and vaults. The earliest use of the term so far traced is in Sir Christopher WREN, the medieval word being *form-pieces* or *forms*.

In windows of more than one light in Early Gothic churches the SPANDREL above the lights is often pierced by a circle, a quatrefoil, or some such simple form. This is known as *plate tracery*. Later, and first at Reims (1211 etc.), the circle is no longer pierced through a solid spandrel; instead the two lights are separated by a moulded MULLION and the mouldings of this are continued at the head forming bars of circular, quatrefoil, etc., forms and leaving the rest of the spandrels open. This is called *bar tracery*, and throughout the

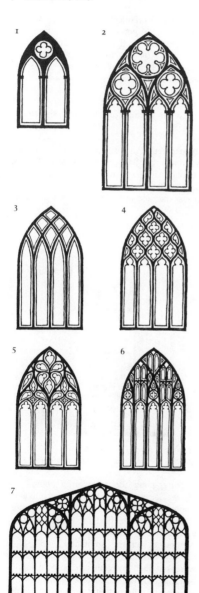

Tracery: Milan Cathedral, c15

later Middle Ages it was one of the principal decorative elements of churches. The patterns made by the bars were first the simple geometrical forms already indicated (*geometrical tracery*), later fantastical forms including double curves (*flowing tracery*), and later still – at least in England – plain, vertical, arched panels repeated more or less exactly (*panel tracery*). In Germany, France, and Spain forms similar to the English flowing tracery became the rule in the late Middle Ages. With the end of the Middle Ages tracery generally disappeared.

Bar tracery, introduced at Reims and brought to England *c*. 1240, consists of intersecting ribwork made up of slender shafts continuing the lines of the mullions up to a decorative mesh in the window-head.

Flowing tracery is made up of compound or OGEE curves, with an uninterrupted flow from curve to curve; also called *curvilinear* or *undulating tracery*. It was used from the beginning of the c14 in England, and throughout the c15 in France, where it rapidly became fully developed and FLAMBOYANT, with no survival of the geometrical elements of the early flowing tracery of England.

Geometrical tracery is characteristic of *c*. 1250–1300 and consists chiefly of circles or foiled circles.

In *intersecting tracery* each mullion of a window branches into curved bars which are continuous with the mullions. The outer arch of the window being of two equal curves (*see* ARCH), all subdivisions of the window-head produced by these tracery bars following the curves of the outer arch must of necessity be equilateral also. The bars and the arch are all drawn from the same centre with a different radius. Such a window can be of two, or usually more, lights, with the result that every two, three, or four lights together form a pointed arch. Additional enrichment, e.g., circles and CUSPING, is always of a secondary character. The form is typical of *c.* 1300.

Kentish tracery is FOILED tracery in a circle with barbs between the foils.

Panel tracery is Perpendicular tracery formed of upright, straight-sided panels above the lights of a window, also called *rectilinear*.

Plate tracery is a late C12 and early C13 form where decoratively shaped openings are cut through the solid stone infilling in a window-head.

Reticulated tracery, a form used much in the early to mid C14, is made up entirely of circles drawn at top and bottom into OGEE shapes resulting in a net-like appearance.

In *Y-tracery* a mullion branches into two forming a Y-shape; typical of *c.* 1300.

(For additional illustration *see* FOIL.)

Trachelion The neck of a Greek Doric column, between the SHAFT-RING and HYPOTRACH-ELION.

Tramello, Alessio (*c.* 1470/5–*c.* 1529). He worked for most of his life in and around Piacenza in a style which owes much to the Milanese buildings of BRAMANTE. His more notable buildings include S. Sisto (1499) and the centrally planned Madonna di Campagna, both at Piacenza. In 1525 he was consulted about the Steccata at Parma which had been begun in 1521 by Giovanfrancesco Zaccagni who resigned in 1525.

Lit: P. Gazzola, *Opere di A. Tramello architetto piacentino*, Rome 1935; J. Ganz, *Alessio Tramello*, Frauenfeld 1968.

Transenna An openwork screen or lattice, usually of marble, in an Early Christian church.

Transenna: S. Vitale, Ravenna, mid-c6

Transept The transverse arms of a cross-shaped church, usually between NAVE and CHANCEL, but also occasionally at the west end of the nave as well, and also doubled, with the eastern arms farther east than the junction of nave and chancel. The latter form is usual in English Gothic cathedrals.

Transitional architecture A term usually referring to the period of transition from the ROMANESQUE to the GOTHIC, or in Britain from the NORMAN to the EARLY ENGLISH style. Sometimes details of the later styles are used on the general forms of the earlier.

Transom A horizontal bar of stone or wood across the opening of a window or across a panel.

Transparente An illusionistic device developed in Spain by Baroque and C18 architects, notably Narciso TOMÉ whose *transparente* in Toledo Cathedral of 1721–32 is a masterpiece. Catholic orthodoxy objected to people

Section: choir of Toledo Cathedral, showing the light source for the transparente

walking along the ambulatory behind the Blessed Sacrament. So it was placed in a glass fronted receptacle – hence the name *transparente* – which enabled it to be seen from the ambulatory as well as the nave or chancel. Around it, on the ambulatory side, altar scenery was built up and illusionistic effects were obtained by elaborate and ingenious lighting. At Toledo Cathedral all the masonry between the ribs of half a Gothic vault of the ambulatory was removed by Tomé and, above it, a dormer with a window was erected, the latter being invisible from below and flooding the altar with light as if in a theatre. When viewed from the altar the source of light becomes visible – Christ Himself seated on clouds, with prophets and the Heavenly Host, in stucco and illusionistic painting.

Transverse arch, *see* VAULT.

Tread, *see* STAIR.

Trefoil, *see* FOIL.

Trezzini, Domenico (Andrei Petrovich Trezini, 1670–1734), the first of the Western European architects employed by Peter the Great of Russia, was of Italo-Swiss origin. He is first recorded in 1700 working on the palace of Frederick IV in Copenhagen. In 1703 he was invited to become architect of the new city of St Petersburg. He was employed mainly to design small wooden houses, also the Summer Palace (1711–14, superseded by RASTRELLI's Summer Palace of 1741–4, also destroyed) in a predominantly Dutch style and the rather gawky Dutch Baroque Cathedral of St Peter and St Paul, St Petersburg (1714–25). His main work was the terrace of twelve pavilion-like buildings to house the government ministries, each with a colossal order of pilasters and a high hipped roof (1722–32, later altered).

Lit: G. H. Hamilton, *Art and Architecture of Russia,* Pelican History of Art, Harmondsworth 1954.

Triangulation The achievement of rigidity, or at least the prevention of completely free relative movement, in an assembly of struts and ties, by arranging them in a continuous series of triangles in one or more planes.

Tribune I. The APSE of a BASILICA or basilican church. 2. A raised platform or rostrum. 3. The GALLERY in a church.

Triclinium The dining-room in an ancient Roman house.

Triconch A building composed of three 'conches' (i.e. of three semicircular niches surmounted by half-domes).

Triforium An arcaded wall-passage facing on to the NAVE, at a level above the arcade and

Triforium

below the CLERESTORY windows (if there are any). The term is often wrongly applied to a TRIBUNE or GALLERY.

Triglyphs Blocks separating the METOPES in a Doric FRIEZE. Each one has two vertical grooves or glyphs in the centre and half grooves at the edges. If the half grooves are omitted (as occasionally in post-Renaissance architecture) the block is called a diglyph. (For illustration *see* ORDER.)

Trilithon A prehistoric monument consisting of a horizontal stone resting on two upright ones, as at Stonehenge.

Trilithons: Stonehenge, near Salisbury

Trim The framing or edging of openings and other features on a façade or indoors. It is usually of a colour and material (wood, stucco, or stone) different from that of the adjacent wall surface.

Triumphal arch A free-standing monumental gateway of a type which originated in Rome in the C2 B.C. in richly decorated temporary structures erected by Roman magistrates for such festive occasions as the triumphs decreed to victorious generals. From the late CI B.C. similar structures were erected in stone, and often richly decorated with sculpture, as city gates or as entrances to *fora* but also frequently as urban decorations with no more than a commemorative purpose: some twenty survive from the reign of Augustus, mostly in Italy and Gaul. They were built throughout the Roman Empire and numerous C2 and C3 A.D. examples survive in N. Africa. There are two main types – those with a single archway (Arch of Augustus at Susa, Piedmont, 9–8 B.C., Arch of Titus in Rome, *c.* A.D. 82) and those with a large archway flanked by two small archways (Arch of Septimus Severus in Rome, A.D. 203 and Arch of Constantine in Rome, A.D. 315). Sometimes they seem to have been designed primarily as richly ornamented bases for gilt bronze statues. The form was revived in the Italian Renaissance, once again as a type of temporary festival architecture, which remained popular until the late C18. Many were built in stone during the C18 and C19 often in direct imitation of Roman prototypes, e.g. Arco di S. Gallo, Florence by J.-N. JADOT DE VILLE ISSY (1739), Arc du Carrousel, Paris, by PERCIER and FONTAINE (1806–7), Arc de Triomphe, Paris,

Arc de Triomphe, Paris, 1806–35, by Chalgrin

by CHALGRIN (1806–35), the Marble Arch, London, by J. NASH (1828), etc. By extension the term Triumphal Arch is sometimes applied to structures with one large and two small doorways, e.g. the choir screen in a medieval church. A Chinese type of triumphal or commemorative arch is called a P'AI LOU.

Triumphal column A massive column erected as a public monument. The first were set up in Republican Rome but these appear to have been relatively small and simple in comparison with Trajan's column completed A.D. 113

Trajan's Column, Rome, A.D. 113

and 125 ft high. It is adorned with a continuous spiral of low relief carving illustrating Trajan's two Dacian wars. This and the similar Antonine Column (or Column of Marcus Aurelius), probably completed in A.D. 193, set a pattern for such monuments. Their progeny included the columns of Theodosius the Great of 386 and of Arcadius of 403 both in Constantinople (and both destroyed), and in much later times the pair of columns flanking the Karlskirche in Vienna by FISCHER VON ERLACH (begun 1716) and the Vendôme Column in Paris with bronze reliefs (1806–10, thrown down 1871 and re-erected 1874). The majority of commemorative columns, though often on bases imitated from the Roman prototypes, have plain shafts, e.g. The Monument, London (1671–7) by WREN, the Washington Monument in Baltimore (1814–29) by Robert MILLS, and the Nelson Column, Trafalgar Square, London, designed by William Railton (1839–42).

Trophy A sculptured group of arms or armour used as a memorial to victory, sometimes with floreated motifs intermingled to form a FESTOON.

Trumeau The stone MULLION supporting the middle of a TYMPANUM of a doorway. (Illustrated next column.)

*Trumeau: Porch of Saint-Pierre,
Moissac, c12*

Truss A number of timbers framed together
to bridge a space or form a BRACKET, to be
self-supporting, and to carry other timbers.
The trusses of a roof are usually named after
the particular feature in their construction,
e.g., king-post, queen-post, etc. *See* ROOF.

Tudor flower An upright ornamental motif,
rather like a formalized ivy leaf, often used in
English Late Gothic and Tudor architecture,
especially for BRATTISHING.

Tufa The commonest Roman building stone,
formed from volcanic dust; it is porous and
grey.

Türbe This is the commonest term for ISLAMIC
secular mausolea (Arabic *turba*). Mausolea
were discouraged in early Islam for theological reasons, and the first surviving example, at Samarra in Iraq, is datable in the
late c9. Two basic types predominate in
medieval Islam: the domed square chamber
and the tomb tower. The origins of the domed
square probably lie in the late classical and
Early Christian mausolea of the Near East.
The fire temples of Sassanian IRAN are sometimes cited as possible models, but though
architecturally similar they are functionally
unrelated to Islamic mausolea. The domed
square is found in Islam from Morocco to
India, but the greatest concentration of the
type occurs in Egypt and Syria, especially
from the c13 onwards. It is equally well
adapted to both small and very large buildings.
While such mausolea with four axial entrances
are known, those with a single entrance are
more numerous. The domed square generally
has an octagonal zone of transition, corresponding to an external drum, between the
dome and the square base (Ayyubid *turbas*
in Syria, c12–c13). Common variations include projecting arched portals in a rect-

angular frame; a double zone of transition
with spectacular stalactite vaulting; ambulatories; internal staircases; galleries; and
subsidiary corner domes or minarets (Taj
Mahal, Agra). In a typical variation the
square ground plan was replaced by an
octagon (Sultaniya, Iran). Tomb towers are
found principally in Iran (from the c11 onwards) and Turkey (from the c13 onwards).
The type is distinguishable by its emphasis

Türbe at Radkan, Persia, 1281

on height and by its conical or polyhedral
roof covering an inner dome. The ground
plan may be circular, square, polygonal,
flanged or lobed. Turkish tomb towers
feature a crypt with a sarcophagus containing the body; this is crowned by an empty
upper chamber sometimes reached by an
external staircase. Many mausolea were intended for family and multiple burials. They
are often attached to mosques, *madrasas* and
minarets and some even have *mihrabs*. The
interior is generally simple, but the exterior,
especially in Turkey and the Iranian world, is
often richly decorated in the local style. [RH]

Turkish architecture The ISLAMIC ARCHITEC-
TURE of Turkey may roughly be divided into
only two styles: pre-Ottoman, loosely but commonly called Seljuk (c12–c14), and Ottoman,
which flourished from the c14 to the c18.
Closer study naturally reveals numerous local
variants of these two styles, but the homo-
geneity and strong sense of direction of Turkish
architecture remains. In this summary the

architecture of areas which were intermittently under Turkish domination (Central Asia, Iran, Iraq, Syria and Egypt) is excluded, not least for reasons of space. Few CII–CI2 buildings survive.

Mosques. The earliest dated Turkish MOSQUE, the Great Mosque of Diyarbakr (1091–2 onwards), reproduces the transept plan found in the Umayyad mosque at Damascus. Its ornament, both classical and classicizing, is partly explained by the lavish use of *spolia* in the courtyard façades; their engaged columns in two tiers echo the *scenae frons* of the classical theatre. In later mediaeval Anatolian mosques the courtyard rarely dominates; instead Turkey evolved the covered mosque, which of its very nature permitted the development of a more integrated and compact style.

Hospital and Great Mosque, Divrigi, 1228–9

The early Anatolian mosques (Konya; Sivas) were basically no more than an extension of the QIBLA side of the a mosque of 'Arab plan' – i.e. a courtyard surrounded by covered arcades which are deeper on the qibla side. Inevitably the scope for further development in this direction was small; a major disadvantage of large-scale extension of multiple-columned naves was lack of light. Simultaneously with the building of these CI2 columned flat-roofed mosques – later variants of which had wooden columns and ceilings – experiments were being made with domed mosques, which were to dominate the Ottoman period. One variant was the arrangement of three domes on the qibla side, with two or three aisles running parallel to the qibla (Ala al-Din mosque, Nigde); in other variants a single large dome replaced the three small ones (Great Mosque, Bitlis), or the mosque became a series of triple-domed aisles (Gök madrasa and mosque, Amasya). Sometimes the dome crowns a central transept (Silvan). Iranian influence dominates in the brick-built Great Mosque of Malatya (1247) with its central courtyard, portal iwan and qibla iwan preceding the domed chamber – a composition which also recalls Anatolian madrasas. In the CI3 the concept of a courtyard reappeared in novel form: the central bay of the mosque, sometimes enlarged, was covered by a skylight with a fountain directly beneath. The idea of giving the mosque another major focus besides the MIHRAB thus regained currency. Contemporaneously with these buildings smaller mosques were erected which consisted simply of a square domed chamber. Mosques of related plan, but open on all four sides, were built in many caravanserais. Thus the CI2–I3 was largely a period of experiment, in which no one type of mosque dominated. The handling of interior space differed considerably from one mosque to another; for no coherent guiding principle had yet been evolved for this problem. By contrast, the concept of an elaborate articulated façade had early taken root. Its cynosure was the monumental PISHTAQ, or projecting entrance IWAN, a feature of Iranian origin also found in MADRASAS and CARAVANSERAIS. It usually has a semi-dome with stalactite vaulting. Most mediaeval Anatolian MINARETS derive from the slender cylindrical minarets of Seljuk Iran, even to their polygonal plinths and engaged columns; but their pencil-shaped tip is a local development. In eastern Turkey square minarets of Syrian type are common. Most Seljuk mosque types continued in the c14, a period when the seeds of Ottoman architecture were sown. One of the key monuments is the Great Mosque of Manisa (1376), a rectangular structure in which the qibla side, dominated by a single dome, takes up almost half the surface area; the remaining part has a large arcaded courtyard with a portico. At Bursa, the Yildirim and Yeşil

Yeşil Mosque, Bursa, completed 1423

mosques (both early c15) illustrate a further development: the central axis is marked by two large domes and a complex vestibule and a 5-domed portico on the north side leads into the mosque. The almost contemporary mosque of Dimetoka is even more important, in the use of a perfect square for the domed mosque itself (excluding the 3-domed portico); the dome, which rests on four piers, is placed in the centre of the square and flanked by vaults on the main axes and diagonals. With this mosque the decisive step towards a single integrated interior, dominated by the dome, has been taken. The Uç Şerefeli Mosque, Edirne (1437–47) has a large arcaded courtyard enclosed by 22 adjoining domed bays, a favourite device of later Ottoman architecture. Thus in plan the major characteristics of the Ottoman style had been established before the capture of Constantinople in 1453. In elevation, too, certain significant features such as the semi-domes flanking the main dome, flying buttresses, a multiplication of low domes and the slender pencil-like minaret with a circular balcony, had all been introduced. But these elements had not yet been fused into an integrated style. Ottoman architects still had difficulty, for instance, in matching the impressive interior space of a large dome

chamber by a correspondingly effective exterior. In many cases the drums are too high and the domes unnecessarily squat; indeed, the ratio of architectural elements to each other is often eccentric and makes these buildings look badly proportioned.

The mature Ottoman style developed soon after 1453. Thus the Fatih mosque (1463–70) already has a huge semi-dome buttressing the main dome, while the mosque of Bayazid II (completed 1506) has two such semi-domes to north and south, with a row of four domed bays to east and west. But parallel to this continuous expansion of the central domed space is an increasing emphasis on the surrounding structures, which are reorganized and harmonized with the principal axes of the mosque. These clusters of subsidiary buildings – mausolea, madrasas, soup kitchens (or imarets) and so on – can be parallelled in roughly contemporary mosques in Egypt and Iran. Wherever possible, dramatic sites were chosen. Internally, the main features of these imperial mosques are the huge niches which billow out from the central space, and which themselves enclose further niches; and a carefully calculated fenestration, from the multitude of windows at the collar of the dome to superposed groups of three and five windows further down. These windows are about the height of a man, thus providing a ready index of the proportions of the interior. The massive piers, with spherical pendentives between them, which support the main dome are placed so close to the walls as to seem part of them and thus create an extensive but unified interior space. Externally the principal accent

Sokullu-Mehmet-Pasha Mosque, Istanbul, 1571

is on a dramatic but ordered stacking of units, a feature which was notably lacking in earlier Ottoman architecture. The crown of the whole composition is the central dome, and from this peak the subsidiary domes, semi-domes and domed buttresses cascade downwards, forming a rippling but tightly interlocked silhouette. An arcaded courtyard precedes this concentrated mass. The minarets customarily placed at the outer corners of these mosques bind the building together. Ottoman architecture reached its peak in the later CI6, in the mosques of the court architect SINAN (Suleymaniye,

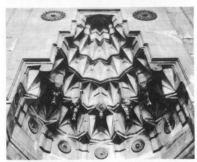

Mosque of Selim II, Edirne, c. 1550–70, by Sinan

Istanbul, 1550–57; Selimiye, Edirne, 1569–74). Many of the internal and external features of mosques built after 1453 are found in Hagia Sophia, and the Turks, who converted the building into a mosque, were naturally not blind to its many unique elements. But before 1453 Ottoman architecture had already evolved independently a number of forms which only received their final and most elegant statement later. It seems more just, therefore, to see Hagia Sophia as the challenge which inspired Ottoman architects to their greatest creations rather than as their source. Certainly the exteriors of the great Ottoman mosques surpass that of Hagia Sophia. Although great buildings were erected after Sinan's time (indeed, the mosque of Sultan Ahmed, 1609–16, is both the synthesis and climax of Ottoman architecture), the style declined into repetition and pastiche. A fascinating epilogue is provided by the Turkish Baroque style of the CI8, which exhibits some ingenious adaptations of European architecture vocabulary to traditional forms.

Madrasas. Sixty-seven medieval MADRASAS, dated CI2–CI5, survive. This institution quickly developed various individual archi-

tectural forms, ultimately inspired by madrasas elsewhere. Thus the PISHTAQ flanked by minarets originated in Iran, while the earliest domed madrasas are in northern Syria. In Anatolia the domed square chamber is preceded by an elaborate pishtaq and flanked by cells and other chambers (Karatai and Ince Minare madrasas, Konya), or by two iwans

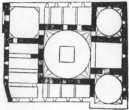

Plan of Madrasa, Büyük Karatai, Konya, 1251–2

with cells on the remaining sides. Other variations are known. The commonest madrasa had a pishtaq leading into a courtyard terminated by a large qibla iwan and flanked by cells for students (Sirçali madrasa, Konya). Sometimes only one iwan is used, at other times as many as four, though the 4-iwan madrasas lack the spaciousness of Iranian buildings with this plan (Çifte Minare madrasa, Erzurum) and may even have a vaulted courtyard (Yakutiye madrasa, Erzurum). The single-iwan madrasa of Ertokush near Isparta (1224) shows a developed axiality in the progression from porch to domed fountain to iwan to mausoleum, a sequence recalling Seljuk mosques in Iran. Many medieval madrasas are composite foundations which also include mosques, mausolea and hospitals. Most Turkish madrasas of architectural importance are of pre-Ottoman date; the same is true of mausolea and caravanserais. In Ottoman architecture these building types were often incorporated in the great mosque complexes (Suleymaniye, Istanbul).

Caravanserais. The surviving medieval caravanserais or hans number about 100 and are almost all of CI3 date, a largely unexplained phenomenon. They were built primarily for trade – including perhaps the important slave trade from Southern Russia to Egypt, which might explain the great size of some hans – and line the major routes at intervals of a day's journey. They served also as charitable institutions. Some are heavily fortified and all are of solid and monumental

Sultan Ahmet Mosque (Blue Mosque),
Istanbul, 1609–16

construction. Most of them display a marked
axial emphasis; the outer pishtaq leads into a
courtyard which terminates in another pishtaq preceding a longitudinal vaulted hall. This
is divided into two aisles flanking a raised
central nave lit by a vaulted lantern. The
travellers, together with their animals and
equipment, were lodged partly in the vaulted
cells flanking the courtyard and partly in the
vaulted hall. The Sultan Han near Kayseri
illustrates this classical plan, with the addition of a domed mosque in the centre of the
courtyard, and domed baths. In other hans
the courtyard is reduced, with rooms opening off it, and the two types of accommodation are integrated by placing the rooms and
stables back to back (Alara Han).

Mausolea. The majority of the MAUSOLEA
erected in the C12–C14 are tomb towers (TÜR-
BES or kümbets) on the Iranian model, consisting of a cylindrical or polygonal body with a
pyramidal or conical roof. The more elaborate
Iranian ground plans with flanges and engaged columns are not found, nor is the great
height of some Iranian towers rivalled. But
the apparent height and monumentality of
many Anatolian tomb towers is increased by
the use of a high socle, which contains a
crypt, and the ground plans are quite varied –
circular, octagonal and dodecagonal among
others. Elaborate flanged and ribbed roofs
occur, and some towers even have an open
arcade placed half-way between the cornice
and the plinth. Their form and decoration

suggest strong Armenian influence. Other categories of mausoleum include the domed square chamber and the iwan type, in which the façade is dominated by the iwan preceding the tomb chamber. Ottoman mausolea rejected the Seljuk tradition of the pointed roof in favour of a dome, which was sometimes ribbed; but they too are often octagonal in plan. Others are square, with four axial arches, or hexagonal. A novel feature is the arcaded portico marking the main entrance or surrounding the entire mausoleum.

Palaces. The two-storeyed C13 Ala al-Din Kiosk formerly crowned the city walls of Konya; it apparently has nothing in common with the C13 palace at Kubadabad, which partly recalls Umayyad palaces. This is a rectangular enclosure containing numerous non-communicating rooms distributed around an irregular court. Other Seljuk palaces may well have resembled Ottoman palaces quite closely. These consist of miniature cities whose various elements are linked only by a sur-

ARCHITECTURE) – domes, conical and pyramidal roofs, vaults, including stalactite and rib vaults, and iwans. Mostly the material is finely dressed stone; in the east especially, the malleable TUFA of Armenian architecture was popular. Marble was used sparingly. Seljuk decoration is unusually eclectic. Here, too, forms which Iran developed in media such as brick and stucco reappear in stone, subtly transmuted by influences from Armenian architecture and painting, from Syrian stone and marble carving and even from Gothic ornament. To this predominantly geometric, arabesque and epigraphic decoration is added zoomorphic ornament, a new element essentially of nomadic Turkish origin. The scale of the ornament is often badly proportioned to the surface which it covers. The high development of glazed decoration – glazed bricks, tile mosaic and whole tiles – was perhaps partly due to Iranian craftsmen fleeing from the Mongol invasions. Ottoman architecture at first combined brick and stone

Baghdad-Kiosk in the Top-Kapi-Saray,
Istanbul, 1638–9

Kiosk of Sultan Mohamet II in the garden
of the Top-Kapi-Saray, Istanbul, 1472–3

rounding wall. Numerous detached pavilions or kiosks alternate with the private apartments of the Sultan and his harem, kitchens, throne and council halls, arsenals, stables, and gardens with canals and fountains (Edirne; Topkapi Saray, Istanbul). This loosely-knit, open-plan type of palace is typical of Islamic architecture.

Turkish Seljuk architecture translates into stone the basic forms of the brick architecture of Seljuk Iran (*see* IRANIAN ISLAMIC

Sultan Ahmet III Fountain in front
of the outer gate of the Top-Kapi-Saray,
Istanbul, 1728

but by the c16 dressed stone was preferred. This architecture has one central theme – the dome, which was not accorded a similar prominence or developed in such multifarious ways elsewhere in Islam. The fugal complexities of Sinan's buildings depend ultimately on experiments begun three centuries before and developed tenaciously and unswervingly by generations of architects. Hence the concentration and logic of the great c16 mosques, and hence the justice of describing them as architects' architecture. The latter judgement applies equally to the careful detailing of external features such as windows, recessed panels and mouldings – all executed with a matchless sense of interval and so precise that they give the illusion of being architectural drawings. This external decoration, with its expanses of empty space, is in strongest contrast to Seljuk decoration, where the reigning principle is usually *horror vacui*. Certain decorative features, such as bands of masonry in alternating colours, are common to both styles, but the Armenian, Iranian and zoomorphic elements which were important earlier are wholly absent in Ottoman architecture. By contrast, the Seljuk tradition of ceramic decoration for interiors continued and entire walls were sheathed in Iznik tiles.

[RH]

Lit: A. Gabriel, *Monuments turcs d'Anatolie* I and II, Paris 1931, 1934; U. Vogt-Göknil, *Türkische Moscheen*, Zurich 1953; S. K. Yetkin *et al.*, *Turkish Architecture*, Ankara 1965; K. Otto-Dorn, *The Art of Islam*, New York 1968; O. Aslanapa, *Turkish Art and Architecture*, London 1971.

Turret A very small and slender tower.

Tuscan Order, *see* ORDER.

Tylman van Gameren (before 1630–1706). Dutch architect chiefly responsible for introducing the Baroque style into Poland where he settled in 1665. His three centralized churches in Warsaw – Holy Sacrament (1688), St Casimir (1688–9) and St Boniface (1690–92) – reveal him as a somewhat stolid, classicizing master of the Baroque. St Anne, Cracow (1689–1705) is livelier, but this may be due to collaboration with Baldassare Fontana. Tylman rebuilt the palace of Prince Sanguszko, Warsaw (enlarged c18), designed Castle Nieborów (1680–83) and completed the Krasiński Palace, Warsaw (1682–94).

Lit: E. Hempel, *Baroque Art and Architecture in Central Europe*, Pelican History of Art, Harmondsworth 1965.

Tympanum The area between the LINTEL of a doorway and the arch above it; also the triangular or segmental space enclosed by the mouldings of a PEDIMENT.

Tympanum

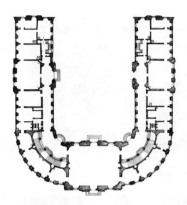

Undercroft A vaulted room, sometimes underground, below an upper room such as a church or chapel.

United States architecture The *incunabula* of New England's domestic architecture, dating from the C17, are of no more than strictly local interest, first Dutch in inspiration, then English. A monumental scale was only rarely achieved (William and Mary College, Williamsburg, 1695, much restored as is the whole of Williamsburg). Churches are entirely Georgian in the C18, often influenced in their spires by GIBBS. Houses are equally Georgian, in the country as well as the towns. But in both houses and churches timber plays a prominent part alongside, or instead of, brick. Among the best churches are Christ Church, Philadelphia (1727 and 1754) and Christ Church, Cambridge (1761 by HARRISON). The finest early Georgian houses are Westover, Virginia (c. 1735) and Stratford, Virginia, of about the same date. From the mid-C18

Westover House, Virginia, c. 1735

notable examples are Carter's Grove, Virginia (c. 1750), Mount Airey, Virginia (1758), Mount Pleasant, Philadelphia (1761) and Whitehall, Maryland, with its giant Corinthian portico. Later porticos tend to have attenuated columns (Homewood, Baltimore). Verandahs of giant columns along a whole façade are characteristic of Louisiana (Oak Alley, c.

Colonial Style street in Nantucket

1835). As town *ensembles* Salem and Nantucket, Mass., Charleston, South Carolina, and Savannah, Georgia, may be singled out. The United States has still quite a few C18 public buildings: Old State House, Boston (1710); Independence Hall, Philadelphia (1732); Faneuil Hall, Boston (1742), and so to the Capitol in its original form by Dr THORNTON, LATROBE, BULFINCH, etc. (1792 etc.) and the Boston State House by Bulfinch (1793–1800). The earliest university buildings are also Georgian: at Harvard (1720, 1764 etc.); at Yale (1750–52); and then Thomas JEFFERSON's University of Virginia at Charlottesville (1817–26), the first Ameri-

King's Chapel, Boston, 1749–58,
by Peter Harrison

University of Virginia, Charlottesville,
1817–26, by Jefferson

building he also submitted a Gothic design; a country house of his (Sedgeley, Philadelphia, 1799) was Gothic too. However, except in church design, Gothic made slow progress, and the most thoroughly Grecian years are the 1820s and 1830s, with the big government buildings in Washington by MILLS (Treasury, 1836 etc.), by STRICKLAND (Merchants' Exchange, Philadelphia, 1834 etc.) and by Town & DAVIS. Davis's is protean architecture. His state capitols of Connecticut (1827), Indiana (1831) and others are Grecian, his New York University (1832 etc.) is collegiate Gothic, Lyndhurst, Tarrytown (1838) is Gothic too, and many villas are of the COTTAGE ORNÉ type with steep barge-boarded gables. The most prominent Gothic churches are RENWICK's Grace Church, New York (1846) and UPJOHN's Trinity Church, New York, of the same years. Henry Austin deserves a special mention; if ever there was rogue architecture, his New Haven railway station (1848–9) was it. Its style cannot be derived from any direction.

can campus, i.e. with buildings composed round a spacious lawn and the library rotunda as its climax. By Jefferson also is the Virginia State Capitol of 1785–92, the first with a temple front, and Monticello of 1770–1809, with its ingenious mechanisms inside.

The Greek Revival starts with Latrobe's Ionic Bank of Pennsylvania of 1798 with its beautifully shallow Soanian dome and his Doric Water Works of 1812. From 1803 he did much in a Grecian taste inside the Capitol in Washington, notably the Senate Rotunda and the semicircular House of Representatives. His finest work, again comparable with that of SOANE in elegance and originality, is Baltimore Cathedral (begun 1805). But for this

Baltimore Cathedral, 1805–18,
by Latrobe

Trinity Church, New York, 1839–46,
by Richard Upjohn

Already in the second quarter of the century certain American specialities began to appear. One is certain types of buildings and the plans that suit them. HAVILAND'S Eastern Penitentiary at Philadelphia (1821–9) was the most influential prison in the world, and Tremont House, Boston, and Astor House, New York, (by Isaiah Rogers, 1828–9 and 1839–46) established the superiority of American over English hotels. As to size, the Astor House had about 300 rooms. In the fifties the Fifth Avenue in New York and the Cape May Hotel had about 500. Europe knew nothing like it. Americans were equally go-ahead with equipment such as lavatories and bathrooms and later lifts. To building materials the attitude was just as enterprising. Whole façades of cast iron can be found in England as well but with nothing like the same frequency. The earliest surviving example is James BOGARDUS's Laing House in New York of 1849, the finest early example the Haughwout Building also in New York of 1857 (by J. P. Gaynor). The style is Italian Cinquecento.

The sequence of most-favoured styles during the second third of the century is much as it was in Europe: Grecian, domestic Gothic, Gothic or Norman for public buildings (the Smithsonian Institution in Washington, by Renwick, 1846–55), the Italianate Villa style (Morse-Libby House, Portland, Maine, by Austin, 1859), the French Renaissance with pavilion roofs (Washington Old Corcoran by Renwick, 1859; State War and Navy Building, by A. B. Mullet, 1871–5). Odd men out are the Moorish Longwood, Mississippi, of 1860, the French Louis XI Biltmore, N. Carolina, of 1895 (by HUNT for a Vanderbilt), the crazy, steep-gabled, overcrowded no-style-that-ever-was of Eureka, California, of 1885 (by S. & J. C. Newsom).

The United States moved from a marginal to a central position with the work of H. H. RICHARDSON, both in the field of the massive uncompromising commercial building for which his style was a French-inspired Romanesque (Marshall Field Wholesale Warehouse, Chicago, 1885–7) and in the field of the informal, comfortable, moderately dimensioned private house (Sherman House, Newport, 1874–6). Equally informed and influential were his Romanesque small branch libraries

The Crane Library, Quincy, Mass., 1880–83, by H. H. Richardson

(North Easton, 1877). His most original works are the Brattle Square and Trinity Churches both in Boston, and of 1870 etc. and 1872 etc. Even more independent are some of the houses designed in their early years by McKIM, Mead & WHITE, notably one at Bristol, Rhode Island (1887). Otherwise that firm is principally remembered for their Italian Renaissance Revival (Villard Houses, New York, 1885; Boston Public Library, 1887), Colonial Revival, and also Palladian Revival, the latter on a grand scale (Pennsylvania Station, New York, 1906–10).

The W. G. Lowe House, Bristol, R.I., 1887, by McKim, Mead & White

Guaranty Building, Buffalo, 1894–5,
by Dankmar Adler and Louis Sullivan

Meanwhile, however, Chicago had established a style of commercial architecture all her own and vigorously pointing forward into the C20 (CHICAGO SCHOOL). It started from the principle of iron framing in the Home Insurance Building by JENNEY of 1883–5 and with the Rand McNally Building of 1890 by BURNHAM & ROOT achieved the all-steel skeleton. Aesthetically the climax was reached in such buildings as the Tacoma (1887–9) by HOLABIRD & ROCHE, the Marquette (1894) by the same firm, and, most personal, the

Carson, Pirie & Scott Store, Chicago,
1899–1904, by Sullivan

Philadelphia Savings Fund Building,
Philadelphia, 1930–32, by Howe & Lescaze

Wainwright at St Louis (1890) by SULLIVAN. With Sullivan's Carson, Pirie & Scott Store, Chicago (1899 etc.), a totally unhistoricist style of unrelieved verticals and horizontals was reached, though Sullivan was perhaps at his most original in his feathery, decidedly ART NOUVEAU ornament. This comes out most delightfully in the Auditorium of 1887–9 which externally is the immediate successor of Richardson's Marshall Field Store.

Sullivan's principal pupil was Frank Lloyd WRIGHT, whose work, chiefly in the domestic field, bridges the whole period from *c.* 1890 to nearly 1960. But his brilliant style of

velopment of C20 architecture in the United States belongs entirely to the years after the Second World War. The flowering was fostered by such distinguished immigrants as GROPIUS, MIES VAN DER ROHE, NEUTRA and BREUER. The first stage belongs to the rational, cubic, crisp so-called INTERNATIONAL MODERN and culminates in Mies van der Rohe's houses and blocks of flats of *c.* 1950 onwards, and most of the work of SKIDMORE, OWINGS & MERRILL. The second stage is that of the

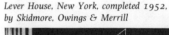

Lever House, New York, completed 1952,
by Skidmore, Owings & Merrill

Ward H. Willits House, Highland Park,
Illinois, 1900–1902, by Wright

sweeping horizontals and of intercommunication between spaces inside a house and between inside and outside spaces found little recognition in his own country. In fact, the C20 style on a major scale had to be imported from Europe: the pioneer building was the Philadelphia Savings Fund Building by HOWE & LESCAZE (1930–32 – a relatively late date in European terms), but the spectacular de-

Guggenheim Museum, New York, 1946–59, by Frank Lloyd Wright

Amon Carter Museum, Fort Worth, Texas, 1961, by Johnson

St Paul's Lutheran Church, Sarasota, Florida, 1959, by Victor Lundy

neo-sculptural, anti-rational, highly expressive style current in many countries while this dictionary is being produced. The United States is richer than any other part of the world in such buildings, from a love of novelty as well as from a prosperity that encourages display. Trends within this trend cannot here be separated: they run from the powerful concrete curves of Eero SAARINEN to the

The TWA Terminal, Kennedy Airport, New York, 1956–62, by Eero Saarinen

First Presbyterian Church, Stamford, Connecticut, 1959, by Harrison & Mills

Sarasota High School, Sarasota, Florida, 1958–9, by Rudolph

dainty eclecticism of Edward STONE (Huntington Hartford Museum, New York, 1958–9), and include such mercurial and controversial figures as Philip JOHNSON, Minoru YAMASAKI (St Louis Airport), and Paul RUDOLPH.

A postscript on American technical achievements: First FULLER'S geodesic domes, of which the largest has a diameter of 384 ft. Second the even higher SKYSCRAPERS of New York: Woolworth by C. GILBERT, 1913, 792 ft; Empire State by Shreve, Lamb & Harmon, 1930–32, 1250 ft; World Trade Center by Yamasaki, 1970–74, 1350 ft. Thirdly and finally road-works. The American freeways, parkways, trunk roads, turnpikes have no competitors. Their boldness and their intricacies of junction are stupendous. But they place the motor vehicle above man. Man, unless he is engaged in driving, suffers in both the country and the city – in the country by neglected landscape, in the city by ruined townscape.

Lit: J. Burchard and A. Bush-Brown, *The Architecture of America,* London 1967; W. Andrews, *Architecture, Ambition and Americans,* New York 1947; H.-R. Hitchcock, *Architecture: Nineteenth and Twentieth Centuries,* Pelican History of Art, Harmondsworth 1969, paperback edn 1971; F. Kimball, *Domestic Architecture of the American Colonies and of the Early Republic,* New York 1922; T. F. Hamlin, *Greek Revival Architecture in America,* New York 1944; H.-R. Hitchcock, *American Architectural Books,* Minneapolis 1946.

Unwin, Sir Raymond (1863–1940). The leading English town-planner of his day and the man who – in partnership from 1896 to 1914 with Barry Parker (1867–1941) – translated into reality the garden city scheme conceived by Ebenezer HOWARD. The 'First Garden City', as the company for its realization was actually called, was Letchworth in Hertfordshire (begun 1903). However, while the growth of Letchworth did not progress as rapidly or as smoothly as had been anticipated, two garden suburbs did extremely well, the Hampstead Garden Suburb outside London (begun 1907), and Wythenshawe outside Manchester (begun 1927). The Hampstead Garden Suburb in particular must be regarded as the *beau idéal* of the garden city principles of domestic and public planning, with its formal centre – the two churches and the institute designed by LUTYENS – its pattern of straight main and curving minor vehicular roads and its occasional pedestrian paths, its trees carefully preserved and its architectural style controlled in no more than the most general terms of a free neo-Tudor. Unwin also showed his sense of subtle visual planning effects in his *Town Planning in Practice,* first published in 1909, and a textbook to this day.

Lit: W. L. Creese, *The Search for Environment,* New Haven 1960; W. L. Creese, *The Legacy of R. Unwin,* Cambridge, Mass., 1967.

Upjohn, Richard (1802–78), was born at Shaftesbury, where he was later in business as a cabinet-maker. He emigrated to America in 1829 and opened a practice as an architect at Boston in 1834. His speciality was Gothic churches: the first came in 1837, and the principal ones are Trinity Church, New York (1841–6), an effort in a rich Anglo-Gothic, and Trinity Chapel, W. 25th Street (1853), also Anglo-Gothic. He built in other styles as well (Trinity Building, New York, 1852, is Italianate). Upjohn was the first president of the American Institute of Architects. (For illustration *see* UNITED STATES ARCHITECTURE.)

Lit: E. M. Upjohn, *Richard Upjohn, Architect and Churchman,* New York 1939.

Urban renewal The replanning of existing towns or centres to bring them up to date and to improve amenities and traffic circulation. *See* TOWN PLANNING.

Utzon, Jørn, *see* SCANDINAVIAN ARCHITECTURE.

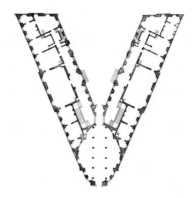

Vaccarini, Giovan Battista (1702–68), was born in Palermo. He studied under Carlo FONTANA in Rome and settled in Catania (1730), where his exuberant Sicilian Rococo style is seen in the façade of the Cathedral (begun 1730), Palazzo Municipale (1732), Collegio Cutelli (1754), and S. Agata (begun 1735).

Lit: F. Fichera, *G. B. Vaccarini*, Rome 1934; A. Blunt, *Sicilian Baroque*, London 1968.

Valadier, Giuseppe (1762–1839), archaeologist, town-planner, and a prolific though rather reactionary architect. His main buildings are neo-Palladian rather than neo-classical, e.g., interior of Spoleto Cathedral (1784), interior of Urbino Cathedral (1789), and façade of S. Rocco, Rome (1833), though the boldly simple S. Pantaleo, Rome (1806), is more in tune with his times. His masterpiece is the reorganization of Piazza del Popolo, Rome, for which he published a design in 1794 and which he began in 1813. It was executed 1816–20.

Lit: P. Marconi, *G. Valadier*, Rome 1964.

Vanbrugh, Sir John (1664–1726), soldier, adventurer, playwright, and herald, was also the outstanding English Baroque architect. His father was a Flemish refugee who became a rich sugar-baker and married the daughter of Sir Dudley Carleton. He was brought up as a gentleman and commissioned in the Earl of Huntingdon's regiment in 1686. In 1690 he was arrested in Calais for spying and imprisoned for two years, part of the time in the Bastille. After his release he took London by storm with his witty and improper comedies *The Relapse* and *The Provok'd Wife*. Then he switched his talents to architecture – 'with-

out thought or lecture', said Swift – having been invited by the Earl of Carlisle to try his hand at designing Castle Howard (1699). Lord Carlisle also had him appointed Comptroller at the Office of Works (1702), and thus he became, without any training or qualifications, WREN's principal colleague. But he turned out to be an architect of genius. The Tories later deprived him of his Comptrollership, but he was reinstated after the death of Queen Anne and knighted (1714). Witty and convivial, a friend of Tonson and Congreve and a member of the Kit Cat Club, he lived on terms of easy familiarity with the great men who became his clients.

His style derives from Wren at his grandest – e.g., Greenwich Hospital – and probably owes much to HAWKSMOOR, his assistant from 1699 onwards. But every building he designed is stamped with his own unique personality – expansive, virile, and ostentatious, more Flemish than English and often rather coarse and theatrical. Castle Howard (1699–1726) is an amazing trial of strength by a young undisciplined genius. His great opportunity came in 1705 at Blenheim Palace, the nation's gift to Marlborough in honour of his victories. Here he had almost unlimited funds at his disposal and the whole megalomaniac conception suited his temperament perfectly. He was always at his best on the largest possible scale, and his genius for the dramatic and heroic, for bold groupings of masses and for picturesque recessions and projections and varied skylines had full play.

His style reached sudden maturity at Blenheim – indeed, English Baroque architecture culminates there – and it changed little afterwards. The best of his surviving houses are Kimbolton (1707-9), King's Weston (1711-14), Seaton Delaval (c. 1720-8), Lumley Castle (entrance front and interior alterations, c. 1722), and Grimsthorpe (north range only, c. 1723-4). He said he wanted his architecture to be 'masculine' and to have 'something of the Castle Air', and nowhere does his peculiar version of the Baroque come closer to the massiveness of a medieval fortress than at Seaton Delaval. Sombre and cyclopean, this extraordinary house is unlike any other building in England or anywhere else. His strong sense of the picturesque led him to further and more explicit medievalisms elsewhere, notably at his own house at Greenwich (after 1717), which is castellated and has a fortified-looking round tower. He seems here to have foreshadowed the romantic spirit of later Gothic revivals. (For illustrations see BAROQUE ARCHITECTURE, ENGLISH ARCHITECTURE.)

Lit: G. Webb in *The Complete Works of Sir John Vanbrugh*, vol. IV, London 1928; L. Whistler, *Sir John Vanbrugh, Architect and Dramatist*, London 1938; L. Whistler, *The Imagination of Vanbrugh and his Fellow Artists*, London 1954; K. Downes, *English Baroque Architecture*, London 1966.

Vanvitelli, Luigi (1700-73), was born in Naples, the son of the painter Gaspar van Wittel, studied painting with his father in Rome, and emerged as an architect only in the 1730s. He worked at Pesaro, Macerata, Perugia, Loreto, Siena, Ancona, and Rome (monastery of S. Agostino and remodelling of S. Maria degli Angeli) before he was summoned to Naples by Carlo III in 1751 to build the enormous 1200-room palace at Caserta. This is the last great Italian Baroque building. Its immense internal vistas, ceremonial staircase, and central octagonal vestibule rival the most extravagant stage-set in scenographic fantasy, though the exterior already veers towards neo-classical restraint. Almost equally impressive are his Chiesa dell'Annunziata (1761-82), Piazza Dante (1757-63), and twenty-five mile long Acquedotto Carolino (1752-64).

Lit: F. Fichera, *L. Vanvitelli*, Rome 1937; F. Bologna, *Settecento Napoletano*, Turin 1962.

Vardy, John (d. 1765). Friend and close associate of KENT, whose designs for the Horse Guards, London, he carried out (with W. Robinson, 1750-8). His most important surviving work is Spencer House, London (1750-

65), an excellent example of PALLADIANISM freely interpreted.

Lit: J. Summerson, *Architecture in Britain, 1530-1830*, Pelican History of Art, Harmondsworth 1969, paperback edn 1970; H. M. Colvin, *Biographical Dictionary of English Architects, 1660-1840*, London 1954.

Vasari, Giorgio (1511-74). A painter and author of the famous *Vite de' più eccellenti architetti, pittori e scultori italiani* (1550, revised 1568), which by its eulogistic account of MICHELANGELO exerted an important influence on architectural taste. As an architect he had a hand, with VIGNOLA and AMMANATI, in designing the Villa di Papa Giulio, Rome (1551-5). His only important independent work is the Uffizi, Florence (begun 1560), with a long narrow courtyard stretching down towards the river and closed by a range with two superimposed Serlian arcades – an adaptation of Michelangelo's Laurentian Library to external architecture. In Arezzo he designed SS. Fiora e Lucilla (1566) and the Logge Vasariane (1573). In Florence he modernized the interior of S. Maria Novella (1566-72) and S. Croce (1566-84) in accordance with the ideas of the Council of Trent, removing the medieval screens, monks' choirs, etc. and replacing the old altars in the aisles with uniform, large aedicules.

Lit: P. Barocchi, 'Il Vasari' in *Atti dell' Accademia Pontaniana*, VI, 1958.

Vauban, Sébastien le Prestre de (1633-1707). Architect, town-planner and the most famous of all military engineers. According to Voltaire he constructed or repaired the fortifications of 150 'places de guerre' and he was said to have directed some 53 sieges. A close friend of Louvois (minister of war 1666-91) and of Colbert, he became *Commissaire Général des Fortifications* in 1677. In 1703 he was made a *Maréchal de France*. His genius as a military engineer lay in the resourcefulness with which he used and adapted traditional means rather than in the invention of new ones. His ingenuity is well displayed at difficult sites, e.g., Mont-Louis in the Pyrenees and Mont-Dauphin and Château Queyras on the Savoy frontier. But his most famous fortifications are those of Lille (1668-74), Maubeuge (1683-5) and Neuf-Brisach (1697-1708). Some of his fortresses were in effective military use up to the 1914-18 war, notably Langwy (built 1678). He laid out the new towns he brought into being, such as Neuf-Brisach, and occasionally designed individual buildings, e.g., the governor's house, church and arsenal at Lille and churches at Givet and Briançon. He restored the *châteaux* of Auney and Ussé. But his merit as an architect is best appreciated in the massive simplicity of such ramparts as those of Oléron, Gravelines and Bayonne and in his monumental gateways which range from the Baroque splendour of the Porte de Paris at Lille, enriched with columns, entablatures, trophies and sculptured panels, to the simple grandeur of the Mons Gate at Maubeuge. In these Vauban approached the noble severity and grandeur achieved by his contemporaries Libéral BRUANT and François BLONDEL. His memoirs, *Plusieurs maximes bonnes à observer pour tous ceux qui font bâtir,* contain a complete treatise on building. (English translation by G. A. Rothrock was published 1968, Ann Arbor.)

Lit: R. Blomfield, *Sebastian le Prestre de Vauban, 1633–1707,* London 1938; M. Parent & J. Verroust, *Vauban,* Paris 1971.

Vaudoyer, Léon (1803–72). French architect. His *chef d'œuvre* is Marseilles Cathedral (begun in 1852) which combines convincingly a Romanesque plan with a Byzantine elevation and the polychrome horizontal striping of e.g. Siena Cathedral.

Lit: L. Hautecoeur, *Histoire de l'architecture classique en France,* VII, Paris 1958; H.-R. Hitchcock, *Architecture: Nineteenth and Twentieth Centuries,* Pelican History of Art, Harmondsworth 1969, paperback edn 1971.

Vaudremer, Joseph-Auguste-E. (1829–1914), after a training under the sober utilitarian architects Blouet and Gilbert, started with the large Santé Prison, Paris (1862 etc.), in the same spirit. However, in 1864 he was commissioned to build the church of St Pierre de Montrouge in Paris (1864–70), and here his very sobriety and directness made him choose the Romanesque rather than the Gothic style. The building must have impressed H. H. RICHARDSON. Romanesque also, but internally with much grander stone vaults is Notre Dame, rue d'Auteuil, Paris (1876 etc.). The much larger and more famous Sacré Cœur on Montmartre is by Paul Abadie (1812–84) and was started in 1876. It is inspired by St Front at Périgueux, which Abadie disastrously restored.

Lit: L. Hautecoeur, *Histoire de l'architecture classique en France,* VII, Paris 1958; H.-R.

Hitchcock, *Architecture: Nineteenth and Twentieth Centuries,* Pelican History of Art, Harmondsworth 1969, paperback edn 1971.

Vault An arched ceiling or roof of stone or brick, sometimes imitated in wood or plaster.

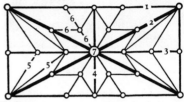

Vault	4. Longitudinal ridge-rib
1. Transverse rib	5. Tiercerons
2. Diagonal rib	6. Liernes
3. Transverse ridge-rib	7. Boss

Barrel vault, see tunnel vault.

Cloister vault, see domical vault.

Cross vault, see groin vault.

Domical vault A dome rising direct on a square or polygonal base, the curved surfaces separated by GROINS. In America called a *cloister vault.*

A *fan vault* consists of solid concave-sided semi-cones, meeting or nearly meeting at the apex of the vault. The areas between are flat and, if the cones meet, form concave-sided lozenges. The cones and centres are decorated with panelling so as to give the appearance of a highly decorated rib vault.

A *groin vault* is produced by the intersection at right angles of two tunnel vaults of identical shape.

Groin vault: Corvey Abbey church, westwork, 1146–59

Lierne A tertiary rib, that is, one which

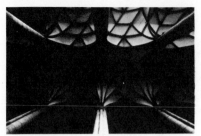

Lierne vault:
St Georg, Nördlingen, 1427–1505

Stellar vault: Monastery church,
Bebenhausen, c. 1500

does not spring either from one of the main springers or from the central BOSS. A *lierne vault* is a ribbed vault with liernes.

A *net vault* is one whose ribs form a net of lozenges.

A *ploughshare vault* or *stilted vault* has the wall ribs sprung from a higher level than the diagonal ribs, in order to increase the light from a clerestory window.

In a *quadripartite vault* one bay is divided into four quarters or CELLS.

A *rib vault* is a framework of diagonal arched ribs carrying the cells which cover in the spaces between them.

A *transverse arch* separates one bay of a vault from the next. It can be either plain in section or moulded.

Tunnel vault (also called *barrel vault* and *wagon vault*). The simplest form of vault, con-

Tunnel vaults: Store building near Temple of Rameses II, C13 B.C.

Ribbed quadripartite vault:
Palazzo dei Consoli, Bevagna, c. 1270

Pointed tunnel vault:
S. Maria, Bominaco, 1263

Ridge-rib The rib along the longitudinal or transverse ridge of a vault, at an angle of approximately 45° to the main diagonal ribs.

In a *sexpartite vault* one bay of quadripartite vaulting is divided transversely into two parts so that each bay has six compartments.

A *stellar vault* is one with the ribs, liernes and tiercerons arranged in a star-shaped pattern.

Tierceron A secondary rib, which springs from one of the main springers, or the central boss, and leads to a place on the ridge-rib.

Ring vault:
Fort Tilly, Ingolstadt, early C16

*Umbrella vault: Eglise des Jacobins,
Toulouse, CI3–14*

sisting of a continuous vault of semicircular
or pointed section, unbroken in its length by
cross vaults. BUTTRESSING is needed to
ground the thrust, which is dispersed all along
the wall beneath. Tunnel vaults can be subdivided into bays by transverse arches.

Wagon vault, see tunnel vault.

Vaulting shaft The vertical member leading to
the springer of a vault.

Vaux, Calvert, *see* DOWNING.

Vázquez, Lorenzo, to whom the earliest works
of the Renaissance in Spain are now attributed,
was master mason to Cardinal Mendoza. For
him the Colegio de Santa Cruz at Valladolid,
begun in 1486, was transformed in 1491 by
Vázquez, with its Quattrocento frontispiece
medallion. The next buildings in order of date
were also commissioned by members of the
Mendoza family: the palace at Cogolludo
(probably 1492–5), with windows still floridly
Late Gothic; the palace at Guadalajara (before
1507); and the castle of La Calahorra (1509–
12). In the latter case, however, it is known
that Michele Carlone of Genoa was called in to
take charge. For other early major Renaissance designs in Spain *see* EGAS.

Lit: F. Chueca Goitia, *Arquitectura del siglo
XVI* (*Ars Hispaniae*, vol. XI), Marid 1953; G.
Kubler & M. Soria, *Art and Architecture in
Spain and Portugal and their American Domi-
nions, 1500–1800,* Pelican History of Art,
Harmondsworth 1959.

Vázquez, Pedro Ramírez, *see* MEXICAN ARCHI-
TECTURE.

Velde, Henry van de (1863–1957). He was
born at Antwerp of a well-to-do family and
was first a painter influenced aesthetically by
the Neo-Impressionists (Pointillists), socially
by the ideals which at the time also inspired
van Gogh. About 1890, under the impact of
RUSKIN and MORRIS, he turned from painting to design and in 1892 produced the first
works that are entirely his own and at the
same time entirely representative of ART
NOUVEAU, the anti-historical movement just
then emerging. They are works of typography
and book decoration, with long flexible
curves, and an appliqué panel called *The
Angels Watch*. Their stylistic source seems to
be the Gauguin of Pont Aven and his circle,
especially Emile Bernard.

In 1895 van de Velde designed a house and
furnishings at Uccle near Brussels for his own
young family. It was his first achievement in
architecture and interior design, and both
now became his principal concerns. He was
commissioned to design interiors for Bing's
newly established shop L'Art Nouveau in
Paris (1895) and then showed most of this
work at an exhibition in Dresden (1897). In
both centres its impact was great, but whereas reactions were largely hostile in France,
they were enthusiastic in Germany, and so
van de Velde decided to leave Brussels and
settle in Berlin. In the next years he did much
furnishing work for the wealthy and the
refined, including the shop of the imperial
barber Haby (1901). In 1901 he was called
to Weimar as a consultant on the coordination of crafts, trades, and good design. He
furnished the Nietzsche-Archive there (1903),
and rebuilt the Art School and the School of
Arts and Crafts (1904, 1907), of which latter
he became director. He also did the interior
of the Folkwang Museum at Hagen (1901–2)
and the Abbe Monument at Jena (1908).

His style is characterized by the long daring
curves of Art Nouveau, endowed by him with
a peculiar resilience, and in architecture also
by the use of the curve rather than the angle
– e.g., for roofs. For the Werkbund Exhibition
at Cologne in 1914 (*see* GROPIUS; TAUT) he
did the theatre, also with curved corners and
a curved roof.

Being Belgian he left his job in Germany
during the war, lived through restless years of
émigré life and only in 1925 settled down
again, now back in Brussels. However, the

years of his great successes and his European significance were over. His late style is less personal, close to that of the School of Rotterdam (see OUD). Its finest example is the Kröller-Müller Museum at Otterlo in Holland, beautifully coordinated with the heath scenery around (1937–54). (For illustration *see* ART NOUVEAU.)

Lit: H. van de Velde, *Geschichte meines Lebens*, Munich 1962; K.-H. Hüter, *Henry van de Velde*, Berlin 1967; A. M. Hammacher, *Le monde de H. van de Velde*, Antwerp 1967; *Exposition Henry van de Velde, 1863–1957*, Exh. Cat., Brussels 1970.

Venetian door An adaptation of the SERLIANA to a doorway, i.e., with the central opening arched and flanked by tall narrow square-topped windows.

Venetian window, *see* SERLIANA.

Veranda An open gallery or balcony with a roof supported by light, usually metal, supports.

Vermiculation Decoration of masonry blocks with irregular shallow channels like worm tracks.

Vertue, Robert (d. 1506) and **William** (d. 1527), were brothers and both masons. Robert, the elder, appears at Westminster Abbey from 1475. About 1501 both brothers were master masons for Bath Abbey, begun at that time by Bishop King. This grandly Perpendicular building has a fan VAULT which, so they told the bishop, would be such that 'there shall be none so goodly neither in England nor in France'; and as at that moment neither the vault of King's College Chapel, Cambridge, nor that of Henry VII's Chapel in Westminster Abbey, or that of St George's Chapel, Windsor, existed (though the latter was building), the claim was just. The Vertues' precise connection with these three works cannot be proved, but as they were jointly the King's Master Masons, with Robert Janyns and John Lebons (*see* REDMAN), it is likely that a connection existed. William, in any case, signed a contract with another (John Aylmer) to vault the chancel at Windsor, and visited King's College Chapel once in 1507, once (with Redman) in 1509, and once (with WASTELL) in 1512, if not more often.

In 1516 William appeared at Eton (with Redman), where he made a design (the design?) for Lupton's Tower. From 1510 he

was King's Mason (after 1519 jointly with Redman). In 1526 he probably designed the fan-vaulted cloister chapel in the Palace of Westminster.

Lit: J. Harvey, *English Medieval Architects*, London 1954.

Vesara architecture, *see* INDIAN ARCHITECTURE.

Vesica An upright almond shape; found chiefly in medieval art to enclose a figure of Christ enthroned.

Vesica: San Pedro, Moarbes, Palencia, Spain, late C12

Vesnin, Alexander (1883–1959). Vesnin took an engineering degree in 1913. He did important theatrical work, but also the setting for the May-Day celebrations in the Red Square in 1918 (with his brother) and the Karl Marx Memorial, also in Moscow, in 1920.

Lit: M. A. Iljoin, *Vesnin*, Moscow 1960; V. Quilici, *L'architettura del Costruttivismo*, Bari 1969.

Viaduct A long series of arches carrying a road or railway.

Vice A winding or spiral staircase.

Vicente de Oliveira, Mateus (1710–86), the leading Portuguese Rococo architect, began under LUDOVICE but forsook his grandiose manner for one more delicate and intimate. His masterpiece is the Palace of Queluz (1747–52, interior destroyed), where a large building is disguised behind an exquisitely frivolous façade swagged with garlands of carved flowers. He also designed the very large Estrêla Church in Lisbon (1778).

Lit: G. Kubler & M. Soria, *Art and Architecture in Spain and Portugal and their American Dominions, 1500–1800*, Pelican History of Art, Harmondsworth 1959.

Vietnamese architecture, *see* SOUTH-EAST ASIAN ARCHITECTURE.

Vignola, Giacomo Barozzi da (1507–73), the leading architect in Rome after the death of MICHELANGELO, was born at Vignola, near Modena, and studied painting and architecture at Bologna. In 1530 he settled in Rome. He seems to have played the leading part in designing the Villa di Papa Giulio, Rome (1551–5) in collaboration with AMMANATI and VASARI. It is a masterpiece of Mannerist architecture and garden design, with much play with vistas from one courtyard to another, hemicycles echoing each other, a curious rhythmical use of the ORDERS, and very shallow relief decorations applied to the surfaces. In 1559 he began work on the Palazzo Farnese at Caprarola, which had already been started on a pentagonal plan. He designed the rather stern façades, the elegant circular interior courtyard and the ingenious arrangement of rooms. The famous circular staircase is also his, and he probably designed the gardens as well.

In 1558 he designed the plan for the Palazzo Farnese in Piacenza on which work stopped soon after 1560 so that barely a third was built. He may also have designed the Portico dei Banchi at Bologna. In about 1550 he built the little Tempietto di S. Andrea, Rome, for Pope Julius III, using for the first time in church architecture an oval plan. He was to repeat this in 1566–7 on a larger scale in his design for S. Anna dei Palafrenieri, Rome (begun 1573), and which was to be used extensively by Baroque architects. His most influential building was the Gesù, Rome (begun 1568); it has probably had a wider influence than any church built in the last 400 years. The plan, which owes something to ALBERTI's S. Andrea, Mantua, combines the central scheme of the Renaissance with the longitudinal scheme of the Middle Ages. The aisles are replaced by a series of chapels opening off the nave, and various devices – e.g., lighting and the placing of the nave pilasters – direct attention to the high altar. (The façade was designed by Giocomo della PORTA

and the interior was redecorated in High Baroque style in 1668–73).

Vignola was architect to St Peter's (1567–73) and continued Michelangelo's work there faithfully. In 1562 he published *Regole delle cinque ordini*, a simple MODULAR interpretation of the architectural Orders which, on account of its straight-forward approach, enjoyed immense popularity. It became the architect's alphabet, and one of the most important textbooks ever written. (For illustration *see* ITALIAN ARCHITECTURE.)

Lit: W. Lotz, *Vignola-Studien*, Würzburg 1939; M. Walcher-Casotti, *Il Vignola*, Trieste 1961; L. H. Heydenreich & W. Lotz, *Architecture in Italy, 1400–1600*, Pelican History of Art, Harmondsworth 1974.

Vignon, Pierre (1762–1828). French Empire architect famous for the Madeleine in Paris (1806–43), his one important building. He was trained under J.-D. Leroy and LEDOUX and in 1793 became *Inspecteur général des bâtiments de la République*. His Madeleine is an enormous peripteral Corinthian temple on a high podium, as imposingly and imperially Roman in scale as in its slightly vulgar ostentation. It superseded a building designed by Pierre Contant d'Ivry in 1764, revised by G. M. Couture *c.* 1777. This had hardly begun to be built when Napoleon called in Vignon in 1806, having decided that it should be a *Temple de la Gloire* and not a church. But he reversed this decision in 1813 after the Battle of Leipzig and the loss of Spain. Vignon did not live to see his masterpiece completed and it was finished by J.-J.-M. Huvé (1783–1852).

Lit: M. L. Biver, *Le Paris de Napoléon*, Paris 1965; L. Hautecoeur, *Histoire de l'architecture classique en France*, V, Paris 1953.

Vihara An Indian Buddhist monastery consisting of a central courtyard surrounded by

Vihara at Ellora, 700–750

cells for the monks. Surviving examples, dating from the c1–c7 A.D., are caves hewn out of rocky hill-sides e.g. Ajanta, Ellora, Elephanta, etc. The façades closing the entrance to the caves are richly ornamented with sculpture.

Villa In Roman architecture, the landowner's residence or farmstead on his country estate; in Renaissance architecture, a country house; in c19 England, a detached house 'for opulent persons', usually on the outskirts of a town; in modern architecture, a small detached house. The basic type developed with the growth of urbanization: it is of five bays, on a simple corridor plan with rooms opening off a central passage. The next stage is the addition of wings. The courtyard villa fills a square plan with subsidiary buildings and an enclosure wall with a gate facing the main corridor block.

Lit: B. Rupprecht, 'Villa, Zur Geschichte eines Ideals' in *Probleme der Kunstwissenschaft*, Munich 1966.

Villanueva, Juan de (1739–1811), the leading Spanish neo-classical architect, was the son of a sculptor under whom he trained. He began in the CHURRIGUERESQUE tradition, then became a draughtsman to SACCHETTI in Madrid and adopted an Italianate Baroque style. He was sent by the Royal Academy to Rome (1759–65), and on his return his brother Diego (1715–74) published his *Colección de papeles críticos sobre la arquitectura* (1766), the first neo-Classical attack on the Churrigueresque and Rococo to appear in Spain. Rather tentatively he began to put these ideas into practice in the Palafox Chapel in Burgo de Osma Cathedral (1770), Casita de Arriba at the Escorial (1773), and Casita del Príncipe at El Pardo (1784). His outstanding work is the Prado Museum, Madrid, designed (1787) as a museum of natural history but later adapted to house the royal collection of pictures. With its sturdy Tuscan portico in the centre and its boldly articulated wings with Ionic colonnades at first-floor level it is an effective and undoctrinaire essay in neo-classicism. (For illustration *see* SPANISH ARCHITECTURE.)

Lit: F. Chueca Goitia, *La vida y las obras del arquitecto Juan de Villanueva*, Madrid 1949.

Villard de Honnecourt, a French architect who was active around 1225–35 in the North-West of France and was probably master mason of Cambrai Cathedral, which no longer exists. Villard is known to us by the book of drawings with short texts which he compiled for the learners in his lodge, the masons' workshop and office. The book is in the Bibliothèque Nationale in Paris and contains plans of buildings (both copied and invented), elevational details, figure sculpture, figures drawn *al vif*, foliage ornament, a lectern, a stall end, a *perpetuum mobile*, and in addition many small technical drawings, more of an engineering kind, which were added to the book by two successors of Villard. From the text and the examples illustrated it is certain that Villard knew Reims, Laon, Chartres, Lausanne, and that he travelled as far as Hungary. The sculptural style of his figures connects him with work of about 1230 at Reims. Villard's book gives us the clearest insight we can obtain into the work of a distinguished master mason and the atmosphere of a lodge.

Lit: H. Hahnloser, *Villard de Honnecourt*, Vienna 1935; R. Branner in *Art Bulletin*, XXXIX, 1957.

Vingboons or **Vinckeboons, Philips** (1614–78), was the leading exponent of van CAMPEN's Dutch classicism for middle-class domestic architecture in Amsterdam. He worked for the prosperous merchants while Pieter POST was patronized by the upper class. Being Roman Catholic he obtained no commissions for public buildings or churches. He created a new type of town-house, sober, unpretentious and eminently practical, with strictly symmetrical planning and severely simple elevations. His designs, published as *Oeuvres d'Architecture* in two volumes (1648 and 1674), were very influential, especially in England. His brother **Justus** (*fl.* 1650–70) designed the façades of LA VALLÉE's Riddarhus in Stockholm (1653–6) and built the imposing Trippenhuis in Amsterdam (1662).

Lit: E. H. ter Kuile in *Dutch Art and Architecture, 1600–1800*, Pelican History of Art, Harmondsworth 1966, paperback edn 1972; Fockema Andreae, R. C. Hekker & E. H. Ter Kuile, *Duizend Jaar Bouwen in Nederland*, Amsterdam 1957.

Viollet-le-Duc, Eugène-Emanuel (1814–79), was born into a wealthy, cultured, and progressive family. His opposition to the 'establishment' began early: he helped to build barricades in 1830 and refused to go to the École des Beaux Arts for his training. In 1836–7 he was in Italy studying buildings with industry and intelligence. His future was determined by his meeting with Prosper Mérimée (1803-70), author of *Carmen* and Inspector in the newly founded Commission des Monuments Historiques. Viollet-le-Duc, inspired by Victor Hugo's enthusiasm on the one hand and by Arcisse de Caumont's scholarship on the other, now turned resolutely to the French Middle Ages and soon established himself both as a scholar and as a restorer. His first job was Vézelay (1840). He then did the Sainte Chapelle in Paris with Duban, and Notre Dame with Lassus. The number of his later restorations is legion.

As a scholar he developed new and highly influential ideas on the Gothic style, which to him is socially the outcome of a lay civilization succeeding the sinister religious domination of the earlier Middle Ages. The Gothic style to Viollet-le-Duc is also a style of rational construction based on the system of rib vault, flying buttress, and buttress. The ribs are a skeleton, like a C19 iron skeleton; the webs or cells are no more than light infilling. All thrusts are conducted from the ribs to the flying buttresses and buttresses, and so walls can be replaced by large openings. These ideas were laid down and made universal property by Viollet-le-Duc's *Dictionnaire raisonné de l'architecture française* (published 1854-68). A comparison between Gothic skeleton and C19 iron skeleton building was drawn, or rather implied, in Viollet-le-Duc's *Entretiens* (2 vols., published 1863 and 1872), and especially in the second volume. Here Viollet-le-Duc appears as a passionate defender of his own age, of engineering, and of new materials and techniques, especially iron for supports, for framework, and for ribs. The plates to the *Entretiens* are extremely original, but aesthetically they are none too attractive. As an architect Viollet-le-Duc had in fact little merit. Time and again one is struck by the discrepancy between the consistency and daring of his thought and the looseness and commonplace detailing of his original buildings, e.g., Saint-Denys-de-l'Estrée, St Denis (1864-7).

Lit: P. Gout, *Viollet le Duc*, Paris 1914; Exh. Cat., *E. Viollet le Duc, 1814-1879*, Paris 1965; N. Pevsner, *Some Architectural Writers of the Nineteenth Century*, Oxford 1972.

Viscardi, Giovanni Antonio (1647-1713). He was born in the Grisons and went, like his compatriot and bitter rival Zuccalli, to work in Munich where he became master mason to the Court in 1678 and chief architect in 1685. Zuccalli helped to oust him from his post in 1689, but he was in charge of enlarging Nymphenburg palace from 1702 onwards (he began the saloon and added pavilions etc.) and he was reinstated as chief architect 1706-13. His most important building is the Mariahilfkirche at Freystadt (1700-1708) with a very high central dome, on a plan that was to have widespread influence even beyond Bavaria (Bähr used it as a model for the Frauenkirche in Dresden). He also designed the Cistercian church of Fürstenfeld (1701-47). His last works were the Jesuit assembly hall or Bürgersaal, Munich (1709-10) and the church of the Holy Trinity in Munich (1711-14).

Lit: K.-L. Lippert, *G. A. Viscardi*, Munich 1969.

Vitozzi, Ascanio (c. 1539-1615). He began as an officer and military engineer, serving at Lepanto in 1571 and later in Tunis and in Spain and Portugal. In 1584 he was called by Duke Carlo Emanuele I of Savoy to Turin where he built S. Maria del Monte or dei Cappuccini (begun 1585) and the Trinità (begun 1598), but his masterpiece is the enormous centrally planned pilgrimage church at Vicoforte di Mondovì, in Piedmont (begun 1596).

Lit: N. Carboneri, *Ascanio Vitozzi*, Rome 1966.

Vitruvian opening A doorway or window of which the sides incline slightly inwards towards the top, giving it a heavy, Egyptian look. It was described by Vitruvius.

Vitruvian scroll, *see* RUNNING DOG.

Vitruvius Pollio, Marcus (active 46-30 B.C.), a Roman architect and theorist of slight importance in his own time but of enormous influence from the Early Renaissance onwards. He served under Julius Caesar in the African War (46 B.C.), built the basilica at Fano (destroyed), and in old age composed a treatise on architecture in ten books *De architectura*, written in a somewhat obscure style and dedicated to Augustus. This is the only complete treatise on architecture to survive from Antiquity. Several manuscript copies were known and used in the Middle Ages. In 1414 Poggio Bracciolini drew attention to a copy at St Gall, and the treatise soon came to be regarded as a vade-mecum for all progres-

sive architects. Both ALBERTI and FRANCESCO
DI GIORGIO derived much from it for their
writings and buildings. The first printed text
was published in Rome *c.* 1486 and the first
illustrated edition by Fra GIOCONDO in 1511;
an Italian translation was prepared under
RAPHAEL's direction *c.* 1520, and another
translation was printed in 1521 with an
extensive commentary by Cesare Cesariano
and numerous illustrations. A vast number
of subsequent editions and translations in
nearly all European languages appeared. The
obscurity of the text, which made a strong
appeal to the Renaissance intellect, enabled
architects to interpret its gnomic statements
in a variety of ways.

Volutes used decoratively,
S. Pietro in Vincoli, Rome, C16

Lit: A. Boethius & J. B. Ward-Perkins,
Etruscan and Roman Architecture, Pelican
History of Art, Harmondsworth 1970.

Vittone, Bernardo (1704/5-1770), a little-
known architect of real if rather freakish
genius, worked exclusively in Piedmont where
he was born. He studied in Rome and edited
GUARINI's posthumous *Architettura civile*
(1737). His secular buildings are dull; not so
his numerous churches, mostly small and
scattered in remote villages, in which the
unlikely fusion of Guarini and JUVARRA had
surprising and original results in a gay Rococo
vein. Of his structural inventions the penden-
tive-squinch (e.g., S. Maria di Piazza, Turin,
1751-4) and the fantastic three-vaulted dome
are the most successful. His churches at
Vallinotto (1738-9), Brà (1742), and Chieri
(1740-4) show his structural ingenuity at its
prettiest. Later churches – Borgo d'Ale,
Rivarolo Canavese, Grignasco – are larger,
less frivolous, but suavely calm and sinuous.
He had several followers and disciples in
Piedmont, but no influence whatever farther
afield.

Lit: R. Pommer, *Eighteenth Century Archi-
tecture in Piedmont,* New York–London 1967;
N. Carboneri & V. Viale, eds., *Bernardo Vittone,*
Exh. Cat., Vercelli 1967; P. Portoghesi,
*Bernardo Vittone: Un Architetto tra Illuminismo
e Rococò,* Rome 1966.

Volute A spiral scroll on an Ionic CAPITAL;
smaller versions appear on Composite and
Corinthian capitals. (Illustrated next column;
for additional illustration *see* ORDER.)

Voronikhin, Andrei Nikiforovich (1760-
1814), one of the leading figures in the neo-
classical transformation of St Petersburg, was
born a serf on the estates of Count Stroganov,
who sent him to study in Moscow, then on a
European tour (1784-90), and finally employed him to design the state apartments in
his palace. His main works are in Leningrad,
e.g., Cathedral of the Virgin of Kazan (1801-
11), the most Catholic and Roman church in
Russia, and the Academy of Mines (1806-11)
with a dodecastyle Paestum portico.

Lit: G. H. Hamilton, *The Art and Architecture
of Russia,* Pelican History of Art, Harmondsworth 1954.

Voussoir A wedge-shaped stone or brick
forming one of the units of an arch. (For
illustration *see* ARCH.)

Voysey, Charles F. Annesley (1857-1941),
worked first under Seddon, then with Devey,
and set up in practice in 1882. He was at
once as interested in design as in architecture,
under the general influence of MORRIS and
of MACKMURDO in particular. The earliest designs for wallpapers and textiles are of 1883
and are indeed very reminiscent of Mackmurdo. His first commissions for houses date
from 1888-9, and from then until the First
World War he built a large number of country
houses and hardly anything else. They are
never extremely large, never grand, never
representational; instead they are placed in
intimate relation to nature – perhaps an old
tree preserved in the courtyard – and developed
informally. They spread with ease and, having lowish comfortable rooms, are often on
the cosy side. The exteriors are usually
rendered with pebbledash and have horizontal
windows. They are no longer period imitations at all – in fact, more independent of the
past than most architects ventured to be before
1900 – but they never lack the admission of
a sympathy for the rural Tudor and Stuart

traditions. Voysey designed the furniture and all the details, such as fireplaces, metalwork, etc., himself, and the furniture is again inspired by Mackmurdo's (and in its turn inspired MACKINTOSH's). It is reasonable, friendly, and in the decoration not without a sweet sentimentality; the same is true of textiles and wallpapers.

Among his houses which had a tremendous influence at home (right down to the caricatures produced between the wars by speculative builders) and abroad, the following may be listed: Perrycroft, Colwall, 1893; Annesley Lodge, Hampstead, London, 1895; Merlshanger (Grey Friars), Hog's Back, 1896; Norney, Shackleford, 1897; Broadleys and Moor Crag, both Gill Head, Windermere, 1898; The Orchard, Chorley Wood, 1899. After the war Voysey was rarely called upon to do any architectural work. (For illustration *see* ENGLISH ARCHITECTURE.)

Lit: J. Brandon-Jones, 'C. F. A. Voysey' in *Architectural Association Journal*, May 1957;

N. Pevsner, *Studies in Art, Architecture and Design*, London 1968.

Vries, Hans Vredeman de (1527–1606), began as a painter, settled in Antwerp, and published fantastic ornamental pattern-books – *Architectura* (1565), *Compertimenta* (1566), *Variae Architecturae Formae* (1601) – which had enormous influence on architecture all over Northern Europe including England (e.g., SMYTHSON's Wollaton). His style lacks FLORIS's grace and wit but well represents the Flemish and Dutch contribution to MANNERISM and expresses the northern feeling for flat pattern in strapwork or carved decoration of interlaced bands and forms similar to fretwork or cut leather.

Lit: H. Gerson and E. H. ter Kuile, *Art and Architecture in Belgium, 1600–1800*, Pelican History of Art, Harmondsworth 1960.

Vyse A spiral staircase or a staircase winding round a central column.

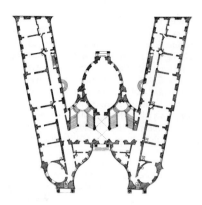

Wagner, Otto (1841–1918), became professor at the Academy in Vienna in 1894, and delivered an inaugural address pleading for a new approach to architecture, for independence of the past, and for rationalism ('Nothing that is not practical can be beautiful'). Before that time he had himself designed in the neo-Renaissance style. His most familiar achievement is some stations for the Vienna Stadtbahn (1894–7), ART NOUVEAU with much exposed iron, though more restrained than Hector GUIMARD'S contemporary ones for the Paris Métro. But his most amazingly modern and C20-looking job is the Post Office Savings Bank, Vienna (1904–6), the exterior faced with marble slabs held in place by aluminium bolts and the interior featuring a glass barrel vault realized with a clarity and economy hardly matched by anyone else at so early a date. Wagner had a decisive influence on the best younger architects of Vienna (*see* HOFFMANN, LOOS, OLBRICH). His most monumental building, close to the style of the Secession, is the church of the Steinhof Asylum, outside Vienna, with its powerful dome (1906). (For illustration *see* AUSTRIAN ARCHITECTURE.)

Lit: H. Geretsegger & M. Peintner, *Otto Wagner, 1841–1918: The Expanding City,* London 1970.

Wagon roof, *see* ROOF.

Wagon vault, *see* VAULT.

Wainscot The timber lining to walls. The term is also applied to the wooden panelling of PEWS.

Wall plate, *see* ROOF.

Wall rib, *see* FORMERET.

Walter, Thomas U. (1804–87), was of German descent, and was born in Philadelphia where his father was a mason. He studied under STRICKLAND and started on his own in 1830. As early as 1833 he was commissioned to design Girard College, Philadelphia, an ambitious, wholly peripteral (and thus functionally dubious) white marble building. In 1851 he began the completion of the Capitol in Washington: he added the wings, and the dominant dome on a cast-iron framing is his. He also completed MILLS' Treasury. Like nearly all the leading American architects, Walter was also capable of major engineering works – see a breakwater he built in Venezuela (1843–5).

Lit: T. Hamlin, *Greek Revival Architecture in America,* New York 1944.

Warchavchic, Gregori, *see* BRAZILIAN ARCHITECTURE.

Ward The courtyard of a castle; also called a *bailey.*

Ward: Gravensteen Castle,
(Château des Comtes de Flandre),
Ghent, 1216

Ware, Isaac (d. 1766). A protégé of Lord BURLINGTON and a strict Palladian. His buildings are competent but uninspired, e.g., Chesterfield House, London (1749, destroyed), and Wrotham Park (c. 1754). However, his *Complete Body of Architecture* (1756) was very influential and became a standard textbook.

Lit: J. Summerson, *Architecture in Britain, 1530–1830*, Pelican History of Art, Harmondsworth 1969, paperback edn 1970; H. M. Colvin, *Biographical Dictionary of English Architects, 1660–1840*, London 1954.

Wastell, John (d. c. 1515), lived at Bury St Edmunds and, though evidently highly appreciated, was not in the King's Works. He had probably started under and with Simon CLERK, and followed him both at the abbey of Bury and at King's College Chapel, Cambridge, where he appears from 1486 and was master mason throughout the years when the glorious fan VAULT was built and the chapel completed. The vault can therefore with some probability be considered his design, though the King's Masons, William VERTUE and Henry REDMAN, visited the building in 1507, 1509, and 1512. Wastell was also Cardinal Morton's mason and then the master mason of Canterbury Cathedral, where he was presumably the designer for Bell Harry, the crossing tower of the cathedral (built 1494–7). Other buildings have been attributed to him on stylistic grounds.

Lit: J. Harvey, *English Medieval Architects*, London 1954.

Waterhouse, Alfred (1830–1905), started in practice at Manchester in 1856 and moved to London in 1865. In Manchester he won the competitions for the Assize Courts (1859) and Town Hall (1869–77), both excellently planned and externally in a free, picturesque Gothic which yet does not depart too far from symmetry. Soon after, his style hardened and assumed that odd character of sharp forms and harsh imperishable materials (terracotta, best red brick) which one connects with him. He remained a planner of great clarity and resourcefulness and used ironwork freely for structural purposes. But he was a historicist all the same, happiest in a rigid matter-of-fact Gothic, but also going in for a kind of Romanesque (Natural History Museum, London, 1868 etc.) and for French Renaissance (Caius College, Cambridge, 1868 etc.). Of his many buildings the following may be mentioned: some very interestingly plan-ned Congregational churches (Lyndhurst Road, Hampstead, 1883; King's Weigh House Chapel, 1889–91); the headquarters of the Prudential Assurance in Holborn (1876 etc.); the City and Guilds Institute in Kensington (1881); St Paul's School (1881 etc.; demolished)); the National Liberal Club (1884); and a number of country mansions (Hutton Hall, Yorkshire, 1865; enlargement of Eaton Hall, Cheshire, 1870 etc.).

Lit: H.-R. Hitchcock, *Architecture: Nineteenth and Twentieth Centuries*, Pelican History of Art, Harmondsworth 1969, paperback edn 1971.

Water-leaf A leaf shape used in later C12 CAPITALS. The water-leaf is broad, unribbed, and tapering, curving out towards the angle of the ABACUS and turned in at the top. (For illustration *see* CAPITAL.)

Water-table, *see* OFF-SET.

Wattle and daub A method of wall construction consisting of branches or thin laths (wattles) roughly plastered over with mud or clay (daub), sometimes used as a filling between the vertical members of TIMBER-FRAMED houses.

Wave moulding A compound moulding formed by a convex curve between two concave curves: typical of the Decorated style.

Wealden house A timber-framed house peculiar to England. It has a hall in the centre and wings projecting only slightly and only on the jutting upper floor. The roof, however, runs through without a break between wings and hall, and the eaves of the hall part are therefore exceptionally deep. They are supported by diagonal, usually curved, braces starting from the short inner sides of the overhanging wings and rising parallel with the front wall of the hall towards the centre of the eaves.

Weatherboarding Overlapping horizontal boards covering a TIMBER-FRAMED wall; the boards are wedge-shaped in section, the upper edge being the thinner.

Weathering A sloping horizontal surface on sills, tops of buttresses, etc., to throw off water. *See* OFF-SET.

Web A compartment or bay of a vault, between the ribs, also called a cell and a SEVERY.

Webb, Sir Aston (1849–1930). In England perhaps the most successful of the providers of large public buildings in suitable styles around 1900. His favourite style, especially earlier in his career, was a free François I. Later there are also buildings in the Imperial-Palladian of the years of Edward VII. Chief buildings: Law Courts, Birmingham (with Ingress Bell, 1886–91); Metropolitan Life Assurance, Moorgate (with Bell, 1890–3), one of his best; Victoria and Albert Museum (1891 etc.); Christ's Hospital, Horsham (with Bell, 1894–1904); Royal Naval College, Dartmouth (1899–1904); Royal College of Science (1900–6); University, Birmingham (1906–9), Byzantino-Italian; Imperial College, Kensington (1911); Admiralty Arch (1911); façade of Buckingham Palace (1913).

Lit: H.-R. Hitchcock, *Architecture: Nineteenth and Twentieth Centuries*, Pelican History of Art, Harmondsworth 1969, paperback edn 1971.

Webb, John (1611–72). A pupil and nephew by marriage of Inigo JONES, whose right-hand man he appears to have been from the 1630s onwards, e.g., at Wilton. He acquired technical skill and scholarship from Jones, but lacked imagination and originality. His independent work dates from after his master's death and much of it has been destroyed. Lamport Hall (1654–7), the portico and some interiors at The Vyne (1654–7), and the King Charles Building at Greenwich Hospital (1662–9) are the best that survive.

Lit: M. Whinney, 'John Webb's Drawings for Whitehall Palace' in *Walpole Society*, XXXI, 1946; J. Summerson, *Architecture in Britain, 1530–1830*, Pelican History of Art, Harmondsworth 1969, paperback edn 1970.

Webb, Philip (1831–1915), hardly ever designed anything but houses. Among the architects of the great English Domestic Revival, he and Norman SHAW stand supreme: Shaw much more favoured, more inventive, more voluble, more widely influential; Webb harder, more of a thinker, totally deficient in any architectural bedside manner, and perhaps more deeply influential, even on Shaw himself. Webb chose his clients and never agreed to having a stable of assistants. His style is strangely ruthless: from the first he mixed elements from the Gothic and the c18, not for the fun or devilry of it, but because one should use the most suitable motifs regardless of their original contexts. He also liked to expose materials and show the workings of parts of a building.

His first job was Red House (1859) for William MORRIS, whose closest friend he remained throughout. For Morris's firm he designed furniture of a rustic Stuart kind, and also table glass and metalwork. He also joined in the stained glass work. His principal town houses are No. 1 Palace Green, London (1868) and No. 19 Lincoln's Inn Fields, London (1868–9). Of his country houses Joldwyns, Surrey (1873), Smeaton Manor, Yorkshire (1878), and Conyhurst, Surrey (1885) come nearest to Shaw in character – gabled, cheerful, with weatherboarding, tilehanging, and white window trim. Standen (1891–4) is best preserved. Clouds (1876) is the largest and least easy to take, strong no doubt, but very astringent indeed, designed, as it were, in a take-it-or-leave-it mood. Webb's interiors from the later seventies onwards often have white panelling and exhibit a marked sympathy with the c18 vernacular. In 1901 he retired to a country cottage and ceased practising.

Lit: H. Lethaby, *Philip Webb and his work*, London 1935.

Weinbrenner, Friedrich (1766–1826), was born at Karlsruhe and visited Berlin (1790) and Rome (1792). His major achievement is the transformation of Karlsruhe into a neoclassical city, rather like a miniature version of Leningrad. The Marktplatz (1804–24), with balancing but not identical buildings and a pyramid in the centre, and the circular Rondellplatz (1805–13), with the Markgräfliches Palais, are masterpieces of neoclassical town planning. He also built a handsome circular Catholic church (1808–17).

Lit: A. Valdenaire, *F. Weinbrenner, sein Leben und seine Bauten*, Karlsruhe 1919; A. von Schneider, *F. Weinbrenner, Denkwürdigkeiten*, Karlsruhe 1958.

Wells, Joseph Merrill, *see* McKIM.

Westwork The west end of a Carolingian or Romanesque church, consisting of a low entrance hall and above it a room open to the nave and usually flanked or surrounded by aisles and upper galleries. The whole is crowned by one broad tower, and there are occasionally stair turrets as well. In the main upper room stood an altar as a rule. (Illustrated next page.)

Westwork at Abbey Church, Corvey, Germany, 837–85. The towers are later

Lit: D. Grossmann, 'Zum Stand der West-werkforschung' in *Wallraf-Richartz Jahrbuch*, XXIX, 1957; F. Möbius, *Westwerkstudien*, Jena 1968.

Wheel window, *see* ROSE WINDOW.

White, Stanford (1853–1906), was of old New England stock and was brought up in a cultured house. He was a pupil of RICHARDSON and from 1879 a partner of McKIM and Mead. White was a rich *bon vivant*, a man who entertained sumptuously, and exuberant in other ways as well. He was a brilliant and effortless designer, his range stretching from magazine covers to a railway carriage, including Gordon Bennett's yacht, and houses more original than any by anyone anywhere at the time. The temerity of the Low House at Bristol, Rhode Island (1887, recently demolished), with its enormous spreading pitched roof, is almost beyond belief. For other buildings *see* McKIM. White was shot dead during a theatre rehearsal in 1906.

Lit: A Monograph on the Work of McKim, Mead and White, 4 vols., New York 1925; C. Baldwin, *S. White*, New York 1931.

Wilkins, William (1778–1839), son of a Norwich architect, was educated at Caius College, Cambridge, where he was elected Fellow in 1802. He travelled in Greece, Asia Minor, and Italy (1801–4) and published *Antiquities of Magna Graecia* on his return. He pioneered the GREEK REVIVAL in England with his designs for Downing College, Cambridge (begun 1806), Haileybury College (1806–9), and the temple-style country house Grange Park (1809) with its Theseum peristyle and other rather pedantically Athenian references. In fact, he was rather priggish and doctrinaire, and his rival SMIRKE had little difficulty in overtaking his lead in the movement. But Downing College is important historically as the first of all university campuses – separate buildings round a park-like expanse of lawn – preceding JEFFERSON'S Charlottesville. Wilkins's other university buildings in Cambridge were neo-Gothic, e.g., New Court, Trinity (1821–3), and the screen and hall-range at King's (1824–8). He had greater opportunities in London to develop his neo-Greek style but muffed them – University College (1827–8), St George's Hospital (1828–9), and finally the National Gallery (1834–8), which ruined his reputation. Only the main block of University College is his, and though the portico itself is very imposing he seems to have been unable to unite it satisfactorily with the rest of the composition. This inability to subordinate the parts to the whole resulted at the National Gallery in a patchy façade unworthy of its important site.

Lit: J. Mordaunt Crook, *The Greek Revival*, London 1972.

William of Ramsey (d. 1349). A member of a family of masons who worked in Norwich and London from about 1300 onwards, William appears first in 1325 as a mason working on St Stephen's Chapel in the Palace of Westminster (*see* MICHAEL OF CANTERBURY). In 1332 he became master mason of the new work at St Paul's Cathedral, which meant the chapterhouse and its cloister. In 1336 he was appointed Master Mason to the King's Castles south of Trent, which included the Palace of Westminster and St Stephen's Chapel. William was also commissioned in 1337 to give his *sanum consilium* on Lichfield Cathedral. In the early thirties he may have been master mason to Norwich Cathedral also: the cloister there was taken over by one William of Ramsey from **John of Ramsey**, probably his father, who was already master mason to the cathedral in 1304. William was evidently an important man, and what we know from an old illustration and surviving fragments of the chapterhouse of St Paul's indicates that the creation of the Perpendicular style was due to him, or at least that he made a style out of elements evolved in London and especially at St Stephen's Chapel in the decade preceding 1330.

Lit: J. Harvey, *English Medieval Architects*, London 1954.

William of Sens (d. *c.* 1180). Designer and master mason of the chancel of Canterbury Cathedral, rebuilt after a fire had destroyed it in 1174. He was a Frenchman (or else his successor would not have been known as **William the Englishman**) and came from Sens Cathedral, which was begun *c.* 1140 and which contained features repeated at Canterbury (also in the Englishman's work, no doubt on the strength of drawings left in the lodge by William of Sens). He was, however, also familiar with more recent French work, notably Notre Dame in Paris (begun 1163), St Rémi at Reims, Soissons, and buildings in the north-west such as Valenciennes. William, as the true mason of the Gothic Age (*see also* VILLARD DE HONNECOURT), was familiar with wood as well as stone, and with devices to load stone on to ships. He had been chosen at Canterbury from a number of English and French masons assembled for consultation on action to be taken after the fire.

Lit: T. S. R. Boase, *English Art, 1100–1216*, Oxford 1953; G. Webb, *Architecture in Britain, the Middle Ages*, Pelican History of Art, Harmondsworth 1955; P. Frankl, *Gothic Architecture*, Pelican History of Art, Harmondsworth 1962.

William of Wynford (d. *c.* 1405–10) was made master mason of Wells Cathedral in 1365, after having worked at Windsor Castle, where William of Wykeham was then clerk of the works. Wynford remained in the royal service and in 1372 received a pension for life. He also remained William of Wykeham's protégé, and worked for him at Winchester College and from 1394 at Winchester Cathedral, where he probably designed the new nave and west front. New College, Oxford, has also been attributed to him. He was obviously a much appreciated man; he dined with William of Wykeham, at the high table of Winchester College, and at the prior's table at the cathedral, and received a furred robe once a year from the cathedral. On several occasions he appeared, no doubt for consultations, together with YEVELE.

Lit: J. Harvey, *English Medieval Architects*, London 1954.

Wind-brace, *see* ROOF.

Winde, William (d. 1722), was born in Holland, the son of a Royalist exile. He took up architecture in middle age about 1680, and became, with PRATT and MAY, a leader of the Anglo-Dutch school. His Buckingham House, London (1705, destroyed), with its unpedimented attic storey, fore-buildings, and quadrant colonnades, was very influential. None of his buildings survives.

Lit: J. Summerson, *Architecture in Britain, 1530–1830*, Pelican History of Art, Harmondsworth 1969, paperback edn 1970.

Winder, *see* STAIR.

Window 1. An opening made in a wall to light or ventilate an enclosed space. Early windows, from considerations of security and architectural stability, were little more than incisions in the wall. Their SILLS and the REVEAL of the JAMBS might be SPLAYED to increase the flow of light. The spread of glazing and developments in skeletal vaulting both made larger windows possible. These would be divided into LIGHTS by MULLIONS (and later horizontally divided by TRANSOMS), whose heads in Gothic architecture were elaborated into steadily more complex TRACERY. Gothic windows are usually protected externally by a HOOD-MOULD, and the reveals may be enriched by COLONNETTES and MOULDINGS. In classical architecture a window may be framed externally by a simple ARCHITRAVE, with or without a crowning ENTABLATURE or PEDIMENT, or it may be more richly set in an AEDICULE. 2. *Window* is also used to refer to the glass held in wood or metal frames within the opening. Such frames, with QUARRIES of glass held in lead CAMES braced by SADDLE BARS, were originally hinged when required to open inwards or outwards – the CASEMENT WINDOW. When larger panes of *crown glass* became available in the C17, these were incorporated in wooden SASH WINDOWS sliding up and down one in front of the other. These were at first held in place by pegs, and then (the '*double-hung*' *sash*) by cords with counter-balancing weights inside the jambs. These were invented in Holland in the 1680s, and on their introduction to England (first recorded as replacements in the Banqueting House, Whitehall, in 1685) they rapidly replaced casements in all but the smallest houses. In the course of the c18 the *glazing bars* became slenderer and the panes of glass larger, but only in the c19 did the ready availability of large panes of *sheet glass* allow the abandonment of glazing bars, and thus a delicate relationship between the proportions of the glazing and those of the building as a whole.

The need for light in the factories and ever more mammoth office blocks of the c19 and c20 has made windows steadily more prominent in relation to the wall. (Repeal of the excise duty on glass in England in 1845, and of the window tax in 1851.) The development of SKELETON CONSTRUCTION, together with more efficient heating systems and the invention of air-conditioning, have removed the traditional constraints upon this process; and much of modern architecture can be seen as the acceptance, followed by the aesthetic exploitation, of the new relationship of the window to the *skeleton frame*. Modern buildings employ metal-frame windows which, where they open at all, are usually sliding, or of the side and vertical *pivot-hung* type. *Double-glazing* is becoming common.

Special types of window include: *bay*, *bow*, and *oriel windows*, which are all forms of projection from a house front containing fenestration. *Oriel windows* generally project from an upper storey (though not necessarily, viz. college halls), supported on some form of CORBELLING or BRACKET. *Bay windows* are canted projections rising from the ground; *bow windows* are rounded projections, often only of the window frame itself. *French windows* are, as the French name (*croisée*) for them suggests, casement windows carried down to the floor so as to open like doors. They made their appearance at Versailles in the 1680s. *Dormer windows* are windows placed vertically in a sloping roof with a roof of their own. The name derives from the fact that they usually lighted sleeping quarters. For the *Palladian* or *Venetian window*, *see* SERLIANA. The *Diocletian* or *thermal window*, whose use was revived by PALLADIO himself and became another feature of PALLADIANISM, is a semicircular window divided into three lights by two vertical mullions. It derives its name from its use in the THERMAE of Diocletian at Rome. *Picture window* is a name often used to describe a large window in a house, containing a single uninterrupted pane of glass. *See also* CHICAGO WINDOW, FANLIGHT, LANCET, OEIL-DE-BOEUF, SKYLIGHT.   [AL]

Lit: R. McGrath & A. C. Frost, *Glass in Architecture and Decoration*, 1937.

Wit or Witte, Peter de, *see* CANDID, Peter.

Wolff, Jacob, the elder (*c.* 1546–1612). Master mason to the city of Nuremberg. His most notable work was the *überherrliche* (super-magnificent) house which he and Peter Carl built for Martin Peller in Nuremberg (1602–7, destroyed in the Second World War but partially rebuilt). Martin Peller had been a consul in Venice and the Pellerhaus is a curious compromise between Venetian and German taste, its three heavily rusticated storeys being crowned with a rich three-storey German gable. On the Marienberg, above Würzburg, he connected the wings of the existing castle to make a vast elongated rectangular court (1600–1607), very sparingly decorated. His son **Jacob Wolff the younger** (1571–1620) travelled and studied in Italy and brought back a more highly developed Italian Renaissance style which he used in a striking manner in his additions to the Nuremberg Town Hall (1616–22, destroyed in the Second World War but rebuilt).

Lit: E. Hempel, *Baroque Art and Architecture in Central Europe*, Pelican History of Art, Harmondsworth 1965.

Womersley, J. L. (b. 1910). City Architect of Sheffield 1953–64 and a pioneer in England of large-scale housing in high and ingeniously interlocked ranges of flats (Parkhill Housing, 1955–60; Hyde Park Housing, 1962–6).

Lit: R. Maxwell, *New British Architecture*, London 1972.

Wood, John, the elder (1704–54), a competent exponent of PALLADIANISM (e.g. Prior Park near Bath, 1735–48), revolutionized town planning with his scheme for Bath (1727 etc.), unfortunately only partly executed. He began with Queen Square (1729–36), treating the north side as a palace front with a rusticated ground floor and attached central pediment. (This had recently been attempted in Grosvenor Square, London, *c.* 1730, by Edward Shepheard, but only partially realized.) Entirely original was the Circus (1754 etc.), a circular space with three streets radiating out of it; the elevations have superimposed Orders so that it looks like the Colosseum turned outside in. He intended to follow the Circus with a Forum, of which North and South Parades are fragments, and an enormous Gymnasium (unexecuted), and thus make Bath once more into a Roman city. He died soon after placing the first stone of the Circus, but his work was carried on by his son **John Wood the younger** (1728–81), who took it a step further towards open planning with his Royal Crescent (1761–5), the first of its kind and an artistic conception of great originality and magnificence. It has been widely copied ever since. His other buildings – e.g., the Assembly Rooms (1769–71) and Hot Baths (1773–8) – are excellent late examples of Palladianism. (For illustrations *see* CRESCENT, ENGLISH ARCHITECTURE.)

Lit: J. Summerson, *J. Wood and the English Town-Planning Tradition,* London 1949.

Wren, Sir Christopher (1632–1723). The greatest English architect. His father was Dean of Windsor and his uncle Bishop of Ely, both pillars of the High Church. He was educated at Westminster School and at fifteen became a demonstrator in anatomy at the College of Surgeons; then he went to Oxford. Experimental science was just then coming to the fore, and he found himself in company with a group of brilliant young men who were later to found the Royal Society. He was entirely engrossed in scientific studies. Evelyn called him 'that miracle of a youth' and Newton thought him one of the best geometricians of the day. In 1657 he was made Professor of Astronomy in London, in 1661 in Oxford; but two years later his career took a different turn with his appointment to the commission for the restoration of St Paul's. After the Great Fire of London he was appointed one of the Surveyors under the Rebuilding Act (1667) and in 1669 became Surveyor General of the King's Works. Then he resigned his Oxford professorship and was knighted (1673). He was twice M.P. (1685–7 and 1701–2) and, despite his Tory connections, survived the Whig revolution of 1688, but on the accession of George I in 1714 he lost his office. He was twice married, first to a daughter of Sir John Coghill, and secondly to a daughter of Lord Fitzwilliam of Lifford. He died aged ninety-one having, as he wrote, 'worn out (by God's Mercy) a long life in the Royal Service and having made some figure in the world'.

If Wren had died at thirty he would have been remembered only as a figure in the history of English science. His first buildings, the Sheldonian Theatre, Oxford (1663), and Pembroke College Chapel, Cambridge (1663),

are the work of a brilliant amateur, though the trussed roof of the Sheldonian already displays his structural ingenuity. In 1665–6 he spent eight or nine months studying French architecture, mainly in Paris, and may well have visited Flanders and Holland as well. He met BERNINI in Paris, but learnt more from MANSART and LE VAU, whom he probably knew and whose works he certainly studied. French and Dutch architecture were to provide the main influences on his own style. The Fire of London in 1666 gave him his great opportunity. Though his utopian city plan was rejected, every facet of his empirical genius found scope for expression in the rebuilding of St Paul's and the fifty-one city churches. The latter especially revealed his freshness of mind, his bounding invention, and his adventurous empiricism. There were, of course, no precedents in England for classical churches except in the work of Inigo JONES. Wren's city churches were built between 1670 and 1686, nearly thirty being under construction in the peak year of 1677. Plans are extremely varied and often daringly original, e.g., St Stephen, Walbrook (1672–87), which foreshadows St Paul's, and St Peter's, Cornhill (1677–81), in which his two-storeyed gallery church with vaulted nave and aisles was first adumbrated. This type was later perfected at St Clement Danes (begun 1680) and St James's, Piccadilly (begun 1683). But his originality and fertility of invention are best seen in the steeples, which range from the neo-Gothic of St Dunstan in the East to the Borrominesque fantasy of St Vedast and St Bride.

More scholarly and refined in detail than his sometimes rather hastily conceived and crudely executed city churches is his masterpiece, St Paul's Cathedral. Nothing like it had ever before been seen in England. It was a triumph of intellectual self-reliance, and the dome is one of the most majestic and reposeful in the world, purely classical in style. Baroque influences are evident elsewhere in the building, notably in the towers, the main façade, and such illusionist features as the sham-perspective window niches and the false upper storey in the side elevations to conceal the nave buttresses. The interior is ostensibly classical, but contains many Baroque gestures. It was begun in 1675, and Wren lived to see it finished in 1709.

His secular buildings range from the austere Doric barracks at Chelsea Hospital (1682–92) to the grandest and most Baroque of all his works, Greenwich Hospital (1694 etc.), where the Painted Hall (1698) is the finest room of its kind in England. Of his vast and elaborate additions and alterations to Whitehall Palace, Winchester Palace, and Hampton Court only a fragment of the latter survives (and this was probably revised and altered by his assistant William TALMAN). Like nearly all his work, these great schemes were carried out for the Office of Works. Of his few independent commissions the best are Trinity College Library, Cambridge (1676–84), and Tom Tower, Christ Church, Oxford (1681–2). Apart from Marlborough House, London (1709–10, now much altered), no town or country house can be certainly attributed to him, though his name has been optimistically given to many. HAWKSMOOR was his only pupil of note, but he had a wide and profound influence through his long reign at the Office of Works. (For illustrations see ENGLISH ARCHITECTURE.)

Lit: A. T. Bolton, ed., *The Wren Society*, 20 vols., London 1924–43; E. F. Sekler, *Wren and his Place in European Architecture*, London 1956; J. Summerson, *Sir C. Wren*, London 1952; M. Whinney, *Wren*, London 1971; K. Downes, *C. Wren*, London 1971.

Wright, Frank Lloyd (1869–1959). The greatest American architect to date. His *œuvre* ranges over more than sixty years and is never repetitive, routine, or derivative. He first worked with SULLIVAN, whom he never ceased to admire, and was responsible for much of his master's domestic work. The first type of building he developed as an independent architect is what he called the prairie house – low, spreading, with rooms running into each other, terraces merging with the gardens, and roofs far projecting. Houses of this type are located in the outer suburbs of Chicago (Oak Park, Riverside, etc.). The development was extremely consistent, ending up with designs more daringly novel than any other architect's in the same field. The series was heralded by houses before 1900 and was complete by about 1905; its climax is the Robie House, Chicago (1908). Concurrently he had done one church, Unity Temple, Oak Park (1905–6), and one office building, Larkin Building, Buffalo (1904) – both with the same stylistic elements and the same freshness of approach as the private houses. The Larkin Building might well be called the most original office building of its date anywhere.

Some bigger jobs came along about the time of the First World War: Midway Gardens, Chicago (1913), a lavish and short-lived entertainment establishment, and the no longer surviving Imperial Hotel at Tokyo (1916–20). He was aided here by Antonin Raymond, who then settled in Japan. Both these buildings were very heavily decorated, and the elements of this decoration, polygonal and sharp-angled forms, are entirely Wright's, favoured by him from the very beginning, but less in evidence in the prairie houses, at least externally. The houses of the twenties introduced a new technique which allowed Wright to use surface decoration on the outside as well: precast concrete blocks.

In fact, from then onwards, Wright went more and more his own way, and it is very rare for his work to run parallel to international developments and conventions. One exception is Falling Water, Bear Run, Pennsylvania (1937–9), which is as brilliant as anything he ever designed yet closer to the so-called INTERNATIONAL MODERN of Europe (and by then of America) than anything else by him. His own work which, about 1914–17, influenced GROPIUS as well as the Dutch De Stijl Group (see OUD) is not represented in Europe at all, as his harmless little Memorial Hostel for Venice was prevented from being executed. In his autobiography Wright tells of many such calamities, but as a writer he was biased and monotonously convinced that he was always right and blameless. This attitude seems to have distinguished his Taliesin community in Wisconsin from the fraternity ideals of RUSKIN: it was more of a master-and-disciples than a guild relationship. Wright built at Taliesin three times (1911, 1914, and 1925 etc.), and then added a Taliesin Winter Camp in Arizona (1927 etc.), eminently fantastical and very exciting.

World-wide recognition came late to him, and only in his last twenty years or so, that is from the time when he was nearly seventy, did large commissions come his way fairly evenly. The first was the Johnson Wax Factory at Racine, Wisconsin (1936–9). Here he built an office block with walls of brick and glass tubes, and an interior with reinforced concrete mushroom columns (see MAILLART). The laboratory tower was added in 1949. The chapel of Florida Southern College dates from 1940, the Unitarian Church at Madison from 1947, the design for the Guggenheim Museum in New York from 1942 (completed 1960), and the office skyscraper at Bartlesville, Oklahoma, was completed in 1955. The museum, designed as a spiral ramp on a circular plan, is functionally indefensible but formally certainly startling. The skyscraper and the two ecclesiastical buildings display Wright's inborn passion for sharp angles more radically than any of his earlier buildings, and it is interesting to observe that the recent turn of architecture towards aggressive sharp angles (see BREUER, SAARINEN) has given this pre-1900 passion of Wright's a new topicality. He lived through three phases of free decorative play in international architecture: the Arts and Crafts, Expressionism, and the most recent anti-rationalism. (For illustrations see UNITED STATES ARCHITECTURE.)

Lit: H.-R. Hitchcock, *In the Nature of Materials: the Buildings of F. L. Wright*, New York 1942; V. Scully, Jr, *F. L. Wright*, New York 1960; O. Lloyd Wright, *F. L. Wright, His life, his work, his words*, New York–London 1970; H. Allen Brooks, *The Prairie School, F. L. Wright and his Mid-West Contemporaries*, Toronto 1972.

Wyatt, James (1747–1813), the most successful architect of his day, rivalled the ADAM brothers and even overshadowed CHAMBERS, whom he succeeded as Surveyor-General in 1796. But his brilliance was superficial, and his reputation now rests mainly on his neo-Gothic extravaganzas, though the best of these have been destroyed. The son of a Staffordshire timber-merchant and builder, he went to Venice for six years in 1762, studying there under the painter-architect Visentini. He leapt to fame on his return to London with the Pantheon in Regent Street (1770, now destroyed), an astonishing neo-Classical version of Hagia Sophia in Constantinople. He was inundated with commissions from then onwards, despite his outrageously bad manners to clients and his general unreliability. His classical houses, very smooth and elegant, include Heaton House (1772), Heveningham (1788–99), Castle Coole in Northern Ireland (1790–7), and Dodington (1798–1808), the latter very solemn and severe, owing much to the Greek Revival. His neo-Gothic work ranges from the exquisite miniature Lee Priory (1782, destroyed, but one room survives in the Victoria and Albert Museum) to the fabulous Fonthill Abbey (1796–1807, destroyed) for William Beckford and the almost equally extravagant Ashridge (1806–13).

His numerous and ruthless restorations and 'improvements' to Gothic buildings include work at Salisbury, Durham, and Hereford Cathedrals, and earned him the name of 'Wyatt the Destroyer'.

Lit: A. Dale, *James Wyatt*, Oxford 1956.

Wyatt, Thomas Henry (1807–80), and his brother **Sir Matthew Digby** (1820–77), are not related to James WYATT. Thomas Henry's *chef-d'oeuvre* is Wilton Church, Wiltshire (1842–3), in an Early-Christian-Italian-Romanesque manner; it is perhaps the finest example of that style of the 1840s, rarer in England than in Germany. He also designed many Gothic churches (for a time in partnership with David Brandon). Sir Matthew Digby belonged to the circle of Henry Cole and Owen Jones, who were responsible for much of the work on the Exhibition of 1851; Wyatt himself was Secretary of the Executive Committee. He was a poor architect (see the architectural parts of Paddington Station, 1854–5), but an extremely intelligent and far-seeing architectural journalist, a believer in the new materials of his century and the possibilities of machine production.

Lit: N. Pevsner, *Studies in Art, Architecture and Design*, London 1968.

Wyatville, Sir Jeffrey (1766–1840). He was the nephew of James WYATT under whom he trained and whose work at Ashridge he completed in 1817 (adding the north entrance, east wing and stables). Although a competent classical architect (e.g., his entrance hall and stable court at Longleat 1801–11), he specialized in neo-Gothic and 'Tudor collegiate' mansions. His masterpiece is Windsor Castle which he remodelled for George IV between 1824 and 1837, giving it a picturesque silhouette by raising the Round Tower 33 ft to make it a dominant feature around which to group his newly battlemented and machicolated towers. He added the George IV Gateway and Lancaster Tower and rebuilt the Chester and Brunswick Towers. His Waterloo Gallery and new royal apartments are still in use. He changed his name to Wyatville when he began work at the Castle and was knighted in 1828.

Lit: D. Linstrum, *Sir Jeffrey Wyatville, Architect to the King*, Oxford 1972.

Wynford, see WILLIAM OF WYNFORD.

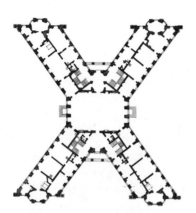

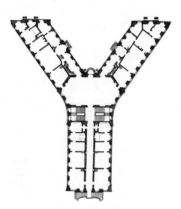

Xystus An AMBULATORY. In Greek architecture, a long portico used for athletic contests; in Roman architecture, a long covered or open walk bordered by colonnades or trees.

Yamasaki, Minoru (b. 1912). His most important building is St Louis Airport (1953–5), designed with Hellmut and Leinweber. Its crossing concrete vaults are eminently impressive. Later buildings tend to be playful and weak; American Concrete Institute, Detroit, 1958; Reynolds Metals Building, Detroit, 1959; Conference Center and Education Building, Wayne State University, Detroit, 1958 and 1961; Michigan Consolidated Gas Company, Detroit, 1962; School of Music, Oberlin College, 1964; World Trade Center, New York, 1970–74.

Lit: I. McCallum, *Architecture – U.S.A.,* London 1959; M. Manieri Elia, *L'architettura del dopoguerra in U.S.A.,* Bologna 1966.

Yevele, Henry (d. 1400), was admitted a citizen of London in 1353, became mason to the Black Prince about 1357, to the King (for Westminster, the Tower, and other palaces and castles) from 1360, and to Westminster Abbey from 1388 at the latest. It is probable that he had designed the nave of the abbey (as begun *c.* 1375), and the nave of Canterbury Cathedral, built in the 1390s, has also been attributed to him. He designed Westminster Hall in 1394. He was a wealthy man with property in many places, and he engaged in business both in connection with and apart from his duties as the King's Master Mason.

Lit: J. H. Harvey, *Henry Yevele,* London 1946.

Yorke, F. R. S. (1906–62), one of the pioneers in England of the INTERNATIONAL MODERN style of the twenties and thirties, started with a number of white cubic private houses in 1934. He was in partnership with Marcel BREUER 1935–7, and later the name of the firm became Yorke, Rosenberg & Mardall; it has been responsible for flats, housing, hospitals, schools (e.g., Stevenage, 1947–9) and for Gatwick Airport (1957 etc.).

Lit: The Architecture of Yorke, Rosenberg and Mardall, 1944–1972, London 1973.

Yorkshire lights In a mullioned window, a pair of lights, one fixed and the other sliding horizontally.

Yoshisaka, Takamasa, *see* JAPANESE ARCHITECTURE.

Zakharov, Adrian Dmitrievich (1761–1811), the leading Russian neo-classicist and perhaps the greatest Russian architect, was trained at the St Petersburg Academy of Arts, then in Paris under CHALGRIN (1782–6), and travelled in Italy. His masterpiece is the Admiralty, Leningrad (1806–15), vast, bold, and solid, with a façade a quarter of a mile long, a huge columned tower supporting a needle-like spire over the central gate, and dodecastyle Tuscan porticos at the ends. To give expression to such an immense frontage without breaking its unity was a major achievement. But the end blocks are still more successful, the nearest approach to BOULLÉE's architecture of geometrical shapes on a grand scale: each is in the form of a cubic pavilion capped by a low cylindrical drum, pierced by a vast semicircular portal, and flanked by colonnades. Another of his notable works is the church of St Andrew in Kronstadt. (For illustrations see CLASSICISM, RUSSIAN ARCHITECTURE.)

Lit: G. H. Hamilton, *The Art and Architecture of Russia*, Pelican History of Art, Harmondsworth 1954; H.-R. Hitchcock, *Architecture: Nineteenth and Twentieth Centuries*, Pelican History of Art, Harmondsworth 1969, paperback edn 1971.

Zapotec architecture, *see* MESOAMERICAN ARCHITECTURE.

Zehrfuss, Bernard, *see* Jean PROUVÉ.

Zen Buddhist architecture, *see* JAPANESE ARCHITECTURE.

Ziggurat (or **Zikkurat**) An Assyrian or Babylonian temple-tower in the form of a truncated pyramid built in diminishing stages, each stage being reached by ramps.

Ruins of Ziggurat of the Moon God Nanna at Ur, built by King Ur-Nammu (partially restored)

Zimbalo, Giuseppe (active 1659–86). The chief exponent of the wildly exuberant and rather coarse Baroque style developed at Lecce, e.g., Prefettura (1659–95), Cathedral (1659–82), S. Agostino (1663), and Chiesa del Rosario (1691). His pupil Giuseppe Cino carried his style on into the C18.

Lit: M. Calvesi & M. Manieri Elia, *Il 'Barocco' Leccese*, Rome 1966.

Zimmermann, Dominikus (1685–1766), one of the greatest South German Rococo architects, but a craftsman before he was an architect. He retained to the last his peasant vitality, spontaneity, and unquestioning piety. Perhaps it is significant that his masterpiece, die Wies, was built neither for a great prince nor for the abbot of a rich monastery but for a simple rustic community. Born at Wessobrunn, Zimmermann began there as a stucco worker, then settled at Füssen (1698), and finally at Landsberg (1716), where he eventually became mayor. He continued to work as a stuccoist after becoming an architect and frequently collaborated with his brother Johann Baptist (1680–1758), who was a painter. His earliest building is the convent

church at Mödigen (1716–18), but his
mature style first becomes apparent in the
pilgrimage church of Steinhausen (1728–31),
which is also the first wholly Rococo church
in Bavaria. It broke away decisively from its
Baroque predecessors, the mystical indirect
lighting and rich velvety colour of ASAM giving place to flat even lighting and a predominantly white colour scheme – bright,
brittle, and porcellaneous. The colours used
are all symbolical, as are the motifs in both
painted and carved decoration. At the Frauenkirche, Günzburg (1736–41), he adopted an
oblong plan, and at die Wies (1745–54) he
combined an oval with an oblong, using the
former for the nave with its wide ambulatory
(necessary for a pilgrimage church), and the
latter for the rather long chancel, which is
treated with an intensified, predominantly
pink colour scheme. Here stucco work, white-
painted wooden statues, and frescoes combine with architecture to delight and instruct
the pilgrim, be he never so humble or so
sophisticated. In more ways than one it is the
meeting-place of the courtly Rococo style and
an ancient tradition of craftsmanship which
stretches back to the Middle Ages. (For illustration see ROCOCO ARCHITECTURE.)

Lit: H.-R. Hitchcock, German Rococo: The
Zimmermann Brothers, London 1968.

Zoophorus A frieze with animal reliefs, as on
the Theseum in Athens.

Zuccalli, Enrico (1642–1724). Baroque architect, born in the Grisons, who settled in
Munich where he and his rival Giovanni
Antonio VISCARDI dominated the architectural scene for several years. He succeeded
Agostino BARELLI as architect to the Elector
in 1672. In Munich he completed Barelli's
Theatine church of St Cajetan, reducing the
size of the dome. He supervised the decoration
of the Residenz (Imperial suite 1680–1701;
Alexander and Summer Suite 1680–85) and
built the Porcia Palace (1694). Outside Munich, at Schleissheim, he built the Lustheim or
Banqueting House (1684–9) and began the
main palace (1701, completed by Joseph
EFFNER). In 1695 he began rebuilding the
palace at Bonn but this was completed after
1702 by Robert de COTTE. He also rebuilt the
abbey church of Ettal (1709–26, partly burnt
and rebuilt 1742). His kinsman **Gaspare**
(active 1685) built two Italianate churches at
Salzburg: St Erhard (1685–9) and St Cajetan
(1685–1700). (For illustration see BAROQUE
ARCHITECTURE.)

Lit: E. Hempel, Baroque Art and Architecture
in Central Europe, Pelican History of Art,
Harmondsworth 1965.

The publishers would like to thank all those who have helped in the preparation of this volume by making available precious originals, supplying rare photographs, granting reproduction permissions, or assisting with general inquiries. Special thanks are due to the Institute for Art History and the Archaeological and Byzantine Institutes of Munich University.

The illustrations, where they are not the authors' or from the archives of Prestel Verlag, originate from the following sources:

Aerofilms Limited; Wayne Andrews; Architectural Association; *Architectural Review*; Lala Aufsberg; Milli Bau; Bavaria-Verlag, Gauting; Brecht-Einzig; *Country Life*; Heinrich Decker; Eric de Maré; Deutsche Fotothek, Dresden; Foto Alinari, Florence; Foto Marburg; Professor Dr Friedrich Funke; Klaus Gallas; Professor Dr Roger Göpper; Hatje-Verlag, Stuttgart; Hedrich-Blessing, Chicago; Hirmer-Verlag, Munich; Irish Tourist Board, Dublin; Josef Jeiter; A. F. Kersting; G. E. Kidder-Smith; Franz Klimm; Kohlhammer-Verlag, Stuttgart; Rainer König; Leonard von Matt; National Monuments Record, London; Werner Neumeister; Tomio Ohashi; Orszagoe Müemleki Felügye-löseg, Budapest; Hans Patzelt; Pressehuset, Copenhagen; Paul Rickenbach; Jean Roubier; Dr Arthur Schlegel; Helga Schmidt-Glassner; Toni Schneider; Henri Stierlin; Wim Swaan; U.S. Information Service; Corporation of USSR Architects, Moscow; Dr Andreas Volwahsen; Eduard Widmer; Dr Dietrich Wildung; Professor Dr Otto Zerries.

The drawings were executed by David Etherton and Klaus Gallas.